On reading The Lotus People *by Aziz Hassim, I could not help pondering again about how place is an inescapable denominator in South African writing. It was Es'kia Mphahlele who observed that our literature is marked by a tyranny of place. In the South Africa of the past, living in a particular place was the result of who you were in racial terms, and also determined your experience and identity as a person. If character is fate — how might we think of "place as fate"? In Hassim's compelling narrative, we are confronted again with the geographical dividedness of apartheid South Africa.* — Mail & Guardian

Durban-born Aziz Hassim, now a retired accountant, spent most of his early years fraternising on the streets in Durban's Casbah. Durban, and particularly the Casbah area, had a kind of romance and bittersweet lifestyle during the fifties and sixties which, in spite of the apartheid laws (or perhaps because of them) lives on only in the minds of those that inhabited it at the time. Hassim's debut novel ... spans the events and moods of this era and served as a form of catharsis for the 66-year-old Hassim. While he calls the cleansing process his "personal TRC", he also wished to record a past he is convinced has disappeared forever for the younger generation who think he is "making up stories" when he tells them about the era. — 6th International Festival of Writers, Durban

The Lotus People *may well have been divided into two volumes, such is its wealth ... the first real novel written by an IndoSafrican that has been published.* — The Post

The Lotus People, *though not autobiographical, is really a product of its times, actually lived through which needs to be conveyed to the present generation. It is important to record the history of those days as Aziz Hassim says that "We, all of us, need to know where we come from and where we are going." The author's thorough research and background makes the novel a highly engaging read.* — Ajit Kumar, Consul General of India, Durban

"Crimson League, the notorious gang that ruled Durban's underworld and struck fear into the hearts of many in the 1950s and 1960s was ironically the protector of the town's community and in many instances helped finance the struggle against apartheid." This is just one of the amazing revelations illustrated in Aziz Hassim's first novel, The Lotus People, *a book that South Africans should read if they wish to gain a rare insight into happenings of the past.* — The Leader

The book, spanning 1882 until the late 1980s and revolving around the lives of fictional and real people like Dr Kesavaloo Goonum, is obviously politicised. At times vehemently so, as it uses the instigation of the Group Areas Act, the forced removals of blacks from their homes, the 1949 race riots and the increasingly violent anti-apartheid movement in the 1980s as the backdrop for most of his characters' movements and motivations. — Sunday Tribune

AZIZ HASSIM

publishers

publishers

STE Publishers
4th Floor Sunnyside Ridge,
Sunnyside Office Park,
32 Princess of Wales Terrace,
Parktown 2143
Johannesburg, South Africa

Copyright © Aziz Hassim 2003

First published in 2002
Reprinted in 2006

ISBN 1-919855-07-6

Cover design by Adam Rumball

Book design by Mad Cow Studio

Set in Ehrhardt 11pt

Printed and bound in South Africa by Interpak Books

Sculpture used on cover: Indian Flower Sellers by Mary Stainbank, 1970
Corner of Gardener and Pine Street, Durban

For
Kesavaloo Goonum
lest we forget

No work of this nature stands entirely on its own.
My grateful appreciation to the following people is noted:

Mr Vasi Nair, retired educationist, guru and mentor of my
early years.
The late Mr MG Pillay, of Australia, educationist and
ex-inspector of schools; and his son Bala, for their warm
encouragement and faith in my abilities.
Professor Rajendra Chetty for his unstinting support and erudite
back cover blurb.
Jeff Jhaveri and Suren Patel, for providing me with the space
to work undisturbed and in peace.
Razia Amod, who typed, retyped and then typed once more —
always with a lovely smile and the patience of a saint.
My early readers: Babs Amod, Yasmin and Shaquir Salduker,
Yasmin and Afzal Khan and, especially, Rashida Mulla.
Thad Metz of the University of Missouri, St Louis (USA),
and Adila, for their constructive comments, suggestions and for
encouraging me to "hang in there" whenever my enthusiasm waned.
Andrew Verster, who was there for me when I needed a boost.
Arvind Sardar for his unstinting devotion.

I salute them all.

chapter one

Durban: January 1882 — Yahya/Pravin

In the year 325, before the birth of Lord Jesus Christ, Alexander the Great, conqueror of half the known world, was finally stopped at the borders of the North West frontier Province of India. His disciplined army, the most feared fighting machine of the time, could advance no farther. The warrior Pathan of India had stopped him in his tracks.

For almost two years Alexander camped on the barren land between Afghanistan and Greater India, initiating occasional forays against a formidable opponent before finally conceding that the Pathan was a warrior that could be neither intimidated nor defeated. Severely wounded, weakened in spirit and facing a revolt from his terrified commanders, the great General bowed graciously to a superior enemy, saluted the heroic Pathan and turned back towards Macedonia.

Yahya Ali Suleiman was a descendant of that fierce tribe of India, a man who asked for no quarter and gave none. He considered himself beholden to no one except God, requested no favours and bestowed no largesse. Mingled within his Pathan blood was a drop of the Great Mughal who had, at some time in the dim past, taken one of his ancestors in marriage. The mixture of those great warrior tribes, the Pathan and the Mughal, was reflected in his bearing and his posture as he quietly waited in the stifling reception room. The inherent arrogance, however, seemed tempered by some recent event although, even then, it was barely held in check.

Pravin Naran was a Hindu from the State of Gujerat, the offspring of a gentle, cultured people. His father and his father's father, who was his

11

dada, as much as his maternal grandparents, had inculcated in him the strong belief that "he who throws the first punch loses the argument". Violence was contrary to his nature, his religion and his existence.

Naran was, by profession, a *Bunya* — a businessman. His philosophy was steeped in the concept of *Ahimsa*, a way of life that precluded harm to any living creature. In his dealings with his fellow men he was guided by the principle of courtesy and honesty, his motivation a reasonable profit for his goods or services.

The cut and thrust of business afforded him his greatest pleasure, to best a worthy adversary in a transaction was a matter of pride and achievement — though never at the expense of another. If both parties to a deal failed to derive a benefit, Naran simply refused to participate. This was not to suggest that he was a saint of sorts, not by any stretch of the most fanciful imagination. He was simply a man of his word who expected others to subscribe to the same standards.

Amongst Naran's people there was a crude saying: "To be a man, a real man, you must have arse." Conversely, a man who retreats in the face of any opposition or takes a backward step is contemptuously referred to as having had his arse torn: "*Guyn fati gai.*" Such a reference was usually exchanged in mock humour, occasionally with extreme crudity, hardly ever in anger.

The tragedy was, as is common in such cases, that people of other races sometimes misinterpreted the *Bunya* philosophy as a sign of weakness or the stance of a coward — they seldom did so with impunity and almost always to their great regret.

The concept of a *real man*, in the make up of a *Bunya*, had nothing whatsoever to do with physical strength or the ability to wage war: any fool can inflict violence and the more primitive the man the greater the tendency to do so. Sheer guts in business, on the other hand, where fortunes could be made and lost overnight, presented a challenge worthy of a civilized individual. Best these people in a business transaction and they responded with delight. Cross them and you would see another side to their character, often after many years had passed and the infidelity was all but forgotten. Insult a *Bunya* in public and very likely he'd turn his back in contempt. Slap his face and his lower lip would tremble in anger and he would simply walk away. However, to make the cardinal error of trying the same tactics on his family or towards those he loved would be an act of stupidity. Fools, emboldened by the *Bunya's* Christ-like response, occasionally made such a mistake. They seldom went on to brag about it.

Pravin Naran was such a man. And he now had to face the wrath of the

Pathan seated in his outer office, a man whom he had only vaguely heard of and known to him only by his first name: Yahya.

❧

For a long while Naran remained motionless, lost in thought as he attempted to recall everything he knew of the psyche of the infamous Pathans. "*Hai Ram*", he muttered over and over again: How does one deal with this savage, this product of the arid North West of India, this descendant of the arrogant KHANS whose traditional solution to any problem was the knife — or the rifle — whichever was nearest to hand? He subscribed to no laws of what Naran considered civilized behaviour. He came from a land that was the world's wildest and harshest frontier. In that rugged, mountainous region, bloody tribal vendettas were a way of life, a daily dance with death.

Famed for their fierce independence and ethnic pride, they subscribed to one law only: *Paktünwali* — the way of the Pathan. The chief obligation of this code of honour, its binding force, was *Badal*, or revenge, which stipulated an eye for an eye, a tooth for a tooth. In many ways it was this very quality that was so revered by all Indians, for the Pathan was the natural guardian of the Khyber Pass, the gateway through which many times in the course of history invading armies had attempted to breach its defences on their way to the conquest of the Indian subcontinent. Their success was measured only in the degree by which they failed.

Naran dug deeper into the recesses of his mind. There was another aspect to *Paktünwali* and he dredged his memory to recall the salient details. Slowly, from the folklore of his youth, the word *Maelmastya* emerged, and then he had it — the second code of the frontiersman's custom: the right to hospitality, which extended to an enemy as much as a stranger. Naran realised that it would have to be this aspect that would have to form the basis of their discussion — dealing with a Pathan is a gentleman's game. He sighed heavily. His delicate nerves were not soothed by the decision.

Naran clapped his hands, the sharp echo resonating off the walls of his office. Ramu, who served as his general factotum, responded to the summons, followed closely by the lean and rangy Pathan who was attired in the everyday dress of his people: long shirt, short waistcoat and the loose fitting *shalwar*. Only the turban was missing. Naran, who expected the visitor to remain where he was until called, was mildly annoyed by the man's presumption. With an angry gesture he quietly dismissed Ramu.

13

Immediately, even as he stood up, Naran felt intimidated by the man's presence. He was still contemplating the manner his greeting should take when the Pathan embraced him and, in a voice as soft as melted butter, said, "*Namasté bhai*". Naran, somewhat disconcerted by the unexpected warmth, returned the greeting and indicated a chair across from his own. In an attempt to regain the initiative he raised his right hand and began to speak in Gujerati, his voice firm but controlled.

"You dealt with *Dakus*, parasites of the business community. You were no more than grist for their mill. The world over, the purchase or sale of land is subject to certain set rules which must be observed before payment is made. You entered into negotiations with dishonest people and you failed to reduce your agreement to writing. You paid cash for a valuable piece of land without completing a document recording the transaction. With the utmost respect to you, that was foolish."

Naran paused for breath and to ascertain the man's reaction. The Pathan's face was impassive. He was listening intently, taking in every word.

"I subsequently bought the land," Naran continued evenly, "And through the correct channels. You must believe me when I say that I did so in all sincerity and completely unaware of your previous dealings, let alone your interest in the matter. Now you come to me, believing no doubt that I am somehow responsible for your misfortune. I assure you nothing could be further from the truth. My first intimation of your involvement was when our mutual friend Madhoo Daya informed me of the situation an hour ago and requested that I grant you an audience."

Naran sighed. The encounter was both distasteful and unnecessary. He spread his arms wide and addressed the warrior again, choosing his words with care, reluctant to offend the other's quick temper.

"What I now have to say to you gives me no pleasure. You must believe that. The world of business is not your world. You are totally out of your element. Your people have protected the borders of our motherland from foreign invaders from time immemorial. That was your function, a job in which you were accomplished. When you venture into business you enter a world alien to your nature. The world of commerce is governed by many and complex rules. Whilst you acted honestly you were nevertheless either unaware of those rules or you chose to ignore them.

"I acknowledge that your lack of experience in these matters should not be the basis for exploitation. But that is the reality. In a court of law you can prove nothing. And, of course, this is South Africa. Your traditional methods of obtaining satisfaction will not serve you here. And there is even less I can do for you.

"There is a saying that the people of my village are fond of repeating. Experience, they say, is the best teacher. People often forget the rider: but the fees are high. Consider that you have paid those fees. You are a poorer but a wiser man for it. All you can now do is learn from the experience.

"Come to me again, on any other matter where my knowledge is useful, and I promise you my counsel and at no cost to you. But in this particular situation I cannot help you."

Naran was aware that throughout his speech the Pathan had looked him straight in the eye, had not interrupted once, neither by manner nor by words. Anxious now to bring the meeting to a conclusion, he began to rise.

The Pathan quietly raised his hand, the rest of his body absolutely motionless, restraining the movement Naran had made. Well, Naran thought, here it comes. He had to consider himself fortunate in that he had been allowed to finish his speech. What needed to be said had been said. From here on it was in the lap of the gods. He folded his hands over his stomach and leaned back in the chair. He was damned if he was going to allow this savage to intimidate him.

When the Pathan spoke, Naran received his first surprise. The man's voice was soft, no hint of anger or recrimination in it.

"I am aware that this is not your problem. I have no quarrel with you. I accept that you acted honourably when you made your purchase. There is no reason why you should be talking to me, but you are and for this courtesy I will be eternally grateful to you. A Pathan does not say such things lightly."

The Pathan had paused, as if allowing the implication of what he had said to be absorbed, then continued: "Whatever the outcome of this discussion, I will bear you no malice, now or in the future. I wish you to understand that I say this in all sincerity. You are under no obligation to hear what I now wish to say but I request that you do so, if for no other reason than simply as a gesture of goodwill to a fellow countryman in an alien land."

Naran was intrigued. He was hooked and he knew it. He couldn't have terminated the conversation if his life had depended on it. For a short second longer he contemplated the fierce countenance of the man who sat across from him, his appearance in complete contradiction to the words. Finally, he nodded.

"Thank you. How I resolve my problem," the Pathan continued in his strange monologue, revealing for the first time a touch of emotion, "and deal with those who have taken advantage of my ignorance of the rules is an issue that, in all fairness, does not concern you. Let me be the first to acknowledge that." The peculiar timbre in the man's voice, the way in which it dropped an octave, sent a shiver up Naran's spine. He silently thanked the heavens above that he was not the recipient of the threat that was implied in the tone.

"I have a proposition to make to you. If my request does not meet with your desire I promise you that will be the end of the matter and I will not bother you again. You have my solemn word on it.

"On the other hand, if you are generous enough to come to an arrangement with me, you will have made a friend for life. In the years to come it is possible you may have occasion to call upon that friendship, in matters that are beyond the scope of your abilities. You will not find me wanting. I must stress, however, that any such concession from you can only be given of your own free will and without any fear of retribution should you refuse. For what I have just said I expect no credit nor do I expect you to be grateful — to refuse my request is your right. Allow me now to proceed with what I have to say or show me the door."

Long before the Pathan had ceased to speak Naran had begun to straighten up and was now leaning slightly forward, a hint of admiration in his eyes. He could not have said it better himself. Somewhere in the genes of the Pathan there was the mystic quality of *Vaniagiri*, the ability to cope diplomatically with adversity and turn it into an advantage.

This was no simple frontiersman. Unversed in the ways of commerce perhaps, but far from a fool. What Naran had initially assumed was no more than an ingenuous buffoon was proving to be a man to be reckoned with, behaving with a wisdom and restraint that even the Great Akbar would have been proud of. Not trusting himself to speak lest he give his thoughts away, Naran indicated with a nod of his head that he wished to hear the Pathan's proposition. That was when he received his second surprise.

"You know that I cannot relocate my small store, nor do I wish to suffer the insecurity of a tenant. I ask simply for this: sell me a quarter of the rights to the property, only the portion on which the store stands, at the full price that you paid for all of it. And trust me to pay you within the time period that we agree upon now. I am a Pathan, my word is my bond. You know this. But I do not expect you to rely on that alone."

He had barely finished speaking when he reached into the sleeve of his *kameez* and, from a hidden pocket, extracted an old leather pouch. The material was almost black with age, and worn to a fine shine from repeated handling. And it was heavy, that much was obvious from the thud it made as it was placed on the table, within reach of Naran.

"This is my security," Yahya said. "I am prepared to leave it with you, in trust, until I have paid you in full."

Naran picked up the pouch and hefted it a few times before untying the leather thongs. With unnecessary care he unfolded the bundle. When he inserted his hand into the deep pocket his fingers felt the warmth of the metal within it. He sensed, even as he extracted it, that it was a weapon of some sort. What he wasn't prepared for was the beauty of the dagger as it lay in the palm of his hand. That was the final surprise.

Naran placed it on the table between them and gazed at it in awe. It was an antique from the Mughal period, moulded more than a hundred years ago, at the very least. The scabbard and hilt of the dagger were of solid gold, studded lavishly with emeralds, rubies and rose-cut diamonds. It was an item created by several specialist craftsmen working as a team, the precious stones set in the *Kundan* style. The curved blade, in the distinctive shape of the Gurka *kukri*, was of the finest tempered steel and slid easily out of its protective sheath.

Naran, who had visited the best museums in the world, had never seen the likes of it anywhere. It was a thing of immense beauty and was absolutely priceless, the intrinsic value alone sufficient to pay for the property under discussion a hundred times over. As tempted as he was as it lay glittering in the lengthening shadows of late afternoon, it was nonetheless a weapon of destruction, conceived for no other purpose than to inflict death. It conflicted harshly with his sensibilities. Some of that revulsion must have been reflected in his face.

"It has been in my family from as far back as anyone remembers," Yahya said quietly, misinterpreting Naran's reaction. "It was handed down to my father by his *dada* and before that by his *dada's dada*. I have sufficient proof ..."

"No! No! I do not doubt its authenticity or its rightful ownership. But I cannot accept it, in trust or otherwise. It clashes with my belief, please put it away. But do not allow my rejection of it to dismay you. I am honoured by the trust you place in me and I have a proposition to place before you which, if you find acceptable, can resolve the problem you face."

Yahya's normally impassive face was a mixture of hope and confusion as he carefully returned the leather pouch into his shirt.

"I will sell the entire property to you, at exactly the price at which I purchased it, on one condition: from this day on, and until you have made full settlement of the debt, five percent of your gross profits will be handed over to me. Any losses will be for your account only. You will compute the amount on a monthly basis and pay it over as *uplung*. I take it you understand the concept, the meaning of *uplung*?"

"Yes. Any monies I pay over will be in cash. I will obtain no receipt in exchange."

"Good." Naran was pleased. The man was not totally unversed in elementary business concepts. "You appreciate that the profit portion of the payment will not be utilised towards a reduction of the capital sum. It merely represents a form of compensation for the money I have outlaid. Call it interest if you wish."

"I understand," Yahya responded, speaking slowly now, his mind working at a speed it was not accustomed to. "And the capital, you expect a lump sum payment?"

"That is up to you. As long as any instalment is a reasonably substantial amount."

"And am I correct if I assume that the percentage profit calculation will remain unchanged, regardless of any reduction in the initial capital?"

"That is correct."

"Then it would be to my advantage to retain such amounts, perhaps use them to increase my stocks and generate a greater turnover, expand my business ..."

Naran was delighted. The man was full of surprises, any doubts regarding his Mughal background were rapidly disappearing; such wily reasoning could only be the product of an illustrious background. How, in the name of all gods, did such an individual fall into the clutches of the *dakus* who had cheated him? Yet, Naran was fully aware, the man had genuinely been deceived. There was no doubt about that. He put the thought aside, to be reflected upon later. There was an aberration in the Pathan's character, it would be useful to know what it was. Aloud, he simply said, "You learn fast, my friend."

"Then we have an agreement?"

"Yes."

"You referred earlier to a transfer document. I do not mean to give offence but have no wish to make the same mistake twice, although I can see that as things now stand I have nothing to lose."

"That's not quite correct. You could build up the business swiftly, create a goodwill value. Without a written agreement to effect transfer in your name I could eject you at any time and retain such value for myself. Leave the agreement to me. Trust me to be fair in its content."

"The matter of the profit payment, will that also be a part of the document?"

"That won't be necessary. We are honourable men. Let's leave that part of it as a *bhai-bund* understanding, a gentlemen's agreement. I require no proof of sales or whatever. You alone will compute that amount and I will accept your word as the final arbiter concerning that item. If you require any assistance regarding the manner in which you should be making the calculation please feel free to call on me. But that is your decision. And if you haven't thought of it yet, there is no question of any rental payable by you."

Yahya was nodding his head, a little slowly. It dawned on Naran that he was moving too fast and that the Pathan, quick as he was, was having difficulty absorbing what was being said.

"Leave it at that. By this time tomorrow I will have prepared a written agreement for us to discuss and settle upon."

"*Atcha*! Fine. But there is a little matter I wish to settle in my mind." Yahya was speaking extremely slowly, choosing his words with care. He seemed to be formulating the sentences in his mind before articulating them. "We are men of honour but who knows what the future has in store for us. So long as I live I will honour this agreement. I understand the concept of *uplung* and why you do not wish to reduce it to writing. But what is your security? Once we sign the papers I could take forever to repay the capital and renege on the *uplung* payments."

"My security is your word of honour. If you don't keep to it ... well then ... that is my *karma*. I will only lose money. But you, my friend, your *karma* will manifest itself in the years to come. That is not a thing to treat lightly. You could also destroy what I believe is beginning to turn into a mutually valuable friendship. Only you can decide what that is worth."

"Forgive me if I upset you. I just needed to know the rules. What you call *karma* and my *Paktünwali*, there is little to separate them."

When they parted neither was aware that the foundations of two great dynasties had been put in place, over a simple embrace. The Gujerati, whose cardinal rule governing any business transaction was to give nothing for nothing, had made a monumental exception. The Pathan, who believed in taking possession of what he considered was his, by violence if necessary, had humbled himself against what was tantamount to a tribal conviction.

A bond had been forged between two families, one that would outlast both their lifetimes and extend well into the next century.

And long before the year 1882 drew to a close, Naran was forced to call on the Pathan for assistance, on a matter of life and death.

chapter two

Durban: 1986

It was an old face, ravaged by time. The full flowing beard was snow white. The eyes, in contrast, were bright and piercing, frightening in the intensity of the emotion reflected in them. The fanatic glare held his small audience and locked it into a hypnotic embrace. Something, perhaps the manner in which he moved his leonine head, the tone of his voice, sent a shiver up the spines of one or two of the younger members of his family.

Dara Yahya Suleiman cleared his throat as he surveyed the room. He had been speaking for some time and had broken off in mid-sentence, drawing air heavily into his lungs. In the silence that followed not a soul dared to speak. They were totally intimidated, he commanded their absolute attention. Deliberately, his hand trembling slightly, he stretched a huge gnarled paw and folded the knotted fingers around a glass of water. He took several long sips, coughed once, then lowered the glass. When he spoke again his voice was hoarse, tired.

"It is not my intention to frighten you," he said softly. "You are my flesh and blood. But you must face the facts. To hide from the truth is to behave like a barren woman dreaming of some day becoming pregnant. I must ask you to look at what will certainly happen, through my eyes.

"I see blood being spilled in the streets, the blood of my children and that of their children. I have no stomach for it. We are the descendants of a warring people but we have learnt to despise violence. We now prefer the route of arbitration, of negotiation, to reach an amicable solution. I regret that the time for that has now passed."

Dara had been speaking in English, in a slight guttural accent, choosing his words with care. In spite of having spent a lifetime in the country, never once leaving its shores, the language was still somewhat foreign to him. On occasion he was reduced to painstakingly translating his thoughts from the old vernacular before giving voice to them.

"The Afrikaner is obstinate, stubborn and unyielding. They are a people who have not lived long enough, have not yet developed the philosophy of reason. I say this with the greatest of respect for their achievements, but the truth remains that their culture is steeped in violence. They have sunk their roots deep into this land and those roots are nurtured by their ability to wreak havoc upon whoever opposes them. Theirs is the most efficient army on this continent and their police force could give lessons to the Nazis.

"They have taken this country by force and they retain that which they have looted by utilising the weapon of terror. They fear now that they are about to lose that which, in their misguided sincerity, they believe belongs to them alone and to no other race. They will not give up the smallest part of it, preferring to die rather than divide. They won this land through war. If they lose it, it will only be through another such encounter. This is not because I say so, these are the facts ... you may choose to believe whatever you wish. That is your right, but be careful that it is not also your greatest stupidity.

"The black man is now more militant than ever before ... and justifiably so. He no longer seeks equality. That concept was stillborn the day they threw Mandela in jail. It is my belief that he truly considers himself superior to any other race group and will not settle for less. I have no dispute with this — without pride in his origins a man is less than an animal. To believe himself to be above all others is his birthright. To dictate this opinion on others is oppression. My quarrel is with his methods, the manner in which he now goes about obtaining his freedom. And, regrettably, his past too is immersed in bloody conflict and he is prepared to lay down his life for what he also believes is rightfully his."

He lifted his head and glanced around him, his thick silver mane bristling as it flowed over the back of his head. His hand shook slightly as he once again raised the glass to his lips and took several sips.

"I do not speak of what will happen in the days to come. It has commenced — the great confrontation between these two mighty races. The country is going up in flames. There are those who believe, because they do not have the courage to face the reality, that the deaths and mutilations are restricted to the townships. They prefer to delude themselves into thinking this is a black-on-black thing. The more complacent amongst you may seek solace from similar delusions. Perish the thought, you cannot afford such luxuries.

"Always remember, before two mighty forces engage in battle, they first test their opponent's will by attacking the weak. That is already happening. Even as I speak the blacks are once again looting and pillaging our homes and businesses in Inanda — not much further from here than the distance a bullet travels. For us, it is like 1949 all over again."

Dara's neck had sunk deep into his shoulders, his eyes all but closed. For a brief moment he felt the old, long suppressed bitterness course through him. He tasted the bile that filled his mouth and threatened to seep through his clenched lips. With a supreme effort he subdued the emotion and swallowed heavily, slowly subsiding into the soft leather of his chair. In spite of himself, his mind was beginning to drift.

With startling clarity Dara recalled the brutal savagery of the Zulu hordes that had rampaged through the Indian ghettos of the city, systematically plundering and destroying every Indian property and leaving a trail of destruction and scores of dead and dying. The sounds and sights of the carnage wreaked on a defenseless section of the population overwhelmed him, cruelly beating through his mind like crude jungle drums. The massacre had continued for three days and two nights, without respite or relief and with a curious apathy displayed by the forces of law and order.

When it was over Dara had gathered his family around him, buried his dead, and stoically picked up the threads of his life from the smouldering ruins of his hard-earned possessions. The treasured acquisitions garnered over more than half a century had been wiped out virtually overnight. With a resolute will, born out of a primeval need for survival, he had started again with nothing and painstakingly built an empire which, though still under his absolute control, now vested in the three sons that sat before him. This time around he was determined that not one tiny portion of that fortune would ever be looted from him.

Dara shook his head, straightened his wasted body, and forced his thoughts back to the present. When he spoke again his voice was even, balanced, revealing nothing of the horror his mind had relived.

"Nothing has changed. Neither of these two powerful antagonists has any love for us. Like the Jew throughout the world, the Indian in this land is despised for the very reason that he is admired. Even as they seek to emulate us, they denigrate our culture, our education, our self-sufficiency and the fact that we look after our own.

"Why are these things held against us? When our forefathers came to this country they came as pioneers, unlike the early whites who landed here as a smug and snivelling bunch of parasites demanding handouts. Unlike those arrogant colonialists with their mighty European empires providing military support, nothing we own has been obtained by force or from behind a cannon or a rifle. We sweated for what we have and we paid for it far beyond the value we obtained. And we do not, in the manner of the Boer, claim to be God's chosen people, with the divine right to impose our will on honest people and usurp for ourselves what rightfully belongs to others.

"Like our ancestors, you and I made this country our home, we worked hard in a hostile land and we prospered. We have been fair, we have given more than our share to charity. Even our enemies are the first to acknowledge this. We built our own schools, hospitals and old age homes. And we opened them up to all races. It was not our laws that denied the black man access to these facilities. Our factories and trading houses provide employment for a great many of those very people who choose to consider us as their natural victims. And then, even as they enjoy the fruits of our efforts, at the cunning instigation of the very people who oppress them they claim that we are the real exploiters.

"When the riots of '49 failed to break our spirit, the State resorted to more overt measures, such as the Ghetto Act, which it implemented with a ruthlessness that would have shamed a ganglord. And to this day they continue to do so with impunity and with a shameless disregard of all the civilized nations of the world. Throughout all this, our people joined the blacks in the politics of resistance, holding high the banner of justice whilst their majority suffered in silence. In resisting and protesting against the State's infamy, we shed not a drop of blood, choosing instead the now world-renowned weapon of Passive Resistance, which we ourselves learnt at the feet of the great mahatma.

"There is a saying among wise men that when you fail to learn from your past you are condemned to repeat it. There is also a saying that when a man victimises you he should bow his head in shame. When he repeats that action you should bow yours.

"I believe there are those among us, including one or two in this very room, who are convinced we can still contribute more, that our rulers are on the run and are making the last-ditch stand of the mortally wounded animal. This may be true. I prefer to be more realistic. It is not in my nature to be cast as driftwood, subject to the vagaries of the wind and the tides. If we allow our responses to be dictated by events as they unfold, we will be judged by our descendants as a recreant generation, too weak to avoid the treacherous waters ahead.

"I prefer to learn from the past. I have no appetite for what it now tells me about the future. But do not take my word for it. Look around you, at this continent of Africa. What has it taught you? In country after country the white man has been the exploiter and has enriched himself. The Indian the victim who has been bludgeoned into paying the price, by the incensed indigenous inhabitants whose memories are short and their greed to emulate the now defeated rulers greater than their powers of logic. And where are those countries today? Where are the Indians who stood at their side and hoped to provide the economic base from which those countries could prosper? Am I now to be their meal, the bones off which they partake their last supper? I refuse to bury my head in the sand and trust to the folly of idealists who believe otherwise.

"The time has come for us to honour the pioneer spirit of our ancestors. Whilst I live I am the head of this family. By the will of God, you and yours are my responsibility. I have searched my soul. I have considered the options. The conclusion is inescapable. *We must leave this country. Now!*"

Dara was prepared for the reaction that followed his last sentence, had braced himself for it. In the immediate angry silence preceding the inevitable protest, his eyes had looked into those of his eldest son, from whom he expected the greatest opposition. As Jake slowly straightened up, his strikingly handsome face flooded with anger, Dara held up both his hands in a placating gesture.

"Sit down, Yacoob. Hear me out. I am aware you disagree with much of what I have said. I do not hold that against you. I have granted you the courtesy of explaining in lengthy detail what our future here will be. I ask you for a display of the same courtesy now." Dara paused to sip more water, deliberately concentrating on the act of swallowing, allowing Jake to save face and concede the request. The confrontation would come later. For now he merely wished to finish what he had to say.

"Most of you," Dara continued, "have comfortably accepted the African way of life. The culture of Africa, its lifestyle, its struggle, has become a part of you. You cannot conceive of any other existence. I have not agreed with you, but I have learned to live with it."

"You are no longer young men and, without the resources to start again, you will end up as *dakus*, back to where, but for my efforts and the grace of the Almighty, you have extricated yourselves from. Without the energy and strength of youth you will not survive in such an environment.

You particularly, Yacoob, should not need to be reminded of that."

Dara's voice had gone up a little, the index finger of his right hand pointing accusingly. He sighed and lowered his hand.

"Let that be on your conscience. God will judge you when your time comes. I have no desire to usurp that function and judge you now. But I am an old man, my days are few. Before I depart this earth I wish to have no regrets, no cause for unhappiness at having failed to act in the best interests of my family.

"Delay your departure from this land if you wish. Pursue your heroic endeavours to achieve that which cannot be achieved. Those are not things that are within my control. But the women and children, yours and mine, will not be sacrificed to your romantic dreams. It is a matter on which I will brook no interference. And I will not enter into any discussion regarding the future of our business enterprise — as the controlling shareholder the final decision is mine.

"The necessary arrangements have been made. For several years now I have been manipulating our liquid resources and the structure of our fixed assets. We will lose much but there will be sufficient to commence again, in another more hospitable place, where our talents will be appreciated.

"I have initiated the first stage of the final move and the nature of these negotiations demand the utmost discretion. That is all I can disclose to you and all you need to know. You will act and behave accordingly. Discuss what you have heard today with no one and make no long-term commitments. There will be no further debate on this matter.

"Go now and join your families in celebrating the conclusion of the Fast."

With that, Dara stood up, signaling the end to the meeting. He was the patriarch again, the martinet whose decision was by tradition the final word and not subject to any further revision.

"Salim, join me in my study, in exactly half an hour."

Without so much as a backward glance Dara left the room.

⚭

"The old man's talking *kuk*!" Jake was on his feet, the suppressed anger reflected in his contorted face. He glanced at the open door through which his father had left and, out of a lifetime of imposed discipline, he instinctively lowered his voice. "His days are over anyway. He's running cold, like a real *chacha*. We belong here, we are part of the struggle. Damn it, Sam, this is our country. We can't just forsake the cause and ..."

"You disagree with him then?" Sam asked, his voice clipped, cold.

"It's not the issue," Jake responded, reluctant to enter into a verbal duel with Sam. "But shit, man ..."

"Jake, please cool it. This isn't the time for ..."

"Listen Sam," Jake interrupted, the anger resurfacing. "I've spent all my life being dictated to by the old man. It stops now. Hell, *bru*, he didn't even ask for our opinion. I'm sorry, but I can't go along with him this time."

"That's fine by me, Jake," Sam said softly. "But a little bit of the advice, okay? Right now he's calling the shots. If we decide to play hardball we simply don't have the ammunition to stand up against him. Think about it."

"Tell me something," Jake asked, his voice still angry, "Did you know of this, before today?"

"I knew something odd was going on. But this? No, Jake. It's the first time I heard of it."

"Ah, to hell with it," Jake said in a conciliatory tone. "You deal with it. You always were his blue-eyed boy. But Sam, listen to me. Negotiate whatever sweetheart deal you wish with him. I'll back up whatever you do. But don't talk to me about leaving. And you know I speak for Hannah too. That, my *bra*, is non-negotiable."

Jake strode out of the room, slamming the door behind him.

Sam turned to his younger brother, Rashid, and to his sisters, Ayesha and Hajra. When he spoke he sounded curiously like his father, radiating the same authority, a touch of the arrogance.

"All of you, please join Jake and the others. I won't be long. And not a word of what took place here."

Sam stepped up to Ayesha, smiling for the first time that morning, his love for her reflected in his eyes. "*Ben*, Ahmed will be curious. Say nothing. When the time is right, I'll speak to him." He leaned forward and kissed her on the cheek. "Sally," Sam continued, looking at his wife, and then at Jake's wife, Hannah, "I know I don't have to say this, but it's important that you keep this to yourselves. I'm sure *Baji* has discussed this with Ma already. She won't ask any questions. Go with God."

The greeting was softly returned, but Sam had already turned his back on them and was standing with his arms folded across his chest, looking through the large picture window at the activity in the garden below him. As soon as the room had emptied he dropped his hands to his side. "So," he mused aloud, "It begins." He took a deep breath, strode across the room to a corner table and reached for the phone, dialling from memory. He heard a click at the other end, then a quiet voice, "Yes?"

"He has made up his mind. It's exactly as you suspected. I'll need your help soon."

"Of course, Sam. Give me a call when you're ready."

∞

In his late forties, Salim Suleiman was in superb condition. A shade over six feet, lean and angular, he appeared at first glance deceptively thin and mild, a pushover — an assessment many an opponent had swiftly revised. His nut-brown skin was flawless, a natural tan that blended smoothly with his light brown eyes. A daily routine of thirty minutes in his private gym, followed by a brisk hot shower, had made his muscles rock hard with a tensile strength that manifested itself in his agile, quick movements.

It was accepted, without dispute or rancour, that he would, in time, be the obvious successor to the Suleiman empire, to whose fortunes he had contributed in no small measure. He had the uncanny ability to get to the heart of a problem swiftly and without any apparent thought. He implemented his decisions ruthlessly, seldom conceding to the opinions of his advisors and deferring only to his father, who was the final arbiter in all matters.

Sam loved his wife and children with the same single-minded devotion that he bestowed in caring for his body. His business life was his private affair. It was only on momentous occasions that he deigned to discuss his decisions with his wife, and then grudgingly and with scarcely concealed impatience.

He had married Salma when she was barely sixteen and just beginning to turn into the statuesque beauty that she retained into her middle years. She had borne him two girls and a boy, in the early years of their marriage, and all three had inherited the best qualities of both parents. Sam's attitude towards his children was that of the strict disciplinarian. In truth he could deny them nothing and they exploited the weakness shamelessly whilst pretending, at the same time, to be submissive and dutiful.

In reality, which Sam acknowledged privately, the anchor was his wife who was not deceived by the wiles and guiles of her daughters or the arrogance of her son. She brooked no nonsense from them. Nor was she averse to grabbing the nearest article to hand and slamming it against her children. She had attempted in vain, and by her own admission failed, to inculcate Eastern traditions and customs in any of them. That, however, had not deterred her and she continued relentlessly, at every opportunity, to extol the Indian way of life.

Salma herself was not, by any measure, orthodox in either dress or manner. She subscribed, nonetheless, to the highly valued concept of *izzat* — which not only governed an individual's standing in the community, but also determined the rules of respect and deference towards an older person. She could, at short notice, switch personalities and was equally at home with all race groups as she was with the community elders.

Sam had, in a manner typical of a large number of his generation, struck a delicate balance between his father and his own family, between tradition and a tolerance for change. He always dressed impeccably in stylish three-piece suits during normal working hours, shedding this in the evening for casual loose tops and jeans when at home.

He was dressed that morning in a deep cream v-necked cotton shirt, beige brushed-wool trousers and tan leather moccasins. He crossed the wide expanse of the well-tended lawn, walking loosely and with a welcoming smile on his face. As he joined the throng of family and close friends gathered around the braaivleis stands, the aroma of meat and spicy kebabs assaulted his nostrils. Instantly, he was enveloped in the festive atmosphere. The sound of disco music drummed into his ears and he could see the happy children, who outnumbered the grown-ups by three to one, moving their bodies to the rhythm of the sound, their gay clothes and mod hairstyles contrasting outrageously with the conservative garb of the more sedate older generation.

Sam was about to turn around when Ahmed, Ayesha's husband, stumbled towards him, his portly figure dressed in a ludicrous and badly cut off-white suit. He embraced Sam, hugging him first on the right shoulder, then the left, and once again on the right. The faint sour smell of whisky floated towards Sam who wrinkled his nose distastefully. A surge of anger flared through Sam and he was on the verge of pulling away when, over Ahmed's shoulder, he caught the pleading look in Ayesha's face, a forgotten plate of bread rolls in her hand. Sam smiled warmly at her, noted the grateful acknowledgment of relief as she silently thanked him and sadly turned away.

"Sam!" Ahmed gushed, "Well over the fast."

Sam returned the greeting coldly, then whispered angrily, "Where did you get the booze?"

"There's a bottle in my car. Come and ..."

"Go and wash your mouth and eat something that will take the *klunk* away. If I catch you having another drink ..."

"Sam ... I'm sorry ... I ..."

"This is not the time or the place for it. If you can't control yourself then leave this house."

Sam's face did not betray the menace in his voice. Outwardly, he was relaxed, smiling, ostensibly having a friendly chat.

Sam moved on, stopping from time to time to kiss a cheek in greeting; to clasp hands in the old way, gripping first the palm, then the thumb and finally the palm again, using his left hand to cover the handshake as a mark of respect. He followed strict protocol, seeking out the eldest and working his way down to the youngest — family first, then friends.

Someone had changed the music to a classic Hindi number, the singer a legendary artist who enjoyed immense popularity in the Indian community. Most of the children, eating and laughing merrily, had clustered into little groups. The lilting melody soothing his battered ears, Sam was pleased at the change.

He paused for a moment, running his fingers through his mostly intact salt and pepper hair. He heard a soft chuckle, turned in the direction of the sound and saw Karan Naran. They smiled warmly, pure pleasure reflected in their faces. They moved towards each other, arms stretched wide.

"The gods will be pleased," Karan said, his eyes twinkling. "Thirty days of abstinence are over. The body cries for sustenance."

"There is only one God," Sam replied mockingly, his grin belying the retort.

They embraced each other, the bond between them apparent even to a casual observer.

"Where's *bhabi*?" Sam asked, his hand lightly draped around Karan's shoulders.

"Devi's in the kitchen, where she belongs," Karan laughed, "helping your mother with the dishes."

They continued talking as they moved in the direction of the sparkling pool at the far end, the squeals of the younger children as they jumped in and out of the water growing in volume. As soon as they were out of earshot of the others Sam lowered his voice, his expression suddenly serious.

"Are they still rioting in Inanda?"

"I don't know for sure," Karan replied softly. "Only rumours reach us. I believe the Gandhi settlement has been totally destroyed, all the historic archives and documents lost in the fire."

"Your father's store?"

"Gone up in flames."

"Will the insurance cover you?"

"Are you joking? Those honkies never pay. They take the premiums with both hands and then hide behind some ridiculous statute that the courts happily enforce. They claim we do not have riot cover, that this is not an act of God ... so on. They refer us to some government department or other and continue to grow rich on our misery. It's an old story. The irony is that, in spite of dishonouring our claims, they immediately raise the premiums to cover what they sneeringly call an increase in the risk they are exposed to."

"Then why take out insurance at all?"

"Because the law demands it and the associated banks that the insurance cartels are shareholders of will not open an account for any company that does not have the necessary cover. You should know that, Sam."

"I suppose I should, but your office handles that side of my affairs. I seldom bother with the details and I have never had occasion to claim."

"Well, just make sure you don't have a fire, or a flood, or a theft, or ..."

"Okay! Okay! I get the message."

"Anyway, Sam, the store in Inanda was no great loss to us. It was only a small outlet with little stock, the premises rented on a monthly tenancy. The others were not so lucky."

"Your cousin ... ?"

"Home safe. He got out yesterday, before things got too bad. On the way out he saw several hotheaded Indians riding shotgun on a truck and traveling in the opposite direction, determined to rescue their friends and relatives."

"I hear there were many deaths on both sides."

"There's some truth in that. There's a story going around that some guy went crazy, shouting 'never again' over and over as he pumped bullets into the looters."

"What the hell are the cops doing!" Sam almost shouted. "They're never around when ..."

"Sam, take it easy," Karan interrupted.

"The hell I will. If that was a white area the whole damned army would have been there so fast ..."

"Sam, listen to me," Karan cut in harshly. Sam's voice had gone up several octaves, causing one or two heads to turn in their direction. "We can talk freely here but you can never tell. Perhaps we should go in the house where we can't be overheard."

"Okay," Sam said, lowering his voice. "But not yet. I have to join my old man in a few minutes. Let's rather meet at your place this evening. I need to talk to you urgently. My father has something up his sleeve. I'll know more about it by then."

"Fine. In the meantime I'll find out whatever I can about what's going on in Inanda. The unrest may be isolated and could soon blow over. And Sam ... listen, I don't want to sound heavy, it's not the day for that, but this new State of Emergency is different from anything we've been through before. Please be careful. They can lock anyone up, without access to legal representation, without visiting rights and with no recourse to the courts. Even the newspapers aren't allowed to publish any such detentions. What you said earlier, about the cops, that alone is enough to put you away for as long as it suits them. The best connections in the world wouldn't be able to help you then."

Sam's lips twisted into a caricature of a smile, his eyes bleak and lifeless. When he spoke his voice was hollow. "When they talked of Nazi Germany we wondered why the people didn't stop them. Now we're asking the same question again. Tell me, Karan, does freedom have a price or is it a right?"

"Determine first the nature of the battle. Survival before freedom. History merely records events, it seldom teaches us how to respond to them. Perhaps that is what is meant by civilization — to the extent that you fail to learn from your past, to that extent you remain rooted in history."

"My father's philosophy is different. He says he is civilized, therefore he must uproot himself and take a walk." Sam forced a chuckle. "I'm torn between two dictatorships — that of the State, which is based on hatred and committed to my destruction; and my father's, which is based on love and could destroy me nevertheless. And within the two your philosophy advocates survival. And what is it that I am surviving for? Which of the ashes will taste less bitter?"

Sam had expected to find his father alone. He was mildly surprised that Dara had a visitor. He was already backing out when his father beckoned to him. "Come in, Salim. Meet a friend of mine."

Sam entered the study and shook hands with a short, thickset man of indeterminate age. At first glance he appeared quite ordinary and Sam automatically assumed it was a casual visitor who had stopped by to offer the customary festive greeting. It was a routine that would be repeated often during the course of the day and he was about to retire to a far corner, giving Dara a chance to graciously remove the caller. Dara's subsequent introduction caught him by surprise.

"Salim, this is Vis Kander, of the Metalworkers' Union."

Caught off-guard, Sam barely concealed his surprise from showing on his face. The name had been enough. Kander was, without any doubt, the most powerful union boss in the country. He had featured prominently in all the newspapers and periodicals as an arch opponent of the government, until the stringent curbs on the press had all but removed him from the public eye. Men of Kander's stature seldom made casual calls and Sam instinctively knew that his presence was somehow a part of the overall plan that Dara had alluded to during the meeting earlier.

"My son is fully in my confidence," Dara said. "Please speak freely."

Kander nodded, settling comfortably in his chair. "As I've already told you, our source of funds has completely dried up. The government has blocked the receipt of development aid from Europe and our survival now depends on formulating alternative strategies. Depending on the size of your available resources we can strike a mutually beneficial deal, one that can solve both our problems.

"I must stress, though, that the sums involved are immense and may be beyond your reach and you may find it necessary to call on some of your associates to put together a consortium of sorts. My colleagues and I would have no objection to any such arrangement, provided always that our only line of contact does not extend beyond yourself ...," he jerked his head towards Sam, pointing with his chin, "... and your son here, but only if absolutely necessary."

Dara was listening intently, his elbows on the desk, his chin resting on his fist. His eyes had narrowed almost to slits, and when he spoke there was a slight edge to his voice, barely noticeable.

"I appreciate your concern. It is sad when honest businessmen are reduced to the level of *dakus*, forced to act like thieves in the night." He sighed, shaking his head briefly. "Do not misunderstand me, Mr Kander. What I said is not meant to cast any aspersions on you or your friends. I am, however, fully aware of the dangers inherent in what we propose to do. I, too, would require that we deal only with yourself at all times. But I am an old man now and must lean heavily on my son. Who can say how many days are left to me? It would be foolish of both of us to tempt fate unnecessarily. Besides, my son will take over from me in a few weeks. It would be wise to involve him at the outset, in both our interests." Dara spread his hands apologetically, palms up, in the age-old gesture of a man who has no alternative, who is helpless in the face of matters beyond his control.

Kander inclined his head, indicating acceptance. "I'm sure it's only a minor problem. You can take it from me that my colleagues will go along with whatever I recommend. With luck we can tie everything up pretty fast."

Dara visibly relaxed, satisfied with the way the discussion was proceeding. He smiled as he said, "Luck, my friend, is for gamblers. We can leave nothing to chance. You mentioned a large sum of money. Exactly what amount do you have in mind?"

"Three million," Kander replied, then added almost deprecatingly, "In American dollars."

Dara made a rapid mental calculation, his fingers curling slowly into his palms. "At current exchange rates that's roughly seven million rands. A consortium will not be necessary. I can handle that on my own."

Sam was startled. The magnitude of his father's resources had caught him unawares. He began to wonder what else he was not privy to. He was careful, though, not to give any indication of his surprise, realising instinctively that Kander could, at a later stage, exploit the knowledge if the opportunity afforded itself. Without Kander being aware of it, father and son had briefly glanced at each other, Dara's face registering approval at Sam's composure.

Kander had slowly straightened up in his chair, a look of dawning respect reflected in his attitude. "Excellent! Then we only need to run through the *modus operandi* and set up a system for the swop."

"I take it," Sam said, sensing that it was time he stepped in, "This will be a one-off deal, at the end of which we will have no need to stay in touch with each other?" It was a calculated manoeuver by Sam. If Dara remained silent, Sam had the answer to the extent of Dara's cash assets. If Dara intervened Sam would know that Dara had other funds secreted somewhere.

"I would like it that way," Kander replied, pre-empting any response from Dara. "It may be necessary to structure it over several tranches, spread over intervals of a few days between each transaction. Say a million rands at a time."

"Naturally, you will expect payment in cash, in banknotes."

"Yes. Preferably in fifty-rand notes. It will take time to count and balance such large sums, even with a team of operators."

"I can't guarantee that," Dara interrupted. "I mean the fifty-rand notes. You will appreciate that this is *uplung* money, hot money that the taxman knows nothing about, accumulated over a long period of time. A fair portion has been converted into notes of large denomination, but not all."

"I understand that and I'm sure we can live with it. Can we agree now, on the procedure?"

Sam looked at Dara, seeking permission to continue. Dara moved the index finger of his right hand and gave a slight nod of agreement.

"We will need a trustee, someone we have mutual faith in, whose function will be to hold the cash pending confirmation that the equivalent sum has been deposited in an overseas account specified by us. As each deposit is effected by your European contacts, the trustee will receive a call from our agent in London, whereupon he will immediately hand over the cash to you. Arrangements can be made for you, together with the trustee and ourselves, to count each tranche in advance and the package can be sealed in any manner specified by you. That way no time will be wasted during the handover."

"Your agent, then, will maintain a close relationship with the overseas labour union funding our local operations?"

"Only if necessary. All we require is confirmation that the funds have been deposited in our account and have been received by our bankers."

"Of course. I'm merely ensuring that I get the procedure correctly set up at our end. I understand that deals of this nature normally carry a premium, a form of commission payable by, in this case, yourselves. Can we talk about that now?"

"Normally, that is the standard procedure. A premium, currently ten percent, is usually added to the converted amount when payment is made locally. However, that is only paid when a local owner of foreign funds enters into such a deal. In your case you need the funds here as desperately as we need it overseas. There is a mutual benefit, a common need, and the question of commission does not arise. However, if my father feels otherwise ...?" Sam's voice trailed off, leaving an avenue open to Dara.

This was where the negotiations normally became somewhat sticky. The earlier part, the actual exchange of the monies, as complicated as it appeared, was really the simplest. It was when an agent attempted to obtain a personal benefit, settling on a percentage at one end and disclosing a lower rate at the other, with the hope of retaining the difference for himself, that problems usually arose; Sam was preparing to ease out of the discussion, signaling Dara with his eyes, when, to his astonishment, Kander seemed to capitulate.

"I have no dispute with what you said. Let us dispense with it. Now, as to the conversion rate, what is the basis of its determination?"

"The spot rate from time to time," Sam replied. "as each tranche is effected. Or we can agree on it now, as it stands at present. The choice is yours."

"I prefer to fix it now. I have no head for figures."

Sam looked at Dara, who moved in smoothly. "The fluctuations will be for our account, whichever way they go. I suggest we settle on it at whatever the fix is at noon tomorrow."

"As to the question of a trustee," Kander added, "we would be perfectly satisfied that you yourselves occupy the role. The procedure of counting the money and so on can be done in exactly the manner set out by you. Would you consider that fair?"

"We are honoured by your trust. You may be sure that you will have no cause to regret it."

"Then our negotiations are complete and we can shake on it. I will return to you at nine in the morning and we can set the ball in motion."

Kander paused, then asked, "I'm curious. You don't have to answer if you so desire, but are you not interested in the use your money will ultimately be put to?"

"You should know better, Mr Kander," Sam replied. "We are businessmen. This represents no more than a simple transaction conducted secretly by honest traders who are precluded from acting openly by an unjust government that makes a mockery of the free enterprise system. In any other country we can do these things without fear of prosecution, through any legitimate banker. We are simply buying dollars from you. What you do with your proceeds of the sale is entirely your affair. The morals of the transaction do not enter into the discussion."

Sam had been talking fast and he paused now to take a deep breath. Before he could continue Kander quietly cut in. "Mr Solomon, it was an idle question. I'm a union official, concerned with the welfare of my members. The money will be utilised toward training the workers and promoting their advancement. I merely mention it in passing. I appreciate your comments, that you have no interest in its eventual distribution. Please forgive the curiosity of a layman."

The apology was sincere, free of sarcasm or innuendo. They shook hands and Sam walked Kander to his car. As Sam headed back to the study he was thinking: now comes the interesting part. The old man is a wily fox indeed. Seven million! There is no way he could have amassed such a fortune without my knowledge. There has to be an explanation ...

When Sam reached Dara's study his father had already left, retreated to the left wing of the house where his quarters were located. Pursuing him there was a waste of time. Dara did not suffer intrusions into his privacy. There was nothing to do but wait until Dara himself decided it was time to disclose further information.

∞

The dining room was huge, sumptuously furnished. One wall was almost entirely covered by an oriental carpet of pure silk, interwoven with a religious motif depicting the blue-skinned Krishna, playing a flute whilst the Gopis frolicked around him. An accurate, miniature reproduction of the famous Taj Mahal, carved out of a block of marble a foot square and placed on an ornamental fretwork base of contrasting colours, adorned a far corner. Interspersed around the other walls were ivory and brass figurines of various sizes and in distinctive poses. In pride of place was a copper statuette, almost three feet high, of a nautch girl frozen in the act of completing an intricate movement. The overall effect was opulent without being cloying.

Karan sat at the head of the table, with Sam on his left and Salma on the right. Karan's widowed sister and her sixteen-year-old daughter, Darika, were seated opposite Sam. Alongside Sam was his youngest daughter, Azra, together with a fifteen-year-old, a school friend of Darika's who was spending the holidays with Karan's family.

An empty chair, directly across from Karan, was reserved for Devi, who only occupied it intermittently as she hurried back and forth between the kitchen and the diningroom. On each trip she rapidly filled the bowls with steaming curries, faster than they were emptied. Karan had long ago given up any attempt at pinning her down, reluctantly accepting that it was the traditional role of the Indian housewife whose prime concern was her guests.

The three teenagers were dressed identically, in jeans and loose tops. They were impatient to get away, to be done with the meal and escape from the watchful eyes of the parents. They giggled occasionally at some private joke, flashing their doe eyes at each other in mock sufferance, the fact that their antics were completely ignored having no effect on their behaviour.

The main course, which consisted entirely of spiced vegetable dishes, was expertly prepared and a tangy aroma wafted up from them and enveloped the diners, whetting their appetites.

The table overflowed with a variety of dishes that would have been bewildering to anyone other than those accustomed to Indian cuisine. Dhals, beans, lentils, fresh vegetables, peas and potatoes, cauliflower and cabbage — all individually cooked and superbly presented. Piles of roti, the circular unleavened bread without which even the simplest of meals would be incomplete, fresh rolls and the inevitable savoury rice, were surrounded by tiny containers of a dozen different varieties of pickles: mango, lime and carrot among others. Crispy wafer-thin papadum and lightly tossed salads, together with tiny thimbles of fiery chutneys, were placed within easy reach of everyone.

Young and old used the tips of their fingers only, an art in itself, cultivated since early childhood. For dessert there was rice pudding, sweet and sour buttermilk *lassi*, fruit in season, followed by tea and coffee. The meal was consumed in an atmosphere of convivial bliss, the conversation flowing smoothly.

At last the men fell back in their chairs, Sam letting out a whoosh of appreciation. While the elders laughed the girls were quick to jump up, hurrying to clear the table, after which they would wash the dishes and clear the kitchen. Only when that was over could they gracefully escape.

Sam and Karan quietly withdrew to the den, a male preserve which the women only entered at the expense of a sharp rebuke.

"So," Karan asked, "How forthcoming was the old *topee*?"

Sam sighed and shook his head. "Like so many others who think like him, he is joining the chicken run. And, in his usual blinkered way, he's taken it for granted that the rest of the family will tag along with him whether they like it or not."

"Jake will never agree to such a move."

"He's made that pretty clear already. I'll say this much, Karan. The old man makes a damn persuasive case. Not even Jake can refute one word of his argument."

"And you?"

"What can I say against such clear and logical conclusions. He paints a bleak future for us in this country and I must admit that he behaved completely out of character. Before he laid down the law he spelt out chapter and verse of our history in this country. It's impossible to discard his reasoning, there are no grounds on which I can ask him to reconsider. On the strength of what he said it would be tantamount to asking him to commit suicide — and take the whole family with him."

"So there's no hope of dissuading him."

"None. All I can do is play the dutiful son and go along with him, win his confidence and hope he'll play open cards. He's cagey as hell though and playing it close to his chest. All I know so far is a large sum of money will soon be siphoned out of the country. What I don't know is where it's coming from."

"If it's reached that stage it may be too late to stop it."

"I don't intend to. With the way the exchange rate is going the rand will be down to thirty US cents before the year is out. I can always arrange another swop, bring it back and make a killing in the process. The trick is to obtain control of it at the other end, win my father's confidence and gently ease him out of the driver's seat."

"Easier said than done, Sam."

"I know. I can only try. As far as the local operations are concerned, once he has stripped the property companies of their assets he'll simply transfer all his shares over to me. He'll want to keep the retail outlets going as long as the cash flow is as large as it is now. He'll probably keep one foot in this country for a while, move the women and children out and settle them into a new life only God knows where. And, when things become intolerable, as he is convinced they will, he'll move whoever is still here at a moment's notice."

"Is there any hope at all of diffusing his plans?"

"Without knowing what they are? Look how far he has gone and he hasn't even approached you yet. You are our legal and financial man, your office has always attended to these things, from the time of our respective grandfathers. He trusts nobody."

"I know him. He'll probably present me with a file when everything is neatly signed and sealed. When it's a *fait accompli*."

"I have a few ideas as to the direction in which he is moving. More so now after today's discussion with Kander, but I have to know where the money is coming from. I had a hint from an old friend of ours who picked up something in the marketplace. He suspects Dara is making a package deal to sell the properties. That makes sense when you consider that he was raising loans on the security of our fixed assets. You pointed that out to me more than a year ago."

"It was a casual observation. I assumed that Dara, in his usual obtuse way, was building up a kitty to buy something big, like a shopping centre or some such thing."

"We know better now. The only purpose that makes any sense is that he wanted to facilitate the eventual sale, make it easier for the buyer to take over the bonds and come up with the difference. It's a delicate but well thought out manoeuver. Dara must have transferred the proceeds from the bonds to a private account somewhere. If I recall correctly, he reduced all the shareholders' loan accounts pretty close to zero. But even then the amount is nowhere near the sum under discussion with Kander."

"It's the sort of devious manipulation that Pravin-dada was expert at."

"He was obviously Pravin-dada's star pupil, all those cosy evenings they spent together were not wasted. Whilst you and I laughed at what we thought was the cackle of two old men in their dotage they were thirty years ahead of their time."

"Pravin-dada," Karan mused. "Your grandfather and mine, they were quite a team."

"So were my father and Pravin. After your old man died in the riots, Dara was all Pravin had. He took the place occupied by your dad. He certainly learnt well at Pravin's feet. Anyway, my problem was to find out who Dara was planning to sell the properties to and for that purpose I needed the services of somebody who could ferret out the information for me without raising Dara's suspicions. That way I could step in with a false front before Dara could conclude a deal, and secretly buy back our assets myself. I also needed to put the funds in place to enable me to effect the purchase. Immediately after the meeting this morning, I made a phone call and took the first step in that direction."

"What worries me is how the hell did your dad expect to suddenly make the money disappear from his asset and liability statements. The bond funds, together with the residue from the sale of the properties, have to be accounted for somewhere."

"He wouldn't give a damn about such things. You know Dara, he is accustomed to sailing close to the wind. But he is shrewd as hell too. You can be sure he's covered all the angles."

"Who did you speak to?"

"The person who first gave me the hint that Dara was preparing to sell out."

"You said it was a mutual friend of ours."

"Yes. Nits Vania."

"What!" Karan looked shaken. "You're dealing with 'The Fixer', after all these years ..."

"Why not? We have always been very close, even after I walked off the streets. And Jake and Nits, you know how tight knit they are. And what about you, Karan? There was a time when we were inseparable: you, Nits, Sandy, Jake and I. Have you forgotten?"

"No, Sam. I do still see Nits, at a few social functions. Sometimes we even throw around a few memories from the old days. But that's as far as it goes. When it comes to business I draw a line."

"Why? In his own way Nits is more honourable than any businessman I can think of at the moment, though that may not be his public image."

"But Sam, the guy's a thug, a master of the subtle strong-arm tactic, his tentacles stretch so far into the underworld that even some of the *Motas* are wary of him."

"That depends on who he is dealing with. Visit him at home, socially. You'll be surprised at how warm he can be. Kathy literally pushes him around and he just smiles and ..."

"Kathy is a real lady. I'll never know what she saw in him. And that goes for Maliga and Hannah, in spades. How the hell did those *dakus* have enough sense to choose so wisely? Maliga and Sandy? Hannah and Jake? It's a bloody mystery to me."

Sam burst out laughing. "You know what's wrong with you, Karan? You never really were on the streets. A year or two would have done wonders for your outlook on life."

"No thanks. You had it, Sam. I'll draw on your experience when I need it."

"Then do so now. Let me tell you something that is not generally known. Nits has moved up in the world. You'd be surprised at the kind of people he mixes with these days. He's the confidante of some of the biggest names in the Indian business world and very little happens without him knowing about it. He no longer finances bail money for the thugs. He is a big wheel now and is virtually a banker in his own right, with one big difference — he can step in at short notice and provide enormous sums of money without requiring any underlying security. Where do you think that kind of money comes from? On his own he is not so fabulously wealthy. You'd be surprised at some of his partners, many of whom you venerate as pillars of society"

"Okay, so I misjudge him. But tell me, is there any truth in the rumour that he is an ANC man?"

"A man like Nits is as surrounded by rumour as a mangy dog is by fleas. If it is true, though, then I reckon it's a big plus for him. It confirms my estimation of his integrity."

"Enough of this, Sam. Let's get back to the main issue. What do you think Jake will do?"

"He has made it pretty clear. He'll go along with me. He is right about one thing though — the days of men like Dara are over. Their fires are beginning to burn out. They act on instinct, born out of years of insecurity and nurtured in the fear generated by political impotence; the death rattle of frightened old men unable to come to grips with the reality of life. I'm not saying their analysis of the situation here is faulty, I've already admitted that Dara makes a hell of a lot of sense. It's his solution to the problem that I object to."

"One can't blame them ..."

"I don't, especially when we see the thousands of whites packing up and leaving the country. But those are people who never belonged here anyway. The majority of them were freeloaders. In comparison, our numbers are negligible. But we know no other country, Karan. Like the Afrikaner and the Coloured, we are here to stay. We made our money here, it must remain here. We must continue fighting until we emerge victorious and then help build a new world for all our people."

"That is up to the Afrikaner. He wields the mighty sword. Whether or not this land goes up in flames is entirely a decision only he can make. The rest of us can merely indulge in the politics of protest. So far that has not achieved a thing."

"Up to a point, yes. But the descendants of the Voortrekkers are not inherently evil. No man of the soil is. Forget about the mavericks among them. The rest want for their people exactly what we want for ourselves. The real catalyst here is their leaders who will plunge this country into chaos. They're like a bunch of gamblers playing Russian roulette with somebody else's life. They can afford to be reckless. What do they have to lose?"

"If that's true, that the majority of the whites are basically decent people, tell me why the Nats repeatedly get voted into power, with ever-increasing majorities?"

"Because they frighten their constituents into believing there's a bogeyman around every corner and only they, the State, stands between them and destruction. It's a plot of Machiavellian duplicity, the old story of absolute power corrupting absolutely."

"So you're saying that all those whites who gobble up with both hands the bounty that the State heaps on them are just whitewashed, misguided poor souls who have lost even the power of reason. I don't think they will be pleased by that theory. It reduces them to the level of slavering animals, salivating at the mere thought of all the free lunches they receive."

"Then tell me, how do you account for what Hitler was able to do, the way he turned the Germans against the Jews, set them off into a mass killing spree against decent, honest citizens?"

"It hasn't quite reached that stage here."

"No it hasn't, or perhaps we just don't know yet if it has. Remember, it was many years later that the truth of Nazi atrocities dawned on an unsuspecting world. But you still haven't answered the question, you haven't accounted for Hitler. Mass hypnosis is no longer a theory, many eminent scientists suspect there is a basis for such a technique."

"So get someone to snap a finger," Karan scoffed. "I'm tired, Sam. This country does that to you."

"Then you're a candidate for Dara's exodus. I've never run in my life. I'm too old to start now. As Pravin was fond of saying: 'No man can escape his *karma*!' It's not something you can run from."

"I'm no good at this, Sam. We are not intellectual giants."

"Of course. I'm merely indulging in a bit of catharsis, getting if off my chest."

chapter three

Durban: 1882 — Yahya/Dara

Yahya crossed the dusty street and stepped into Madhoo Daya's tiny workshop, which occupied the display window of a store selling farm implements and sundry hardware. Yahya greeted Mr Essack, the owner, and pulled a chair close to Madhoo, who sat on the slightly raised platform.

"You look satisfied," Madhoo said, his fingers flying as he handstitched a new waistcoat.

"Pravin Naran is a reasonable man," Yahya replied. "We have come to a happy arrangement. I will be able to retain the store and buy it in time to come."

Madhoo nodded, not lifting his eyes as he concentrated on the sewing. "And the *dakus*? Do you know where they are?"

"No." Yahya shrugged his broad shoulders. "Our *hajam* from across the road, Nathoo *bhai*, says he heard they had left for Mombasa a few days ago. I believe him. The barbers always know what's going on."

"So the ring is lost forever."

"Perhaps. But our paths will cross again one of these days. I will recover the ring, or its value in money. It's just a matter of time."

"Men like those two, they always come back looking for more *gharachs*. You will join me for meals later?"

"Yes," Yahya said, as he stood up. "Now I must see to my store."

For the next three months Yahya pushed himself to the brink of exhaustion, opening the store at seven in the morning and seldom closing his doors until after six in the evening. Even after that, the long summer

45

days gave him almost a full hour of daylight during which he hurried to the suburbs and bought old pots and pans which he worked on at home till late at night. With infinite patience he mended, restored and polished them till they shone in the moonlight, only stopping for a short break when he joined Madhoo for meals and, occasionally, a cup of tea.

By the end of April the stocks in Yahya's store had grown considerably. He lived frugally and, without the expense of having to pay rent, he ploughed back every penny into the business. His reputation for honesty and the quality of his repairs ensured a steady stream of satisfied customers who called on him to mend their damaged articles and simultaneously purchased a few items of new goods. His white customers, particularly, liked his silent manner and quiet dignity and often made the trip simply to watch him as he worked, his brawny arms rippling as he struggled with the heavy steel utensils. Yahya was content in the knowledge that things were at last beginning to look up.

On a Friday, early in May, Yahya was about to retire for the night when there was a timid rap on his door, followed by several loud knocks. He glanced at the clock, noted that it was almost ten, grunted as he opened the door, raising the Coleman lamp high above his head. Ramu, Pravin Naran's servant, stood trembling in the doorway.

"*Saab*, I have a note for you from Pravin *seth*."

"Are you cold?," Yahya asked, as he unfolded the paper and held it close to the lamp.

"*Jaldi, saab*! Please hurry."

Yahya squinted as he strained his eyes to read the rough scrawl: "Come quickly. I need your help." He lowered the lantern to the floor, reached behind the door for his *achkan* and slipped his arms through the wide sleeves. As he shrugged the knee-length overcoat onto his shoulders he asked, "*Kiya*? Pravin *bhai* is okay?"

"Please *saab*. The *seth* is in trouble. There are men in the back yard."

"Come!" Yahya said, snuffing out the lamp and shutting the door.

"Yahya?" It was Madhoo's voice, from his open window.

"It's nothing, *bhai*," Yahya said. "I'll be back in a while."

Ramu was panting as he struggled to keep up with Yahya's long strides, almost trotting as he gasped, "It is better if we go through the passage in Grey Street. The men are at the back."

Yahya simply nodded, immediately changed direction and crossed over towards the narrow lane. Within minutes they were at Naran's door, which swung open as they reached it.

"Yahya, thank you for coming." Even as Naran spoke Yahya could hear angry shouts as several voices hurled insults towards the interior and taunted Naran to step into the yard.

"They are *kalassis*," Naran said. "From the crew of the Indian vessel that came in today."

"What do they want?" Yahya's voice was calm, radiating a quiet confidence that immediately reassured Naran. Even the frail Ramu stopped trembling.

"I received a parcel of gold sovereigns from home, delivered by a trusted crew member. Somehow his mates must have found out about them and followed him to my office. When he left they came in and demanded a share of the coins, as their reward for its safe passage to me. I asked them to wait in the outer office whilst I slipped out the back door. I thought the police would take care of them but you know how it is ..."

"They waited till I closed up, *Saab*," Ramu said. "No police came and they left. They have come back now and I think they are drunk."

"Your wife, she is here?" Yahya asked Naran.

"Behind that door, in the bedroom."

"You two stay here. Guard her door."

Yahya strode across the room, crossed a narrow passage, and opened the door leading to the back of the house. For a moment he stood there, casting a long shadow in the bright moonlight. He could see the sailors clearly, four of them, in their loose calico pants and thin vests. Their leader, a tallish man with a scruffy beard and heavy shoulders took several steps forward.

"You are not Naran," the man said gruffly in Hindi, "We want that *mader chod*! Now!"

Yahya surveyed the vast yard, noted the timber stacked high along the edges and, satisfied that no one was lurking in their shadows, stepped onto the hard sand. He walked unhurriedly towards the speaker.

"*Kiya?*" The sailor angrily asked, "Who are you?"

When they were less than a yard apart, Yahya stopped, his hands at his sides. "Go back to your ship."

The shippee was an experienced street fighter, a survivor of many encounters in the back alleys of hundreds of dockyards around the world. The soft menace in Yahya's tone, his easy stance, alerted the man and made him sense the potential danger posed by what he realised, instinctively, was a dangerous opponent. One of his younger mates, a short and wiry individual, perhaps less perceptive, possibly lacking in experience and deceived by the shadow cast by Yahya, stepped around the leader and stuck his face into Yahya's bristling beard.

"*Tu ghee khane wala*" he spat. "You won't eat *ghee* again ..."

Yahya's massive hand caught the youngster in the chest and sent him flying through the air. He landed in a heap several yards away, his body doubled up in pain as he gasped for air. Yahya's eyes remained fixed on the ringleader's face.

"*Acha!*" the man quickly called out in surrender as he turned away. "We go. Karrim? Prem? *Chalo!*" He had barely finished speaking when he spun on his toes, his right hand raised high, the long blade of the deadly *chaku* glinting as he prepared to sink it into Yahya's face.

Yahya's left hand shot out, caught the knife wrist in a vice grip, his right simultaneously locking his opponent's free hand to his side. For a moment frozen in time they remained motionless, a macabre tableau sketched in charcoal by a surreal artist. Almost imperceptibly, Yahya's grip began to tighten as his fingers curled inwards.

The *kalassi*'s jaw dropped, his eyes glazed over in agony. The dagger fell to the ground and a thin wail began to emanate from the open mouth, a steady stream of spittle drooling across his chin.

Yahya, his eyes blazing mercilessly, continued to apply pressure. Suddenly, in the deadly silence, there was a loud cracking sound as the wrist bones splintered. Blood seeped between Yahya's fingers, the seaman's knees buckled as he lost consciousness and hung in the air, held up only by Yahya's raised hand. When Yahya finally released his grip, the man collapsed to the ground soundlessly.

"*Maaf! Maaf!*" the remaining two in the background were on their knees, pleading for mercy, bowing repeatedly and touching their heads to the ground.

"Go" Yahya said. "Take your friends with you."

The two jumped up, sobbing with relief, each half lifting, half dragging the wounded duo as they hastened out of the yard. It was only then that Yahya noticed the blood on his hand. When he looked up Pravin and Ramu were walking towards him, Pravin's arms stretched wide.

"Come inside," Pravin said. "For what you have done ..."

"No, bhai," Yahya interrupted quietly. "Not tonight. Your wife needs you now. Go to her and comfort her. I'll see you tomorrow."

Yahya washed his hand at a nearby tap, then walked home. As he approached his door he saw Madhoo Daya waiting for him.

"Yahya, is everything okay?"

"Yes, Madhoo," Yahya said wearily. "I'll explain in the morning."

Yahya dozed fitfully that night before sinking into a deep sleep. He was roused several hours later by a loud banging and Madhoo's voice shouting his name and calling to him.

"Madhoo, what ...?"

"Your shop, Yahya," Madhoo screamed, "it's burning."

Yahya jumped out of bed and flung the door open. "My shop?"

"Yes. It's burned to the ground."

Long before Yahya reached the store he could see that it was completely gutted. Five or six men had gathered around and were talking amongst themselves. As Yahya approached them Ramu came up to him, wringing his hands in despair.

"I've been asking around. The *kalassis* did this, friends of the men you beat up last night. Their ship has already sailed."

"It's the way of cowards," Yahya said quietly. "We'll never see them again." Yahya began gathering together the more durable items in an attempt to salvage what little of his stock that he could, Madhoo and Ramu assisting him. He was busy examining a steel frying pan, blackened by smoke, when Pravin Naran came over.

"Leave it, Yahya," Pravin said. "We can obtain fresh stocks. And the store itself was nothing, just old wood and iron. We can replace it in a week with a better and bigger structure. The value is in the land and you can't burn that."

Yahya looked up, his eyes bleak. "No, Pravin *bhai*, this is where it stops. If I continue this way it won't be long before I become an object of charity."

"Yahya, I feel responsible."

"Don't. What I did for you last night was my duty. You exercised a neighbour's right when you called on me. That's all there is to it. Let us never refer to it again."

With Madhoo and Ramu helping him, Yahya made several trips between the charred remains of the store and his room. Finally, after thanking Ramu and sending him off, he settled next to Madhoo on an old log and shared a cup of tea with him.

"What will you do now?" Madhoo asked.

"I'm not a cripple, Madhoo. I'll do what I'm good at. I'll start hawking again."

Madhoo, not a man given to much talk, simply nodded and stood up. "I'll see you later, then."

After Madhoo had left Yahya lowered himself to the ground and sat with his back resting against the heavy log. The morning sunshine was pleasantly warm and he closed his eyes. Instantly, his mind was transported back to India and to the day, almost a year ago, when his father had called him and his brothers together.

Yahya was barely twenty when his father had gathered the family together in the large room that fronted their spacious bungalow in Porbandar. He could still see, vividly, in his mind's eye, the huge table around which he had stood with his three brothers and listened to the gruff voice in which their father had addressed them.

"We make a good living from our small *dukan* but our numbers are increasing and soon the income from it won't be enough to feed all of us. We must look for new opportunities. I have been told that the place called Natal offers many. They say that our people are welcome there and it is, after all, a part of the British Empire. Many years ago the English rulers of Natal had written to Sir George Grey in London and begged for his help in asking us to settle there. They claimed that the future of Natal depended on us Indians and our abilities and that without our help it will be ruined within a few years.

"I have personally read a copy of that letter in an old newspaper and, since then, many of our people have settled there. I do not know how things are over there today but we know the devil who rules our own country and have learnt to live with him. I think that the time has come for one of us to again seek our future in a different environment. This is not new to us. My father migrated south to this very State when things in our own Province became intolerable. We can do it again."

His father, having spoken, invited no comment and encouraged no response. It seemed, Yahya thought now, as if he were merely asking one of them to seek employment in a nearby village and not proposing a journey to a distant country over the ocean.

Whilst he had been speaking Yahya's father had removed a ring from his right index finger. He handed it to Yahya.

"Slip it on," he said quietly. "Turn the stone towards your palm and always keep it hidden, let only the band show. It is very valuable. Sell it when you reach the place called Durban. It will fetch more than enough to buy a small property and set you up in your own *dukan*. Don't rent if you can own, and don't own if you can't pay cash."

His father, after signaling to Yahya and his brothers to remain where they were, went into an inner room. When he returned he carried a bundle of rags wrapped tightly with thin strips of cotton. The knot was sealed with wax. He handed the bundle to Yahya and stepped back.

"That is our most valuable possession. It is a family heirloom and has been handed down to me by my father, who received it from his father who had previously received it from his own father. There are ancient documents inside a pouch, certifying ownership of this item. Guard it with your life. I have no idea what it is worth but I have reason to believe the value is enormous.

"When all else fails, when all hope is gone, open the bundle and do whatever you have to. God has given you a wisdom far beyond your years, He will guide you if such a time comes. If things go well and you don't have to resort to the final option, hand it to your eldest son. Repeat all I have just said and trust to God that your son will be equal to the inheritance. Only give it to him if an occasion such as today arises, or when you realise that your days on this earth are numbered and the angel Gibreel is on his way to you."

And so it was settled.

Yahya was the oldest and unmarried. He would be the forerunner on whose success the others would follow. Within days, his head still reeling, he had boarded the Courland and was on his way to Durban.

Yahya opened his eyes and sighed. He was enjoying the warmth of the sun and was reluctant to move. He could hear, in the distance, the sound of carts and, occasionally, the whinny of a horse as it trotted across the hard ground. Perhaps I should go back, he thought. Immediately, a deep feeling of shame suffused him, the thought of returning to his family and admitting he had failed, that he had sold the valuable ring and subsequently lost the cash through an act of foolishness, was too much to bear. He jumped up and went into his room.

After he had washed and changed into fresh clothes, Yahya spread the prayer mat across the floor and, for the next hour, was oblivious of his surroundings. When he finally re-emerged from the room his confidence was restored and he was ready to face the day.

∞

"This country," Yahya said to Madhoo Daya, "has not been kind to us. Look at me. I'm an educated man, I can read and write fluently, I take nothing that does not belong to me. Yet I am reduced to a level below that of even a manual labourer. Surely there must be a better way of earning a living than walking the streets and being insulted by illiterate fools each time I try to sell my goods."

"Your Gujerati education is of no value here," Madhoo said quietly. "Outside of our tiny community the only language that is spoken is English; without it we always appear stupid and dumb."

"Then I will learn it," Yahya said. "But my priority will always be to save enough money to open my own store again. My future depends on it."

That was the last time Yahya complained to anyone about the shortcomings of his life. He stubbornly ignored the limitations placed on his race by the rulers of the land in which he had settled. He wrote copious letters to his family in India without once mentioning the hardships of his existence. He stoically accepted every indignity heaped on his once proud bearing and made a covenant with himself that he would, ultimately, overcome the vicissitudes of his capricious fortunes.

Over the next few years he made no new friends and led a fairly humdrum existence, spending most of his evenings either in desultory conversation with Madhoo Daya or writing long letters to his family. He took great care, whenever he wrote home, to sound optimistic, choosing to lie rather than give his family cause for anxiety. He little realised that his carefully maintained charade would soon result in consequences which would give him cause for extreme trepidation.

Encouraged by the good news from Yahya, and oblivious of the true circumstances of his impecunious state, his father directed missive after missive in which he insisted that it was time for Yahya to marry and begin a family. Yahya sought refuge by claiming that the colony had no suitable young ladies befitting his station in life but promised to make efforts to scout around for a prospective bride.

When his father made no further mention of the matter in his subsequent letters Yahya sighed with relief, secure in the knowledge that his explanation had been accepted. As time passed he relaxed and gave it no further thought.

Yahya's relationship with Madhoo began to intensify and soon matured into a strong bond of friendship. Unlike Yahya, Madhoo made a fairly good living at his craft, there being very few tailors around at the time. When he offered to teach Yahya the trade he was surprised at the sincerity with which Yahya turned him down, explaining that he had no wish to encroach into his friend's monopoly of the market. The refusal forged an even stronger affinity between the two and they rapidly reached a stage where they became inseparable and began to share the evening meals on a regular basis. Yahya, being a bachelor, soon began to eat with increasing frequency at Madhoo's place and, after a while, stopped cooking altogether. In many ways they became a family and, in spite of the startling difference in their size and appearance, were often mistaken for brothers.

On most evenings the two strolled across the road and passed the time talking to their countrymen who unfailingly gathered in the large courtyard directly behind the mosque. On one such evening the barber, whose shop served as an unofficial post office and to which address all the incoming correspondence was directed, handed Yahya a thick envelope. The postmark was almost a month old although it had, only that very morning, been delivered to the barbershop. Yahya absentmindedly stuck it in his pocket and it was only much later, when the conversation around the courtyard began to pall on him, that he became aware of its bulk and decided to read what he was sure was the usual news from home.

Yahya read the letter out aloud for Madhoo's benefit, commenting occasionally on the contents as he turned the pages. Madhoo listened with his eyes closed, head tilted back, a vivid picture of the village playing on his mind. Suddenly Yahya's voice stopped in mid-sentence and Madhoo opened his eyes. Yahya's own eyes had gone wild and he was beginning to shake with agitation.

"What is it?" Madhoo asked, alarm and consternation mingling in his voice. "Is something wrong?"

"What is the date today?" Yahya almost shouted.

"Bhai, what is the matter? Has someone ...?"

"Madhoo, what is the date?" Yahya cut in impatiently.

"The fourteenth of August," Madhoo replied, then added lamely, "1887." Yahya grimaced painfully, then said in a barely audible voice, "I am getting married tonight."

Madhoo looked at Yahya incredulously, was about to laugh, when Yahya thrust the letter in his hand. "Here, read for yourself."

The first thing Madhoo noticed was the date, the 14th of July. His eyes skimmed over the pages, swiftly absorbing the contents. Towards the end he read out aloud, more to convince himself of its accuracy rather than any other reason "... and the two families have agreed, theirs and ours, that there be no further delay. The date has been mutually set for the fourteenth of next month. Your wife will sail for Durban a week later and will arrive there on the twenty third of September."

What followed was a list of instructions to Yahya on what he was to do and how he was to conduct himself. A specific condition was that immediately the girl set foot in Durban and before he took her to his home, he was to go to the local priest and undergo a proper marriage ceremony.

Yahya was instructed to arrange everything in advance. A set of documents were attached to the letter, all correctly signed and witnessed for the priest's benefit. Amongst these were statements from the bride's father consenting to the marriage, together with notarially certified affidavits from three respectable elders of the village confirming that the bride had agreed to participate in and willingly consented to the ceremony about to be concluded in India.

"Everything has been taken care of. I wasn't even consulted," Yahya said thickly.

"It is the way we have always done these things," Madhoo said bluntly. "Do you know this girl? It says here her name is Nadia."

"I seem to remember a child by that name. Madhoo, what am I to do?"

"Follow the instructions in the letter, what else?" Madhoo replied.

Later that evening, as Yahya lay in bed, he tried to visualise the scene in Porbandar, the festivities and the folk dances, and his eyes grew misty. He couldn't deny to himself that he felt a certain pleasure at the thought of having a companion and easing the loneliness of his bed. Then he thought of the state of his finances and groaned aloud, "How will I manage?"

Initially, the days flew by. Then began to drag as his impatience grew. On the day the ship docked, Yahya was waiting at the pier with Madhoo and Kantha, Madhoo's wife.

When he first saw Nadia as she stepped off the ship, Yahya's heart jumped with excitement. The child had grown into a beautiful woman, slender and tall, with the serene arrogance of a true Pathan. In place of the simpering, giggling little girl he was dreading the thought of meeting was a determined, assured young lady who descended the stairs with a calm dignity and unruffled poise. Yahya was completely disconcerted and if it hadn't been for the Dayas he would have forgotten why he was there that day.

Kantha took control immediately. She thanked the family that had travelled with the girl and acted as unofficial escorts, then took Nadia by the hand and led her to a waiting ricksha, leaving Yahya and Madhoo to commandeer another and follow as best they could. When they reached home a priest and two witnesses were waiting outside Kantha's door, sweating in the hot sun.

The ceremony completed, Kantha dragged Madhoo into their room and left the couple to themselves. Bereft of the support of his friends, Yahya, for the first time in his life, lost his confidence as he gazed at his bride in confusion. When she smiled at him and bowed her head he grew angry, pulled himself together and, with a proprietary air, led her to his room and shut the door.

Within a week Nadia had taken control of his mundane existence and turned his single room into a home. She was, in addition, a superb cook and Yahya gloried at being able to reciprocate the Dayas' past hospitality and having them over for regular meals.

It took another nine years, however, before Nadia agreed that it was time to plan the first child. She had avoided pregnancy in ways that Yahya found bewildering, colluding with Kantha in preparing various herbs and roots which she religiously consumed daily and the efficacy of which had proven itself until she had, for her own mysterious reasons, decided it was time to discontinue their use.

As the baby in Nadia's stomach slowly grew, Yahya was suddenly and without prior warning forced to discontinue his hawking business, out of which he was just beginning to make a decent living and even saving a little each month.

In the last decade of the nineteenth century the whites of the colony had whipped up anti-Indian sentiments that verged on hysteria and were determined to put even the lowliest of traders out of business. All hawkers' licences were withdrawn at the whim of the Licencing Officer. The right to appeal to any court of justice was expressly forbidden. The Indian merchants were themselves at the mercy of the authorities who threatened to discontinue the issuing of further licences and refused to renew existing ones. Virtually overnight, the Indians were in danger of being reduced to near poverty.

Yahya became a tinker, making petty repairs and earning a few pennies wherever he could. Madhoo was somewhat fortunate in that, as a tailor, he could just as easily operate from home; he continued to receive the patronage of his white customers who admired the quality of his workmanship and paid a mere pittance for his services. Once again Yahya, this time with Nadia at his side, began to share the contents of the Dayas' kitchen. Somehow, they existed.

Pravin Naran came over regularly. His repeated offers of assistance were gratefully acknowledged and graciously rejected by Yahya, and in his turn by Madhoo. Neither was aware that Kantha, in blissful ignorance, was obtaining groceries at a massive discount from the local store, the owner of which was secretly recompensed by Naran.

Within a few months, the authorities relented in the face of massive opposition by influential Indian merchants, who threatened to take their case to London. Life slowly reverted to normal. Yahya resumed his occupation as a hawker.

When at last things began to improve, the Dayas, together with their small daughter, Heera, moved to a flat a short distance away and Yahya took over their vacant room. The parting, as such, was highly emotional although their lives, in effect, barely changed. Kantha came over every evening and fussed over Nadia while the men passed the hours at the courtyard behind the mosque.

∞

Early in November Nadia gave birth to a bouncing, pug-nosed little girl who entered the world with a lusty cry. Yahya, overjoyed, redoubled his efforts and often worked late into the night, taking on even the most menial of repairs and gratefully accepting the few additional pennies. During the day, from early morning till late evening, he hawked his wares to a larger and more distant clientele.

One such night, when Fatima was barely a year old, Yahya was in the yard repairing a metal bucket when Nadia came over and squatted next to him, the dim light of the lamp casting huge shadows around them.

"You are pushing yourself too hard, Yahya, you must rest."

Yahya grunted, his biceps bulging as he strained to straighten the dent in the heavy steel container. "I'll rest when I'm dead. Time enough for that. The living must eat."

"We have enough to eat and we have saved a few pounds for the future."

"The future? In a country where they can order us to stop work tomorrow? How far can a few pounds take us? Do you want us to become charity cases, like those lazy *mafetyas* who loiter outside the mosque on Fridays with their hands outstretched, palms open to every merchant that goes in to pray?"

"They have more mouths to feed than you have."

"They should have thought of that when they were grunting over their women's bodies."

"Did you?"

Yahya sighed and looked at Nadia with angry eyes. "Woman, I agreed to wait a long time before Fatima ..."

"I'm not talking about Fatima."

"Then what in the name of the Rana of Gujerat are you babbling about? Go to Kantha. I don't have time to gossip ..."

"Then find the time to listen."

"There's no future in idle talk."

"*Gadha!*" Nadia almost screamed, "I'm trying to tell you ..."

"So now I'm a mule? Good! Write to your mother ..."

"I'm pregnant."

"What!" Yahya dropped the heavy bucket. "How ...?"

"How? How? *Sala!* You always knew how. You were so good at it that ..."

Suddenly, Nadia blushed and covered her face, sniffling into her fingers. Yahya quickly enveloped her in his huge arms and gently patted her shoulder.

"It's God's will," he mumbled. "You took all the precautions. It was written."

"We can't afford another child."

"Let me worry about that," Yahya said softly. "To provide for us is my job."

On a night several weeks before the baby was due, a few minutes after nine, Nadia suddenly went into labour and shouted at Yahya to fetch the midwife. Hastily pulling his pants over his nightshirt Yahya ran, in his bare feet, the legs of his trousers flapping wildly at his ankles, praying under his breath that Nadia would hold on until he returned.

In less than five minutes, he had turned the last corner into Cross Street and was within a hundred yards of the midwife's home. Yahya was about to put on an extra burst of speed when he saw, too late, the native constable's foot shoot out and trip him. He flew through the air, somehow landed on his feet and stumbled as he attempted to regain his balance. He had barely straightened up before the constable had him by the shirt. In an effort to balance himself he reached out and the constable, misunderstanding Yahya's intentions, brought his baton down with a thud on Yahya's head.

Stunned, barely able to see clearly, Yahya thought of Nadia and roared in anger as he lifted the constable and raised him high above his shoulders. The constable, ideally placed, swung the baton desperately and connected with the base of Yahya's neck.

When Yahya regained consciousness he found himself in a filthy cell, one ear caked in blood and his neck throbbing with pain. He dragged his body along the ground until he reached the bars of his cage and pulled himself upright. As the reality of his position and the danger Nadia was in seeped through his brain, he grew agitated and began to shout loudly until an officer came over and told him to shut up.

"Please," Yahya shouted, "Why am I here?"

"Curfew laws," the sergeant replied. "You Indians know you are not allowed on the streets after nine at night."

"My wife," Yahya said, "she's having a baby. I must get the midwife to her."

The sergeant looked at him carefully. For the first time in his life Yahya began to plead, begging to be let out. Finally, more in disgust than out of human charity, the sergeant shook his head wearily and opened the cell door.

"Bloody Indians," he said with a grimace. "Get out of here. Don't let me see you on the streets at night again." He shoved Yahya towards the exit.

It was after midnight when Yahya stumbled home, midwife in tow. But it was too late. Nadia had already lost the baby.

∞

It had taken another five years before Nadia reconciled herself to the unhappy experience and agreed to conceive for the third and final time. The loss of the second child, within minutes of entering the world, had wiped the last traces of laughter from her eyes and had made her permanently bitter against the rulers of her adopted country. It was only Yahya's infinite patience and soft cajoling that had coaxed her once more into motherhood.

Dara's birth had an auspicious beginning and was the stuff of which legends are created — he had not only cried out from his mother's womb, but had also been born with a caul. In their home village of Porbandar such a twice-blessed birth was popularly believed to be associated with a glorious future and, had they been in India, the boy would have been feted for months and visitors from distant towns would have called on the lucky couple and participated in their good fortune. However, on the night of the fifteenth of August 1903, in the town of Durban, only the midwife was present to hear Yahya exclaim, "*Allaho-Akbar*" — "God is Great" — and to whisper the soft rejoinder "*Ameen*".

His heart almost bursting with joy Yahya, leaving his wife in the care of the *dai*, stepped through the door and closed it softly behind him. He stood in the rough cement courtyard, the cold penetrating his bare feet, his crude cotton trousers six inches above his ankles, and looked up at the sky. His face solemn, he slowly raised his hands chest high, palms facing inwards in supplication, and began to pray.

In the still, starry night, alone with his God, his body swayed gently to the soft cadence of the Arabic words. He prayed for a long time, oblivious of his surroundings and feeling close to his Creator, before he lowered his hands to his sides.

"*Baji*, it's cold."

The voice startled him, shook him out of his reverie and jerked him back to his harsh surroundings. He peered into the darkness.

"*Baji* ..."

Yahya saw the outline of his daughter, standing forlorn and lost in a nightdress several sizes too large for her frail body. He took a few steps forward, then bent low and scooped her up in his arms, hugging her tightly to his chest.

"You should be sleeping," he said gently, ruffling her tousled hair.

"What are you doing, *Baji*?" she snuggled into him and wrapped her arms around his neck.

"God has given you a little brother," Yahya said.

"I would have liked a sister," she said drowsily. "Can I see him?"

"Later. The *dai* is still busy with your mother."

"Do you also have a brother, *Baji*?"

"Yes. I have three brothers, but they are far away."

"In India? I would like to go there someday."

"If God wills it."

"If God wills it," she responded, her voice musical. "*Baji*, were you praying?"

"Yes."

"Like they pray?" she asked, pointing to a steeple barely visible through the darkness in the distance.

For a moment Yahya was silent, unsure how he could explain to a child the complexities of different religions.

"Do they pray like you did?" she persisted.

"Yes ... a little ..." Yahya began reluctantly. "Not a lot. They pray to Jesus and say that he is the son of God. We call him Isa and he is the messenger of God, a prophet. But they are good people. The Koran says they are people of the Book and we must respect them."

He heard her sigh, already confused. With a light shrug he said, "Come, Fatima. You must go to bed." But she was already asleep, breathing evenly against him. He carried her indoors and tucked her in, drawing a worn blanket around her thin shoulders. Gently, he patted her shoulder a few times, then walked across to a shaky table set against a wall and lowered his body onto an old wooden chair.

From a drawer he extracted a few sheets of yellowed paper and a stubby pencil. "My dear brothers," he started to write, the curves and loops of the Gujerati letters filling the pages as his pencil swiftly flew over the paper, his face glowing with pride as he imagined the pleasure his news would give his family in India.

His brothers would be grown men now, he smiled as he paused to gather his thoughts; their families complete, their children grown up. More than two decades had passed since he had last seen them. Already their faces had begun to blur and he put the pencil down, concentrating all his efforts in an attempt to recall what they had looked like. He realised, with a shock that momentarily stunned him, that he could no longer visualise their features and didn't even remember the names of their children. He reached into the drawer again, pulled out a bundle of old letters and frantically poured through them, picking up a name here, another there. He stopped when he realised that his eyes had gone moist, that he could no longer read clearly. He pushed his chair back, stretched his long legs and closed his eyes.

This country, Yahya thought, has nothing to offer. Why do I stay here? Have I become so much a part of it that I can no longer consider leaving? They lied to us, he almost said aloud, when they first convinced us to settle here. Could anyone have even imagined that we would be punished for the very abilities through which we hoped to succeed, to build up this colony and make it flourish? How different, he almost cried with bitterness as he picked up the letter he had just written, would my life have been if my father had only taken the trouble to check his facts in advance.

He heard a door open and knew it was the midwife, her work finished. Yahya jumped up and went outside. The old woman was waiting for him, her small saffron coloured bundle at her feet. Yahya reached into his pocket, extracted a half-crown coin and handed it to her.

"I wish it could be more, old mother," he said, "but it is all I have."

"It is enough," the woman replied. "Your wife and son are well. They will sleep now."

"Can you stay?" Yahya implored. "Just till morning, when I can ask Mrs Daya from across the road to come over. I'm alone and don't know what to do if the baby ..." his voice trailed off helplessly.

The midwife considered Yahya's request, then nodded. "*Acha*! I'll stay."

Before he could thank her, she turned and went back into the room.

By the time he was three years old Dara had become a familiar sight around the town. He accompanied Yahya on his daily rounds, sitting precariously amongst the kettles, pots and pans scattered loosely in the tiny cart, which was no more than several wooden boards knocked together by Yahya to form a rough base to which he had attached two bicycle wheels.

Yahya, muscles bulging with strain, hauled the contraption from street to street, delivering and collecting metal utensils that had either been mended by him or required to be repaired. As a tinker he earned an uncertain and indeterminate income which depended entirely on the fickleness of the housewives he called on. On a good day he could earn enough to feed his family for a week, on others all he had to show were his aching bones and blistered feet. He never complained, refused to accept the charity of his countrymen and continued to plan for the day when he had saved sufficient capital to open his own store. In the meantime, whenever he spotted a bargain, he bought an item or two and resold it at a tidy profit. Nadia quietly salted the money away for the time when there was enough to realise what had now become their joint dream.

"You are a stubborn man," Pravin Naran said to him one evening. "There is nothing wrong with accepting help from your friends."

"I manage," Yahya said simply.

"But you don't have to do it this way. I can provide the little capital you require to open your shop. Pay me back when business picks up."

"And if it fails?"

"Then consider it a present from me. Yahya, we are family now ..."

"Present, charity, it's one and the same."

"But don't you see, Yahya? You are getting old now. The way you're going your health ..."

"My health is fine. And I'm not that old. I'm not ..."

"*Acha!*" Pravin said in exasperation. "Madhoo, you talk to him ..."

"I have tried." Madhoo replied dejectedly. "But you know these Pathans. Even after settling for almost a hundred years in Gujerat they haven't learnt a thing from us. His arrogance is his worst enemy."

"No, *Bhaiyo*," Yahya interrupted, "Pride in my abilities, yes. Arrogance? Only when it's an asset. Look, when I first came here I truly believed that I was coming as a free man. A pioneer. On the first day that we docked in Durban they held all the Indians on board our ship as virtual prisoners, on the pretext that the ship was in quarantine. The European passengers who had traveled so closely with us had been happily welcomed and allowed to disembark. It was only after several days of the utmost privation, and when the port authorities had run out of every excuse they could think of, did they allow us to set foot on solid land. Why? If they didn't want us here why did they not simply send us back? Why did we not insist on going back ourselves? Did we stay here out of arrogance?

"And when you took me in, Madhoo, and emptied the only other room you had for me, took your little daughter into your own room with you, was it arrogance that enabled me to accept your kindness? And you, Pravin bhai, when you so generously entered into a form of partnership with me, was it out of arrogance that I came to you? You are both aware that your help was gratefully accepted by me. But I can accept such kindness only once. If I allow it to be repeated it becomes charity. If you now persist in helping me, and I continue to accept what I know is sincere assistance from you, where does it stop? In time I will be reduced to no more than a beggar. Then the time will surely come when people will say: 'Here comes the Pathan. Let's go before he asks for help!' And what will our friendship be worth then?

"No, my friends, I must make it on my own or admit failure. Or I must pack my bags and go back to India. There is no law that stops us from doing that. I stay because I believe in myself. If that is arrogance, then only God can save me from it."

In the face of Yahya's argument Madhoo and Pravin could offer no response.

∽

The years inexorably crept by and, by the time Dara was six years old, he had become his father's constant companion. He unfailingly accompanied Yahya each evening, much to Nadia's annoyance, when they joined Madhoo Daya in the usual meeting place at the rear of the mosque. Long before it was time to leave home Dara would begin to grow impatient, jumping up and down and shouting that it was time and that "Madhoo-kaka" will be waiting.

Early one such evening Dara was playing with several boys of his own age whilst Yahya, Madhoo and a dozen other men from the Grey Street area sat around and conversed in low tones. After a while Dara, bored, drifted over to his father and snuggled into his lap.

"The boy is growing up too fast," Yahya said to Madhoo. "He prefers our company to those of his own age."

In spite of Yahya's concern over his son's serious attitude to life, whenever Dara plied his father with a million questions, Yahya went to great lengths to try and explain the gist of whatever the elders had been discussing. And Dara, who had an extremely retentive memory, seldom forgot.

On that particular evening a younger man, barely in his twenties, was doing most of the talking and Dara listened with his eyes wide and his brow wrinkled with concentration. He could follow little of what the man was saying, most of it way above his head. He could see, though, that the speaker had gripped the attention of everyone around him. Dara knew that his name was Jammu and that he had, according to Madhoo-kaka, simply walked into their group a few years ago, shivering with cold and on the verge of starvation. The men had immediately pulled the exhausted boy close to the glowing embers of the *bhowla* and seen to his needs. Since then he had wandered in and out of their lives, often staying away for months before returning once more. He seldom stayed for long and was something of a mystery to all of them.

"What is it that the English are afraid of?" Dara heard Jammu say.

"They accuse us of unfair competition while at the same time they charge exorbitant prices for their own goods. We are a small community, our numbers are negligible, and yet they claim that we are overrunning the Colony. They forget that they themselves are no more than settlers who came to this country and usurped it by force of arms and with a glib tongue. We came here at the express invitation of their own government, they begged us to settle here, pleading that our presence was necessary to save the colony from ruin.

"Once here, they immediately locked us into slavery and persecuted us with trumped up laws that wouldn't stand up under the scrutiny of that little boy there." He had pointed at Dara at that moment and Dara felt a delicious tremble run through him.

"And," Jammu continued, "If you so-called free Indians think you are treated badly, go and see how our people live on the sugar estates." When he paused, eyes blazing, every one present nodded his head in silent agreement. They were not ignorant of the plight of their fellow countrymen at the hands of the colonists.

"The white sugar barons help themselves to our women and make them into concubines while their husbands are out in the fields. They insist on the right to sleep with every new bride that enters their domain, on her very first wedding night. Is it any wonder that the first child in many of our homes there is fair of skin and light of eye? And who can our people turn to for help? The Protector of Indian Immigrants? Each of those officers is in the pay of the very lechers against whom we wish to complain. And there is nowhere else we can go, either to complain or to escape these swines. To travel anywhere off the lands of the farmer requires a pass. And who do you think issues these passes?" Jammu gave a short, harsh laugh that sent a chill down the spine of each man that heard him.

"They use a system of punishment and reward to set our people against each other. They whip them like animals in a cage, and then spit on them when they don't have the strength to work. Even those of their own kind, the few whites who treat their workers decently, are repelled by the behaviour of their brothers. But these are things that all of you should know, you hear it every Sunday when some of our countrymen whisper them to you, in anger and fear. Those few, who are given a pass to come into town — like pariah dogs that cannot be trusted to roam freely — are only allowed out on the understanding that they will keep their mouths shut or face the consequences.

"But do not believe that all of our people take this lying down. Many fight back even though they know that they can't win. They prefer to stand up in pride rather than swallow it in despair. And a large number commit suicide. Let me tell you something. A year ago it was proven that the highest suicide rate in the world was in France and that the rate amongst the indentured workers on the sugar estates was twice as high. Remember that — twice as high.

"And some, of course, just run away."

Jammu paused, running his tongue over dry lips. Someone passed him a metal cup which he accepted gratefully, emptying it in one long draught. For a long minute he looked around him, like a man who is in possession of some great secret and is not sure whether he should divulge it. The men sensed his hesitation, knew he was on the verge of saying something important. Finally, one of them prodded him gently.

"We know that what you say is true. But, brother, you speak like a man who has lived on the farms. Tell us about things we do not know."

Jammu chuckled, a crooked smile on his face. "I have been with you, on and off, for many years. You took care of me when I thought I could no longer go on. You are people I can trust." He seemed to hesitate again, then suddenly made up his mind.

"I think I owe you an explanation. You have been good to me and it's time I was open with you. The day when I first came here was not long after I decided that freedom was not something that others granted to you as a gift. I realised that it was my birthright, bestowed upon me by God and could only be taken away by Him, in the form of death. I had to choose between suicide and freedom. I concluded that suicide was no more than the abrogation of another right — the right to live. I chose to exercise both those rights."

"My family, which consisted of my parents and myself, were indentured to a man by the name of Meikle. He still owns the estate by that name. Remember it, tell it to your children and to your children's children.

"This man Meikle, and his wife, are truly evil. They pay no wages and feed the labourers weevil-infested mealie meal, the portions so meagre that they were insufficient to keep us on our feet. They whip the workers daily and quite often even their children join in. Because I was a shepherd I was a little fortunate. I was out most of the day with the sheep and only returned in the evening.

"One evening one of the sheep went missing and, although I searched everywhere, there was no sign of it. I sat on a hillock and shivered in the dark, more out of fear at having lost the animal than through the cold. And

I can tell you the winter on the farm bites through the bones even when indoors and covered with a blanket.

"The next morning, just as the sun came over the horizon, the miserable animal returned. I laughed happily and hurried back, leading the flock carefully to make sure none strayed again. The sun was already in the sky when I reached the farm buildings and the first thing I saw was this man Meikle and his wife standing at the door of their huge house. Without a word they bundled me into their dining room and tied my hands together. Then they stripped me naked and hung me by my wrists from a beam in the ceiling. While the woman shouted encouragement, the husband thrashed me with a whip. I fainted when the bitch squeezed my privates. After they tired of the sport they lowered me to the ground and revived me by kicking me on my legs. They then screamed at me to take the sheep out again.

"I was a boy the night before. On that day I became a man. And when I ran away that afternoon I left that farmer with a few scars that will remain with him till he dies. But I know nothing has changed on the farms. I have slipped in and out of there often since then.

"I also learnt something else — abuse, in any form, is a denial of freedom. And remember this also, that they have no mysterious power of their own — their strength is derived from our weakness. Refuse to co-operate with them and they are helpless. Of course, they have weapons against which we cannot fight. Let them use these weapons. Expose them for what they are. If we value freedom then that's the only form of death that can uphold it."

When he stopped speaking Dara felt as if the first person that Jammu had looked at was Dara himself. He hadn't understood much of what Jammu had said but the message had nevertheless osmosed itself through his skin and a little of the anger that surged into the men around him now permeated through his own body. And because of that he didn't notice the sudden tension in the air nor sensed the presence of the new man who had just joined them. It was only when the men began to stand up out of respect and reached out to shake the newcomer's hand that Dara became aware of him.

Dara's first thought was: he is so skinny, maybe he also ran away from home. When the visitor spoke his voice belied his frailty. The voice was strong, resonant, and yet no louder than was necessary to reach the furthest of those who clustered around him. He was speaking directly to Jammu.

"Although you were not aware of it I heard everything you said. It is men like you who give me hope, make me feel that my time here has not been wasted."

Jammu was delighted, almost delirious at the sight of the newcomer and fussed over him as he cleared a space and drew a bench for him to sit on. The visitor, however, seemed to be totally unaware of the adulation of his fellow countrymen and simply lowered his body onto a grass mat and sat cross-legged on the floor. Yahya, Madhoo and the others immediately drew closer and began plying him with questions, wanting to know what was happening in the Transvaal and the Cape. Most of those present, many of whom were considerably older than the visitor, accepted his answers without question and deferred to him in every respect.

"Are they still moving the Indians out of the city centre and into locations in the Transvaal?" one of the men asked.

"Yes," the visitor nodded. "We have tried everything but have not succeeded in stopping this inhuman practice."

"And they're not allowing any more of our people to settle in this country," another said. "We are not even allowed to bring our wives and children over."

Mahomed Khan, a burly individual with hulking shoulders, sat up on his haunches and, eyes blazing with anger, launched into a long tirade that ended with the words: "It's time we fought back like men. When the British go to war they call on us, the Pathans and Sikhs and Gurkhas, to lead the charge. And when it's over this is how they treat us. The trouble is very few of us fighters settled here. Nearly all of our people here are those that prefer to talk. Well, I'm tired of the insults. None of these whites dares to call me a coolie to my face, they know who to pick on."

"Mahomed is right," another growled "They tax us indiscriminately for all sorts of ridiculous things. As a businessman I pay the same taxes as anyone else and, on top of that, because I'm an Indian I have to pay additional fees and commissions that the English trader does not have to pay. And all these revenues are channeled towards helping only the white people. I agree that it is time we stopped talking and started fighting. They are already beginning to treat our civility as the act of cowards."

Jammu's speech seemed to have fired them into defiance and the arguments flew back and forth as each grew more militant and bellicose. At last, the visitor raised a hand in a request for silence.

In the hush that followed his gesture he took a deep breath and, choosing his words with extreme care, began a speech that not one person present that day would forget as long as he lived. They would repeat it in the years to come with pride and the knowledge that not only were they the last to be thus addressed on South African soil but were the only ones who were privy to that particular speech. Whilst Jammu had earlier spoken to them entirely in Hindi, which all of them were fluent in, the newcomer addressed them in English. They understood him equally well.

"As a nation," the man began calmly, "our culture has now reached the stage where we have outgrown violence. We prefer to settle our disputes by rational debate, at the end of which the only victor is the concept of justice and fairness towards all men, regardless of colour or religion. We subscribe to the principle which states, quite simply, that violence only begets violence and solves nothing.

"Every man, however lowly his station in life, is entitled to his opinion. It is only when one group of men chooses, at the expense of another, to dictate its opinion, that it becomes an agent of the devil. Whether such a transgression of man's basic right is enforced by the use of superior muscle power, as in the case of an individual, or the utilisation of the machinery of war, as in the case of nations, does not alter the fact that it is the act of a bully. It is this belief, that might is always right, that reduces man to the level of the animal in the jungle.

"The Indian in this country has always been committed to the highest principle of civilized behaviour, namely, that man's God-given right must always remain inviolate. And he has conducted himself in accordance with this belief. You cannot redress injustice by resorting to physical retaliation against those that transgress the precepts of freedom. You cannot obtain liberty by violent rebellion — the one negates the other — you cannot destroy civilization in order to save it.

"It is only by appealing to the intellect that you can obtain an intelligent and just response. You must stand firm in the pursuit of truth, but truth is not a physical thing, it is a belief that is central to all religions. You cannot uphold a belief by physical retaliation. The first concept is a creative emotion, the second a destructive force.

"Do not for a moment assume that what I ask of you is a weapon that the weak employ against the mighty. On the contrary, it is what civilized man resorts to as his most powerful weapon when dealing with primitive behaviour. I am saying to you that, even from a position of strength, brute physical force has no place in our thinking.

"Do not misunderstand me. I am not asking you to patiently suffer oppression until, by some miracle not of your own making, all your problems suddenly disappear. Oppose it, certainly, but do not sink into the dangers of hatred for your oppressor. That will only beget a similar response and achieve nothing."

He spoke well into the night and Dara began to doze. The men, however, continued to listen with rapt attention, not even daring to cough for fear of breaking the spell.

Dara awoke when he felt his father move as he stood up, to hear the final words of the speaker who was shaking hands with each one and saying, "The unity shown by the Indian in this country is the greatest legacy you can leave to your children."

On their way home Yahya carried Dara in his arms and the boy, his head buried in his father's neck, began to doze off again. As they crossed the street Dara asked drowsily, "*Baji*, who is that man?"

"You are lucky," Yahya replied, "to have met him. One day he will be a very great man."

"But *Baji*, what is his name?"

"Mohandas Karamchand Gandhi," Yahya answered, almost reverently.

❧

The next morning, Yahya pulled the cart up the gentle incline of Berea Road, Dara at his side munching a rare apple that a passing hawker had given him. Father and son had settled into the routine pattern of their working day, with Dara asking numerous questions and Yahya answering them as best he could. They conversed throughout in Gujerati.

"What did that man say last night, *Baji*? You told me he was a great man."

"He reminds us of our culture, which we can so easily forget in this place. And you must always remember that you are an Indian, you must never covet that which does not belong to you."

"Is it like religion?"

"Yes."

"Do all religions teach the same things?"

"All religions teach only what is good. They do it their way and we do it our way. There is no reason to fight over the methods."

"What did he mean when he said that we must not act like animals?"

"What he was saying," Yahya grunted patiently, leaning forward a bit as he strained against an upward slope, "is that if parents behave like *dakus* then their offspring can only be *dakus*. Maybe even worse because the children live longer and have greater experience in looting from others. In the same way, when governments behave like thieves they reduce the people who benefit from such theft to the level of *chors*, to no more than *dakus*."

They had reached a stretch of the road that was fairly steep and Yahya began to breathe heavily as he pulled mightily, his muscles bunching. Dara had gone to the rear and was pushing with his back against the cart, his tiny calves already beginning to knot into hard lumps.

It was a long time before the road leveled out again and they stopped for a breather, Yahya wiping his neck with a clean piece of cloth. They rested for no more than a few minutes before resuming their journey. The wheels were turning freely now as they descended towards Lancers Road. In the first hour they made several sales and obtained reasonable prices, then delivered some items that Yahya had repaired and collected a few that required mending. Just after one, they pulled into an open park and sat in the shade of an old tree as they ate the lunch Nadia had prepared for them.

"The whites in this country," Yahya said as he slowly chewed the hard roti, "are from Europe. For centuries they have looted the world and have now become the biggest *daku* nations on earth. Their people have the highest standard of living, enjoying the luxury of consuming what others have produced. They can go on like that for a long time but in the end they will have to pay for it. It is God's law and they cannot escape its justice."

"Do they not believe in God then?" Dara asked, his eyes squinting.

"Of course they do, but many of their leaders forget about God when they get tempted by the devil. Unfortunately, the children and perhaps even the grandchildren will pay the price. When you breed *dakus* you condemn them to a hell that is not always the fault of the children. They will do well if they remember the words in their holy book, that the sins of the fathers will be visited on the sons."

"Mother always says that there is good and evil everywhere."

"Yes. God and the devil. And when you pursue the devil's work you must eventually breed a devil yourself. Europe will one day breed such a devil who will turn on his own people, many of whom are innocent but will pay the price for the folly of their ancestors."

"How can that happen, *baji*?"

"It is God's law, my son. Some of us call it *kismet*, the Hindus call it *karma*, the Christians something called fate. It is all the same. It can only be avoided by giving back what does not belong to you. Why take it in the first place?"

They finished the rest of their meal in silence, drank a little water from an earthenware pot they carried with them, then set off once more.

And so it went on, year after year. The bond between father and son strengthened to the point where neither could stay away from the other for long. By the time he was fifteen, Dara had grown into a strapping, broad

-shouldered young man, resembling Yahya as he had looked in his youth. The role between father and son had been reversed, with Dara now pulling the cart and Yahya walking alongside him.

The cart had been extended considerably. They now carried a larger variety of goods and could afford to charge a little more for their efforts. And Nadia continued to add to the pile of coins and notes. They still occupied the same run-down, two-roomed structure in Queen Street, although in every other way their lives had improved considerably and three solid meals each day were no longer a rarity.

Dara's sister, Fatima, had married a few years ago and Yahya had been able to save face and give her a wedding that had at least some of the trappings that the occasion warranted.

Fatima had settled happily with her husband and his family in Victoria Street and Yahya was content at having adequately fulfilled his parental duty. He continued to write unfailingly, once a month, to his brothers in India and had fatalistically accepted the loss of his parents, replacing his grief with the joy of seeing his daughter and son grow into adulthood. And he continued to plan for the day he could open his own store, to which was now added the longer term plan of taking Nadia for a visit to the land of their birth.

Dara's days were full of activity, with little time for play. The lack of such pastimes, however, never troubled him — his father provided him with all the companionship he required.

At precisely three o'clock in the afternoon, on each day except Saturday and Sunday, he hauled the cart into the yard and, leaving Yahya to see to its unloading, ran into the house, greeted his mother, washed, grabbed a hasty meal and rushed off to his *madressah* classes. For the next two hours he received his religious lessons, together with a modicum of instruction in the English language. At exactly five on the dot he presented himself to Kantha, who supplemented Madhoo's earnings by running a small Gujerati school.

By six thirty he was back home, to wash once more and follow Yahya to the mosque to perform the evening prayers. Only after that did he have a little time in which he could indulge himself, laughing and joking with one or two boys his own age. He had to be careful, though, not to abuse the privilege lest he incur Nadia's wrath and his father's displeasure.

The evening meal was light and eaten quite late. Nadia made a point of ensuring that the three of them sat together, without fail, and insisted that Fatima and her husband came over twice a week, on Tuesdays and Fridays. By the time that was over, Dara was usually too tired and simply tumbled into bed.

In January 1920, Yahya at last fulfilled his dream of owning his own shop. With Pravin's assistance he negotiated with the owners of the Porbandar Arcade, which stretched from Grey Street through to Cathedral Road, and secured a small shop not much larger than a stall. Nadia handed over all their savings, the princely sum of thirty pounds, and Yahya went into business.

Dara continued the rounds by himself, sorely missing his father's company and the lengthy conversations as they moved from street to street. On Saturdays, however, the monotony was relieved when he joined Yahya in the store and assisted him with the customers.

Within a year Yahya's natural business acumen, long suppressed, began to bear fruit and the goods overflowed the entranceway and spilled over into the public area. "Always buy for cash," Yahya repeatedly instructed Dara. "And sell for cash. Owe no man a penny and you will be beholden to no man."

Dara was an apt pupil and soon discontinued hawking to join his father and the two were together again daily, only this time around Dara did not realise that he would soon rue the decision.

Yahya watched his son, the fullness of his body, and noticed the way he eyed the girls as they passed by. Dara was too good-looking for his own safety and when the girls began coming over to the shop on the flimsy pretext of looking for items that Yahya obviously did not sell, giggling and flashing their eyes at Dara, his father finally put his foot down and said, "Time you got married."

∞

On a Sunday evening, a week later, Yahya was in the yard sitting on an ancient wooden rocking chair that was in danger of falling apart, its base rotted and cracked. Years ago, when he had first received it in lieu of payment from a grateful white housewife for whom he had done some work, it had been in reasonably good condition. It had now settled at an unnatural angle, no longer capable of serving its original function. It did not worry him. He was quite comfortable.

Nadia sat a short distance away, on the straw *chatai*, cleaning vegetables for the next day's meal. It was a balmy evening and a hush seemed to have settled over their world. Both, in their own way, were content. They conversed intermittently, with long silences in between. From time to time, Nadia lifted her eyes and glanced at her husband. On each occasion an infinite peace fell over her and she smiled inwardly. He doesn't say much, she thought, hardly ever loses his temper and seldom enters into an argument, except when I provoke him. He is a good man, the stars were certainly well placed when we married.

Nadia sighed and, lifting the huge enamel bowl from her lap, placed it on the floor next to her. When she straightened up she caught him staring at her, a questioning look in his eyes.

"Well," Yahya asked, "What are you thinking of now?"

"Not of you," she retorted. Then said quietly, "I was thinking of Dara, of what you were saying to me a few days ago."

"And?"

"I agree it's time for him to marry. We must find the right girl."

"From our village."

"*Tchah!*" Nadia spat dismissively. "A girl from India? The boys these days are not like you, they like to see the girl before ..."

"He will do as he is told," Yahya said with feeling. "It is not a matter that concerns him. We decide, we select the girl, we set a date. Then we tell him. *Kalaas*! End of discussion."

"Yes," she responded placatingly. It was not the time to push too hard. The girl would be chosen by her, someone from a local family. But she would have to tread carefully. She must never abrogate her husband's authority.

"I watch him in the morning," Yahya said, "before he wakes up, His *dunda* is always pointing at the ceiling, the bed sheet like a tent around him."

"Like his father," Nadia said automatically. Embarrassed, she quickly changed the subject. "At least let me look around, do some visiting. There may be someone you could approve of, one of our own kind ..."

"There is no other kind," Yahya said bluntly. "I will write to my brothers. What was good for me is good for my son."

"You know the government will not allow us to bring a girl over from India."

"There are ways," Yahya said. "I have heard some stories. The white officials at customs are quick to accept a bribe."

"And what would you pay with? You talk like the Nawab of Petaudi."

"Leave that to me," Yahya said with finality, brooking no further discussion. "The girl will be from our village."

Nadia dropped the topic. She knew her man, knew that in time she would manipulate him to her way of thinking. In the meantime she would make her rounds, look around ...

"You are planning something, woman," Yahya said. "I know you. Don't try to get around me."

"*Acha*!" Nadia said, suddenly very angry. "Have you thought about what happens afterwards? For you it was very easy. You lived alone. Your parents were over the ocean. But we are here, and so is Dara."

"What is the difference?"

"What is the difference? *Gudha*! When they are married they will live here, in this home, with us. Isn't that also the proper thing for them to do?"

"It has always been so. I see no problem ..."

"Yahya, listen. I want a daughter in law that I can live with, not some simpering village maiden who will come here expecting to rule the roost. And certainly not some conniving little thing who will constantly nag our son to move out and live elsewhere on their own. With a local girl we can set the rules in advance, leave no doubt about what is expected of her. These things are easily arranged, all the girls know the terms of marriage."

"The girls in the village don't know this?"

Nadia sensed that her husband was weakening. He had left India as a boy, with no thoughts of what marriage entailed. It was time to educate him.

"They know it," Nadia replied with total honesty. "The difference is in the selection, and the choice of the right family who will always be here to correct her. And for Dara, the job of selecting the right family must be done by me, not by some relative in India who would go around bragging in the village about her grand mission and end up choosing a girl from some family keen on getting rid of her. Matchmakers are easily bought and not always interested in doing the right thing."

"So," Yahya asked, smiling, "how much did my family pay for you?"

"*Sala*," Nadia retorted, "you were lucky. The girls were in no hurry to leave their homeland and settle in this godforsaken place."

"But you did," Yahya said, still smiling.

"Yes, I did," she replied, returning his smile with one of her own. "But I had seen you before you left for this country."

For the first time in years, Yahya actually laughed, loudly and with unrestrained mirth.

"I will start tomorrow," Nadia said. "When I settle on the girl then you can speak to your son."

It didn't quite work out that way, but it wasn't much different either.

∞

Fortunately for Dara, Nadia had no intention of choosing a bride for him without his participation, and when Yahya protested that she was breaking with custom and insisted that Dara be excluded from the process, she refused to even consider the idea.

"Don't you see," Nadia told her husband. "This way, if he has problems with his wife he can't blame it on us. He will have to admit he had some choice in the matter."

Dara, who had not expected to find an ally of sorts in his mother, flattered her cruelly and used her as a buffer to buy time. He knew, however, that he could not delay the decision forever, that eventually he would have to submit to his mother's insistence that they set out on their search.

Towards the middle of 1922, Dara finally gave in and joined his parents in the search of a bride for him, and the interminable Sunday routine was underway. They began to call on various families, ostensibly on a social visit but in reality to assess the family and give Dara an opportunity to see the girls. Nobody, however, was fooled by the elaborate pretence and the girls were always dressed in their finest clothes and waiting long before the Suleiman family was due.

The weeks passed. A month went by, then another, and still Dara could find no one that raised his slightest interest. Nadia became irritable and then angry with him. "Is there no pleasing you? Who do you think you are? The Maharajah of Jodhpur?"

Dara refused to be swayed. He had no intention of being lumbered with a girl whose nature would clash with his own. He was not given to easy laughter and often sank into long bouts of silent introspection during which he was tight-lipped and uncommunicative. He was fully aware of the trait in him and knew that marriage with any of the frivolous, preening girls he had seen thus far would, at best, be intolerable.

The lacklustre visits continued with the options growing narrower and the field beginning to peter out. By the last Sunday of August Dara decided to put an end to the charade. It had only taken one glimpse of the eldest Jamal girl to satisfy him that, once again, he would end up facing Nadia's usual recriminations as soon as they were back home. Suddenly, his patience snapped. He had had enough of looking at overdressed and insipid adolescents with long hair slicked down and glistening from an over-application of coconut oil. He had been sitting in the stifling flat in Beatrice Street, eyes lowered to the ground and sipping the revoltingly sweet tea, when it all became too much for him and he stood up.

It was the lowest form of insult, a violation of the strict rules of protocol that governed such meetings. Dara had failed to observe a basic act of courtesy which required him to empty the cup and await a decent interval thereafter before taking his leave. And, to make matters worse, he had pre-empted Nadia, whose function it was to give the lead and for him to dutifully follow in her footsteps.

Dara had barely caught the look on his mother's face, saw the flash of anger in her eyes, when the younger sister walked in to clear the table. Dara froze, every fibre in his body tingling with excitement. He forgot where he was, all sense of reality vanished. He was aware only of the girl and the welter of wild emotions surging through him. He gawked, his whole being fixed on the vision before him, unconscious of his scandalous behaviour or the fact that he was displaying the worst form of bad manners. For Dara the quest had finally ended. The olive-skinned, bright-eyed beauty before him, dressed in a simple *kurtah*, hair loose around her shoulders, was the epitome of his dreams.

He heard someone cough, the sound loud in the abnormally quiet room. Dara tried, and failed, to take his eyes off the girl. He continued to stare at her fixedly until she looked up proudly, the beginning of a smile stretching her full lips apart.

"Shaida!" the girl's mother said, a little too loudly. She looked at her mother, the smile suddenly vanishing and, forgetting what she had come for, she fled the room in confusion.

The spell was broken and Dara turned to his mother, unsure of what to do next, feeling foolish as he stood there with his mouth still open and looking dazed. He blinked, focused his eyes, and was surprised to see that his mother was smiling with pleasure. He was about to sit down again when Nadia said, "Come, Dara. It's getting late."

He met the girl again for the second time, three months later, on the day they were married.

❧

By 1938 Yahya's business had progressed to the point where he had expanded considerably. In addition to his original store in Madressa Arcade he now had a second, considerably larger outlet in a busier area in the heart of Queen Street. In spite of his advanced age he was still robust, with the energy of a man twenty years younger and the strength to lift his eldest grandchild at arms length as he tickled her with his beard.

Dara was, by then, a father of three children — two boys and a girl. Lack of space had forced him to move out of the family home and buy a comparatively spacious house in Verbena Road, about a mile away. Their eldest child, a girl, had been named Ayesha in honour of Shaida's grandmother. The first boy, Yacoob, was named after Dara's maternal grandfather. Salim was the name chosen for the second, after days of agonising over a list a page long and after careful reference to the Koran.

With both his children happily settled and with families of their own, Yahya was satisfied that his duty to God was adequately fulfilled and he asked Nadia to prepare for the final requirement: the pilgrimage to Mecca. And, after well over half a century, the urge to visit what was left of their families in India had become an obsession with both of them.

Neither Yahya nor Nadia was destined to make either journey. Each time they were on the verge of departing, Yahya was called upon to contribute towards some cause or another, and each time Yahya felt that the needs of the community were greater than his own longing to fulfil his dreams. On the first such occasion he donated his entire savings towards the construction of a school for Indian children.

"I have to do this," Yahya said to Dara. "You know the government refuses to allocate any funds for the betterment of our people. I owe it to the thousands of our children who have no schools to go to. Think of all the children in the sugar plantations, think of your own little ones. What chance will they have in a world such as this? Did the Prophet himself not say that we should seek education above all else?"

A year later, when once again a sufficient amount had been accumulated for the journey, Yahya handed over a fistful of notes to the trustees of a bursary fund which had been created specifically for the purpose of sending several students overseas to complete their law studies.

"They have stopped Indian students from attending classes at the University of Natal. Some woman called Mabel Palmer has done her best and failed to make them change their minds."

"But *Baji*," Dara asked hoarsely, "how can they do this? What are they afraid of?"

"Ask the man called Sweeney, of the Department of Law at the university," Yahya answered bitterly.

"But these are public servants. Their salaries are paid out of the money they collect from us in taxes What gives them the right ...?"

"The colour of their skins, Dara. And don't shout, it's not like you. Anyway, everyone knows it's the decision of the Natal Law Society that wants to keep the profession exclusively for whites."

"Then the time will come when they will have to pay for this crime against us. Or their children will pay."

"That is God's law," Yahya said, closing the topic. "Not for you to decide."

And so it went on, year after year. With perverse regularity and uncanny timing, fate and its fickle nature continued to intervene. Yahya and Madhoo, together with scores of their contemporaries, continuously and with monotonous repetition handed over their meagre savings towards the construction of clinics, hospitals and whatever other facilities the community needed and which the government should normally have provided.

"It's a test," Yahya said. "The money in our possession does not belong to us. It is entrusted to us by God for the benefit of the people. To break that trust would be to break faith."

"But what about you," Dara grumbled. "Are you not a part of the people? Is it necessary to give it all away? Surely you are allowed to keep a portion of it for yourself?"

"Yes," Yahya conceded. "But only sufficient for us to live decently and not be objects of charity ourselves. Beyond that money is an evil that corrupts the soul. We become misers and the store of wealth benefits nobody. True wealth is what is contained between your ears. With a good brain and a healthy body who needs money?"

"But *Baji*," Dara cried in frustration, "to make the Haj is not a luxury. To retain sufficient to visit your family is not forbidden."

"Who is talking about what is forbidden?" Yahya retorted. "There is no compulsion in religion. God does not impose a responsibility that we cannot fulfil. It is written. If He wills it, I will realise my wishes. If not, then I won't. *Kalaas*! The matter is ended."

"No!" Dara said angrily, displaying open rebellion for the first time. "We have to talk. You have done your share and earned the right to make this journey. I will take over from here, continue your work and contribute on your behalf. There is a limit to what is expected of any man."

"Then you place a limit on God's word. I have no desire to face up to that question when the *fareeshta* Gibreel calls on me when my time is up."

"*Baji*, please. I am not asking you to ..."

"*Choop*! Enough!" Nadia shouted from the kitchen. "Dara, you show disrespect for your father. How he lives is not for you to question. Now go. I heard the *azaan* whilst you two *gudhas* were arguing. It is time for prayer."

By 1945 Dara had over fifteen thousand pounds worth of stock, all paid for in cash and free of any encumbrances. Yacoob, barely thirteen years old, had become a part of the business and accompanied Dara daily to the stores, only leaving at two in the afternoon to attend special classes. All normal schools were overcrowded and had doubled up to provide lessons in the afternoons, the teachers offering their services free of charge as their contribution to the community.

Hardly a day passed when Dara was not vexed by the constraints placed on his business endeavours, both by the government and by the white business houses. On most evenings, as soon as he had shut the door to the Queen Street shop, he rushed over to the arcade, collected Shaida and the two of them walked across the road to Yahya and Nadia. By then his children would also have joined their grandparents and, after supper, Madhoo and Kantha Daya unfailingly came over and everybody gathered in the familiar yard, passing the evening in pleasant conversation. At every opportunity, Dara engaged the two older men in deep discussions regarding the restrictions placed over them and their future growth, leaving only late at night when he grew weary of hearing depressing news.

"We are not politicians," Madhoo Daya always said. "We can only support our leaders, who are very capable people."

Dara began to follow the news by reading the newspapers extensively and, in the process, obtaining a good grasp of the English language. Most of his day to day conversation, however, was still conducted in Gujerati and it was still the language in which he did all his thinking. It was only when dealing with his customers that he spoke in English and, occasionally, in Zulu.

Initially, Dara's relationship with Yacoob followed a similar pattern as the one that existed between his own father and himself. However, in spite of Dara's efforts, he failed to inculcate a philosophical outlook in Yacoob who grew increasingly rebellious as the years passed. Yacoob could see nothing noble in the attitude of the Indian people and saw little merit in the concept of non-violent resistance.

On Yacoob's fourteenth birthday Dara bought him his first complete outfit — navy blazer, grey shorts, black shoes and woollen socks that reached up to his knees. He looked extremely smart as he went off to school that afternoon, his cheek still burning where Shaida had kissed him.

When he came home that evening the coat was torn at the shoulder, one eye almost completely closed, the lower lip split open. Shaida almost screamed when he walked through the door and when she tried to hug him he roughly pulled away. He refused to tell her what had happened.

By the time Dara closed his shop, saw to Nadia who was filling in for the day at the arcade store, and reached home it was already quite late and

Yacoob had gone to bed. Over dinner, Shaida told her husband about it. Dara listened silently, his face expressionless. When he had completed his meal he walked into Yacoob's room and stood over the bed, looking down at his son who was breathing deeply as he slept. Gently removing the blanket, Dara studied the naked body, noted that the bruises were superficial and that no serious damage had been done. He reached over and lifted his son's right hand. The knuckles were swollen, the skin broken in several places. He laid the hand down and replaced the blanket. When Dara left the room there was a tiny smile hovering at the edge of his mouth.

"The boy fought back," Dara said to Madhoo the next morning. Madhoo had stopped by for a routine visit and had been shocked to see Yacoob's battered face.

"But he refuses to talk about it," Dara added.

Madhoo shuffled over to Yacoob who was standing with his back to a display case, looking sullenly out the door.

"Yacoob?"

"*Ji*, dada?"

"What happened?"

"Nothing."

"Yacoob, nobody is cross with you. Please tell me what happened."

"They beat me up, *dadaji*."

"Who?"

"The white boys at the Grand tearoom."

"Why?"

"One of them, a big boy, called me a coolie and I punched him."

"And?"

"His friends piled into me."

"Did the shopkeeper do nothing?"

Yacoob shook his head sideways, his lips tight with anger.

"Who is he?"

"A white man. Mr Ramsay."

Madhoo nodded, closed his eyes briefly, then placed a hand on Yacoob's shoulder.

"Come with me."

"*Dadaji*, I don't want to go there with you. I'll go again alone."

"We're not going there. Now come."

They walked side by side as they crossed the wide street and entered a passage between two buildings. At the far end of it, on huge double doors leading into a basement, was a neat sign: Patels' Physical Culture Club, 90 Queen Street. Established 1929. Madhoo opened the door and walked in,

Yacoob close on his heels. The smell of sawdust and stale sweat assailed their nostrils almost before they entered the cavernous hall, most of which was in darkness. There was no one in sight but Madhoo didn't hesitate, leading the way to the rear with a confidence that suggested he knew his way around the place. They approached a door marked "Office" and, before they reached it, it opened and a husky man walked towards them.

"*Namaste*, Madhoo-kaka," the man said, a wide welcoming smile spreading across his face.

"*Namaste*, Chico. Things look quiet today."

"Still early. We'll start filling up soon. What do we have here?" Chico had an amused look on his face as he sized Yacoob up, noting the eye.

"Dara's boy. From across the road."

"Oh yes, Yahya's grandson."

"And as good as my own."

"Looks like he's been in a fight and got the worst of it."

Yacoob's face went red, his good eye blazing, his fingers curling into fists. Chico saw the blood encrusted knuckles and laughed again.

"I see you fought back," Chico said, respect dawning in his eyes. "Good for you."

"Take him on, Chico," Madhoo said, "Teach him a few things."

"*Kaka*, we have too many members already ..."

"As a favour to me, then," Madhoo pleaded.

"We have a big waiting list, it won't be fair," Chico said reluctantly.

"It's the *Goras* that did this to him, ganged up on him."

Yacoob didn't understand what it was that brought about the change.

Suddenly, the smile vanished from Chico's face, his eyes narrowed to slits, the muscles in his massive shoulders bunching tightly.

"Leave him here," Chico said, so softly that Yacoob barely heard him.

❧

Over the next two months all Yacoob did was pushups, chin lifts, sit-ups and climbed a pair of ropes hanging from the rafters. Each day Madhoo Daya came over for a while, watched Yacoob, and chatted with Chico.

Unable to stand the monotony any longer Yacoob finally went over to the Daya home one evening and, over a simple meal of roti and beans, poured out his frustrations.

"I'm not learning to fight, *dadaji*," he said. "All I'm doing is silly exercises on the floor for two hours a day, every day. I can't carry on any longer."

"Chico knows what he is doing. He is the best in the business, and that includes the white trainers."

"But I'm not learning anything."

"He has his reasons and his own system of training. I also know that he is treating you as a special case, you do exactly as he says."

"Yes, *dada*." Yacoob's voice was sullen, unhappy.

"I'll tell you what," Madhoo said, "I'll come over tomorrow as usual and I'll have a word with Chico. *Teek*?"

"*Teek*, okay."

The next morning Yacoob was doing his umpteenth sit-up when Madhoo Daya walked in. For a few seconds Yacoob stopped where he was, his shoulders raised, caught Chico eyeing him and quickly commenced again. From a corner of his eye he watched the two as they talked in low tones. A moment later Chico flicked his thumb and forefinger, making a loud snapping sound. It was a signal of some sort and suddenly the gymnasium was quiet, the grunts and groans silenced.

"Suresh," Chico called, "come here. You too, Yacoob."

Yacoob jumped up and hurried towards Chico. He passed a group of advanced bodybuilders and wrestlers. They were smiling, faces lit up, almost as if in anticipation of some great sport that they were about to witness.

By the time Yacoob reached Chico, Suresh had joined them. He was slightly built, much lighter and about the same age as Yacoob, but wiry and supple. He was bouncing lightly on his bare feet and slapping his hands together.

"Madhoo-kaka," Chico said, "I think you should leave now." Then he leaned close and whispered, "You don't want to see this. Let the boy save face."

Madhoo Daya nodded, turned and walked out.

Chico took Yacoob by the right hand, Suresh by his left, and led them to the centre of the gymnasium where a wide space had been miraculously cleared for them. The others had all stopped whatever they had been doing and formed a square, their arms folded across their chests. The younger members were jostling in the rear and climbing onto benches and stools to obtain a better view of what was to follow.

"Street rules," Chico said, "Anything goes. Use your elbows, knees, fists, whatever. There will be no break, no rest periods. Whoever is standing at the end is the winner. Move!" He slapped his hands loudly, then pushed the two into the centre.

Yacoob rushed forward, aimed a punch at Suresh's jaw and swung with all his might. Even before he had completed his swing he knew he had missed. There was no one in front of him and he went stumbling into a group of athletes who gently steadied him and pushed him forward again. He began to advance, careful now, concentrating on his timing. When he was close to his opponent he set his feet, the legs wide apart, and swung again. His fist swished through the air. Unbelievably, he had missed again. He couldn't understand it. His opponent had hardly moved!

Yacoob planted his feet firmly and tried again, failed to connect, and went flying through the air. Suresh had swiped his right foot from under him, effortlessly. Somebody caught him by his shoulders before he hit the ground and steadied him. Humiliation and anger coursed through Yacoob. Of the two, he knew instinctively that the former was more debilitating, would sap his courage and reduce his resolve. He allowed the anger to surface, then moved forward. He began to circle the boy, moving in a sharp arc to his left. Suddenly, he dropped his right shoulder, feinted to his left, raised his right fist and, with careful timing, aimed an uppercut at Suresh's solar plexus. It was a good move, perfectly executed and precisely timed, the weight of his body behind the swing. A split second before the blow connected Suresh moved to his left, caught Yacoob's elbow and flicked it upwards.

He was off balance again, one foot in the air, hurtling towards the floor. Even before he hit the ground he knew, in a moment of sudden revelation, that he was outclassed. His smaller, lighter opponent was toying with him, could finish him off whenever he wished.

A helping hand reached out and he grabbed it. When he was on his feet he noticed that Chico was standing in front of him and had been the person who had assisted him.

"You okay?" Chico asked gently. "Shall we try again?"

"No. I know when I'm licked. I guess I have a lot to learn."

"That's a good attitude. You're one of the few who have walked through my door and had the courage to admit it. You have to know your limitations before you can make progress. You can't learn what you don't know without first knowing what you do."

Chico clapped his hands, dismissing the spectators and sending them back to their routines.

"Suresh, take Yacoob into a corner and teach him the moves. Hold nothing back. I'll check on you two later."

For the next six weeks Suresh taught Yacoob how to bob and weave, to swerve and feint, to sidestep and swipe, to economise on his movements and not telegraph his punches, and how to use his opponent's weight against him. He showed him the importance of a correct stance and the trick of using his feet as additional weapons and his shoulders to cushion his face.

A senior colleague took over from time to time and gave Yacoob lessons on infighting: the power of the elbow over the fist, the knee over the feet and the knack of butting an opponent at close quarters.

Chico supervised him when he moved on to weight training and explained the advantage of light weights with greater repetitions over heavier weights with fewer repetitions.

"You don't want to become muscle bound," Chico explained. "Retain your agility and remain supple. To be able to move fast, to react swiftly, is preferable to great strength and bulging muscles."

For another three months Yacoob went through routine after routine, Chico constantly at his side, until he was ready to drop. His body grew hard as steel, the muscles clearly defined, and he could leap through the air, from a standing position, to almost half his height and to kick way above his head.

Finally, on an evening before closing time, Chico called Yacoob over to his office and asked him to sit down. Yacoob lowered his sweaty body onto a chair and sat forward expectantly.

"I've taught you all I know. It's time for you to move on. Before you leave I have a few words of advice. Listen carefully. Forget about the boys that beat you up. I have been preparing you to cope with such a situation in the future, not to seek revenge for past injustices. If you can't triumph at the first encounter don't go looking for a second chance. Revenge is a petty emotion.

"Don't ever get into an argument. When you speak you give yourself away and allow your opponent to assess your abilities. Make your point and hold your tongue thereafter. If you can't reason with your opponent turn around and walk away. Your strength must be reflected in your confidence, not on the things you say.

"What you learnt here, the day you faced Suresh, was that there is always someone better than you. Remember that. Don't ever allow anyone to test your abilities lest you be found wanting. When you can't avoid a fight, don't hesitate. Move first and move fast. A bully has a sixth sense about these things and knows how to capitalise on your weak points. Don't give him the advantage and never give in to him. It only increases his meanness and encourages his cruelty.

"There are only two more things I have to say to you: not all whites are bad and not all Indians are good. Don't prejudge all people on the behaviour of a few. And don't ever use your fighting skills against innocent and defenseless people, never initiate violence against those who do not resort to that option. If I ever hear that you have acted differently I'll come looking for you."

Chico stood up and held out his hand. Yacoob jumped up, shook his hand firmly and gave a slight bow.

"Go with God," Chico said. "Come and see us now and then. You'll be welcome."

Yacoob walked out of the gym, a pupil of one of the best gurus in the country.

Though still not much more than an adolescent he talked and behaved with the maturity of an adult, spent most of his time listening to the political debate conducted by the elders, and kept his own counsel. Only with Madhoo Daya did he open up, demanding answers to questions that vexed him. He read extensively, devouring every book he could lay his hands on.

Madhoo, who had no son of his own, was elated at the newfound confidence displayed by his protege and exploited every opportunity to advance Yacoob's informal education. In one respect, however, he failed miserably: Yacoob refused to accept that the concept of non-violence had any merit.

"It suits them perfectly," Yacoob countered every argument that Madhoo advanced. "Talking to people who don't listen achieves nothing. Show me one good thing that your philosophy has achieved in the almost one hundred years that we have been in this country."

"You cannot fight evil with evil," Madhoo said in despair.

"But you can fight it with justice. When a man consistently refuses to listen to reason he deserves to be punished. You can't go on forever appealing to his better nature when he repeatedly proves that he does not possess one. If that applies to an individual why should it be different with a government?"

"But how can you punish a government?" Madhoo asked, "we don't have the vote. We can't throw it out at the next election."

"We squash it, like any other monster. The longer we allow it to suck our blood, the fatter it gets and the more it enjoys the taste."

"Where do you get these ideas?" Madhoo asked despairingly, shaking his head. "It must be the Pathan in you. There is no other answer."

"No, *dadaji*, that's not true and you know it. Am I initiating violence? I am simply saying that we must respond to it. When our words are silenced by their guns, we have to shut up and obtain guns of our own.

Your way, and that of my father's and my grandfather's, has failed. Until you admit that, we will remain in bondage forever."

"You are talking like a man advocating war. All it does is kills people. It is better to talk it over."

"Would talking have stopped Hitler? How many more Jews would have been murdered in the meantime? How many lives were saved when they squashed him?"

"Leave it," Madhoo said, giving up. "You are still a boy. When you grow up, you'll understand."

"What, Madhoo *dada*? What will I understand? If you can't tell me now how will I suddenly find the answers when I am as old as you?"

"Yacoob, I can't answer you," Madhoo Daya said, his voice reflecting his futility. "I only know you're wrong."

⚭

"I have no answers for him," Madhoo said to Yahya and Dara the next morning. "He makes my blood run cold when he talks. And I fear most of our children of that age think like him. They should be out enjoying themselves, not talking politics."

"This country does that to them," Yahya said. "From the time they are in our laps all they hear is how this government suppresses us. As they grow up they experience the tyranny themselves. You can't hurt people and expect them to smile at the pain."

"It has gone on for too long," Dara said. "When people lose their patience it happens very quickly. This government is very stupid if it can't see that."

"When we talk like this what can we expect from the young ones," Madhoo said. "And yet, you are right. As Yacoob says, they begin to enjoy the taste of their stolen fruit and grow fat on it. Listen to me now! I'm beginning to quote him."

"I don't think they're all that bad," Yahya mused. "After all, the whites also produce, look at their farms."

"By riding on the backs of their labourers, who are treated like slaves," Dara cut in. "Or obtaining interest-free loans from the government, which they seldom pay back. You can't subsidise the one, suppress the other, and then hold up the white man as a shining example of productivity."

"Who knows where the real truth lies," Madhoo said. "Your father and I, Dara, are old men now. Our philosophy of reason as the basis of all disputes will die with us. Perhaps you and your contemporaries will prevail a little longer. After that Yacoob's age group will take over. If our rulers have not made substantial changes by then I'm afraid this country will immolate itself."

"I know of no place in this world," Yahya said sadly, "where power has been relinquished without a war being first waged."

"Hopefully India will be the exception soon," Madhoo said wistfully.

"But even there," Yahya said, "there are those who demand partition of the country. I'm afraid even our civilization has degenerated to the point where violence rules over reason."

"And then everybody loses," Dara said. "At least our leaders here are still talking of peaceful change."

"And the women are gossiping as usual," Yahya grumbled. "Your wife has dragged Yacoob to some silly tea party or other. Nadia and Kantha are gone only God knows where. We'll have to make our own tea and probably get our own lunch too."

There were close to thirty women present at Julie Rawat's rambling house in Mitchell Road, clustered in groups of four or five. Most of them were in their mid-thirties, a few somewhat younger. Nearly all were dressed in neat saris or colourful punjabi outfits, one or two strikingly beautiful and elegant.

The talk, in the main disjointed and lacking cohesion, was mostly of children and marriage. Occasionally recipes were exchanged and notes compared on the latest fashion trends. The atmosphere was generally of a festive nature, except when the conversation revolved around the high price of food and the activities of the black-market traders, especially those selling traditional Indian groceries and condiments.

"I paid two shillings for a pound of ginger," Shaida Suleiman said. "And even more for some dried chillies."

"You were robbed then," one of the ladies said. "Go to Bhoolas in Queen Street. Their prices never change."

"I always pay sixpence for a pound of beans at Haribhais," an old lady in a white dress said.

"Sixpence!" someone exclaimed. "I paid double that only yesterday. Where is this shop?"

"Down the passage in Victoria Street. Actually, most things there only cost sixpence for a pound. Even peas and coffee."

"Can we talk about something else?" a young woman said. "After all, we came here to get away from such things."

"I'm not sure why we're here," Shaida said. "Julie insisted I come over and bring a few others with me, but everyone refused to leave home without their mother-in-law's permission. So I dragged Yacoob along with me to avoid being accused of walking the streets alone. Now look at him. He is so miserable by himself that he'll run away at any minute."

"That bunch in the corner doesn't seem to be worried about anything," the young woman said. "Look at them. You'd think they own this house."

The group of four that was being discussed had hived off to a far corner and was keeping a haughty distance from the rest. Related to each other by marriage or blood ties, they were dressed in fashionably expensive clothes and were wearing heavy gold jewellery around their necks and on their flashing hands. By their attitudes, they gave the impression of being somewhat superior and acted as if they had merely condescended to grace the occasion as a courtesy to their host.

If fine feathers make fine birds, the quartet was indeed an apt example that justified the proverb. One of them, a descendant of one of the fair skinned northern tribes of India and the wife of a wealthy businessman, appeared to be the pivot around which the other three revolved. She gave the impression that she was patronising those around her and once in a while moved her hands with a superior air, underlining the obvious esteem in which she was held by her little group and revelling in the deference with which her every utterance was greeted. Occasionally she made a slight *moüe* of annoyance and the recipient of her displeasure hastily fluttered around her to give reassurance and avoid being relegated to less favoured status.

The annoyance in Julie Rawat's face was obvious as she studied the prima donna from a distance and she made no effort to disguise her contempt. When her sister, Farida, passed by with a tray of sweetmeats Julie laid a hand on her shoulder and asked in an angry undertone, "Did you have to invite Rabia and her moths to my house? This display ..."

"Please," Farida said, keeping her voice low, "I have my reasons. I promise you their presence is very important. Just bear with me a little longer."

"But what is this all about?"

"You'll find out in a minute," Farida said, quickly walking towards another group and giving them a wide smile. "How are you, Premilla? Try this, ladies, it's really very nice."

"And get fat like your mother-in-law?" Premilla smiled back good naturedly, taking the sting out of her words. "Give it to the queen bee in the corner, she looks like she could do with some sweetening."

At that moment the door opened and two women in their late twenties walked in. Both were simply dressed in conservative clothes, and wore very little make-up or jewellery. There was a dignity about them and a sense of such overwhelming confidence that they immediately captured the attention of everyone in the room. The meaningless chatter died down abruptly. Farida handed the tray to Premilla and turned towards the newcomers.

"Hello, doc ... Zainub."

"How are you, Farida?" the shorter of the two, the one who had been greeted as "doc", asked in reply.

Without waiting for a response she stepped deeper into the room, her eyes flicking appraisingly over the guests. There was a studied casualness about her that belied the seriousness of her expression. The force of her personality was so compelling that even the frivolous four in the corner were frozen into immobility. There was nothing particularly arresting about her features, but such was the dynamism emanating from her that it immediately made the "queen bee" and her minions look insipid by comparison. Her companion complemented her to perfection and the two women, without having uttered a single word, had effortlessly taken complete command of the room.

"Doc, let me introduce you to everyone," Farida began.

"No, my dear. That won't be necessary." She took a backward step, ensuring that no one was behind her, and then started to speak.

"My name is Goonum," she said simply and without further ado. "I have not come here for a social visit," she continued bluntly. "Nor am I here to win your friendship. I have neither the time nor the inclination for such frivolities. If, by the time I leave you, I am satisfied that you are fully aware of the level to which you will soon be reduced, I will have served my purpose.

"In any normal society the function of the government is to act on the will of the people, to obtain the greatest good for the greatest number. In civilized communities every individual has the right to a vote, the right to choose who will represent that individual in Parliament. We as Indian, together with the African and the so-called coloured, have been denied this basic right. A single race group, the white, has made a mockery of democracy.

"When, in addition, an illegitimate government such as exists in this country utilises the product of our labours to expressly benefit their own people, the evil is compounded beyond the proportion in which it was conceived.

"Greed is never a finite emotion. It's an insatiable monster whose coffers have no capacity for fulfilment. It feeds on those who have been denuded of any power with which to protect that which they have honestly acquired.

"To the white looters in this country, you are their natural victims. They will not rest until they usurp everything of value that you possess and redistribute it to their own people. And they are not the least bit concerned with the manner in which they go about it. The issue of morality, even in its widest sense, does not bother their conscience.

"Even as I speak to you they are in the process of formulating even more unjust laws to give a so-called legitimacy to their usurpation of our wealth. They call one such Act 'The Asiatic Land Tenure and Indian Representation Bill'. My colleagues and I choose to call it 'The Ghetto Bill'. The ramifications of this Act are horrendous in the extreme. It will give them the right to grab your properties and your businesses, at a price arbitrarily determined by them and them alone. You will have no say in its compilation. It will be done without consultation and without your participation.

"As a people, our civilisation predates that of Europe by several millennia. After having looted the rest of the world, including India, these barbarians, many of them no more than recent immigrants to this country, are now spreading their sticky tentacles over everything their avaricious eyes covet.

"Their arrogance knows no bounds. World opinion, which will always be just that and no more, does not deter them. They will extort from us all they can. They will feed on us like parasites until we are reduced to penury. And then they will mock us and refer to us as a burden on their so-called charity.

"Well, I have a message for them: I have no defence against the superior weapons of war with which you hope to achieve your decimation of my people, but you are grossly mistaken if you believe that a mere display of your military might is sufficient to reduce me to a cowering mouse. You will have to fire those weapons and you will have to destroy me. And then, perhaps, you can help yourself to my possessions.

"That is my message to them. To you here today I have a different message — you can join my colleagues and I in resisting these tyrants or you can be their lily-livered victims. That decision is yours. But do not believe that you can sit on the fence, that somehow you will escape the horror that awaits you. I refuse to believe that any Indian can be that stupid."

For a brief moment she paused, eyes flashing with anger, her jaw grim. Then, nodding a silent farewell, she took a backward step and was about to turn away when she hesitated and faced her audience again, eyes now twinkling with mirth. In that short moment she was, without any doubt, the most beautiful woman in the room. And when she spoke again there was a lilt to her voice that added to her allure.

"Incidentally, you may be interested to know that I personally possess very little. I own no property and have little wealth of any significance."

Goonum turned to her companion, cocking an eyebrow questioningly. She received an acknowledging nod and took a discreet step to the side.

"My name is Zainub Asvat," the tall, fair woman said, her voice soft and even. "I have come down from the Transvaal, together with several other women. I want you to know that we had no objections from our husbands regarding this journey. And even if there had been, it would not have stopped us.

"There were obvious risks associated with the journey and we were constantly abused by rude comments from the white rabble. That is unimportant. What matters is that we are here to support Goonum and to make you aware of what is happening.

"Throughout the country Indian women are mobilising. Our men, leaders such as Doctor Dadoo and Doctor Naicker, are already marked men. They are not deterred by the threat to their lives. We women, and that includes each of you, are made of equally stern stuff.

"You are Indian, descendants of a great nation. You are women and you are mothers. Do you wish to see yourselves and your children consigned to some bleak and distant ghetto? Do you wish to see everything you toiled for taken from you and handed on a plate to some white *chinal?*"

She paused, allowed her words to sink in, then continued angrily.

"The arrogance of these contemptible fools," she said, her voice rising, "is equalled only by their enormous stupidity. In their smug complacency they truly believe that we are a politically insignificant and powerless minority, that we can by pushed aside with impunity.

"They never stop to think, in their headlong rush to grab everything in sight, that if that were true we would never have achieved what we have so far. In ignoring this reality they are making a massive error of judgment.

"I am not certain of how your husbands will react. But I am sure of one thing: in the final reckoning you, each of you, is the real decision maker in your homes. Ultimately, your men defer to you. Regardless of their posturing and self-important strutting around the family home, they always concede to your better judgment. They may not openly admit it but they know that ours has always been a matriarchal society.

"The time has come for you, the wives and mothers, to show our rulers that they are making a terrible mistake — they haven't taken us and our innate strength into account. It is time to open their eyes, remove their delusions and teach them that we are more than the simple 'basket Marys' that they are so good at sneering at."

She had struck the right chord. Even the "queen bee" had stepped forward, her eyes blazing.

"Okay," Zainub Asvat continued, "Let's show these people what we are made of. There will be a mass rally on Sunday at Nichol Square. Come over. Coerce your neighbours, your friends and your husbands to join you. The Indian Congress needs your support to enable it to support you."

She folded her arms, joined Goonum and waited for a response.

"We will be there!" Surprisingly, it was the "queen bee" who had spoken and, typically, assumed the role of leader. "We will all be there. Nobody, not even the government, takes what belongs to me."

"Well," Goonum said drily, "It'll take a lot more than a rally to stop them. You'll have to fight them tooth and nail, and God knows, they could take it even then."

Nobody noticed Yacoob standing by himself, a little way off, his fists clenched till the knuckles shone white with anger.

∞

"I am going to that rally," Shaida said bluntly. "And you are coming with me. There is nothing to discuss."

"But I have to know what it is about," Dara said. "We can't just go there because some silly woman says so. Did you say she is a doctor?"

"Yes. And I told you why we are going."

"All I heard was some *lawara* about this ghetto thing."

"So it's all nonsense?"

"Okay, maybe not. I just want to know more about it."

"You want to know more? Come to the rally."

"*You* inviting *me*?"

"*Sala*, I'm asking you. But stay at home alone if you wish. We are going."

"Are you taking my children? Ayesha also?"

"Yes."

"And if I say no?"

"Then you say no. We still go, and you come with us."

"Woman, you ..."

"Dara, listen. Just come to the rally. Only after that can you decide what we should do."

"And if I decide not to do anything? After that?"

"Why, then we do whatever you say."

"Okay, maybe we should go ..."

"Now eat. After I wash the dishes I want to talk to *Baji* and Madhoo-kaka and ..."

"*Ben chod*!"

"Dara!"

"*Acha*! *Acha*! Go now. *Ben chod*!"

On the morning of the rally, the last Sunday of March 1946, a hint of an early winter was in the air. By midday the sun had reasserted itself and spread its warmth over the city. Hours before the appointed time sombre groups of Indians could be seen heading towards Nichol Square, the men leading the way with the women and children not far behind.

By two that afternoon the square was packed to capacity and still the crowds poured in, from Pine Street, Commercial Road, Grey Street and Albert Street — the roads that flanked the island venue.

The speakers, standing in the rear of an open lorry, looked down on the huge crowd and surveyed the scene. Hundreds of women were standing in rows before them, a sea of men and boys immediately behind them. A few folding chairs were provided for the old and the frail and most of them were already occupied. When the square could accommodate no more, the latecomers lined the pavements and spilled over onto the streets.

At 2.30pm, without any formal introductions, the speakers walked up to the mike and identified themselves. The first, a poet and playwright by the name of Dhlomo, took the speaker's stand.

"The fight for justice," he said in a clear baritone, "should not be the sole responsibility of the Indian people. The fight for freedom is a fight in which we are all participants. We all want to be free. The young people in the African National Congress support your struggle."

He had barely resumed his seat when a coloured, a Mr Smith from the Durban branch of the APO, walked up to the mike.

"The coloured people of Durban have pledged to support the Indians in this fight. If so-called white civilization requires a Bill of this nature it has no right to exist. It should itself perish. We endorse the decision of the Natal Indian Congress to launch a concerted campaign to defeat these measures of the government."

When Dr Naicker, the President of the Natal Indian Congress, stood up, shouts of "yay" and cheers could be heard from the audience.

"My friends," he began simply, "this is not a time of joy nor a time for celebration. We are here to decide whether we wish to be reduced to serfs in this land of our birth. The scale is weighed against us, but we also know our strength and we are determined to end this exploitation by the whites once and for all.

"Speeches full of rhetoric and anger will achieve nothing. The defiant tone of General Smuts, when he moved the second reading of the Ghetto Bill last Monday in the House of Assembly, will not be softened by what we say today. He is not a man who listens to us.

"What Smuts is glibly telling the world does not fool us, and it should not fool the great nations who honour him. To the leaders of those nations I have a word of advice: read the Bill, study its contents, and then tell us it is not in accord with the doctrines of the tyrannous Hitler whom they fought so fiercely. If just one leader of repute, wherever on earth he may be, refutes my statement I am prepared to concede defeat and allow its passage into law. This is how certain I am of my facts.

"Recently, Mahatma Gandhi, that great apostle of peace, in his usual courteous way, asked, 'Field Marshal Smuts is a great soldier and statesman. Will he not perceive that he will be taking the white people of South Africa down a precipice if he persists in the policy underlying his measures?'

"I would like to add my own comments to that of the Mahatma. If Smuts pushes this Bill forward he will harm us grievously. But, in the years to come, it is his own people who will be called upon to pay the price, in exactly the same manner as Nazi Germany is now being asked to do.

"Yesterday we received a cable from Mr Sorabjee Rustomjee who is presently in India. It contained a statement made by Srinivasi Sastri, the former Indian Agent-General in South Africa. Sastri, in a sick-bed statement said, 'The Field Marshal and his sonorous hypocrisy should be exposed to the gaze of all honest men. That the new world, reborn after the terrible struggle of the past few years, should witness and quietly tolerate this monstrous progeny is a tragedy of the blackest order. This fact should be made known to the United Nations, in all its hellish character, and their intervention invoked in all solemnity.'

"Those were the words of Sastri," Naicker continued, "who has had an opportunity to study Smuts' Bill. You heard the words of the Mahatma. Throughout the world the press is quoting leader after leader in its condemnation of Smuts. Here, in South Africa, the white-owned newspapers remain, to be generous to them, strongly muted in their condemnation of this outrage.

"It is time to add your voice to that of the world because it is you who will pay the ultimate penalty."

On the lorry Dr Goonum, her back against the cab, unfolded her arms and reached out. She took the hand of a young woman and led her to the mike. She was solemnly lovely, not much more than a girl, her angry eyes in stark contrast to her face.

In the front row of spectators Shaida Suleiman turned to Kantha Daya and asked, "Who is that?"

"Fatima Meer," Kantha replied, "Watch her."

"But she's just a schoolgirl!"

"She's a hell-raiser. Heera heard her in the school-grounds and claims she's a firebrand, a real fighter. Let's hear her for ourselves."

When Fatima Meer spoke her voice rang clear as a bell, her posture defiant, her tone conveying a challenge that sent a thrill up the spines of all who heard her that day.

"Who do these people in government think they are? They have the nerve to tell the African that he cannot exercise the franchise because he belongs to a barbarous, uncivilized people. Then they have the bloody cheek to tell the coloured that he has no place in the human race. And now these arrogant idiots tell us that our culture is a threat to them. Smuts, that supreme hypocrite, argues that the purpose of the Bill is justified to maintain European culture.

"When I close my eyes and listen to him why is it that I hear the voice of the Führer expounding the supremacy of white culture?

"And when we refuse to curl up and say 'yes, baas' they are shocked at our impertinence. They cannot believe that we, whom they love to call 'black bastards', have the temerity to oppose them.

"Twenty years ago, before I was born, Dr Malan, that repugnant little turd, said similar things in a similar voice when he attempted to justify his Areas Reservation Bill. Well, I wasn't around then to answer him. I am here now."

She raised herself to her full height, almost on tiptoes, and pointed at a contingent of white policemen standing at the edge of the crowd, silently making notes.

"You there! Are you listening? Put your pencils down. I'm going to make it very easy for you. Go back to your masters and ask them to tell Smuts I have a message for him. Are you ready to hear it?"

"Oh my God!" Kantha cried: "She's worse than I thought. May the Lord Krishna protect her."

At the rear of the crowd, at its very edge, Yacoob jumped onto a milk crate and strained forward to hear the next words.

"Go to Smuts," Fatima continued, her voice rising to a crescendo, "and tell him this. Tell him that we, the majority who has had no say in electing him, now say: TO HELL WITH THE GHETTO BILL AND TO HELL WITH HIM!"

As the mike resonated to her words Yacoob, high on his milk crate, shouted back. "TO HELL WITH THE GHETTO BILL!"

It was immediately picked up by over seven thousand throats that shouted back, as one voice: "TO HELL WITH THE GHETTO BILL!"

It was a cry from deep within the hearts of a community.

"Now we march," Fatima shouted, "down the lily-white West Street. The time for speeches is over." She nimbly jumped down from the lorry and led the way. The women, ten and twelve to a row, followed her with their fists in the air, the men and children immediately behind them. Yacoob forced his way to the front and pushed himself between Fatima and Goonum, smiling grimly.

"Hey Jake," a boy called Sandy shouted from somewhere close, "make place for me."

As they passed the police contingent Fatima said loudly, "Get the bloody hell out of our way."

Suddenly Jake, Sandy, and a whole bunch of young boys had formed a protective barrier around her. "Watch that big Boer there, Nits," Jake said to a tall youngster. "*Khup* the bastard if he makes a move."

"Take it easy, you boys, whoever you are," Fatima said. "This is a passive march. Keep it that way. Just keep walking."

That was the beginning. Rally followed mass rally. Grey Street and the roads leading off it became the focal point of the Resistance Movement. Throughout the country, from every Indian area, money poured into the coffers of the Natal Indian Congress and was utilised towards furthering the cause of the Passive Resistance Campaign.

In Durban, at schools and community halls, paid for and erected by Indian charitable foundations over which the government had little control, volunteers in their thousands signed up as members of the Resistance. And, for the first time, Indian women presented a unified front as they led their men in the fight against the repressive laws that were being promulgated on an almost daily basis. The previously disjointed grouping, consisting of a few but determined professionals, was swelled by women from all walks of life. The housewife and the factory worker, the market gardener and the hawker, the wealthy and the peasant, the labourer and the socialite, rubbed shoulders and cast aside their interpersonal differences in the face of a common threat to their future.

In the Transvaal, over a thousand women, led by Fatima Asvat, marched in protest from the Natalspruit grounds to the City Hall.

In Johannesburg several thousand staged a mass demonstration, then walked through the centre of the city. The procession, half a mile long, disrupted traffic and drew vulgar comments from the white pedestrians.

In Durban, at the Avalon Theatre, the doors of which were thrown open by the Moosa Family, Zainub Asvat addressed a thousand women and concluded with the words: "Let us pledge that we have now sown the seeds of our struggle. We will not let it perish. If necessary we will water it with the blood of our hearts."

At the Gandhi Library in Queen Street Dr Goonum, Fatima Meer and the wives of wealthy businessmen held repeated mass meetings. And when they deemed that English would not be sufficiently understood to drive their point home, they reverted to the vernacular. Mrs NP Desai, speaking in Gujerati, asked the women to swear an oath that "No sacrifice, however great, will be an obstacle in our pursuit of freedom. We place our wealth and our lives at the disposal of our leaders."

Old and frail women, many of them veterans of the Passive Resistance from the days of Gandhi, suddenly appeared from nowhere and re-enlisted into the movement. Their presence fired the resolve of the handful that had stood on the sidelines and debated the extent of their participation.

On one such occasion, a ravishing beauty dressed in fashionably Western clothes with a thick mane of hair cascading around her shoulders, silently walked up to the speaker's platform and, with a flourish, placed her gold earrings on the table.

"That was Fatima Seedat," Goonum said to a colleague. "A loyal member for some time now." She called out to the woman as she was returning to her seat, "You sure Dawood won't object, my dear?"

"Why should he?" the lovely lady shouted back. "He has already donated more than half his life to the people. The earrings are nothing in comparison."

One by one, the others followed her lead. Gold earrings, necklaces, bracelets and chains, piled up in front of Goonum.

"Oh dear," Goonum cried, "now we'll be forced to call on some of the men to escort us out of here before some thug attacks us."

∞

By late May of 1946 Durban was firmly established as the focal point of the campaign. Huge contingents of supporters from the Cape and Transvaal poured into the city and the general public welcomed them into their homes and provided them with accommodation and food.

"The time has come," Fatima Meer said to Goonum, "to leave the talking to the men. Now we take our bodies to where our mouths haven't reached."

"And where is that?" Goonum asked her fiery protegé.

"Into the white enclaves. We invade the public parks and open fields. Let's find out if they support the atrocities of their leaders."

"We'll do it!" Goonum said with shining eyes. "It's time to open the minds of those smug racists."

The women formed into groups. The ladies from Johannesburg: Zainub Asvat, Zohra Bhayat, Amina Pahad and Zubeida Patel, who were already being sought by the police for their militant speeches, were joined by Lakshmie Govender and Veeramah Pather of Durban, both firebrands with a price on their heads. With a dozen others they pitched several tents in a municipal ground, at the corner of Umbilo Road and Gale Street, and awaited arrest. An hour later more than a hundred Europeans arrived, jostled them and hurled verbal abuse.

"Don't respond," Mrs Pather said. "Hold your ground and stand firm."

Frustrated by the dignified behaviour of the protestors, a bunch of white men dumped a bucket of human faeces over the tents and made rude sexual gestures to the women. Suddenly, one of the men unbuttoned his fly and bared himself. Whilst his friends guffawed, the women averted their eyes and silently continued the vigil.

After a while the whites, tired of the sport and angered by the contempt of the protestors, prepared to leave, threatening to return later and beat, as one of them said, "the hell out of you bitches."

"They'll be back," Lakshmie Govender said. "And when they do you can be sure that they will resort to violence."

"They already have," Amina Pahad said, ineffectively attempting to staunch the flow of blood from her forehead, where a deep gash had been opened up by a blow from one of the men who had jostled them.

Zainub Asvat, a medical student from Wits, quickly tore a bandage from her scarf and, as she wound it around Amina's head, said, "Okay. If this is how it has to be, fine. We are in it now and we shall face it to the bitter end."

Within the hour the howling mob returned, armed with bicycle chains, belts and knuckle dusters. Whilst they circled the defenceless women, two police vans and an ambulance pulled up and parked across the street. With the police looking the other way, the mob waded in. Lakshmie Govender went down from a blow to her head. Zubeida Patel bent over to assist her when the steel buckle of a belt caught her on the temple, spouting blood over her attacker. "You're a big man," Mrs Pather said mockingly. A second later a huge fist split her lips apart.

In a few minutes the ground was littered with bodies. As suddenly as they had arrived, the whites dispersed, jeering and screaming as they disappeared in the distance.

"That'll teach you a lesson," a straggler shouted.

"Teach me another tomorrow," Lakshmie shouted back. "We'll be here again. Same time, same place."

Five of the injured women were loaded into the ambulance. Those who could walk were arrested by the police and herded into the vans.

"Why are you arresting us?" Zohra Bhayat asked.

"For travelling without a permit," a policeman replied with a laugh.

As Zainub Asvat entered the van, she turned around and saw several policemen laughing and joking with some of the men who had returned and were busy pulling the tents down and taking them away.

It was an incident that had been repeated throughout the city that night.

The women were not intimidated. The sit-in continued, for weeks on end. The men, unable to deter their wives, resorted to the only option open to them. They joined the determined protestors and, at the same time, provided them with the protection that the police refused to give them.

∞

On the thirteenth of June Indians throughout the country downed tools and declared it a national day of mourning. On that Thursday morning, "Hartal Day", the Indian quarter of Durban resembled a Sunday. The streets were empty, the stores and offices closed. The children refused to go to school and these also closed down for the day. Sastri College was deserted, as was the Durban Indian Girls High School.

It was also the day on which the Ghetto Bill was rushed through Parliament and passed into law. The same afternoon India severed its diplomatic relations and recalled its High Commissioner.

The next morning Dr Goonum was picked up by a police van as she crossed Queen Street and, by that very afternoon, sentenced to three months of hard labour. Her crime? Disturbing the peace!

The following Monday, Zainub Asvat took the platform and addressed a massive gathering of angry Indian citizens.

"If you are looking for an example of the saying that those whom the gods wish to destroy they first make mad, you only need to look over your shoulder. And if there is such a thing as madness being contagious, then it appears as if our rulers have infected their own people with the most virulent form of that disease.

"It is the prejudice, the intolerance and the colour madness of white South Africans that must now accept the responsibility for what must follow. And it is the protection of this civilisation that Smuts uses as an excuse for enacting the Ghetto Bill. It is a strange civilisation that operates through the law of the jungle.

"I ask every member of the ruling race to search their consciences and reconcile the high principles that their leader so hypocritically expounds at the United Nations with the laws he enacts here at home in their name. They should consider whether this treatment of their fellow human beings is in keeping with the tenets of their religion, their civilisation and the ideals of democracy for which they, in comradeship with other dark races, fought a horrifying war.

"Whilst they're about it they must also examine the attitude of their police force. As upholders of the law their duty is clear. The actions of Hitler's storm-troopers and those of our police are so identical one wonders whether these men are recent immigrants from Nazi Germany.

"As far as the rest of us here are concerned, our task by comparison is relatively simple — in the pursuit of truth, it is impossible for us to compromise, we are now more determined than ever before to carry the banner of justice."

When she paused for a sip of water a lady in the back row raised her hand.

"Yes?"

"Miss Asvat, what will happen to your medical studies? Will you be allowed to return to Wits? I ask because the girls at Durban Girls High have been threatened by their white headmistress with expulsion for participating in Hartal Day."

"I have probably been expelled already. That is the least of my concerns. Education, without the freedom to exercise your knowledge, is like a marriage between two members of the same sex. It is a farce that cannot be consummated.

"I do not believe in participating in such farcical charades."

∞

With the Resistance Movement engaging a higher gear and entering the international arena, the illegitimate regime of Smuts and his cohorts bared its fangs. It moved in with a vengeance, ignoring the isolated and ineffectual voices of its somewhat liberal members. At a stroke of the pen, overnight and with breathtaking audacity, it declared the affluent sections of the city as exclusive areas for White occupation. Thousands of gracious and beautifully maintained homes, constructed and owned by Indian residents in the quiet suburbs of First Avenue, Mitchell Road, Florida Road, Cowey Road and their adjacent environs, were expropriated and their occupiers given thirty days in which to vacate the premises. Compensation, determined solely by the government, would be decided on at some future date. It was a looters' paradise. The white financial establishment, in cahoots with the State, rubbed its collective hands in gleeful anticipation of enormous profits.

Mortgages on properties owned by Indians were arbitrarily called up, leading to foreclosure and forced sales to European buyers at prices that were a fraction of the market value. Even in cases where the owners were able to come up with the money to liquidate the debt, they were turned away at the door and sent packing. Needless to say, the law specifically prohibited any Indian from attending such auctions. Suddenly, every white could afford a ready-made mansion. Railway shunters and office workers were elevated to the middle class whilst the middle class Indian was reduced to penury. The new rich acquired airs and graces that would have made an English lord blush with embarrassment.

A specially created corp of enforcers, known as "The Investigators", accompanied by the CID, invaded Indian homes to check on contraventions of the Ghetto Bill. Their powers of entry were as wide as their filthy mouths and roving hands — they could enter any Indian occupied property, without notice and without seeking permission, at any time of the day or night, and demand proof of occupation and seize documents that, in their opinion, indicated a contravention of the infamous Act.

In terms of the law, this new band of lecherous looters, who had the express right to summarily interrogate anyone, became a law unto themselves. Any refusal, the slightest show of defiance, was subject to a fine of £100 and imprisonment of one year. Premises which the investigators, in their sole opinion, considered as being illegally tenanted resulted in the occupants having to pay a fine of £5 per day for each day of such occupation.

The investigators' report on the matter was sufficient evidence for the courts to ensure compliance with the Act and to pass sentence.

The reign by terror had begun.

∞

Dara grew increasingly morose and irritable. The hitherto paragon of dignity argued with Madhoo Daya constantly, stretching their relationship to its limitations. Every rumour, each morsel of an unjust action, caused him to fly into a rage.

"Look at this!" he shouted, slamming his huge fist into a copy of *The Leader* that was spread over his knees. "Read this! They've cancelled this chap's taxi licence because he is a member of Congress. And look here, thirteen Indian-owned properties in Umbilo Road have been expropriated, without any compensation. Tell me, Madhoo-kaka, is this not daylight robbery?"

"It's daylight robbery," Madhoo said, trying to placate him.

"So what do I say to Yacoob? He asks me these questions daily, demands to know what our policies have achieved so far. I have no answers for him."

"I know, Dara, I know. The young ones are growing increasingly rebellious. Passive Resistance is not a concept that they have any faith in. Who can blame them."

"And yet he is besotted with those Resistance people. He follows Dadoo and Naicker around the city, attends every rally at which they speak. Now he speaks with more authority than a veteran politician. Our children are becoming rebels, losing out on their education and their youth."

"We cannot hide the truth from them. Your father and I are now too old to be of any use to anyone. It's Yacoob and his age group that will bear the brunt of these vile laws. It would be wrong to delude them into believing differently, that our rulers will suddenly see reason and act as decent human beings."

"But what about their own people? Are they so blind that they cannot see what is being done in their name? How can they vote monsters like these into power?"

"They are the products of those you refer to as monsters. They are inundated with handouts. They live in homes they never dreamed they would ever own. They receive free medical care, they enjoy huge state pensions, given to them by a government growing rich on our looted wealth and on the labour of the black men on the farms and the mines. Their children have magnificent playing fields, swimming pools, free schooling and open universities. Their businesses grow rich on slave labour, which in turn allows them to pay their own kind a salary several times in excess of what they produce. They have been spoilt beyond redemption. Can you see them voting their benefactors out of power?"

"Then there is no hope."

"There is always hope. Evil cannot last forever. In time the forces of good always triumph."

"When? Another hundred years later?"

"You tire me, Dara. I have no other answers for you."

"And the answers you have given me do not help anymore. Neither does *Baji*, who has retreated into a shell of his own."

"I'm afraid he is beginning to lose faith in the principles of non-violence."

"Then it may be time for us to listen to our children for a change. If we have no answers for them then it's fair that we ask them for a solution."

"Their solution will result in a bloodbath."

"It will lead to that anyway. I will never understand the white race. They divide the world into two camps, then say white is right and black is bad. If they believe that why don't they just stay at home and stop exploiting black assets?"

"Greed is always more palatable when it is justified in some manner. Whether the facts support their theory is not important."

"*Baji* once told me, many years ago, that Europe and its greed will spawn a devil, a monster with an insatiable need, and that he will be spawned from amongst his own kind. I believe *Baji* was right and Hitler was that monster."

"And they turned to the very countries that they exploited for help in pulling him down. India had to send its men to assist in what was, really, a white-on-white conflict."

"So do we wait until Smuts turns on his own colour before we stop him? Perhaps Yacoob is right when he says that appealing to their reason only encourages them to exploit us further. After all, they know they are safe from our vengeance."

"Dara, you are trying to justify a physical retaliation."

"I am trying to understand how my son and his contemporaries think.

I have to at least admit that if our approach consistently fails, then it must be discarded and replaced with something that is effective and can stop this blatant looting."

"The only alternative to peaceful protest is a violent uprising. I have already told you the end result of that is a bloodbath."

"That may be preferable to the gradual draining of our lifeblood, which only weakens us."

"Dara, what is happening to you? Do you know what you're saying?"

Dara buried his head in his lap in frustration. Madhoo Daya looked miserable and ancient beyond his years. Shaida, in the kitchen, listened and hugged herself in despair.

∞

"They can't do that to him," Yacoob said to Sandy. "Do you know who that is? That man is Moonsamy Govender, the one they call 'Katmarandi'. Chico told me he fought almost sixty bouts, drew once and never lost."

"I know, Jake. I've spent a lot of time at his home in Grey Street. I've even been to his old home in Mount Edgecombe. He taught me a lot about fighting."

"But Sandy, he's an old man. He earns his living as a confectioner, working from home. He won medals for those wedding cakes that those bastards threw on the floor!"

"They've been known to do worse things."

"They wouldn't have tried that on him thirty years ago."

"Look, Jake, not even Katmarandi, in his prime, could have stood up to their guns. And no man, no matter how tough, can take on a gang of thugs who have the law behind them."

"Shit on that jive, buddy. The day those cowards come to my place I'll blow their heads off and to hell with their fucked up laws."

"That's the day they'll hand your body to us."

"That's fine too. If enough of us do that you can be sure they'll back off."

"Maybe. And that's a big maybe, Jake."

"At least we'll be doing something instead of just whining about how inhuman their behaviour is."

"They'll simply call out the army and wipe us out. You're wrong, buddy, your answer is not the way to handle it."

"What's the alternative? Plant a bomb in the investigators' basements?"

"It's certainly a better solution. Jake, I'm hungry. Let's get something to eat."

"You go ahead. I'm going to catch a bus to Overport to hear Dadoo. Want to come along?"

"No. I'm on the way to the market to make a few bucks. See you tonight?"

"Ja. Say around seven."

On the bus Yacoob squeezed next to two middle-aged men who were sitting on the wide bench seat. As the rickety vehicle rattled up Old Dutch Road, he idly listened to their talk, his mind still on Katmarandi.

"I had to take the afternoon off," one of the men said. "They'll dock me half a day's pay. But what can I do, our families were very close, used to be neighbours in Warwick Avenue for many years."

"You should have become a teacher, Ismail. We have all our afternoons off. What did you say his name was?"

"Michael — Michael Abrahams."

"Hey! I know that name. Michael Gabriel, wasn't it? A real dandy, always dressed in a suit and bow tie, centre parting, short hair. Saintly looking fellow with a long thin face."

"That's not a bad description of him, Vasi."

"Wasn't he a violin tutor? I think his daughter was Annie Lawrence."

"That's him. One of the best families in Durban. Came from Kimberley, actually. A top all-round sportsman in his younger days."

"I think he represented Griqualand West in the Sam China Cup."

"Among other things. He was quite a brilliant billiard player. Pretty tasty boxer too, turned pro for a while."

"What happened to him?"

"Didn't have the killer instinct. He had too gentle a nature and loved his music too much to remain a pugilist."

"What I mean, how did he die? Natural? I'm sure he wasn't very old."

"Early sixties, I suppose. I hear his heart gave in when they threw him out of his house. He built it himself, brick by brick. But you know how it is. People make these stories up ..."

"Who threw him out, then?"

"Agents of the Group Areas Act. The investigators."

"Fucken shits!" Yacoob spat out as he jumped up. "Fucken shits!"

"What did you say, boy? Did you hear that, Ismail. These youngsters, what do their fathers teach them?"

The bus had slowed down and Yacoob jumped off before it stopped, ran alongside it for a few seconds, then hopped onto the pavement. He was still seething with anger as he crossed the overgrown field and headed towards a huge crowd massed at the far end. When he heard Dr Dadoo's voice he knew he was late, had missed some of the speech. He pushed his way to the front, close to the speaker.

"... so don't talk to me about the British coming to our aid, or anyone else for that matter. And let me tell you something else: In the House of Commons, when Pritt of the Labour Party, asked Prime Minister Attlee if he had considered the cable that was sent by us, concerning racial discrimination here in South Africa, do you know what Attlee said? His answer, word for word, was 'as stated on previous occasions, the position of Indians in South Africa is not considered proper for interference by His Majesty's government.'

"This Bill is now the law of the land. It will lock up our people just as Hitler locked up the Jews. It's only a matter of time before they confine us to limited areas and then you can be sure death won't be far off. And Attlee has said he is not interested!

"It has already brought about our economic and social deaths. Give them time and the rest will follow.

"Sieg Heil, Herr Smuts! You have indeed donned the mantle of the Führer. Your hero didn't last long enough to see his pure white new world. Can you now succeed where he failed?

"Those of you who hear me, think very carefully. If you do nothing your children and your grandchildren will call you a recreant generation and spit on your graves. To go to jail is preferable to such a legacy."

Dr Dadoo was about to step down from the crude, makeshift platform when Yacoob asked, "Do you really believe that this policy of Passive Resistance will do any good?"

Dadoo smiled and said to one of his colleagues, in a low voice, "See, already the children are doubting us." To Yacoob he said, "Only time can answer that question. But the key word is resistance. I'm warning against doing nothing."

"If I'll die anyway," Yacoob said loudly, "I may as well die fighting. I haven't seen your way achieve anything yet."

Before Dadoo could respond, Yacoob walked away.

∽

"Will you listen to me?" Sandy lectured Jake that evening. "You can't fight an army with your fists. What was it you told me Chico said? 'Don't let anyone test your abilities lest you be found wanting!' Was that it? That was good advice. How come you have such a short memory?"

"Because good men are already dying, Sandy ..."

"And you think that by adding to their number you'll solve the problem?"

"How come nobody has any answers, only questions?"

"Jake, take it easy. Listen, let the Resistance build up. Already it is a formidable force. The hatred for the white man is festering and getting worse as the days go by. The time will come when the fires of our leaders will burn out and they call on us. It won't help if we're six feet under then."

"We can't just sit and wait while these bastards ..."

"You're not listening now. I'm saying we learn all we can, add to our knowledge of the politics of the situation. With that comes conviction and strength. Right now you're reacting in anger and that is a dangerous emotion that takes away your reason. Listen to people like Dadoo. They've given up their livelihood, lost their wealth to talk to us. They've been to jail simply for exposing the looters. You can't call them stupid; do you really believe that they are cowards, or less angry than you? They are realists, my friend. They know that farting against thunder raises nothing but a big stink. Learn to bide your time, keep your anger in check, and when the moment is right move in with a vengeance. If that takes another hundred years, that's okay. Any other action will simply kill all hope."

"And what makes you so clever?" Jake asked. "I seldom see you at the rallies."

"I get around. And look, *lighty* ..."

"I'm a *lighty* now? How much older are you?"

"We grow up fast around here. Anyway, all I'm saying is first we survive, then we fight. Now, are you game to try your luck with the bioscope racket? There's money to be made."

"I guess *lighties* like money too," Jake grinned.

Much later, at just after eight that night, Jake walked into his grandfather's yard. Dara and his mother were sitting cross-legged on the floor. Yahya was dozing in his rickety wooden chair. Jake's grandmother, Madhoo Daya and his wife were conversing in low tones not far away. The inevitable copy of *The Leader* was in Dara's lap.

"Did you read this, Madhoo-kaka? Some young chap called TM Moodley told a group of students in Maritzburg exactly what he thinks of Smuts. You know what worries me? The whites don't read *The Leader* and the white-owned dailies don't report on these things. Do they really know what's going on?"

"He's at it again," Nadia whispered.

Madhoo nodded and said, "The whole country is at it. But there are times when you have to relax. Dara hasn't learnt that yet." Turning to Dara he said, "I know that tone, Dara. You start with a very reasonable question and end up arguing with me. I'm not in the mood for you tonight."

"I'm only saying," Dara continued, unfazed, "that this chap, the editor of *The Leader*, doesn't pull his punches. He says here, 'Smuts, the apostle of tyranny in South Africa, will don the mantle of the prophet once again overseas.' To say that, in print, takes a lot of courage."

Suddenly, Dara threw the paper on the ground. "But only we Indians read this. I don't think a single white cares how they get their benefits."

"That may be so," Madhoo said, drawn in spite of himself. "But you're wrong about the whites. Many of them are beginning to condemn Smuts."

"Name one?" Dara demanded. "Just one."

"I can name many. The Bishop of Pretoria, the Reverend Wilfred Parker, openly denounced white supremacy and asked Smuts to give up what he called the *Herrenvolk* attitude. Those were his exact words."

"He did? I didn't hear about it."

"That's because you've closed your mind to anything that's good about the whites. In that, you're not alone."

"That's because Dara," Shaida said, "like all our men, talks too much. They never stop to listen."

"I should have married your sister," Dara said. "She had more respect."

"Respect does not put food on the table," Shaida retorted. "Have you ever been to any of our stores? They're always short of milk, bread and rice. There's so little rice we have to stand in queues, for hours, to get just a handful. There's plenty of it if you pay the black-market price. A few weeks ago I paid just two shillings for a bottle of oil. Now they are demanding five shillings and sixpence! What am I supposed to pay with? Respect?"

"Did I ask you to give your jewellery to Congress?" Dara demanded.

"Wait! Wait!" Madhoo cut into the argument. "Shaida, why don't you go to the white stores?"

"Do you know how they treat us there? When we walk in the white assistants look at us as if we are dirty. They just ignore us and refuse to serve us. And when they sometimes do serve us it's even worse. They call us 'Mary' and short change us."

"Then they insult the mother of their god," Dara interrupted. "Why should that upset you?"

"I told you he's looking for an argument," Nadia said.

"Yacoob?" Dara suddenly shouted, "Why are you hiding in the shadows? Come here!"

Yacoob approached his father and folded his hands across his chest. Nadia smiled and asked, "Have you eaten, *dikra?*"

"First you greet your elders," Dara ordered. "Then you tell me why you haven't been to school lately. And why you haven't been to your *madressah* classes. Then you eat."

By the time Yacoob had finished greeting everyone, Yahya had jerked awake and pulled Yacoob to him, rescuing him from Dara's accusations. In spite of his advanced age, Yahya was still a powerful man. His heavily veined arms were like steel bands that crushed Yacoob to his side.

"You grow tall, like a Pathan should," Yahya boomed through his long white beard, his barrel chest heaving. "Don't worry about your father. First you eat, always. How can you think straight and show respect on an empty stomach? Look at Madhoo Dada. He eats beans and roti all day and grows shorter."

"And who sleeps all day?" Madhoo asked, "with his stomach full of meat."

"Sleep! Who was sleeping? Was I asleep when I heard Dara scolding my grandson?"

"Go back to sleep," Nadia said, "between you and Dara poor Madhoo ..."

"Me?" Dara asked. "I have never shown any disrespect to ..."

"*Choop, sala!* Shaida cut in. "Don't be rude when *bai* is speaking."

"You see," Dara said to Madhoo, spreading his hands. "This woman that all of you were so anxious to marry me to ..."

Nadia burst out laughing. "We were so anxious? Who was shaking like a leaf when he first saw Shaida? You're right, you should have married her sister. Maybe then your big mouth would have remained shut for ever and the rest of us could have lived in peace."

Shaida blushed and disappeared into the kitchen. Yacoob grabbed the opportunity and escaped into the streets.

∞

The Casbah on a Saturday morning was like no city anywhere on earth. The streets and pavements were clean, the shop windows freshly washed and glittering, the shoppers dressed in festive gear and wearing anything from the sari to the Hawaiian sarong. Old men in turbans and long shirts shuffled alongside the younger generation in jeans and colourful T-shirts.

They came from everywhere, from the suburbs and the country towns, from distant villages and tiny hamlets; white, black, brown and all shades in between smiled at perfect strangers and strolled on the pavements with gay abandon, some looking for bargains, a large number simply out to enjoy the day and meet friends and relatives before moving on to restaurants and bioscopes.

Each street served a specific function. The eastern end of Victoria Street was theatre-land, the western half reserved mainly for the markets and grocery stores. Grey Street, from the racecourse to the West End Hotel in Pine Street, was the clothes-horses' paradise, offering an array of the most recent fashion trends from virtually every major centre in the world, the garments carefully copied and faultlessly reproduced in local sweat shops and factories. Queen Street was a street of barbers on the one side and hardware and timber merchants on the other. Pine Street housed the best family-owned tailor shops in the world; Prince Edward Street the neatest sari houses and craftsmen jewellers. In between and at every corner was the inevitable tea-room, serving the best in chilli-bites and confectionery.

It was a day reserved exclusively for pleasure. It seemed to provide a catharsis for body and soul and primed the spirit for the week ahead. It was also the day on which Jake, Sandy and their mates made more money than the average bank manager earned in a week.

The numbers racket, or *Fah Fee* as it was called, was played by nearly everyone who could spare a tickey or more and provided a lucrative source of income for the streetwise operators, which was supplemented by the sale of black-market cinema tickets, always in short supply and available only from sharp-eyed operators who had cornered the market. They were bought and sold with a cheerful smile and a gambler's abandon. It was simply a part of life in the Casbah.

And life in the Casbah was about politics too. Children were weaned on it, as children elsewhere were weaned on mother's milk. It was the logical outcome of the policies of repression, the common denominator around which their lives revolved. Spectators watched sport and simultaneously talked politics, diners enjoyed their meals and discussed the latest developments, young couples impressed each other with their awareness and the depth of their knowledge, and street sweepers picked up pamphlets and debated the merits of protest as a force for peaceful change. There was no other area of under one square mile that could equal it for the intensity of its emotions and its pursuit of justice.

Elsewhere, in the corridors of power, the government of General Smuts was equally determined in its refusal to bow to world pressure. When the Resistance arranged for Sorabjee Rustomjee to go to America and the UNO and present its case, he was promptly arrested on a trumped-up charge that the courts gleefully pounced on, and smugly sentenced him to three months imprisonment. The Resistance responded with equal speed. It nominated Ashwin Choudree as its new spokesman and swiftly flew him out of the country. It was fast learning the tactics of evasion.

But the Resistance was, nevertheless, considerably weakened. Under a ludicrous law called the Riotous Assemblies Act, its leaders were unceremoniously arrested and carted off to jail. And, in cases where the Act was too obviously inapplicable, the prosecutors simply resorted to an equally ridiculous seventy-year-old trespass law and arrested individual leaders as they walked down the street.

Together with Rustomjee, RA Pillay and MD Naidoo were locked up. Doctors Naicker, Goonum and Dadoo were picked up the next day and hauled off to jail. A further three hundred and twenty registered members were arraigned before the magistrates and arbitrarily fined the sum of £5 each. When they chose to go to jail instead, they were informed that their assets would be attached to cover the fines. They simply nodded, refused to pay anyway and dared the courts to do their damndest.

Suddenly, support came from an unexpected quarter. A clergyman from the Rand, the Reverent Michael Scott, stepped onto the platform at Nichol Square — renamed the Red Square by the white press — and gravely announced, "It is not the resistors who are on trial. It is my religion and my race that stands condemned."

He had barely finished speaking when Mrs Lavoipierre, the Chairperson of the Council for Human Rights, declared in a firm voice, "The aim of my council is to see that freedom does not represent an empty word." When Benny Sischy mounted the platform, the police moved in. The three, together with a dozen white supporters, were arrested and escorted to prison.

In a packed court the next morning Dr Dadoo, grey-faced and unshaven, smiled grimly and said to the magistrate, "Impose the maximum sentence your warped minds can conjure up. Go ahead. Do it! All this is a farce anyway. Every piece of legislation you now fall back on is a mockery of justice, a travesty of decency, democracy and human rights. We both know it. Don't ask for my participation to salve your troubled conscience."

"Impose it," Dr Naicker said, "The maximum sentence."

"My people have had no part in forming your laws," MD Naidoo said. "We have no vote in what you choose to call a democracy. Why do you now ask me to plead my case? Just act on it. Pass the sentence!"

"There will be no peace on earth," Dr Goonum cried, "until colour as a measure of civilization is abandoned. There are nine million people in this country, ten times more than you represent, who had no stake in electing your government. You, sir, are a symbol of that government's laws. I, too, am a symbol — of all that is decent. I will never submit to you. Pass the sentence. Let's hear it!"

The magistrate, Mr LI Cohen, found them all guilty and sentenced them to six months' imprisonment.

When Benny Sischy was found guilty under the trespass laws and fined the sum of £5, he refused to pay. Turning to the magistrate, he said, "Although these laws exclude the Jewish people from their operation, it's an insult to you and I as members of the Jewish community. It is a violation of all that South Africans fought for in the war and of all democratic principles. It segregates the Indian people into ghettos, obstructs their social and economic development and denies them the most elementary human right — the right to live."

That weekend Dara was somewhat mollified to find that some whites at least were beginning to stand up and be counted on the side of justice.

"There may be hope after all," Yacoob said to Sandy. "I was beginning to believe all whites were moochers."

∞

By January 1947, the family owned weekly, *The Leader*, stood out as the only paper anywhere in the country that dared to openly defy the government. The white press, when it bothered to comment at all, glossed over the facts and made little mention of the massive resistance displayed by the Indian community. The majority of the whites continued to enjoy life in blissful ignorance of the source of their munificence.

"THE GESTAPO WALKS AGAIN" the headlines in *The Leader* screamed. In issue after issue it attacked the government, reported extensively on the horrendous actions of the investigators and the police, and exposed the courts for their duplicity and the agility with which they responded to ensure that the despicable laws were fully invoked. Over 1 500 resistors were in jail by then, for crimes the democracies of the world would have laughed at.

When, in February 1947, *The Leader* reported that King George VI had bestowed the Order of Merit and honoured Smuts at a gala function in Durban, Dara almost had a heart attack.

"*Ben chod*!" he repeated unbelievingly, over and over again. "Is there no end to British duplicity? They honour the re-incarnation of Hitler! Have they forgotten already, in less than two years?"

When Madhoo Daya refused to respond, Dara became enraged. "Have they forgotten that India sent the cream of its armed forces to support them in their battle against that madman whose protegé they now treat as a hero? The Indians gave their lives so the British could live. It was they who were being invaded, their country that was facing destruction, not India."

Madhoo remained silent, his head bowed, desolated by the British betrayal and their disregard of the entire world's condemnation of Smuts' devious behaviour. "Do you remember, Madhoo-kaka, how proud we were when we read that the Indian armies had won over six thousand awards for gallantry? It says here, in *The Leader*, that they received no less than thirty one Victoria Crosses, two hundred and fifty two DSOs, one thousand three hundred and eleven Military Crosses, four George Crosses and three hundred and forty seven of the same Order of Merit that they now hand out so freely. This same George, this Royal buffoon, this bloody idiot ..." Dara spluttered, ranted and raved at Madhoo, swore repeatedly and slammed his massive fist on the sturdy table, splitting it apart and sending it crashing to the ground.

"Enough," Shaida said, her eyes blazing. "Madhoo-kaka, call *Baji* before this *gadha* hurts himself."

"It's okay," Madhoo said. "I don't blame him." Then, for the first time in over forty years, Dara saw Madhoo Daya lose his temper. It was an awesome sight and it shook him.

"Dara," Madhoo said, furious with an anger that shook his small frame, "Britain is a country of hypocrites. You talk as if you expect some loyalty from them. When will you realise that it is a nation in decline?"

"Madhoo-kaka, I ..."

"*Choop*! Go to your store. Leave now!"

Dara turned and walked away, his shoulders slumped.

"That was unfair," Kantha said. "This is his father's home. You have no right ..."

"Don't you speak to me about rights, woman."

"I'm sorry, Madhoo-kaka," Shaida said apologetically. "I've tried to hide this paper but ..."

"No, Shaida, don't ever do that. It's not why I'm angry. *The Leader* reports the facts. We cannot live in ignorance."

Madhoo took several deep breaths, brought himself under control, then smiled sadly. "I'm cross because Dara ignores his business, his turnover is dropping. If he doesn't pull himself together he'll be in serious trouble. But I understand his frustrations. His behaviour may be extreme, but it is the mirror image of what every Indian is going through in this city today. I hear the talk on the street corners. There is a mood of anger everywhere and there's always the danger that it could break out into general violence. I pray that our people's respect for law and order is not overcome by emotion. We may be able to contain Dara's generation. As for the younger ones ..."

Madhoo shook his head and shuffled out, Kantha following. Shaida watched them till they disappeared from sight, then slumped into a chair, her heart heavy as a lump of lead.

❦

At the Queen's Tea Room, across from the mosque, Jake and Sandy were having a late lunch. Shanti, the owner, was standing close by, talking to a customer.

"My grandparents came here long before many of these whites," he was saying, "from Rajputana. We are members of the Kshatriya, the warrior class. Neither the Mughal, nor the British after them, ever succeeded in ruling us for long. They preferred, ultimately, to enter into an alliance with us rather than attempting to subjugate us. If there were enough of us Rajputs in this country, things would not have been allowed to go so far. But we're only a handful, we are forced to go along with the rest. This Passive Resistance, it is stupid. The two words negate each other."

Mr Gani, who occasionally managed Mad Mullah's gambling school down the passage next door, walked in and joined Sandy and Jake at their table. "Gani–dada", as he was universally known, was immaculately dressed in his usual dark blue pin-striped suit and navy tie. He was an incredibly handsome man who bore a strong resemblance to the actor Errol Flynn.

Gani–dada had caught the tail end of Shanti's statement and smiled. "Not even all the Rajputs, the Gurkhas, the Pathans and the Sikhs put together stand a chance against the might of this State."

"I was told that they are great warriors, brave men who never show their backs to an enem,." Jake said.

"They are that and a lot more. They are also masters of the art of guerrilla warfare. They are skilled night fighters, darkness is their friend,

113

their ally. They become one with the shadow and a few can decimate a whole battalion with no more than a knife. But they are the advance guard who soften the enemy's defences and clear the way. Without the back-up of tanks and artillery their efforts would be wasted. Anyway, as Shanti says, it's not the warrior clans that came to this country. The majority of Indians here are either of peasant stock or from the business class. Such people do not make very good fighters."

"So they talk," Jake said.

"Quite right. It's the only option open to them."

"It's an option that the other races see as the act of a coward."

"Then they are stupid, or ignorant. Take your pick."

"And you, Gani-dada?" Sandy asked with a grin, eyeing the jack-razor sticking out of Gani's vest pocket. "Which of these mighty tribes are you from? You don't hesitate to use that weapon. I've seen you wield it with telling effect against some of the whites that come here looking for easy pickings."

"I only use it when they initiate the action and when all other reasonable avenues fail."

"And the cops?" Jake asked. "What do you tell them when they see it?"

"Simply that I am a barber, which I am, and the razor is a tool of my trade, which it is."

"Look who walked in," Jake said.

Sandy stretched elaborately, pretended to ease his neck muscles, then casually turned around. "Crazy Killroy," he laughed. "Ignore him or he'll come over and pour water into our food."

"Not everyone thinks he's crazy," Jake said. "Have you seen him when he discards those filthy rags, has a bath, shaves and puts on decent clothes?"

"He's crazy alright," Sandy said. "But he has his lucid moments from time to time. Do you know his story?"

"I've heard some vague rumours about how he ended up on the streets."

"Forget what you heard. I know all about him and his family. Killroy there, and I forget his proper name, was the most brilliant student at Sastri some years ago. Remember Mr Bengali, the maths wizard? He couldn't keep up with Killroy. Once, under a fictitious English name, old Bengali forwarded a postal entry on behalf of Killroy to some maths olympiad that was open to whites only. Killroy not only walked away with the first prize, the judges came looking for him to meet the genius personally. When they finally traced him to Sastri and saw our black boy there, the South Indian upstart, they had him expelled for trying to pass himself off as a white.

Poor Mr Bengali almost lost his job. They accused him of an act of duplicity and called him a son of a bitch in front of his entire class. Of course, they withdrew the award that Killroy was so proud of. But that's not what broke him.

"A few weeks later they threw his family out of their home, which they had owned for over forty years. But that didn't stop the bastards. The family is still waiting for compensation and living in a shack in Tintown. As for our friend there, his school days were over. No educational institute dared to accept him. Unable to find any joy amongst the derelicts in Tintown, Killroy sought solace on the streets. Finally something in him snapped, as it was bound to. In a fit of anger the normally placid genius beat up a white cop who was harassing some female hawkers. They threw him in jail. What you see now is what came out of prison. Nobody knows what they did to him when he was inside."

"Tell that story to any white man and he would call it far-fetched," Gani-dada chuckled.

"There are some of our own who think so," Sandy said drily. "But those are the facts. Talk to anyone who was in Sastri that year. Talk to Mr Bengali."

"That's our biggest problem," Jake said. "Look around you. Everyone here, and all over town, what are they doing? Talking! Our leaders go overseas and talk. The United Nations passes resolutions and then talks some more. And Smuts? He tells the UNO to mind its own business, literally slaps it in the face, and carries on regardless. *The Leader* says it is all reminiscent of Hitler in his hey-days, when he defied the League of Nations. By the time the world stopped talking and woke up to Hitler's tricks, millions of Jews were dead — ask them how all the talking helped."

"When there is no other option," Gani-dada said, "all one can do is resort to reason. What did the poet Iqbal say? 'The pen is mightier than the sword'."

"Pure crap," Jake said. "Try pointing a pen at a man who wants to shoot you. If you're lucky he'll probably die laughing before he pulls the trigger."

Sandy grinned and clapped Jake on the shoulder. Gani-dada, unamused, smiled wanly. "You *lighties* haven't lived long enough. There are subtle nuances to the poet's words."

"Words, Gani-dada, words. That's what we keep coming back to. But okay, so tell me why only the Indians are so good with them?"

"When you say that you display your ignorance. The African has been trying to reason with the whites for over a hundred years."

"And when you say that," Jake interjected, "you fight my argument."

"Okay, Jake. I give up. I'm a barber, not a politician."

"I'm not finished. What about the coloured?"

"What about him?"

"There are five times more of them than us. How come they're so silent?"

"You really believe that? That they're silent?"

"Oh, they talk all right," Sandy butted in. "But what do they say? One of their leaders, the Chairman of the Coloured Advisory Council, chap by the name of Marcus Goulding, openly stated that, 'at my instigation General Smuts has declared that the coloured people must be looked upon as an appendage to the human race'. Can you understand the implication of such a statement? But then he goes on to say 'salvation of the coloured people did not lie in a non-European front'. He not only spurns the idea of an alliance with us and the African, he goes on to insult us by saying: 'But I am not anti-Indian. My wife is an Indian'. What is he trying to do, suck up to the whites?"

"You *lighties* are clued up. But there is something you have to learn, you must look beyond the statements of one man, no matter whom he claims to represent. I haven't heard of him but he sounds like a government lackey. We have one or two like him amongst us."

"Like hell," Jake said. "Our people will tear him apart in the streets."

"Listen, you two," Gani-dada said. "It's time you spread the horizons of your knowledge a bit further. If you think the Indian is hounded I suggest you examine what the coloured is going through."

"I know what he is going through," Sandy said. "We are talking about his politics."

"I'm no expert there. I'm a hustler and a barber. But I'm twice your age and I can teach you a thing or two. The coloured is a descendant of mixed races, he is constantly torn between two worlds. The race classification laws splits their families up, tears them apart. Go and speak to them. Many of them are your friends and neighbours. Instead of blindly condemning them on the strength of one man's statement, talk to them. Don't fall in the government's trap of divide and rule."

"All we're saying is they're strangely silent," Jake said. "Look, they're not all descendants of a white ancestor. Many are the result of unions between the African and the Indian. And why do they anglicise their Indian surnames, as if they're ashamed of their origins. Perhaps it's an attempt to pass off as white, if only on paper."

"You're talking sociology now, not politics. And you are also displaying your stupidity. Answer the question yourself. How come you're called Jake? Why did you anglicise?"

"Okay, okay," Jake grinned. "I think the word is touché. Point taken, Gani-dada."

"That's what I like about you guys, you're quick to learn ... but hang on, here comes someone better qualified to answer you. Hey, Moses, over here!"

Moses Renton, a principal at a coloured school and a cueist of great repute, ambled over.

"Hello, *dada*. You treating today?"

"Why not. Grab a chair. These boys have some questions for you."

"Who hasn't? The streets are full of kids, most of them only ten or twelve years old. They should be in school instead of distributing pamphlets and asking questions. You know what my barber just asked me? You all know Mahomed from across the street at the Embassy. 'Tell me, Mr Renton, does evil have a lifespan?' How do I answer that? Now you lighties want to pick my brains. Give me a break. Questions I answer in school. I come here to relax."

"Well, relax while you answer this one," Gani-dada said. "You'll love it, if I know you. Go ahead, Sandy."

"We were wondering why the coloured community is so silent," Sandy said.

"You *lighties* don't ask easy questions," Renton answered. "And you are far wiser than those of your age a generation ago. Perhaps that's one good thing that's come out of all this. I can guarantee there's not one white kid as politically advanced as those I meet in the Casbah. And your command of the language, I doubt any English-speaking boy of your age can even come close to you. Must come from all the reading you do.

"Anyway, back to your question. There is no quick answer. But I'll try. This Act, the one we call the Ghetto Act, is aimed specifically at the Indian and it's prime purpose is to ruin him economically. The coloured owns little by the way of property and no businesses worth mentioning. They are mainly artisans, with a sprinkling of academics.

"They are busy fighting a unique battle of their own, one initiated by our common enemy. They are struggling to hold their families together, to stop brother from being separated from brother, mother from daughter, father from son. They are victims of a different Bill, the Racial Classification Act or something like that. And the government's agents use the pencil — which was invented solely for the purpose of reproducing man's thoughts on paper — as a tool that determines who is white and who isn't. If the pencil slides smoothly through your hair you're home and dry. You're white, brother, come and enjoy all the privileges. If it catches, even slightly, then that's your lot and off you go, to the nearest bush.

"I could go on. Like the dark child being sent to play in the garden when the white cousins visit. Or the one sister who gets a plum job in a white company while the other, better qualified, has to make do as the tea-maid. I'm afraid that, in a nutshell, will have to satisfy you for now.

"I'm not saying the Ghetto Act won't affect us. It will. When they take you out of your home and hand it to a white, do you think that white will tolerate a coloured neighbour for more than a few days? But the Indians are property owners, the coloured is a tenant. When he is pushed out he can move on without any great financial loss. The fact that the issue goes beyond such monetary considerations is of lesser importance to people who are battling to keep body and soul together and their families intact."

"Okay, let's drop that for a moment," Sandy said. "Why are the whites trying to break the back of the wealthy Indian? After all, eighty percent of our people live below the poverty line. Those are their statistics, not mine."

"That's an easy one, my boy. Your wealth is a threat to them. You can use it to mobilise the other deprived race groups, for one thing. But wealth is only one issue. Ask any Jew why the Nazis persecuted him. Greed is one of the motivators, jealousy another, your academic achievements a third. Your pride in your culture, the fact that you scorn their culture, could also be a part of it. I could go on. Spare me the agony. It will only spoil my appetite."

"Mr Renton," Jake asked. "Do you think passive resistance will achieve anything?"

"Honestly? No, it won't. But neither will its alternative."

"So where does one go from here?"

"If I could answer that I wouldn't be a school principal. I'll be the head of this country."

∞

When Dara and Shaida turned into Wills Road, on their way to visit the Narans, it was just beginning to get dark. The Pather house, and its neat garden, was ablaze with lights. A festive atmosphere emanated from it and loud music spilled into the streets. People were moving in and out, laughing gaily and shouting congratulations.

"What's going on here?" Shaida asked Dara. "Looks like they're having a party."

"They would have invited us. Let's go in and find out."

"Dara! It's not decent to barge in like that."

At that moment Mrs Coovadia, from a few doors away, stepped onto the pavement. "Shaida, how are you?"

"Okay. What's going on?"

"Haven't you heard? Dicky and Maisie Rogers have appeared at a Royal Command Performance, at the London Palladium. They also performed, as Koba and Kali, before five of the Royal families of Europe. The Pathers only received the news yesterday from a friend of Dicky's who came over from London and brought the press cuttings. Dicky and Maisie are on their way to Hollywood now."

"And the Pathers only found out today?"

"They believe the government has been suppressing the news and intercepting Dicky's letters. Don't forget, they had to run away from here to avoid prosecution under the Immorality Act."

Shaida was excited. She wanted to go in and congratulate the family but could barely get past the garden gate. The crush of well-wishers was so large that Mrs Pather's beautiful garden was all but ruined. When someone stepped on a rose bush Dara pulled her away.

"We'll come back tomorrow," he said, grumbling. "Look at what they have done to the poor woman's garden."

"Don't blame them," Shaida said. "They're all so happy. Aren't you excited?"

"About what? That boy always had it in him. I'm just happy that he rubbed the government's nose into its own shit."

"But it gives us all cause for hope."

"Hope? What hope?"

"That there is a better world, that there are decent whites."

"*Ben chod*!" Dara exclaimed. "That's overseas, woman, not here. You want to settle there? I don't mind."

"There you go again," Shaida sighed. "In a minute you'll start an argument." In a show of humour, for the first time since they had married, Dara actually began to fool around with her.

"Okay, Mary," he leered at her, "Now, how much for those lovely to-may-toes?" He was mimicking a white female at the Indian market, getting the accent just right. "Did you say sixpence! For those shrivelled old things? You coolies are nothing but rogues!"

Shaida looked up, saw Dara's wide grin, smiled and reached out to him.

"Come, *baas*. For you I make cheap."

"Shaida, are you mad! In public too!"

"Oh, shut up," she said. "I only wanted to hold your hand."

As they crossed the road Dara took her hand in his, still smiling.

∞

It was the last day of 1948 and Yahya sat in Pravin Naran's lounge and sipped his tea, then poured a saucerful and blew on it. He drank deeply and sighed as he sat back.

"Something is worrying you," Pravin said. "I know you too well. Now, are you going to tell me or keep me guessing?"

"Who can know me better than you do?"

"Madhoo Daya, I expect."

"Madhoo is my brother. Like you and I, we are family. But there are some things about me that only you know. What I have to discuss with you is not within the scope of Madhoo's abilities."

They had been talking in Gujerati, in their own quiet way. Nevertheless, Naran stood up and closed the door, ensuring their privacy. He did it more to reassure Yahya rather than a need for secrecy.

"Pravin, before I get on to more important things, I must first discuss Dara with you. I am concerned about him and his business. He neglects it and unless he does something he will reach a stage where it will no longer sustain him."

"I have repeatedly offered to help, set him up wherever he wishes. You keep turning me down. You don't know how painful I find that. Perhaps now, at last ..."

Yahya made a sweeping gesture, dismissing the offer once again. "If he cannot run his little store profitably anything bigger will be a waste of your money. I've always believed he had to find his own way in the world and, until recently, he was doing well, even bought a little place in Verbena Road a few years ago. But now he seems to have become unhinged, argues constantly and tries Madhoo's patience to the limit. In the meantime, the business suffers. In every other way he is fine. Together with Shaida and my grandchildren he spends a great deal of time at my place. For this I thank God daily."

Yahya had lapsed into silence and had withdrawn into his thoughts. Naran waited. With Yahya, he knew, patience was a virtue that was often tested to the extreme.

"It is this Resistance business," Yahya finally continued, "The crazy politics of this country, that are eating him up and making him doubt his reason. You and I, we grew up under the Raj, we know the British and their tricks. But this is something new, something terrible."

After lapsing into another of his silences, he muttered, "At least, in our days the British had some dignity. Now, as their Empire crumbles, so does their sense of decency. Their Royal family hands out medals the way we hand out charity on Thursdays to whoever comes to our door. *Tchah*! They are *chootyas*. Their days, like mine, are numbered."

Just as Naran was beginning to think that Yahya was going to withdraw into himself again, Yahya straightened up and began to speak in a firm voice.

"Pravin bhai, the time has come for me to prepare myself for the final journey. No, wait! Hear me out. We live here but we were born in India, we know these things. We see the signs and we read them, the way no Westerner can. Like the *Sufis*, we hear the tread of the messenger of death long before we hear the knock. When he comes we are not surprised, we need no extra time to put our affairs in order. He finds us prepared.

"And that is why I am here.

"I have no regrets. That which I could do nothing about, I learnt to live with. *Kismet, karma*, call it by whatever name. What is written decides how we live and how we die. All I have left undone is to wrap up my affairs and close the book. To do this correctly I need your assistance."

Pravin Naran's face was sombre, sad but composed. The inevitability of death did not disturb him. The fact that his friend would soon be gone forever pained him, but it was a pain tempered by acceptance, it was the salve that assuaged the grief he felt. He simply nodded and waited for Yahya to continue.

"Dara is my only son and I believe I have taught him well. With time I am confident he will come around again. But this country warps our character, brings the Pathan in us to the fore, makes us sometimes think that violence, which we foreswore years ago, may be our only hope after all. If Dara slips into that frame of mind, if he reverts to the way of his ancestors, he will perish.

"Who does that leave? Yacoob? I fear I have lost him already. But watch Salim, Pravin. That boy is mature beyond his years. He has a strength of character which, if allowed to develop, will exceed my highest expectations."

Yahya reached into his coat and extracted a small package.

"That is the problem I leave in your hands, together with this."

Even before Pravin touched it he knew what it contained.

"So, we come a full circle. Life does play some funny games."

"The value of the dagger must be immense today."

"Yahya, the only people who can come close to attaching a price to it are Sotheby's of London."

Pravin unwrapped the parcel, for only the second time in almost seventy years, and gazed at the glittering object in awe.

"I know a lot more about these things than I did when you first brought it to me. At a rough guess it's worth a million pounds, sterling. And if that shocks you prepare yourself for a bigger shock. My estimate is based on its intrinsic value only, purely on the size and quality of the diamonds, rubies and emeralds. This huge stone here, in the centre, is of a quality and clarity I have seldom seen before. It alone must weigh over ten carats. Every major collector in the world will covet this masterpiece, for his private pleasure and to thumb his nose at his rivals. At an auction it could possibly exceed my valuation several times. The Royal families of Europe will clamour for it.

"It is a unique example of its period. Nothing that even comes close to it exists. If it does it has disappeared into some tycoon's private museum."

"Do you feel the time has come to sell it?" Yahya asked.

"No. Never! Hopefully, it will remain in your family for a long time."

"Then I leave it in your good hands. When the time is right make the decision I would have made."

"It will be secure in my vault, to be held in trust until a decision is reached. I will give you a receipt for it, together with a photograph."

"I require no receipts or photographs."

"But Yahya, I am as old as you are. If something happens to me ..."

"Then you must make your preparations, as I have made mine."

"It's a great responsibility," Pravin sighed.

"And you are equal to it. Now, do you see a future for our people in this country?"

"Yes."

"In spite of what is happening?"

"Yes. I have faith in the belief that truth always triumphs in the end."

"And the properties in Grey Street?"

"They will remain ours, unless we willingly sell them. The government will not loot those, as a sop to world opinion. I could be wrong but I strongly believe that."

"What will a fair-sized store, with a warehouse and one or two large flats above, in a prime position, cost?"

"Around ten thousand pounds, depending on the size."

"Would one such be available for purchase?"

"It shouldn't be a problem."

"I am prepared to gamble on it then. I would like to secure a base for those I leave behind. But I do not wish them to know of it until one of them is equal to his inheritance."

"And the money to purchase the property?"

"You have everything I possess. Handle it however you wish."

"Here's what I think we should do," Naran said after a few moments reflection. "I will buy the property for cash. I will maintain it, pay all rates and taxes and let it on a monthly tenancy. I will use prevailing interest rates on long-term money as a guide and keep an account of all income and costs. On the day I hand it over I will pass a bond on it and recover my capital. Now, how do I register the property if you wish to keep it a secret from Dara?"

"Find a way around it," Yahya simply shrugged.

"The answer may lie in the formation of a company, with a blank share certificate. I'll speak to my accountants."

"Pravin bhai, don't bother me with the details. I'm tired now."

"*Acha*! Now this," Pravin said, pointing to the parcel that lay between them.

"My father instructed me to hand it to my eldest son, but only if he is equal to his inheritance. I assume that, in the event Dara does not qualify, my father's wish does not exclude his grandchildren."

"And that decision you leave to me?"

"If you accept it, in the name of our friendship. If not ..."

"No! No! I accept the responsibility. God help me to do the right thing."

"He will. When the time comes he will guide you."

"*Teek*! His will be done."

"Now I must go. Tonight concludes my preparations. God willing, I'll see you again."

"You don't look like a dying man to me," Pravin laughed. "You look as strong as a horse."

"There are many ways a man can die," Yahya said as he stood up. "*Khuda Hafeez.*"

"Go with God," Pravin echoed. "And I pray you read the signs all wrong."

"You know the signs are never wrong," Yahya said, as he hugged Naran.

"Gently, my friend, gently," Naran cried. "You bloody Pathans don't know your own strength, not even when you're about to die."

Dara was up before dawn. He had showered, changed, completed his Fijr prayers and was ready for breakfast by the time the sun peeped over the horizon. When he entered the kitchen Shaida was bending over the new coal stove, the latest from "Welcome Dover". The fire was already going well, warming the room. When she brought him his first cup of tea he was leaning back, the Globe chair tilted against the wall.

"You'll break the chair," Shaida snapped.

"What's for breakfast?" Dara asked, straightening up.

"It's getting warm. Learn to have *sabr*."

He looked up quizzically but Shaida had already turned away and was fussing at the stove.

"The boys are not up yet?" he asked.

"It's Sunday. They always sleep late. You want to wake them?"

"I only asked."

"Don't ask about things you already know."

"But the sun is already out. What is the time?"

"Look at your wrist. You're the one with the watch."

Dara was confused. It was obvious Shaida was angry about something, but he couldn't put his finger on it. If she thinks I'm going to ask her, he said to himself, she can wait forever.

"Looks like it'll be a warm day," he volunteered.

"It's summer. All days are warm."

"Nice day for a walk."

"You want to go now, or wait for your *nasto*?"

"You know I never leave home without having breakfast. *Ben chod*!"

Dara had tried to provoke her into an outburst, hoping the vulgarity would elicit a response and force her to make her point. Whatever it was, from her attitude he knew an argument was brewing. If she brought it up first he would have the edge later. When she ignored him he began to grow angry.

"You going to take all morning?" he demanded to know.

"This is Patel's tea room? I'm the waiter?"

"Did I say that? Am I a customer here who ..."

"No," she said sweetly, "you're the big boss, the *seth saab*."

"I did something wrong?" Dara burst out, unable to contain himself any longer.

"Why did you scold Yacoob last night?"

"So that's what it's all about."

"Yes. You don't know? And you slapped him. We don't do those things in this house."

"He's my son. I have the right to discipline him."

"And I'm his mother, not the maid. You don't think you should talk to me first?"

"Woman, you ..."

"Why did you slap him?"

"He goes around with the Vania boy. That boy is a bad influence."

"Nithin?"

"Yes, Nithin."

"What's wrong with him?"

"Look, woman, I don't spend the day in the kitchen. I hear things out there that ..."

"I hear things too. Why don't you ask me?"

"What do you hear? In this kitchen?"

"Nithin is a good boy," Shaida said, ignoring the jibe. "I know."

"Then why doesn't he get a job?"

"You got a job for him?"

"No, but ..."

"There are no jobs, Dara. You know it."

"So what's so good about him?"

"Now you want to discuss it? I'll tell you. He pays the rent, buys the food, and he gives his mother money to get the girls married."

"Where does the money come from?"

"He doesn't steal it. He sells newspapers and works at the docks. Nobody complains about him. And when he isn't working he's home early."

"Yacoob gets in late every night."

"So who is the bad influence?"

"Okay. Maybe I shouldn't have blamed Nithin last night, but Yacoob still needs disciplining."

"But you were wrong in the way you went about it," Shaida said, closing the subject and placing a fresh cup of tea and a plate of *Puree* and *Patha* on the table. Dara's eyes lit up, he began to smile, the bad humour vanishing. It was his favourite dish, a rare delicacy, the preparation of which was an art in itself that took several days of careful and time consuming labour. He began to wolf it down, pausing occasionally to sip his tea and savour the taste.

"When did you make this," he finally said as he slowed down. "I don't remember buying the *madhumbi* leaves."

"Nithin's mother made it," Shaida said sweetly. "He brought it over himself."

"*Acha*!" he said placatingly. "Maybe his father should ..."

"That *sharabi*! When is he ever sober? Don't talk to me about that *katchra*, that rubbish."

Dara resumed eating, reluctant to spoil his pleasure. At last he stood up, sated. "That was good. You want to take a walk with me?"

"What! You want to go for a walk, with me?"

"Something wrong with that? You my wife or what?"

"You've never asked me before, just to take a walk to nowhere."

"Woman! Will you stop babbling. You coming or what?"

"I'm coming. Let me fetch my scarf."

By the time they stepped into the street it was already quite warm. They strolled to the end of Verbena Road, walked alongside the bamboo trees and turned into Duffields Avenue, crossing over Carters Avenue and entering the park. For a while they moved aimlessly, leaving the pathway several times and crossing the tidy lawn to inspect the colourful flowers that were just beginning to bloom in profusion.

A little later they crossed over Old Dutch Road and entered Puterman's neat little store at the corner of Leathern Road. It was empty of customers and Puterman was reading the morning paper.

"Hello, Solomon," he said, looking up. "Morning, Mrs Solomon."

Shaida acknowledged the greeting with a smile and moved to the far end, examining a display of fresh fruit on a stand.

"Have you seen this," Puterman said to Dara. "Heaton Nicholls, the South African representative at the UNO said, 'There is no legal colour bar in South Africa. All there is is custom, which cannot be set aside by the government.' Can you believe this man's nerve? To lie so blatantly ..."

Please God, Shaida prayed, closing her eyes. Not now. Not this morning.

"It also says here," Puterman continued, "that the government announced last week that the building of Indian schools and Indian education itself is not a responsibility of the State. You know something, Solomon, when Germany ..."

"I'd like some fresh cakes, please," Shaida cut in quickly, distracting Puterman from the subject of politics.

"Sorry, Mrs Solomon. Nothing fresh. I opened late this morning. Try Gardiner down the road, in Ajax Lane."

Shaida hustled Dara out of the store and headed towards home.

"What about the cakes?" Dara asked.

"I changed my mind. I'll bake some scones."

They walked in silence down Wills Road. As they turned into Verbena

Road Shaida asked, "You don't seem to be upset by what was in the paper?"

"I'm upset," Dara said quietly. "But I've learned something. When I get angry I lose my dignity and hurt those around me. It only adds to their pain and takes attention away from the real issue. It achieves nothing."

∞

Dara's store, diagonally opposite the famous minaret, was a mini emporium. It sold just about anything portable, from cosmetics to cutlery, knives to nails, garden shears and stationery, axes, aromatic oils, potions and patent medicines. It was also a tobacconist and newsagent and, deep in the rear, behind huge swing doors, was a neat barbershop. And it had the unique distinction of being the unofficial meeting place of the local habituees, who frequented it the way they would a private club.

On Saturday mornings the spacious barbershop was always full, the benches lining the walls occupied by men who sat shoulder to shoulder, laughing and ragging each other in a mixture of dialects ranging from Hindi, Urdu and Gujerati. However, when a topic of common interest was discussed, English was the only means of communication, the proficiency displayed by the speakers remarkably skilled and authoritative.

Photographs of locally famous sportsmen were in profusion, pasted to the walls and doors. Yellowed and faded newspaper cuttings, many of them sketches by the talented cartoonist, Yusuf Kat, were surrounded by framed portraits of outstanding individuals and by team pictures of cricketers and soccerites: the Oriental Cricket Club, Young Bharat Cricket Club, Stella United, the Young Aces, Berea and a dozen others. In pride of place was a photograph of MI Yusuf, the famous all-round sportsman, above the caption: "400 not out".

On the wall above the mirrors, fronting the heavy leather upholstered steel and porcelain chairs, was a framed notice that read:

NO CREDIT
OLD CHINESE PROVERB
You ask credit, me no give, you sore.
You ask credit, me give, you no pay, me sore.
BETTER YOU SORE

Next to the notice was a faded cartoon of two men, one corpulent and obviously wealthy, his open safe overflowing with money. Below it were the words:

THIS MAN SOLD FOR CASH.

The other showed an emaciated and tattered old man, next to a safe with rats scampering in the interior. The writing below it read:

THIS MAN SOLD ON CREDIT.

At eye level, pinned to the swing-door, was an elaborately hand-painted notice, carefully written in deep black India ink:

IN GOD WE TRUST
EVERYONE ELSE MUST PAY CASH.

It had been affixed by a precocious youngster who now occupied a chair in the far corner and who, from time to time, interjected imperiously whenever he disagreed with any statement made by the older patrons.

Dara operated on a simple principle. The barbers retained half of what they charged, as theirs to keep. The other half they handed over to Dara, as his share towards the overheads and his profit. The arrangement was fair and suited everybody. It was the duty of each barber who manned one of the six chairs to ensure the floor was swept immediately after each haircut. Before the next customer occupied the chair, the clippers had to be sanitised, the jack-razors washed in warm water and carefully stropped. As a result, Dara's was the tidiest barbershop in town, even on the busiest day, and no one ever complained of skin rash or a failure to observe elementary rules of hygiene.

Even some of the *Motas*, the feared gangleaders, were not totally immune to being ragged now and then by one or two of the local wags who made certain, however, to steer clear of the true nature of the gangsters' activities.

The barbershop was an area of free speech and freedom of opinion. The slightest hint of a recourse to violence resulted in the guilty individual being banned for life, regardless of his status or standing in the community. It was a rule that had never been invoked, Dara's looming presence alone sufficient to ensure its observance.

It was a typical Saturday morning. All the barbers' chairs were occupied, the benches packed as usual, the few easy chairs in each corner taken. The drone of voices rose and fell, depending on the topic and the interest it generated.

"Old Nat Moodley is at it again," someone said. "He's arranged for

PM Pillay to take on Michael Twala. I hear Tommy Logan, young Veeran and Fareed Shaikh will also feature in the bill."

"I'd rather watch Bud Gengan and Seaman Chetty," Ramjan Khan, an old man, said, waving his hand dismissively. "Talk about world class to me. Talk to me about Moti 'Kid' Singh and Kid Sathamoney. Talk boxing, man. Not brawling."

"You old guys live in the past," the first speaker said. "It's scientific action now, not showmanship."

"You call them showmen? *Sala*, if one of them hits you you'll run crying to your mother, only she won't recognise you."

There were hoots of laughter and one or two of the patrons ducked under an imaginary blow and shouted "Mama" as they stomped their feet.

"I see Braima Osman of Orientals is in form," Pappy Timol, a cricketer, said. "He took six Sparks United wickets for only ten runs. Any Sparks United fans here?"

"They're busy giving batting lessons to the teams," James Oliver, the Aces star forward, said.

A youngster by the name of Bubla Jhavery, sitting in a corner, waved an old copy of *The Leader*. "Any of you read this? It says here that Indian waiters were fired by a local hotel to make way for Italian immigrants."

"So what's new?" Gani-dada asked, as he carefully shaved a customer. "A few weeks ago they kicked a whole lot of our people out of a block of flats in Berea Road to make place for German and Italian immigrants. The government even chartered a special ship to bring them here."

"I heard about that," Bubla said. "The block was owned by an Indian family. The government arbitrarily expropriated it and threw the tenants out into the street. Dadoo gave the full details at a rally. The cops locked him up the next day but he's a tough one, when they took him away he shouted, 'Hail, Führer Smuts!' He spends more time in jail ..."

Suddenly, everyone joined in. Comments and opinions flew fast and loud. Nearly everyone had a story to tell, many from personal experience or as eye-witnesses to some horror or the other.

"Dadoo gives us hope," Ahmed Randeree of the famous resistance family said. "When the cops threw Ramdeen in jail for calling them the henchmen of the looters, know what happened? When Goonum called for more volunteers his mother walked up and signed the register."

"Happens all the time. They lock up one member of the family, two others sign up."

"Last year the store belonging to Dadoo's family in Krugersdorp was burned to the ground. When the nightwatchman said he saw some

Europeans sprinkling petrol and setting it on fire, they locked the poor man up."

"Don't know how it helps, all this resistance business. Even the UN is helpless. It rules against Smuts and he goes ahead anyway and simply rejects their resolutions."

"If it wasn't for the Resistance," Bubla retorted, "you would never have known about it."

"Sure. But when Ismail Meer mentioned it they threw him in jail, one month's hard labour. You talk, you go to jail."

"Keep talking like that and the magistrate will give you a bouquet," Bubla jeered. "You're doing his job for him."

Someone hooted loudly and they burst into laughter, the chagrined individual joining in and saying, "How do I argue with little boys like that? Dara should have an age limit."

"Age limit my bum," Bubla said. "With over two thousand resistors in jail now, you want to shut me up?"

"But this chap Dadoo," James Oliver said, "They keep locking him up and smashing his face. And what does he do when he comes out? Heads directly for the nearest rally, before even going home."

Bubla, who had been rummaging through a pile of old newspapers, said, "Here's what I was looking for, listen to this. When the Ghetto Bill was passed in the senate Dr Dadoo said: 'Senator Clarkson, in winding up the debate, outdid Goebbels in adopting the deplorable tactics of bluff and buffoonery. He stated with a temerity that would have made even Goebbels blush that ninety five percent of the Indians agreed it was giving them a security that they never had before.' That takes guts, saying that."

"I suppose," Randeree said, "that is why Smuts refused to go to the United Nations. He couldn't face the UNO when it called him over. After all his big talk about human rights and all that he would have looked pretty stupid. He just ducked out and sent one of his ministers, Henry Lawrence, in his place."

"I hear the Aga Khan called Smuts a hypocrite right here in South Africa."

"They'll find a way of locking him up too."

"Talking about that," Ramjan Khan asked, "Whatever happened to Debi Singh's request for a judicial inquiry into the treatment of prisoners?"

"A chap called Sullivan, an MP, said it was all nonsense."

"Nonsense!" Bubla was outraged. "They strip the prisoners twice daily and cane them. Even the women are abused and made to walk naked in the courtyard and when they complain they dose them with castor oil and feed them in rusty tin dishes. There are hardly any toilets and they provide them with no sanitary paper. There are more than five hundred prisoners in each block. Do you know how it stinks?"

"Hey, how do you know all this?" another youngster asked.

"You stupid or something?" Bubla replied. "If you don't know about it then you must be the Yankee Doodle of this town. There are hundreds of sworn affidavits made by the prisoners when they come out. Ask Mrs Rabia Docrat. Ask Sooboo, ask Patel, ask anyone in town who has been inside. There are plenty of them. There are even a few right here who ..."

"Wait a minute," Gani-dada said, as he wiped his customer's face and removed the towel. "You were in jail, Narainsamy. Is this true?"

Narainsamy Reddy stepped out of the chair and looked around. His gaunt face, shining from the hot towel, was set in a grim mask. He was still young, in his late twenties, and favoured his left leg as he stood before them.

"They locked me up last year, not long after I returned from the war in the North. What that boy said is true, and that was not the worst of it. But let me tell you something else."

Narainsamy spun the chair around till it was facing his audience, then sat down. "When they mobilised us and asked us to join the Union Defence Force of South Africa, they told us that we were being sent to fight the Axis Powers. We were to fight, they said, for the freedom and liberty of all civilised people, regardless of race or colour. That was good enough for me. We joined up.

"My comrades and I went through four years of hell up there. Many of my buddies died. We fought on, believing that the end of the war would herald a new world. And when we were there, in North Africa, Field Marshal Smuts talked glowingly of our sacrifices and our heroism against the enemy.

"Some of us survived the horrors of that war. When we returned we believed we were coming back to a better South Africa, unlike the one we had left. What did we find instead, almost from the first day? The fucking Ghetto Act! It was like a stab in the back. We would have expected such an Act would have been passed against the enemies we fought, not against ourselves.

"The irony is that now the Germans and Italians are welcomed with open arms. Our homes are taken from us and given to them. Did I hear one of you say that someone called Smuts a hypocrite? Well, that person knew what he was talking about. And when Dadoo calls Smuts the agent of Hitler, he knows what he is talking about. To me, and my fellow veterans of that war, he is just a son of a bitch. And we know what we are talking about. They locked me up for calling him that. They can do so again for repeating it."

Bubla gave a low whistle as Narainsamy limped out. "You should have said that in court, when they charged you for joining the Resistance."

"I tried to," Narainsamy said over his shoulder. "My statement is still there. The magistrate looked at it once, then refused to allow me to read it."

Jake, his face flushed, ran after the ex-soldier as he disappeared through the door.

The barbershop had gone still, the silence complete. Only the swing doors, through which Narainsamy had left, moved as they swished past each other.

Dara's voice, when he quietly announced that it was time for him to close up, sounded abnormally loud. No one was in the mood to talk as they filed out, heads bowed.

∞

To the casual observer, especially a non-Indian, Persadh would have given the impression of being an illiterate and a fool. The truth was quite the opposite. When he chose to do so, he could speak fairly good English, but it was a language he could barely read and not write at all. That he was highly educated in Bengali and an expert on the writings of Rabindranath Tagore was not widely known.

Persadh was a scholar of *Sadhu-Bhasa*, the classical Bengali language of literature which bore little resemblance to *Calit-Bhasa* — the colloquial form of speech. His private life was modelled on the teachings of the great poet who had won the Nobel prize for literature in 1913. When the mood was upon him he could quote, from the top of his head, sections of the original *Gitanjali* — the English version of which had won Tagore the coveted award.

The name Balram Persadh was not the name given to him at birth. In 1919, when in protest against the Amritsar massacre, his guru surrendered the knighthood awarded to him in 1915, Balram concluded that a contribution of some sort was expected from him. In a fit of anger he blew up a British garrison, was spotted by some sepoys, and his life on the run began. After narrowly escaping capture on several occasions, he finally secured a job in the galley of an ocean liner and jumped ship in Durban. He settled amongst a group of Hindi-speaking people in Newlands, assumed the fairly common name of Balram Persadh, and conveniently forgot his Bengali origins.

Lacking in skills of any sort and unable to find a job that could sustain him, he tried his luck at market gardening. It wasn't long before he realised that it involved a lot more than planting seeds in the ground and watering them daily. He gave up in disgust and fell back on his small hoard of gold coins. In 1922 he met Kalavathee at a neighbourhood function, approached her family for her hand in marriage, and was happily accepted by them.

With his resources rapidly dwindling, and with a wife to support, the need for gainful employment weighed heavily on him. By a stroke of luck one of his wife's family, a municipal worker, secured a job for Balram as a cleaner at the Town Gardens. It wasn't long before his dignified bearing and general appearance caught the eye of a councillor who moved him into the City Hall where he became a tea-maker and general office cleaner.

"You have to be very careful, Balram," his wife's uncle told him. "If you want to keep your job in that fancy place you'll have to learn the rules of the game. Act stupid, don't ever quote Tagore or display your knowledge of his works. Always look at the floor and keep your mouth shut. It's the only way you will survive there."

Almost from the first day Balram surpassed even the most obsequious of his co-workers in the art of self-effacement. He took his cue from Tagore's famous work *Galpa Guccha*, which contained stories of the misery and debasement of humble people, and emulated a character from one of the tales. He had acted the part many times in village plays back in India. It came easily to him.

With quiet efficiency he went about his work of serving tea to the councillors and mopping up the mess in their offices. He never, not even in their absence, referred to any of them by any term other than "sah" — it was his private form of protest against the manner in which they addressed him. He was never called "mister". He was simply "Ram". It was always "Ram, fetch a pot of tea" or "Ram, empty the wastebasket" or "Ram, wipe these stains off my desk". "Ram" was not his name, he simmered inwardly. Ram was God and to refer to him in this manner was, in his opinion, nothing but blasphemy. Outwardly, he simply said, "Okay fine, sah," and smiled.

Balram quietly went about his work and, like the character in Tagore's play, he pretended to be somewhat deaf. He found this gave him certain advantages and made his life easier. Even when he heard them clearly the first time, he continued to look foolish and acted as if they were not there, until they shouted at him in exasperation. However, he responded so quickly and humbly that they soon overcame their anger and forgave him. His behaviour not only restored some of his pride in himself, it was also a private source of great amusement and enabled him to retain his sanity.

There were other distinct benefits flowing from his act. The councillors preferred to leave him alone most of the time, turning to one of his colleagues rather than going through the tiresome routine of addressing him. As a result he was almost invisible to them and they seldom noticed him, a virtual nonentity. In his presence they spoke freely and never lowered their voices. This suited him perfectly. Their conversation bored him and he preferred not to listen to them. It left him free to indulge his thoughts and dwell on Tagore's wisdom.

Balram's standard response to any instruction was always "Okay fine, Sah". They were the only words he spoke, and he did so with an alacrity that always raised a smile. After a while the younger councillors mimicked him when they responded to an unwelcome request from a colleague. "Okay fine, sah", they replied with a smile and everybody unfailingly laughed. It took the edge off any angry exchange and restored the good relationship.

And so Balram, always attired in a spotlessly clean khaki shirt and trousers, went about his duties as the "nobody" he was. And the councillors went about theirs. And, after twenty five years in the job, the act came so naturally that he didn't even have to try anymore.

And he finally got his own back, for all the years of abject humiliation, in a telling way. In 1947 and 1948 he became the eyes and ears of the Passive Resistance Movement. And he was more adept at it than in his moronic pose. He simply donned the mantle of another of Tagore's characters, the one he had emulated in real life when he destroyed the garrison in India. And he enjoyed the challenge it provided, playing both characters at the same time, switching from one to the other with consummate ease.

Balram caught the eye of the Resistance at a rally in early 1947, at the Red Square. Towards the end, as the crowds were dispersing, he found himself standing next to a young woman who had been one of the speakers.

"Excuse me," Balram said tentatively.

"Yes, uncle?" the girl responded with a smile. "Can I help you?"

"These speakers, do you think the government listens to them?"

"We're sure they do. Their stooges are always taking notes."

"But do you think it'll change anything, put a stop to their vicious tactics?"

"What else can we do? Protest is the only route open to us."

"Yes," he said softly. "Yes, of course. You're a brave girl. What is your name, *beti*?"

"Fatima," she replied. "Will you excuse me now?"

"Yes, go. And God help you."

She was turning away when he added, "Maybe I'll speak to the mayor tomorrow, when we have tea."

She whirled so fast that she almost collided into him. As she steadied herself she asked, "Did you say the mayor?"

"Yes," Balram replied, enjoying himself. "I see him every morning. In the City Hall."

"In the City Hall?"

"Every day," Balram couldn't help teasing her. "And I listen to them talking. But I didn't hear anything about this Ghetto Bill. Maybe I wasn't listening."

"You hear them talking? Every day? How do you get in there?"

"I work there, *beti*. I'm the tea-boy." His upper lip curled a little as he said the last word. He started to move away.

"Father, wait!" she said, her voice excited. "Please, come with me." She took him by his hand and led him to an older woman. "This is Dr Goonum," the girl said. "I'm sorry, I didn't ask you for your name."

"That's because you have good manners," he said. "My name is Balram Persadh."

Goonum stretched out her right hand, then quickly withdrew it when she realised her mistake. "Hello, Mr Persadh."

"Please tell the doctor what you do," Fatima said.

"Goonum. Just call me Goonum."

"I work at the City Hall."

"And he listens to their conversation," Fatima said pointedly.

What Balram had started off as a joke ended up as a clandestine operation in which he became the key player. Almost overnight "Ram the moron" became "Balram the Rana of City Hall."

∞

Persadh didn't attend any future rallies. Twice a week he stopped by at the Congress offices in Saville Street, on his way to the bus rank. Though he couldn't read English, he had an innate sense of what was important and occasionally reported on items he had overheard that got the Congress officials all excited. Once or twice he even filched documents that he thought were important. Although there was nothing momentous in them it gave the Resistance an idea of how the councillors thought and acted.

He got to know Dr Dadoo and Dr Naicker and surprised them with the level of his intelligence and the depth of his knowledge. Whenever they had the time they enjoyed a brief discussion, on Tagore's philosophy and his works, and he amazed them with his ability to quote verbatim from the great man's writings.

It was the doctors who nicknamed him "Rana of City Hall".

Back home, after his two girls had gone to bed, Balram discussed his activities with his wife and commented on the leaders' commitment to justice and concern for the future of their people. It drew them closer and gave them something to talk about, an activity which had hitherto been lacking in their lives.

"So many doctors," he muttered to his wife. "Who is looking after the sick?"

For Balram 1948 passed very swiftly. Early in November he sensed a change in the atmosphere and began to fear that his days at the City Hall were short-lived — the attitude of two of the senior members had become secretive and they often stopped talking when he served tea. In the beginning it was quite subtle, just the occasional rudeness. It wasn't long before the brusqueness became pointedly overt and, when they began to snap at him for no apparent reason, he knew it was a matter of time before he was pushed out altogether.

On a Friday evening he discussed it with his wife.

"I have always been very careful, especially with those two. They are the most powerful men there and I have always stayed out of their way, there is no way they can suspect what I am doing."

"Maybe they are angry with the passive resistors and are taking it out on you."

"No. They've always hated the passive resistors. It's nothing new."

"But now that the Bill is passed and the resistors haven't stopped ..."

"It's not like that. Something is going on, it's only these two that seem to have changed. The others are okay. Oh, they hate anything Indian, except our food and our girls, but otherwise they haven't changed."

"It could just be your imagination. Maybe you feel guilty that you're spying on them."

"I don't feel guilty! I tell you something is going on there."

"Then talk to the doctors. Tell them how you feel."

Balram slept badly that night. Early the next morning he took the bus to the city and called at the Congress offices. He was pleased to see that Dadoo, Naicker and Goonum were all present. In a quiet voice he told them his fears.

"There may be a simple explanation," Dadoo said. "Our increasing militancy and our attacks against the racist City Council is probably beginning to irk them. The fact that we have recently become vociferous in our condemnation of them may finally be penetrating their arrogant facade. Up to now they were quite immune to our criticism, considering us as no more than lesser minions amongst the general rabble in this city. Now that we are exposing them internationally, their infamous indifference is beginning to crack. And our Rana here is always right there, pricking their consciences by his presence."

"You may be right," Goonum said. "He may be no more than a target for their frustrations. On the other hand, there may be more to it." She turned to Balram and asked, "You kept saying something is going on, why do you say that?"

"It's just a feeling I have. And it's not only because of the way they treat me. Those two councillors sometimes stop talking even when some of their own kind are around. And there's a look on their faces ... it's like ... you know ... that they're planning something bad."

"Something bad?"

"I don't know how to say it, to put it into words, but I don't like it."

"Nothing else?" Goonum asked.

"No, nothing else."

"Okay," Dadoo said. "All you can do is wait it out, and keep out of the way of those two. It may just be a passing thing."

∞

During the course of the following week Balram followed Dadoo's advice and kept his distance, making sure he stayed as far away from the offices of the angry councillors as he could. He busied himself on the cleaning detail, leaving one of the others to attend to the function of making and serving tea. There was nothing unusual in the arrangement, the workers often agreed amongst themselves to swop activities for a few days. Apart from the change, those on the cleaning team had an opportunity to slow down for a few hours and laze the day away.

What Balram accidently saw during that week sent him rushing back to Saville Street on Friday evening, the one evening when he knew all three of his Congress contacts would be present and planning the weekend's rally. As soon as he was alone with them in a back office he blurted out, "They're meeting some rough looking characters."

"Rough characters?" Goonum asked. "Where do they meet?"

"Secretly, in the back near the storerooms. They talk to them at the big doors near the parking lot, in the lane that runs through Smith Street and West Street."

"What do they talk about?"

"I don't know. I am always too far away to hear them and I make sure they don't see me."

"The same councillors who are rude to you?"

"I can't say for certain. I have no business being there. But it's always empty and ..."

"Okay, hang on a bit. You say that they are rough looking chaps?"

"Yes, like *dakus*."

"How could you say that?" Naicker asked. "You said you couldn't even see the councillors clearly."

"The councillors had their backs to me. But I could see the others clearly."

"Could you see their faces?"

"Not really," Balram said, a little angry now. "There are always some Africans and one or two whites, Look ..."

"Africans?" Goonum asked. "Wait a minute, just hold on. Let me think about this."

"I think I'm beginning to get the picture, Goonum," Dadoo said. "They're recruiting a bunch of toughs to serve as rally-busters."

"Good thinking," Goonum said, snapping her fingers.

"But why all these cloak and dagger methods?" Naicker asked. "They could easily ask the cops to hire ..."

"You're being simplistic, Monty," Goonum replied. "It widens the circle of conspirators."

"Now you're being simplistic. These guys are on record as being racists. Why should they care now?"

"Because if it gets out they won't look so good. Don't you see, things could get ugly, people could get hurt, badly."

"You're right," Naicker conceded. "They won't want to be associated with that."

"And it'll suit their purpose," Dadoo said. "To make it appear as if it's a spontaneous thing. Isolate us from the rest of the population. Use it as propaganda to make us look bad ..."

"We'll have to find an answer for it," Naicker said. "There's a rally this Sunday."

"We'll think about that later," Dadoo said. "What about Balram?"

Dr Naicker turned to Balram and smiled, "I'm sorry. I didn't mean to sound as if I was cross examining you."

"It's okay," Balram said, mollified. "I'm just glad the information was useful."

"You'll have to stop coming here," Goonum suggested. "If they begin to suspect you in some way they could have you followed."

"But why should they suspect him?" Dadoo asked. "After all, they didn't see him ..."

"I'm not too sure," Goonum replied. "Why is he the only one they're rude to? There must be some reason for it."

"Okay," Naicker said. "Balram, stay away from here. Is there any way you can phone us?"

Balram shook his head.

"When you reach home?"

"There are no phones on my street."

"If we send a car to fetch you, after work."

"No good," Balram shook his head. "There are no cars in Newlands. If my neighbours saw a car outside my house ... too many questions ... what will I say ..."

"I have a better idea," Dadoo suggested. "Look through the glass there. You see that chap at the filing cabinet?"

Balram nodded.

"He's seen you here often. Give us the name of your corner store. He'll be there every evening at seven. Ignore him if you have nothing to report. If there's something we should know head in a direction away from your home. He'll pick you up and bring you here. Is that okay?"

"I'll have to explain it to my wife. But it's okay."

"We understand. You're not worried? All this ducking and dodging?"

"I'm not worried. If Tagore can reject his knighthood, this is a small thing."

As soon as Balram left, the doctors discussed the implications of what he had told them. Suddenly, Goonum clapped her hand to her forehead and groaned loudly. "Damn! I keep forgetting to ask the Rana the names of the councillors who are so rude to him."

"What difference does it make," Dadoo said, stretching his legs. "Isn't it obvious? Who else can it be? Think about it. Whose public utterances have been the most racist?"

"Smith and Osborne!" Naicker said sharply.

"You could be wrong," Goonum said. "There are some there who are even worse. Let's not be unfair."

⚭

The rally went off without incident. With the exception of the usual contingent of police taking notes and recording the registration numbers of cars parked in the area, nothing untoward marred the day and the protestors dispersed peacefully. A group of young pugilists from Sonny Moodley's gym waited until the speakers were ready to leave. Finally, at a nod from Dadoo, they too moved on.

As the summer days grew longer, and after several more rallies went off without disturbance, the Resistance leaders grew confused.

"We're missing a point here," Goonum kept saying. "They must be planning something else."

"They could be gunning for us personally," Naicker mused. "If they can decapitate the head, the body will cease to function."

"You flatter yourself," Goonum laughed. "The body functioned very well when we were all in jail. The Resistance is like the legendary Hydra, each time they cut off a head, two grow in its place."

"And do you know how Heracles finally destroyed the Hydra?" Dadoo asked with a smile. "He simply burned the roots. And, as we are so fond of saying: *Kalass*! *Kaput*!"

As it happened, Dadoo was not far off from the truth. But even he couldn't have contemplated the enormity of the Machiavellian plot underway in the hallowed corridors of the august monument to white supremacy.

Balram plodded on in his usual manner, pretending a bonhomie that he didn't feel. He made certain he stayed out of the way of the two councillors but continued to covertly watch their movements, hoping to get a solid lead on what the doctors suspected was happening.

Early in December he became aware of a subtle tension in the air. Even those who had ignored his presence had now stopped talking whenever he was around. Balram carried on in his usual manner, continued saying "Okay fine, sah" whenever he was addressed. But his senses were alert, forever probing, seeking a hint of whatever was in the air.

Just after nine one morning, Balram was in the small boardroom that led off the private offices of a senior member, preparing the table for morning tea. The office leading to the boardroom had been unoccupied and, as was his usual routine, he had simply walked through. A few minutes later he heard angry voices in the outer office.

"Don't you dare question me, young man, on matters that don't concern you!"

"But it does concern me. Everything in this city concerns me. The Indians ..."

"Fuck the Indians! The bastards are taking over the bloody city, buying every piece of land in sight."

"That's not true, sir. We both know they own far less than five percent of the real estate around here. That's hardly owning everything in sight. And in any case, they're restricted to the Casbah. The law doesn't allow them to buy property or to trade in the CBD. How can they possibly ..."

"Listen, you young pup! I don't need a champion of the coolies here in my office."

"I'm simply stating the facts, not taking sides."

"Fine! Now get out."

"I will, sir. But won't you reconsider ..."

"I already told you. I don't know what you're talking about."

"I'm not the only one that suspects there's a plot to break the Indians."

"*You don't hear too good, boy.*" There was a menace in the voice, a threat that, although not directed at him, made Balram's blood run cold. He began to shiver. A second later he heard footsteps, then a door banged loudly.

Balram remained rooted to the spot. He hardly dared breathe. If he was discovered now there was no way he could go into his act, his face would give him away. He clenched his hands tightly as he attempted to control the wild trembling that coursed through his body.

The minutes passed. As he subdued his fear, he became aware of the silence. He gathered his courage, thought of Tagore and began to move. He risked a peep into the office. It was empty. He quickly walked out and disappeared down the corridor. The rest of that day he pretended he wasn't well, allowing one of his colleagues to take over. The pretence was not far from the truth.

Balram didn't dare show his face or leave the building. He kept himself busy sweeping the empty balconies and keeping out of everybody's sight. Just after four that afternoon he went onto the first floor balcony overlooking the Town Gardens, aimlessly pushing the broom in front of him. The experience that morning had unnerved him and for a while he simply stood in the warmth of the sun and stared at Queen Victoria's statue. It was then that he heard the voice again, from below him, on the stairs leading to the wide public walkway.

"... questions are being asked. I don't think we should delay much longer. Everything is almost in place. It's time we blasted these coolies to hell."

"You're sure it can't be traced back to us?"

"Not a chance. It will be put down to a spontaneous uprising by the kaffirs. All it needs is a catalyst and it will snowball on it's own after that. Our recruits are well paid and there will be rich pickings for them."

"Let's do it, then. But wait a few weeks, until after the festive holidays. We don't want our own businesses to be disrupted. And we will be away on our annual vacations."

They were still talking, secure in the knowledge that they were alone, as Balram edged back from the parapet. His body had started shaking again.

∞

Long before seven that evening Balram was at the corner store, mixing with the customers. By seven fifteen his contact was nowhere in sight and he was becoming edgy. By seven twenty he knew he had to move out before he became too conspicuous. He bought a pint of milk and left.

As he stepped onto the dusty pavement, he saw the filing clerk hurrying over. Balram waited until their eyes made contact, then turned and headed in the opposite direction, away from where he lived.

In less than five minutes a car pulled up and Balram jumped in. It was a noisy old Pontiac and he had to slam the door several times before it held.

"Get me to the doctors, quickly."

"Something's happened?"

"Just get me there, *bhaya*."

Only two of the doctors were present — Naicker and Dadoo. They made him repeat, several times, as much as he could recall of both the conversations he had overheard. When they were satisfied that he had told them all he could remember, they sat back and silently considered the implications of what Balram had said.

"No more," Balram said. "I won't come here again. I'm not a young man anymore and this business frightens me. And I can't afford to get caught. If I lose my job ..."

"We understand," Naicker said. "You've been very helpful."

"I thought I could handle it, just run away if they found out what I was doing. I was stupid. I'm married now and I have to think of my wife and two daughters. What happened today made me realise that I'm not so brave now, not like when I was a single man in India ..."

"We appreciate your fears," Dadoo said kindly. "None of us knows his threshold until he is confronted with it. And now that we know that their behaviour towards you was not personal, you can easily slip into your normal routine and forget all about what you have done for us. But we will always remember the help you gave us. You need have no fear of exposure."

"You've been invaluable, Balram," Dr Naicker said. "You've done your share for our people, you can always be proud of that."

For a while they exchanged a few pleasantries, then shook hands and arranged for the driver to take him home.

"Don't know what to make of it," Dadoo said when they were alone again. "That bit about 'rich pickings' is what worries me. What do they expect to get at the rallies, unless they plan to snatch the gold chains off the women's necks."

"What were the Rana's exact words? Did he say something about 'all over the city'?"

"And something about disrupting their own businesses. That makes little sense. Our rallies are held after business hours."

"And they are well advertised, held at a fixed venue. That bit about 'rich pickings' is worrying me."

"They talked about blasting us to hell. Who? You and I? The other speakers?"

"There's something else, Yusuf. This Rana of ours, do you think his imagination is beginning to run wild? He reads Tagore a lot. Apart from being a great poet, the man was a bit of a mystic too. Is it possible that Balram is so immersed in this role of his that he is losing touch with reality?"

"He looked really shaken, frightened out of his wits. There was little of his usual bravado today. And he wants out, he made that clear. That alone suggests ..."

"Yes, okay. It was just a thought. I agree it's a bit far-fetched. But, you know, people sometimes get carried away by their self-importance, need to come up with something impressive, and we have been quite generous in our praise recently. I'd hate to think this cloak and dagger thing went to his head and he decided to dramatise his role."

"Anything's possible, Monty. Let's see what Goonum has to say tomorrow. She's usually pretty good at these things."

The next morning, both the doctors were picked up and imprisoned. It was a routine matter — 'to prevent them from rabble rousing' the charge read. Goonum went off to the Transvaal to participate in a few rallies and support her colleagues in that province. Balram returned to work satisfied with his input and pleased to be out of it for good.

Christmas was a little more than a week away. The city went into festive mode.

∞

On Wednesday the twelfth of January 1949, Dara and Shaida decided to spend the evening in Queen Street. Fatima had come over for a few days to escape her in-laws. It was a sultry night and they had spread a few straw mats in the yard and settled down to a leisurely evening. Salim and Ayesha were playing a short distance away and Rashid, still barely a toddler, was in Nadia's lap. Yahya was in his usual chair and Yacoob, at his grandfather's specific request, had joined the family and was sprawled on the floor close to him, his head resting in his palms as he looked at the sky and listened to the noises around him.

A little later Madhoo and Kantha came over and apologised for their daughter's absence. Heera, who had married and settled in Tongaat, had failed to show up, phoning to say that her husband was unable to obtain use of the family car that day.

"Time you got rid of that cart, Yahya," Madhoo said, pointing to the wooden contraption that lay abandoned in the yard.

"Never," Yahya responded vehemently. "It can rot but as long as it's in front of me it reminds me of the bad times."

"You're too sentimental, *Baji*," Dara laughed.

"Sentiment has nothing to do with it. You must remember your past before you can build a future."

"Listen to the old *chacha*," Nadia said jokingly. "One foot's in the grave and he talks of building a future."

They all burst out laughing.

"Madhoo-kaka," Dara said, encouraged by the easy banter, "I think it's time you and *Baji* took Kantha kaki and my mother for a visit to India."

"*Tchah*!" Yahya spat out dismissively. "Who is left for us to visit? Nephews and nieces we have never known? I'm happy to pass my days with my grandchildren."

"They will still be here when you return," Dara persisted.

"I wouldn't manage," Yahya said. "Too tiring for my age."

"*Sala*," Nadia said. "You don't have to walk there."

When they laughed again, Yahya closed his eyes and pretended to sleep.

When Madhoo Daya, in his usual quiet way, said, "There is nothing there for us anymore, the things and people we love are right here," the subject was firmly closed.

Dara's thoughts drifted into the past, to the happy days behind the mosque and the lazy hours of talk and laughter; to Gandhi and his philosophy of *Satyagraha* — conceived initially during his stay in South Africa and carefully nurtured in India — and wondered what it had achieved. He actually became a victim, he thought bitterly, of the violence that he preached against. Dara must have said the last sentence aloud because Yahya said, "What? What did you say?"

"I was thinking of Gandhi and the day he spoke to us."

"Yes ..." Yahya said softly. "We knew even then that he was a great man. He died a Mahatma, a great soul."

"I sometimes feel," Dara said, "that his philosophy has suited our rulers more than it benefitted us. They laugh as they persecute us, knowing that we will never revolt against them."

"Then you haven't understood a thing," Yahya said. "Why does the alternative to reason have to be war? If you lose your sight do you cut off your head?"

"But *Baji*, we are worse off now than ever before in our history. We have fewer rights than a stray dog, who at least can wander about freely."

"Unlike the dog," Madhoo said, "you have a higher level of logic. That dog also has the ability to piss on the street. Would you aspire to that?"

"I don't understand the connection."

"Then think. What you ask for is more than the simple right to wander freely. When you achieve more than the next man you are envied. Success and enemies are inseparable, you can't have one without the other."

Yacoob suddenly sat up and said, "That is a rule that applies to individuals, Madhoo dada. The State cannot behave that way. And there were times when even Gandhi told us to fight for our rights, when he stated that we could not claim the rights of citizenship without agreeing to defend the State against its enemies. He himself took part in a war, fifty years ago."

"As a stretcher bearer, Yacoob. Not as a soldier," Yahya said.

"The moment he participated, in whatever way, he accepted that he was an active player. You can't agree to defend anything against someone without fighting back."

"You're wrong, Yacoob," Madhoo said. "Gandhi was advocating passive resistance. He was asking us to state where we stood in the war."

"And what happened? We made our stand clear, and the two enemies, the Boer and the English, got together and formed a partnership that now rejects us."

"But that is their crime", Madhoo cried. "In time they will pay for it."

"They haven't paid for it in your time. What makes you think that they'll do so in mine?"

∞

The following evening Dara was sitting on the porch in Verbena Road, chair tilted back against the wall, his feet crossed at the ankles as they rested over the low railing. Shaida, busy embroidering a tablecloth, was conversing with him in low tones.

"Both of them are very old now, but they are still healthy. If you can convince them to go for a holiday it would do them a lot of good. And they'll enjoy travelling with the Dayas. If they can take Yacoob with, it'll give him something to do, maybe even change his attitude to life."

"Yacoob's okay," Dara said. "There's nothing wrong with his brain. He asks questions that I often ask myself. If I can only convince him to stay at the store and learn the trade."

"And his education?"

Dara was about to respond when Yacoob came running up the road, still dressed in his gym clothes and breathing heavily.

"*Baji!*" Yacoob shouted as he jumped onto the porch. "I just heard that a lot of Africans are fighting in Grey Street."

"Stop screaming," Dara ordered, looking at Yacoob sternly, "And say your salaams first."

Yacoob took a deep breath, filling his lungs with air. "*Baji*, listen ..."

"You finished your workout long ago," Dara said crossly, "were you fooling around again?"

Yacoob turned to his mother, the strong muscles of his arms rippling, his deep chest bursting out of his thin shirt. "Ma, there is trouble in town."

"What kind of trouble?" Shaida asked absent-mindedly.

"The Africans are attacking the Indians!"

Dara's chair hit the ground with a thud as he jumped up, clearing the porch in one giant leap. He landed on the balls of his feet and spun around swiftly as he broke into a run.

"Dara!" Shaida screamed after him, but he was already out of earshot.

Yacoob dropped his kitbag and, without a glance at his mother, ran after Dara, his long muscular legs pumping furiously. Within minutes he had caught up and father and son paced each other silently. In spite of his age, Dara's years of pulling and pushing the cart had left him in admirable condition and he moved smoothly, breathing evenly and holding his elbows close to his sides.

A few minutes later they crossed the Victoria Street bridge and sprinted alongside the Brook Street cemetery, Dara's breath loud as he gasped for air. They entered Queen Street together, side by side in the darkness, eyes darting all over for signs of danger.

When they reached Yahya's house Dara bent down to open the rickety and badly rusted iron gate. Yacoob, without a break in his stride, rose high in the air and cleared the picket fence with at least a foot to spare and arrived at the front door ahead of his father. As he reached for the doorknob it opened and Nadia almost collided with him as she stepped out.

"*Gadha*!" she said, "what is this nonsense?"

Dara had caught up with them and was looking around foolishly at the peaceful scene, relief flooding through him when he saw that his mother was unharmed.

"*Dadima*," Yacoob began, his voice ragged. "There was trouble earlier and we thought ..."

"*Tchah*! A little trouble and you come running like *dakus* in the night. Come in before you collapse."

Dara, his energy all but spent, leaned against a wooden post and took a deep breath. "Is everything alright?"

"Can't you see?" Nadia said crossly. "Or are you blind as well as stupid."

Yacoob was smiling. It always amused him when his grandmother scolded Dara and treated him like a boy. Dara rounded on him in anger.

"You said there was a lot of trouble, that ..."

"*Baji*, I heard it was bad," Yacoob said quickly, his smile vanishing. "I was told ..."

"There was trouble," Nadia said, in Yacoob's defence. "Many people were hurt. But it's over now."

"*Baji*," Dara asked, "Is he okay?"

"Yes. He went across the road to check on Madhoo-kaka."

Just then Yahya shuffled into view. As he entered the yard Dara was shocked to see how old he looked, as if overnight the years had suddenly pounced on him.

"Madhoo is okay," Yahya said in a low voice.

"What happened?" Dara asked.

"Who knows," Yahya replied. "They just climbed into the Indians, with sticks and iron bars, and for an hour they beat up everyone in sight."

"Didn't anyone fight back?" Yacoob asked.

"With what?" Yahya asked angrily. "Shopping baskets and groceries?"

Yahya lumbered through the door, moving sluggishly, and lowered his body onto the bed with a sigh.

"Ma," Dara said. "Come home with us, both of you."

"This is our home," Yahya said gruffly. "We stay here."

"The trouble is over, my son," Nadia joined in. "Go home to your family."

"But mother ..."

"*Choop*! Go now, we are tired. Nobody will harm two old people like us."

"Then one of us will spend the night here," Dara said firmly.

"There's no need to do that. We're safe. Nobody attacks old people."

Still Dara lingered, reluctant to leave them alone, until Nadia gently turned him towards the door and led him out, closing it softly behind her.

"Your father needs to sleep, Dara. He is used to his little luxuries. You and Yacoob can come in the morning." She kissed them both on the cheek and sent them on their way. At the gate they turned around and she waved at them, grey hair shining in the moonlight.

The next morning Dara, as usual, stopped by on his way to the shop and joined them in the ritual cup of tea. Before he left he promised to come over for lunch immediately after the Friday prayers were over at the mosque.

The Casbah was abnormally quiet as Dara opened his store for business. There were few shoppers in sight. When Yacoob stepped in Dara walked over to Mr Govender next door. The old man, a herbalist, was applying a match to a clay lamp in preparation for his morning prayer, his back to the door. Dara waited until he had finished, taking a few backward steps and waiting at a respectful distance. Finally, the old man turned around and his face lit up with pleasure as he hurried over, smiling widely.

"Hello, Dara," he said, in his soft cultured voice.

"*Namaskarum, tata*. Are you okay?"

"Yes, fine. And your father?"

"He's okay. I hear there was trouble last night."

"It was bad. Very bad. But no one knows how it started or what it was about."

"We've always had a good relationship with the Africans," Dara said. "Why should they attack us?"

"Nobody understands it, *thumbie*."

As they chatted they stepped out onto the pavement. With no customers around most of the shopkeepers were outside their shops and standing around in little groups, discussing the events of the night before in hushed voices. After a while Dara excused himself and went back to his store.

"I think I'll go to the mosque early today," he told Yacoob. "Make sure you lock up carefully. Your grandmother is expecting us for lunch. Be there."

Yacoob, who had taken to ducking the Friday service, nodded. Dara grunted and moved on. When the other Muslim shopkeepers began to close their doors, at precisely twelve noon, Yacoob locked up and crossed the street, hoping to leave the keys with his grandmother. He knew that both his father and grandfather would go to the store together after lunch and, in the meantime, he had almost two hours to while away in Victoria Street. With luck his father would fail to notice his absence in the mosque.

Nadia, however, was in an unusually talkative mood and Yacoob was only able to escape when his grandmother looked at the time and exclaimed, "Yacoob, you've missed the sermon! Go, quickly, before you miss the prayer too."

By the time he was back on the street the prayers were over and the congregation was streaming out. Yacoob cursed under his breath and decided to cut through an alley before his father spotted him. He had barely entered it when he heard the roar, like distant thunder, that seemed to be coming from the far end of the road, near the railway lines.

For a moment he was disorientated, not sure what it was. He could see Mr Govender peering up the street as he shaded his eyes with one hand, a pint of milk in the other. Mr Khuzwayo, the only African shopkeeper on the block, left his music saloon and joined the herbalist. Together they looked up the road and squinted into the distance.

At that moment a horde of several hundred Africans, armed with a variety of deadly weapons, turned the corner from Grey Street and entered Queen Street. Their blood-curdling yells stopped the Indians in their tracks, many still in the act of greeting the worshippers as they emerged from the mosque.

Yacoob's first thought was that it was a group of boisterous gumboot dancers, from the dairy down the road, indulging in a bit of horseplay. Then he saw old Mr Govender go down, his skull split open and blood spurting around him; the portly Khuzwayo fell to his knees, his white shirt red with his own blood. There was the sound of shattering glass as a shop window caved in, the deadly shards flying through the air. A child screamed in agony somewhere, the sound suddenly choking off in a gurgle.

Yacoob was pushed back into the alley by a group of Indians as they sought refuge from the sheer mass of Africans who had descended on them. Using his shoulders and his elbows he shoved his way forward, tripped over a young woman lying on the pavement, her sari almost torn off her shoulder, the deep cut of a panga running diagonally across from her neck and disappearing into her waist.

He rose to his knees, lost his balance as he slipped over the contents of a shopping basket, steadied himself again before going down once more under the weight of a dozen bodies. He lay on the ground, stunned, the human shield over him writhing painfully as the blows rained down from above.

There was a momentary lull as the first wave swept beyond them and Yacoob struggled up and looked around. The street before him was in shambles. Men, women and children were sprawled across the road, their faces convulsed in grotesque masks as they groaned in pain. Many simply lay on the ground, unmoving and silent in death. Several were moaning in anguish as they pulled themselves across the tarmac, eyes wild with fear.

A little girl ran towards him, panic-stricken, tears streaming down her face. Yacoob moved towards her, arms outstretched, when the second mob from the railway lines descended on them. The Indians who were still on their feet scattered in every direction, someone scooping up the girl in mid-stride and disappearing into the mosque.

A handful of youngsters made a stand, there was a brief scuffle before they were battered to their knees by the heavy cudgels that smashed into them, their heads bloody from the blows.

"You have no weapons!" a voice screamed. "There are too many of them. Don't try ..." It was suddenly cut off and lost in the melee.

Yacoob turned back, made a move towards the alley, when his feet left the ground and his body flew through the air. He landed with a thud, the breath knocked out of him, legs flailing above his face. He went into an automatic roll, pulled his knees close to his stomach, tucked his chin into his chest and coiled into a human ball that spun around several times of its own volition. His back slammed against something and he shuddered to a halt. His mind blank, he instinctively unwound his limbs and sprang to his feet, oblivious of the blood that seeped from his torn skin and saturated his clothes.

Miraculously, Dara was before him! Father and son locked fingers and headed for the alley. Halfway through it a door opened and someone shouted, "In here, quickly." Dara pushed Yacoob through the opening, then followed. There was a narrow stairway in front of them and, together with their unknown saviour, they sprinted up it until they reached a wide landing that led to a spacious balcony overlooking the street.

There were almost twenty others already there, one or two seriously wounded. Dara was unharmed apart form a tiny bump on his forehead. His eyes were searching Yacoob's face in an attempt to determine the extent of his injuries.

"I'm okay, *Baji*," Yacoob said, pulling his shirt over his head. Dara saw the scratches on the muscular frame, noted that the cuts, though still bleeding, were superficial and not deep. Yacoob pressed the sodden shirt against a slightly deeper scratch, staunching the blood.

"Dada?" Jake asked Dara.

"I'm sure he is okay. He always leaves the mosque after everyone else, usually the last one out. Even these madmen won't invade the house of God."

They moved to the edge of the balcony and looked into the street. Yacoob couldn't believe the scene below him. Wherever he looked, hordes of Africans were smashing shop windows and glass doors, breaking in and attacking those who had sought refuge within, mercilessly clubbing their screaming victims. The animal cries of the wounded were drowned out by the deafening sound of breaking glass and splintering wood.

From somewhere close by, the wild howl of a hurt woman rose above the clamour; cut off abruptly, it was followed by a low moan. It sounded as if it was immediately below the balcony, in the gutter, but the resounding din had started up again and Yacoob couldn't be sure he had heard it at all.

In the middle of the street a small group of Indians was fighting back, outnumbered and empty handed. In less than a minute they were overpowered, their faces tramped into the hard concrete. Yacoob looked at Dara, who nodded at him. They looked around for a weapon as they headed towards the door. Suddenly, Chico was before them, shaking his head.

"No, Yacoob. We have no choice. There are thousands of them. It would be a stupid move, a losing battle. We wait here."

"We can't just do nothing," Dara said, his voice hoarse.

"And we can achieve nothing out there," someone else said firmly. "It's a job for the police."

Someone whimpered behind them and they turned around. A man in a red skullcap had just carried a woman in and was lowering her gently to the floor. The back of the cap, as he bent over, was white and Yacoob realised that the front of the cap was saturated with blood oozing from the man's forehead.

"My husband is out there," the woman moaned in pain. "Dara, *bhai* ..."

Dara, who had stooped to the floor and lowered his face in his hands, sprang up and approached the woman.

"It's me, Neeru," the woman whispered.

It took five of them to hold Dara down, Chico and Yacoob among them. They pinned him to the ground as Dara roared helplessly, "That's Pravin kaka's daughter-in-law. His son is out there."

"We all have someone we care for out there," someone said. "It would be madness to step out now."

Yacoob bent beside Dara and whispered softly in his ear. "Wait, *Baji*. Just a few minutes, then we move."

But an hour passed, then two, and still there was no let up in the carnage. The noise had grown louder than ever and the looting had begun. From the relative safety of their vantage point on the balcony they could see hundreds of Africans, loaded with goods, scurrying about as they carried their booty away. Hundreds more were pouring in from the side streets. The wounded and the dead were still lying on the road.

"Where the hell are the police!" an angry voice asked.

"One of them could be Prakash," Dara said. "I can stay here no longer."

"This is a library, Dara," Chico said. "Without a weapon of some sort we won't last long. If we don't count the women and the old men there are only about ten of us. They'll wipe us out in a minute."

Dara had already started moving in the direction of the stairs. Yacoob turned to Chico and said, "If they decide to break in here you'll have to man the door." Chico nodded and Yacoob followed Dara, ignoring the warnings of the old man in the skullcap. As they emerged into the alley they heard the lock click into place behind them and looked at each other solemnly. There was no turning back now.

Curiously, it was Yacoob who took the lead, with Dara less than a step behind him. When they reached the edge of the alley Yacoob flattened himself against the wall, one arm stretched wide as he restrained Dara from moving ahead.

"We can see clearly from here," Yacoob whispered to Dara. "Did Neeru-kaki say how Prakash-kaka was dressed?"

"In his white Nehru outfit," Dara said. "He is nowhere on the road. I checked that from upstairs. Just look around the pavement and gutter on this side."

Yacoob's eyes were scanning the area that was blocked off from above by the overhang of the balcony. "What was dada wearing?"

"The long black *achkan*, white shirt and trousers," Dara whispered back. They strained their eyes, studying every figure in sight, moving their glances from one body to another. Fortunately, very few people dressed the way Prakash or Yahya did and this made their task considerably easier.

"They're not out here," Yacoob said, keeping his voice low.

Dara nodded, the relief showing on his face.

"Don't move yet, *Baji*. Let's wait for the right moment, then we head for dada's house. If we get separated don't turn back, just ..."

Dara suddenly gripped Yacoob's arm, above the elbow, his fingers digging deep into the bicep. With his free hand he pointed across the road.

"Look," he said in a tight voice, "whites!"

Yacoob was stunned. Several whites, their faces and hands crudely covered in what looked like black shoe polish, were coming out of a store loaded with goods. Not far away, a few more were heading in the opposite direction, similarly loaded with merchandise from the Indian shops. It was their hair that gave them away.

"*Mader chods!*" Dara spat out vehemently. "Fucking dogs!" The crude words spilled from his lips with an animal viciousness.

"Hush, *Baji*," Yacoob said thickly, blood rushing to his face. He peeked around the corner, then pulled his head back. He looked across the road, his hand still holding Dara back and waited, watching the looters.

"Now," Yacoob said. "Follow me. Don't run."

They took a few steps, still hugging the wall, then Yacoob darted through the smashed door of a shop and pulled Dara in after him. Just inside the door he tugged Dara down and they knelt there, peering into the road. Nobody had noticed them. Safe for the moment, Yacoob began to remove his shoes, rolling his pants up to his knees.

"Take your shoes off and pull your pants as high as you can."

Dara looked at his son questioningly, then wordlessly followed the instructions. Yacoob stood up and looked around. The inside of the ransacked shop was littered with merchandise strewn all over, dresses and clothing scattered on the ground. On a shelf just above his head was a stock of huge Basuto blankets. He grabbed two of them, passing one over to Dara. Then he quickly gathered everything within easy reach and made up two light but bulky bundles, each with a long grip that allowed the bundles to trail close to the ground.

"Cover your head and shoulders with the blanket, let it hang to your feet," Yacoob said as he draped himself in similar fashion. He was about to pick up a bundle when a thought struck him and he lowered it to the ground. He signalled Dara to wait, then disappeared into the interior. Dara heard him rummaging around, then saw him returning with a pair of long handled cane machetes.

Yacoob stood in front of his father, a questioning look in his eyes. He knew it was a decisive moment, a time for Dara to make a final commitment, to choose between survival and philosophy. It was one or the other, he could no longer indulge in the niceties of the issue. Father and son stared at each other for a few seconds, then Dara grimly reached out and grabbed a handle. He hefted it once, nodded, then said, "The time for talking is over."

"Let's go," Yacoob said, throwing a bundle over his shoulder. "Walk, don't run. Act like a looter."

They moved out, bent low, pretending they carried more than what was actually in the pile over their backs. Fortunately, Yahya's house was on the same side of the street and, by hugging the shop fronts they were less conspicuous to the looters who were blindly swarming everywhere. Twice they ducked into the gutted shops to avoid coming face to face with mobs brandishing pangas and tyre levers, in each case emerging only after the warring mob had passed by. On both occasions they saw several whites, roughly disguised, egging on the crazed gangs to even greater destruction. Dara swore under his breath repeatedly and vowed vengeance.

A hundred yards from their destination, at the point where Cathedral Road opened up into Queen Street, they glimpsed two European women singing and dancing as they encouraged a bunch of Africans to break down the ornate gates leading to the Porbandar Arcade.

"Keep moving, *Baji*," Yacoob implored Dara, whose stride had faltered at the sight. "Even if they break through, Madhoo-kaka is safe on the upper floor, the steel gates leading to the flats are unbreakable."

Still Dara hesitated somewhat, then the thought of how vulnerable his mother and father were made him move faster and restrained him from acting foolishly and endangering their own lives.

"Look, *Baji*," Yacoob said from under the blanket, "They've given up and moved on. Even the outside gates have held out."

In another minute they were in front of the house and Yacoob, who was still leading and was slightly in front, stopped dead in his tracks. His heart sank at the sight before him.

The two-roomed cottage was razed to the ground, clothing and furniture thrown into the yard. The overhanging roof, its wooden support posts knocked from under it, was tilted and swaying dangerously.

Dara let out an inhuman cry and, throwing caution to the winds, dropped his disguise and darted forward. Yacoob looked up and down the road, in the same motion picking up Dara's camouflage and quickly entering the comparative privacy provided by the many mango trees that his grandmother had planted as a young bride. Dara was demented, overturning tables and chairs as he waded through the wreckage, his hollow eyes seeking some sign of his parents' fate. Yacoob stood helplessly, the machete at his side, numbed by his father's agony.

After what seemed an age Dara rejoined his son, a hint of relief mingling with his anguish.

"They must have escaped to safety, possibly to Madhoo dada," Yacoob said, more to himself than to Dara. "Maybe someone gave them a lift home."

"Shaida!" Dara almost screamed. "My children!"

Once again it was Yacoob who brought sanity to their fears, holding Dara in check and re-introducing the element of caution to their movements. He made Dara don his disguise again, checked that it was safe to emerge on the street once more, then led the way.

They were running now, away from the shopping district, emulating the looters who were scurrying with their spoils towards the bridge under which they were stashing their booty. And they were all too busy to look twice at another pair of their own kind.

They crossed the bridge safely, passed scores of burnt-out vehicles that were still smouldering in the bus rank, and crossed over Warwick Avenue. When they reached Wills Road they discarded their bundles and blankets. The road ahead of them was deserted, the houses undamaged, and they moved forward at a half-trot.

At each corner there was a gang of Indians and coloureds, armed with an array of improvised weapons, who greeted them as they passed. Most of them seemed to know Yacoob, addressing him as Jake and calling him to join them. Yacoob returned their greetings and promised to return in a few minutes.

They were still a short distance from the house when they saw Shaida on the porch, Salim and Ayesha on either side. When they were close Shaida stepped onto the pavement and took her husband into her arms, for the first time displaying her love for him openly in front of the children. They hugged silently, then Shaida saw the dried blood on her son's body and quickly pulled away.

"I'm okay, Ma. Just a few scratches."

Shaida turned to her husband and looked at him questioningly, the unspoken query on her lips.

"I don't know," Dara said softly. "They were not at home. We think they went over to Madhoo-kaka's flat where it would be safer."

He did not tell her that the house was destroyed.

⊗

They spent an apprehensive night, unable to raise any of the numbers in town that they repeatedly dialed until their fingers grew tired. The house, like the street itself, was comparatively safe from attack. The few raids that had been attempted by the Africans had met with furious resistance by the residents and had been repulsed swiftly. In the absence of the element of surprise the roving mobs concluded it was prudent to move to tamer areas.

Yacoob, who had joined the vigilantes on the street, came in a little after nine the next morning, red-eyed and tired. He repeated that all the outlying Indian areas had been overrun in an orgy of destruction, hundreds of homes reduced to ashes and a larger number of Indians murdered. He had heard, however, that the Casbah, stripped of everything valuable, was now fairly quiet. There was no guarantee, though, that another raid would not be launched later in the day.

Dara refused to wait. "Stay here," he instructed Yacoob. "I must find out what happened to your grandparents."

When Dara reached Queen Street it looked as if it had been hit by a tornado. His shop, together with most of the others, was completely gutted. None had escaped intact. There wasn't a single person on the streets, not even a solitary policeman. He had to rattle the gates to the arcade before someone showed up and allowed him in. As he climbed the stairs leading to Madhoo Daya's flat, a low keening reached his ears and, when he emerged on the landing, he saw people standing around in groups, talking in whispers in the manner of people attending a funeral.

Dara stood still, a sinking feeling in his stomach. He felt an arm encircle him, looked down and saw Heera. She buried her face in his chest, her body shaking as she sobbed loudly. Immediately, he wrapped his arms around her, his eyes moving from face to face, seeking an explanation. When no one met his gaze he gently disengaged himself and, holding the grief-stricken girl by the waist, stepped through the door.

Madhoo was in a chair, hands limp at his sides, eyes closed. The normally peaceful face was shattered by grief. Dara quietly went to him, knelt at his side and placed a hand on the bony knees.

Madhoo seemed to have sensed Dara's presence. Without opening his eyes he groaned and began to shake his head from side to side, his lips trembling soundlessly.

"Kaka, what happened?" Dara asked gently.

Madhoo was beyond hearing, had retreated deep within himself. His chest heaved from the effort of containing his grief. He was on the edge of a breakdown. Dara patted his knees a few times, comforting the old man as he looked around him. A neighbour came over and whispered in Dara's ear. "They are gone — murdered. Your mother and father and Kantha kaki."

Dara was stunned. He felt his legs turn to jelly, the floor beginning to cave in below him. A hand reached out, steadied him, then helped him to his feet.

"Where are they now?" Dara asked, his mouth dry, the words barely audible.

"At the mortuary," a voice behind him answered.

Someone led him to a window and offered him a glass of water. Heera's husband came over and said woodenly, "Kantha kaki had gone over to visit your mother. When the trouble broke out they all decided to come here. Their old legs couldn't carry them fast enough and they were massacred as they crossed the streets. A neighbour saw it all through his window."

"The neighbour saw a passing car stop," a familiar voice took over. "The driver rushed them to hospital. Your father lived long enough to give him this telephone number. The phones only started working an hour ago. The driver got through to us to give us the news and to say that he had stayed with them through the night and done his best to get the doctors to see to them. He left his name and telephone number."

Dara listened in silence, his head bowed in misery, his mind numb. After a few seconds he nodded several times, absent-mindedly.

"We must bury our dead," he said at last, raising himself with an effort.

"The driver of the car has offered to help us with the authorities, to get the bodies released. He seems to be an influential man, a white man."

Dara's head jerked up. "Did you say a white man?"

"Yes, his name is Van Rensburg."

"I must go to my family," Dara said, as he stumbled out of the room.

When Shaida saw him walk through the door her hand shot to her mouth, stifling the scream.

Dara lowered himself to a sofa, pulling her close to his side.

"They're gone," he said. "Kantha kaki too. We must make the funeral arrangements."

It was another two days before they could venture out of the house. The rioting had escalated beyond all proportions, the State not lifting a finger to halt it.

chapter four

Durban: 1986

W hat the hell did you expect, Sam?" Nithin Vania almost shouted. "This is no penny-ante stuff you're talking about. When you first spoke to me you merely asked me to keep my ears close to the ground and find out who your old man was negotiating a sale with. I got that information for you."

"I know, Nits," Sam said. "And I'm grateful to you. But I need to know ..."

"What you just asked me for are full details of the deal and copies of the documentation. Who do you think I am? Some sort of invisible man who can walk in anywhere and take what is needed without being seen? And you want to zilch the deal by using me as your front man! On top of it all you want me to provide you with the finance. You must be crazy, man."

"Slow down, Nits, and don't pull that outraged act on me. You forget how well I know you."

Nits smiled ruefully and reached into his pocket. He extracted a slim, solid gold cigarette case with a built-in lighter, his movements slow and deliberate. He appeared to be lost in thought.

Sam folded his arms and waited. As close as they were, Sam knew this was business and there was no better negotiator than Nits Vania. He was obviously playing for time whilst he planned some manouevre or another. The trick, Sam knew, was to find out what Nits wanted for himself out of the transaction. He was sure it wasn't money. Nits had plenty of that. He decided to wait it out.

"Sam," Nits said at last, "we have come a long way, you and I. From the gutter to the boardroom is a pretty big jump and we've learned a lot along the way. We're not like those milksops out there who simply walked into their fathers' money. We're a different breed, men with ass, we don't get a running stomach when things begin to get hot. But our numbers are small, there are too few of us. If we combine our forces we could be a power to be reckoned with."

Sam felt something click in his mind. He had a pretty good idea what Nits was after. He decided to get straight to the point.

"We've always respected each other, Nits. I haven't forgotten that in the old days Jake and Sandy wouldn't have survived without the information you passed on to me. But, from the first day I went into business, I made a point of never turning to my old mates for help. It was a way of life that was over and done with. With the backing of the Crimson League can you imagine the muscle I could have commanded? Those milksops would have been no more than *garachs* bending over backwards to please me. I would have made a lot of money, but I doubt whether I would have survived up to now. With respect to you, I don't think the way you do. I was never comfortable in that world and I would be less so now. Whatever you have in mind, I'm asking you to forget it."

"Hold on, Sam. I think you underestimate me. When I walked off the streets I didn't look back either. The only difference between you and me today is that you're a trader and I'm a financier. Sure, you've achieved a great degree of so-called respectability in the market place and, because I moved out much later, I have a bit of a 'reputation' that's not easy to shrug off."

"I have never, and I swear by everything that's sacred, held that against you. But now I prefer to operate on a moral base that ..."

"Crap, Sam! And if you don't know it's time you learned — there are no morals in business. Look into the history of all the big business houses, companies that are registered on the Stock Exchange, that are so big we can't even hold a candle to them. You'd be surprised at how they achieved their growth. Do you think the white man got where he is today by being ethical? Do you think that the Group Areas Act and all its restraints on free trade are based on moral principles? I'm a product of their system, my friend. I can't lick it so I operate within it. They prop up their calculated violation of all that is fair by hiding behind laws created by them as they go along. That is their henchman, the strong-arm that represents *their* muscle. Do you think it's much different from what *you* could have called on?"

"You're delving in the area of semantics, Nits. There may be little difference between the function of the forces of law in this country and a bunch of thugs. But the concept of law, fairly applied ..."

"You still don't see the point, do you? Okay, let me ask you a question closer to home. Do you, in your assessment of what is moral, consider the practice of *uplung* as legally acceptable?"

Sam was stumped, and he knew it. If he claimed that it was the answer to the government's double standards in the manner in which it framed its laws, he would be admitting that the practice was no different to the way in which Nits himself operated. It would be a justification of his entire argument. If he maintained that it was an unacceptable and illegal avenue of evading taxation then his own argument would be shot to hell.

"Forget I asked you that, Sam. It was a bit under the belt. I was just making my point, not demanding an answer from you."

"It's a fair question and it deserves an answer," Sam said slowly. "I don't have one for you. I guess one sometimes just grows into these ..."

"To hell with it, Sam. What I was going to suggest we enter into was only an idea. It changes nothing between us."

"Nits, let's be honest. What you really want, if I'm not mistaken, is a haven for your illegal funds and a safe place to launder it. Solomon Brothers, with its enormous cash flow, would be the ideal base for your operations. For me, it would be too high a price to pay for what I am asking from you. But please understand this, I do not stand in judgment on the manner in which you operate. I am merely acting within the dictates of my own conscience. What you do is entirely your own affair."

"But you don't hesitate to call upon my services, in spite of your so-called high values," Nits said, his voice dry. Then he smiled, and Sam couldn't help noticing the touch of sadness in it. "Any port in a storm, Sam? Or a genuine appeal for help from an old buddy?"

"The information I'm asking you to dig up for me will hurt nobody. No one will lose a cent because of it. As for any port in a storm? You can answer that better than anyone else. In a matter of life and death, I'd risk everything I have to back you up and I believe you know that. If you don't then it's time you learned something."

"No need to, buddy. I believe you and I mean that sincerely. I guess that was twice below the belt. Shit! Let it ride. I'll do what I can to help you, all the way down the line and no strings attached. Let's just say it's for old times sake."

"Like hell it is," Sam said laconically. "You'll wait your turn, for the day you need me, and balance the books. All other things being equal, that's a fair expectation."

"That's what I've always liked about you, Sam," Nits laughed spontaneously. "You were never one to bullshit around. I'll give you the dope you need, but I'm curious — unless I'm missing a point your dad can't really tie up the deal without your signature."

"He'll simply conclude it and present me with a *fait accompli*. That's the way Dara always operates. I can hardly take my old man to court and charge him with breaking the Company's Act and failing to obtain a Shareholder's Resolution."

"That would be his style. All the old guys don't have much respect for the rules ..." his voice trailed off. He looked at Sam speculatively for a while, then, on impulse, asked, "What are you going to do about Jake?"

"Nothing. He won't raise any dust over the sale."

"I'm not referring to that. I'm talking about his other activities."

"What other activities? He seems quite settled. Sure, he sees his old buddies from time to time, to spend a few hours ..."

"You really don't know? About his political ..."

"Jake? In politics?"

"In some ways, for all your sophistication, you're quite naive. I guess that's not your fault. You've been fairly protected from ..."

"Nits, what the hell are you talking about?"

Nithin gave Sam a penetrating look, his dark eyes boring into Sam's own. He gave the appearance of a man torn between conflicting interests, as if he were privately debating issues that were concerned with more than a passing discussion and went beyond the realms of friendship. Sam had the clear impression that Nits was trying to make a decision that went beyond loyalty and into areas of self-preservation.

Sam felt a mild fluttering in his stomach and a creeping fear of something very unpleasant that was about to enter his life, some knowledge that would be way beyond his control and cause an upheaval in his already disturbed business affairs. And there was nothing he could do to ward it off. All he could do was wait and hope that his fears were unfounded, that whatever Nithin said would not be too unsettling. When Nithin spoke, the tone of his voice alone increased Sam's trepidation.

"Jake and Sandy are the only guys I've ever completely trusted. I've never doubted Jake's loyalty to me. I value him above the brother I never had. He's into activities that even I cannot extricate him from. And you know Jake, trying to dissuade him from a course of action he is committed to is like trying to reason with a religious fanatic. The argument is lost before the first word is spoken."

Sam inclined his head in agreement and braced himself for what was to follow. He knew that his worst fears were about to be confirmed.

"Sam, I would like you to forget that I was the one who told you this. Jake is a senior member of Umkhonto, has been for many years. And he isn't only on the decision-making team, he's out in the field and active in acts of sabotage, any one of which could destroy him. He's out to blow this government to hell and he doesn't give a damn about the methods. And he leads a charmed life. He's escaped certain death so often they've nicknamed him '*Aza Kwela*' — the man who dances in and out of the Security Branch's clutches with impunity and mocks them with devilish abandon."

"Oh my God!" Sam groaned. "I've heard of him — I mean this chap *Aza Kwela* — I always thought he was some fictional pimpernel, a creation of some weird imagination. That my own brother is one and the same person ... you have to be mistaken, Nits. I live in the same house with him, I see him every day at the office, we eat at the same table. No! You're dead wrong. I ..."

"Sam, in the last year, how often has Jake been away from home, for longer than a night or two?"

"Quite often, but those are business trips, man. He ..."

"You're quite sure?"

And then Sam knew, with a certainty that could not be denied, that Nits had to be right. Sam had never questioned Jake's reasons for his regular absences, even when the occasional doubts had surfaced. At first he had assumed Jake was having an affair with some woman, then had quickly discounted it whenever he saw the look of intense devotion that Jake bestowed on Hannah. But he couldn't deny that he had been concerned, more than a few times, whenever Jake returned after a few days away, with hollow eyes and the strange glow of triumph that nothing could account for.

"Nits," Sam almost moaned, "What can I do?"

"Nothing, Sam. Not even Hannah could divert him. I know where he comes from, he is the classic product of an environment that breeds revolutionaries like him. And he is not alone in that — he may be unique in his daring behaviour — but there are a damned sight more like him than the general public believes."

"Is Sandy a part of ..."

"Sam, don't ask questions that I will not answer. But no, Sandy is not in this. I doubt he even knows the extent of Jake's involvement. But I could be wrong. Those two are very close. I can't tell you more, please don't push me. What I've told you so far may have been a mistake, but I truly believed you could not have been so completely ignorant of his activities. I also wished to save you from the shock of hearing it from some other, less concerned source. I'm also afraid, Sam, that the net is closing in on him, that it won't be long before he is either captured or shot to death. And I'm not the only one who thinks so."

Sam, not normally easily shaken, was stunned into silence. Nithin simply looked at him, then said quietly, "You'll have to learn to live with it, Sam. Jake is fighting a just cause, many of us believe it's a noble one. This is the reality of life in a country that callously abuses the majority of its citizens. If you choose to live here you must accept the hazards of life — or death — in a tyrannical environment."

"You're right, Nits, I have been naive," Sam said, taking a grip on himself.

"I wouldn't have told you if I thought you couldn't handle it," Nithin responded. "And here's something else for you."

Nithin reached into his briefcase and extracted a slim package. "I must be getting old," he said, throwing a sheaf of papers on the table.

Sam only had to look at the first page to realise what it was.

"I never do things in half measures," Nithin stated bluntly. "What you now have is a photocopy of the brief to the buyer's attorneys, with a full list of all the properties and their descriptions, together with the purchase price applicable to each of them. The last page is confidential and not part of the documentation given to the attorneys. You'll find it interesting."

Nits closed the briefcase with a bang, snapping the locks in place.

"When you're ready give me a call. I'll front for you and finance it if necessary, but you'll pay my usual rate of interest. It'll cost you. You can bet on it."

"It'll be a pleasure," Sam said, as Nits stood up. "I owe you a few, Nits. And thanks for telling me about Jake. I won't forget this."

"Sure. Just don't pay me back with another speech about morals."

They shook hands warmly and Sam walked Nits to the door, then shut it behind him. He glanced at the last page of the document. Each of the properties was listed, one below the other. There was an additional column, hand written after the rest had been typed. Against each property there was an amount, the effect of which was an increase to the purchase price.

In spite of the distraction caused by the danger Jake was in, Sam couldn't help saying aloud, "*Uplung!*" He had the answer to what had been worrying him. He now knew where the balance of the money for Kander's deal was coming from.

chapter five

Sam: 1946-1986

*I*mmediately following the termination of the World War II, whilst the Allied armies were engaged in rounding up the remnants of the ruthless Nazi, in South Africa a new regime of terror, not unlike the one that had so recently been defeated, was in the process of being initiated. Those members of the South African government who had vehemently opposed their country's participation in the war against Germany were now in their element. After all, only a small majority of thirteen had prevailed in the South African Parliament when it voted on the issue of entering into the war against Hitler. With the war over the Nazi sympathisers were resurfacing.

The wily Jan Smuts, known even amongst his own people as *Slim Jannie* — the shrewd one — had learnt wisely and well from his supreme position as commander of the South African contingent. He had the cunning to appreciate that, where the Führer had failed, he himself had less than the proverbial snowball's chance of succeeding. He was also aware that, unlike the late and unlamented dictator, he had a lot going for him: He had been amongst those who had voted in favour of his country's support of the Allied cause; he had distinguished himself as a general in the Allied forces; he was highly respected and had the sympathetic ear of virtually all the leaders of the Western nations; he was viewed as a moderate, certainly had no bloodthirsty ambitions, and was a man of great charm. It could not be held against him for wanting no more than to assure the future of his own people — the Afrikaner — who had suffered grievously at the hands of the British at the beginning of the century. And he had no ambitions beyond the borders of South Africa. Most important of all, Britain was still a Great Power and he knew the English mind, perhaps better than the English themselves did.

In his early years, as a brilliant student at Cambridge, he had pursued his legal studies with distinction whilst his subtle and sophisticated brain probed the psyche of his English colleagues. In later years he had added to this knowledge. In the war between Great Britain and the colonies of Transvaal and the Free State, during the years 1899 to 1902, he had been a General in the Boer army ranged against the British forces. He had learnt then, with telling advantage, the shortcomings of the English soldier when waging war on foreign soil.

The Boer War, as some called it, was a totally uneven encounter between English forces, numbering in excess of 500 000, against less than 90 000 Boers. Smuts and his valiant men turned it into the largest and most costly war that Britain had engaged in from the time of the Napoleonic wars right up to World War 1. In spite of its overwhelming might, Britain suffered one reversal after another, with debilitating frequency. The Afrikaner, fighting for his land and his freedom, with the rightful banner of justice held high, gave the well-equipped and numerically superior British armies a salutary lesson in the art of war. Finally, and in utter desperation, the British General, Kitchener, resorted to the only option left to him: the scorched earth policy.

Soon after the war it was Smuts' intellectual vigour that secured for the Boers their political rights. With stunning panache he, together with other white delegates who represented a mere fraction of the total population of South Africa, unified the British colonies of the Cape, Natal, Transvaal and the Orange River. The constitution governing these colonies, signed in Durban, was to a large extent the work of Jan Smuts himself. And he made certain that power, where it counted most, was concentrated in the all-white Union Parliament. Neatly, and in one fell swoop, the political colour bar was enshrined in the new constitution.

Britain, after the disastrous Boer War, had no stomach for further hostilities. The once-proud British tradition of upholding the rights of the underdog was ignominiously consigned to the dustbin of history. The draft constitution, reeking of racism and known as the South Africa Act, was meekly passed as an act of the British Parliament in 1909, notwithstanding the fact that many members of the British Parliament objected to the discriminatory nature of the document.

If the simple Afrikaner, the honest man of the land, perceived it as a betrayal of his own principles, he failed to notice it in the aftermath of the suffering he had so recently experienced.

Now, in 1946, with the knowledge culled from those historic events, Smuts suddenly realised that what he had achieved in 1909 was insignificant compared to what was so glaringly obvious to his calculating mind. History, in its relentless need to repeat itself, had provided him with a further opportunity, a glorious moment in which to entrench, even more solidly, his perverted dreams of a white South Africa. And, for the second time, he led his people down a precipice from which escape could only come at the expense of their own political destruction.

For Smuts the time had come, once again, to capitalise on the simple fact that Britain and the free nations of the world had had their bellyful of warmongering. The will to enter into further acrimonious accusations, immediately following the carnage of a war where the dust had barely settled, was weak to the point of being non-existent. It presented a daunting prospect, even for those nations deeply committed to upholding the rights of man.

It was a point in time that was an opportunist's dream.

Unlike Hitler, who was an arrogant dictator and had dared the world to do its damndest, Smuts utilised his charm and diplomacy to achieve, intentionally or otherwise, what would ultimately and not too far in the future resemble with startling similarity the Nazi state that had flourished in Germany. It was regrettable that a man of his immense international stature had found it necessary to stoop to a level where he had to resort to devious methods to ensure the continuation of white supremacy: on the one hand he was busy drafting the preamble to the United Nations Constitution on Human Rights, on the other, and back in his own country, he was promulgating racial laws that would have shamed some of his staunchest colleagues in the UN.

In the process of suckering the leading nations of the world into a massive double dealing confidence trick, it's a fact that he succeeded beyond even his own wildest expectations. It was a duplicity of horrifying proportions that culminated with a document which the Indians in South Africa appropriately called the "Ghetto Act", and which would remain on the statute books for almost fifty years.

In the pursuit of enforcing that infamous Act and the myriad racial edicts aimed at keeping South Africa lily white, the forces of law and order were stretched to the limit. As a consequence criminal activity in the specifically demarcated non-European areas was not only a low priority — it was to be tacitly encouraged. After all, in an environment where the energies of the inhabitants were devoted solely towards keeping the body and its meagre possessions intact, the inclination to protest against moral issues was bound to be diluted. All that was required was to police the edges of the ghettoes, to ensure the violence within did not spill over into the exclusively white areas and impinge on the safety and the sensibilities of the master race.

As a consequence, within each of the boundaries of the black residential areas, a token police force comprising exclusively of non-European constables headed by a white official was allocated the function of maintaining a modicum of law and order. In reality, their mandate was to obtain the maximum revenue for the country's coffers. And to ensure its success, the hapless policeman's remuneration and promotion was determined by the zeal with which he pursued this objective. Fines for the simplest transgressions, often on trumped up charges, were freely issued and with scant regard for justice. It was not surprising, therefore, that the black constables in these areas were treated with little respect and were susceptible to the minutest bribes. The petty thieves, thugs and ganglords flourished; the honest and hardworking citizens their obvious victims.

In addition, the demarcation of exclusive settlement zones, restricted to the sole occupation of a specific race group, acted as a neat hindrance to racially unified political resistance and fostered a degree of friction amongst the African, coloured and Indian citizens. Such animosities suited the State admirably, the concept of divide and rule was a useful tool indeed in keeping those marginalised people occupied with narrower issues and out of the mainstream of real politics. To the hardcore white politicians such tactics were old hat, to the poorly educated majority it was a sophistication beyond its grasp.

The error of the whole plan was that it was based on a concept that was evil and unjust and, by its very nature, was bound to fail eventually. Sadly, that was a sophistication beyond the ken of the white rulers of the land.

It was in those times, and in that environment, that the young Salim Suleiman emerged one fateful morning.

In the late forties Grey Street, and the roads bisecting it, were a miniature replica of a major city in India. Rows of neat double-storied buildings, consisting of stores on the ground floor and residential flats above, stretched from one end of the road to the other. Occasionally, in between the colonial-styled structures, was the odd cottage with mock Grecian columns and sash windows. The Casbah, as it was often referred to, was inhabited almost exclusively by Indians, with a fair sprinkling of coloureds. It was owned and developed in its entirety, and from its inception almost a hundred years before, by Indians who had automatically settled within its confines before spreading out into the suburbs. It was a vibrant and energetic community that was representative of the second and third generations of the early settlers.

At the corner of Grey and Queen Streets, occupying almost half a block, was the magnificent and architecturally famous Jumma Mosque, with its minarets and many domes. The largest of its kind in the Southern hemisphere, it was a natural landmark for both the local residents and the out of town visitors. Adjoining the mosque, fronting onto Cathedral Road and directly opposite the historic Emmanuel Cathedral, were a row of cottages that had been consolidated into a large unit that served as a *madressah* for Muslim children.

Religious tutors, for the Cathedral Road *madressah* and other similar institutions throughout the country, were as rare as fish trotters and the search for this scarce breed was conducted as avidly as the ancients sought the Holy Grail; and with similar results. The failure to obtain the services of a single teacher, even one who could impart only a rudimentary knowledge of religion, forced the small Muslim community to extend its quest to foreign shores. Consequently, any individual who even loosely contemplated a trip to India was earnestly enjoined to be on the lookout for a suitable incumbent to fill one of the many vacant posts.

The vacuum, especially in Durban, was a charlatan's paradise.

The Cathedral Road *madressah* was in the dubiously fortunate position in that it had acquired the services, some months earlier, of a self-styled theologian from Delhi whose qualifications, as such, were accepted without question and with the most cursory scrutiny.

On that fateful morning in 1950 the spurious purveyor of religious instruction was at his oily best as he paraded before his class of eager children, strutting with a magnanimous benevolence that bordered on what could only be described as ludicrous. He had chosen, as his topic for that day, the normally simple concept of what was considered as *halal* — suitable for consumption by a Muslim. The rules governing the topic were elementary. However, for the arrogant impersonator they presented problems that required a fair degree of improvisation which, in the absence of an invigilator, were easily overcome. He had barely concluded his trumped-up presentation when a young boy raised his hand, an expression of total confusion evident on his bright young face.

"*Masterji*," he asked solemnly, adjusting his tiny knitted skullcap, "You said that all meat must first be made *halal*, before the animal loses its life, otherwise we cannot eat it?"

"That is correct. Good!" the teacher replied, beaming with approval at his star pupil. "As always, you learn good."

"And *Masterji*, you said we make it *halal* by saying a prayer to God. We ask God to forgive us for taking the animal's life. We say that we do that because we are hungry and not for sport."

The teacher smiled widely, peering over his horn rimmed spectacles as he pointed his wooden ruler at the boy. "You been paying careful attention. I will speak to your father. Now, you remember exact prayer?"

The boy intoned, by rote, the phrases from the Koran, his tongue tripping fluently over the Arabic verses.

"Excellent! Now ..."

"Sir," the boy persisted innocently, unaware that his simple pursuit of a vexing problem would unleash a cataclysmic response that would alter the course of his life forever. "*Masterji* ... you see ... last Sunday my father took me to the bay, to fish ..." He was grasping for the right words, his face serious and a little apprehensive.

"Yes, yes. That very interesting. But we not here to learn to fish. We here to learn to be good Muslims, heh?" He was still smiling but was no longer looking at the boy. His eyes darted around the classroom, twinkling as if at some great joke that he had just heard, encouraging a response from the other pupils.

A girl dutifully tittered, someone in the back row guffawed loudly and the whole class joined in.

"But sir," the boy said, slowly standing up. "I didn't mean ..." he stumbled over the words once again, his confidence gone, face red with embarrassment. Quickly, he straightened up to his full height. "You see my father caught a fish and it died and he didn't say the holy words and we took it home and ate it." He had said it all very fast, in a rush, almost angrily. He turned to face the class, eyes blazing.

The teacher slapped the ruler on the desk behind which the boy stood, the loud crack resulting in an immediate hush. "Oho! So now we know what is worrying you. You think your father did wrong? By eating the fish?"

"I don't know, master."

"Okay. Orright! But that a good question. Your father didn't say the holy words before fish die. Anyone know why?" He was playing for time, fully aware there was a perfectly logical explanation. That, however, was as far as his knowledge went. His mind began to work swiftly. He had to come up with some explanation, shut the boy up. He breathed deeply, strutted pompously to and fro on his spindly legs with an exaggerated air of being the possessor of great wisdom. Suddenly, he stopped dead in his tracks, pointed the ruler at the boy and gave a cunning smile.

"The fish already *halal*!" he said loftily.

The class was as one now, in unison with the boy, their fresh eager faces earnest as they marvelled at the miracle inherent in the statement. All eyes were wide, they looked up trustingly, awaiting in wonderment the revelation they knew was about to be disclosed.

The sanctimonious fraud nodded approvingly. He was in his element. This was how he had always envisioned himself — the Great Master, a man of infinite wisdom. For a moment he wished the parents of all his pupils were there to see how well he conducted his lessons. Perhaps, he speculated, the fees could be upped another notch. After all, private tuition was not easily obtained. If they wanted the best they would have to pay for it. For the time being he put the thought aside, to be re-appraised at a later date.

"The fish," he continued grandly, "is favoured creature. Long, long time in past the prophet Abraham decide to make life of man little easy. He also know fish feel no pain. What he do? He throw sword in sea and say holy words, one time for all time."

And, as the wonderment grew, so did his confidence.

"You, boy, you see side of fish where neck would be? You notice cut there? In shape of sword cut? Orright! Now you know why fish already *halal*."

He looked around triumphantly, saw a timid hand, half raised, posing a question.

"Yes, speak up! We must all ask question."

"*Masterji*," the little girl who had raised her hand asked, "did he not miss any of the fish?"

"None. He get them all. Just like that."

"Is such a thing possible?" asked another wonderously.

"With man of God all things possible," he replied cuttingly, with an air of reproach.

"But sir ..." It was the boy again, back on his feet, his face perplexed. "I'm confused."

"What is there you confused about? It all very clear."

"Yes sir, but they taught us in school, the other school, in the biology class, that the cut on the fish's side is its gills."

"So? Fish has gills! Thank you for educating us. You want to be master now?" He was the friendly schoolmaster once more, encouraging laughter from his captive audience. The voice in the back row guffawed again, on cue. This time, however, the boy was not daunted by it.

"What I mean, master, is that the fish breathes through its gills."

"You think I don't know this? You think you only one that went to this other school? Enough! The fish already *halal*. Subject close. Now we prepare for tomorrow's lessons." His voice had an edge to it. Something was wrong. He sensed it in the faces before him, they appeared unhappy with the explanation. He began to regret his earlier decision to humour the boy. It was time to put an end to all questions, forever. The boy, however, remained standing, refusing to be cowed.

"Sir," the voice was still respectful, genuinely confused. Now it was the teacher who was beginning to be apprehensive, dreading what could only be another conundrum that would draw him deeper into the mire of his own fanciful creation. He had to act fast, intimidate his little tormentor into silence. He narrowed his eyes, tugged at his sparse beard, pointed the ruler angrily at the seat and demanded instant obedience.

The boy slowly obeyed. As he lowered himself he asked loudly, "How did the fish breathe before the sword was thrown into the sea?"

"What? What?" he spluttered, visibly upset. Specks of saliva flew from his lips and a thin line of spittle dribbled onto his beard. His features suddenly twisted grotesquely, all previous resemblance to the benign holy man completely erased.

"You dare to question word of God?" he screamed dementedly, advancing furiously, angered by his own impotence in the face of the logic thrown so impudently back at him. "Unbeliever! Dog! Less than dog!"

The ruler whooshed through the air, the thin edge catching the boy on the side of his head, a glancing blow that nevertheless broke the skin and splattered blood across his cheek. The tiny skullcap flew off the boy's head and landed on a desk some rows behind him. Oblivious to the horror on the faces before him, aware only that he was in danger of being exposed as the fraud that he was, he hurled verbal abuse as his cowering victim fell back in the chair, hands raised in fear.

Just as suddenly as he had started, he stopped. Through his manic fury his deranged mind somehow sensed the stupidity of his actions. Through the fog of his wrath he saw the blood seeping between the small fingers and he drew back. For a second, an expression of abject fear abruptly crossed his face and he dropped the ruler to the ground. He mumbled incomprehensively as he took a backward step, then another, overcome by panic and unsure of his next move, his nerves jumping as he attempted to control his trembling body. He was in the act of turning around, in the grip of an overwhelming desire to flee the room, when he noticed the boy calmly wipe his face with the tail of his shirt. The bleeding seemed to have stopped and no other visible signs of damage were apparent. Reassured, his confidence returned, and with it the hope that he could still save the day. A cunning look spread across his face. There was still a chance. If he could restore order, diffuse the situation and somehow win over the pupils before they went home ...

"Orright! okay! What you looking at? Open your *kitabs* and study your lessons. You, boy, come with me." He was fast reverting to form, pretending it was all a minor disturbance, an unavoidable accident, nothing to be upset about. He began to fake a smile and was about to reach out and take the boy by the hand when he saw the look in the youngster's eyes, the intense hatred reflected in them, and his nervousness returned.

"Salim Dara Suleiman," he said, feigning benevolence, "you have sinned. You must make *maaf*, seek forgive ..."

The edge of the slate caught him on his forehead, above the left eye. The force of the blow literally shaved off his bushy eyebrow and plastered it to his temple, exposing the white flesh below. He felt his legs give way, begin to fold under him. As he lifted his hands in a feeble attempt to break his fall the boy streaked past him and dashed through the door.

⁓

It was Friday morning, the day before the Hindu festival of *Diwali*, and Grey Street was teeming with thousands of shoppers jostling each other as they darted in and out of the shops and the few departmental stores, their interior brightly lit and crammed with goods. With the exception of the so-called restaurants, the tea-rooms and the take-aways, every other outlet had huge banners spread across the entrance.

"Give Away Sale" a large calico hoarding proclaimed. "Smash and Grab Sale" screamed another. "Knock Down Sale" flashed a third in letters so large they could be read a block away. The "sales" were ongoing affairs and never changed from one month to the next, year in and year out. It was a way of doing business and it worked.

On the pavements in front of each store were the street vendors selling combs, razor blades, cosmetics and a variety of trinkets and toys. These were the hustlers, the local sharks who moved from one street to another, always a step ahead of the law. A privileged few had permanent spots, trading under licence from the merchants whose shopfronts they occupied and to whom they paid a nominal rental. They were more cocky, shouted at the top of their voices as they called out the prices of their goods, safe in the knowledge that the law couldn't touch them.

Spivs, pickpockets and the occasional mugger insolently drifted through the throngs, looking for an easy mark. Their arrogance was complimented by the way they dressed — the latest in fashion — charcoal grey trousers and shocking pink shirts, glossy patent leather shoes. The more prosperous flaunted a pink designer shirt and a waistcoat in the same fabric as the trousers, the buttons invariably undone. They swaggered with a proprietary air, shoulders swaying cockily as they passed by, eyes sharp and darting all over, their faces hard and challenging.

Rising above the noises of human activity, the hooting and mechanical sounds of cars and trucks, was the deafening blare of music as Hindi signature tunes competed with the latest Western hits. Sudden laughter, its joyous peal, was just as suddenly replaced with a shout of anger and cries of "keep your hands to yourself, you bum!" and immediately followed by a chortle and a mocking comment. It was almost always a short-lived incident. Nobody paid much attention to it. This was the Casbah. It was accepted as naturally as a passing greeting.

At the corner of Grey and Victoria Streets, outside the renowned Victory Lounge, Salim paused for a deep breath. He chewed the last morsel of *bhajia* and swallowed it, savouring the taste of the spicy spinach as it lingered on his palate, his hunger unsatisfied. Reluctantly, he crumpled the greasy paper packaging from which he had extracted the last crumb and threw it in a bin. For a while longer he inhaled the pleasant aroma of freshly cooked Indian food as it wafted through the door and stimulated the juices in his belly. He had spent his last penny. As ravenous as he was, hunger was preferable to returning home.

Salim was still smarting from the beating he had received from his father the previous night, the angry berating still echoing in his ears. He had hardly begun to give his side of the story when a neighbouring shopkeeper had walked in and recounted, in vivid detail, the incident in the *madressah*. For Dara it was enough, scandalous in the extreme. That his son had reacted like a thug was bad in itself. Worse was sure to follow — all outstanding fees would have to be paid, immediately, together with a suitable donation towards "school funds" — as a penitence for Salim's blasphemous behaviour. And then there would be medical bills incurred by the poor teacher, followed by charges raised by the *hakim* for all the potions and liniments and poultices required to aid the healing process.

"I'll be ruined," his father had shouted, "bled dry for years to come." It had not occurred to him to examine his son's head or attend to the split in the scalp.

Salim idly crossed the road, passed "Dhanjee's Fruiterers" and headed towards the penny arcade, lured by the sound of raucous music as it spilled onto the street. The single word, "Funland", in huge garish letters, was emblazoned above the entrance, with tiny colourful lights flickering on and off above it. Through the wide plate glass windows he could see the viewing machines, jukeboxes and gaming tables. At the edge of the pavement a young and surprisingly light-skinned African held a penny whistle to his lips, his feet in the gutter. Between his ankles was a soiled beret in which nestled a few coins thrown by passers-by.

He walked into the funland a little diffidently, unsure of himself. The place was packed, noisy with laughter and the sound of whirring machines and rolling balls. Nobody paid any attention to him. A small group of Africans, snapping their fingers, approached a jukebox and one of them inserted a coin into the slot. The sound of Glen Miller's *In the mood* rose above them. "That's my number, man," one of them called out as he swayed to the rhythm. They played it several times, referring to it as "It's what you do tonight" and ecstatically swinging to its beat.

For a while he wandered around, then stepped out again. Several young boys, their behaviour suggesting they were on home ground, had gathered at the entrance and were making lewd gestures as a girl walked past. An older boy, about sixteen or seventeen years old, was strutting around, his knees slightly bent and spread at an angle, one hand cupping his genitals. "Hey there," he sang at the girl, "you with your ass in the air." When he winked knowingly at his mates and made as if to touch her, she neatly sidestepped and continued without a backward glance. The boy rolled his eyes and his pals exploded into fits of laughter, enjoying the exhibition.

An older woman, in her early thirties and quite good looking, crossed over the road and stepped onto the pavement. Her tight dress accentuated her buttocks and they jiggled saucily with each step. The boys eyed her impudently, licking their lips in an obscene manner. At that moment a portly old man drew alongside the woman, apparently in a hurry, his left hand swinging in an exaggerated arc. As he overtook her, his palm brushed her behind, seemingly by accident. When he repeated the movement the boys hooted and began to ululate. One of them shouted, in a lilting voice, "Hey guys, the dead hand brigade is in town." The man glared at them and quickly disappeared into the crowd.

Sam moved on, not quite understanding what the boys had meant by the comment or the significance of the charade executed by the lecher. He instinctively knew, though, that there had been a sexual connotation attached to it. He dug his hands deep into his pockets, his fingers curled into fists. Pangs of hunger gnawed at his belly and he sucked in his stomach. He had to get something to eat.

Directly across from the amusement parlour was a record shop, its interior packed. The inevitable "sale" was on. It appeared though, that on this occasion, there were genuine bargains on offer. The customers spilled over onto the pavement where, in a space of his own, a young boy did a soft shoe shuffle, his dagga-glazed eyes fixed on the movement of his feet. It was a solo performance of which Sam was the only spectator. No one else paid any attention to it.

As Sam stood and surveyed the scene, the activity around him intensified. Skin shades from fair to pitch black, with virtually every variation in between, abounded; the pure white noticeably absent. Whites, as a rule, rarely ventured into the area. The few who were brave enough to do so came in tight little groups, mainly tourists and sightseers, looking for bargains whilst they absorbed the unique atmosphere of the famed Casbah. And yet, the reality was that there was little to fear.

Over the years the Casbah had acquired a highly exaggerated reputation for violence which was belied now by the easygoing attitude of the shoppers as they moved around, unperturbed by its notoriety. The occasional fight between the local thugs seldom, if at all, interfered with normal activity and was over almost as soon as it had started, with police activity minimal and restricted in the main to the issuing of traffic fines.

In spite of his hunger Sam was dazzled by everything around him, for the first time feeling incongruous in his old fashioned handed down trousers and scuffed shoes. He decided to head for an arcade across the road, which was also a thoroughfare into the next street. It was far busier and he would feel less conspicuous. He had barely moved when a heavy hand landed on his shoulder and turned him around. A tall, thin man, dressed from head to toe in green clothes and a green beret tilted rakishly over his head, snarled at him, "Where you from, *lighty*?"

Sam twisted his shoulder and slipped out of the grip. Before he could move again the man had caught him by the front of his pants and half lifted him off the ground.

"You going to the bio, *lighty*?"

Sam nodded, not sure what was expected of him.

"Gimme a sassy, *scarpie*. Shine up!" he snarled.

"I don't have any money," Sam said, struggling.

"Don't give me that jive, you little shit." The thug held him easily as he expertly riffled Sam's pockets with his free hand. Finding them empty, he released Sam and stepped back, losing interest. Sam was about to walk off when he heard a soft voice behind him.

"What's going on here?"

Hearing the familiar voice, relief flooded through Sam and he turned around.

"This guy handling you, Sam?" Jake asked, his voice quietly menacing.

"He asked me for a sixpence," Sam replied, looking at the thug nervously.

"Cut a line, Blade," Jake said. "This is my *lighty* bro."

"Sure, Jake, sure. Hey, I didn't know." He took several backward steps, then quickly disappeared into the arcade.

"Sam, what are you doing here?" Jake asked.

"I had to get something for *Baji*," Sam lied.

"Hey, c'mon. You don't have to tune me false." Jake was smiling.

"Schools closed today for *Diwali*. I didn't want to go to the *madressah*."

Jake burst out laughing. "I heard about yesterday. That old shit had it coming."

For a moment Jake looked at Sam speculatively.

"You hungry?" he asked Sam.

Sam nodded.

"Let's go," Jake said, leading the way.

The Casbah was Jake's district, his home ground, where he spent most of his time. He seemed to know everybody and stopped often to talk to an acquaintance before moving on. Jake was almost seventeen, tall with wide shoulders and slim hips. He walked with catlike grace, rolling his hips like some of the cowboys Sam had seen on the screen. There was a street-wise alertness about him that contrasted glaringly with Sam's gawky appearance and outdated clothes.

They entered a narrow passage, between two blocks of flats, and emerged a minute later onto a wide and busy intersection, not much different to the one they had just left. Jake turned to his left and approached the open doors of a café, using his elbows to cut a path for them. The place was noisy and not particularly clean. Most of the tables were occupied and those that weren't hadn't been cleared, greasy plates and stained cups and saucers still lying where the previous diners had left them.

Jake walked to a table in the far corner and pulled up a chair and sat down, his back to the wall, facing the entrance. He indicated a chair next to him and Sam joined him. Jake caught an apron-clad waiter's eye and jerked his head, beckoning him over to them. The waiter, who was about twice Jake's age, hurried over and made a show of cleaning the table, balancing plates, cups and saucers on his wrists and arms with the agility of a trained juggler. He disappeared through a swing door through which Sam could hear loud voices and the clatter of crockery and cutlery.

The waiter was back in less than a minute, wiping the table with a damp, soiled cloth. A thin film of moisture, stale-smelling and offensive, spread across the worn oilcloth covering the wooden top. Sam pulled back, raising his elbows, his nostrils dilating with distaste.

"Howzit Jake," the waiter fawned.

"Two specials," Jake snapped, ignoring the greeting. "And make sure the plates are clean."

"Sure, Jake. Got you."

Sam looked around. A few feet away, immediately above a hobo noisily sipping tea, was a huge blackboard suspended from the ceiling. Chalked in large black capitals it announced "Bunny chow today. 6d for half".

"What are your plans for later?" Jake asked.

"Go home, I guess."

"Want to spend some time with me?"

"Ja," Sam nodded eagerly, his eyes lighting up.

The food arrived, thick lentil curry with beans and thin slices of bread together with two cups of tea. Suddenly, Sam's disgust vanished. The plates were washed clean, the food smelt appetising. He dug in with relish, using his fingers for the bread and scooping the curry with a teaspoon. The food was unexpectedly delicious, the aroma pleasing to his nostrils and whetting his already aroused appetite. After a while he fell back, licking his lips as he sipped the tea.

Jake was absorbed in the meal, his head lowered, hair spilling onto his forehead. He ordered two more servings before he was satisfied. Finally, he wiped his fingers with the tissue-thin serviettes, squashed them into a ball, and flung it in an empty plate. He flicked his fingers for the bill. The waiter wrote something on the page of a small pad, using a stubby pencil held stiffly in his thick fingers. When he tore off the page and handed it to Jake, Sam was surprised that all it read was: Two teas. BB. 3D.

Sam glanced at Jake who merely smiled thinly as he placed a tickey on top of the bill. He transferred a few coppers into his left hand and, as he stood up, deftly dropped them into the wide pocket sewn on the front of the waiter's apron. The action was executed smoothly, unnoticed by the sharp eyes of the proprietor who stood behind the counter.

Sam followed Jake as they walked out. For the price of two teas and buttered bread, they had both eaten a princely serving that would normally have cost at least two shillings. Sam no longer wondered why Jake seldom ate at home.

When they emerged onto the street Jake, who had caught the astonishment on Sam's face when he had looked at the bill, smiled as he said, "Sam, around here you'll have to learn to keep a straight face. Don't let it worry you. Come on."

For the next hour Sam was introduced to a colourful world. He met many members of the Victorians, the junior arm of the dreaded Crimson League. Sam, in spite of his limited knowledge of the underworld, had heard of the infamous mob whose name was only mentioned in whispers and who controlled the entire Casbah, and beyond, with blatant disregard of the law. As Jake's younger brother he was welcomed without question and often with a touch of deference.

In the course of that first hour Sam learned that Jake was right up there with the leaders of the Victorians and shared equal rank with the few that called the shots and made the decisions. And Jake was respected, with a solid reputation which he could only have earned with his ready fists and quick responses. Sam positively basked in his brother's popularity and rapidly lost his earlier diffidence. Sometime, during that hour, he knew that he had reached a turning point in his life.

Later that afternoon Sam experienced his first taste of easy money.

The cinemas in the Casbah were all located in Victoria Street. Owned by a handful of wealthy families and run by managers whose only function was to ensure that every show was packed to capacity, more than fifty percent of the ticket sales was in the hands of the Victorians. The owners were seldom in evidence except on Saturday nights, when they pulled up in their expensive limousines and treated their friends to a night out. And on those occasions their seats were reserved. The special "boxes" in the upstairs gallery, their exclusive preserve.

Jake, with Sam in tow, stopped first at the Avalon Cinema. He went into a huddle with the manager, emerging a few minutes later with a handful of tickets. He then led the way to the Victoria Theatre, popularly known as the "Vic", and repeated the performance. From there he crossed the road and entered the Royal Picture Palace and once again bought a large number of the best seats. After that they took a breather, sipping cokes outside a fish and chip outlet, the rear of which housed the Victorian's headquarters.

Jake, normally taciturn, was unusually talkative. "None of the cinema's offer an advance booking service. When the rush starts there'll be large queues and only a few will obtain seats. Once the 'House Full' sign is up the 'runners' will go into action. The tickets we have will sell at twice the price."

Sam was intrigued. "How much can you make?"

"On a good day," Jake said, his eyes everywhere as he spoke, "We can clear anything up to fifteen or twenty quid, net profit."

When Sam's eyes shot up Jake laughed. "It's not all mine to keep. We pool it."

"Jake, can I be a runner for you?"

"Anytime. But how will you be able to get away from home?"

"I'm going to go and tune ma. I'll tell her I'm spending the night at aunty's place. Okay?"

"Up to you, Sam. Here." Jake slipped Sam a half a crown coin.

"Sink it," Jake said with a smile. "An advance for later. If you're coming back make it fast. The action starts early."

"Will you be here?"

"Ja," Jake said shortly. "Just ask around for me. Now dust."

∞

Sam half ran, half walked as he headed home, his head spinning from the interaction of the day's events. He saved time and distance by cutting through the Indian market and the Warwick Avenue bus rank, weaving in and out of the thousands of commuters. A hundred yards from home he slowed down and began to gather his thoughts. A twinge of guilt ran through him as he thought of deceiving his mother, but the weight of the heavy coin in his pocket quickly dispelled it.

When he walked through the door of the cottage in Verbena Road he sensed that his mother was not at home. Ayesha was in the kitchen preparing the evening meal.

"Where's Ma?"

"You're late. You'll catch it when *Baji* comes home."

"Don't tell him, *ben*. Please."

Ayesha's face softened and she ruffled his hair. "I won't. And ma doesn't know. She's been away all day at the Kajee house. They're going to have a baby."

Relief flooded through Sam. His mother could be away till late that night, depending on when the baby was born. He fidgeted around for a while, then twisted a fresh roti into a cone and filled it with a little of the potato curry that was simmering in a pot. He took a few tentative steps out of the kitchen.

"I'm going to spend the night with aunty."

Ayesha frowned. "*Baji* won't like that."

"It's Friday. He'll only come home after eight."

"He'll ask for you if you're not here."

"*Ben*, make a plan for me, please," he pleaded.

Ayesha looked doubtful. Sam changed tactics, lowering his voice.

"There's always a lot to eat at *foy*'s house."

Ayesha relented, placing an arm around Sam's shoulders.

"Okay, I'll think of something. But you'll have to go to the shop in the morning and help *Baji* as usual."

Sam kissed her on the cheek before she could change her mind. "Take a clean shirt for tomorrow," she shouted after him as he rushed off, but he was already through the door and out of hearing.

On the pavement again, Sam stopped and looked around. Some of his friends were playing in the narrow road, kicking a ball around. It was a cosmopolitan neighbourhood with Indian, coloured and Malay families living close to one another. The whites were on the other side, beyond the park that was occasionally used as a common playground.

Sam's house was a maisonette, one of two. His immediate neighbours were the Reids, a coloured family of seven boys and a girl. Sam spent a lot of time with them and was close friends with the younger boys. Normally, he couldn't wait to join them as soon as he came home from school. For once, though, he was in a hurry to get away and didn't stop for them.

"Hey, Sam," he heard Sheila Reid call, "you coming over? Ivan just brought home a puppy."

"Later," Sam shouted over his shoulder as he quickly walked towards Wills Road. Sam had started to run and, as he reached the corner, he nearly bumped into Mrs Reid, a stout motherly woman. She was sweating profusely and wiping her face with a handkerchief and flexing her aching arms.

"Sorry, Isaac," Sam apologised. Like everybody else, including her own children, nobody referred to her by any other name. Sam picked up one of her baskets, holding it in front of him with both hands, and staggered towards her door. He lowered it carefully in the pocket-sized garden, then rushed back and repeated the performance with the second basket. When he returned to the corner again she was still standing in the same spot, breathing heavily.

"Come, Sam. Come eat."

"Thanks, Isaac. But I have to go to town."

"You turning down good food, Sam? For someone that's always hungry ..."

"I ate earlier. Jake bought me lunch."

"That one," she snorted. "He'll come to no good. Does your dad know you're spending time with him outside the house?"

Sam panicked. He had been bragging, showing off at having eaten at a café. If his father found out there would be trouble.

"Isaac," Sam started to say, "you won't tell ..."

"No, Sam. I won't tell your dad. Jake's not a bad boy and he's good to me. But you be careful, you hear?"

"Okay," Sam said, rushing off.

When he was back in Victoria Street he headed directly for the fish and chip shop. Jake was in a large room in the rear, away from the customers and staff. Besides Jake, there were four others in the room, all slightly older than Jake and dressed in sharp, fashionable clothes. At Sam's entrance, they stopped talking.

"It's okay," Jake said. "It's my *lighty* bru." He didn't introduce Sam, merely pointed to a corner a little distance away. Sam sat down self-consciously, his hands under his thighs.

"The *vit ous* are getting heavy," one of them said. Sam later found out that his name was Magua. "We give in now and we're dead."

"Fuck them!" Jake said. "We can't go to their district without catching it. They want to make kuk with us, it's that time."

A short, muscular African, his feet propped up on a chair, lit a cigarette and drew deeply. "I'm with Jake," he said, his voice guttural. "They come here, we take them. We *makelaar* with them."

"I'm not *skrik* of these guys, Vusi," Magua said. "I can make *klaar* with the best of them. But Jeff here *grafts* there sometimes."

"No shit, daddy," the one called Jeff said. "I don't have to go there. No big loss."

"Those whites," Jake said thoughtfully, "they're connected to the Dutchenes. They live near them. We declare with these *ous*, we declare with the Dutchenes too."

"You live there, Jake," Magua asked. "You reckon they're good *maats* with each other?"

"Can't be sure," Jake replied. "The Dutchene boys are like us, all *bruin ous* or *charos*. But I know they mix sometimes, especially when the whites come to their shebeens looking for black *ezie*."

"That's their *indaba*," Vusi snapped. "Jake, this is our territory. They make shit with us we handle them."

"I think we should talk to the *Motas*." The speaker was a tall, lanky Tamilian, his dark skin glowing with vitality. Sam noticed something different about him, an air of confidence and suppressed violence. He had spoken directly to Jake and was now looking at him patiently as he waited for a response.

"We talk to the big boys, Sandy," Jake's voice was low, a little angry, "and they want to climb in for a share of the *paisa*. They already get a bigger cut of the *fah fee* takings than our runners. I always said I don't *tamba* their style."

"Those *Motas* in the League make us do their dirty work," Vusi almost snarled. "Why should they get a cut of our action. They get a tickey for every *kaaitjie* of dagga we sell. That's nearly the same as we keep for ourselves. And we're the merchants. We take the risks."

"I agree," Sandy said reasonably. "You think I like it? But if we take on the West Street Willys we need to do two things. We must keep the Dutchenes out and also square the cops. You guys know how it is. You touch a *wit ou* and the cops move in. And they hear nothing. White is right, as far as they are concerned. It'll disrupt us for days, set us back badly. To avoid that we need the Crimson League. They have the connections."

Sam liked the way he spoke, softly and without raising his voice.

"Okay," Jake seemed to have reached a decision. "Vusi, we talk to them. But we must make a plan, a trade off. There's something else we need from them. Sandy, can we talk later?"

"Sure, I have to pull a number in a few minutes. The runners will be waiting."

"Vusi," Jake stood up and nodded. "Let's check on the ticket sales." He motioned to Sam to follow him.

The street lights were on, the cinemas bathed in the glow of neon tubes. Most of the stores were closed for the day, their interiors gloomy. The entire scene had changed, a more festive atmosphere seemed to be in the air. In place of the shoppers, a leisurely and relaxed crowd had taken over, mostly youngsters and courting couples, with the odd family group. Most of them were gravitating towards the cinemas or converging in the foyers. A fair number were African who, in spite of being precluded, by law, from any place of entertainment, nevertheless brazened their way in. Nobody bothered to ask questions and the law was, in any case, seldom around.

Sam was surprised at how quickly the tickets were taken up and amazed at the high prices paid for them. Jake had introduced him to one of the runners and, between them, they had disposed of their entire stock of tickets in under ten minutes. Sam, who had merely stood by and collected the money, handed the proceeds to Jake. Runners from the other cinemas came over and Jake checked their takings, gave each a few coins and shoved the notes deep into his pocket.

Sam followed Jake as he crossed the road and entered the café again. He bought two cokes and then asked Sam, "What do you want to do now?"

"I'd like to stick around with you. I only have to go to the shop in the morning."

Jake didn't ask Sam how he had managed to get away. "You'll have to rough it," he said. "And keep your mouth shut. If there's any trouble stay out of the way."

Sam shook his head up and down silently.

They moved around for a while, joining little groups that Jake referred to, in an aside to Sam, as local sharks who earned their living hustling for the big boys. "They run around buying food and cigarettes for the gamblers. They're just small time *scotens*, you don't want to be like them."

Jake never stopped in one place for long. He seemed to be restless, on the move all the time, constantly alert. Eventually, he increased his stride and moved purposefully towards the far end of Victoria Street, where it was darker and comparatively quiet. He stopped at the corner of Soldier's Way and Prince Edward Street, in front of a building on which a large neon sign winked on and off. Below the lights there was a sign "The Vineyard" written in red and white flourescent paint. A huge, half naked Zulu, belly bulging onto his thighs, sat on a wooden crate and cracked a long oxhide sjambok against the floor. When he saw Jake his face split into a grin.

"*Hau, Jake, Unjani?*"

"*Lungile, Khati. Bugile Vusi?*"

"*Ja, phagati.* Inside."

Jake nodded and handed him a large coin, patting his shoulder. As he led the way down a narrow passage, towards the rear of the building, he whispered, "Always be on good terms with the *chinglaans*, the guards. They can save your life."

When they reached a pair of huge double doors, Sam heard music from a jukebox. They stepped in.

The interior was done up in mock Roman decor, cheap plastic plants covered in dust crept on the walls and across the ceilings. Earthenware pots, with even more of the imitation fauna were everywhere, providing the tables with a degree of privacy. The place was full of customers, the smell of liquor and stale food rising in the air. A pall of cigarette smoke hung over the whole area. At least thirty or forty people were sitting around the tables and lining the bar counter that ran along the length of the hall.

Jake stood just inside the door and looked around. Sam spotted Vusi and tugged Jake's hand, attempting to draw his attention. Jake ignored him as he surveyed the interior. Finally, satisfied, he moved in. The barman noticed Sam and shouted, "You can't bring the *lighty* in, Jake. He's underage."

Jake saw Vusi at the end of the bar and, ignoring the barman, headed towards him. Sam followed, his eyes on the slim man behind the counter, expecting to be thrown out at any minute. When they reached Vusi the barman came over and slapped his palms on the counter.

"Jake, don't cause it. If the *larnie* comes here I'll catch it."

"Don't come out sideways with me, Jimmy," Jake snapped. "Your boss won't leave his air-conditioned lounge and his white customers until closing time. Now get me a beer and one for Vusi. Get my *lighty* a coke and some boiled eggs. Shift it!"

The barman hesitated, saw the look on Jake's face, and shrugged his shoulders. He uncapped two beers and placed them on the counter, together with a wet tankard that was still dripping with the water it had been washed in. Jake ignored the tankard and drank directly from the bottle. He took several deep swallows before he lowered the bottle and turned to Vusi.

When Sam's order arrived Vusi placed it on a stool, within easy reach of Sam, then said something to Jake who looked over his shoulder. A tall, dark-skinned girl in a tight skirt that seemed too short for her was sauntering towards them. She was quite pretty, in a hard metallic way, and swung her hips provocatively as she approached them. She looked Indian to Sam but could easily have passed for a coloured. When she smiled her teeth shone startlingly white in the dim light.

"I've got a customer lined up," she said to Vusi as she winked naughtily at Jake. "He wants ten *kaaitjies* of the best. He'll pay two shillings for each."

"Two bob!" Vusi scoffed. "For good *zol*? He's a *vit ou*?"

"Ja. White as they come."

"He'll pay a gron at least. Tell him two and six or forget it."

"Okay ... Where's the parcel?"

"You sure he's not a *kerel*, Candy?" Vusi asked suspiciously.

"He's no cop," she laughed. "I know this *ou* well. He's crazy about black *ezie*. Pays me a quid just to sit in the car and play with him."

Vusi laughed, reached into a nearby pot plant and extracted a small paper packet from which he counted the slim rolls of dagga. He handed the tubes to the girl who stuffed them between her heavy breasts.

"Buy me a drink, Jake," she said, leaning heavily against him and pressing her chest against his arm.

"Ask your *pussbhai*," Jake smiled mockingly, pointing his bottle at a burly, shifty-eyed man sitting at one of the tables.

"Shit on that pimp," she said, her voice suddenly hard. "I'm going to drop him. This *garach* is becoming one of my regulars. A real fish. I tune him right I reckon he'll marry me."

"You crazy?" Jake asked unbelievingly. "That's jail bait, baby. Cops catch you with a white man it's seven years for you and back to his mama for him."

"This guy's a good thing, Jake. I got him under control and his old man's loaded. A real *larnie*."

"That makes it worse for you," Vusi said.

"No, Vusi, it makes it easier. He'll swipe his mother's jewellery and take me to the States. Start up a new life."

Vusi shook his head knowingly, impressed in spite of himself. He knew the game. A white guy lusted after a black girl, got a huge kick out of tasting the forbidden fruit, and took the only way out. He whisked her out of the country and indulged himself in safety. It happened often and seldom lasted long. The men always came back after a few months, without the girls.

"You *smark* this *ou*?" Vusi asked. "I mean really love him?"

The girl snorted, finding the question ludicrous. She tossed her head back, pushing her long hair out of her face.

"Who cares about that jive," she sneered. "I just want to get the hell out of this dump, go to the land of milk and honey. No shit, daddy!'"

She paid Vusi and, as she turned to leave, Sandy walked through the door.

"What you say, Candy baby?" Sandy asked with a leer. "Want to make like that?"

"You're too late, honey chile. This here mama's little baby is heading for the big time. You want some you come looking for me in good ole California."

She stepped around Sandy, waving with her fingers. It was the way they always greeted each other, no more than that. Any more would have to be business.

Sam was struck again by Sandy's presence. He seemed to dominate the place with his confidence, creating an aura around him that commanded the respect and attention of almost everyone that he spoke to. Sandy looked at Sam, then at Jake, his face disapproving.

"He'll have to wisen up sometime, Sandy. I don't want him to grow up to be a *garach*."

Sam vaguely understood the meaning of the word. A derogatory description employed in describing anyone that was an easy mark for the hustlers. In its normal Gujerati context it simply referred to a customer in any store. On the streets it had a subtle nuance, a contemptuous appellation synonymous to the word "dupe". To be referred to as a *garach* in the underworld was an insult — you either retaliated physically or forever lost the respect of your equals.

Sandy smiled and ruffled Sam's hair, then turned to Jake and Vusi. "We'll have to talk to the League. The word is out that the Willys want a cut of the takings. They'll make their move soon."

"If it's okay with Vusi," Jake replied, "We can go to the *Motas* now."

Vusi didn't answer for quite some time, his woolly head resting against the wall behind him, his brawny arms folded. When he finally spoke the anger was unmistakable.

"The League better play ball with us. They want something done, we don't give them jazz. We do it. It's their turn now, Sandy. They don't shine up, we do it on our own."

"Let's just talk to them, Vusi," Sandy suggested. "Maybe we can work in a trade off, like Jake said."

"Okay," Vusi said. "You know me, I move when you move. What about the *lighty*?"

"He can sleep at the pad tonight," Jake answered. "Sam, go to the fish and chip hangout and bunk down in the back."

Sam nodded and left. The café was an all night stand and no one questioned him when he walked through and headed for the rear. There was a door at the far end and when he opened it he saw that it led to another, much smaller room. In one corner was a sink and a urinal. Two double bunks lined the other end. He removed his clothes and his shoes, stood for a moment in his underpants, then sank into a lower bunk, suddenly aware of how tired he was.

∞

Someone was shaking Sam roughly and he opened his eyes to see Jake leaning over him. For a moment he was disorientated, believing he was still at home in his own bed. Jake gently slapped him a few times, removing the last signs of drowsiness and forcing him to focus on Jake.

"We must talk, Sam. Let's get some chow."

Sam rubbed his eyes vigorously, then walked over to the sink and washed his face. He dressed fast, then followed Jake into the outer room where two plates of eggs, bread and coffee were laid out.

"What's the time?" Sam asked.

"Seven thirty," Jake replied. He looked tired, eyes red from lack of sleep.

"I have to go to the shop."

"Okay, now listen. Stay at home today, speak to the old man, convince him that you have an evening job here. I'll tune the *larnie* and if *Baji* decides to check on you he'll back you up. That way you won't have to duck and dodge every night."

Sam nodded, eating quickly.

"I won't be coming home for a few days," Jake mumbled, his mouth full. "They don't miss me anyway. When you're ready come over. Sandy and I have something lined up for you."

They finished the meal and stood up simultaneously. Jake patted Sam's shoulder and walked out.

In less than five minutes Sam was in Queen Street. When he entered the store his father was busy with a customer whilst another was studying the label on a metal bucket. Sam immediately turned his full attention to the lady holding the bucket, praying silently that he would make a sale and distract his father. To his delight she bought the bucket, together with several other items, and paid the full price without bargaining for the usual discount.

For the next hour Sam kept himself busy, always on the move. The usual Saturday shoppers were on the streets and it was a busy morning for them. He made several more sales, constantly watching his father out of the corner of his eye, uncertain what to make of the expression on his face. At the first opportunity he surreptitiously dropped the coins that Jake had given him in the cash drawer. For a moment he felt a twinge of regret, then consoled himself with the thought that it was an investment of sorts. The increase in the day's sales would put his father in a good mood and he would perhaps be more receptive to the proposition Sam intended to put to him later in the day.

When he heard his father grunt, a sound that always signified satisfaction, Sam began to relax. After that the day passed swiftly, with customers pouring into the store, although they bought very little. Sam was wondering about that when his father cleared his throat.

"We need stocks," Dara said. "The business is there but we're turning good customers away."

"Can't we get more goods from the merchants?" Sam asked.

"I always pay cash, to get the best prices. You pay too much when you buy on credit and then you can't compete. I must speak to your mother, maybe we can sell the last of her jewellery to raise some money."

"Karan's uncle is a jeweller. We could pawn the jewellery ..."

"Never pawn anything," Dara said emphatically. "You'll be bled dry for your last penny. It's better to sell and buy back later. Remember that, never pawn jewellery."

Sam always listened to his father carefully, especially when the neighbouring businessmen dropped in to chat and pass the time of day. He now considered what he had just been told, his brow furrowed.

"How much interest do they charge?"

"Enough!" Dara almost barked, his voice harsh. "You pay through your nose and end up losing the jewellery anyway. Five percent a month is the minimum."

"Is that legal?"

"Listen, you only get a receipt for the interest they are legally allowed to charge, the excess they take in cash. And if you fall behind once, they confiscate the jewellery and you lose everything."

"But if you sell the goods fast, in less than a month, you can make more than five percent ..."

"A pawnbroker is a bloodsucker and a thief, Salim. Even when you pay him the full amount you never get back your original jewellery. They have ways of stealing some of the gold, removing a few of the links and replacing them with cheap metal. Sometimes they even shave off some of the gold or reduce a portion from twenty two carats to much less. And people like us can't tell the difference. Even when you sell, watch their scales, make sure the balance is right."

"Are they all thieves, then?"

"No. Some, like Karan's uncle, are very honest and can be trusted. But it's better just to sell and buy back when you have the money again."

All the talk about carats and weights made Sam's mind spin in confusion.

"We lost everything in the riots." Dara's voice was bitter. "We took a bond on the house to open this place. But, with a little capital, who knows ..."

"We can build it up again, *Baji*. Like you did before."

"Maybe. When you join the business we could do better. In the meantime, you study. Learn accounting; then we don't have to pay a bookkeeper later. Be careful of bookkeepers, they have ways of finding out your secrets, like *uplung* and hidden stocks that help you save on tax. When the bookkeeper knows about that he can blackmail you by raising his fees, and if you don't pay he causes trouble. And you can't change bookkeepers. They threaten to expose you if you try that. Bookkeepers! They become your partners without introducing any capital."

Dara spoke in a curious mixture of English and Gujerati, switching from one to the other suddenly, in mid-sentence. But Sam listened carefully and stored the knowledge away. It would serve him well in years to come.

As soon as it struck one they prepared to shut down for the weekend. Sam helped his father count the day's takings, making little piles of the coins and straightening the notes.

"Twenty two pounds, eleven shillings and ninepence," Dara said. "Not bad for this time of the month." He wrote the amount on a piece of paper, then did a rapid calculation. "Profit twelve pounds, ten and six." He separated the profit from cost of stock, then pushed the smaller amount towards Sam and handed a small coin bag to him. It was already half full. "Count it again," he instructed Sam.

"Ten pounds, one shilling and a tickey," Sam called out.

"Correct. Put it in the bag and hide it in the usual place."

That attended to, they tackled the second amount. Two pounds, ten and six went into another bag, for rent and lights. That took care of the day's overheads. Dara placed another pound in an envelope that already had some notes in it. "For charity," he told Sam. Another pound he pushed into his back pocket. "*Uplung*," he said, watching Sam carefully, who nodded in understanding. The balance of eight pounds went into another bag and into another pocket. "Net profit," he told Sam. "This weekend we can eat well."

Dara removed an old and frayed book from the money drawer and carefully noted the figures into various columns, meticulously rechecked them and finally closed the book with a satisfied expression. It was primitive, but effective. The balance sheet was updated, on a daily basis. That way he always knew the state of his business and adjusted his lifestyle accordingly.

When they reached home Sam knew the procedure would be repeated: so much towards the bond on the house, so much for lights, for food, for clothes and so on. Sam sighed. It was all too much. He preferred Jake's simple method of doing business.

"Always keep a proper record," Dara said. "That way when the business grows and you deal with large sums you always know where you stand."

It was late that afternoon before Sam had an opportunity to approach his father. He had been judging Dara's mood carefully, waiting for the moment when he would be at ease and least likely to raise objections.

"*Baji*," Sam tentatively raised the topic, making his voice sound casual, "When I was at *foy*'s place last night I heard there's an evening job going at a fish and chip shop in town. I saw the owner and he said I could go over tonight."

"How is your aunt?" Dara asked. "Did you give her my *salaams?*"

"Yes," Sam lied. "About the job ..."

"The town is not a good place at night. Bad influence on a young boy like you."

"But *Baji*, it's only from five in the evening till ten at night, when the bioscope crowd comes out. And I can still help you in the shop after school."

"At night you study. You want to be like your brother, who only comes home to have a bath and change his clothes?"

Sam knew he was on dangerous ground now. He was trying to formulate some sort of reply when his mother joined them. "What's this about Yacoob?" she asked.

"Salim wants to go out and work," Dara said, ignoring the question.

"Only in the evenings, Ma," Sam quickly said. "I can always do my schoolwork on the days when I'm not working and on Sundays."

"What has Yacoob got to do with it?" she asked again, not easily diverted. Shaida understood Jake better than anyone else did and never hesitated to defend him against any form of criticism.

"The shop is in town. *Baji* feels that ..."

"We'll talk about it some other time," Dara interrupted. "What do you need a job for anyway?"

"They pay five shillings an evening," Sam said desperately. "If I work only four nights a week that's almost five pounds a month. It can pay the bond on the house."

"Or buy you some decent clothes and help you put aside something for when you go to university," Shaida said with a smile.

That clinched it. Sam knew that Dara would never object to anything that helped further his education. And his mother was obviously not opposed to the idea of the job. And, besides God, she was the only one Dara deferred to. The rest of the questions were a mere formality, establishing the rules that he would have to conform to. Sam agreed to all the conditions, knowing that if he was careful in the beginning most of them would be relaxed after a while. And he could easily stretch the time at which he came home at night by claiming the cinema had ended later than usual.

They agreed that he could start that night, but only after he had taken a bath, changed into fresh clothes, said his evening prayers and finished his meals. It was almost seven by the time Sam reached Victoria Street and headed directly for Jake's headquarters. The Saturday night crowd had swelled enormously, spilling halfway onto the street in front of the cinemas.

Sam spotted Jake, looking smart and very handsome in a black outfit, the shirt cut in pseudo military style with two breast pockets with flaps and a button-down collar. Jake smiled broadly and punched Sam lightly on the arm.

"You little shark," Jake said. "You made it after all."

"Am I too late to sell tickets tonight?"

"Nah! They're all top shows. Already the 'House Full' signs are up. The runners will take care of it."

When Sam's face fell, Jake said, "I'll see you right later, okay? You won't lose out. Just hang around for a while and watch my boys."

For the next half an hour Sam circulated on the fringes of the cinemas. It didn't take long before all the tickets were sold at top prices. Jake had made a killing and was in an expansive mood. He slipped Sam a crisp ten shilling note and watched with amusement as Sam's face lit up.

"Sam," Jake said. "You remember I told you I had something lined up for you?"

When Sam nodded he went on, "Okay. Come with me. Sandy and I want to talk to you."

They walked side by side, Jake silently leading the way through narrow passages between deserted office buildings. Sam noticed that, for all his engaging and confident ways and easygoing nature, Jake was always on the alert even when there was no one in sight. They were moving through the rear of the blocks, through dark and gloomy areas where Sam could barely see more than a few yards in front of him. Jake, however, knew his way around and moved swiftly, scaling low walls and cutting through narrow gaps that were barely wide enough for one person to pass through.

They were walking in single file now, through a maze that left Sam totally disorientated. He fixed his eyes on Jake's neck and stayed as close as he could without bumping into him. When they entered a narrow courtyard dimly lit by a light from a distant stairwell, Sam thought they had reached the end of their journey. There was nowhere they could go, high walls loomed all around them and several heavily burglar guarded and padlocked gates barred the exits. Jake didn't hesitate. He circled a stack of wooden packing crates, found a gap and soundlessly worked his way forward. In a few seconds they came to a fire escape and began to climb towards the first floor. At the top Jake walked along a narrow wall for a few feet then, hanging by his fingers, jumped down and waited for Sam. Without thinking, Sam emulated his brother and landed on his feet with a thud and went down on his knees. He felt his brains shake and his head began to ache immediately, stunned by the high jump.

He heard Jake whisper, "You okay?" shook himself and nodded. They moved forward again, walked through a wide passage that seemed to go on forever, then suddenly emerged onto Queen Street. Jake barely paused before he crossed over and entered another maze, once again working his way through the rear of the buildings. In a few seconds Sam was lost once more and, breathing heavily, followed as best he could.

Within a few minutes they were back on the street, at the corner of Commercial and Grey Streets. At last, Jake stopped and lit a cigarette. "The Casbah is another world, Sam. Another country. When you know your way around an army of cops wouldn't find you. You could disappear for weeks, move around freely. And don't ever think this is the only such place. You can lose yourself just as easily in the Dutchene or May Street or in any of a dozen other mini Casbahs."

"But we're not ducking from anybody, Jake. Why didn't we just walk on the pavements?"

"It's not wise to be seen all the time. The less anyone knows where you are the better. It's a good rule to follow."

Jake was on the move again. A hundred yards in front of them was the West End Hotel, at the corner of Pine Street, and he headed for it. After a few minutes, they entered the non-European bar. Sam saw Sandy, sitting on a stool. As soon as Sandy saw them he stood up and signalled to the elderly barman and whispered something in his ear. The barman nodded and jerked his thumb over his shoulder, pointing to a room behind him. Sandy ducked under the swing top and Jake and Sam followed.

They settled around a rickety wooden table, the uncomfortable Globe chairs creaking under their weight. Sandy wasted little time on preliminaries, getting straight to the point.

"Sam, there's something we would like you to do for us. It's very important and if you're game we'll make sure you do well out of it. It isn't anything heavy and, if you're sharp, you won't get into trouble. How do you feel about it?"

Sam simply shook his head up and down, feeling a little excited at the prospect of being a part of whatever Jake and Sandy had in mind.

Sandy studied him carefully for a long while before he spoke again, choosing his words with care. "How much do you know about the gangs in town?"

Sam's forehead began to crease as he thought about it. "I've heard of the gangs, we talk about them in school all the time. But I only know some of the Dutchene guys, to say hello to ..."

Sam had led a fairly cloistered life and was still too young to understand the structure of the many street gangs that operated in the various Indian and coloured communities around the city. Their status was clearly defined and, although all of them were of mixed orientation, mainly Indian and coloured, there were a few African members within each grouping. Regardless of which race group predominated, the leader was always the best street-fighter or the most fearless and daring amongst them. In the school-grounds it was these leaders whose names were mentioned in awe and a touch of hero worship.

"I was hoping you'd say that," Sandy said. "For what we want you to do ... it can only work if you're not seen as a part of any gang. Your age, and the fact that you're still in school, is an advantage. But you must learn what the streets are about, and fast. You don't want to be a *scarpie* like most guys your age. Jake and I can help you there, so listen carefully."

For the next fifteen minutes Sandy laid out the scenario for Sam, who listened wide-eyed and in absolute silence.

The Casbah, Sandy stressed to Sam, was the exclusive turf of the Victorians, who had the backing of the infamous Crimson League with its untold resources and many tentacles that spread deep into both the business community as well as into the law courts. However, the Beatrice Street Gang and the Young Americans could not be dismissed lightly; both were fearless and, at a push, were capable of standing their ground. And, to a lesser extent, they too had access to the League.

Farther afield, the May Street bunch ruled the Umgeni Road area with an iron fist, whilst The Dutchenes reigned supreme in the Old Dutch Road and Warwick Avenue complex. There were other less organised groupings, such as the Overport and Sydenham bunch, but they kept to their own territories and minded their own business.

The more feared gangs seldom ventured on each other's turf except when, in street parlance, they set out to "declare", in which case it meant all-out war.

"You had better understand something clearly right now, Sam. These gangs, in whichever area, never interfere with decent people who keep out of their way. An act of violence against ordinary people can only mean one thing. You're out, for good. And without the support of your gang you're a goner, game bait for any member of the underworld who wants to settle an old grudge. Don't ever, when your time comes, violate that rule."

"It's a tough world, Sam," Jake added. "If you want to be a part of it you'll have to be sharp, use your brains before you act. Think first, keep your eyes open, and learn to use your fists like a pro. That we can teach you. We can't teach you how to think."

"Perhaps we're moving too quickly," Sandy said. "But you're family, you need to know how the streets operate if you want to survive. You're lucky. You have us to guide you. Most guys learn the hard way."

"You can walk away now, Sam," Jake said softly. "No hard feelings."

"No! I've made up my mind," Sam said quietly.

"Okay. But you'll have to take it easy for a while. Watch and play. Lead a dual life, spend time with us and also at the shop with *Baji*. You'll understand as we go along."

Sam nodded, happy to be guided by Jake.

"There's one more thing," Jake said. "Sandy, you're the historian. Tell Sam about the League."

"Sam," Sandy said. "You may not understand a lot of what I'm going to tell you. But listen anyway. You have to know your environment, it gives you the edge over the ordinary thugs who think with their fists and last only as long as it takes them to become punch drunk. You want to be a survivor, not end up as an old *scoten* or a barfly, jumping every time some *kachela* shouts at you."

Sandy began to set out how the Crimson League came into existence, talking slowly, his eyes half closed as he recalled the past:

The Casbah, in the early forties, had been in the grip of a crime wave initiated by a wild bunch with a reputation for quick violence and little respect for either the law or the rights of the ordinary citizens. They began a reign of terror that struck fear into the hearts of every shopkeeper, who was extorted beyond his ability to comply to the ever-increasing demands of his merciless and progressively ruthless tormentors. In desperation, and as an act of last recourse, they fell back on their own resources. It was time, in the words of one of them, to get *vilt*.

At a secret meeting one Saturday afternoon they enlisted from amongst themselves four stalwarts whose function it was to form a vigilante committee for the sole purpose of putting an end, once and for all, to the maniacs that were tormenting them. The committee was provided with the necessary funds to hire the services of whomever could aid them and assist in attaining the noble objective.

"Turn the streets crimson with the blood of those parasites," an angry old man, who was at the end of his tether, shouted. "Stamp the bastards into the ground."

The Crimson League was born that Saturday afternoon.

The businessmen made two cardinal errors. They gave no thought to the disbanding of the vigilantes once the objective had been achieved and, in their anger, they gave the task force of four a free hand and made no efforts to monitor it. In a symbiotic act born out of impotence the progenitors of the League took the only avenue that promised success — they recruited from the underworld those who had not allied themselves to the extortionists. With promises of cash rewards, they went into action. In the weeks that followed they fought numerous running battles with an enemy that refused to be intimidated. Whilst each initially underestimated the other, the League had the distinct advantage in that, when the law finally stepped in, it was able to claim that it was on the side of justice. They also derived the added synergy of establishing a degree of rapport with senior police officers and bribed them freely from the substantial funds at their disposal.

After several more skirmishes, late one Friday night they engaged in a massive pitched battle from which the League emerged triumphant, wiping the enemy out of existence. In effect, the vigilante committee had served its purpose. In reality, a new wave of terror, much more sophisticated, was about to begin.

On the Saturday following the epic encounter the leaders of the League met at a rundown cottage in Cross Street. Of the original four businessmen only one was still a member, the others had opted out almost as soon as the fighting had started. Whilst no formal agenda existed, the five top members were clear on one thing: the contributions from the shopkeepers represented a lucrative source of income and the Casbah was under their control. The sole remaining businessman had tasted power and had no desire to return to his previous mundane existence.

Within an hour a committee of five was elected to head up the Crimson League. The Big Five, as they referred to themselves, were now the undisputed crime kings of the Casbah.

And, in the years that followed, they became the kingpins of the underworld. "You can't cough in this town," Sandy concluded, "without the League's permission. Once in a while, though, someone comes along who thinks he can take the League on and secure for himself all that the League controls. Up to now these upstarts have been brushed aside easily and buried in some dump. But now there's a new guy on the scene, far more ambitious and better organised, and the Big Five is beginning to get edgy."

"Sam," Jake said, taking over from Sandy, "You're probably wondering where you fit into all this. Don't get carried away. It's no big deal. These gang wars can be very costly for the Big Five and they don't rush into action until they're satisfied there's a genuine threat to them. They know this guy, it's no secret who he is. They suspect he is busy getting in solid with the other gangs. What's worrying them right now is that he could be trying to *khusa* the Dutchenes into joining forces with him.

"For the League that would be a formidable enemy. They need to be sure which way the wind is blowing. Sandy and I can't help them there. We live in the Dutchene area but are known to belong to the Victorians, and that means we're a part of the League. We've done a few favours for the Dutchenes but that means nothing."

"You're still green, Sam," Sandy added. "Just another *lighty* who lives there and kicks a ball around with other *lighties* your own age. They won't pay any attention to you. If you're still game, after what we've just told you, you can be a sort of scout for us, see what's going on."

"You'll be in no danger at all, Sam," Jake said. "Just keep your mouth shut and carry on as usual. Only keep your eyes open and tell us if you see or hear anything connected to what we told you. You think you can do that?"

"Yes," Sam said softly. "I'm there most days after school anyway. And Dicky, who is a big shot around there, is always good to me. He sees me right now and then, always gives me a few *otties*."

"What you must do," Sandy said, "Is go there in future and stay till late until the last *lighty* is ready to go home. Don't try to play the spy or anything. Just watch what's going on. Then, instead of going home, come here to us. Okay?"

For the next few days Sam went down to Etna Lane daily and fooled around with his friends until it was time for the kids to go home. Usually, by around eight thirty he was back in Victoria Street. And he had nothing to report, in spite of listening, at every chance, to Dicky Delange and his mates as they talked amongst themselves. Finally, just as he was beginning to get bored and starting to miss the bright lights of Victoria Street, he saw and heard things early one evening that he knew Jake and Sandy would give anything to know. He couldn't wait to get away and, at the first opportunity, he ducked out and headed for town.

It took Sam almost an hour before he could locate Jake and when he started to tell him what he had seen Jake stopped him in mid-sentence.

"You may have something," Jake said. "Go to the pad and wait there. I'm going to find Sandy and Vusi."

It was another half an hour before the three walked in and closed the door behind them.

"Okay, Sam," Jake said. "Start from the beginning again."

And, while they listened to him intently, Sam told them.

"I was in Dicky's yard with a friend of mine. We were trying to fix the chain on his bike. Then this car pulled up and a lot of chaps came into the yard."

"What kind of car was it," Sandy interrupted.

"A big car, black and shiny. Very posh."

"You know the make?"

"No. I don't know much ..."

"It's okay. Don't worry about it. Go on."

"Hang on a second," Jake said. "These guys, can you describe them?"

"Well, they were dressed sharp, you know, like the gangsters in the bios. Like that guy in *Street With No Name*, with felt hats and all."

"Okay. Then what happened?"

"Nothing much. They went up to Dicky. He was with Lukey Draai and Lionel Goldman and that tough Indian guy they call Skipper. Foxy Bremner was there too."

"They were all there?" Vusi asked, "These guys you mentioned just now?"

Sam nodded and waited as Vusi looked at Sandy and Jake, saying, "Looks like it was planned, they were having an *Indaba*."

"Let Sam finish," Sandy said.

"Yes, well, they spoke for a long while. Then Dicky said something like, 'Count us out, Michael. We want no part of it,' and Lukey, you know, in that funny voice of his, he said something in an angry voice, but I couldn't understand a thing."

"Sam, think carefully before you answer," Jake said, "you sure you heard the name 'Michael'? Clearly?"

"Yes. I heard the name clearly."

"Okay, what did they do then?"

"They talked for a while, then they left. Those guys, the gangsters, didn't look happy."

"I guess that's all we need to know," Sandy said. "Sam, you did well. It was a long shot, asking you to do this, but it paid off."

Vusi was still looking doubtful and Sandy asked, "What, Vusi, something worrying you?"

"I don't know, Sandy ... could be anybody. And Sam could have been mistaken about the name. We slip up, give the League the wrong ..."

"No, Vusi," Jake said. "We're on the right track here. And look, we didn't mention the name to Sam. We deliberately didn't do that."

"Ya?" Vusi asked. "Okay. I'm satisfied. Let's go."

"Sam," Jake said. "Go home now. Carry on tomorrow as usual. Don't stop just yet."

On the Friday night, when Sam went into town, Jake called him aside and quietly told him to go home. "There's going to be *parrer* later tonight, Sam. The crap is really going to fly. Stay away from here till Monday."

"Can I come over tomorrow, just for a while?"

Jake shook his head firmly, then slipped a pound note in Sam's shirt pocket.

"You won't find any of us around here. Now go. I'll see you on Monday."

The next morning, while Sam was seeing to a customer, he heard the first bit of news concerning what Jake had alluded to. The shopkeeper from next door walked in during a lull and said to his father. "Trouble last night in town. Some gangster called Michael John was killed in a gang war."

"They live by the knife, they die by the knife," his father said dismissively.

"But they killed him in his flat, Dara, not on the streets. How can they do that? Just go to a man's house and kill him."

Sam kept his face averted, his heart thudding rapidly. He needed to know more, find an excuse to leave the shop and go to Victoria Street, for just long enough ...

"Salim, stop dreaming! I can't see to all the customers alone."

Sam had no chance to leave, to duck out even for a few minutes. When they reached home he debated for a while, in his mind, whether he should go to town later in the day. He had almost made up his mind to go, then decided against it. Jake had made it very clear that he had to stay away until Monday.

On the Sunday, as he played with his friends in the park, all they talked about was the big *parrer* in town and how the Crimson League had wiped out some guys that were getting too big for their boots.

"My pa said they're all cowards," Lionel Sebastian told Sam. "They don't fight fair. Without their gang they're nothing."

"My dad can take any of them," Alan Spies said. "One at a time, any time." Sam believed him. Uncle Tainy, Alan's old man, was real tough. A nice man, always good to the boys, but tough, with real muscular arms and big shoulders.

"I reckon my *boet*, Douggie, can take all of them on, *mul* it with anybody." Solly Martin bragged, puffing his chest out.

"You think they call my father cowboy for nothing?" Aby Vahed asked.

"Hopalong Cassidy," Baboo Kajee teased Aby. "When there's trouble, he hops along."

Aby piled into Baboo and while they rolled on the grass Sam quietly went home.

"They know nothing," he said to himself. "I could tell them things that'll make them crap in their pants."

∞

Sam left school early on Monday, on an excuse that he wasn't well. When he reached the fish and chip shop one of the waiters told him that Jake, Sandy, Vusi and a lot of the others were locked up. The cops had picked them up on Saturday night and taken them away. Sam, worried now, walked around for a while, but the glamour was gone from the street and he finally went home.

Jake walked through the door at four that afternoon and headed straight for the bathroom. After he had his bath and changed he went into the kitchen and gave his mother a thick wad of notes. "It's good money, Ma. I earned it at the cinema."

"You earn this kind of money at the cinema?" Shaida asked doubtfully.

"And at the docks, Ma. I go there with Nithin. They pay well. You don't have to tell *Baji*. Buy some clothes for Ayesha, for when she gets married."

While his mother fussed around Jake, refusing to let him go again until he had eaten a solid meal, Sam went outside and waited. It wasn't long before Jake joined him.

"I can't talk now, Sam. Ma's watching. The League bailed us all out. Come over tonight. I'll tell you about it then."

It was a night Sam would remember for a long time. He met some of the *Motas* when they came over to the Victorians' headquarters to see Jake, Sandy and Vusi, and was surprised at how ordinary they were. He had expected to see burly and hulking men, with scars on their faces and dressed in flashy clothes. Instead, they looked like simple businessmen and appeared quite harmless. It was their eyes, though, that sent a shiver up Sam's spine and when they spoke their voices were low and menacing.

The *Motas'* cars, which were all black and huge, glittered as the neon signs from the Avalon Cinema flashed across them. In each car there were two or three sinister looking men, their felt hats pulled low over their faces. Although the parking bays on either side of the road were empty the drivers ignored them and were double parked, almost in the middle of the road, with the engines running. For once, the usually brusque traffic police were nowhere to be seen, and nobody approached or came near the posh limousines. Even the regular denizens of the area, and the *scotens*, who knew everybody, kept their distance.

In a little while the *Motas* left and small groups of curious bystanders began to converge in front of the café and peer into the interior, almost as if they expected to see a celebrity or some such equally famous visitor. Sam basked in the attention and the obvious adulation bestowed on those around him and, once again, began to feel out of place in his worn and ill-fitting clothes. Finally, Jake and his friends headed into the back room and Sam followed them in. As soon as the door was closed Vusi turned to Sandy.

"You were right, *bra*. The *Motas* are shining up."

"We scratch theirs, they scratch ours," Sandy smiled. "No more kickbacks. From now on we keep what we make."

"Ja, and we can score with the schools."

"Sure. Anyway, that was no great concession. The *scotens* and waiters don't gamble at the *Motas'* schools, they only bet a tickey or a sassy at a time."

"But we really climb in now, regulate the show and collect a handy kitty."

While Sandy and Vusi were talking Sam asked Jake, "Did you guys really pull a job for the *Motas*?"

"Nah!" Jake simply smiled. "They have specialists who do that. We just covered the area, kept it clear from interference by any of the other gangs."

"But why did the cops arrest you and ..."

"Sam, the cops have to be seen to be doing their job. They pick up everybody who belongs to the streets. Eventually, they'll pin it on some poor bum and it will be overs-cadovers. Life will be back to normal."

Sam wasn't sure if Jake was telling the truth, but before he could say anything else Sandy came over and handed Sam a five pound note.

"Get some decent clothes, Sam. You look like Huckleberry Finn. Go to 'Ideals' and mention our name, you'll get a huge discount."

"How will I explain it to Ma, Jake?"

"Tell her you just got paid for working here. Ma's okay, she knows you need a few glad rags."

"Let's get out of here," Vusi muttered. "I feel like a goldfish."

For two weeks after that Sam was on a high. He had bought a few trousers and some shirts. Nothing flashy that his mother could object to. Even Dara seemed quite relaxed and happy to see Sam dressed neatly. And Sam made sure he unfailingly helped his father every afternoon and on Saturdays, keeping a low profile as far as his so-called job was concerned. He made it a point of going home early whenever things were quiet and Jake and his pals were occupied with activities that they refused to allow him to participate in.

They didn't object to Sam joining them whenever they gathered at the Vineyard, and on those evenings he felt particularly grown up, listening to their sharp talk and friendly banter. Jake, however, was firm with Sam when it came to liquor — he wasn't allowed to touch it, not even a beer. Sam was not put out by the rule, hated the smell and, if he ever walked into his home with even a hint of it on his breath, his mother would probably kill him. As for as his father, Sam didn't even dare to contemplate what could happen to him.

"You look sharp, Sam," Sandy said one evening as he looked him over. "Those clothes make you look grown up and older than you are."

Vusi, on his usual stool against the wall, said, "Time you dived into a Spanish, Samboy." When Sam said "Huh?" Sandy burst out laughing.

"Maybe not just yet, Vusi. I reckon there are times I can still smell the milk on his breath."

"That's the jismo rushing to his ears, looking for a way out," Vusi smiled, his eyes twinkling.

"Is that why there's a shine behind the ears?"

"Nah, that's only the normal sign of a wet ..."

"Cut it out, you two" Jake said. "Give the *lighty* a break."

"What's jismo?" Sam asked.

This time all three burst out laughing. Sam was still wondering what he had said that had been so funny when the girl, Candy, breezed in.

"Give us a packet of *scaves*, Jimmy," she said to the barman, a little too loudly, ignoring Jake and his friends. Out of the corner of her mouth she whispered, just loud enough for Sandy, who was nearest to her, to hear, "Five jambos at Buttys corner. They asked my *garach* to send me in to check if you guys are here."

Sandy didn't turn to face her. He simply took a swig of his beer and looked the other way. In another second she was gone.

"The Willys are outside," Sandy said to Jake and Vusi casually, his glance raking the tables, checking each face. "They're out to declare."

"Shit!" Vusi snarled under his breath. "I thought the League squared it."

"They did," Sandy replied. "The cops will stay out of it. The rest is up to us."

"The League could have backed us up."

"They offered. I told them we could handle it."

"Save the thee and thy, you okes," Jake cut in. "That guy in the blue shirt, at the corner table, Sandy. I'm sure he works with Jeff, at the Willys club. How come he's here tonight?"

"You sure?" Sandy asked Jake.

"I've seen him with Jeff. He's never come here before. And look at him, he's nervous as hell."

"Gimme a minute," Sandy told Jake. "Keep an eye on the door."

Sam watched as Sandy walked towards the table. The man in the blue shirt stood up quickly, then sat down again when Sandy pulled up a chair next to him. After a few minutes they saw Sandy nod and walk back towards them.

"You're right," Sandy said to Jake. "He claims they threatened to *snay* him, forced him to watch out for us. When we were all here he was to give them a buzz and tip them off. Says he saw us together but couldn't make the call. I believe him."

"Makes sense," Jake said. "That's why they sent the prossie in to check."

"The bastard could have tipped us off," Vusi angrily muttered. "It would have given us a chance to get organised."

"But he told me something interesting," Sandy said. "This guy is sure they're not loaded. The Willys have got the aerial that the cops have backed off. They dare not carry a gat. They're clean."

"So all they have are the usual *guthrees*," Jake smiled thinly, his lips stretched tightly over his teeth.

Vusi jumped off his stool. "Okay, it's that time!"

Sandy turned to the barman, "Six quarts, Jimmy. Empty."

Jimmy reached under the counter and began to line the bottles in front of Sandy, who grabbed two of them by the neck. Jake and Vusi took two each. They headed for the door, Sam following. "Stay here, Sam," Jake ordered. "Don't come out till we call you."

Sam waited till they were out of sight, then ran to the back of the bar and into the kitchen. In a few seconds he was back, running towards the entrance, with two huge kitchen knives and a carcass hook still attached to its chain. He heard the sound of bottles breaking and increased his speed. When he reached the pavement he saw the Victorians, spread out and beginning a cautious advance towards the Willys, one of whom was already on the ground.

"Jake," Sam shouted, then threw the hook towards Jake, who caught it in mid-air. In the slight diversion that Sam had created, both Vusi and Sandy had taken a backward step. Sam placed one of the knives on the ground and slid it, handle first, towards Sandy, then darted to the left and handed Vusi the other. With Sam in the background, away from the action, the Victorians moved forward with more confidence. Suddenly, both Jake and Sandy were in the air, in a flying leap, their feet poised. Vusi bounded forward, went down on one knee and, as he turned, swiped one of the Willys off his feet. A second later the nightwatchman joined in, on the side of the Victorians, his whip singing. Knives and iron bars flashed in the neon lights of the Vineyard. From the first floor of the hotel, just above the Indian bar, several heavy bottles rained down on the Willys, thrown by some of the patrons who had stepped into the balcony.

It was a brief but bloody encounter that left Sam stunned by the intensity of its violence. The Willys, with the odds now against them, began to retreat, then scattered as they fled towards the white sector of the hotel.

"Let's go, Sam," Sandy shouted, and the four of them quickly headed towards Victoria Street. Back safe in their pad, they examined their wounds. Jake had a deep gash on his forehead which he bandaged with an old shirt. Sandy had been stabbed twice in the arm. Vusi's head was bleeding, the towel red as he tried to staunch the flow. All three were grinning widely as they looked at Sam.

"You're pretty *vilt*, *skiddo*," Sandy said. "That was good thinking."

"Sheet!" Vusi exclaimed, looking at the bloody towel, then said, "I guess there's more than jismo between those ears, Sam."

"Jake?" Sam asked, "How can these *vit ous* operate around here?"

"After today, they won't even try," Jake answered.

"But I mean ... how? The darkies here won't deal with them."

"Sure they won't. Anyway ..."

"Wait!" Sandy said. "Hold it a second. Sam, say that again."

"The darkies," Sam said. "They won't deal with ..."

"That's it, Jake," Sandy snapped his fingers. "The runners, they have to play ball."

"Jeff, Sandy! He's their tube," Vusi growled, forgetting about the blood dripping into his neck.

"And that guy in the bar," Jake frowned.

"He pulled a double bluff on us," Sandy said quietly. "He got cold feet at the last minute."

"This Jeff, He's very stupid," Vusi fumed.

"It was a crazy idea, from a dagga-crazed mind," Sandy said, sounding sad. "Well, that's his lot. He's out. Tomorrow, we grill the runners."

From that night onwards, when Sam spoke, they listened attentively.

∞

Over the next three years Sam filled out, put on weight and grew tall, and lost the last vestiges of innocence. He seldom said much, and when he did he unfailingly commanded the attention of his peers. It was an environment, however, in which he was becoming increasingly uncomfortable. His nature was simply not in tune with the violence that the others accepted as normal activity and, as the attraction of the bright lights and easy money palled, so did his commitment. He continued, however, with his dual life. From his father he learned the intricacies of business and the rules that governed the straight trader. On the street he mastered the tricks of turning a shilling into a pound, faster and with less effort than even the most dishonest shopkeeper could have imagined.

Sam also spent a lot of time, especially on Sundays, with Pravin Naran's grandson Karan, and found these hours particularly relaxing. He didn't have to be alert at all times, to continuously watch his back and keep an eye open for potential danger at every corner. And it was Karan, ever the weaver of dreams and with his nose buried in a mountain of books, who helped Sam maintain an even keel and a balance between the two worlds he moved in. Karan seldom failed to remind Sam that, while the street had its own attractions, there was a much larger and more glittering world to explore than the narrow confines of the Casbah.

By the time he was seventeen Sam was already an accomplished veteran of the underworld. He kept his temper under strict control and always weighed each situation before reacting. In this he emulated Sandy, whose reputation for reasonableness was legendary. Jake, on the other hand, said very little and refused to participate in any discussion unless it concerned him directly. However, on those occasions when an appeal to reason failed, both Jake and Sandy exploded into action with a vengeance that resolved any dispute swiftly and with finality. As a team, the two of them, together with Vusi, was an awesome force indeed.

Torn between two worlds, Sam repeatedly considered his options and weighed, whenever he was alone, the relative benefits and disadvantages of the one over the other. In the meantime, he gave each a special brand of loyalty that never placed it in jeopardy or made it vulnerable to the other.

It was, however, a totally unrelated incident that finally swung the scales and sealed his fate.

Around eight on a hot summer evening Sam, both his parents, his sister Ayesha, who had married a year before, her husband Ahmed and his brother Rashid were out on the veranda enjoying a rare family gathering. Shaida had prepared a huge bowl of spiced pineapples, chopped into tiny cubes, and they were digging in with relish. Sheila Reid had come over and was regaling them with the hilarious antics of her youngest brother who had fallen madly in love with a girl almost twice his age and who was totally oblivious of the attention of her young admirer.

"He calls her his koekoebun," Sheila screamed with laughter, "and then disappears whenever she comes to visit me. And as soon as she leaves he runs to the mirror and looks at himself from every angle and puffs his chest out until he goes red in the face."

Sam, who had been in two minds about going into town, finally settled down and said, "Give him a break, Sheila. The next pretty face he sees ..."

The car that pulled up had an official tag attached to the front bumper and the letters GG painted on the doors. On a street that seldom boasted a parked car, it loomed ominously large and forbidding. The kids who had been playing "follow the leader" on the road suddenly disappeared into their homes and a few doors banged loudly as they were hastily shut.

The white man who emerged from the car walked straight up to the veranda and, in a curt voice, announced, "Investigator! You all live here?"

"This is our home," Sam said. "What do you want?"

"The questions will be asked by me, boy. That your father?"

Dara stood up and walked over. "What can I do for you?"

"Inside, everybody," the investigator barked, then walked through the door and looked around.

As they followed him in Sam signalled to Shiela that she should slip away. Once inside they were herded towards a wall and the man turned to Dara, "You own this house?"

"I own it," Dara replied.

"Get the papers!"

"What papers?"

"The title deeds, man. Get them."

"I don't have them. The house is bonded. The deed is at the bank."

"Get the latest rates certificate and the light account."

As Dara left the room, Sam asked, "Don't you need to identify yourself and produce ..."

"Shut up, boy! Keep your bloody mouth shut!"

As Sam took a step forward, his face furious, his mother quickly came between them and said, "Salim, go to your room."

"I'll wait here, Ma."

"No. I want you to go to your room. Now, Salim."

There was no question of disobeying her and Sam, red with anger, turned to leave, dragging his feet and delaying his departure.

"That's good thinking, Mary," the investigator said amiably, then seemed to stumble slightly. His hand reached out and, seemingly by accident, his palm enveloped Ayesha's breast. It remained there for a second, then, incredibly, began to fondle her.

Sam whirled around, hissing between his teeth, on the verge of launching himself on the man when Shaida swiftly hugged him and whispered, "Salim, think of *Baji*. He'll end up in jail."

Sam was simmering, his face dark with fury. The investigator, for the first time, lost his confidence and, in a quivering voice, mumbled, "It was an accident, I tell you ..."

"Try that again," Sam said harshly, "And I'll break your damned neck."

"Salim, *choop!*" Shaida ordered.

At that moment Dara returned to the room and, unaware of what had happened, handed some papers to the investigator, who quickly busied himself with examining them. Sam saw the mute appeal on his mother's face, silently pleading with him not to aggravate the situation. He pulled himself together and nodded, his eyes not leaving the official.

The government man pulled up a chair and removed a pad from his briefcase. His pen flew as he wrote on it, then tore off the top copy and, together with his card, handed it to Dara.

"Sign here."

When Dara had signed it, the investigator said, "You have sixty days to vacate this house. You're lucky. Everybody else has only thirty." He gave Sam a wide berth as he walked out.

Sam followed him to the door, still fuming with suppressed anger. He watched as the official entered the Reids' yard, then slammed the door. Ayesha had disappeared into her room; his parents, stunned, were still looking at the eviction notice, Dara holding it by the tips of his fingers.

"There's nothing we can do," Dara said at last. "I knew our turn would come. I've been dreading this day for over a year." His voice sounded hollow.

Sam went out, lit a cigarette and took several pulls on it, dragging the smoke deep into his lungs. He had just flicked the cigarette onto the road when he saw the investigator emerge from the Reids' house and cross the road, heading for the Kajees. He heard Isaac wailing loudly, then the sound of her voice as she said to someone, "I just paid the last instalment. They can't do this to me."

Sam left the veranda and headed towards town. As he passed Nithin's house he saw Mrs Vania peering through the curtains, her face startlingly white. Sam could have sworn he saw her cheeks trembling with fear.

When Sam walked into the Vineyard Jake, Sandy and Vusi were laughing at some joke, but clammed up immediately they saw Sam's face. Sam told them what had happened, his voice emotionless, leaving out nothing. Jake's eyes went flat when he heard what had been done to Ayesha, his jaw muscles bunching into knots.

"Let's go home," Sandy said, his voice icy.

When Jake and Sam reached Verbena Road nearly all the residents were out, talking in groups as they clustered on the pavement. The GG car was gone. Every home on the road had received a similar notice, sixty days in which to pack up and leave. Jake walked up to Dara and put his arm around his father's shoulders. Sam couldn't remember when last he had seen Jake do that. It was the first night in several weeks that Jake slept at home.

The next morning Jake was up early. He shook Sam, rousing him. "Get dressed, we've got work to do."

They had a quick breakfast, Shaida pleased to see both her sons together at the table.

"I'll walk Sam to school, Ma," Jake said over his shoulder as they left the house.

"Jake, what did you mean when you said we had work to do?"

"You'll find out. Forget about school today."

Jake set a brisk pace and when they reached town he headed straight for the Victorians' headquarters. He pulled up a chair, placed the investigator's card in front of him and dialed a number.

"Is *Meneer* Botha in?" Jake asked, in a heavy Afrikaans accent. "Okay, *dankie*. Could you give me his home number?" he listened for a few moments, then said, "It's fine, thank you. I just found it. I'll ring him there."

"They don't give out the home number," Jake swore under his breath, then flicked through the telephone directory. "The bastard isn't listed here."

"Jake, what are you thinking of?"

"Making him pay for what he did to Ayesha."

"But, Jake, the cops will terrorise us, maybe even throw *Baji* in jail and ..."

"There's no way he'll be going to the cops. Just gimme a minute to think. Get us some cokes."

When Sam got back Jake was pacing the floor, deep in thought. Sam sipped his coke as Jake tapped the card against his teeth, then said, "Okay, let's go."

They walked all the way back to Warwick Avenue. Jake approached a stout wooden gate attached to a high corrugated iron fence that they couldn't see over, and pressed the bell. It was a while before the gate opened and a reedy coloured man stood before them, holding a fierce Alsatian by its leather collar. Two other equally vicious dogs growled in the background.

"Yo Jake. Howzit?" He stepped back to allow Jake and Sam to walk in.

"Ya, Ace. How you doing?"

"*Lekker*, my man."

"Akie in the *pozzy*?"

"Sure. He expecting you?"

"No. But I have to see him."

"Hey, Jake? This time in the morning?"

"It's important, Ace."

"I dunno. It's early bells. Who's the *lighty*?"

"My *bra*. He's okay."

"Lemme check it out. Come. These guys only bite when I do."

They entered the spacious yard, the dogs prowling around them. Ace unlocked a door and led the way into an airy sun room, beautifully furnished with sofas and chairs and a low coffee table in the centre. It was spotlessly clean and smelled as if it had just been aired.

"Wait here, Jake."

Jake leaned his back against a bar counter and, his hands in his pockets, said, "Akie is one of the Big Five. We came through the back entrance. You can get anything you want here except women and liquor."

They waited for almost ten minutes before a grey-haired man, of average height, dressed in a silk gown, walked in. Ace was nowhere to be seen.

"Hello, Jake." he said, amiably. "This your brother Sam? Sit down. What can I do for you?"

Jake handed Akie the investigator's card. "I need this guy's home address."

Akie looked at the card, then placed it on the bar counter. "What's going on?"

"It's personal, Akie."

"You don't want to tangle with those guys, Jake. The League can't help you here."

"All I want is the address. You're the only one I know that has the connections to get it."

"And then?"

"On this matter you won't hear from me again."

"How serious is it?"

Jake simply looked at Akie straight in the eyes. For about fifteen seconds they just stared at each other, then Akie broke the silence, "Ya? Like that?"

Jake didn't say anything.

"Okay," Akie said abruptly. "It's your shit. You're on your own. How soon you need this info?"

"I'm going to Victoria Street now. I won't move till I hear from you."

Akie turned around and disappeared into the interior. A second later Ace came over and let them out.

As soon as they were back on the road Sam asked, "Jake, what the hell are you thinking of doing?"

"Nothing that will bounce on us. Just take it easy."

Jake was walking fast, not giving Sam a chance to ask many questions.

Back in town, Jake prowled around for a while and Sam reluctantly kept up with him. The morning matinee show at the Avalon was about to commence but there were very few patrons around, mainly schoolkids playing hooky and going to the cinema to smooch and grope in safety. Sandy joined them at around eleven, complaining bitterly about the poor takings from the morning bank. "I had to pay out heavily on top of it. Somebody actually played a whole buckskin on the number I pulled. That's fifteen quid down the drain."

"Sandy," Jake asked, "when you got home last night ..."

"Ya. There was a whole squad of the bastards doing the district, road by road. Wills Road and all the side lanes. And this morning, around nine, their cronies were already swarming like bees around honey, checking out the houses and writing down the numbers of the ones they liked. And some of them looked like they didn't have two black pennies to rub together."

"It's *bonsella* time again," Jake said. "*Khup* the coolie and fatten the leech."

"They call it Christian charity," Sandy snarled. "We keep the bible and they snatch the bucks."

"Keep it low, you *ous*," Vusi warned from behind them. "The area's crawling with *byfores*."

"What the hell do they want now?" Jake asked.

"Nits mumbled something about a raid, asked me to pass it on. But he said it's not the Vice Squad this time. It's the State Security guys."

"Probably just a show of strength," Sandy said dismissingly. "Anyway, we're ordinary crooks, third cousins to them. They're not interested in us."

"Let's get something to eat," Sam suggested. "I'm starving."

"*Hai*!" Vusi exclaimed. "This *lighty*, he's been hungry since the day he came here."

They were in the middle of their meal when Ace walked in and handed Jake a piece of paper. "The man said memorise and destroy."

Jake looked at it, then reached for a match and applied the flame to the paper. Ace watched it burn, then walked out.

"What was all that about?" Sandy enquired.

"The address of the investigator that jazzed us last night."

"What's on your mind?"

"Plan to teach the *gamoola* a little lesson, maybe tonight."

"Jake, let's talk it over first."

"No, *boet*. I stopped talking a long time ago. What he did to Ayesha has a lot to do with it, but it's more than that. Comes a time when you have to start shoving back. We talk, they thrive. Let's see how they like a bit of their own medicine."

"I think you're making a bad move, Jake."

"Maybe, Sandy. I reckon you want to get somewhere you have to move. Talking is not moving. You guys cover my beat tonight?"

"Sure. But if you won't change your mind, then I'm coming with you."

"Me too," Vusi insisted.

"That would be a bad move. Too many of us in a white area will only attract attention. All I need is a car and a good driver. For that Nits is the best. And Sam will have to come with too."

"Why involve Sam?" Sandy asked, a little crossly.

"He saw the guy and can point him out. I don't want to *neuk* the wrong *oke*."

Jake had disappeared for several hours. When he returned at around five he appeared to be somewhat relaxed, though his jaw was still tight and his eyes grim.

"I checked out whitey's house," he told Sam. "It's perfect. Big plots, lots of privacy between the neighbours and the roads are nice and wide. And quiet. We can *julate* in and out very fast."

Sam kept quiet. He had decided it was pointless asking Jake what he was going to do. Whatever, Sam thought, the bastard deserves it. And if Jake was satisfied that it couldn't bounce on them it was good enough for Sam.

Nithin arrived at seven, driving a nondescript car with up-country number plates. Jake opened the back door for Sam, then jumped into the front next to Nits. There were two huge bunches of flowers on the back seat, next to Sam.

"The *chootya* will be too busy *vrying* with his *chinal* till well after nine," Nits told Jake as he smoothly engaged the gears. "He won't miss the car till then."

"No trouble hot-wiring it?" Jake asked.

"It was easy, took less than a minute. John Farley is a master. And I can remove the contacts just as fast."

"Where'd you get the flowers?"

"John again."

"The way back to town? You covered it?"

"No problem. I checked it carefully when we were there earlier. Know it as well as my chick's *ezie*."

"Okay. We play this *lekker* we can *jidiga* out of there faster than a *scoten* can pipe a card."

"How you plan to handle it?"

"Depends on who opens the door. If our *gamoola* comes to it, it'll be that time for him. If not, we deliver the flowers and call it a day."

"If he's at home."

"I'm betting on that. These *madars* like to eat well before they set out to hound us."

As soon as they were out of town, Nithin pulled up on the side of the road. From the floor between his feet he collected a small bottle of what looked like ordinary cooking oil. He went to the front of the car and splattered a few drops on the registration plate while Jake collected a handful of soil from the side of the road and sprinkled it over the oil, covering the numbers. They repeated the process at the rear, then Nithin flung the bottle into the bushes and they were back in the car, driving off again.

They were in a quiet, tree-lined suburb with large gardens and wide driveways. Sam had never been there before and he was completely lost. Nits, however, drove confidently, taking extreme care at the stop streets and crossroads. Pretty soon they were cruising down a wide boulevard separated by a centre island on which massive ancient trees and hedges completely blocked off the opposite side of the road and provided total privacy to the houses on either side.

Nithin had slowed to a crawl when Sam said, "There's the GG car, in front of that house."

They pulled up in front of the parked car. "Grab the flowers," Jake told Sam.

On the pavement Jake said, "Keep your face covered by the flowers. Hold them high. If you recognise the investigator put your foot on my shoe. If anyone else comes to the door let me do the talking."

Jake took the second bunch and held the bulky flowers in front of him, then adjusted the back of his shirt with his free hand.

Jake ignored the ornate wrought iron entrance gate and walked up the paved driveway. A few yards away, on their left, was a flight of stairs leading to the front door. At the top, Jake pressed the bell and they heard a muffled gong somewhere in the house.

"Keep your face covered," Jake whispered, as he half covered his own.

The door opened and Sam saw the arrogant face of the man who had come to his house.

Jake was speaking unnaturally loudly, in a thick Afrikaans accent, and sounded more like a Boer than a Boer himself would have sounded. Sam realised that Jake was making sure that whoever was in the house heard him.

"And they asked me to deliver these flowers to you," Jake was saying in Afrikaans when Sam tramped Jake's toe.

Jake's hand was a blur as it reached behind him and came up with a revolver.

Before either Sam or the man at the door registered the movement, Jake fired twice, rapidly, the bullets hitting the investigator in the face and flinging him backwards.

Sam, stunned, his ears deafened, almost dropped the flowers.

"*Kom!*" Jake said loudly whilst the echo of the bullets was still reverberating around them. Sam, hanging on to the flowers, was pulled forward as Jake ran to the car. As they reached it the doors were flung open by Nithin and they dove in. Before Sam had fully grasped what had happened they were already turning a corner, Nithin driving at a moderate speed, one hand in front of his face.

A few minutes later they emerged on the road leading to the city and

Nithin accelerated, going much faster but not exceeding the speed limit. At the corner of Victoria and Albert Streets Nithin pulled up. As Jake left the car Nithin said, "I'll see you as soon as I dump the car."

They were still carrying the flowers as they headed for the fish and chip shop. When they passed a dustbin Jake dumped his bunch in it, Sam following suit. Vusi and Sandy were waiting in the back, pacing the floor. Jake handed Vusi the revolver.

"Stash it, Vusi."

Vusi shoved the revolver inside his shirt and left the room. Jake went up to the sink and began washing his hands, working the soap into a thick lather. As Sam slumped into a chair, Vusi returned.

"Any problem?" Sandy asked Jake.

"Nix," Jake replied. "Not even a dog saw us."

Vusi looked at Sam and said, "You okay, *lighty*?"

Sam shook his head up and down dumbly. He couldn't trust his voice at that moment.

"He'll be okay," Jake said, drying his hands. "He was cool as ice."

"And Nits?" Vusi asked.

"Should be here any moment. That guy's like the sphinx. Nothing shakes him."

The three of them were having a drink when Nits walked through the door and closed it behind him. "Took me a few moments to clean the number plates. The gods must have approved of us. I was able to park the car in exactly the spot it was in earlier."

"You reckon it was a clean hit?" Sandy enquired of Nits.

"It was like we hadn't been there," Nits laughed. "I timed Jake from the moment he fired the shots to the second we drove away. Twenty five seconds. Pity we can't claim a new world record."

Whilst they talked, Sam was thinking that all four of them had known in advance exactly what was going to happen. He was the only one that had been ignorant up till the last minute. Even as the thought ran through his mind he knew that he would have done nothing to stop Jake. Men like the investigator enjoyed terrorising simple people and didn't deserve to live. Whilst he himself would never have been able to pull the trigger, there was no way he could condemn Jake for his actions. How a man died was often the result of his own choosing. The investigator should have known that one of his victims would someday turn on him.

"You guys can calm your nerves with the liquor," Sam said with a smile. "I'm hungry. I'll see you around."

That night, as Sam made his way home, he finally made the decision to walk away from the Victorians.

∞

For the next three days the headlines screamed about the cold-blooded murder of a dedicated State employee, saying nothing about the work he did or the department that paid his salary. One newspaper quoted his wife as saying, "He was a gentle man who loved his family and would never have harmed a soul. He even fed the dogs in the streets and always saved the bones from his table for them. I can't understand why his own people did this to him."

Another paper claimed it was a sinister plot planned and executed by a group that was incensed at the official's inability to allocate to them certain houses in a new white Group Area. "It wasn't up to him to decide," his wife had told the reporter. "He didn't even know which houses were available. Even our own son had to wait for months before he was able to get a house. And I know it was an Afrikaner, I'll never forget that voice as long as I live."

When one newspaper snidely commented that the man was the epitome of decency and that even when he occasionally dealt with the Indians "these law abiding citizens welcomed him into their homes and offered him tea and samoosas", Sam squashed the paper and muttered "for citizens" read "victims". He never read that particular paper again.

In spite of the eviction notice and with the knowledge that in less than sixty days he would have to find alternative accommodation for his family, Sam's father stoically plodded on. In the past couple of years he had slowly built up the business and, with every cent going into the purchase of stocks, he was cramped for space. When he heard that the shop next door to him was up for sale Dara, ever the optimist, decided it was time to expand. His problem, however, was that any such extension of his business would require Sam to discontinue his schooling and join him on a full-time basis. After careful consideration he concluded that his son's education was, in any event, unlikely to progress to the point where it would be an asset, more so when viewed in the light of certain rumours regarding Sam's activities that had filtered back to him.

In direct contrast to Jake, Sam unfailingly joined his family at dinner several times a week. He was devoted to Ayesha, who was expecting her first child, and he loved his mother to the extent that her happiness took precedence over his own. Neither father nor son was aware that fate had, for once, decided to be kind to the luckless family.

In the past week, from the day following the shooting of the investigator, Sam had only spent an hour or two each day in Victoria Street and had made sure he was at home in time to share the evening meal and enjoy the warm family environment that he had often missed in recent years. Apart from the impending loss of their home, which they had, characteristically, accepted as an inevitable part of existence, the only thing that somewhat marred these otherwise perfect evenings was the presence of Ayesha's husband.

Ahmed was a short, portly man of twenty eight. His parents had, on his behalf, come over with a proposal and Ayesha's parents had, in the traditionally arbitrary manner, accepted it. Ayesha met him for the first time on her wedding day. Since then he had cunningly inveigled his way into the family, currying favour with Dara at every opportunity and complaining about his miserable lot with a firm of import agents. In recent months, he had begun to bring Ayesha over on most nights and was quietly ensconcing himself in Jake's room, which was seldom occupied.

Sam had disliked Ahmed from the very beginning. However, for Ayesha's sake he was always scrupulously courteous and carefully polite towards him. Ayesha, though, who had inherited her mother's soft good looks and none of her patience, treated him with ill-concealed disdain that bordered on contempt. Sam had often wondered, more so in the past week, how she had consented to allow him to father her child. Looking at her now, and the cool aloofness with which she leaned away from her husband, he knew with certainty that duty, not passion, had been the motivator. Duty, tradition and obedience, Sam thought, it holds us together and tears us apart. It's the cement that binds us and, like Siamese twins joined inseparably by a common heart, allows us only sufficient room to ineffectively kick at each other from time to time.

Ayesha caught Sam's speculative look, smiled as she held his glance, then tossed her head back. She's read my mind, Sam said to himself, and that's her answer — having complied with the rules she could now afford to be arrogantly difficult. Watch my smoke, little brother, she seemed to telegraph to him, while I reduce this pathetic excuse for a prince to the toad he so obviously resembles.

Sam mentally shrugged. She deserves a Pathan in whose embrace she could bloom, he told himself, and she has ended up with an oily creep whose breath alone is sufficient to slay the mightiest dragon. With the kind of games lady luck plays with my family even the State can't compete.

They had almost finished their meal and Sam sighed, for once eager to escape to some haven where he could be alone for a while. His father, however, cleared his throat loudly and settled back in his chair. Sam recognised the signal. It was his father's way of indicating that he was about to talk on an important matter and they were expected to remain in their seats. Sam silently sighed again and folded his arms. *If he tells me he has found a girl for me, this house will witness a miracle that will be the talk of the town for years to come. I'll grow wings before their very eyes and fly out of here so fast even Malikul Mort, the Messenger of Death, won't find me in a thousand years.*

The Toad, still unfamiliar with Dara's ways, was noisily slurping his tea, oblivious of the look of disgust on Ayesha's face. They waited in silence until, sensing some change in the atmosphere, he looked up and then hastily lowered the cup.

"Business has been good over the past few years," Dara began, his eyes fixed on Sam. "I have bought back your mother's jewellery and put aside a little capital. It is time to expand, to acquire another outlet. I have heard that Laloo Bhai, whose shop is next to ours, wants to sell out. The goodwill he is asking is a little high, but with whites throwing all our businessmen out of the suburbs the price for shops in the Grey Street complex will soon skyrocket."

Dara paused, inviting a response from Sam. In the absence of any reaction from Sam, Ahmed opened his mouth, a sly smile on his face. When he saw the look of scorn that Dara suddenly directed at him, he shut his mouth with a snap.

"It is not possible for me to control two shops at once," Dara continued, still directing all his observations at Sam. "You must decide whether you wish to continue with your present life or join me full-time in the business."

"But Salim's education ..." his mother began, when Dara cut her short.

"I hear many things in my little shop. I do not wish to discuss them at this time. I have lost Yacoob to the streets. I have no desire to lose Salim. Perhaps I was too lenient after the riots and was distracted by the need to see to more urgent matters. That was my *kismet*. Allah's will. Things are different now, I have learnt from that experience. Salim must choose now, tonight. Family or friends."

Sam said nothing, knowing instinctively that his father was not finished. If he had learnt one lesson from Dara, it was the patience to remain silent until he had heard all the facts. His father would view a hasty response as being worse than no response at all.

"It is a question of my *izzat*," Dara explained, "my respect, without which I am nothing. And I must make this clear, if you choose the path of the thuggie, follow in the footsteps of your brother, then my door is closed to you for good. You must leave us, never to return. Speak now, Salim. *Daku* or *Dukan*! One or the other, for now and forever."

Shaida was devastated, close to tears. Her world was beginning to fall apart, to shatter around her: Yacoob was no longer a part of her life; Ayesha married to a bumbling idiot forever seeking handouts; her home about to be taken away from her; and now Salim, her dearest and most caring, pushed into a corner from which he too could only go one way. In desperation she turned beseechingly to her husband, her eyes begging him to recant, to say something to ease the tension. The look on Dara's obdurate face destroyed whatever hope was left — she knew her man, the ultimatum would not be revoked. Dear God, her heart cried out, what more is left for me to still suffer, is there to be no end to my grief?

And then Salim spoke, and hope was reborn from the grave of her dashed dreams, her wilted heart soared, and from the smouldering ashes of her charred aspirations, his voice was a song of deliverance and a release from the pain of her agony. She closed her moist eyes, her face radiant, and silently sent a prayer of such intense devotion that not even the distant and remote heaven could fail to hear.

"*Baji*," Salim said softly, his right hand raised before him as he addressed his father with a maturity far beyond his years. "I have never shown any disrespect to you or any of the elders in our community. My life, like yours, has been dictated by the need for survival in a country that considers us as slaves whose only function is to contribute to the well-being of the white man. It is you, in your wisdom, who taught me that in such an environment the observance of a law that is unjust in the eyes of both man and God is in itself immoral. In this I have always been guided by you and my conscience is clear. Not one penny of what I have earned was acquired by force or contrary to the willing participation of those I dealt with. I have always given value in exchange, greater than the payment I received. That too, was a rule I learnt at your feet."

As Shaida listened, her eyes still shut tight, she thought: he is his father's son. Flesh of his flesh and bone of his bone. A Pathan to the core, the Dara of my youth, the voice of destiny.

"You now request a commitment from me. You give me a choice where you have the right to demand. The courtesy with which you have addressed me tonight deserves an equally courteous response. '*Daku* or *Dukan*?' That is not a choice, it is a moral imperative. Let us embrace on it."

"Spoken like a Pathan," Dara said with deep emotion as he stood up, and father and son hugged each other. Dara was stunned beyond belief by what he had heard, the voice so curiously like his own that he swelled with pride.

"Every father should have a son like you."

"And every son a father such as you. And perhaps a mother who keeps her eyes open."

"*Choop, gudha!*" Shaida said. It was the first time she had uttered those words with a smile.

∞

When Sam and Dara walked into Mr Lalloo's store the elderly Gujerati welcomed them with the dignity and refinement that was characteristic of his people. Sam, leaving his father to attend to the usual preliminary matters that preceded any serious discussion, casually looked around. The store was considerably larger than their own, almost twice the size, with the added advantage of a mezzanine floor that covered half the rear and served as both a storeroom and an office.

The two senior men had drifted off and were engaged in earnest conversation, their voices muted and barely audible to Sam and the owner's son, who was sullenly ignoring Sam. Sam quietly wandered around, discreetly assessing the stores potential for conversion to their own traditional trade. The possibilities were exciting and Sam was considering the feasibility of knocking down the dividing wall when he heard Dara clear his throat.

"Mr Lalloo is being very reasonable," Dara said. "We have agreed on a price of five thousand pounds, lock, stock and barrel. Twenty percent of it is *uplung*. We will have no problem with the landlord, who knows us well and also owns the shop we trade from. Both the stores are part of the same building."

"We don't know the landlord personally," Mr Lalloo said. "We have always dealt with the letting agents."

"So have we," Dara replied. "But they are decent people and I am sure they will agree to the change in tenancy. There is no reason why we cannot take over on the first of next month."

"Then we've agreed," Mr Lalloo smiled. "The *uplung* in cash. The balance over twelve months."

"No way," Mr Lalloo's son butted in belligerently, "I have had a much better offer."

Both Dara and Lalloo turned to him in surprise. Lalloo was the first to react. "When did you receive this offer?"

"I ... last night."

"You did not tell me."

"I forgot ... there were other things ..."

"What is the offer?"

"Six thousand. In cash!" the son spat it out, his voice lacking conviction.

"Who made the offer?" Lalloo asked, a hint of anger in his voice.

"Some people I know. They are coming to see us tonight."

It was patently obvious to Sam that it was a lie and Sam looked at him speculatively, attempting to fathom the motivation behind it. Father and son were clearly in contra-positions, Mr Lalloo considerably embarrassed.

"Is this a firm offer?" Dara asked, his voice a little sharp.

"They will talk to us tonight," the son answered petulantly.

Lalloo continued to stare intently at his son until, finally, the boy looked away and began to fidget with a display of shirts. Lalloo shook his head and turned to Dara, clearly distressed by the turn in events.

"*Maaf, bhai,*" he said, spreading his hands. "I honestly did not know of this."

"It is not the way we do business," Dara said accusingly. "We agreed on a price. Our word has always been our bond."

"These children," Lalloo said helplessly, "They embarrass us ..."

"They have learnt the twisted ways of the white man," Dara retorted angrily. "The decision is still yours to make. We shook hands on it."

Sam felt it was time he stepped into the discussion, to diffuse what was beginning to take on the tones of a dispute. He addressed Lalloo with extreme courtesy, modulating his voice and displaying the utmost respect. "Kaka, I understand your problem. Let us not quarrel over it. Permit us to leave you on an amicable basis, with no ill feeling. Discuss the matter with your son when we are gone. We know you are an honourable person. My father will accept whatever you say to us tomorrow. Can anything be fairer?"

Mr Lalloo was visibly upset. He was a man of impeccable character, of the old school of thinking. It was obvious that Sam's words, couched in the manner that they were, had a profound effect on him. Sam was sure that, had the son not interrupted at that moment, the old man would have reconfirmed the deal immediately.

"Business is business," the son said with a hint of triumph, totally oblivious of the predicament he had placed his father in.

Dara was on the verge of saying something when Sam nudged him and quietly inclined his head towards the door. As they walked out Sam was astounded to see the look on the son's face: he seemed to be seeking his father's approval at the way he had conducted the negotiations.

Back in their own shop next door, Dara threw his hands up in despair. "We cannot afford to pay any more. You should leave these things to me. You are not yet ready to handle delicate ..."

"*Baji*," Sam interrupted. "I do not believe Mr Lalloo will go back on his word. It was necessary to give him an opportunity to save face, to deal with his son in private. Let's see what happens."

That evening Sam explained the position to Sandy who, in his usual manner, quietly listened until Sam had finished speaking.

"Perhaps we should let the League handle it," Sandy suggested. "One call from them would turn this guy Lalloo to jelly."

"I would prefer to keep them out of it, Sandy. I have a feeling that things will work out okay. This Mr Lalloo is very much like my father, they believe in the old way of doing business. And you know how the League operates. Once they get their clutches into a businessman they'll bleed him dry. I don't want to expose Mr Lalloo to them. He is an honest man and he knows he is receiving a fair price, one set by himself. His misfortune is that he has a fool for a son."

Sandy nodded. "How about you, Sam? You sound as if you're tuning into your old man."

"I've been doing a bit of thinking. I reckon life on the streets is not for me. The really big money is in business and maybe it's time I moved on. How do you feel about it?"

If Sandy was surprised he did not show it. In all the years Sam had known him he had never heard Sandy answer a question without careful thought. He was not disappointed now.

"Sam," Sandy said, "right from the beginning, when you were still a shit *lighty*, I knew there was something different about you. Perhaps it's just that you play too fair. Even in a street fight you refuse to kick a man when he's down. You just don't play dirty. I'm not sure that sort of an attitude will help you in business but you definitely can't make it big on the streets that way. You'll survive, sure. But that's about it."

"And you, Sandy. How long do you think guys like you and Jake can last? You're far too intelligent to keep on this way."

"Not much choice, *boet*," Sandy smiled wryly. "Did you know I spent a year at varsity?"

"No!" Sam was genuinely surprised. "But now that I think about it ..."

"Two things put a stop to that. The first was lack of money. The second was the realisation that there was no future in it. Sounds funny, doesn't it?

Anyway, I grew up on the street and I reckon there is no better university than the gutter. The education system's geared to keeping us down in the gutter. Well, that's where I chose to be, but on my terms and of my own free will."

"Do the guys out here know about your time at university?"

"I'm not too sure. I don't think so. With Jake and Vusi, who know about it, it doesn't make any difference. With the others you have to be careful. Some of them think that being educated means you're a pushover. You can waste a lot of time proving them wrong. Anyway, you're still young, Sam. Pull out now. Join your old man while you still can, before your reputation starts to spread in the business community. Once that happens none of them will deal with you."

Sandy glanced at his wristwatch, then stood up. "Let's go. Time to make the rounds. And Sam, get out now, straight away. It's a good time for you to split. There's something big brewing. There's going to be mob violence worse than anything you've seen so far. The Big Five is about to make a move on some guys, rivals who are an offshoot from their own ranks. The Victorians will automatically be drawn into it. You can avoid being a part of it by taking a walk."

"What about you and Jake, and Vusi?"

"We don't have much choice in the matter. This is our life. The only way we know of making a living. We're too far in now to back out."

They moved around for the next hour, stopping from time to time and collecting Sandy's takings from the runners. Sam spent a few minutes with Nits Vania, who ran a loan shark racket and operated on the fringes of the various gangs. Nits was a loner who gave allegiance to no one except his partner John Farley. He settled his disputes personally and without recourse to assistance from any particular mob. He was known to everyone in the underworld as a straight dealer whose rates were reasonable and who had pretty solid connections quite high up. He walked freely in and out of the Magistrates' Courts and was on good terms with most of the cops. In an emergency, Nits could always be depended upon to provide bail money and his "clients", as he called them, never defaulted willingly knowing that any such action would leave them out in the cold the next time around. And for them, there was always a next time.

To the casual observer Sam and Nithin were no more than strangers who happened to be standing next to each other, watching the crowds rushing by. Even a trained operative would have had difficulty ascertaining whether any conversation passed between them. And yet, in those few moments, Nithin always tipped Sam off on when and where the

Vice Squad planned to make their next raid. It was information that was valuable to the Victorians and allowed them to contain their "pay offs" to a minimum.

Nithin was speaking now to Sam, without moving his lips and looking elsewhere. "All clear. No raid tonight. They're headed out of town."

Sam turned and walked away, nonchalantly greeting a perfect stranger with a wide smile. When he rejoined Sandy he passed on the information and Sandy, who had been on edge all evening, visibly relaxed.

A little later, as the night crowds began to converge around the cinemas, Sam turned to Sandy and held out his hand. He was surprised when Sandy grabbed him by the shoulders and roughly hugged him.

"Play it safe, *lighty*," Sandy said, keeping his voice deliberately casual. "And if once in a while the bug bites, you know where to find me."

"Sure, Sandy. And hey, thanks."

"Anytime. Just remember this. When you belong to it the street is your best friend. It's a cocoon that's safer than a mother's womb. Walk away and it's your greatest enemy. You're no more than game bait. From here on always watch your back. The *kachelas* will think you've gone soft, reckon you're an easy mark. The first time that happens, hit hard. Tramp his face into the dirt, make an example of him. They'll get the message."

"I'll remember that."

"You do that. See you around."

Before Sam could say anything more Sandy turned his back and walked away. For a little longer Sam wandered around Victoria Street, absorbing the sights and sounds, bittersweet emotions surging through him. For one last time he wanted to immerse himself into the night, revel in the power and savor the respect accorded to him by the denizens of the underworld who went out of their way to greet him. Up till now he had always responded to their deference towards him with a flippant nod of his head. The realisation that this would soon be replaced with contempt and speculative looks of just how far he could be pushed removed the gilt from his gingerbread. He realised, with mild regret, that Sandy's parting advice held more than was apparent in the words. From now on, and without the backing of the Victorians, he would be just another Joe, a target for the hustlers and the wide boys.

As Sam crossed over onto Grey Street he shrugged his shoulders, his lips stretching into a tight smile, eyes suddenly hard and merciless. He'd been there, he was not likely to forget where he came from. The punks could try their luck with him. He'd make sure that the first time they did so would be the last time. As Sandy had said, they'd get the message. Fast!

Sam looked at his watch. It was still early and he wanted to make one more call. He headed towards Karan's place.

Karan's mother fussed over him, chiding him for not coming over often enough and scolding him for being too thin and not eating good food. Karan smiled widely, his eyes twinkling. It was a regular routine, whenever Sam visited them. When at last she left the two alone and headed for the kitchen, still grumbling under her breath, Karan burst out laughing.

"Some big deal you are," he mocked. "You want to swim with the sharks but can't handle an old woman."

"When in Rome ..." Sam started to say.

"Don't talk to me about Rome when you haven't even crossed the street yet."

"Maybe I have, only not in the way you think. Seriously, Karan. Are you planning to go to varsity next year?"

"Yup. The old man wants me to take up law."

"Is there really a future in that?"

"Why all the questions?"

"I've just been talking to Sandy. He thinks varsity is a waste of time."

"He's right. With the limited openings offered to us a degree is pretty near useless."

"But you just said you're going to study law."

"In my case there's a big difference. My grandfather has wide business interests and a legal background will be very useful in his various trading activities. I know I have no hope of getting an opening to serve my articles but I won't have to anyway. I'll simply walk into my grandfather's trading house and occupy any desk I want."

"I don't understand these whites," Sam said, more to himself than to Karan. "Why do they hate us?"

"Hate has nothing to do with it," Karan responded. "According to my grandfather it's the natural fear of an inadequate person for a man of ability. They do the same to us in business, raising all sorts of obstacles to free trade. At the same time they heavily subsidise their own kind, making certain that whatever restrictions they place on us confer a direct benefit to the white race."

"I've heard all this before, especially when Jake gets going. I'm not too clear though about specific ..."

"Let me give you a simple example," Karan butted in. "You've heard of that new club our business guys opened up in Prince Edward Street. What's it called? The Club Lotus? It's no more than a social centre, an answer to the exclusively white Durban Club which we are not allowed to enter. You know what the authorities did? They insisted that the liquor licence would only be granted if they hired a white licensee. So the club had to employ some white bum, give him a fancy office and pay him a fat salary. In other words, no white licensee, no club. Get the message?"

"I guess so."

"That's it, Sam. You dance to their tune or they switch off the music. All very neat and tidy. Some democracy!"

"So it's a question of the greatest good for the smallest number. It's not what I came to talk to you about. But you answered my questions anyway."

"What exactly are you talking about?"

"I guess I'm going into business," Sam replied, standing up and heading for the door. "I needed to be sure there was no future in the academic world."

∞

The next morning Sam was up earlier than usual. After breakfast he collected the store keys from the usual place in the kitchen cupboard and, without a word, waited for his father to lead the way. It was a normal schoolday and Sam would, under any other circumstances, have been preparing for school. Dara asked no questions. They left home together.

When father and son arrived at the shop they were surprised to see Pravin Naran walking towards them carrying the inevitable briefcase in his left hand.

"Salaam, Dara," Pravin said as he followed them through the door.

"You're early, Pravin kaka," Dara said quizzically. "Please come to the back where we can sit. Salim, keep an eye on things."

When they had settled down, Naran looked around him. "I hear you are doing quite well."

"*Ji*, kaka," Dara answered. "The riots set us back but we survived. God has been good to us."

"You have been good too. In obeying His laws. Out of good only good comes."

"Somebody should tell that to the government."

"They have been told, my son. Unfortunately, their leaders choose to ignore the Bible, the rules of which are no different to your Koran — or my Gita, for that matter."

"Then they break God's laws."

"For which their *Karma* will speak for itself."

"There are those amongst them who claim publicly that the Bible gives them the right to enslave us."

"They are the ones who distort their holy book, for their own enrichment. There have always been men like that throughout history. There are many more who protest against such blasphemy. Sadly, they are powerless against the might of the State."

"And there are even more who quietly enjoy the benefits that the same State confers upon them."

"I think the Bible has a message for them also. Their sons will pay the penalty."

"It's not a legacy I would ever leave to my children. And how do they think they will answer on the day of the great reckoning? Time is running out for them. The Koran says that God cannot forgive us for crimes we commit against our fellow men. We must first obtain forgiveness from our victims before we turn to Him."

Naran slowly nodded his head, the deep lines on his face growing more pronounced as he pondered Dara's words. "I have read portions of all the Holy Books. My memory is no longer what it was. But somewhere in the Koran there is a verse which says something like 'only to you, oh man, of all my creations, have I given the power of infinite reason. Why then do you not use it'. If I am right then I'm afraid that even God is sometimes frustrated by the behaviour of those he placed on this earth. We mortals have little hope of making sense out of people like that."

"I remember my father once said to me that where God is prepared to wait until the Day of Judgment before he condemns us for our folly it would be blasphemous of us to pass judgment on them now. It would be like placing ourselves above Him."

"Judgment, Dara, and protest, are two different things. To remain silent in the face of injustice is the same as perpetuating it — you become an ally of the perpetrator. But enough. I have other matters to discuss with you."

"But first we have some tea, Pravin kaka. Can I order some *bhajia*?"

"No. Tea will be fine."

"Salim," Dara shouted. "Arrange for tea. And make sure it's hot."

"I understand," Naran said, "That you are negotiating with Mr Lalloo next door to take over his store."

"Yes. We should finalise it today."

"Then you have not yet signed any papers?"

"No. Not yet."

"Good. Then I am in time to tell you some things that may influence your decision. Ah, Salim. Thank you.

"Now," Naran continued, as he sipped from the saucer. "I have a confession to make. Please hear me out without interruption. I'm afraid I have been guilty of the sin of judgment that you so nicely defined earlier. However, I may be forgiven because I was acting on orders from your father. On his instructions I have been watching your progress for several years now. I am pleased to say that you have removed any reservations there may have been in the past."

Naran paused, waiting for a response from Dara. When Dara remained silent he grunted with approval.

"Prior to his death your father bought a property and registered it in the name of a private company. The shares have been held in my name, in trust until the time I, in my sole opinion, am able to decide whether it can be handed over to you. That time has come."

Naran paused again, watching for Dara's reaction. The face before him was composed, reflecting nothing beyond respectful curiosity. He is another Yahya, Naran thought with satisfaction. He reached into his briefcase and pulled out a thick envelope.

"The title deeds are in there. You will also find an updated balance sheet of the company" Naran handed the envelope to Dara, who tentatively took it and placed it on the table in front of them.

"You will notice that a sum of £980/12/9 is owing to me. Don't be concerned by it. Pay me as and when you can. The original amount was considerably more but rentals in the past few years have shot up and have rapidly reduced the indebtedness."

Naran settled back into his chair, inviting comments from Dara.

"I'm confused," Dara said, his brow knitted. "My father had no money ..."

"Yahya and I had an arrangement. It need not concern you now. The property is, of course, worth far more than the price paid for it. The balance sheet reflects only the cost at the time of purchase."

"And the property itself," Dara asked. "Where is it?"

"You are sitting in it," Naran replied simply.

Dara was stunned. For the first time that morning he lost his composure as the enormity of Pravin Naran's statement penetrated his mind. He lifted the heavy envelope, then quickly lowered it as he realised his hand was trembling violently. He was still struggling to absorb the implications of his good fortune when Naran stood up.

"You need to be alone, Dara," he said gently as he prepared to leave. "You are a wealthy man now. Make certain you are equal to your inheritance."

"So we don't have to pay Mr Lalloo the goodwill after all," Sam said, "Or buy any of his stocks. We simply give him one month's notice to vacate and take over."

"No, we don't have to," Dara replied. Then, choosing his words with care, he continued, "But it would be wrong. A bucket of pure water, Salim, can be completely polluted by a single drop of urine. So it is with money. What we have now is honest money, all of which can be tainted by a single act of dishonesty. Let us not be guilty of such an act. We have a deal with Mr Lalloo, entered into before we knew we owned this property. We have to keep it."

"But isn't that exactly why Pravin-dada told us about it today? So we don't end up paying for what we already own?"

"We own the property, not the goodwill. And Pravin-dada told us now because he is an honest man himself. He also mentioned that I must make certain I am equal to my inheritance. To me it was a warning against greed."

"I'm still not sure I agree we should pay Mr Lalloo, even if the amount is now insignificant compared to what we own. And he himself did renege on the deal, didn't he?"

"That was his son's stupidity, not Mr Lalloo's fault."

"And if Mr Lalloo now asks for more than the price you agreed on?"

"Why do you suddenly doubt him? Yesterday you called him an honourable man, today you feel differently. You see what money does?"

Before Sam could reply Mr Lalloo walked in, his face drawn and lined with weariness. He greeted them with a voice that was barely audible and, without going into the usual preliminary courtesies, launched into the topic of the sale. He barely looked at Sam, his words directed at Dara.

"I slept little last night. I am ashamed at the way my son behaved and I apologise for that. There is no other buyer and I must tell you that in all fairness. My son ... *Tchah*! These youngsters sometimes try to be too clever."

"Times are changing," Dara said sadly. "We may be the last of our kind."

Lalloo gravely nodded his head in acknowledgment. "Some people chase after money the way others chase after women. Not for pleasure but for power. They little realise that neither of these pursuits confer any value, they only erode their strength and eventually destroy them."

"Whilst we are still in charge the decision is ours. So, what do we do now, Bhai?"

"That is up to you. I would want to conclude the sale, exactly as we agreed, if you still want to do so. But my son's actions reflect on me and I have to make a gesture of good faith and restore our relationship. I am willing to retain my old stock and transfer it to my shop in Commercial Road. They are not the goods you normally deal in. We can adjust the price accordingly."

Mr Lalloo had been speaking entirely in Gujerati. He now turned to Sam and repeated, in English, the words with which Sam had concluded their last discussion: "Can anything be fairer?"

Dara held out his hands, arms wide, and embraced Mr Lalloo. "You have honoured the terms of our deal. I can do no less. Come, let us have tea and settle the details. Now that Salim is fully a part of my business he can help us with the agreement."

Dara had smiled when he said that, acknowledging Sam's perspicacity of the day before and his accurate summation of Mr Lalloo's moral commitment.

∞

Over the next two years the fortunes of Suleiman and Sons underwent a phenomenal change. Three more stores were swiftly acquired. Sam, under Pravin Naran's guidance and contrary to Dara's strict insistence on always buying for cash, stocked up to the ceilings, obtaining long terms from his suppliers and selling for cash. He turned over the creditors' money as often as three or four times before payment was due to them, using the flow of funds to pick up large parcels at bargain basement prices. He was steadfastly punctilious in paying his bills and never asked for an extension of time.

It wasn't long before notes signed by Dara circulated freely in the market place, had a reputation for being as good as gold and were accepted without question by the most prudent merchants who discounted them several times before payment was due. On occasion, using Pravin Naran as an intermediary, Sam even bought back his own paper for cash and at less than face value, thereby reducing the eventual cost of his purchases even further.

Dara, unable to keep pace with Sam's machinations, simply moved around from one store to the other on an arbitrary basis, which was facilitated by the fact that all the stores were virtually adjacent to each other. Only a small haberdasher stubbornly remained in between Dara's row of retail outlets, refusing to budge in spite of several tempting offers to buy him out. Sam bided his time, secure in the knowledge that sooner or later the recalcitrant old Urdu-speaking tenant would succumb to the carrot Sam kept dangling under his nose.

Before long, the opportunity presented itself. The owner of the property that housed the haberdasher's store indicated his desire to sell. With stunning speed Sam moved in, offered a sum far in excess of what the property was worth, and within twenty-four hours concluded the agreement. Sam summarily ejected the haberdasher, retained a firm of architects and, within a matter of a few months, removed all the internal walls and created a modern, glittering departmental store that was the envy of every trader in the Casbah.

The luckless haberdasher, out on the street and with nothing to do, complained bitterly to whomever would listen to him. With Sam moving around in a frenzy and seldom in one place long enough for Dara to confront him, Dara finally and in despair employed the poor man and placed him in charge of the company's own haberdashery department. Securely occupied once again, the complaints stopped and a modicum of peace returned to Dara's disturbed world.

By late 1955, Sam, barely twenty one years of age, was already a veteran trader with a solid reputation. Dara retained full control of the business and over finances generally and Sam was perfectly content with the arrangement, concentrating his energies on buying and selling. It was an atmosphere he thrived in, playing one supplier off against the other, buying in bulk and at the cheapest price possible, reselling subsequently at a small margin but turning the goods over swiftly before his competition had time to catch up with him. By the time his rival traders received their stocks Sam was already offloading the same items at below their cost and moving on to new products. It wasn't long before the general public realised that a "sale" at Suleiman and Sons was always a genuine sale and not the usual trumped up affair which prevailed at other stores.

It was Karan's idea that the time had come for Sam to import his own goods, cutting out the middleman and increasing his margins. Pretty soon Sam had established contacts with manufacturers in India and the Far East. Pravin Naran guided him on the intricacies of the new venture, helping Sam through the welter of documentation connected with international trade. Pravin patiently explained the importance of forward cover and the effect of exchange rate fluctuations on the final cost of the commodities. He introduced Sam to Manech Randeria, the head of a reputable firm of shipping agents who in turn assisted Sam when he purchased a small warehouse to store his goods.

Literally overnight, turnover jumped enormously and it wasn't long before Sam was both an importer and an exporter. With Manech's contacts Sam exploited the huge markets in the neighbouring countries, most of which lacked the infrastructure and expertise required to produce their own goods or to buy directly from the foreign suppliers.

Dara, although grumbling continuously, accepted that he was out of his element and, in the face of Sam's phenomenal success, conceded that his system of business was outdated and not suited to what he reluctantly admitted was the new dynamics of the business world. On one point however, he remained firm: the properties they traded from had to be owned by them to provide the security of tenure so vital to their future success. "Don't rent when you can own," he insisted. "And don't buy unless you can pay cash." In that, father and son complemented each other, with Dara the visionary and Sam the opportunist.

When Sam began to make regular trips overseas, on one buying expedition or another, Karan smiled delightedly and reminded him, "Can you recall what I said to you once? It seems so long ago now and you've come so far in such a short time. I told you that there is a far more glittering world out there than the streets of the Casbah could ever hope to compete with. What do you say now?"

"Like you said at the time, Karan," Sam replied nostalgically, "The street has its own attraction. Once it gets its hooks into you it never lets go. But you're right, it's a narrow world that can confine you and close your eyes to the wider horizon. Still, although they are two different worlds, they have a common denominator: their methods of doing business are exactly the same — you find out what people want, then supply it. Like with the cinema tickets, you have to corner the market and hang on to it. In the one case you use your fists or a gun, in the other you work around the law by using your bankers or the shippers. The only difference is in how society perceives the two methods of operation."

Sam occasionally met Sandy, equally at home in the sordid bars and backrooms as he was in the boardroom. Although he refused to touch any liquor he enjoyed the brief respite from the routine of wheeling and dealing that had now become a way of life for him and provided little excitement and lacked the glamour that he had initially revelled in.

On one such evening, Sandy, in a rare mood, did most of the talking and regaled Sam with hilarious stories of incidents concerning some of the fawning businessmen who liked to delude themselves into thinking they were a part of the underworld simply because they were allowed once in a while to talk tough and brag in loud voices about their dubious exploits.

"As long as they pick up the tabs," Sandy laughed, "the boys are happy to indulge them. A few weeks ago one of the *scotens*, a real small fry, actually strung one of them along so beautifully it was a delight to watch him in action. He played the poor fish so deftly that by the end of the day the *garach* had bought him a new outfit — suit, boot and choot. They're constant companions now, with the poor sucker swaggering around his own mates and acting as if he is one of the inner circle and an important member of the League. In a little while one of the sharper *kachelas* will move in and brush the *scoten* aside and before the stupid mutt knows what's happening he'll be wrung dry. Happens every once in a while, but what the hell, if these guys like the reflected glory they have to pay for it."

"You're a natural raconteur, Sandy," Sam observed. "I wish sometimes you could sit in on one of my negotiations. I reckon we'd fleece those manufacturers faster than they can deliver the goods."

"Seriously, though," Sandy continued, no longer laughing, "The League is really big now. There have been a few minor changes. It's not quite the unified entity it used to be. There's a new player on the scene now. You know Mo Govender, he's one of us, and he's got his own team. But there's no real quarrel between him and the League. Together they totally control the underworld, throughout the country."

"Mo was always a straight dealer," Sam commented. "Always there for the small guys. And he can be trusted, unlike some of the okes in the League."

"That's for sure," Sandy agreed. "Anyway, they've formed a syndicate with Sheriff's boys in Jo'burg and the Globe Gang in Cape Town. Nearly half the judges in the country are owned by them, together with every big name in the police force. Besides yourself and perhaps a handful of others, a businessman can't even sneeze without their permission. Anything you want — from dagga to dames, from guns to gambling, from fixing a football game to foreign currency — they can provide at a moment's notice and at a flick of their fingers. And, for the right amount of money, they can put anybody away without batting an eyelid. They're now only a step away from linking up with the international mobs. When that happens they'll move onto the highest circles and entrench themselves more solidly than ever before."

"What about the white underworld? Surely they have certain advantages?"

"White is nothing, Sam. They haven't evolved along the same lines, haven't been subjected to the same restraints. In a way the lack of policing in our areas gave the locals a platform to commence from. Once on the way, and with the bucks at their disposal, they could bribe anybody no matter how highly placed the official was. As they say, buddy, money talks."

"And in every language, Sandy. I've learnt that by now. And what about Jake and Vusi — and yourself? Where do you guys fit in?"

"Oh, we do okay," Sandy said flippantly. "The street is still our turf. The *Motas* may pull the strings higher up but we still rule on the ground."

"I noticed the snazzy Ferrari. Do Vusi and Jake swank around in similar style?"

"They have different tastes, Sam. Those two are oddballs, disappear for days every once in a while and don't talk much about what they're up to. But they're okay. Still loyal as all hell to me and straight shooters. The three of us have more control at our level than the Big Five have. It's an arrangement that suits both sides. The one hand shakes the other. In that, nothing has changed. It's the same as in the old days, except now the stakes are higher."

"I've noticed, though, when I drove down Victoria Street, that there are quite a few white faces around now."

"Sure, we still call the shots but unlike a few years ago the white boys are beginning to line up in our territory. We don't mind. They're like us. They don't give a damn about politics or apartheid. Apart from their skins, they're no different. They think black, talk and act like any of us. And they play it clean, unlike some of our own runners. And, in some areas, like Greyville, they're indispensable. They can move in and out of their own suburbs freely, they open up markets for our dagga and *fah fee* banks that never existed before. Again, it's an arrangement that benefits everybody."

"And Jake?" Sam asked. "Is he still playing it cool?"

"Jake is ice. And the best street fighter anywhere. But there's an anger in him, Sam, some kind of hatred that's lurking close to the surface. The day it explodes even the Big Five would have difficulty restraining him. You can sense it in his every movement, the feeling of some great violence barely held in check. I've seen some good guys actually shiver when they catch the smouldering rage in those eyes. And he's fearless. Nobody, not even those that hate him, would ever call him a coward."

"But what is it, Sandy? Where does this anger come from?"

"I have an idea, Sam. It's something that's been building up in him since we were *lighties*. But I could be wrong. Maybe it's more recent, since the riots. You may not know it but he was in the thick of it. Whatever, the day it erupts there'll be no stopping him. I just hope his natural ability to hold himself in check is stronger than any impulse to run wild. But Sam, you sound as if you don't see much of him. Does he come home at all?"

"Not much. He drifts in and out. He adores the old lady and sees her once in a while. There's a peculiar relationship between him and the old man, a strange bond that stops my dad from completely disowning him. But they keep their distance and Jake seems to avoid coming face to face with him. He's never been to the store, not ever. The last time I saw him must have been almost a year ago."

"Jake's the best buddy I ever had. Still is. I guess what he needs is a good woman, someone who can tame that fury in him. But Jake never lets anyone get too close to him so there's not much hope there, even if such a chick existed."

"And Nits? Still the loner?"

"Nits is something else. You'd never think we all grew up together. Like Jake, his loyalty is always there but he hardly says much. Him and that chap John Farley, I don't know what they talk about. He's a deep guy, Sam. And he's all for Jake, you can see it in their faces when they're around each other. Goes back to the old days, I guess. But he keeps pretty much to himself."

"I suppose we're all funny that way, Sandy. You say howzit to them for me, especially Vusi. And that reminds me, I'm beginning to feel hungry. I'll see you around. Just take care."

"Sure, you too. Come around when the bug starts to bite again."

∞

Pravin Naran's office was on the sixth floor. It was large, spacious and full of antique furniture, most of which he had brought over with him from India over seventy years ago. It was musty, untidy and cluttered with dusty photographs and odd bric-a-brac. Old newspapers, yellow with age, were stacked five and six deep on a huge desk, the wood of which had darkened with age and lost its original lustre. Over the years he had resisted every attempt by his grandson, Karan, to upgrade and modernise it in keeping with the rest of the building.

The Naran businesses occupied the first six floors. The ground and two floors above it housed one of the most up-to-date departmental stores in the city; on the fourth floor was Naran's wholesale, the fifth a warehouse, with offices on the sixth. Pravin Naran no longer took an active part in the businesses, had indeed ceased to do so many years ago. The office was simply a feeble effort to stamp his authority and a convenient hideaway, which he occupied for no more than an hour or two each day.

In March 1956 he was six years short of his hundredth birthday, was extraordinarily well preserved and possessed a memory that, on his good days, was the envy of his family, his grandson and three great-grandsons who headed the family empire. Pravin had always eaten sparingly, was a lifelong vegetarian and, up to a few years ago, had concocted his own Ayurvedic foods, until a mild bout of arthritis had forced him to hand over its preparations to his eldest great granddaughter whom he supervised carefully and with ill-concealed patience. More often than not he slapped her wrists in irritation when she failed to follow his instructions to the letter, pushed her aside and took over himself, only to delegate the function to her once again when his fingers failed to respond to the task. He had discontinued his yoga exercises the year before although he continued to meditate daily at a fixed time. Almost without fail he simply dozed off in the middle of it.

He rose now from his chair, patted the latest issue of the *Hindustan Times* and stuck the Nehru cap on his head, at exactly the right angle. For a full minute he rummaged through his desk, looked around him distractedly, finally searching his pockets until he found his small bunch of keys. He grunted to himself, sighed, and prepared to leave. At the door he hesitated, looked around again until he located the light switch. It was in the off position. He looked at the ceiling, noted that he had not turned the lights on in the first place, nodded and left the room. He locked the door carefully, rattled the handle a few times, then walked towards the lift.

He emerged on the third floor, surveyed the activity around him for a while, then re-entered the lift. He repeated the process on the second floor, lingering a while longer. When he reached the ground floor he stepped up to the nearest till and motioned to one of the staff to open it. The saleslady smiled, rang up "no sale" and stepped aside. Pravin grabbed a handful of one shilling coins and pocketed them, patting the assistant on her shoulder. As he walked towards the main exit the saleslady reached for a piece of paper, wrote "Pravin Naran" on it and dropped it in the till.

When Pravin emerged onto the pavement in Grey Street he turned to his right. Along the way he stopped from time to time and dropped one of the coins into a delighted beggar's tin, then continued on his journey. He turned right again into Queen Street, went on distributing the coins until they ran out. At the entrance to Dara's store he paused in front of a beggar, patted his pockets absent-mindedly, then motioned to the unmoving mendicant to remain where he was. He entered the store, went behind a counter and randomly pushed several keys on the till until it opened and the tray slid out. He extracted a coin and stepped out. The dumbfounded counter assistant behind the till looked at Rashid, who happened to be close by, in astonishment. He smiled, nodded his head and continued perusing the folder before him.

Pravin re-entered the store, passed the lady at the till, stopped, then retraced his route. He patted her on the shoulder, mumbled something indistinct, then turned back.

"*Mota Bapu*," Rashid said. "*Namaste*."

"*Salaam*, Rashid. Are you well?"

"*Ji, bapu, Tame?*"

"*Teak*! Take me to *Baji*."

Before Rashid could lead the way, Pravin left him behind and headed towards Dara's office. Dara's door was closed. Without knocking, Pravin opened it and walked in. Dara, who was in discussion with two other men, jumped up. "Kaka! You honour me. Come in."

Pravin had already passed him and had stopped at the desk, waiting for Dara and oblivious of the visitors. Dara smiled apologetically and indicated to the men that they should leave, then led Pravin towards an easy chair near a coffee table. Pravin lowered himself carefully and settled back.

"Tea, kaka?"

"No! Can't take it any longer. Bladder, you know."

Dara was about to occupy the chair at the opposite end when Pravin said, "Close the door."

Dara closed the door and rejoined the old man. For a few minutes they enquired after children, grandchildren and, in Pravin's case, great grandchildren. They conversed exclusively in Gujerati.

"Dara," Pravin said abruptly, "I am here on important matters. Please listen."

Dara sat back and folded his hands over his stomach.

"My time has come," Pravin Naran said emotionlessly. "I have read the signs and noted the days left to me. You understand?"

Dara's face fell. He leaned forward and touched the old man's knee silently. Pravin patted Dara's hand. "It is nothing. It's good that you know about the signs. It's not something we can teach our children. They are too Westernised and have lost the touch. When their time comes they'll be caught unawares. It is one of the reasons we can no longer depend on them on matters of importance. It is not surprising they are busy making out their will when they should be making money. *Tchah*! We became fathers to *chootyas*.

"When he knew his time was up your father visited me. He had no need to make out a will. I was his instrument. He left with me a valuable item, a family heirloom, to be held by me in trust until it could be passed on. Before I hand it over to you I must inform you that there is a condition attached to it, which you will have to observe when your time comes. The condition is very simple, the requirement onerous. You must make sure that, whichever of your descendants you pass it on to, qualifies without reservation. It is your job now to see to it that whoever receives it is equal to the inheritance.

"At the time when Yahya gave it to me he was not sure of the state of your mind. You were acting rashly and were in danger of behaving unreasonably. Yacoob he discounted for obvious reasons and his behaviour to date has justified that estimation. He asked me to watch Salim, for whom he had high hopes.

"I was entrusted with the responsibility of making the final decision."

Pravin's mouth seemed to have dried up. He passed his tongue over his lips and swallowed a few times. Dara jumped up, poured water into a glass from a carafe on his desk and handed it to Naran, who took a few small sips, sighed gratefully, and then continued speaking.

"It was an onerous responsibility, a most difficult task. For a while Salim seemed to be following in Yacoob's footsteps, effectively removing himself from consideration. As you know, Salim and my grandson Karan have always been very close, he has been a regular visitor to my house. There were times when I was tempted to intervene, to discipline him. It would have been the wrong thing to do. Fate must be allowed to take its course.

"At one stage I was beginning to lose hope for Yahya's male descendants. You must understand. It was not a responsibility I could treat lightly, simply to relieve myself of its burden. I began to consider the female line. Shaida qualified in every way. However, it was an option that did not please me. I decided to wait.

"Subsequent events have justified that decision. Salim, and you, have both progressed to the point where either of you qualifies to take possession of this extremely valuable treasure. Naturally, as first in line it is to you that I must hand it over. The responsibility, from this day on, becomes yours."

Naran reached into his pocket and extracted a bunch of keys. From an old-fashioned clip he removed a single key and handed it over to Dara. Attached to the key was a grubby piece of leather on which were written some Gujerati numbers. The numbers themselves had been highlighted so many times that the leather was deeply indented with them.

"That is the key to my safe deposit box at my bank. Arrangements have been made with the manager, a Mr Henry, to let you have undisturbed access to it. In the box is a bundle that contains your inheritance, together with an envelope from Sothebys of London. You will find in the envelope two pieces of paper. The earlier dated one is a valuation, prepared at my request, some years ago. I was not surprised that it exceeded my own estimate, made at the time Yahya left it with me. The second is a recent offer, through Sothebys, by a private museum in the United States. You will find their offer exceeds Sothebys' valuation many times over.

"The value is, of course, of passing interest to you, you are sufficiently wealthy now to find it unnecessary to give the offer any consideration. I have, on your behalf, rejected it. It is also time to bring your inheritance home, where it belongs.

"Now Dara, my preparations are complete and I am ready to meet my maker. It has been said that 'those whom the gods are pleased with die young'. I have often wondered what sin I have been guilty of to have offended them to the point that they made my stay on earth so lengthy. Still, they granted me good health during these many years so hopefully my crime may have been a very small one. Perhaps they only remembered me now — the gods often do that, play their little games. Whatever, the answer should be most interesting, don't you think?"

Pravin Naran died in his sleep two days later, peacefully and with a smile on his face.

∞

"Prompt as usual," Karan commented as Sam walked through the front door.

"I suppose you're entitled to act superior," Sam retorted. "As my tutor for the evening you must feel quite important."

Devi, Karan's wife, entered the room and smiled widely when she saw Sam. She was accompanied by a girl of about nineteen, dressed in a Punjabi suit. "Salim bhai," Devi said. "This is an old friend of mine, Salma Khan."

Sam inclined his head in greeting, then turned to Karan. "I can't stay long. Can we get into it straightaway?"

"Sure, let's go into my study."

Karan immediately went into an involved explanation concerning the merits of converting a business from a partnership to a limited liability company. " .. In that way you separate your personal assets from those of the business and, provided that you do not issue any personal guarantees, you would be able to protect them from any action your creditors institute against the company. Naturally ..."

Karan's voice trailed off. Sam, normally reticent by nature, was even quieter than usual. And he wasn't paying attention, his eyes glazed over in the manner of a person emerging from a drug-induced stupor. Karan sighed.

"Maybe we should go a little slower," he began to suggest when Sam shook his head, as if to clear it.

"Who is she?" Sam asked in a hoarse voice.

"Who? Who the hell are you talking about?"

"That girl. Who is she?"

"What girl? Oh, you mean Salma. As Devi said, she's a friend ..."

"With a name like that she must be a Pathan?"

"Of course she is. What the hell is the matter with you?"

"I want her."

"What! You *want* her? Just like that?"

Suddenly, Karan noticed that Sam's face was grim. He looked as if he was preparing to go into battle with some powerful adversary. A slow smile began to spread across Karan's face.

"*Murigiyo, Sala.*" Karan said. "You're dead, buddy."

"I have to talk to her, Karan."

"Then why did you behave so abruptly when Devi introduced you?"

"I was scared," Sam replied, now clearly embarrassed.

"You? Scared?" Karan burst out laughing. Then went to the door and shouted, "Devi, come here for a minute!"

When Devi came into the room Karan said, "Now tell Devi what you just told me."

"*Bhabi*, I ..." Sam began sheepishly.

"He says he wants her," Karan chuckled. "He wants to buy her. You know ..."

"Buy what?" Devi asked.

"Karan, please ..." Sam pleaded.

Devi looked at the two of them quizzically, then asked, "Have you been drinking?"

"No! No! Devi," Karan was beginning to chortle, "We're talking about your friend Salma."

"I just want to meet her," Sam said softly.

"But Salim, that's why I called her over today. But you acted so off-handedly that she left."

"She's gone?"

"Not for good, you idiot," Karan said, still ragging Sam.

"She lives almost next door, Salim," Devi said. "I can always call her over."

"Now?" Sam asked eagerly.

"Okay. But not for long. Let me try."

It wasn't long before Devi returned with Salma. Once again Sam was absolutely tongue-tied until Devi helped him along by suggesting, "I'll leave you two alone for a little while."

The little while stretched into half an hour, then an hour. By then Devi was beginning to get agitated. "Karan, if Salma's mother finds out she's talking to Salim alone I'll be in serious trouble."

"But we can see them from here."

"It makes no difference. You get Salim back to your study. I have to walk her home. Now!"

"Give them another minute."

"And what if Ba walks in?"

"I'll explain to her ..."

"Your mother will never forgive me." Devi walked into the room decisively and almost dragged Salma back. "Enough! It's time you went home."

"*Bhabi* ..." Sam began.

"Salim, *buss*! Enough! You'll cause serious problems."

"Can I phone you?" Sam asked Salma desperately, trying to follow them. When Salma nodded, Karan held Sam back and said, "Take it slow, Sam. If you get caught now her parents will marry her off to someone so fast ..."

"Devi said she lives a few doors away. How come I've never seen her before?"

"They just moved in. Devi's family and the Khans are old friends."

"What do I do now?"

"Wait. Let my mother handle this."

From that point on the rules set by tradition took over. The romance of courtship was superceded by the mundane routine of so-called "negotiation" between the two families involved. The weeks stretched into months whilst Sam fretted and fumed at the restrictions placed on him and Salma. Once or twice during that time he was able to snatch a few minutes alone with her, always at Karan's place and under Devi's watchful eye.

Devi became Sam's intermediary and confidante and she seemed to enjoy playing the matchmaker. However, they had to be extremely circumspect whenever she could arrange for them to be together as the slightest hint that the couple was in direct contact would have resulted in both families calling off the discussions altogether.

Sam continued to chafe at the bit, pushing his mother to speed matters until she snapped at him in irritation. Eventually, almost four months after Sam first met Salma, they were formally engaged. It was a simple function. Sam's parents, together with Ayesha and Ahmed and Karan's mother, visited the Khans. The Khans themselves had called over a handful of their immediate family. Gifts were formally exchanged — jewellery and some clothing for Salma, a watch and a shirt for Sam. The evening ended with everybody taking a small bite of some sweetmeats — the "mouth-sweetening" event. Sam had to remain at home, his presence not required. Salma remained in her room.

The following evening Sam dressed in his best casual clothes in preparation for a visit to Salma. His mother, when she saw him, asked, "And where do you think you're going?"

"To see Salma," Sam replied happily.

"Are you mad!" his mother shouted, horrified.

"But Ma, it's okay now for me ..."

Shaida slapped her forehead with her fingers. "Salim, you can't see her."

"But Ma, we're engaged now."

"So? Do you know nothing about these things? How could I have raised an ignorant ..."

"Ma, what's wrong with visiting her? I'm not going to take her out or anything like that."

"She has her reputation to think about."

"What can happen to her reputation? We're engaged. I'm the one she'll marry."

"Engagements can be broken. Do you think any other family will look at her if they know you've been seeing her?"

"But why should the engagement break off?"

"Those are the rules. This is not one of your big business deals. You see her on the day you get married."

"This is silly, Ma."

"*Choop*! Now go to your room."

Sam went to Karan instead, expecting some assistance and a degree of sympathy. What he received instead only frustrated him even more. Devi refused to listen to Sam's pleas and simply said, "You are engaged. What more do you want?"

In the end, Sam had to be content with a few snatched telephonic conversations with Salma, whenever she was alone at home and could ring him at the office.

Finally, on Sam's twenty-third birthday, he entered the mosque and, at an all-male affair, participated in the marital vows. Witnesses from both sides of the families signed the register and solemnly shook hands. Sam was now free to call on the Khans and formally take his wife home.

From the moment they left the mosque the celebrations started. Amid much hooting of cars and shouts of ribald laughter from family, friends, relatives and neighbours Sam entered the Khans' front gate, surrounded by a dozen best men, and attempted to gain access to the front door. But it was not to be. Several young girls from Salma's family surrounded him and demanded what they called "access money". It was all in good fun, though, and after mock negotiations by Sam's official representative, a handful of notes was distributed amongst the girls. A glass of almond milk was handed to Sam, who took a few sips, saw Salma shimmering in white and surrounded by her bridesmaids, and walked towards her.

"Don't do anything stupid now," Karan whispered. "You're not supposed to kiss her or even hug her. Just stand next to her and let the photographer take over. He'll tell you when to put the ring on her finger." Sam, king for the day, did exactly as he was told.

At last, after hundreds of photographs had been taken, an equal number of hands shaken and even more words of good fortune had been gracefully acknowledged, Sam and Salma entered the bridal car and left for home, followed by a procession of cars hooting in unison as balloons were burst and ribbons fluttered in the air.

∞

Dara had bought the home that he had been renting in Reservoir Hills and Shaida had extended and renovated it. Sam had his own quarters, with an en suite dressing room and bathroom. A similar section had been added on for Jake, in spite of Dara's objections. It had never been occupied. Dara and Shaida occupied a complete wing, with Rashid's room down the corridor. The kitchen, lounge and dining room was a communal area. Shaida, however, reigned supreme in the kitchen, with Salma relegated initially to the mundane function of preparing the meals and seeing to the dishes. It was an arrangement that worked perfectly.

Sam's life settled into a routine of business during the day and quiet evenings with Karan two or three times a week. On Fridays, when Salma spent the afternoon with her parents, Sam worked late in the office until it was time to join her for supper at the Khans. They were a nice family, but too easygoing and boisterous for Sam's normally quiet nature and he usually took Salma home before nine.

In March 1963, on Karan's advice, Sam converted the business into a limited liability company, changed the name to Suleiman Bros (Pty) Ltd, with an issued share capital of one hundred shares. Dara, canny as ever, insisted on registering fifty one of the shares in his own name, assuring himself of the majority voting rights. The balance of forty nine shares he left to Sam's discretion, to be dealt with as he saw fit. Thirty of them Sam registered in his own name, five in Rashid's and four in Ayesha's name. Ahmed who had by then inveigled his way into the family business and achieved his long-standing ambitions, was delighted. Sam didn't bother to tell The Toad that there was a special condition attached to the shares and that his marital right was specifically excluded, totally nullifying his participation in any meeting of the shareholders.

The remaining ten shares, representing an effective 10% of the business, Sam held back in reserve. Not even to his mother did Sam admit his secret dream of one day coercing Jake into the business and into the family fold.

Jake drifted in and out of the family home, remaining at times for the whole afternoon and spending hours seated in the kitchen while Sam's mother and Salma prepared the day's meals. Shaida had, by then, given up on asking Jake any questions on his activities, content with spending the few hours with him. Jake always left before Sam or his father came home.

There were periods when Jake would, suddenly and without prior notice, disappear for weeks on end, only to reappear and carry on as if nothing had happened. Dara had long given up on Jake, never enquired after him or mentioned his name. He lived as if Jake had never existed.

As Sam's business expanded, his leisure hours contracted. Rashid had failed to measure up to Sam's standards and The Toad was content to live with his in-laws like an adopted son. Ayesha, even in her early middle age a ravishing beauty, kept to herself, read a lot and, on those evenings when she stayed over, relegated her husband to the guest quarters. With her daughter, she spent the night in Jake's room or in deep conversation with Salma, with whom she had developed a strong bond. Life, as far as Shaida was concerned, was close to perfect.

On a Tuesday morning in 1966, whilst Sam was busy in his office, his secretary buzzed him on the intercom. "There's some guy here, Sam, who is hassling the girls at the cosmetics counter. I think you should come down."

"Get security to throw him out," Sam ordered.

"I can't. I mean, it's not as if he is being rough or anything. But he's a nuisance and refuses to leave."

"Is he drunk?" Sam asked.

"Far from it. Quite charming in fact and damn good looking. The trouble is the assistants are flocking around him and ignoring the customers."

"How long has he been there?" Sam asked, irritated by the interruption.

"About ten or fifteen minutes. And Sam, I think he's carrying a gun. I'm sure I caught a glimpse of it when he reached for a cigarette."

"I'm on my way."

Sam strode towards the counter where a few of the girls were giggling at the man in front of them. All Sam could see was a tall, slim figure in a grey chalk-striped suit, the face turned away. Sam, his jaw set in angry lines, increased his pace. When he made a detour to avoid a group of shoppers, the profile came into view and he stopped dead in his tracks. The lines around his chin began to relax and he broke into a smile.

"Jake!" Sam shouted.

"Hey, my *bra*," Jake shouted back as he moved towards Sam. The ladies at the counter quickly turned away, suddenly busy.

"Nice to see you," Sam said as they hugged. "Come on. Let's go to my office."

When they passed his secretary Sam stopped and said, "Rushda, meet my brother, Jake."

"Your brother?" Rushda said, flustered. "I didn't know ..."

"I was beginning to forget too," Sam said over his shoulder.

When they entered his office Sam closed the door and they settled on a pair of easy chairs. "Jake, I meant what I said. It's really nice to see you."

"Good to be here. Hey, this is really plush" Jake was looking around the large office appreciatively.

"A big change from 'Dara's Hardware', huh?"

"It's another world, Sam. You've moved fast and done well."

"We had a lot of help from Pravin-dada."

"He was a good man. Him and grandfather, and Madhoo dada, they were good guys. Especially Madhoo dada. I miss him sometimes."

"Men of principle. They don't make them like that anymore. It's a nice time to grab a bite, Jake. What do you say? I'll take a few hours off."

"Thanks, Sam. But I'm here for a favour."

"Sure, whatever I can. Just name it."

Jake began to hedge, looking embarrassed. "Only if possible, Sam. I don't want to put you in a spot."

"Don't even think about it, *boet*. You need some cash? Something else? It's yours."

"Well, you better hear me out first. As I said, no hard feelings if you can't see your way ..."

"Jake, cut the cackle. Tell me what I can do."

"Okay. I need a job."

"What!" Sam said incredulously. He couldn't believe he'd heard correctly. "Just say that again."

"I need a job."

"Here? At Suleiman Bros?"

"As I said, only if ..."

"No! No! There's no problem. But you actually want to work? A seven to five day?"

"Longer, if necessary."

"I refuse to believe this," Sam said. "Now, tell me ..."

"I mean it, Sam. I'm coming home."

"Ya? Well, okay. Look, do you need some bucks? You in some kind of spot?"

"All I need is a steady job. Anything. Stick me anywhere."

"Well, I suppose you could take control of security."

"Set a crook ... so to speak."

"So to speak. Let's start from there. When do you want to move in?"

"I'm coming home tonight. Can I join you in the morning?"

"Why not. We can leave home together. I better warn you, I'm here before seven each day. *Baji* usually comes in a little later."

"Doesn't bother me," Jake replied, getting to his feet. "See you later."

Before Sam could say another word, Jake was gone. Sam felt as if the breath had been knocked out of him. He was wondering if Jake would really show up at home when Dara flung the door open and entered the office.

"What was he doing here?" Dara asked, his voice tight.

"He's your son, *Baji*," Sam said with a small smile. "He belongs here."

"He belongs in the gutter."

"He's coming home tonight."

"Why?"

"It's his father's house. He belongs there too."

"Salim, talk straight. Why are you smiling?"

"Jake ... Yacoob's joining us for meals tonight. I thought I'd call Ayesha over. The whole family will be together for a change."

Sam could see the conflicting emotions on his father's face. He was
sure Dara would have raised strong objections but the words "the whole
family together" seemed to have swung it.

"*Tchah!*" Dara spat and walked away.

∞

Although Dara didn't say much at the table, the dinner was a huge success.
Jake was in a happy mood, his eyes soft and he looked somehow mellow and
relaxed. Sam hadn't told either his mother or his father that Jake was
moving back for good, or at least that was what he'd said. He'd privately
asked Salma to prepare the room and had left things to develop from there.

Sam couldn't help but marvel at the way his mother was behaving. In
everything she did, the way she talked, it was as if there had been no
interruption in their lives. She carried on as if it was a normal evening, no
different from any other. For a second Sam wondered if Jake had already
spoken to her, then immediately discarded the thought. It just wasn't his
style. To Jake, it would be an underhand act and he just didn't operate that
way.

Salma, who had gotten to know Jake a little better after his visits, was
pleased to have him at home and Sam could see she genuinely liked him.
Ayesha, who probably hadn't seen Jake in years, fussed over him and, in
spite of her "iron woman" facade, Sam could see her eyes were moist with
ill-disguised happiness. The Toad, on the other hand, looked hostile and
uncomfortable, possibly seeing Jake as a rival to his ambitions. Sam
couldn't help being amused. If he knew Jake at all, he was certain the new
resolve was a short-lived weakness. Before the week was out Jake would
probably disappear, perhaps for another few years.

Ayesha began to serve the rice pudding and, as she bent over Jake's
plate, he affectionately held her hand and detained her. With an arm
around her waist he looked around the table, his eyes finally settling on his
father. His Gujerati, when he began to speak, was still faultless, the words
tripping over his tongue effortlessly.

"*Baji*, I have no wish to deceive you. I have decided to come home for
good and have asked Salim to give me a job at your store. But I would like
the decision to be made by you. If you cannot see your way to granting this
request I will not hold it against anyone. I understand that I cannot just
walk in and expect to carry on as if I have never given you cause for grief.
Whatever you decide, I would like to spend the night in my room, with
your permission. I only ask that, at this stage, you do not demand any

answers from me. Perhaps later. But for now please grant me that courtesy. It's not much to ask.

"I'll leave you now and, if you have no objections, retire to my room. Please discuss my request and, in the morning, Salim can give me the answer. *As-Salaamu-Alaikum.*"

For the second time that day Sam couldn't believe his ears. Jake had already left for his room, Ayesha following him, their arms around each other's waists. In the silence that followed, Dara cleared his throat, then did so again. When he cleared his throat for the third time Shaida stood up. "Salma, do the dishes. Salim, help her. Come, Dara. Let's go to our room."

When his father simply nodded and followed her, Sam shook his head in disbelief. "Everybody seems to have undergone some kind of a change," he said to Salma. "It's like the angels have been working overtime on this family. Maybe I should say a little prayer of thanks before they change their minds."

"It's time you did. When last did you unfold your mat?"

"I get tired in the evenings, Sal. The business ..."

"You're never too tired to eat."

"I have to replenish my energy."

"And your soul? Do you expect it to function without prayer?"

"Why do you sound more and more like my mother?"

"*Choop, sala*! Go perform your prayers."

∞

At the end of the first week Sam was intrigued. Jake tackled his job with enthusiasm. He had a way about him that won over the security personnel and streamlined the detail into an efficient force. And he dressed in keeping with his job. The flashy suit he had worn when he had called on Sam was gone, replaced by simple trousers and cotton shirts.

The more Sam tried to draw him out, the tighter Jake's lips became. He deftly avoided Sam's questions and when Sam became insistent he simply said, "Talk about how I'm shaping up. You got any complaints?"

"None. You're doing a good job."

"Then think of my salary."

"Name it. Whatever you ..."

"No. Pay me the going rate. No more."

"Jake, if you need any money ..."

"I'm okay. Just make sure you pay me at the end of the month. I want a cheque, made out in my name."

"Consider it done. If it's not enough, just say so."

"The going rate, Sam. If you pay me an *ottie* more I won't cash it."

"Okay," Sam sighed.

When another week went by Sam's curiosity got the better of him. He decided to call on Sandy. He could contain himself no longer.

When Sam walked into Sandy's club he was welcomed with a wide grin and led to a far corner where they could talk without being interrupted. They chatted for a while about the usual things, Sam commenting that Sandy was beginning to move up in his world. The club was a far cry from the old fish and chip shop.

"Things change, Sam. Nothing remains the same. How's Jake?"

"That's why I'm here."

"I expected you two weeks ago. What kept you?"

"I guess I couldn't believe it. I had to give him time, be sure he meant it."

"He means it all right. Make no mistake."

"What's happened, Sandy? What brought this about?"

"The most powerful emotion in the world, buddy. The type that sets a thousand ships out to sea."

"You mean ..."

"Quite. Our boy is in love. Hopelessly and helplessly. And, if I may add, desperately."

"Tell me about it, Sandy."

"What can I say? He's gone, head over heels. Trouble is, the chick doesn't want to hear about him."

"She doesn't care for him?"

"She's crazy about him. But when she found out what he does for a living she dropped him, just like that. Refused even to take his phone calls."

"You're going too fast, Sandy. Tell me all you know, but slowly."

Sandy flicked a finger at one of his *scotens* and gave some kind of a sign. In less than a minute a bottle and two glasses were on the table. When Sandy raised an eyebrow enquiringly, Sam shook his head and Sandy nodded. "I guess some things always remain the same. Coke?"

"No. Just give me the story. All of it."

Sandy reflected for a few moments as he sipped his drink.

"Jake met her at a political rally. Some ANC thing," Sandy said slowly. "I don't know much about that part of it. You know Jake, his left hand never knows what his right hand is doing. Anyway, he turned on the charm and prepared for an easy conquest, a quick fling. From what little he said I gathered she contemptuously spurned his advances and refused even to go out to dinner with him. He grew desperate, at every political meeting tried every trick he had learnt over the years to win her over. When everything failed he changed tactics. He got some of the runners to follow her around, find out where she lived, where she worked, that sort of thing. A lot of what I'm telling you now I found out from Vusi.

"Eventually, she gave in to his relentless pursuit of her and agreed to have dinner with him, just once. It must have gone off well because she went out with him again soon after that. It wasn't long before they were inseparable. She was good for him, I can tell you that. The rage is still there, but it's a little muted, more focused. I don't even imagine she would try to tame him that way. Nobody can. And in any case, they're both into some political thing so I suppose they share the same anger. Whatever, they became a team.

"It was something to see, Sam. Those two were so crazy about each other that no one else seemed to exist when they were together. And they talked all the time. God, how they talked! And then they settled into some kind of pattern. Went to the movies most evenings or just held hands and strolled around town. Over the weekends they took long walks around the avenues, picking up a bite to eat at quaint cafes or take-aways. Jake kept her away from us, never brought her around to meet the boys or see him in this environment. We understood, of course.

"I met her once, when he insisted I join them for dinner. It was a lovely evening, I took Maliga along and we enjoyed ourselves immensely. Vusi, who was closer to the two of them, because of the political activity, joined us for a while. But it was obvious Jake was a little uneasy, which is understandable. I guess he was reluctant to expose her to his normal world. After all, she comes from a good home and, apart from her ANC connections, seemed to have led a pretty cloistered life.

"For the whole of that year we only saw Jake during the day. As soon as it was close to five he disappeared, off to meet her. It must have been the happiest time in Jake's life, and I've known him for most of it. I reckon my car saw more mileage then than at any other time over the years I owned it.

"And then the wheels came off. At first I simply thought it was one of those things, that their affair was too intense and they needed some space away from each other. I was wrong. As the weeks went by Jake was absolutely distraught. I was sure he was going to hit the bottle. Fortunately, he was made of sterner stuff.

"One evening he finally poured his heart out. He admitted he had made a big mistake in the image of himself that he had created for her. Whatever garden path he had led her up he had made certain that she knew nothing of the way he earned his living. Jake is too well known. It was stupid of him to imagine he could hide it from her forever. She was bound to find out about it and somehow she did. Whoever gave her the lowdown must have painted a damned bleak picture. The initial shock must have been replaced by a feeling of disgust and anger. She viewed it as an act of treachery on Jake's part.

"I happen to know all this because I set Maliga the task of effecting some sort of reconciliation. It was uphill all the way. The chick, her name by the way is Hannah, refused to even consider a meeting with our man. But Maliga, if anything, is not easily dissuaded. She is far more practical and knows the good side of Jake, she hung in there until she was able to extract a small concession. If Jake walked away from all this, found himself a steady job and held onto it for long enough to satisfy this paragon of virtue, then perhaps, only perhaps, she would reconsider meeting him again.

"Well, as far as I was concerned, that was the end of it. Jake hates ultimatums, and a steady job to him is like asking him to chop off his pecker. When Maliga repeated it to him I expected Jake to write Hannah off and get on with his life. We both know now how wrong I was."

Sam just sat there, a silly grin on his face. As things began to fall in place, he finally asked, "This girl, Hannah, she's really got him where he lives, huh?"

"That's saying it mildly."

"What can you tell me about her?"

"As a person, not a lot. Maliga's the one to talk to. As for where she comes from, depending on how you look at it, there's the usual good news and bad news. How do you want it?"

"Let's hear the bad news first."

"Her father's a *wit ou*, a Jew. That's about all I know. Now here's a real bouncer for you — the mother. She's a true blue Pathan!"

"You have to be joking!"

"Nope. She's one of those fair ones, with blue eyes. Takes after some of your Northern people, you know, with all that ancient Greek blood ..."

"But we know all the Pathans in this country. There aren't that many of us. How come I've never heard of this couple?"

"Maliga tells me the two first met in London, while she was studying something or the other. She had gone there direct from India. The *wit ou*, a local *gamoola*, had gone over to visit his parents. However it developed, they got married. She couldn't take him to India and he couldn't bring her here openly. In the end they went underground, settled in some coloured area around Sydenham and kept a low profile. It happens often."

"Shit! Leave it to Jake to complicate things."

∞

Over the next few weeks Jake surprised everybody, including Dara who was beyond any such emotion where Jake was concerned. He was ready and waiting for Sam in the morning, stayed in the store till late each evening and went home with Sam after he'd finished his paperwork. Once home, he stayed there. When Sam left a small company car at Jake's disposal he only used it for a few hours over the weekend when he felt cooped up and had to get out for a while.

Sam phoned Sandy a few times each week to find out if there were any further developments at Maliga's end. All he learned was that Jake phoned her daily, promptly at eight in the evening, to make sure she was still working on Hannah. About Hannah Sam found out nothing more. He was amazed, though, to find that Jake had a natural talent for business and a keen sense of the latest trends in men's clothing, often making suggestions that initially seemed outlandish but subsequently turned out to be very wise recommendations. And he knew how to motivate people around him, the staff liked and trusted him and he spoke their language.

When Sam transferred Jake to "Menswear" and gave him a free hand, even Dara approved without any reservations. Within months Jake reshuffled the department, employed several young salesmen with a good dress sense and paid them more than the going rate. He insisted they always dressed in style, sold them goods from the store at far below cost and made certain they wore them all the time, both in the store and out of it. "It's the way to go," he told Sam once. "Just watch the Sharks in the street, they're the trendsetters."

Business began to boom and sales climbed every month, beating all previous records. "It's nothing clever," Jake said flippantly. "The guys out there see our boys swanking in their new outfits, looking sharp as hell, and want to know where they buy them. Word gets around and they make a beeline to Solomon Brothers."

"I don't know how long this will last," Sam told Karan a few days later. "If this girl doesn't give in soon Jake may just chuck it all in and go back to his old ways. It'll kill my old lady."

"Does your mother know about the girl?"

"Not yet. Where's the point in it? Nothing much is happening and there's the question of religion. I know nothing about her family. Sandy says her father is Jewish. As far as my mother is concerned that won't speak too highly of the wife. Perhaps she has even converted to the Jewish faith. I guess I'll just have to leave it be and trust in luck."

"You don't know your mother, Sam. I also think you're being unfair to her. We all have this stereotype image of Indian mothers. Let me tell you, when the chips are down they can be quite versatile. Try talking to her."

"Not a chance. I wouldn't know where to start."

"Talk to Devi then. Tell her all you know and let here work on it. It can't do any harm."

"Karan, I don't want to interfere in Jake's affairs. He's on a knife-edge as it is."

"Why should he know about this? Think about it, man. Don't you think your mother would like to know what brought about this transformation? She must be on tenterhooks herself, fearing the day Jake could revert to his old ways. When she realises how much depends on this girl that Jake is crazy about, that she is responsible for his about-turn, she'll look at it differently. I reckon she'll settle for her rather than Jake back on the street, anytime. But it's time you moved. Mobilise the reserves, so to speak."

"Ya, okay. Let me think about it."

After several days of vacillating on the matter, Sam finally took the plunge and told Devi everything he knew about Jake's affair, leaving nothing out. When Devi asked Sam about the girl's surname and where she lived, he admitted his ignorance and smiled sheepishly.

"How can you be so indifferent," Devi berated Sam angrily. "And you will be a father yourself someday. Have you learnt nothing from your own parents? Get it for me, today."

"Devi, look, I'm not his father ..."

"*Choop, Sala!*"

"Better do as you're told, Sam," Karan grinned.

⚭

On a Saturday afternoon, after the store had closed and Sam was alone in his office preparing to leave, the phone rang. He was on the verge of ignoring it and calling it a day when he noticed that it was his private line and decided to answer it.

"Sam?"

"Yes ..." The voice was unfamiliar and Sam couldn't place it.

"This is Hannah."

"Who?"

"Hannah. Hannah Friedman."

"Yes, yes, of course." Sam was shaken, not sure of what to say next.

"Did I get you at a bad time?" She spoke very softly, in a pleasant tone.

"No, it's fine. I mean ..."

"I'd like to see you, Sam. If that's okay with you?"

"Sure. Anytime. Just say when."

"Today?"

"Today is fine. Can you come to the office? I can send a car to ..."

"That won't be necessary. I have my own car. But I'd like to meet you alone. I don't want to bump into Jake ..."

"Jake's gone home. Would you like to come over now?"

"I'll be there in half an hour," she said, cutting the connection.

Shit! Sam muttered to himself. What the hell do I do now? He quickly picked up the receiver and dialled his secretary at home. "Rushda? Something's come up. Can you come over straightaway? Thanks. I'll leave the front door open. When you get here wait at the entrance. I'm expecting a lady to visit me. Can you bring her to my office? You're a star. I'll make it up to you later."

Sam began to pace the floor, not knowing what do to next. "I didn't ask for this," he said aloud. "Damn it! I should never have answered the phone." He was standing at the window when he heard the tentative knock, then the door opened and Hannah walked in. Rushda seemed to have discreetly disappeared somewhere into the store.

She was in her mid-twenties and quite pretty. Not pretty, Sam quickly revised his estimation — good looking, in a very assured way. She had an olive complexion, was quite tall for a female, with dark shoulder-length hair. She was simply dressed, in a two-piece costume that reached below her knees. The usual handbag was missing, all she carried was her car keys and a tiny purse. Apart from a pearl necklace, she wore no other jewellery.

As she stood there smiling at him, Sam suddenly realised he looked foolish and quickly stretched out a hand. "Hello. Come in, please." He pulled out a chair for her, then settled behind his desk.

"I understand now why the leopard changed his spots," Sam said. "Can I get you something? A coke?"

Hannah chuckled softly, then smiled warmly. "No thanks. I just thought we should talk, for a few minutes. Has Jake told you about me?"

"He's not much of a talker. But I know a little about you from Sandy. I like what I've heard so far."

"I'm glad. Sandy's a gentleman. Jake's lucky to have him for a friend."

"You really think so?"

"Yes. Whatever Sandy told you about the reasons why I broke up with Jake, he was not one of them."

"It's good to hear that. We go back a long way."

"I've heard about that from Maliga. And a few other things too. But Sam, I don't want to spar with you about Jake's past. We were very close for about a year. You get to know a person well in that time. I loved him during that year, madly and to the exclusion of everything else. I still do."

"But then you dropped him."

"Maybe I was hasty. I should have talked it over with him. But the shock of finding out that he was a gangster, a streetwise thug, was too much for me. I suppose I felt betrayed, badly let down. I was carrying around this image of him, of a gentle person whose only anger was directed at the system. It was a bit too much to suddenly discover that there was another Jake, who lived in a world of gambling and racketeering and only God knows what else. I was devastated. The only thing I could think of was to run, as far from him as possible."

"I grew up in the same world. So did Sandy."

"I know that now. Maliga's quite a talker, a really nice person. She told me many things and I don't mind admitting they had quite an effect on me. And marriage to Sandy has worked for her. With Jake and I it would be different. It would be short-lived and would go sour very quickly."

"But you were prepared to reconsider if Jake changed his ways."

"I agreed to give it a try, especially when I realised that it in every other way Jake had been absolutely honest with me. But I truly didn't believe such a change was possible. At least, not until Maliga told me about you."

"And now? Are you less doubtful?"

"That's why I'm here, Sam."

"Would you mind telling me how you obtained my private telephone number?"

"I thought you knew. That you expected my call."

"I didn't, honestly."

"Your mother gave me the ..."

"My mother! Where does she fit into ..." Suddenly Sam burst out laughing, he couldn't contain himself. It took him a few seconds before he could pull himself together. At last, his eyes still twinkling with mirth, he said, "Mothers! They never fail to amaze me."

"I thought you two had ... I mean, you and your mother ..."

"We've never spoken about you. But I know what happened. A good friend of the family had a hand in it. I'm just surprised at the way my mother went about it. Can you tell me how she got in touch with you?"

"She just walked through the front door one afternoon and introduced herself to my parents. I have no idea what they talked about except that Jake and I figured in it. I know that my parents were quite receptive to whatever she said and I had never made any secret of my association with Jake. He used to pick me up from home and they liked him a lot. They were confused when I broke up with Jake. When I refused to talk about it I guess they simply blamed him for the split and cooled off towards him."

"She came over to your place, just like that?"

"Your mother is quite a formidable woman, Sam."

"And then?"

"When I got home from work she was still there, all three very cosy and comfortable. And she didn't lie to me. Laid it straight on the line. Called Jake every kind of name she could until even I almost wanted to defend him. But she said some good things too, in a very forthright way. She also told me all about how he was a different person now, working in the store, that sort of thing. I knew it all, of course. Maliga made sure she kept me in the picture, do you know she even showed me photocopies of his salary cheque?"

"That explains why he insisted I pay him by cheque. He wanted to prove that it wasn't simple nepotism, that what he earned was on merit."

"I've accepted that. But your mother! I've never met anyone like her. You want to know what she said, her exact words? 'Grow up, girl. Grab life with both your hands and live. You don't know what grief is. When it hits you, you'll need a man around, not some simpering *garach*. And no matter how lucky you are, there will be bad times. That's when a real man like Jake will protect you.'"

"She actually used that word, '*garach*'?"

"Exactly. Why?"

"It's an underworld term. Where the hell did she pick it up?"

This time they both laughed, easy with each other, the tension gone.

Sam suddenly jumped up. "Give me a minute. I almost forgot about Rushda."

When he returned he smiled mischievously. "I've told her to go home. Give her something to talk about over the weekend."

When Sam was back in his chair he looked closely at Hannah for a while, as if considering something.

"I think you should give it a try, Hannah," Sam suggested.

"I can't deny that I miss him, every minute of the day. But I'm scared too, Sam. I've never believed in half measures. It's all or nothing. Jake's the first guy I've gone out with and he swept me off my feet. I wasn't thinking straight. But now that I've met your mother I realise that there is a lot more involved. Any cultural differences, especially after talking to your mother, can be overcome. But there is the religious problem and I can't ignore that."

"Is it important to you? I mean, the question of religion?"

"I've never given it much thought up to now. My father is a practising Jew. My mother I'm not too sure of. She says her prayers and observes the fast of Ramadaan. The two of them have some sort of understanding and I guess it works for them, which is all that matters. They've left me pretty much to make up my own mind. I feel as if I can't sit on the fence any longer."

"This religious ... problem, is it because of Jake?"

"Yes and no. I've seen what it has done to my parents, separated them from their families. I've never known any of my grandparents, my uncles or aunts. I feel a deep void in my life which would not have existed if either of them had made a decision and embraced the other's religion. I don't want to subject my own children to such traumas."

"I understand perfectly," Sam said slowly, his face grave. "I sometimes think religion causes more unhappiness than the solace it provides."

"And you, Sam. Are you strong on it?"

"I've never had to face the decision that you are confronted with. Actually, it has never affected my dealings with the people around me. My best friends are not Muslims. That was not the result of a considered decision, it's just the way things happened. They pray their way, and I mine. That is, whenever I get down to it. Of course, we were not setting up home together so I suppose that helped."

"And you didn't have to worry about having children with them," Hannah smiled.

"That's true and I guess that's the crux of your problem. On a one-on-one basis it should never be cause for dissension. I'd never dream of asking my best friend the details of his marital bed. It's a personal thing, a private matter. I look at religion in the same way. It would be presumptuous and rude of me to even question it, let alone judging them on their beliefs. It hasn't altered our relationship or commitment to each other. There's no reason why it should."

"Not many people look at it quite that way."

"Sure. They'd rather go to war over it. In the name of religion more lives have been lost than through all other causes put together."

"Sam, just talking to you has helped a lot and made me see things differently. But I can't take up with Jake again until I sort myself out. It's no longer an issue of his past, I have to be honest about that. I'll just have to leave things as they are and hope that ..."

Sam held up his had, cutting her off. "Please. I have a suggestion. Hear me out before you decide on what to do. Okay?"

Hannah inclined her head. "Okay, Sam."

"I think," Sam continued, "it's sensible that you should have these reservations. And now that I've met you I like what I see and hear, for whatever that's worth. I believe you are very good for Jake and I'm beginning to understand the reason for the remarkable change in him.

"Jake has undergone a metamorphosis that has delighted my family, even my father who is not easy to please. I'd hate to see him revert to his old way of living, which I'm certain will be inevitable if he begins to accept that he has lost you for good. With Jake, that can happen overnight.

"My brother and I have not had it easy. Jake especially. Someday I'd like to tell you of these things. I was fortunate in that I had a few friends who took an interest in my future and guided me in the right direction. Jake was not so lucky. Or perhaps he had been through too much to be receptive to any persuasion.

"I am not sure what it is that Jake contributes to your relationship. Your own intelligence and way of reasoning things out impress me. Anything else is your private affair. If I can act as an honest broker between you and my family, create an environment where everyone can live on an amicable basis, I would be honoured to do so. You have met my mother and you know how she feels. My father is quite different. He is a staunch Muslim and very rigid about it. So is my mother, but she dotes on Jake and takes a more realistic view of things. Over the years I have learnt one thing — my mother can swing my father around to her way of thinking.

"I can't guarantee anything. That would be foolish. But I honestly believe you and Jake could be truly happy together. I've never known Jake to want anything as much as he wants you. And whatever else his faults, Jake is not a liar. I'm asking you to give both of yourselves a break, to take a chance on life. Sometimes, what you call problems have a way of resolving themselves. We're talking about your future now. If any children you may have disturbs that equilibrium then it would be better not to have them. It would be like introducing the serpent into the Garden of Eden."

"You're very persuasive, Sam," Hannah smiled.

Sam's lips split into a grin, his strong even teeth white against his tan skin. "Go with the feeling, Hannah. My mother was right about there being both sunshine and rain in our lives. My family has had its fair share of grief. When I see something like what there is between you and Jake I don't like to analyse it. This is what I'm suggesting to you. Nobody will be hurt if you two get together again."

"Okay," Hannah said suddenly. "You're right. Jake has made the effort. I should do the same."

"Then do it now. Whenever I mention Jake your face lights up. And I saw the immediate pleasure a second ago, when you decided to go for it. Now, I'm hungry and I know someone who is dying to treat us to a meal. Give me the word and he'll be here in two minutes."

Sam placed his hand on the receiver of the phone and waited. When Hannah nodded he dialled the number. "*Ben*, can you call Yacoob for me?" A naughty twinkle came into his eyes while he held on. "Jake, I need you at the office urgently. Nothing serious but I need you here fast to close a difficult deal. This is your department and this person insists the goods are not returnable ... good. .. You have your keys? Hurry, will you?"

Sam replaced the receiver and began to chuckle. "He'd better have a strong heart when he walks through that door."

"I'm actually beginning to get excited. Thank you, Sam. And your mother too. She's some lady."

"I've never known anyone like her. Even Salma, my wife, is beginning to emulate her. With my mother on your side a major war is reduced to a small skirmish. I just know the two of you will get on famously."

"You must be a lot like her. You act fast."

"No. The men in my family take after my dad. Whilst we spend an age analysing everything, she just gets on with it and in the end her will prevails."

"I'd like to meet all of them. Your wife, your sister and even your dad, in spite of what you call his rigidity."

"And you will. You know, I can't help thinking how things change with time. Neither my parents, nor Salma's, would allow us to as much as talk to each other, even after we were engaged. And now look at what's happening."

"It wasn't so radically different during Victorian times in England."

"Possibly. On the other hand my mother may have convinced herself that she was simply calling on your folks with a proposal on her son's behalf."

"Well ... considering that she practically ordered me to see Jake ..."

They were still laughing and talking about customs and rules when the door opened and Jake walked in. He looked pretty sleek in his blue jeans and white T-shirt and, because Hannah had her back to him, he didn't immediately see her.

"Make sure you log me for overtime," Jake started to say when Hannah turned around. He stopped, took a hesitant step forward, then smiled broadly as she stood up and moved towards him. When she fell into his arms Jake crushed her to him, his head buried in her neck. They held the clinch for almost a full minute, then Jake asked in a muffled voice, "How you doing, babe?"

"Okay. I missed you."

"Ya, me too. We going to make time now?"

"I want to ..."

Sam heard the breath leave Hannah as Jake held her tightly.

"I'm hungry," Sam said.

When they didn't answer or turn towards him, Sam repeated, "I'm hungry. I thought we could go to ... oh hell! Lock up when you leave."

He left them alone, pulling the door after him.

∞

In spite of Shaida's efforts, Dara remained tight-lipped and refused to concede over the question of Jake's marriage. "Why does he require my permission?" he asked stubbornly. "He has always gone his own way. What's stopping him now?"

"Hannah would like your blessing."

"Am I God? How can I bless what is forbidden?"

Surprisingly, it was Hannah's father who finally swung Dara around. He came over one evening, with his wife, Noorjehan, and confronted Dara with a simple question: "Why do you confuse custom with religion?"

Dara, who had hitherto never gone beyond a curt greeting, looked at Moses Friedman and asked, "What does that mean?"

"The Koran does not forbid a marriage between a Muslim male and a female of another religion, nor does it require the female to convert to Islam."

"How would you know?" Dara asked scornfully.

"Because I have read the Koran. Provided that the female is from amongst the 'people of the book', in other words a Christian or a Jew, there is no restriction ..."

"Show me where it says that!"

Moses had come prepared. He quoted chapter and verse, then opened a copy of the Koran and placed it before Dara. "Read it — Sura V, verse 6."

Dara read the Arabic words slowly, re-read them, then quietly sat back.

"Perhaps Yusuf Ali's translation will help you," Moses said. "Here, in his commentary, immediately below the Arabic injunction, he says, 'Islam is not exclusive ... inter-marriage is permitted with the 'people of the book'. A Muslim man may marry a woman from amongst their ranks on the same terms as he would marry a Muslim woman ..."

Dara held up his hand, silencing Moses. "I need to think about this."

"Take your time," Moses smiled courteously. "But don't look for arguments against the word of God because it conflicts with ..."

Dara left the room without a word.

"I guess he's in a cleft stick," Sam told Hannah later. "He can't reject what is placed before him and at the same time can't understand how he missed that section previously. He's totally confused."

Hannah, however, obtained her own copy of the Koran and pored over it. She began asking questions at every opportunity and even drew Dara into the conversation. Dara initially participated with reluctance, then, in the face of her insistence, began to thaw towards her. When, eventually, she announced that she had no objections to marrying Jake under Muslim rites, Dara's reserve melted and he joined in with a will.

When the date for the wedding was set, Dara's enthusiasm knew no bounds and Hannah had to restrain him, insisting on a quiet wedding at home, with only a few close friends and family. Sandy and Vusi were counted as close friends and were included in the joint lists, together with Nithin Vania.

"After you are married," Shaida said, "Stay with us. You will have your own private quarters. Try it for a while. If it doesn't work out you can always get your own place."

"It will make life easy for you," Salma added. "You won't have to rush home from work and prepare the meals and see to the washing."

"They'll stay with us," Dara said, pre-empting Jake and Hannah. "Bank your money. Save for the future. You'll have a good start in life."

When Jake looked at Hannah she smiled and said, "Let's try it, Jake."

On the evening of the wedding, after the guests had left and the family was alone, Sam handed Hannah a thick envelope.

"What is it," she asked.

"Open it," Sam answered, looking mysterious and quite pleased with himself. It contained the last ten unissued shares in Solomon Bros, registered in Hannah's and Jake's joint names.

chapter six

Durban 1986

Vusi slipped into Lamontville just after midnight, when the sky was at its darkest. Not a single street light was working and a deadly hush hung over the whole area. He had to step carefully to avoid the tree stumps and rocks that were scattered everywhere, moving warily and ducking into the shadows whenever a pool of moonlight penetrated through the shifting clouds. There was no sign of life, human or animal: even the dogs seemed to have disappeared into the dense bush. He was in a war zone and the silence was beginning to unnerve him. He was on edge and a slight tremor shook his body.

He thought he heard a sound and fell flat to the ground, ears straining. For several minutes he remained frozen, glued to the earth. The silence was complete. He was about to move, his palms beginning to take his weight, when he heard it again and his body tensed, suspending all movement. His eyes moved wildly as he tried to locate the origin of the sound.

Then it came again, the shuffling of many feet. Vusi frantically rolled his body towards the wreck of a burnt car that had been reduced to no more than a shell. It provided little concealment but allowed him to blend into its bulk, the twisted metal casting grotesque shadows. As his eyes focused he made out, in the darkness ahead, what appeared to be a barricade constructed from forty-gallon drums. Several had toppled over, spilling their contents of sand and rubble. In the distance he could see the movement of a group as it disappeared over a hill. He remained rooted to the ground, careful to avoid any sudden noise.

"Vusi?"

The voice was barely a whisper. He wasn't sure he had heard it.

"Vusi?" It was slightly louder now.

It came from somewhere behind him and he tucked his head in, peering from under the crook of his arm. A shadow moved over him and a heavy hand fell on his shoulder, pinning him to the ground. Vusi gasped, fear coursing through him. He was about to struggle to an upright position when a soft voice commanded, "Quiet. You are with friends."

Vusi turned over on his back, relief flooding through him. He made out Sipho's familiar features.

"What took you so long?" Sipho asked, his voice barely audible.

"I lost my bearings. Nothing looks the same here." Vusi's voice sounded like a croak.

"A few of our men are waiting up ahead. Follow me."

Vusi stayed close to Sipho. They were moving fast and in a few minutes joined several other men armed with pangas and kierries. There were about ten of them. In the dark Vusi could only make out shapes and shadows. They moved forward together, travelling with a sense of urgency. Sipho led the way, stopping them occasionally as he went on to scout the terrain ahead.

Soon they were deep in the heart of the township and Vusi noticed a change in his companions, a lessening of tension. They emerged onto a gravel road, a thin stream of refuse water flowing through the middle of it. Sipho held up his hand, then indicated with a sweep that they should spread out. He signalled to Vusi to stay close to him, then cautiously advanced on a house that stood slightly apart from the other dwellings. When he reached the door he held his ear against the wood, listening. Apparently satisfied, Sipho knocked once, softly. He paused for about ten seconds, knocked twice, rapidly, then opened the door just enough to squeeze through. He pulled Vusi in after him.

The interior was dimly lit, the only source of light the flame of a candle that stood on a small oil drum. Apart from two battered chairs, the room was unfurnished. Both the chairs were occupied. One of them was set far back and Vusi could only see the outline of its occupant. From the one nearer to him a heavy set man stood up and held out his hand.

"Vusi," he said simply.

"Phineas," Vusi replied. "You are well?"

"Yes. So far. But the government stooges are everywhere, ready to sell us out to the police. We have to keep moving."

"How long will this carry on?"

"Who knows? This time there will be no turning back. What you see here is what you'll find in every township throughout the country."

"There's very little in the papers."

Phineas snorted. "We don't have time to talk about that. Did you bring the stuff?"

Vusi reached into a pocket and removed a small box and handed it to Phineas. "That's all?" Phineas asked, disappointed.

"There are fifty bullets in there, .38 calibre. That's all we could get. We're expecting a much larger quantity in about a week, could be as big as Jake's last consignment."

"Ah, Jake! He's okay?"

"He's being careful. He thinks they're watching him."

Phineas looked startled. "We can't afford to lose Jake. He takes too many risks. If something happens to him ..."

"Jake's cool," Vusi said.

"Ja," Phineas agreed, "but we can't lose good men now." There was both admiration and affection in the tone. "A few more like him ... Anyway, fifty bullets! Less than two per revolver. How the hell can we fight a war with that ..."

Phineas shook his head in despair, his face suddenly bleak, the box in the palm of one hand, as if he were weighing it.

The shape in the corner stirred and came to life. As the figure rose Vusi saw that the man was quite short, although in the dim light he loomed large and appeared to fill the room. There was something vaguely familiar about him and Vusi strained his eyes in an attempt to make out the features. At that moment the flame of the candle shot up briefly, fed by some sudden burst of oxygen, and Vusi gasped.

"Doctor!" Vusi burst out, then, controlling himself, whispered, "I thought you were out of the country?"

"I am wherever I'm needed. It's good to see you, Vusi."

"Thank you, *nkosi*. I'm pleased that you are well. There are rumours that you had been wounded and moved out of the country."

"There are always rumours. But now, there is something you can do for me."

"Anything, *nkosi*."

"Thank you. I would like you to arrange a meeting between Jake and me. It's also important that Sandy is there. And, of course, yourself."

"It will be done. When?"

"Today is Thursday. I'll meet you on Saturday at around three in the afternoon, at the old fish and chip shop."

"It may be better to meet at the club ..."

"No. I prefer the fish and chip shop. It's still there?"

"Yes. There won't be any problem."

"Then leave now. We must all go. It won't be long before the Caspirs are on the roads."

"Yes, *nkosi. Shala gachle, baba.*"

"Stay well, my son. Phineas will guide you out."

∞

The old hangout had undergone a remarkable change. It was tastefully furnished and carpeted, the dining area offering a greater variety of foods. The management still vested in the same family, except Mr Moodley's two sons had now joined the business. Sandy and Vusi continued to move in and out freely, the room at the back their private dining area whenever they wished to use it.

Outwardly, the trio had barely changed, except for the way they dressed and the expensive watches and rings that flashed in the light. Vusi was beginning to grow anxious, jumping up every now and then to peer into the main dining room. He was about to get up again to take another look when Sandy said, "Take it easy, Vusi. He'll get here."

"He's late," Jake said. "I don't like it ..."

Jake cut himself off as the door opened and a scruffy waiter walked in, carrying a tray with several cokes and a plate of burgers.

"Who ordered that?" Jake asked the waiter angrily. "Nobody comes in here without ..."

"Hi Doc," Sandy said softly.

Jake's mouth hung open in surprise, then he smiled.

"Hello, Sandy," the doctor replied. "Got you, Jake."

"I should have known," Jake said. "Mr Moodley would never send a new waiter in here."

"*Baba!*" Vusi hurried over and shook hands.

"I've been out there for several hours, long before you guys walked in. I had to be sure that we were safe."

They made small talk for a while, eating the burgers and sipping the cokes.

"We can't be too careful," the doctor said.

"What is it like in the townships?" Sandy asked.

"Absolute chaos. Our people are dying by the hundreds, and not only at the hands of the police."

"This business of the 'necklace'," Sandy added, "our own people killing each other. How can you win a war when there's so much infighting."

"An unfortunate side effect," the doctor said, spreading his hands helplessly.

"Anyway, you asked for my presence here today?"

"Yes. We require your help."

"Depends on what you want from me."

"The whole country must be turned into a battlefield, it's time we moved out of the townships and into the city centres. This is what I am here for. There are others throughout the country on a similar mission."

"What does this have to do with me?" Sandy asked.

"The cities are difficult to target. The reasons are obvious — the security forces are virtually on the spot. This limits our ability to make any significant penetration."

Sandy said nothing, his long legs stretched out in front of him, arms folded. He listened respectfully, eyes hooded. Both Vusi and Jake remained silent.

"We feel that if we can mobilise the street people, especially the runners employed by you, our success will be considerably enhanced. They are used to police harassment, know all the alleys and backyards intimately and can move from one end of a street to another without appearing on the pavement. If you will pardon the analogy, they are like hounded rats that can disappear into the gutters, only to reappear again at some other safe place. It's their normal lifestyle, their natural environment."

The doctor had stopped speaking and was searching Sandy's face for a reaction. Sandy was looking at the floor, his face conveying nothing except that he was listening intently.

"The waiters especially," the doctor continued, "are invaluable. They, together with the cleaners, are the only ones who can move freely in the white areas, especially the beachfront and the flatlands. They are a part of that landscape."

"For whatever you have in mind," Sandy spoke up finally, "let us assume that such a thing were possible — that they can be mobilised — what makes you think that they can be motivated to carry out your instructions? They are not political animals. And who would control them?"

"Their motivation," the doctor replied, "is money. As for discipline, well ... the method of payment will take care of that, reward for results.

What we have in mind is a short term thing, after which they can revert to their usual activities and be considerably richer in the process. With one or two pace-setters to lead them we can simplify ..."

"Such ringleaders are available, to spearhead whatever you need done?" Sandy cut in.

"It's a further matter that I wish to discuss with you."

"And the money to induce them to work for you?"

"It's available," the doctor said confidently, "with enough for yourselves."

Something in Sandy's face made the doctor realise he had said the wrong thing. "We can do what we have to on our own," he hastened to explain. "It's just that time is against us. All we require is reliable men to place some items in strategic buildings, at specified times. People like waiters or cleaners are always carrying things. No one will even ask them any questions. It's an opportunity for them to do their bit for freedom."

"Why do I feel that you're talking of time bombs? In blocks of flats and hotels?"

"It's the white man who has declared war. Why should only our people pay the price," the doctor said angrily. "Let them get a taste of what their own police are doing to our people."

"One second, my friend," Sandy said with a smile that only twisted his lips, his eyes expressionless. For a long moment that stretched into eternity he looked directly into the doctor's eyes.

"Up to now," Sandy finally said bluntly, "there were things I was happy to do. When you wanted bullets, we found them. You asked for revolvers — we obtained a few. From time to time you asked us to nick a car and leave it at a specific spot, we did that too and no questions asked. What you are now asking for ... one moment, please. Let me finish.

"You called this a short term thing, as if when it's over we can all de-mobilise and go home. There is no such thing. Look at what's happening in the townships, there is no control over the mobs ..."

"I told you that's an unfortunate by-product," the doctor interrupted Sandy.

"Okay. But there is something else. I no longer have any idea who the various groups of revolutionaries in this country are. You make it appear as if there is an oppressor and a liberator and that you represent the latter. I'm not convinced."

"Sandy, hold on!" the doctor was angry. "You are going off at a tangent. In the interests of the majority ..."

"Shit on that!" Sandy replied, equally angry. "My actions have never been governed by such considerations. Number One in my life is myself. If I can't live for myself how the hell can I live for others, especially when I don't even know who they are. And who are you, Doc? I know you are a revolutionary, but I don't even know your name, or what group you belong to. ANC? UDF? PAC? Some other movement? Don't tell me. I don't care to know."

"Okay, Sandy. I hear you. Until last week we had a plan that was ready to roll. Then the cops picked up Mo Govender. He was the lynchpin on which everything depended. Mo has been a part of our movement all along. When they removed him we were up the creek, without a paddle. That's when we decided to turn to you."

"I know nothing of Mo's political affiliations. My information is that he was nabbed whilst conducting some drug deal."

"Maybe so. Maybe there was a leak and they picked him up on a trumped-up charge. The reason makes no difference. We're asking for your help now."

"And I'm telling you the answer is no."

"Fine," the doctor said, his eyes narrowing dangerously. "You want no part of it?"

"None," Sandy replied.

"Do you speak for the others as well?"

"I speak for myself. Vusi and Jake can decide for themselves — they always have. I will do nothing to influence their decision and I will not stand in the way of any of your plans. But don't ask for my participation. I have no sympathy for the white man, he has blindly followed his leaders in suppressing us. Each of us responds to them in his own way. I do not question your methods nor do I judge your actions. I'm only asking that you count me out of your plans."

"That's fair enough," the doctor said, somewhat mollified. "I appreciate your directness. Vusi? Jake?"

"*Baba*," Vusi said, "all of us respect you. We know enough about you to realise that you are a man of the people. When you ask us for help we jump to it. But this is different. We need to talk to our own people and hear what they say."

"We can't act independently," Jake said. "Up to now what you asked for was small potatoes. I went along with Vusi when Phineas approached him. Any enemy of the white man is my friend. When I help him I do not see it as an act of disloyalty to the ANC. But you are now asking for a commitment to you and that's something else. What you propose, does it have the approval of my organisation?"

"They will not object to it. Check it out."

"Why have I not been briefed on it by them?"

"Because we are all fragmented and the real leaders are out of the country or in jail. We have to act independently sometimes. Make decisions on the spot. You yourself often do things on your own. The legend of *Aza Kwela* did not result from orders that came from the top. You are a maverick, the people on the ground love you. Men like you belong to all of us."

"Thank you. But I belong to no one. As for *Aza Kwela*, you are mistaken. I have never heard of the man."

Suddenly, the doctor stood up. "Think about it. I will make contact with you again soon." He left before they could answer.

Jake looked at Vusi enquiringly. When Vusi simply shrugged, Jake said, "I don't know. We've met this oke a few times and, in his own way, we know he's committed. But how does he know so much about me?"

"Not from me, Jake," Vusi replied. "But he's got me worried."

"Yes. He sounds very convincing. But something doesn't gel here. What is your opinion, Sandy?"

"He didn't sound as if he was certain about you being *Aza Kwela*. I got the impression he was trying to draw you out, using a bit of flattery."

"He sounded serious about this business of creating chaos in the cities."

"No doubt about it," Sandy said. "But it's your scene. You figure it out. I have my own business to see to."

"Okay, I'll see you guys," Jake said, a little absent-mindedly, his thoughts elsewhere.

∞

The entrance to the abandoned railway station, at the corner of Pine Street and Soldiers Way, was a black hole as forbidding as the gates of hell. The once-stately building, erected in the last century, retained little of its former glory. The interior, which in its heyday was packed with commuters and holidaymakers, was now occupied by a different species of the human race — the dregs of society, the despised down-and-outers whose permanent home was the cavernous concourse and the wide platforms. It was an alien world, smack in the centre of the city and less than a hundred yards from the glittering central business district.

From the pavement a dozen concrete stairs, filthy with pigeon droppings and human debris, led to shattered glass doors that still displayed glimpses of their ancient heritage; the heavy, carved wooden framework badly scarred but standing upright in silent protest at its degradation. On the topmost stair, dimly visible in the faint light of a distant streetlamp, a filthy figure dressed from neck to ankles in old sacking lay sprawled in what appeared to be a drunken stupor. The feet, bound with straps of the same sackcloth that covered the body, twitched occasionally and temporarily dispersed the mosquitoes that swarmed around the otherwise inert body.

A bird, its wings rustling loudly in the silence, flew over the drunkard and disappeared into the high ceiling. A second later there was a loud belch, followed by a rasping cough. The derelict sat up, swayed a little, then lifted a brown paper packet to his lips and took a deep swallow from the bottle inside it, smacked his lips noisily as he stood upright, taking a few uncertain steps towards the pavement.

When he reached the lamppost he hugged it with his left arm in a feeble attempt to maintain his balance, holding the paper bag high over his head like a precious trophy representing victory in some hard fought sporting event. For a while he held the pose, humming loudly and intermittently belching deeply from his ample stomach. Then, with a supreme effort, he straightened majestically and surveyed the street in front of him, like some decrepit lord of the manor standing at his castle doors. The face, streaked with grime, was in sharp contrast to the clear and intelligent eyes that darted from corner to corner, surreptitiously taking note of the unusual number of cars parked near the kerbs, each facing in a different direction.

He stumbled across the road, the filthy rags covering his feet occasionally flapping as he carefully placed one foot in front of the other before moving forward. When he reached the opposite pavement, in front of the Main Post Office, he contemplated the single low step that gave access to the walkway, raised one foot higher than was necessary, then quickly pulled it back. He tried again with the other foot, began to lose his balance, and pulled back again. For a full thirty seconds he considered his predicament, his body moving slowly from side to side. He waited a second longer, then lined his feet next to each other and, with a movement as ludicrous as his appearance, he hopped onto the pavement and landed heavily a foot away from the edge. He gave a triumphant bellow, took a celebratory swig from the bottle and cackled with joyous abandon. He began to hum again as he staggered forward.

After some thirty odd steps he stopped, bathed in the glow of several light bulbs that shone from the interior of a side entrance. As the bright lights hit his eyes he lifted a grimy paw to shield them from the glare. From under his covering hand, as he rolled drunkenly from side to side, he saw the dull glint of rifles and grim white faces. He began to move closer towards the interior, hugging the bottle tightly to his chest.

"*Fock off, yulle!*" someone shouted angrily from inside.

"*Ho, kerels, ho,*" the hobo slurred, "*a bietjie doppie, ou maat.*"

"*Gaan huistoe, dronkie!*" the voice hissed. "*Nou!*"

"*Ya, ya, ek is a dronkie. Lekker ou pellie, lekker.*" He backed off, almost tripped over his legs, then staggered towards the road. Halfway across he began to sing in an off-key baritone, the bottle high over his head.

"*Gozia, oh lekker Gozia*
Won't your mommy be surprised
when she sees that belly rise ..."

He danced a little jig in the centre of the road, scratched his head vigorously, took another swig of the liquor and careened wildly towards a store window. At the last moment, just when it appeared as if he was about to fall flat on his face, he suddenly stopped and began to chortle madly. In front of him, deep in the shadows of the entranceway to a tobacconist, were two more heavily armed men, their pale faces glistening in the darkness. He closed one eye, cocked the other and squinted at the soldiers, head lolling loosely on his neck. Then, grinning grotesquely, he put the bottle to his mouth and gurgled deeply. As he lowered his hand he burped and stepped forward, offering the bottle to the hidden men. When the stench of body odour, stale liquor and dry urine assailed the nostrils of the soldiers, they recoiled in disgust and swore at him, shooing him away furiously.

He danced another jig for their benefit, bowed deeply from the waist, gave an elaborate military salute and turned back in the direction he had come from. After a few steps he stopped, scratched his neck, then moved towards West Street. A low voice from somewhere behind him muttered, "*Sies!*" after which there was a hawking sound followed immediately by a spitting noise.

"*Lekker, manne, lekker.*" He waved his precious bottle with both hands and continued drunkenly on his erratic course. He started to sing again:

"*Ma sez, pa sez*
I must buy her stock-ings."

At the corner he crossed the road once more, headed towards the main entrance to the post office and reached inside his filthy garb, removed a loaf of mouldy bread and bit deeply into the crust. Over the top of the loaf he saw another clutch of camouflage uniforms, the shining faces, the glint of firearms. This group too was carefully hidden in the shadows, visible only from the position in which the hobo stood. He ignored them, placed his feet close together and attempted for a second time the monumental hop onto the pavement. He barely cleared the hurdle, staggered forward drunkenly, then fell to his knees. He dropped the loaf, hanging on to the precious bottle as he landed on his elbows, clutching the valuable cargo against his chest.

"*Hai!*" he yelled victoriously, the spittle flying from his lips as he laboriously got back onto his feet. "*Hai!*" he shouted again, then cackled drunkenly, belched, cackled again and moved forward, the loaf of bread forgotten as he gave another victorious jig.

> "*Chingola, hey bokkie*
> *one cigarette, two toffee ...*"

He stumbled on and, at the corner of Church Street, turned left towards the railway station from which he had commenced his journey. As he passed St Pauls Church he touched his forehead solemnly, shouted "Praise the Lord!" and then, at the top of his voice, screamed, "Ha-lee-luya!"

He crossed over Pine Street for the second time, on a zig-zag course towards the concrete stairs, singing:

> "*Someday, you will seek me and find me,*
> *Someday, of the days that shall be ...*"

He continued singing as he laboriously negotiated the stairs, adding words of his own creation in a parody of the original version of the hit song of the mid-fifties. A second later he disappeared into the darkness.

The moment he stepped onto the filthy platform a remarkable transformation took place. With a swiftness that belied his appearance, he unwound the rags from around his body, reached under the sackcloth garment and pulled out wads of towelling from around his waist. As he passed a sleeping *outie* he placed the bottle in the crook of the man's arm, then padded on bare feet in sure, long strides. As he ran alongside the high brick wall that separated the rails from the street he was breathing easily with no sign of strain in his face.

In less than a minute he noticed a glow in the sky, knew it was from the bright lights of the ageing Hotel Grosvenor, and slowed down. He was directly across from the corner of Soldiers Way and Queen Street. He stopped, bent his knees and, with a magnificent leap hauled himself to the top of the wall. When he saw the combi parked at the kerb his lips spread in savage satisfaction — all the windows were open, giving the "all clear" signal that had been agreed upon earlier in the day. He effortlessly scaled the wall, landed lithely on the balls of his feet, and with two huge strides reached the door, which slid open even as he reached out his hand. He dived in, pulled the door shut and began divesting himself of the stinking garment.

"Go Vusi! Get the hell out of here!"

∞

Twenty minutes later, after a quick shower and fresh clothes, Jake met Vusi at the corner of Victoria and Albert Streets. As they merged into the shadows Jake asked, "Did you ring the doctor?"

"Ya. Here he comes." Vusi took a step forward, waved his hand and stepped back again. The doctor sidled up to them and they moved deeper into the darkness.

"Vusi told me something went wrong?" the doctor asked.

"We were sold out," Jake snapped. "The place was crawling with riot cops in full camouflage gear."

"But how could they have known about ..."

"You tell me, buddy," Jake whispered angrily, "and make it sound good, my friend. I don't like being set up."

"You're suggesting I'm a SB stooge?" the doctor said, his voice rising. "Jake, come on, after all we've been through you can say this to me?"

"What we've been through means fuck all. Only the four of us knew about tonight. You, or your *maat* Phineas, is the SB's bumboy. Gimme some answers, Doc. Make it fast. Your time's running out!"

"Jake, please, cool it. I'm telling you there's no way I'd betray you. You have to know that."

"They were waiting for me, Doc. Their unmarked cars were facing in strategic positions. At this time of the night nobody parks there, there's nowhere for anyone to go. If I had driven up as planned I would have been plastered all over the place by now."

"You didn't drive up to the target?"

"No. I do things my way, buddy. It's why I'm still alive."

"But we agreed ..."

"And I went along with you. Vusi and I made our own plans."

"So you suspected ..."

"I suspected nothing. I simply took my usual precautions. When I got there at eleven they were already in place, an hour before I was supposed to drive up. You telling me this was a routine manoeuvre?"

"Jake, listen to me. I agree they were tipped off. There's no doubt about it. But when you accuse me like this, all you're doing is giving the real culprit space to get away. Can we just consider this coolly?"

"So be cool. I'm listening. And I don't have all night, Doc."

"This is not helping," the doctor began to say when Vusi cut him off with a chopping motion of his hand.

"Phineas," Vusi said quietly.

"No way. He's my most trusted lieutenant."

"Phineas, *baba*," Vusi repeated. "You, me, we know *Aza Kwela* and Jake same person. Phineas, he don't know this."

"So?"

"I say this: if you wanted to betray Jake you could do that long ago. The SB, they give anything to *bamba Aza Kwela*. Why they wait till tonight?"

"I think you're onto something, Vusi," Jake said softly. "They wouldn't have risked a gunfight tonight if they had a chance to get me alive."

The doctor was silent, gazing into the distance. Then he nodded, once, clapped a hand to his forehead and groaned. "I did something stupid this afternoon. When I was talking to Phineas I slipped up and said something like 'after *Aza Kwela* plants the bomb ...' Phineas is not stupid, he knows now that you're *Aza Kwela*."

"Shit, *Baba*!" Vusi growled.

"I should never have agreed to working with you," Jake said coldly. "I've always been a loner. Only Vusi ever ..."

"Jake, I'm sorry," the doctor said abjectly. "But it's not too late. Phineas has not been out of my sight since that slip up, except for the last few hours. I left him at Mashu. There's still time. Leave this to me."

"You'd better move it, pal," Jake snapped.

"Jake, before I go ... the bomb?"

Jake grinned crookedly, then gave a harsh laugh. "*Aza Kwela* never fails, my friend. The loaf of bread and the bomb in it is less than ten feet from a bunch of *Jahvers*. When it blows ..."

The post office clock boomed, the first of twelve strokes signifying midnight. As Jake and Vusi disappeared into an alley the muffled sound of an explosion rolled down the street.

∞

At first it was no more than a mild sensation on the back of his head. Half a minute later the nerves at the base of his neck began to bristle. When he felt the familiar pressure between his shoulder blades Jake knew he was being followed. Imperceptibly, he slowed down, located an angled shopfront and gazed into the glass. What he saw gave him no clue of any unusual activity behind him — there were far too many shoppers to distinguish a suspicious face.

Without significantly reducing his pace, he reached into his shirt pocket and extracted a cigarette, then patted his pockets in search of something with which to ignite it. When a man puffing on a cigarette came abreast of him, Jake gently touched the man's sleeve and indicated his need for a match. As he applied the fire to the tip of his cigarette he flicked his eyes across his cupped hands. Nothing. No sign to support his apprehension.

When he came to the wide entrance to the mosque he unhurriedly turned into it, then swiftly headed for the gates that led to the internal walkway. Hidden behind the high wall he considered his options. He could go left, alongside the rear of the shops and towards a second broad passageway from which he could exit onto Queen Street once more and emerge a hundred yards behind whoever was following him. The other alternative was to turn right, skirt the ablution area, take another quick right through the narrow passage and out into Cathedral Road. There was a further possibility — he could make a wide half circle to the rear walkway and slip along the patio towards the Grey Street entrance. He was about to move when he heard a shuffling behind him.

Cursing himself for leaving it too late, he quickly dropped onto a bench and bent over, fumbling at his shoelaces, ready to spring forward at the slightest hint of danger. From the corner of his eye he saw Applesamy, the caretaker, walking towards him. He gave a sigh of relief and began to straighten up. He was on the verge of greeting the old man, a staunch supporter of the Resistance and a good friend, when he saw the warning look in the stalwart's eye.

"Two men, Yacoob," Applesamy said out of the corner of his mouth as he pushed a broom in front of him. "They talking outside, maybe come after you. I see them behind you in Grey Street, see what look like guns inside their jacket. I follow."

Jake nodded, silently thanked the old man, quickly removed his shoes and socks and went into the interior of the mosque. He rapidly circuited the ablution area, padded across the tiles in his bare feet and entered the anteroom to the main prayer hall. He paused as he stood on the soft carpet and once again considered the several routes open to him, Applesamy's warning lending a new urgency to his movements. On impulse he headed for the huge doors that opened onto the courtyard.

As he crossed the rough cement ground and walked towards a pair of steel gates leading to Madressa Arcade, Jake reviewed his situation. Whether the men Applesamy had seen were SB enforcers was not a certainty, that they were trailing him was — his instincts had never failed him.

For two full days, since the night of the post office debacle, Jake had been on the move, stopping only to ring Hannah and reassure her. He hadn't gone near the store, kept his distance from Victoria Street, and spent the nights amongst the graves surrounding Badsha Peer's shrine. The regular devotees of the saint had no love for the cops, and, by extension, of the Security Branch. Jake had roped in Uncle Vallah, who maintained the shrine on a voluntary basis and whose credentials were faultless, and set up the communication line with Sandy. During the day he kept off the streets, only emerging for a few seconds before going underground again. Until Sandy obtained the all-clear signal from the doctor and confirmed that Phineas had been reached in time to silence him, Jake's safety was not guaranteed. He now regretted the restless urge that had caused him to hit the street and had placed him in his present predicament.

In Madressa Arcade Jake entered a store, went to the rear and lowered himself into a chair. It was a good vantage point, he had a clear view of the activity outside without being clearly visible to whoever was out there. Surrounded by musical instruments of every description, he took several deep breaths as he brought his pulse under control. The owner, Nad Pillay, was carefully tuning a grand piano that occupied nearly half the store. Jake was on safe ground, most of the shopkeepers knew him. The piano tuner, ancient beyond his years and the last of his breed, ignored Jake — all his senses were glued to the sound that emanated as he pressed the keys.

Jake had no qualms about remaining where he was, for hours if necessary. The old maestro was a veteran of the Casbah, had learned early in life that one of the essentials of survival required that no questions were asked of the likes of men like Jake — they came, they hung around for a while, they left. A routine affair.

Half an hour later Jake grew restless, wriggled his toes, then stood up and left the store, merging into the throng of shoppers, his eyes darting in all directions. Almost immediately his hackles began to rise, the sense of being watched intensified. He looked around casually, adrenaline surging through him as he prepared for fight or flight. He couldn't discount the remote possibility that the men Applesamy had seen were members of some street gang intent on seeking revenge, out to settle an old score. He realised then that it was pointless taking evasive action. The need to know if the SB was onto his number was overpowering. He decided to settle for a confrontation and establish once and for all who was pursuing him.

Having made the decision, a calmness settled over Jake and the feeling of uncertainty left him. He moved forward boldly. At the corner of the arcade and Cathedral Road he entered Langry's store, tried on several shoes until he found a pair that felt comfortable. He dusted his feet, thanked Goolam for the generous discount, paid, walked out again and almost collided into Louie Pullman, the legendary leader of the West Street Willies and an old enemy. Jake almost laughed with relief as he looked into the slitted eyes of his ancient foe and attempted to locate the back-up, the second man.

Louie was reaching into his jacket when Lang, an old timer with hundreds of street fights behind him, walked over with one hand behind his back. Louie dropped his hand, grinned mirthlessly as he took a step sideways and nodded several times.

"Okay, Jake. You live again. Not for long, *charkie*! Keep watching your back."

Jake shrugged as Louie disappeared into the crowd. He gave the thumbs up to Lang, said, "I owe you one, dad," then walked towards Brook Street.

The incident threw Jake off his stride. For the first time in his life he let his guard down. For three nights he had slept on the hard ground in the graveyard, he was tired, needed a shower and change of clothes. The thought of Hannah and a decent meal was tempting. On a whim he threw caution to the winds, changed course and headed towards home.

It was the first and last mistake he would ever make.

∞

Sam's eyes flew open, straining in the darkness. He wasn't sure what had woken him, but he was sure he had heard something. He turned his head sideways and looked at Sally. She was asleep, breathing regularly. Then he heard it again, a voice near the open window.

"Sam!" someone whispered.

Sam jumped out of the bed and pulled the curtain aside. Through the burglar guard he saw a shadow. "It's me, Sandy."

"Sandy! What the ..."

"Let me in. Through the back door."

Sandy's voice sounded urgent and Sam let the curtain drop without another word. He swiftly crossed the room, throwing a passing glance at

Sally, who was still sleeping. Sam had barely opened the door before Sandy quickly slipped through and closed it. "We have to talk."

"Are you okay?"

"Yes. But Jake's in trouble."

"Jake? He's asleep in his room. I ..."

"Sam, let's sit down. It's a long story."

Sam led the way to the kitchen and switched on the kettle. As they settled down around the breakfast nook, Sandy said, "The cops picked up Vusi an hour ago."

"Is it serious? I'll help, of course. But what has Jake to do with that?"

"You better hear me out. What do you know of Jake's political activities?" Sam suddenly had a sinking feeling in his stomach. Nithin's words flooded through his mind as he looked at Sandy apprehensively.

"Okay. You're not completely in the dark then."

Sandy took it from there, filling Sam in on the details of the conversation with the doctor. "Jake and Vusi must have been satisfied with his credentials. I'm not certain, but I think last week's bombing at the beachfront restaurant was a test case. Jake didn't tell me much about what was going on, which was fair enough, considering I was not a part of that bit of his life. But I know that Jake had reservations about this doctor character. Either the guy was a double agent or had some weakness, perhaps for money or women. Whatever it was, the Security Branch finally hauled him in, and in a short time they came for Vusi. Now the word is out that they're looking for Jake. Vusi would never rat on Jake, so I reckon this doctor oke is suspect."

"They haven't come around here yet," Sam said.

"Get him out, Sam. Now. There's very little time. Look, I'm going around the corner to the Asoka. Rabbi Bugwandeen's boys will help me to hustle Jake away, get him to a safe place. Start moving it. Bring him there fast."

Sandy was already out of the kitchen before Sam could say another word. In a few seconds he heard the door shut as Sandy let himself out.

"What is it, Sam," Sally asked sleepily as she walked into the kitchen. "I thought I heard voices in here."

"I can't talk now, Sal. Go into your room and stay there."

"Sam, I can see something is wrong, your face ..."

"I have to get Jake out. Don't ask any questions. I'll explain later. Tell you what, you get Hannah up. Ask her to tell Jake to get ready and grab a few clothes. He'll understand. I'm going to my room for some cash. Please do as I say. Quick!"

Sam rushed to his room and went straight to a cupboard. He grabbed a bundle of notes, dropped his shorts and slipped on a pair of trousers. He was lacing his shoes when he heard the banging on the door. He felt the walls shake from the heavy thuds. Sam ran towards Jake's room. They met halfway, in the passage. Jake was fully dressed.

"Too late, *boet*," Jake smiled.

"Through *Baji*'s annex ..."

"Sam, these guys are not amateurs. The house is surrounded." Jake was calm as he inserted a cigarette between his lips. "Better open the door before the bastards break it down."

Salma was already at the door. As she opened it a half dozen men pushed her aside and rushed in.

"Take it easy, *kerels*," Jake said. "Have some coffee."

As they roughly handcuffed him, Jake turned to Hannah and said, "Play it cool, babe."

When they bundled him out the door they heard Jake say, "Anybody got a match?" There was a loud thud, then silence.

∞

"There is no power on earth that can help you now," Karan said. "Jake has no access to anyone. No lawyers, no family, no court. Nobody."

They were sitting in Sam's office, a few hours after Jake had been taken away. Sam's face was tight with anger as he listened to Karan explaining Jake's position.

"But he has to be formally charged."

"Nope. And there won't be a trial either."

"But Karan, even a murderer has a right to legal representation."

"A murderer has a better chance than any political detainee. Look here, Sam. I'm as furious as you are. I'm a lawyer, I realise how they have subverted the legal process."

"So what do we do? Just sit here like political eunuchs?"

"Sam, we are absolutely impotent. We don't even know where they've taken him. It could be a week, a month, a year, before we hear anything."

"I can't tell my parents that. I spoke to Hannah earlier. She understands. Although she's been out of politics since they married, Jake hid little from her. But I have to do something, Karan. I can't just sit on my hands."

"I'll try, Sam. Perhaps somebody from the Legal Resources Centre, who know the ropes, may help. I'll also contact some of the big boys, guys with connections. But don't hold out any hopes. There are thousands of detainees that no one can trace. And Jake's a big fish, from what you just told me. Don't expect any results."

"I can't accept that there is no one we can turn to ..."

"I'm trying to be practical, Sam."

"I know. I'm sorry. I guess I'm a little emotional still."

The buzzer on Sam's intercom went off. He pressed a button, silencing the machine, then reached for the direct line to his secretary.

"Rushda, I told you I didn't want to be disturbed ..."

Whatever she said had silenced Sam, the blood draining from his face. The hand holding the telephone shook a little. He listened intently, then simply said, "Thank you," and replaced the receiver.

"They just arrested Hannah," Sam said blankly.

"Where ..."

"She was on her way here, crossing the road, when they bundled her into a car."

"Are you sure ... I mean ..."

"It was an official car. One of my girls saw everything."

Sam and Karan sat on the phone for the next few hours, trying everything they could think of, including calling a few of the better-known government stooges in the Indian community. All of them shied away from the subject, in a hurry to get off the phone.

They went to the CR Swart Square, where political detainees were normally taken. They were met with blank stares and blunt silence. When they persisted with their enquiries they were brusquely told to leave. One of the policemen, a senior official, pointed at the door and screamed, "Fuck off, coolies, before I lock you up too!" Sam was about to shout back when Karan pulled him away and pushed him through the door.

Back in the office, Sam said, "We're going about this the wrong way." He picked up the phone and rang Nithin Vania, asking him to come over urgently. He made a second call, to Sandy, and repeated the request.

Sandy was the first to join them. "When you didn't come over I drove past your home and saw the cops. I was waiting for your call this morning. Did your secretary give you my message?"

"I asked her to hold all messages," Sam replied. At that moment Nithin walked in. In a few words, Sam told him what had happened and how far they had gone.

"You're wasting your time," Nithin said. "These guys are like the Nazi stormtroopers. Not even God can get through to them."

"If you and Sandy can work on your contacts ..."

"This is not a criminal thing, Sam," Sandy said. "My connections don't extend to the Security Branch. These guys are unapproachable. They move in a closed circle. Even the *Motas*, with all their muscle, would not dare to try their luck at this."

"That's not what I'm suggesting," Sam said. "I'm beginning to appreciate just how insular these people are. I think we should use the guys on the street, the hardened criminals, the habituals who spend a lot of time inside. They are the guys who know the wardens and the prison staff. We should work from the bottom up, instead of the other way around. It's a long shot but it's all I can think of."

"Give us a few days," Nits said. "It's worth a try."

The few days stretched into a week. Just as Sam was beginning to give up hope Nithin made a breakthrough. "Come over to my office. Make it quick."

Sam didn't bother with the car, knowing he would make better time on foot. He was in Nithin's office in Short Street in under five minutes and his heart sank when Nits introduced him to a scruffy, wizened old man of indeterminate race who looked undernourished and out of work. Sam had expected to meet a prison official.

"This is Mousey," Nithin said. "He works at the Point Prison. Tell Sam what you told me."

Mousey sat up, puffing his chest out importantly. He spoke in colourful street jargon which neither Sam nor Nits had any difficulty with.

"Man's *simmer* the chow honcho, you know what I mean. No shit, daddy. If I don't move, nobody moves. I got the kitchen unders, like, you know. I tell you, *ek se*, nobody don't tune me false in this *tronk*. I got my aerials all over the joint ..."

"Do you meet the prisoners?" Sam interrupted. "Do you talk to them?"

"Hey, *ek se*, you okes are too much. I mean, they gotta chow, you know. Like a man said, I'm the *sarang, ou pellie*. Not even the *larnie kerels* jive me."

"Tell Sam about the lady," Nithin said.

"Ya, man, ja. You already *koosaad* me about her. Her name's on the chow list. Solomon! That's it!"

"Describe her," Sam said.

"*Lekker* thing. Tight little *ezie*. *Simmer* tunes la di da. Thee and thy style. Looks like a *bruin bokkie*."

"Okay, now look, I want you to do something for me. You do it properly and you can make some money for yourself."

At the mention of money a cunning look came over Mousey's face. "You see me right, *larnie*, and a man can *simmer* organise extra chow for your cherry. You leave it to Mousey. No shit man!"

"I want you to hand her a note from me. Can you do that?"

"Hey, *my maat*, you making *kuk* for me now? They *simmer* watch her all the time. The aunty in charge takes the chow from me. I only sight the *bok* now and then, you know what I mean."

"I thought you said you talked to her?"

"What's with this *larnie*, Nits?" Mousey complained, turning angrily to Nithin. "A man listens to the *bok* tuning with the aunty. I don't *simmer* get close to her."

"Okay, okay," Sam said. "Can you slip a note in her food?"

"Nay, *ou maat. Gott*! That aunty that's in charge, she's got *simmer* like searchlights. Don't miss nothing. If they *drik* a man doing that they can *simmer* turn me into a moffie, you know what I mean?"

Sam thought about it for a minute, then decided that Mousey was probably no more than a kitchen hand. He was convinced, though, that the man had seen Hannah. It was too much of a coincidence to be otherwise. And he was sure that there was some way he could get a message to her. He just had to figure out a plan. He decided to handle Mousey at his own level.

"Mousey," Sam said, "Just hold *kop* and don't come out sideways with me, you scheme what I'm saying? You play me for a *garach* and I'll *slaan* you stupid, *ou pa*."

Mousey's jaw dropped. His mouth hung open in amazement. "How come you jive a man all this time?" Mousey asked, without offence. "You give me your thee and thy for what?"

"Listen, Mousey. You sure you can't get a message to her?"

"No, boss. No way," Mousey replied respectfully, his whole attitude had changed and he sat up straight in his chair.

"But you see her? How often?"

"Two, three times a day, boss."

"Does she look alright? Any marks on her?"

"She looks *lekker*, boss. No shit."

"Does she see you?"

"She sees a man, ya. She knows me like, you know what I mean."

"Okay. What about the woman who is in charge of her?"

"Hey, *larnie*. That aunty is bad news. She's full of shit, boss. Don't talk to nobody. A real fuckin' *boer*, *ou pa*."

"Fine, I understand. You want to make some bucks?"

"How much?" The sly look had returned to his face.

"Plenty. Say a hundred bucks."

"A whole clip? Hey, daddy! For that kind of *marcha* a man can declare for you."

"Right. Come here tomorrow. We'll work a plan."

"Ya, boss. Sure. I'll be here. Same time, same place. No shit, daddy!"

Nits waited till Mousey left, then turned to Sam. "What's on your mind, Sam? We don't know where Jake is yet and you can't get a message to Hannah. That's obvious."

"I don't think Hannah knows that we are aware that she has been detained. Somehow, I must establish contact with her. It will boost her spirits tremendously. She won't feel so isolated and vulnerable. Once she realises that we're batting for her, have actually traced her, it'll do wonders for her morale."

"Worth a try, Sam. If we could find a way to bribe her guard ..."

"We have till tomorrow to come up with something."

"How's your old man doing? Is he still fixed on the sale?"

"Probably more so now. Jake's and Hannah's arrest has thrown him off his stride."

"Well, ... if you need me ..."

"Thanks. I'll see you tomorrow."

That evening, when Karan and Devi came over for supper, Sam told them about his meeting with Mousey. They started throwing around a few ideas on how they could get a message to Hannah, none of which seemed practical. It was Salma who finally came up with the answer, stunning them with its simplicity.

"Sam, you remember that yellow lambswool jersey you bought for me in Hong Kong?"

"Sally," Sam said irritably. "What has that ..."

"Do you remember it?" Sally demanded.

"Sure. Now, can we think of something sensible?"

"Do you remember how crazy Hannah was over it?"

Sam sighed in exasperation. "Yes, Sal. I remember."

"Well, that's it!" Sally shouted exultantly.

Sam looked at Karan and shrugged his shoulders, dismissing the subject for the time being and began to rise from where he was lounging on the floor.

"Sam, listen," Salma said. "Just listen. Give the jersey to this Mousey character. It's a unisex item so he shouldn't mind wearing it. Tell him to make sure Hannah sees him in it."

Sam was halfway up, on his knees. He lowered himself to the carpet, a smile playing at the edges of his mouth.

"Hannah couldn't find another like it anywhere," Salma continued. "She even embroidered the large red 'S' on the pocket for me. She was devastated when she accidentally scorched it with the iron. She can't fail to recognise it."

"And Hannah is no fool," Karan said. "She'll know it's a message from us. Sally, you're a genius."

The next day Sam briefed Mousey carefully on what had to be done and sent him off with the jersey.

The following afternoon Sam waited with Nits. Mousey was due to report back at any minute. Sam filled in the time by updating Nits on Dara's plans to sell off the Solomon Bros assets.

"He's stubborn as hell about it. Of course, he doesn't know that I have the details of the sale and who he is negotiating with. I don't want to cut things too fine. I must tackle him this weekend, before he signs the papers. I haven't quite worked out my strategy. Whatever, I'll see you on Monday with the figures and the financing."

The door opened and Mousey strutted in, the jersey rolled up in a tight ball and squashed under his arm.

"I did it, pally," Mousey said triumphantly, placing the jersey on the desk.

"Are you sure she saw you wearing it?" Sam asked anxiously.

"Ya, *ou maat*. She didn't see a man the first time but I just *simmer* coughed and she sighted it *lekker*," Mousey crowed.

"Did you do what I asked you?"

"Ya, boss. Man put his hand on the pocket, just like you said, and rubbed that 'S'. When she sighted that, I tell you, she *simmer* started smiling, like in the movies. I tell you, boss, that cherry looked like she was coming in her pants, you know what I mean."

"Did she give you any sign or something?"

"Nah, *larnie*. She just *simmer* shook her head and winked, you know, like this." Mousey began to demonstrate and Sam couldn't help smiling.

"But that cherry, she's got guts, boss. When the aunty asked her to eat her chow she said something like 'shopseller' and kept shaking her head at me, like she was saying yes. I think she was swearing the aunty."

"Mousey, you're a star," Sam said, his voice excited.

"Ya boss. That's me. Hey, you gonna make like that now?"

"What! Oh sure." Sam reached into his pocket and pulled out a roll of notes. Mousey eyed him greedily as Sam counted out a hundred rands and passed them over. As Mousey grabbed the money, Sam saw the hungry look on his face and passed over another ten rand note.

"That's the way, boss. The more you *spookoolate*, the more you *coomoolate*."

"Well," Sam commented drily, "You certainly didn't speculate much so far. But thanks. You've helped a lot. Keep the jersey too. Come over again in a few days. We'd like to know how she's doing."

"A man can do that, boss." Mousey said, snatching up the jersey. "We all darkies here, you know what I mean. United we stand, *ou pa*. Divided we still don't fall."

"Thanks Mousey," Nits cut in, walking him to the door. "Come over the day after tomorrow, okay?"

Mousey bowed profusely several times as he backed out of the office.

"What were you so excited about?" Nits asked Sam. "When Mousey said Hannah swore at the guard your face lit up."

"You didn't catch it? She sent us a message!"

"What message? I heard nothing."

"Hannah said: '*Choop, sala!*' It was her way of letting us know that she understood that we were communicating with her."

∞

It was Sam's second visit to the Friedman's since Hannah had been taken away. His mother went over daily and spent an hour or two with them. Moses welcomed him with his usual grave courtesy. Jehan, Hannah's mother, brought him a cup of tea as Sam set out the latest developments.

"It's not much," Sam said gently. "But as least we know she's well and in good spirits."

"And Jake, Sam?"

"Nothing. Only the devil knows where they've taken him. But we're trying."

Sam placed the cup on a stand next to him and leaned back in his chair, crossing his ankles. He looked worn out, dark rings around his eyes.

"Sam," Jehan said, looking at him with concern. "You must rest. There's a limit to how much a body can take."

"I'll be okay. It's just that with both Jake and Hannah away from the business the pressure is really on. And I'm worried about what's going to happen to them."

"Is there any way we can help?" Moses asked. "I used to be a financial consultant before I retired. If there is anything ..."

"You certainly can!" Sam replied, his face lighting up. "You can take control of the cash and the banking, and the paperwork. You too, Mrs Friedman. I'll rest easier knowing there's a family member on the shop floor."

"It'll be a pleasure, Sam," Jehan said.

"Come over tomorrow. I'll take you through the ropes. And I appreciate the offer."

"We are living through bad times," Moses replied. "Only God knows how it will all end. We were hoping to spend our remaining years in quiet retirement. Now the country's imploding and no one seems to be able to stop it. This government! It is stupid. Stupid!"

"There are none so blind as those who refuse to see," Sam said. "There's also the other saying about those whom the gods wish to destroy they first make mad. Seems to me this government is already stark raving mad. And whether we are all destroyed, together with them, is in the lap of the gods."

By the time Sam reached home he had made up his mind to finally confront Dara on the issue of the sale. He found Dara in his study, pouring over some documents.

"*Baji*," Sam said, getting straight to the point. "We must talk."

Dara folded his hands across his chest and leaned back in his chair.

"Sit down, Salim. I agree it's time to make the final arrangements."

"Is there any possibility of a rethink on the matter?"

"My decision is final. All that remains to discuss is the timing and the actual move. Everything is ready at Vis Kander's end. He has been patient. He knows the family is upset at the moment. I can't keep him waiting."

"The rest of the family may not be prepared to go along with you."

"It's not for them to decide. But speak for yourself. Are you against it?"

"*Baji*," Sam answered cautiously, "We are an integral part of this country. All of us, including yourself, were born here. It's the only life we know."

"You cannot talk about life without considering death. And you cannot perpetuate life by exposing yourself to destruction."

"But isn't giving in to evil, walking away from it without offering any opposition, in itself a form of destruction of all that is good?"

"Do you believe I haven't considered that? Our people have opposed the white devil for over a century now. What have we achieved? There comes a time when you must be realistic and concede the futility of any further resistance. In the final confrontation the Indian will be the scapegoat. Both sides are already mustering their forces. I see nothing noble in being the victim of someone else's stupidity."

"There is a huge majority of Indians who disagree with that conclusion. They see themselves as a part of the black struggle."

"Then they must act within the dictates of their beliefs. What is a majority anyway? The rabble always follows the most convincing speaker and who can say he is right and I am wrong. At least I have the satisfaction of knowing that I have no ulterior motive of my own, that my only concern is the welfare of my family. Can these weavers of dreams, who go around preaching some mythical non-racial future, claim the same motivation?"

"I don't know father ..."

Sam felt immensely tired, the weariness coming over him in waves. Every ounce of energy seemed to have been sapped out of him. He began to sink in the comfortable leather of the chair, overcome by a need to close his eyes and drift off to sleep.

"Salim," Dara said with feeling, "I understand what you are going through. But think of what lies ahead. If we don't act now we will be failing in our duty to our family. What is Solomon Bros without you and me? What will happen to those who depend on us to protect them? Can you stand to see the combined efforts of three lifetimes go up in smoke? Your grandfather, then me, and now you. We built this business. No one gave it to us on a plate. I saw the ashes of our hard work once, I experienced the pain. And what use is experience if we don't learn from it?"

"All I've ever wanted," Sam mumbled from the depths of his chair, "was simply to be happy ..."

"It is all I, and my father, ever asked for. It is the birthright of every person. But happiness is not something that is handed to you by someone else. Sometimes you have to fight for the little things. I have lived longer than you. I have seen my parents brutally slaughtered; I have seen terrible things done to our people. Now they have taken my son away. I don't even know if he is still living. They have thrown his wife into some dungeon. Each day their son asks me the questions his father used to ask me when he was the same age. I had no answers for Yacoob and now I have none for his son. Must I now watch him as he grows into a rebel the way Yacoob did?"

Sam could see the pain in his father's eyes, the lines on his face deeper than usual. There was anger there too, and a little despair. Sam had never before seen such a welter of emotions on any face.

"My father lived in hope. He dreamed that there would be a day when all of us would live in peace, black and white. Instead, he was butchered to death. After him I continued the dream. What did I achieve? Two of my children are rotting in jail! And tomorrow? Will they come and take you away too? I would rather dream in some civilized land where my children's ability and not the colour of their skins determines what happens."

Sam had listened to his father without interruption, almost in a trance. All he could think of was: I have no answers for you, father. You are like the Ancient Mariner in whose verbal spell I am helpless. You are very convincing and there's nothing I can think of to counter your arguments or refute your logic, but I am certain that we can cast off this albatross from around our necks and we don't have to go to some greener pastures to do so. Sam shook himself and started to rise, using the armrests to haul his body upright.

"I have been approached by an agent who is acting for somebody very big. Would you care to consider it?" Sam sounded as if he didn't care either way.

"If he can substantially better the present deal. There isn't much time to enter into involved negotiations. When can he see me?"

"I'll know in a day or two."

"Tomorrow, at the latest."

As Sam walked out he wondered why he had been so casual about it. He had approached his father with the intention of either dissuading him from selling out or presenting a firm counter-offer. Instead, he felt as if he no longer cared what happened, as if Dara had finally broken through his resolve and penetrated his defences.

"Perhaps," he muttered, "after I have had a good sleep ..."

chapter seven

Nithin: 1950

Nithin Vania walked briskly down Grey Street, crossed over West and continued along Broad Street until he emerged onto the quiet esplanade. At the edge of the pavement he stopped to catch his breath. That was when he saw them, out of the corner of his eye: three boys and a girl, all white. Two of the boys looked more or less his own age, around sixteen. The third was older and heavily built, with brawny arms and broad shoulders.

Instinctively, he knew he was in trouble.

They were still some distance away and had made no threatening moves towards him. But he was a lone Indian at night and in a white area, and that meant only one thing: he was game bait and in these parts it was always open season towards his kind.

He cursed himself for his stupidity, knowing that he could have taken a safer route. He considered turning back, then heard the laughter behind him as a boisterous group emerged from the brightly lit Plaza Hotel across the road. That avenue of escape was now as effectively closed as the one before him. He debated the possibility of outrunning them, realised he wouldn't get far before someone tackled him, and discarded the option. He decided to brazen it out, pretending a confidence he did not feel, and stepped onto the road. It was a futile gesture.

"Hey coolie! Where do you think you're going?"

He ignored the jibe and stared straight ahead. The sound of running feet reached his ears and he fought down the urge to bolt for it, knowing with certainty that once he turned his back to them he was a goner. In less than a minute he was surrounded.

"I asked you a question, *charkie!*"

Nithin saw the mean expression in the older boy's eyes and took an involuntary backward step, raising his fists.

"Fucken shit!" someone behind him said. A fist slammed into the small of his back. It wasn't a particularly hard blow and the strong muscles around his midriff absorbed some of the impact. The next punch caught him on the side of his face, high up on the cheekbone. The night burst into a million stars. Somehow he maintained his balance and, moving swiftly, aimed a blow at the boy in front of him, hoping to take him out and unnerve his younger companions. But they were too clever for him. With his hand held low he failed to see the sideswipe that kicked his left foot high in the air and spun him around. For a fraction of a second his body was completely in the air. Oh God! Don't go down now. Try to land on your feet. His panic-stricken brain was still shouting instructions when he hit the ground on elbows and knees.

"It's coolie bashing time!" someone from across the road shouted. He could hear the laughter as he tried to stand up. Then they were on him, two on his right, the other on his left. As each boot or knee slammed into him his body shuddered and sank until he collapsed into a heap. He was still conscious when they turned him over onto his back and straightened his legs with a brutal kick.

"Fucken bastard!" The bigger boy grunted as he drew back his foot.

Almost in slow motion he saw the huge boot as it moved towards his face. He tried to raise his hands, to protect his head, but his arms had gone numb and refused to obey him. Once again the stars exploded around him. Tiny lights were flashing in his eyes and performing a macabre dance before him. Nithin tasted the blood in his mouth as it mingled with the saliva and threatened to choke him. He tried to swallow, coughed, and heard his chest wheeze as it pushed the gore through his lips.

"Christ, Larry! You'll kill him!" It was the girl's voice and Nithin was surprised that he could hear so clearly. The pounding in his head seemed to have stopped and his eyes began to focus. They locked onto the dreaded boot, less than six inches from his face, then travelled upwards along the length of the body looming above him.

When his eyes reached the face he saw the vicious grin and the thin lips stretched over gleaming teeth.

The girl was further away, one hand on her neck. He thought he detected a look of sympathy in her eyes, then saw the older boy unzip his fly, the fingers going in. He pulled his penis out and waved it in the air. One of his mates laughed harshly. "Let him have it, Larry. Swazz on the son of a bitch."

The jet of urine struck him full in the face. He tried to turn his face to avoid the spray, only to find that he was virtually immobilised by the beating, his neck muscles refusing to respond. Suddenly it was over and they walked away. The girl lingered a second longer, he thought he saw her lips mouth the word "sorry", and then she too was gone. Somewhere above him he heard a window slam shut, then another, after which the silence reigned supreme.

Nithin lay unmoving for a long time, the humiliation welling up in him and overcoming the pain that was spreading through his body. Anger followed and with it a little energy returned and he tried to sit up. The effort was too much and he turned on his side, resting his head on his wrists and breathing through his mouth. Finally, with a supreme effort he pushed himself to his knees and braced his upper body by digging his fingers into the rough tarmac.

His shoulders swayed from side to side as he gathered his strength. Slowly, he raised his head and saw the lamppost a few feet in front of him. He began to crawl on his hands and knees. Painfully, inch by excruciating inch, he pulled himself upright. For a while longer he hugged the lamppost, the steel cool against his face.

Across the broad width of the road he saw the palm trees and the wide expanse of lawn. He knew there was a tap there somewhere, remembered seeing it on a previous occasion. With the thought came the stench of urine and the fetid smell spurred him forward.

When at last he found the tap he opened it till the water gushed out in force, then crouched below it, his knees screaming with torment. Holding his head under it for a full minute, he carefully washed his face. He felt a lump on his cheek, there was a deep cut on his lower lip and the inside of his mouth was raw. He ran his tongue over his gums, shifted the broken tissue over his inner lips, then spat into the puddle below him.

After a while he removed his shirt and washed it, splashing water over his chest. When he felt sufficiently clean he gargled repeatedly, then drank copiously. Closing the tap, he took several deep breaths, wincing in agony as his ribs protested harshly. Using his shirt as a towel, he dried himself. He ran his fingers over the welts on his upper body and almost bit his lacerated lip when he pressed his fingers against his ribs. He sighed gratefully when he realised that no bones had been broken.

"Hey, *bleksom*," he heard a gruff voice from the window of a block of flats across the road. "You think that's your bathroom? Go on, shake your black arse before I come down. They'll take you out of there feet first." Someone tittered loudly, followed by what sounded like a screech, "You better run, curry guts." This was followed by laughter. Nithin pushed himself away from the tap and headed for the subway under the railway lines.

The long walk to the graving docks loosened his muscles and the cool air cleared his head. When he reached the wharf where the ships were moored he slipped on his shirt. Just ahead of him a group of youths milled around a crane. Most of them were Indian or coloured, a few were African. One of them, a boy called Boya, saw him first and stepped towards him.

"Sheet, Nits! What happen' to you, man?"

The others began to crowd around him, plying him with questions, until someone silenced them with a raised hand and a sharp bark. He was a husky coloured, in his mid-twenties.

"Who gave you the globes, Nits?" he asked softly.

"*Wit ous*," Nits said. The two words were enough. No explanations were necessary.

"How long ago?"

"Fifteen-twenty minutes. Maybe longer."

"Where?"

"Corner of Broad Street."

"How many of them?"

"Three. And a *steckie*."

The coloured studied Nits for a moment, taking in the battered face.

"Let's get them, Jesse," one of the others said angrily.

Jesse didn't reply, he seemed to be thinking it over.

"Those white boys, they sport with us," he said at last. "We go after them we can't come here for a long time. You okes game for that?"

"Fuck it, Jesse," Boya said. "There's no graft here. Let's go *maklaar*."

"Joe?" Jesse asked, turning to a slim Malay. "Want to *neuk* them?"

"It's that time, man."

"Okay. We find them, we *khup* them. Let's move it."

∞

They drove around for the next half an hour in Jesse's battered Chev, trying to pick up the quartet's trail. Five of them were crammed into the car. The others, with little taste for what lay ahead, had backed out at the last minute. Nits was squeezed into the front seat, near the side window. He peered through the glass each time they passed a group of whites milling around a takeaway or nightspot.

Finally Jesse headed for Point Road and cruised around, ignoring the prostitutes that paraded on the pavements in their skimpy outfits. The prostitutes, in turn, shied away whenever they saw the packed car approaching. Their customers were the wealthy whites who drove by in their fancy limousines and paid the highest prices. The Japanese and Chinese seamen came next — they paid well and treated the girls with respect. The likes of those in the Chev was bad news and only meant trouble.

"If we spot them," Jesse said, "we hit hard and fade. Watch out for the *kerels*. You see a uniform you ..."

"That's them!" Nits cut in hoarsely. "In front of Smuggies. The guy in the blue jeans is the *sarang*."

Jesse pulled over and doused the lights. "Spread out. Don't make any moves. Tony, take the wheel. Stay in the car, Nits. Don't let them see you."

Nits smothered the relief that coursed through him. Although still simmering with anger, he hated gang fights. He wanted vengeance but preferred to do it his way. He was also aware that he wasn't really a part of the gang that was now so intent on seeking retribution on his behalf. There were other issues at stake — his beating was incidental to the prime motivation. At different times each of the others had been victims of similar acts; he was merely the spur that had goaded long-suppressed emotions. When the night was over he would be forgotten. He commanded no loyalty and was not deceived into any illusions of belonging.

Nithin looked at the boy at the wheel. Tony ignored Nits completely and concentrated on the crowd across the street. He left the engine running, revving it now and then. Nithin consoled himself with the thought that Tony's indifference towards him was nothing personal — Calcuttans were normally taciturn people and not given to long conversations.

There was a huge crowd of whites milling around the entrance to the Smugglers Inn. Nits could hear the loud rock music pouring through the open windows. Another, smaller crowd, was at the kiosk next door, jostling for service. Jesse, Boya and Joe were sipping cokes on the pavement and surreptitiously eyeing the jeans-clad boy and his friends.

Nits wondered what would happen now. Jesse and his friends couldn't get closer without attracting attention. They had no business being there and were not allowed near the Inn itself. Sooner or later someone would accost them — they would have to decide fairly fast or call it off. Nits couldn't help hoping that they would settle on simply getting into the car and driving off. It wasn't long before Jesse exchanged a few words with the others and headed towards the car.

Joe leaned his back against the door, his arms folded as he surveyed the scene before him. Jesse spoke to Tony through the open window. "Too many whites here," he said. "Let's circle around."

"Hey, Jesse!" Joe said softly, "They moving on."

Jesse casually looked over his shoulder. The foursome was walking away, together with a new girl they had picked up.

"Stay behind the wheel," Jesse said to Tony as he jumped into the back seat. Joe signalled to Boya to join them, then squeezed in next to Nits.

"Let them get well ahead," Joe said. "Then follow them. Use only the park lights."

Tony kept far behind, stopping the car from time to time when they got too close. Much later, when they reached the junction at Pine Street, Jesse stirred. "This is a good spot. When they turn the corner pull up in front of them. I'll take the big guy."

"Not yet, Jesse," Joe warned. "The entrance to the Railway Club is across the road. When those chicks start screaming a hundred *wit ous* will be on us."

"The girl's okay," Nits said. "Leave her alone."

Tony snapped his fingers. "The piecart! They're going to the piecart, man."

"Back up," Joe said. "Quick! Don't rev the engine. Reverse into West Street and go down Gardner. Get to the cart before them."

They parked in front of the Post Office and hurried down Church Street, then crossed over and melted into the shadows. Nithin followed them. In front of the piecart a large number of customers were standing around, eating and drinking; most of them were African night-workers with a sprinkling of Indians and two or three whites. In the distance the noisy group could be heard approaching, the girls screaming with laughter. When they reached the piecart they crowded the counter and addressed the African waiter rudely, the older boy strutting around cockily.

"C'mon, c'mon, kaffir," he snarled. "Give us some curry chow."

"Ja, baas. Indian curry, good curry." He held out a plate of sandwiches, inviting approval.

"What's this shit! Give us curry balls and roti. Shake it, *bleksem*."

"Sure, baas, sure. One mince kebab roll coming up."

"One? You making jokes? Gimme a half dozen."

"No problem, Boss," the Indian cook said as he came forward and joined the counter hand. "Give us a few minutes."

"You got two minutes, meathead. Now move your curry *ezie*."

The new girl laughed loudly, as if at a huge joke. The waiter kept nodding his head and smiling, ignoring the insults. The night-workers turned away, muttering to themselves, careful not to attract attention. In the shadows Jesse turned to Nits and said, "You want to take him, Nits?"

Nits understood what Jesse meant. It was an opportunity to get his own back. Jesse and the others would back him up. It was also a chance to prove himself, get in solid with the gang. He wouldn't have to put up a solo performance although he was undaunted by it. He simply had to initiate the action before it became a free for all. He decided he wanted no part of them. He had gone along with them until now. But it had been no more than a gesture of solidarity with their need to settle old scores. Beyond that, he had no desire to be indebted to anyone. If they wished to obtain satisfaction for whatever they had suffered at the hands of other whites, they could do so without him.

Nits looked at Jesse squarely, then shook his head sideways. Jesse stared at him, then shrugged his shoulders and turned away. "Okay, Boya, go cause it."

Boya grinned, his eyes dancing. Jesse had deliberately chosen him. He was a skinny boy, tall, with long arms and narrow shoulders. When he smiled there was a huge gap where several teeth were missing. He looked harmless, a pushover.

Boya sauntered over to the piecart, walking loosely, one hand digging into his pocket. When he reached the waiter he pulled out some coins and held them in the palm of his hands, making a show of counting them. He stood meekly next to the noisy white boy, continued peering into his hand and moving his lips. Then he looked up, his eyes locked onto the waiter. A signal passed and, without a word being said, the waiter uncapped a coke bottle and passed it across. There was a gleam in the black man's eyes.

As Boya reached for the coke he deliberately nudged the boy, making him spill the coffee he was drinking. The bully turned angrily but Boya was looking elsewhere, shaking the coke bottle, his thumb covering the opening and building up the pressure inside the bottle. Boya straightened up, blew a loud kiss at one of the girls, and gave her a crude sign with his free hand, shoving his thumb between the first two fingers of his clenched fist. He continued shaking the bottle suggestively.

"You little shit! You *fluking* a white girl ..."

"Fuck you, cockroach," Boya said, very loudly, still smiling.

The white boy looked incredulous. He couldn't believe he had heard correctly, then exploded with anger. Boya released his thumb. The jet of coke caught the furious boy squarely in the eye, momentarily blinding him. It was a perfect moment, a well-planned manouevre. Instead of following up Boya handed the bottle to the waiter and stepped back, hands at his sides.

Blue Jeans wiped his eyes, then looked around warily. He saw only the night-workers, none of whom met his glance. His mates looked a little confused, amazed at the Indian's audacity, uncertain of what they should do. Reassured, he turned towards Boya.

"You little bastard!" he snarled. "I'm going to stuff you back into your mother's ..." Before he could finish Boya burst into action.

What happened next was pure magic, a symphony of motion that was an absolute pleasure to watch. Boya's leap into the air would have shamed a professional ballet dancer. His forehead caught Blue Jeans flush on the nose and a spray of blood sprouted into the air. Boya's knee was already coming up, long before he landed on his feet. It connected between the legs, squarely in the crotch.

As Boya came down he pivoted gracefully on his toes and, with the full weight of his body behind him, slammed an elbow into the bloody face. It had happened so fast that those watching the display were stunned, unable to believe what they had just seen. Nits sensed Jesse and the others leave his side and move towards the other two boys. The night-workers were delighted. They shouted at Boya to "*Shaya!*" By then Joe and Tony had caught hold of one of the other two and methodically began to beat him up. The other had started to run when someone tripped him and he stumbled. Before he could fall Jesse caught him and lifted him above his head. He was still shouting, "No, not me" when Jesse slammed him to the ground.

Jesse leaned down, caught the boy by the front of his shirt and pulled him up. When his fist connected on the side of the boy's quivering jaw, there was a loud crack, the sound of breaking bone. The girls began to scream, panic stricken, their hands fluttering in the air before them.

In a few minutes three battered bodies were sprawled on the ground. Jesse and his friends were already across the road and turning the corner, the girls screaming as they ran in the opposite direction. An engine roared to life and the sound of spinning tyres screeched in the night. The waiter, who had scuttled off into the interior of the piecart, re-emerged and leaned over the counter.

"*Hamba!*" he shouted to Nits. "Go! Quickly. You not white. They take you away."

Nits looked around him. The night-workers had disappeared. The few other whites were nowhere to be seen. When he turned to leave he saw the waiter direct a jet of spittle into the face of the unconscious boy lying on the ground. Nithin walked fast along Pine Street, heading towards Warwick Avenue. When he reached Cathedral Road he slowed down. His body was hurting, his lower lip had swelled enormously. He could almost see its outline when he looked down.

He passed the Berea Road railway station, crossed over Lancers Road, then turned into Syringa Avenue. When he emerged onto Wills Road his spirits began to lift. He was on home ground. He knew every backyard and alleyway intimately. Some of the lights in the houses were still on and even the street lamps seemed brighter. He lowered himself onto the pavement, his feet resting in the gutter. He stayed that way for a long time, his mind blank.

Much later, Nithin stood and painfully stretched his body before moving forward again.

When he reached Verbena Road the urge to turn back almost overcame him. He reluctantly lifted the latch of the low iron gate and opened it. He walked along the side of the house and entered through the back yard. He was climbing the stairs that led to the back porch when he heard his mother's voice.

"*Kon che?* Nithin?"

"*Ji, ba.*"

He walked onto the porch and casually sat down in the dark, on the floor. He knew the darkness was sufficient to reveal only the outline of his body, his face hidden from his mother who was sitting on an old wooden chair near the kitchen. An overhead light bulb shone over her as she cleaned some vegetables. Nithin leaned against a wall and stretched his legs. In spite of the lateness of the hour it wasn't unusual for them to meet and converse in this manner.

It didn't surprise him when he saw her crane her head towards him, peering in his direction. He knew from past experience that mothers have an instinct about their children, a sixth sense that took over from the eyes and penetrated into the darkest corner. Her voice, when she asked him if he was all right, was full of concern.

He started to nod, then said in a strong voice, "I'm okay, *ba*. Just tired."

They talked for a long time, conversing entirely in Gujerati, their voices low. Once, from the interior of the house, he heard his father shout something unintelligible in an alcohol soaked voice. They ignored the interruption and carried on as if nothing had happened.

It was a curious relationship. Mother and son empathised strongly with each other. He revered her as a mother but spoke to her as he would a close friend. She in turn discussed things with him that a woman normally only spoke to her husband about. And she was never judgmental about Nithin's behaviour and seldom questioned him about his irregular hours.

Kamla Vania was not a particularly robust woman, with large luminous eyes and high cheekbones. She was thin, almost to the point of emaciation, her body contrasting startlingly with her strong voice and firm, decisive movements. Her skin was milk-white and unblemished, with hardly a wrinkle to be seen. She was not yet forty, and what she lacked physically she more than compensated with her strength of character. With an extra ten pounds in weight and a touch of make-up she would have been a real beauty. Kamla kept her home spotless, maintained an iron discipline over her three daughters, and treated her husband with respect in the presence of visitors and as a boarder when they were alone. Her ambition revolved around the need to ensure stable marriages for her girls and a homely environment for her son. Whatever other dreams she may have had were abandoned years ago.

There was a lull in their conversation and mother and son enjoyed the pleasure of each others presence. Nithin sensed that there was something on his mother's mind and the suspicion was confirmed when she spoke again.

"The Kanjees were here again today," she said simply, and waited for his response. When Nithin said nothing she added, "They're a nice family."

"Yes," he said dully, his voice neutral.

"We can't wait any longer. Daksha is seventeen, Darika eighteen. Soon they will be too old."

"Yes," he said again.

"Nithin ... your father should be involved in this, but ..." She raised her hands briefly, then dropped them on her lap.

"Have you spoken to the girls?"

"Not yet. But they are good girls. They won't object."

"So you will accept the proposals."

"The Kanjee boys are very decent and work hard in the family business. And the girls will be together, in the same house."

"How much will we need?"

"The girls' family pays for everything. And it will be a double wedding. The Kanjees are a big family and very well known. We can expect to feed a lot of guests."

"Don't worry about it. I'll find the money."

"We'll have to buy two sets of jewellery and presents for the boys' family. Clothes for our girls and also pay for the priest and ..."

"It's okay, *ba*. How much do we need immediately?"

"Rings for the boys and some things for the mouth-sweetening when I give them the answer."

"What kind of rings, *ba*?"

"They have to be eighteen carat. Anything less and we lose face. They'll cost at least five pounds each."

"How much time do we have?"

"I asked them to come over the Sunday after next. I suppose I could delay a little longer. But they may not come again if they get the impression that I am looking for a way out, to decently turn them down."

"That won't be necessary. Let them come over. I'll have the rings before then. I'll also have the money next week for the other things. Let's think about the wedding expenses after that. I don't want you to worry about it. Okay?"

Nithin had no idea where the money would come from and he offered no explanation as to how he would go about acquiring it. And his mother asked no questions. He had said he would get it. For her, that was enough.

"Did he find a job yet?" he asked, changing the subject. He never referred to his father in any other way and only spoke to him when he absolutely had to, which was hardly ever.

"No," his mother sighed. "But he tries."

"When he's sober," Nithin snapped. "Which is never."

"It's a weakness, Nithin. They say it's a disease that some men ..."

"It's the only disease I know of that can be bought in a bottle."

"We've been over this before, Nithin. Let it be."

"Where does he get the money from? He never has a penny for us but when it comes to his liquor ..."

"Nithin, leave it. He does odd jobs, when he can get them."

"We're supposed to be *Bunyas*, *ba*. Who ever heard of poor *Bunyas*? The others all have their own businesses."

"It's not his fault," she said, angry now. "After the government refused to renew his licence he opened a small store and carried on until we lost it all in the riots. Even then, he went and worked as an ordinary waiter until they kicked him out and gave his job to an immigrant. Until then he was a good husband and a good father. You blame him for taking to the bottle?"

"That was years ago, *ba*."

"Not everyone has the strength to keep bouncing back. Come. Eat something and go to bed."

"I'm not hungry. You go ahead, *ba*. I won't be long."

He waited until he heard the door to her room being closed, then reached behind an old wooden cabinet and pulled out a crumpled packet.

He extracted a cigarette and placed it in the corner of his mouth, away from the swollen lip. He struck a match and applied it to the tip of the cigarette, wincing in pain as he tried to draw the smoke into his chest. He looked at the flame as it burned down. When it reached his fingers he dropped it and tilted his head back.

Money, Nithin said to himself, is as elusive as the worst bitch in town. And like the bitch it prostitutes itself to the strangest of people. It's loyal to no one, makes great men out of intellectual midgets and reduces giants to insignificant nobodies. It flows to those who least deserve it and deserts those that have every right to possess it. Like the bitch who humbles herself to the filthiest of men, it gravitates towards those who have the courage to grab it forcefully and employ it to acquire even more wealth. Suddenly, his reason rebelled against his logic and he shook his head violently to dispel the thought. A spasm of pain shot through his neck and he forced himself to relax.

Slowly, he moved his head from side to side. Frustration and anger, the most futile of all emotions, twisted his belly into a hard knot. With an effort he contained his emotions by removing his persona from the scene and taking on the role of observer. When he ceased thinking subjectively he directed his brain to the more tolerable aspects of the acquisition of wealth. Whatever the rules that govern it, he thought brutally, I'll master them. Thousands of others have and so can I. Far lesser intellects than mine have amassed it, why should I fail? He sat there for a long time, smoked several more cigarettes, and contemplated his future. As he alternately formulated and rejected one option after another it didn't occur to him that, central to his motivation, was his mother's happiness rather than the need to acquire wealth for himself.

When he finally headed for his room he was certain of only one thing — that he would sleep badly that night.

∞

In the forties and the early fifties, before Nithin decided to claim the Casbah as his personal fiefdom, small family owned tailor shops proliferated in the Indian business centre. They catered to a clientele that was made up of all race groups. Whites, in particular, preferred being fitted out in made-to-measure suits crafted by these superb masters of the sewing needle whose outstanding ability and meticulous attention to detail had spread their reputation throughout the country.

The *darjees*, noted for their scrupulous honesty, charged ridiculously low prices in exchange for what was nothing less than artistic excellence. An additional bonus was that they unfailingly handed over, together with the completed garment, the left over pieces of fabric which they insisted would serve a very useful purpose at some later date. When their shortsighted patrons brusquely pushed aside the off-cuts as valueless and scorned the sage advice, the *darjee* invariably rolled them up carefully and, together with the cut sheets, meticulously filed them away.

"You never know," they always said sadly to such customers, "you maybe damage the suit, the elbows get worn out. Sometime it get torn. Then come back. I repair for you, do invisible mending, very cheap. The cloth belong to you. It always here."

It was surprising how often they did come back, smiling foolishly and regretting their earlier rash behaviour. There was never a problem, they always left with a happy grin, the repairs often effected while the customer waited. And they were never charged for the cloth.

"Come again," the *darjee* repeated with a smile. "You never know. Life is funny."

The *darjees* seldom advertised, except for the neat signs on their windows, usually in gold leaf. There was, however, nothing modest about how they named their businesses or the slogans accompanying those names: "Brittania Tailors — for the world famous BT. drape cut"; "Dattar Tailors — bespoke tailors and costumiers"; "Jagan Bros — for the man of distinction only"; "Regent Tailors — for the look of Royalty"; and "Ranchod Bros — we teach the experts".

One dear old man, in particular, had become a legend in his own lifetime. He operated from a tiny office on the first floor of Lakhani Building — a fair-sized double storey block at the corner of Grey and Queen Streets. A crude hand-written sign at the entrance simply stated: "Bhana Makan — Tailor". If ever a man was brutally exploited by virtually every customer that walked through his door, old Mr Makan was that man. Bhana Makan's charges were the lowest in town, his workmanship better than most. In spite of this he seldom, if ever, received full payment for his efforts. He accepted whatever work came his way, from an elaborate three-piece suit to repairing a minor flaw in a fabric, and remained as poor as a doormouse. Throughout the city he was famous for one simple fact: he was an easy mark. He charged a ridiculously low two pounds and ten shillings for a complete suit and was lucky if he received a fraction of it.

"On account," his customers always said as they piously walked away, after having given him a pittance in payment. However, they never failed to take the garment with them.

"Yes, yes," Old Makan would reply sadly, seldom even bothering to look up from his worktable.

The same customers came back to him, over and over again. And they brought their friends with them.

"Got you a new customer, Mr Makan," they would say, in a tone that implied great friendship towards him. And, as always, he would just say, "Yes, yes," and nod merrily, his round moon face reflecting beatific benevolence. On the very few occasions when his liver acted up and he mildly asserted himself with those whose arrears continued to mount, his customers, who knew him only too well, were cunning enough to act affronted and callously attempted to intimidate the portly old man by shouting loudly: "I said next week, didn't I? My God! After all these years of supporting you, is this how you treat me now?"

"Yes, yes," Bhana Makan would nod absent-mindedly and take on the additional work.

The odd thing about him, though, was that he was neither stupid nor foolish and trusting. It was simply in the nature of the man he was.

"Life goes on," he would say, frustrating those who gave him well-meant advice on how to run his business. "It's their *karma* not to pay. My *karma* not to get paid."

In the last few years of his life he became, what was for him, extremely loquacious. To the simple "yes, yes" he now added, in a quiet sing-song tone, the plaintive statement: "Time and tide waits for no man. Bhana Makan waits for everybody."

For years after his death many astute businessmen always replied, to those looking to pull similar tricks on them and seeking credit facilities, with the famous "yes, yes" and then adding, scornfully, "Who do you think I am? Bhana Makan?" If he was a legend during his lifetime, he became immortal after his death.

Not far from the Makan workshop, at the corner of Grey and Prince Edward Streets, deep in the angle formed by those two roads, was the store owned by the Ranchod family. The glass entrance doors were recessed into the alcove formed by two large plate glass windows, both of which tastefully displayed the latest fabric in vogue overseas. In each window a tailor's dummy rotated slowly on an electronically operated stand. The dummies revolved twenty-four hours a day, seven days a week, and were brightly lit by small spotlights strategically placed around them.

To their more thrifty neighbours, who often shook their heads at what they considered an unnecessary extravagance, the Brothers Ranchod always said, "Not a waste of money. Movement attracts, people stop and look. Good for business." And indeed it was. There was always a customer in the store whenever it was open for business. Equally good for business was the brothers' faultless attention to cleanliness.

Long before the day had commenced, when the streets were still relatively empty, one brother or the other would be busy with a bucket of water and a broom, washing the entranceway and the pavement fronting the store, right up to the edge of it. They even swept the rubbish in the gutter, collecting it in the empty bucket and disposing of it in a bin.

"Mainat ma saram namre," they would say to the early bird that gave them a second look. "No shame in hard work," they would repeat occasionally in English.

The brothers were a dignified pair, extremely prim and proper, even when they were the butt of rude jokes punned around their family name. The local wags, often out of pure envy, would shout *"Ben chod* Brothers!" and sometimes even the cruder *"Raan chod* Brothers!"* — always from a safe distance and would hurry away before either brother could have stepped out. They needn't have bothered. The Ranchods never stooped to the level of such rabble — they simply ignored them.

At night, when the stores had closed down, the spotlessly clean recessed area around the Ranchods front door offered a heaven-sent retreat to the local youngsters who lived close by. It provided comparative privacy on all sides. From early evening until late into the night it was a haven away from the crowded flats and humid residential blocks that dampened the spirits and stifled the creative urge.

On a Friday evening, just after eight, a week after Nithin had been beaten up, several boys were happily ensconced within the spacious enclave, indulging in small talk and laughing merrily. The heat from the ground was still rising and most of them had unbuttoned their shirts to catch what little breeze came their way.

Nithin stood a few feet away, his back against a lamppost. Physically, he was a part of the group. Mentally, he was miles away. His thoughts were jumping all over, unable to fix onto any one item for more than a few seconds. Underlying the turmoil within him was a deep feeling of depression that he couldn't shake off — rent, rings, roti and glad rags, he kept repeating to himself. A few miserable pounds, pieces of paper, was all that he needed to keep his promise to his mother and save her from the unthinkable embarrassment of postponing the engagement and plunging her into despair. All he had in his pocket was just over three pounds, from his newspaper sales. He needed at least another twenty to make up the shortfall. The thought of borrowing the money, which was hopeless in any case, didn't occur to him. The concept was alien to his nature.

He was contemplating the long walk home when Moosa Gani crossed the road towards him. When the other boys saw Moosa their eyes lit up and they began to smile. The boys idolised him and although Moosa, like Nithin himself, only joined them a few times during the month, he was welcomed into the circle with a camaraderie that Nithin had never enjoyed. The difference, Nithin knew, was that Moosa lived across the road, whilst he was from another district and could never be considered a local boy.

"Hey, Moosa," they chorused. "Howzit, man?"

"Hello," Moosa said simply. The boys immediately re-arranged themselves, creating space for him in the centre.

"How you doing, Moosa?" a good-looking boy by the name of Raman asked warmly. "You ducking us these days?"

Moosa laughed softly, his tone warm and friendly. "Never do that, Ray. You know how it is, have to be at the shop early every morning, stay till late. You all know what it's like ..." His voice trailed off as he lowered himself to the ground. The others immediately began to settle comfortably. When Moosa sat down they knew he would stay longer than he normally did. And with a bit of luck he would even give them a few songs.

There were few singers in the country that could equal Moosa's crooning. And he was versatile. He had the unique distinction of being able to belt out the latest Hindi or Western numbers with effortless ease and could switch from one to the other without pausing for breath. Had he chosen to make a career out of his singing prowess, in either genre, he would have shot to the top overnight.

The boys around him were mystified by his refusal to appear in public. The obvious answer, that he was acutely shy by nature, never occurred to them and they would have refused to believe it if anyone had proffered the explanation. Without exception, they were all afficionados of Hindi ballads and highly critical of even the most polished performers. Their deference to Moosa's voice was a measure of their appreciation of his talent.

The fact that Moosa appeared somewhat downcast and a little withdrawn was a big plus for the boys. They knew that whenever he was feeling down the chances of at least one song from him was a certainty. All of them were aware that Moosa had, in the not too distant past, been through a brief but deeply romantic interlude that had ended with crushing finality and left him devastated. That Moosa never referred to it, not even obliquely, only enhanced his stature amongst them.

To Nithin, as he watched them, it was a lot of soppy crap, emotions that people indulged in when there were no forbidding clouds on their horizon. This bunch, Nithin was thinking, and their tomorrows, are taken care of by their parents, whilst my future and that of my whole family is my sole responsibility. Moosa's private source of unhappiness is raw beans compared to what I am faced with.

Although Moosa may indeed have confined his grief to some private corner of his heart, the reality was that there are no secrets in the Casbah — unless they pertained to money. Wealth and the financial worth of any individual was not a subject for discussion, it was strictly taboo. The richest lived as simply as the poor and a family's status was determined only during an engagement or a wedding. It was then that a display of ostentation was not only acceptable, it was obligatory. It sealed forever a family's standing in the community and established its seniority.

And, as in any other place where people live in close proximity to each other, the Casbah was a hotbed of gossip. As long as a topic steered clear of any reference to *paisa* — to money, it was accorded the highest possible form of *carte blanche*. It was a safety valve, a catharsis that made life bearable and added spice to an otherwise mundane existence. High up on the list was the slightest intimation, the subtlest of hints, the barest tinge, of sexual intimacy. And during an interlude when boredom was making the gossips tetchy Moosa had provided them with a glorious opening.

Moosa's so-called "affair" with a girl who lived in the same block of flats as he did eclipsed even the grand passion of the Indian cinema. The fact that the stories doing their rounds contained very little of the reality of the situation was immaterial. The matrons, and of course the spinsters, were in their element. The teenagers were thrilled beyond belief, gleefully responding to every new development as a blow in favour of their own hoped for emancipation. They were careful, though, that they enjoyed no more than a vicarious pleasure from the infamous episode lest they themselves fall victim to the very same notoriety. They had been weaned on gossip and were fully *au fait* with its prime requisite: to survive it had to be constantly fuelled by innovation. And during a lull when no juicy news was forthcoming the accusing finger would commence its search for fresh victims and woe betide the girl who had displayed any sympathy towards the luckless couple.

Moosa, of course, had been the architect of his own misfortune — he had gone beyond the rules of the game. To smile at an unmarried female neighbour, to exchange pleasantries from a reasonable distance, was acceptable only if done in passing and was the outcome of pure chance.

Moosa, however, had foolishly committed the cardinal sin of holding the hands of the girl of his dreams and looked at her with undisguised tenderness. And, what was more, to the scandalised horror of the entire neighbourhood, they had gone beyond such blatant aberration — they had actually touched foreheads and whispered intimately to each other.

"For a very long time!" the devastated woman on the second floor cried when she repeated the incident to the girl's parents, and then proceeded to spread her venom along the length and breadth of the street. "More than a full minute! Saw it with my own eyes."

"Maybe five minutes," she added later. With each repetition, much to the consternation of the two families, the duration of the infidelity was progressively extended. And, like moths drawn to a bright light, more eye-witnesses were coming forward. Naturally, it was unheard of to question the veracity of their observations. Indeed, it would have been an act of social suicide to incur the "righteous" anger of any woman whose story was subjected to even a hint of a doubt.

That was the end of the great romance. Within a month the girl was proposed, engaged, married, and hustled off to an unsuspecting family from the far north. Moosa never saw or heard from her again.

"We were stupid," was all Moosa ever said to the boys in the corner. "I should have asked my mother to approach her folks before the rumours started."

"God's will," Haresh, the oldest in the group had said. "Not meant to be. It's better this way."

"That's a lot of jive," Raman had said scornfully. "Moosa should have *hucked* the *bok* out of town fast. They would have begged him to marry her then."

The debate amongst the boys continued long after Moosa's little dalliance had been forgotten by the gossips, who had latched on to a far juicier topic concerning a married woman who had accompanied her husband to a dinner and dance at a private hotel.

Nithin was on the verge of moving on when Moosa began singing an old classic. He had to admit that Moosa's rendition was flawless, perhaps even outclassing the legendary Mohamed Rafi. As he sang, the fingers of Moosa's left hand tapped out a rhythm on a matchbox. The effect was mesmerising, and had a soporific influence on Nithin. For a while he allowed himself to be drawn by it, obtaining a sorely needed respite from the demons that plagued his mind.

It didn't take long for Nithin's mood to change. The demons returned with a vengeance. A surge of anger coursed through him. I don't need this shit! he swore silently. No one looked at him as he walked away, heading towards Victoria Street.

At the corner of Bond Street Nithin saw John Farley sitting on the boundary wall of the old Methodist Church and stopped to talk to him.

"They seem to be enjoying themselves," John said, pointing to the group in the distance.

"Why shouldn't they?" Nithin scoffed. "The only thing on their minds is which *jol* to go to tomorrow night and whether they'll be lucky and pick up a stray."

Nithin hoisted his body onto the low wall and reached for his cigarettes. He offered John one and they lighted up. Nithin relaxed as he drew the smoke deep into his lungs and felt a little of the tension leave him. In John's company he felt at ease, they were kindred souls who had no need to maintain any false pretences with each other.

"You okay, Nits?" John finally asked, breaking the silence.

"I guess so," Nithin replied, flicking the butt of his cigarette onto the street and watching the shower of sparks as it hit the ground.

"Those dents on your face healed fast," John observed. "They'll be gone in a week, I reckon."

"They're the least of my problems. Right now if I don't lay my hands on some *marcha* fast I'll be in shit street."

"That bad, huh?" John said quietly. "I know the feeling."

"This time it's heavy. I need maybe twenty quid by Monday or I'm sunk."

John gave a low whistle. "That's a lot of *caracas*, pal. Where you gonna get odds like that?"

"I'll make a plan." Nithin had tried to sound flippant but his voice gave him away.

"Nits," John said. "You're not tuning me false? You really in that big a shit?"

"Reckon I am," Nithin replied wearily.

"Don't you have any friends you can hit for a loan? How about those guys down the road."

"When you're *bunse* you have no friends. And those guys there, they wouldn't buy me a beer if I didn't treat them to a few first."

For a while they sat there side by side, each lost in his own thoughts. Then John offered Nithin a cigarette and placed another in his mouth. As he applied a match to Nithin's cigarette he said quietly, "Maybe there's a way out."

When Nithin didn't respond John asked, "You with me, *maat*?"

"Ya."

"Okay. Remember the old Manhattan Music Store in Cross Street?"

"Sure. Old man Soni runs it now."

"Right! Now listen *lekker*. When you go into Fishy's Gulley, behind the stairs that go up to the flats ... you know, where the okes take the strays for a quickie ..."

"I know the place."

"Ya, okay. Well, a little further inside, at the back, there's a burglar gate and behind that there's a low window. That window leads into Soni's store. In the dark you don't see the gate too well. But it's there."

"Well?"

"I reckon we could break in easy. You game?"

Nithin's head snapped up, his eyes searching John's face. "You mean that, John? You're not *charfing* me?"

"I wouldn't jive you, Nits. And I could do with a few bucks myself."

"Is there good stuff there, John? Gold?"

"Ya. And I know a *larnie* in Victoria Street, a pawnbroker. He'll buy anything, no questions asked."

"I don't know ... the cops in this town are fuckin' good."

"Nits, wait. Listen. We take only a few things. Play it cool and don't disturb anything. It would be a long time before they even realise it's missing. That's the trick. Don't be too greedy."

"You've done this before?"

"Nah! But my cousin Googs does it all the time. He's never been caught. He reckons that even if the *larnie* notices something missing he's sure to blame the staff. And they never call the cops. The way these okes underpay their help they're too scared to give them the shits. Anyway, that's what Googs always says."

"Does Googs operate around here?"

"Nope. He lives in Sydenham. He only hits the stores in Overport."

"What about the broken window? When the *larnie* sees that ..."

"Not if we do it right. You remember when I worked for that carpenter? I learnt a few things then. I can open that window easy, no damage. We rub some dust and grease over it afterwards, hide the scratches like ..."

"What about the burglar gate?"

"I've looked at it several times, Nits. The lock's a piece of cake. Googs taught me a lot about opening them, all the different locks. It's big, that's all. With a bent nail and wire I reckon I could crack it. Let me tell you, I've had my mind on this for some time. I just don't have the guts to go it alone."

"What about the okes that go there to bust a pipe."

"It's a favourite ganja spot, sure. But not on Friday nights. Only the locals go in there and on Fridays they all head for the suburbs. But we know them, if they're there we just play it cool and wait till they're gone."

For a long while Nithin didn't say a word. He sat there, slumped forward, his elbows on his thighs.

"Okay," he said finally, snapping his fingers. "What time is it?"

"So who's got a watch," John laughed, raising an empty wrist.

"Around nine thirty, I reckon," Nithin said. "Look John. If we're going to do this it has to be tonight. If I think about it I know I'll change my mind."

"Tonight's okay," John said. "But a little later, after the people in the flats upstairs have settled down. But that's no big deal. They mind their own business and only their lav windows are on that side."

"Let's take a walk past there, sort of size things up."

They jumped off the wall and walked down Bond Street. The narrow lane was virtually in darkness. Most of the street-lamps were faulty and the only illumination was the dull glow cast by the flats on either side.

They turned into Cross Street, passed the deserted entrance to the flats, and as they walked past the jewellery store, they casually glanced at the shopfront. The display window was narrow, the bronze trellis guards rolled down. The interior was completely obscured from the outside by display units on which were arranged a variety of cheap cosmetic jewellery and trinkets.

Nithin and John crossed over Prince Edward Street and continued towards Short Street. At the corner they loitered for a while, smoking cigarettes.

"You think there's good stuff inside?" Nithin asked doubtfully. "The window is full of crap."

"I've been inside, to pay the old lady's account. The real gold stuff is in the back."

"Let's do it," Nithin said decisively.

"Okay. I'll get a screwdriver and some tools. And a torch. It'll be black as a pecky's *ezie* in there."

∞

True to his word, John gained access to the interior without breaking anything. The lock on the burglar gate wasn't as simple as it looked and they hadn't expected to find the bars after they opened the window. For over thirty backbreaking minutes John had battled with the six huge screws that held them in place, working more by feel than sight. After that it had taken another ten minutes before they could, using their combined strength, budge the old stationery cupboard far enough to squeeze in.

Nithin couldn't believe their luck. The back of the store was a burglar's dream.

It was pitch black, except where Nithin shone the torch. The gold glittered as he swept the beam over it. They looked at the dazzling array in awe, holding their breath to contain the excitement generated by the yellow metal. A rivulet of sweat trickled down Nithin's forehead, the torch trembling in his hand.

"*Gott!*" John kept saying in a strangled voice as he peered over Nithin's shoulder.

With the torch in front of him Nithin moved deeper into the store, John close on his heels. They maintained absolute silence, only their heavy breathing betraying their presence to each other. They stopped when they reached an open cubicle. It looked like a tiny office. There was a small desk and a grey metal cabinet in one corner. Nithin tried the handle. It was locked. He shone the beam over it, then whispered to John, "You think you can open it?"

"What for?" John whispered back. "Everything is out there."

"I have a hunch about this," Nithin said softly. "Think about it. None of the display cases is locked, a few of the glass doors are not even fully closed. Could be the really valuable stuff is in that cabinet, one piece could be worth a whole shelf of what's out there."

"Then it would be in a safe."

"I don't see one. And there's something else I just remembered. I've heard of the owner of this place and I'm sure only his family members work for him. He doesn't employ outsiders. So why lock the cabinet? Look, it's worth a try. If we blank out we lose nothing. Okay?"

John shrugged, then reached in his pocket for the thin, flexible file he had used to unlatch the window.

"Careful," Nithin said, "don't leave any scratch marks."

John grunted as he fiddled with the recessed lock, using a combination of thin wires and the file. Time passed and Nithin began to grow uneasy. He had barely said, "Leave it, John," when he heard a click and the door swung open. When John stepped back Nithin directed the beam over the interior and sighed.

"Just old shoe boxes. Probably full of accounting records."

On impulse, Nithin lifted the lid on the nearest box. When he saw the contents his hand started shaking and he dropped the cardboard cover to the floor. He steadied his hand and breathed deeply.

"Fuck me gently!" John said behind him, his voice hushed.

The erratic shaking of the beam passed back and forth over the money, huge stacks of banknotes neatly clipped together. They had been carefully sorted into various denominations, the smaller notes on top, the largest at the bottom. John lifted the lid of the next box. It was full of notes. There were six boxes in all.

Their eyes had grown accustomed to the dark and they could dimly see several more boxes on a shelf lower down.

"There's thousands of pounds in there," John said reverently.

"A hell of a lot more," Nithin said in a shaky voice.

"Let's grab it and get out of here."

"Easy, John. We don't take it all. Remember what you said? Let's not make the mistake of being too greedy."

"Shit, Nits! Why the hell not. This is not stuff we have to sell. It's cash."

"I liked what you said, about buying time. Googs had the right idea."

"We'll never get another opportunity like this. They'll never suspect us."

"Maybe not. Maybe it won't even come to that. You know what this money represents, John? It's *uplung*. Hot money! The owner will never be able to explain it away. His fear of the taxman will be greater than his loss."

"All the more reason why we should huck the lot."

"John, the owners of this store are *bunyas*. They're my people. I know how their minds work. We take a little from each box and he'll only miss it when he counts it. That's a pretty big job and you can be sure he doesn't do that often. But he'll look over the contents regularly, that's for sure. By the time he realises some of it is missing he'll be confused, but he'll never suspect an outside job — no burglar would leave all this behind. He may even suspect his sons, start believing they're messing around. He'll simply thank his gods that his fortune is intact. And that's how far he'll go, apart from moving it to a safer location."

"And if we take the lot?"

"Then all hell breaks loose. He'll know it's an outside job."

"But you said he won't call the cops. What did you say this money is? Hopelong?"

"*Uplung*," Nithin said, smiling. "He still won't call the cops. He'll do something worse. Much worse. He'll call the *Motas*."

They were whispering and standing so close that Nithin could see the fear jump into John's eyes. "The Crimson League?" John was shaking, his voice breaking.

"We'll never get to spend more than a few pounds of it. Every newspaper boy, street vendor, shopkeeper, barman and waiter will be on the lookout. The eyes will be everywhere. Even the cheap hoodlums will be on the prowl. They'll question every tenant in the flat above and across the street. And when the heavies call on them they'll hold nothing back. How sure are we that no one saw us?

"Perhaps from a window as we walked down the street? And the *chinglaans* know everybody that lives around here. They know you. They'll remember we were around tonight. Sooner or later the *Motas* will narrow the field. You can bet they'll get around to us."

While he had been speaking, Nithin had tightened his belt as far as it would go and loosened the top two buttons of his shirt. Carefully, he reached into each box and removed an equal amount of notes without significantly lowering the level of the contents. His fingers moved efficiently. As he finished with a box he shoved the money inside his shirt and lined the box as close to its original position as he could assess. Finally, he buttoned up again.

"Try and lock the cabinet, John. Don't rush it."

Before they left they removed all traces of their presence. It took more effort to pull the cupboard back in place than it had taken them to push it away. By the time they had it in position they were gasping for air. John struggled to replace the bars and tighten the screws. By comparison the window seemed easy. They spread the dust evenly over the frame, secured the lock on the burglar gate and obliterated any scuff marks on the ground. Nithin shone the torch around several times, in wide arcs, seeking any telltale signs. Satisfied, he nodded at John and they walked away.

It was almost two in the morning. They were back in Grey Street, perched on the wall once more. The money was wrapped in an old newspaper and hidden behind some plants near the church door, together with John's tools. It was simply a precaution against any patrolling policeman that decided to search them for ganja or a pipe.

"We did well," Nithin said with satisfaction. "It will be a miracle if anyone in that store finds any signs that someone had broken in."

"It was tough work," John groaned. "My back is killing me."

"Think about the money. The pain will disappear so quickly ..."

"Tell me again," John begged. "How much?"

"Twelve hundred pounds!"

"Each?"

"Each."

"Say it again once more, Nits. This time set it to music."

"One thousand two hundred pounds," Nithin sang, moving his shoulders and snapping his thumb against his fingers. "For each of us, sweetheart. For each of us!"

They shoved each other playfully, laughing as they shadow boxed and almost fell off the wall.

"And we're safe, huh?"

"No doubt about it, John."

"You're a pretty sharp guy, Nits," John said, unable to hide his admiration. "The way you covered all the angles. Pure fuckin' genius! And I'm glad now we only took a little. For a while there the temptation was too much."

"You're pretty good yourself," Nithin said, his voice sincere. "But let's save the compliments for tomorrow. We're a good team, John. There's an idea I've been toying with over the last few days. But it requires capital so I didn't give it too much thought. Maybe now I can give it serious consideration. How do you feel? We can talk about it over a beer at the Globe tomorrow — tonight I guess."

"You're on," John said, looking around. He hopped over the wall and retrieved the two bundles of newspaper, handing one over to Nithin.

"Take care, John," Nithin smiled. "See you tomorrow night?"

"Sure. And hey, if you get mugged on your way home I can always lend you a few bobs." John was chuckling as he walked away.

"Not a chance," Nithin threw over his shoulder. "They'll have to kill me first."

∞

Nithin slept soundly for four full hours, then had a leisurely bath, using several buckets of water and a generous lathering of soap. Back in his room he slipped on his best pair of jeans and prized "Marlboro" shirt. He pulled on his socks and stepped into his moccasins. It was almost seven thirty and he was ready for the day. From the back of a drawer he removed some notes and folded them.

"Nithin, did you get enough sleep?"

"*Ji, ba,*" Nithin answered. "Are the Kanjees coming over this week?"

"Yes. I'm not sure what I'm going to say to them ..."

Nithin smiled naughtily, then said, "Have I ever let you down?"

When she looked at him eagerly he handed her the twenty five pounds. "For the rings and whatever else is needed. Pay the rent too and buy some groceries."

When he saw the look on her face, he quickly reassured her. "There was a lot of work on the ships and the newspapers sold well. I also took an advance from Mr Seedat against the next few weeks' sales. I have to go now, *ba*. Don't worry if I'm late. I think the papers will move fast again today."

"Come here," his mother said, raising her hands. He knew what was coming and leaned forward but she surprised him. Instead of hugging him as she usually did she touched her fingers to his head, then raised them to her own, cracking her knuckles loudly. It was almost a sacred honour, a rare accolade, the ultimate blessing. He started to smile, then saw the solitary tear rolling down her cheek and wiped it away with a forefinger. He turned abruptly and walked out.

Nithin strode briskly down Old Dutch Road, turned into Warwick Avenue and walked along the outer wall of the Squatter's Market. Within ten minutes he was at the southern end of Grey Street. He turned into Saville Street and entered Lakhani Chambers.

The offices of the *Guardian* were already a hive of activity, bundles of newspapers were piled near the door and overflowing into the corridors. Nithin walked into an adjoining office. A tall, bespectacled man looked up and smiled. "My ace salesman," he said by way of greeting. "Bit late today, are we."

"Hello, Mr Seedat. I'll be sending over a friend of mine to collect the papers. I have a few things to do but I'll set him up. Is that okay with you?"

"Sure, Nithin. Everything alright with you?"

"Yes, fine. You may not see me for a while. I have to run now."

He took the shorter route through Cathedral Road into Queen Street and entered the Bottom Market. The stallholders were busy setting up, the fishmongers at the far end rushing around frantically. In less than an hour the market would be packed solid, the customers pushing and shoving each other as they tried to make headway.

The fishmongers, when Nithin passed them, were busy hauling large boxes of dry ice and tubs of frozen ice cubes. Tons of fish were coming in through the massive doors, in trolleys and wheelbarrows. At the Brook Street entrance the seine netters were offloading several truckloads onto the pavement. Nithin gave them a wide berth, then stepped close to a young boy, whispered something in his ear and patted him on the shoulder.

Nithin moved on, a little faster now, heading towards the Indian bus rank. On the bridge itself the noise was almost deafening. The bus drivers were revving their engines, clouds of smoke billowing around the exhausts and rising upwards. Commuters, their baskets pulling their shoulders down, were hurrying onto the ancient buses or joining long queues for the next one to arrive. Newspaper sellers and the usual street vendors darted in-between the shoppers, stopping only to make a sale before rushing off. The bus conductors, their voices rising above all other sounds, called out their destinations from the first step of their vehicle: "Clare Estate, Clare Estate, Clare Estaaate." Others shouted "Duffs Road, Duff's Road, Duff's Rooaad" or "Puntan's Hill, Puntan's Heeeel".

Across from the bus rank, at the edge of the slope behind metal railings, a rangy Indian in tight jeans and a knitted cap did a brisk storage business. Inside a roped off enclosure were hundreds of baskets and huge carrier bags, brimming with produce. On each container was a tag with a number on it. For a tickey per person, regardless of the number of containers, he provided a useful service that enabled the shoppers to continue their purchases of fresh vegetables and fruit without being encumbered by heavy loads that not only made it difficult to move in the crush but was also a strain on their weary arms.

Nithin saw the boy he was looking for and waved at him, beckoning him over.

"Listen Siga," Nithin said as he took his arm and pulled him aside, "I have a present for you."

"That'll be the day," Siga scoffed, "A *bunya* never gives anything for free."

"It's your lucky day. You still want my spot?"

Siga looked at Nithin suspiciously. "You *charfing* me, Nits?"

"I'll make a deal with you. But listen *lekker*. You know how many papers I sell on a Saturday morning?"

"Two, three hundred. You're the only *Guardian* seller ..."

"Double your guess, *maatie*. You still won't be close. The *Guardian* peddles propaganda, not news. It's twice as thick as any other and sells for an *ottie*. It doesn't take the fish long to soak through the flimsy trestle paper. For a penny the *Guardian* is cheap wrapping paper. You can't buy old paper at that price. That's what they're buying, not news. By one o'clock on a bad day I go through six, maybe seven hundred."

Siga looked incredulous, his lips moving as he tried to work out the commission on such sales.

"I have a runner who brings me fresh stocks from Saville Street. I get a tickey for every dozen. I clear at least fifteen bob on Saturday alone. And my runner's a sharp *lighty*. He swipes bundles of them from the corridors each time he goes over. That's all profit. I give him a *gron* at the end of the day, sometimes a little extra. The Friday evening sales are also pretty good."

"You're jiving me, Nits," Siga said. "Don't fuck around.""

"No shit, buddy. And I've already told Seedat you'll be calling on him. If you move fast you'll be back before the rush starts. The runner's waiting for you at my usual spot. Ease your way carefully with Seedat and you'll be okay. He has no idea where his papers end up. You interested?"

"What's the deal?"

"A quarter of all you make. You'll score five times more than you do selling those mags."

Siga's white teeth flashed. "That's a lot of bucks, *maat*. I'm gone."

"Okay. Just one more thing. The runner's my man and I have my aerials at the *Guardian* offices. I'll always know, down to the last *ottie*, what you make. You play it straight, don't sink a few bobs for yourself, and you're in for life. You *toomlela* me and you'll lose those pearls in your mouth."

"Fair, my *maat*. You can trust me."

"We'll see. You better get going. I'll check you later."

They parted, moving in opposite directions, Siga breaking into a trot. Nithin crossed over the bridge, skirted the squatters' market and entered Jailani's Café. He bought two curried pies and a coffee, then stood on the pavement eating and watching the frantic movements of thousands of people as they went about their business. He had two more of the round pies before he was full.

Sated, Nithin walked towards Etna Lane, sidestepping nimbly from time to time to avoid bumping into the dense mass of humanity that covered every inch of the pavements. It wasn't long before he had escaped the throng of people and was crossing over Old Dutch Road and heading towards the extension of Etna Lane. With the exception of a few children playing ball the pavements were empty and Nithin slowed to a leisurely stroll. Halfway down Etna Lane he walked into a cluttered yard.

Dicky de Lange was busy outside a wood and iron out-room, stacking empty beer and cane bottles into a milk crate. Grease-covered wrapping paper and pages of old newspapers were scattered carelessly everywhere and fluttered in the breeze.

"Howzit, General," Nithin called.

Dicky looked up, then smiled crookedly. He was a short, wiry coloured in his late twenties, with compact shoulders and muscular arms. His normally thick ginger hair was cropped close to his skull and he was dressed in a loose T-shirt and khaki pants.

"Howzit, Nits," Dicky said, "You're looking good."

"What's with the *cheese kop*?" Nits asked, looking at Dicky's head.

"Too fuckin' hot," Dicky smiled, running his hand over his head. "Looks like you had a busy night," Nits waved his hand at the litter in the yard.

"You know what it's like. We shebeen okes come into our own on a Friday night after the bars close down."

Nithin nodded. They sat on an old log and chatted for a while. Up to a year ago Nithin had spent a lot of time with Dicky, picking up odd jobs and making a few bobs out of it. It was Dicky who had told Nithin about the job on the wharves and introduced him to the foreman. "You'll be paid about a *blik* a square yard," Dicky had told him, "and you'll have to scrape like mad to get rid of old paint and the barnacles. You graft fast you'll easily clear maybe five square yards in a coupla hours. That's five bob, Nits. A few days a week and you'll make good *marcha*."

Nithin did well and, because the foreman was Dicky's good friend, he made sure the guy with the blowtorch blistered the paint carefully for Nits before he moved on to the others. It was hard work, though, and Nithin's fingers were usually raw by the time he finished, the rough piece of tin that he used as a scraper drawing blood which trickled down his wrist and into his armpits. Even on a bad day he seldom walked away with less than ten shillings in his pocket.

When Nithin started selling newspapers in the early evening and on the weekends, Dicky had said quietly, "Make the bucks, Nits. But look around. You're a brainy *ou*. Don't waste it, you don't want to end up an old bully hustling on the corners. Your *mense* are business people, it comes natural. Give it some thought."

"I'll need big bucks for that, Dicky," Nithin had answered.

"Keep thinking about it. You keep looking for a break and it's sure to come up and surprise you. Don't walk in a dream, keep your eyes open. When you see it, grab it. Don't let anybody stop you. If you're in a tight spot, you get opposition from someone, hit first and think afterwards. Unbalance your opponent. If you can get him mad, lose his temper, you'll have the edge. But keep out of trouble if you can. It wastes good time."

Coming from a man like Dicky, and there was probably no finer street fighter anywhere in the city, it was the best advice Nits had ever received.

"You haven't been around lately," Dicky said now, looking at the cuts on Nits' face. "There are no marks on your knuckles. How come?"

"A few *wit ous* piled into me. I had no chance."

"You saw them coming?"

"Ya."

"Then you had a chance."

"It's history now," Nithin said. "I'm doing well, *boet*. You need anything? Load up on your stocks? I've got the odds if you need it."

"Nah! This is a cash business. I'm set pretty good. Tell me about the *wit ous*. You reckon we could find them?"

"The guys at the docks took care of them. But they were doing me no favours. Forget it. Right now, I need ten *kaaitjies*. The best you got."

"When the hell did you start smoking zol?" Dicky asked angrily.

"It's not for me," Nithin laughed. "I have to return an old favour. What's it now? Still two *bliks* a stick?"

"Not for you. It's a shilling, what I pay for it."

Dicky disappeared into the shack. When he returned he handed Nithin the paper tubes, each about twice as thick as an ordinary cigarette. "This is *rooi* zol, Nits. From the Umgeni Valley. Not some loco weed."

Nithin bobbed his head and handed a pound note to Dicky. When Dicky hesitated Nithin said, "Take it, bro. I've got more of that, whenever you need it." He stuffed the packets into his socks.

They chatted for a few minutes more, then Nithin said, "I've got to make tracks. I'll see you soon." They patted each other on the back when they parted.

Nithin was feeling unusually happy as he sauntered down the lane, the sun pleasantly warm on his back. "Time to repay an old favour," he said aloud. "And settle an old score." The thought of what lay ahead gave him a good feeling. The prospect of rewarding a friend and hassling an enemy was particularly pleasing.

Mansfield Road, when he emerged on it, was free of traffic. Up ahead, in Cromer Lane, he could hear someone banging a hammer against steel. The harsh clang reverberated down the lane and echoed in the distance. When he drew level with the Bhana House he saw several chaps working on a bus.

"Howzit, Nits," one of them shouted and waved.

"Howzit, Dilip" Nits shouted back, without stopping. The Bhanas operated a fleet of buses and were decent people. However, they were not a family you trifled with. They were a tough bunch who gave no quarter and asked for none. They kept pretty much to themselves, avoiding trouble when they could — which, in their business, was almost impossible. They took it in their stride.

Near Curries Fountain Nithin turned left and entered the grounds of Sastri College. Old Soobiah, the caretaker, stood outside his cottage leaning on a spade handle.

"Hello, Tata," Nithin greeted him.

"Nithin? Hey, good to see you, boy. What you doing at your old school?"

"Just passing by and felt like saying hello to you and Mandla. Is he still here?"

"There," Soobiah pointed into the distance. "Near the toilets."

Nithin passed the tennis court and climbed the broad stairs that led to the hall and classrooms. Mandla heard the footsteps and turned around. When he saw Nithin his face broke into a huge grin.

"Neets! *Unjani mkai?*"

"*Sapile*, Mandla. *Wena?*"

"*Lungile, bafana.* You look sharp, Neets."

Nits led the way to a garden bench that was stuck against a wall nearby.

"How's things here, Mandla?"

"For a good kaffir like me?" Mandla laughed. He spoke fluent English, with a street accent, but only when he was in the company of friends. At other times he spoke only in Zulu, kept out of the way and minded his own business. There was no other way he could keep his job — except on that one occasion, the weekend before they threw Nithin out of school for fighting on the grounds.

Even now, almost a year later, the memory of that Saturday was fresh in Nithin's mind. It was why he had come over today. When Nithin looked at the playground he could actually see the events as they had unfolded, it was like looking at a movie screen.

They were playing cricket, about nine of them, taking turns at the bat while the rest fielded. Ratilal Bhagwan, a bright, cheerful boy, was at the crease; Nithin behind the stumps. Farouk Moosa, bowling with deadly accuracy, had just delivered a wide ball that whizzed past before Nithin could catch it. It rolled towards the entrance gate. One of the white boys from the nearby Mansfield High picked it up and, with three others, strutted over, intent on causing trouble. They knew the Indian students would never dare to retaliate, would quietly allow themselves to be bullied, even though they outnumbered the white boys by more than three to one. The boy who had picked up the ball shoved Rati in the chest and snatched the bat from him. His friends began pulling out the stumps and tucking them under their arms. When Nithin walked over the boy with the bat turned to Nithin and smiled nastily.

"You, curry guts, come and kiss my arse."

The boy bent over, lifted his jacket and presented his backside to Nithin. When Nithin didn't move one of his friends chortled, "He's waiting for you to drop your pants. He wants to lick your mudbox."

Nithin just stood there, looking at the pimply-faced boy who was speaking. Nithin knew that if he backed down now and Dicky heard of it, whatever these bullies could do would be mild compared to Dicky's angry response. That clinched it. Nithin's eyes narrowed. *Unbalance your opponent. Make him lose his temper, get the edge on him.*

"Fuck you!" Nithin said loudly, "And your mother too!"

The first boy straightened and turned around, then swung the bat angrily. Nithin waited until the flat wood was so close it looked as if it couldn't miss. At the last possible moment he ducked under it and swung a roundhouse punch that connected squarely on the side of the jaw. As the boy went down Mandla rushed over with his broomstick. Then a funny thing happened. The Indians, who had no need to run, fled in one direction, the white boys in another; the boy on the floor moving sideways on hands and knees like a huge crab looking for a hole to crawl into. Then he jumped up, raised a hand to his jaw and stumbled after his friends who were fast disappearing into the distance.

Mandla burst out laughing. Nithin grinned, pleased with himself. They looked at each other and gave the thumbs up sign.

"Better go," Soobiah said as he walked over. "Those boys will come back. They won't be alone. I'm going to take my family away for the weekend to my brother in Clairwood. Just go before they get here."

Early on the Monday morning a prefect entered the classroom and asked Nithin to go to the staffroom. He followed the prefect and, when the older boy knocked on the door and stepped back, Nithin turned the handle and walked in. As he closed the door behind him he saw the white boy, one side of his face swollen to almost twice its size. There were two men in the room: Nithin's form-master and a tall white man in a green blazer and a green tie. Nithin wondered why the principal wasn't there.

"This the boy?" the man in the blazer asked the boy with him. The boy nodded.

"Nithin," Mr Barsu said, his voice sounding unnatural, "This is Mr Swart. He has come to complain ..."

The visitor raised his hand, brusquely cutting Mr Barsu off in mid-sentence. He held his hand where it was, forbidding any further conversation as he studied Nithin speculatively.

"You don't look like much," he said finally. "I believe you hit my boy with a cricket bat."

"That's not true!" Nithin burst out. "I ..."

"Shut up," Swart spat back angrily, his face contorted. "You only talk when I ask you to. Understand?"

"Yes, shut up," Mr Barsu said.

"Now," Swart said, rubbing his hands together, "we could call the police and have you locked up." Suddenly he smiled expansively. "But we won't do that. Boys will be boys after all."

Nithin sighed with relief. "Thank you, sir."

"He'll be expelled," Mr Barsu said. "No doubt about it."

Nithin wondered what had happened to Mr Barsu's accent. He sounded like a white man, even more so.

"No, no, Barsu, that won't be necessary. We were all boys once," Mr Swart said, smiling and rubbing his hands. "No need for such harsh measures."

"Of course, of course," Mr Barsu said, "Boys will be boys."

"But he must know that what he did was a bad thing. Discipline, hey?"

"Yes, yes, discipline," Mr Barsu agreed profusely, looking sternly at Nithin. "Very important for character building." He was still speaking in his newly acquired accent and looking at the visitor submissively.

"And respect for his betters. He must be put in his place. After all, manners maketh the man."

Nithin was beginning to worry. Something was wrong here. Mr Barsu was smiling too much and agreeing with everything the other said. Why didn't Mr Barsu ask for his version of events? Why had he not called on the other students and asked them what had happened? He had simply accepted that Nithin was guilty and had to be punished in some way. Nithin was still worrying about it and failed to see Swart's left hand as it swung towards him.

The fist caught him above his ear and shook him. He was still reeling when the right hand landed on his temple, the force of the blow turning him around. Swart's kick sent him stumbling forward and he slammed into the far wall. He turned around, totally disorientated, his ears still ringing. Swart was in front of him, smiling cruelly and taking his time. The knuckles landed flush on the bridge of his nose, he felt the bone give, then his legs turned to rubber and he slumped to the floor.

Somewhere far away, he heard voices. "That about squares things up, wouldn't you says so, Barsu? Just a schoolboy thing. The two boys went for each other. Nothing to make a fuss about."

"Yes, of course. A matter of discipline, what! Respect, yes, respect."

Nithin could have sworn there were two white men in the room, having a normal conversation.

He heard the door slam, realised he was alone and painfully stood up. His nose was broken, he was sure of that. His head was still spinning and he felt dizzy. There was very little blood. He thought he heard someone speaking and shook his head, trying to clear it. A drop of blood landed on his wrist and he stared at it, then looked around. He couldn't see anyone, his eyes refusing to focus. But the voice was still there. He could hear it distinctly. He tilted his head to one side, listening intently. From somewhere deep inside him the words surfaced: Hit first, think afterwards. Okay Dicky, he mumbled to himself. Okay. Won't happen again, bro.

"Hey, Neets, you dreaming," Mandla said, nudging him on the shoulder and bringing him back to the present.

"Sorry, Mandla. I was lost in the past."

"Still thinking of that day? You never came back to school. I wondered what happened to you."

"Nothing much, my friend. Forget that day. How's your family?"

"They be okay. I don't see them much but I send them some *mali* each month. What can I do?"

"Sure, *boet*, sure. Hey, I never got around to thanking you for jumping for me that day. You could have lost your job."

"Ya. We sent them boys flying, hey *bafana?*"

"Thanks to you. They would have piled into me."

"*Hau*, Neets! Can't see that happen."

"Anyway. I'm doing okay now. And I got something for you. You still smoke the *sangu?*"

"Ya. It kills the pain in my bad leg. You got some for me? It's hard to get it these days and it's always rubbish, like grass and too many seeds in it."

"I got some for you."

"No? *Hau!* You make jokes with Mandla. *Wena dhlala.*"

Nithin reached into his socks and removed the packets, handing them to Mandla. Mandla's eyes were shining. Slowly, he opened one carefully, then smelt it. With his forefinger he moved the dried leaves around, studying them.

"This be good stuff, Neets. The best. No seeds that can make you lose your head."

"I know. And look, whenever I can, I'll bring some around for you. I got something else too." Nithin reached into his pocket and pulled out a small bundle of notes, counted out ten pounds and handed them to Mandla. "For your family."

"Neets ... *ungazi* ... I don't know what to say. It's more than they pay me in three months."

"Say nothing," Nithin said, standing up. "I'll see you again, my friend."

As he walked down the pathway he said softly to himself: "The favour's repaid. Now to settle the score. Then I can bury the past forever."

∞

Nithin knocked on the door, took a few steps backwards and folded his hands on his chest. The door opened and a tall woman, unusually fair for an Indian and still quite attractive, looked at him enquiringly.

"Yes, Can I help you?" the voice was soft, almost musical.

"Mr Barsu, is he in?"

She looked him up and down, saw the marks on his face and said, "Does he know you?"

"I used to be a student of his, ma'am. I just want to thank him. He did me a favour once. I'd like to repay him."

"How nice of you. Not many students are so grateful. Come in, my boy. Come in. Don't just stand there."

"I'm really in a hurry. Couldn't you just call him to the door? Please?"

She seemed to hesitate, then saw the smile on Nithin's face and smiled back. She left the door slightly ajar and went in. He heard her shout, "Colin, someone to see you. A nice young boy. Says he's in a hurry."

Nithin turned around and faced the street, his back to the door, listening intently. A few seconds later he heard the swish as the door opened wide.

"Yes?"

Just the one word and the hate rose in him, threatening to engulf him.

"Turn around, boy. What's your name?"

Slowly, hands still across his chest, Nithin turned around. The recognition was instantaneous. Barsu's eyes widened, his jaw dropping.

"Close the door. We don't want to alarm your wife."

For a moment Nithin thought Barsu would run back inside and slam the door. Guilt and curiosity won over the fear. With a shaking hand Barsu pulled the door shut and simply stood there, immobilised. Nithin said nothing. Just looked at him contemptuously. Beads of sweat formed on the form-master's forehead. He opened his mouth to say something, failed, and wiped the perspiration with the back of his hand. Nithin suddenly suspected that Barsu had been expecting this call for a long time.

"Were you beginning to relax?" Nithin asked menacingly. "Did you convince yourself that I wouldn't come around after all?"

"Look, my boy. You don't understand ..." Barsu's voice was trembling.

"Just shut up and look at me. And start praying, you skinny bastard."

"Nithin, please ..." Barsu's hand was edging behind him, reaching for the doorknob.

"Don't move," Nithin said. The threat in his eyes froze Barsu.

"That's better. You move again and I'll kick your balls in. I'm going to do that anyway."

Suddenly Barsu's face collapsed. He began to cry. Nithin heard an odd gushing sound and looked down. Barsu's pants had turned dark, the urine forming a puddle at his feet. A tiny stream began to flow towards Nithin.

Disgusted, Nithin stepped back. He had come with the simple intention of telling Barsu what he thought of him and leaving him with the fear that Nithin would be calling again, to even the score. This was infinitely better.

"Keep thinking about me, creep. I might decide to come back and finish the job, when I can find your balls."

As Nithin descended the stairs he knew he would never come back. But Barsu didn't know that, would stew for years to come and jump every time someone knocked on the door.

For months Nithin had waited for this day, had looked forward to it with an eagerness that bordered on the pathological. He couldn't understand why he now felt depressed. But he was beginning to understand something else: vengeance was a cold dish indeed, unpalatable at the best of times.

That evening, over a beer at the Globe, Nithin told John some of it. John was doubled up with laughter, the last swallow of beer trickling out of his nose.

"Shit, Nits!" he spluttered. "You're something else again." He wiped his face with a serviette, then blew his nose on it. "Next time wait till I finish swallowing." Unable to contain himself he burst out laughing again.

"Anyway," Nithin smiled, "I buried that ghost."

For a while they sat in companiable silence. An occasional acquaintance drifted in and they acknowledged the greeting by raising their glasses.

"Remember what I told you last night?" Nithin asked. "You still have most of the money?"

"All of it, except for a quid that I blew today and a fiver I gave my old man."

"Okay. Right now we feel ten feet tall. But the money won't last forever. You can be sure we won't strike it this lucky again. I have a proposition I've been juggling around. You interested?"

"Sure, why not," John replied, taking a deep swallow.

"I like your style, John. And we've both been to high school. Figures don't frighten us. I think we should go into business ourselves."

"Ho, *maat*! What do I know about running a shop?"

"Nothing like that. We can't compete with the Grey Street merchants, they've got the Casbah cornered solid. Besides, we don't have that kind of capital. Also, I'm not suggesting we become partners, I don't go for that. But we can work together, cover for each other, provide support and back-up if required. But we each keep our own books, make our own profits."

"I can live with you, Nits. You play straight. What you got in mind?"

"In a nutshell, we become loan sharks. I can't think of a better way to say it. But don't get me wrong. I have no hangups about it. It's not like extortion or blackmail. The customers come to us, John. We don't force anyone to deal with us. When they do, they act on their own free will."

"I'm not fazed by it either," John added. "Where do we get our customers?"

"That's easy. The factory workers and office staff are our targets. And we only lend to solid, respectable guys. Chaps who have families and secure jobs. We must know where they work and where they stay. Those types don't make waves."

"Sounds good to me."

"We don't lend to whites. If they walk away with our money we can't touch them. Anyway, they earn too well to need us and their employers and bankers look after them. And we don't go near an Af. There's no way we can follow them into the townships and they change jobs more often than we change our pants. We stick to our own, the Indians and coloureds. In other words, we operate in our own environment."

"Makes sense. All we need are a few guys to bring us the leads. After a while I guess it'll simply snowball."

"Exactly. And we stick to the going rate. A shilling on a pound, each week. A thousand will get us fifty. We can double our money in a few months. I have a few other ideas too. But let's start with this. Okay?"

"I'm in. When I worked as a carpenter I hardly ever saw more than six or seven quid a month. What worries me, though, is the competition. They could get heavy."

"I've thought of that. The only guys we need to worry about are the *Motas*, and they're not into this. Requires too much personal attention. They're happy to leave it to the small fry. Any of the others, we attend to it when the time comes. I'm not worried."

"When do we start?"

"Monday. For beginners, we simply circulate, pass the word around. Keep it small until we get a feel for it."

"Like I said before," John said admiringly, "You cover all the angles. And you're cool. You're thinking all the time, even in a tight spot. I saw that last night. You'd make a damn good businessman."

"What's business anyway, John. Buy for five pence, sell for ten pence. Make five percent profit. Nothing clever about it."

"That's not five percent ..." John started to say, saw Nithin smiling, and burst out laughing.

"Okay. I get the picture."

∞

Nithin waited exactly a week before he gave his mother more money. He had to be careful. The slightest suspicion that it was tainted and she wouldn't touch it. He had been setting the scene for several days and finally on Friday morning he handed her twenty pounds.

"It was a very good week, *ba*. Like I told you there was plenty of work at the docks and I also made a few good sales. You can start preparing for the wedding."

"This is a lot of money, Nithin."

"It's only a start. Some of the *kalassis* on the ships will be bringing a lot of watches for me. Quite soon we'll be making real good money. And *ba*, look for a flat in town. We have to be out of here by the end of the month. Most of the others are already gone."

"They ask a lot of key money for flats there. The kind of money we will never have."

"You find the flat, *ba*. I'll find the money."

"But Nithin, the rents in town are very high."

"Haven't I always paid the bond that he took on this house? You always called the instalments rent. What's the difference?"

"Do you think the *sirkar* will pay us for this house?"

Nithin waved his hands vaguely, then glanced at his Cyma.

"I'm late already, *ba*. I must run."

Before she could say anything he was through the door and heading towards Old Dutch Road. A little later he turned into Centenary Road and walked past the new fire station and St Aidans Hospital. A few hundred yards and he was alongside the race course. At Avondale Road he looked at the time and slowed down. It was a quarter to twelve. He still had fifteen minutes on hand and Cowey Road was only five minutes away.

He felt the excitement beginning to build up. With an effort he slowed his pace.

Nithin was in one of the leafiest suburbs of the city, the ancient trees lining the streets casting their shade wide and blocking out the heat of the noonday sun. The houses on either side were large and silent, each set in over half an acre of land. They looked as unoccupied as the deserted road he was traversing, only the neat and well-laid gardens belying the impression. He couldn't help feeling that he was the only living soul for miles around. It was an eerie sensation and had a tranquilising effect on him, laying to rest for the time being the last few ghosts that still plagued him — there were some that even money couldn't dispel.

When he turned into Cowey Road he glanced at his watch again. He was still several minutes early. He had to time it perfectly, he dared not loiter lest someone peer through a window and follow his progress with a curiosity he had no desire to arouse. Casually, he bent down and untied, then retied, the lace on his right shoe. He repeated the process with the other foot, taking his time over it. Then he straightened up, massaging his back and pretending to assuage a pain he did not feel and buying a few more seconds, then moved on.

He passed a low hedge, a high wall that he couldn't see over, then drew abreast of huge double doors, constructed of stout wooden squares. One of the doors was slightly open and he glanced through it casually without slowing his pace. A riot of colour met his eyes: flowers of every shade and shape, the sort he only saw at the flower stalls in Pine Street, stretched into the distance. Out of the corner of his eye he caught a fleeting vision, the shape of a slim girl with a pair of shears in her hand. Then that too was blocked by the other half of the large doors as he walked on.

Within a few seconds he was at an intersection. He turned right and a hundred yards later turned right again, into Tenth Avenue. His pace was more determined now, his stride purposeful. He passed several iron gates, all securely bolted, then reached one that was slightly ajar and slipped through it. Quietly, he shut the gate and engaged the latch. His heart was thudding against his chest and he could feel the heat rising in his cheeks.

"You could have at least winked."

The voice was to his right and close by. Nithin swung around and she was in his arms. They kissed for what seemed like an age before she pushed him away and took him by the hand. They walked over to a secluded gazebo and sat close to each other, his arm around her shoulders, her head buried in his neck. She smelled of soap and some kind of perfume — attar of roses? It wafted up to him and he breathed it in deeply, memorising the different sensations it evoked, to be recalled later when he was alone.

"You passed me by like I didn't even exist," she murmured, not looking up.

"With you acting like Anne of Green Gables," he laughed huskily, "and waving those shears around like a weapon ..."

"They're still close by. If you don't remove your hand from there I'll get them."

He chuckled and straightened up. "We okay? As usual?"

"Yah. My dad and brothers are at the mosque. My mom won't be back till two. We have almost two hours to ourselves."

"Gee, thanks! You're so kind to me." He had started to kid around and she touched his jaw with her fist, silencing him.

"It's the last week of the holidays, Nithin. I'll be in school on Monday. We can meet more often then."

"I can't wait, my love. These past few weeks have been hell, seeing you on Fridays only."

"It's been hard on me too. But you know I can't get out of here alone. My mom or someone is always with me."

Nithin placed a forefinger on her lips, "It's okay, baby. I know how it is."

For a while they sat quietly, savouring their closeness and willing time to stand still.

"My sisters will be married soon," he said.

"I'm happy for them, Nithin. At least the gods are smiling on someone."

"The gods have nothing to do with it, Kathija. I'm the one who is going to see that it happens. When you need the gods they're always sleeping. And even then they cause more trouble than our enemies and then blame it on the devil."

"Are we into that again?" she sighed.

"But look at you and I? We're both Indians, our people came from the same village in India. We could even be related, from some long distant past. Then along came the gods, causing mischief, and some of our people decided to convert and fucked it all up."

"Don't swear, darling. You sound like a thug."

"I feel like I'm becoming one. Look, sweetheart, we didn't choose our religions, we were simply born into them. And even if we had a choice, what does it change? Our blood still remains the same, no one can alter that. Your genes don't change simply because you mumble a few words and give loyalty to a different god. I can't say I'm white, then wake up tomorrow and claim my race has changed, that the white man is now my brother."

Kathija quietly sighed and snuggled into him.

"Don't you see, Kathy love, religion changes nothing. So why should we be subject to its judgment. If someone you love makes you happy then that person has to be good for you. What gives religion the right to interfere. And even if what you are is the result of your religion, well fine. I respect it. I'll thank it for what it has made of you. If it then says that you can't marry me, I say it can fuck off!"

"Will you stop your bloody swearing! And my religion doesn't tell you what to do. What about yours?"

"The same applies. It can ..."

"Nithin, stop blaspheming. What about your parents? What about mine? Would you do anything to hurt your mother?"

"I'd hate to do that."

"And I would never hurt my parents. We could take off now. We'll survive, but it'll kill them, and wherever we are we'll always know that. We'd feel like murderers. No love can survive that."

"So what do we do?"

"We think straight. Our problem is not religion, you've already agreed to convert, whatever that means considering what you just said. Our problem is society, it makes the rules ..."

"So there's no hope. No way we can marry."

"I'm not saying that. I'll play the game, according to society's rules. But I have a few of my own. Want to hear them?"

"There are enough rules already, now you want to make more," Nithin said, exasperated.

"Just listen! For me there are four things that are not negotiable. I'll not go against my religion and I'll do nothing to hurt my parents. I'll never marry a man I do not love and I'll never sleep with any man except my husband."

"That effectively lets me out ..."

"Will you listen! I have rights too. I love you and I will not give you up. Not unless you say it's over."

"That's our lot, then. I can never let you go either. So we keep ducking and dodging until one day the gods wave their magic wand. Boom! We're away."

"Don't Nithin. Don't joke about it. You're too intelligent for that."

"Why do I feel we've been through all this before, been over the same ground."

"Because we have, you idiot!"

"Oh! What happened to my intelligence?"

"You just lose it from time to time. Don't worry, I'll always pull you back in line."

"You're no Indian girl. You're too full of shit."

"Maybe that's why you love me."

"Not maybe. It is why I love you. Kathy, what happens in a few months time? You'll be over your matric exams ..."

"And I intend to pass with flying colours. Six big As. I'll make sure I'm one of the ten Indians they take on at Med School."

"Terrific! And if that non-existent god waves his non-existent wand my non-existent wife, the doctor, can introduce me to her highfaluting friends as Mr Vania. And when they ask, 'What does he do, Kathy?' You can say, 'Oh, he's from Victoria Street.' Nice. Another solid nail ..."

"I'm going to hit you!" She looked as if she meant it.

"You still haven't told me where we go from here."

"We're going nowhere. We see each other when we can. And we wait. And that reminds me, you promised to study accounting. That was a year ago. You haven't even started."

"I have to earn the bucks, Kathy. I told you about my old man."

"You can study and earn the bucks. You have the brains and you're wasting them."

"I can use those brains just as easily making money."

"I know you, Nithin. You won't rest till you make a million. Maybe not even after that."

"Does that worry you?"

"Why should it. I'll help you spend it, as long as it's honestly acquired. You do something wrong and I'll hit you so hard ..."

"Story of my life. Everybody likes to hit me. But you'd better do it now, because those are not the only stars I'll see if I don't get out of here. Look at the time."

"Oh my God!" she said, jumping up.

When they reached the gate she grabbed him by the front of his shirt, the way a thug on a street corner would have, and pulled him close. She kissed him, lingeringly, then pushed him away.

"You make sure you see me on Monday, Nithin Vania," she said, her eyes dancing. "Same place, only early, at eleven. I've made a plan to duck out. How's that for a good Indian girl?"

Nithin was still smiling as he walked down the avenue, his step light, his heart singing. He raised his eyebrows, lifted his eyes to the sky without moving his head and said quietly, "You listening up there? We'll lick you yet, big guy. You may have made us, but the plans we'll make ourselves."

∞

"I need a gun, Jake. Fast."

Jake studied the set face. He had never seen Nithin so angry before. In a voice as soft as the shadows around them, he asked, "How soon?"

"Now if you can. Tomorrow at the latest."

"They're not easy to get, Nits."

"Jake, I don't have the time or the connections. That's why I'm asking you."

"You want to tell me why?"

"I have to clear a problem before it gets out of hand."

"Tell me about it."

"Will you get me one then?"

"I'll do it for you anyway. You're my *boet*. But maybe there's an easier solution, that's why I'm asking."

"You know a guy called Choppers, from Acorn Road?"

"Sure. A real shit. Used to *julate* with the Dutchenes until Dicky threw him out. A mean bastard."

"He's been getting heavy with Daksha. Pulled her into a lane a few times and really handled her. She's so scared she doesn't even go to Puterman's anymore. She's scared to open the door. She tells me he came over yesterday, stood on the pavement for over an hour, just looking at the house. You know his reputation. Daksha says he has already raped one of the girls around here. Everyone's dead *skrik* of him."

"Did he hit Daksha?" Jake's voice had gone cold.

"No. But he handled her something nasty. Pushed his hands between her legs, that sort of thing, then told her he was going to *nye* her. He forced a kiss on her and shoved his hands down the front of her dress. The last time he kept her in the alley for almost ten minutes before she broke away."

Jake's face had begun to harden as he listened. Towards the end his eyes had almost disappeared into their sockets.

"Okay, Nits. Leave the bastard to me."

"Jake, I have to do this myself. It's my sister. You can understand that."

"You mean to put him away?"

"If I can't reason with him, then, yes."

"Reason with that prick! Look Nits, this guy's not the usual bully, he's pretty tasty with his fists. And he's faster than a snake. He'll flatten you before you can pull the gun. Let me at least come with you. And if we have to blow him away it's okay by me."

"I have to do this my way, Jake. I have to see him alone."

"Okay. I understand that. But why rush it?"

"Daksha will be getting married soon. If her future in-laws hear about this they'll call the wedding off. It'll kill my mother. And if that swine even comes on our street again Daksha will probably kill herself. I'm telling you, Jake, she's going crazy as it is."

Jake's eyes were smouldering. "Wait here. I won't be long."

When Jake returned he handed Nits a thick hard-covered novel. "There's a .38 Police Special between the covers. Fully loaded. It's not clean. I used it once before. Get the feel of it, then do whatever you have to. Bring it back to me, okay?"

"Thanks, Jake. I won't forget this."

"It might be better for both of us if you did. You going to take him out tonight?"

"I have to."

"Okay. But tonight's all you have. If he's still walking the streets tomorrow he belongs to me, agreed?"

"There won't be a tomorrow for him, Jake."

∞

Wills Road was as quiet as a bird watcher's hideout, its inhabitants safe indoors and comfortably settled for the night. At the corner of Hampson Grove, deep in the shadows of a thick cherry bush, Nithin sighed again and looked at his wristwatch. It was after midnight. His legs were beginning to tire and his neck ached from the long vigil. It was more than an hour since he had tracked his quarry down to the Lancers Bar and returned to wait for him, convinced that he would take the short route to Acorn Road through Douglas Lane.

Nithin was tempted to go back and peek in but subdued it. He didn't want anyone to see him looking around. He was banking on the option that if his man didn't come this way he could always go to Acorn Road and confront him there — the guy was a known nighthawk and seldom went home before the early hours of the morning. It was not an option he was happy with but it was all he had to fall back on. One way or the other he'd get the bastard tonight. By tomorrow Jake would take over and in all likelihood blow the guy's head off and leave it to the *Motas* to sort it out.

Nithin was about to reach for a cigarette when he heard raucous laughter in Syringa Avenue, followed by a bawdy voice. He froze, his senses alert. When he saw the group emerge into Wills Road he knew the long wait had come to an end. Choppers was in front and berating his companions for refusing to accompany him to a shebeen. There were two others with him and they didn't appear to be too happy in his company. At the edge of the pavement Choppers stopped and began to urinate against a lamppost. The other two continued across the road.

"Hey, you little pricks! Wait for me," Choppers shouted.

Nithin, who was closer, heard the two mutter something and then stop. A surge of adrenalin flowed through his body and, throwing caution to the winds, he left the bushes. Choppers was buttoning his fly as he came over.

"Hello, Choppers."

"Ya? Who are you?"

By then he was only a few yards away and Nithin turned his head, the street light shining fully on his face.

"Hey, it's the Banya boy! How you doing, *lighty*?"

"I want to talk to you," Nithin said, his voice even.

"Sure, *lighty*. Rather talk to your sister, though," Choppers said, laughing loudly.

"That's what I want to talk to you about."

"Ya? Okay. I like to talk about her. I really *temba* that *steckie*, boy."

"I want you to leave her alone."

"Hey, man. That's a nice little piece. I reckon I gotta taste a bit ..."

"You heard what I said?"

"What the fuck, man. You wanna save those juicy parlours for yourself?"

Choppers was openly taunting Nithin, trying to raise a laugh from the other two. They remained silent, not responding.

"Tell you what, man," Choppers leered. "We share that sweet white arse of hers. Just you and me ..."

"I'm going to say it one more time. *Leave her alone*."

"Or what, Banya boy? What the fuck you gonna do?"

"I'll have to shoot you."

"With what, your cock? You little shit ..."

The words ended abruptly as Nithin pulled out the revolver from his waistband and raised it to Choppers' face. They were no more than a yard apart.

"Hey *lighty*!" Choppers said, startled. "That's a big man's toy. Is it loaded?"

"It's loaded."

"Well, fuck-me-gently. Okay, *lighty*, you can have her. Give her one for me."

Choppers raised his hands, signifying surrender, a sly look on his face. Nithin saw Chopper's right leg twitch. *He's faster than a snake, Nits!* Nithin pulled the trigger.

The explosion shattered the silence, reverberating off the houses across the street. The top of Chopper's head burst open as he fell backwards, the right leg jerking upwards as it vainly responded to its last message.

The echo hadn't quite faded before Nithin turned to the other two. It had happened so fast that the shock hadn't registered, there was a silly look on their faces.

"Think fast," Nithin said, his voice flat. "I gave him a fair chance. He was too stupid to take it. I'm giving you the same chance now."

The taller of the two recovered first. "Hey man! He's no friend of ours."

"We don't know nothing! We didn't see nothing, man!"

The first of the lights went on across the road.

"Okay," Nithin said. "If they pick me up for any reason, my *maats* will come looking for you two. Now go!"

Less than a minute had elapsed from the time Nithin had fired the revolver. The other two had disappeared down Douglas Lane. Nithin walked towards Lancers Road, not hurrying, keeping to the shadows. His eyes were alert. Wills Road was still deserted, except for the body lying in the distance. Only the one light had been switched on, from the edge of his eye he saw a curtain move. By then he was turning the corner and heading towards Warwick Avenue.

∞

Nithin was at the kitchen tap pouring water into a glass when Daksha walked in.

"Nithin, did you hear about that man? They found his body in Wills Road."

"What man?"

"That dirty ..." she said, then lowered her voice conspiratorially, " .. rubbish. The one who was worrying me."

"Oh! I didn't know. Well, you know what they say. Live by the knife, die by the knife."

"Someone shot him last night."

"Shot him? I suppose it was bound to happen. He must have had many enemies."

"Nithin, you didn't know about it?" She was looking at him in a funny way.

"Naw, *ben*," he said with a laugh. "I was at the Kathiawad Club last night. You know, the KHYO. I'm sure he got what he deserved. Who told you?"

"Kayroon passed by this morning. She told me."

"Your friend in Wills Road? Did she say who did it?"

"No. She heard a shot but couldn't see anything. And nobody goes out to look, they don't want to get involved. Anyway, most of the people around there have already moved out."

"I guess that's one rotten egg that no one will miss."

The relief on Daksha's face was obvious and she was looking lovelier than ever. "I prayed every day. I even lit a lamp to Kali Mata. Now my prayers have been answered."

"You only lit one lamp?"

"What do you mean?"

"You should pray to all the gods. If you leave any out they could get jealous and cause trouble."

"You really think so?"

"Sure." Nithin's fingers were rubbing his forehead, covering his face. "Now, what do I have to do to get some breakfast around here?"

"Get married! We're not here to serve you." Daksha's voice was actually spiteful. "You walk in and out as you like. If I was *ba* ..."

"It's okay," Nithin said, standing up. "I'm not really hungry."

"When will you give *ba* money for my wedding clothes?"

"I'll get it this week."

"I'll need a few saris. I have nothing to wear. The Kanjee girls ..."

"I'll see to it, *ben*. Okay?"

"I'm sorry, Nithin. Look, I'll get the breakfast."

"No. I'm really not hungry. I'll just get myself a glass of milk."

Nithin was opening the fridge when his mother walked into the kitchen. "You're only drinking milk, Nithin? Sit. Let me warm ..."

"I had a bite, *ba*," Nithin lied. "Daksha saw to it."

"Good. You're looking tired this morning. I didn't hear you come in last night."

"I had to work very late. I'll give you some money for Daksha's clothes tomorrow."

"You can't go on like this. You need to rest. You've done a lot already."

"It'll make Daksha happy. And you need some saris too. Did you pay over the key money."

"We get the flat at the end of the month. It's small. I don't know what we'll do with all the furniture ..."

"Are you happy, *ba?*"

"With my Raja to look after me? It's a long time since I was so happy. Thank you. When I look at you I feel like singing."

"Then do it, *ba*. Now. You used to sing me to sleep. I miss it."

"You still remember?"

They both laughed, hugging each other. "Sell the furniture, *ba*. When I get you a house again we'll buy everything new. Just give me a little more time. Everything's going well."

"I'm happy with the flat ..."

"Then why are you crying?"

"Because I'm happy. You make me happy."

"Then stay happy, *ba*. The good times are only starting."

∞

"Don't go away," Jake said as he took the book from Nithin and disappeared into the house. When he came back they sat on the low boundary wall to Verbena Court and spoke in soft undertones.

"I heard you had to use it," Jake said.

"He gave me no choice."

"I warned you. Anyway, it's done. Any hitches?"

"There were two guys with him. But they weren't his friends. I don't think they'll burn me to the cops."

"You sure?" Jake asked. "Who were they?"

"I've never seen them around before. Didn't look like local okes."

"You're right, then. They'll keep out of it."

"I'm not worried. An old problem has been resolved. If it creates a new problem I'll face it when the time comes."

"You've changed, Nits. Over the past few months you've become hard, almost vicious."

"I'm only responding to events, Jake. I don't start anything."

"I guess you're learning to survive. I also hear you're moving into the rackets now. You and John Farley."

"Just a bit of money lending. Nothing big."

"John's a good guy. And dependable. Can use himself too."

"He's cool. And we trust each other."

"Then go for it. A little capital can grow fast in that game. You come up against any opposition?"

"Nothing yet."

"You won't have any problems. It's a big market, wide open. But watch out for the cops. They'll be looking for their cut."

"Long as they're reasonable I'll cover them."

"Not much choice there, *boet*. If you have any problems with them, or with last night's business, you let me know. I'll get the *Motas* to square it."

"Thanks. You think the *Motas* will want a cut too?"

"No, they won't. They're shrewd that way. They stay out of the small stuff. You know, like bio tickets, selling grass, shebeen running, what you're into now. It keeps us out of their hair. They're into the really big stuff, like extortion and the bucket shops, where the real money is. A few days ago they picked up five grand, just for one call on a guy that wasn't paying his debt to someone in Grey Street. They didn't even rough him up. Just a friendly visit and the oke was falling over himself."

Nithin whistled. "How much did the guy owe?"

"Ten grand. That's nothing. A while back they had to settle a dispute between two families. One of them called the *Motas* and asked them to sort the other family out. You know something? They collected from both families! They came back to the first family and claimed they had been offered more by the second. They kept going from one to the other, upping the ante, until the disputing families had no choice but to make peace and call it a day. But it cost them. The *Motas* cleaned up, to the tune of fifteen grand."

"They get a lot of this sort of thing?"

"All the time. And that's additional to the regular protection money they collect."

"But if their victims get no satisfaction, only end up getting fleeced, why do they go to the *Motas* for help?"

"Because no one talks about it. Those two families are so shit scared of the *Motas* they'll never tell anyone how they were played off."

"So then their stock in trade is fear."

"And connections. They've got the cops in their back pockets."

"Looks like a smooth operation."

"It is. It's like a military hierarchy. The *scotens*, who are way down the ranks, depend on the runners for their living, the runners in turn dance to the tune of the street gangs and the street gangs that make their money from the small stuff have to play ball with the League."

"But Jake, what happens if you get a maverick, someone who begins to expand his operations and starts making real money, like a leader of the street gangs?"

"Then the League expects its cut, a share of the takings."

"And if the oke refuses to shine up?"

"It happens from time to time. A guy gets ambitious and underestimates the *Motas*, who simply nod at the cops and the oke's either out of business or he goes back to them cap in hand for assistance."

"And if he doesn't? If he decides to buck the League?"

"That's been tried too. That's when the League shows its true colours, bares its teeth. They unleash their hounds, their enforcers. Those guys are so ruthless a rabid dog looks tame compared to them."

"So the League is untouchable, huh? Anyway, thanks for the loan of the iron and for your offer to square things if I'm in a spot. I appreciate it."

"For you, Nits? Anytime!"

"I still won't forget it. I owe you."

"There's something else, Nits ..."

"Sure. Name it."

"Nothing like that. But look, *bru*, we grew up together, we're family so I have to say this. I didn't survive in the streets by being stupid. And looking at you I get the feeling you're up to something, you give me the impression you're sort of puzzling, planning and plotting. I don't like what I see in your face these days. I've seen that look before and those guys are no longer around."

"I'll watch and play, Jake. I promise you."

"You do that. In a push, Sandy and I will back you. All the way and against anybody. But we won't like it. It'll be a losing hand, aces and eights."

Suddenly Jake stood up and Nithin joined him. Jake gave him a searching stare, then touched his shoulder briefly and walked away. Nithin looked at the slim figure, the wide shoulders, the cocky walk as he disappeared in the distance. He let out his breath slowly.

No Jake, Nithin said to himself, I won't do anything stupid. But you taught me something today. The *Motas* deal in fear, conquer that and what do they have? The cops and the enforcers. Both are brainless morons who worship money and switch loyalties faster than a bitch changes lovers.

As Nithin stepped off the pavement he cast an eye heavenward. "Hey, you still there? They say you know everything. So tell me, do the *Motas* know how vulnerable they are?"

∞

"It'll take time, John," Nithin was saying, "a good few years. But we set the wheels in motion now. From here on, ten percent of everything we make goes into a special account. We keep a low profile, let the funds build up. No fancy cars, we keep away from the bright lights and the top venues and don't flash the rolls in our pockets. We make it but we don't flaunt it."

"We're each raking in over a hundred a week as it is, Nits. We can double that overnight if we buy the stamps from the construction workers."

"I like that idea, John. I like it a lot. Our outlay is guaranteed and the returns are very good. As long as you're satisfied your cousin at the union offices will play ball ..."

"You can bank on him. And those carpenters and brickies are not interested in the compulsory savings rule that the union introduced. By August their books are nearly full of the investment stamps, worth almost three, four hundred quid. The gambling schools only give them maybe a hundred for the book and they still have to accompany the *ous* to the union offices to cash in at the end of November. We don't have to do that. My cuz will cash it for us, just like that."

"Let's go for it, then. In the meantime we keep moving around, build up an easy rapport with the guys on the streets and do them a few favours. You're already in, because of Googs, with the Sydenham and Overport boys. We have nothing to fear from the Dutchenes and the Victorians. They're committed to me, I grew up with them. If we can get close to the May Street and the Beatrice Street sarangs we're set."

They were sitting on the first floor terrace of Kapitan's Balcony Hotel, overlooking the intersection of Grey and Victoria Streets. For a while they ate silently, then Nithin pushed his plate away.

"When our kitty is big enough we quietly spread the bucks around, but only to the backroom boys, like the guys in charge of the files in the courts. We put a few easy women their way and give them a place to take them. We ask for nothing in exchange. All we do is build up the network. In time we'll get to know the police captains and the magistrates. Like I said, it'll take years."

"You seem pretty sure we won't attract the League's attention."

"Not if we keep a low profile. We must never seem to be a threat to them. We cultivate them but always let them know they're the bosses. You know what I mean? And we don't get too close to them, those dadas are like mind readers."

"But what happens afterwards, Nits? When we're set?"

"At the right time we show our hand, but in a very subtle way. We give them a hint that we have a few friends, that we're useful to them. When they ask us to pull a few strings we jump to do it. We let them believe they own us. We make sure, though, that we keep our distance. They must always respect us. And they'll do that as long as we're not a threat to them. In maybe four or five years we can have a network that's better than theirs."

"It'll cost, Nits. You're talking big bucks."

"Sure. But it's an investment. Like a five-year plan that all the big business houses make."

"So it's all business then. We have no intention of tackling the *Motas*?"

"That would be stupid, John. Why risk our lives for what we can have without double dealing. No, my friend, we don't tackle them. We just get a nice suite of offices and sit back. We wait for them to come to us. And they will, if only to suss out the opposition."

"And what then, Nits. What do we do?"

"We welcome them. And like all good businessmen, we offer them our services. We become the wholesalers, the *Motas* the retailers. We don't merge, we co-exist. Nobody gets hurt and everybody rakes in the *shekels*. If the *Motas* don't accept that we've outwitted them then they would be stupid."

∞

For a Sunday afternoon the Goodwill Lounge was unusually quiet. Only a few tables were occupied and the waiters, in their immaculate white jackets and black trousers, hovered at a discreet distance from the diners. The decor was subdued, the environment spotless; and the soft music, barely audible, complemented the superb cuisine. At the slightest signal from a patron the highly trained waiters glided over with efficient ease and a dignified assurance that made each guest feel exceptionally important and for whom nothing but the best was acceptable.

The Naidoo brothers, Pumpy and Nammy, were proficient restaurateurs whose personal attention to every facet of their operations had created a haven in the midst of the Casbah. Pumpy, the supreme showman whose presence alone was sufficient to elevate the restaurant to a status unparalleled by any such rival establishment anywhere in a city famed for its eating houses, was a man of immense charm and a raconteur of great talent. Nammy, the elder of the two, was a hulking giant who, it was rumoured, had stopped a bullet in his chest without flinching. The rumour, as such, was not without substance. The rowdy Free Stater responsible for the dastardly deed, flushed with both liquor and the arrogance of his race, had found himself unceremoniously dumped into the gutter, after which the redoubtable Nammy had driven himself to the hospital to have the bullet removed. And, if the subsequent reports were to be believed, he was back on duty the next morning, as doughty as ever and as briskly efficient as he would have been if he had spent the night at a pleasure resort.

The "Captain's Table", as Pumpy liked to call it, could comfortably seat at least ten people. It was tucked away in a wing of the old house that had been renovated at great cost. On that particular day it was occupied by Pumpy himself and six of his guests. As Pumpy's private domain, to fill a seat at that table was a rare honour and one that was seldom, if ever, bestowed on anyone except those who formed a part of Pumpy's select circle of friends.

These six guests, flattered by Pumpy's magnanimous gesture, were revelling in the unexpected honour and basking in the covetous glances of the handful of less favoured patrons scattered around the vast dining hall. Their rotund host was in an expansive mood and on the top of his form, gesticulating elegantly with his fastidiously manicured hands as he made a point from time to time.

"It was my father, the restaurateur *par excellence*, who truly deserves the credit for our success," Pumpy was saying in his soft hypnotic voice. "The old Peter's Lounge, as you all know, was situated at the corner of Pine and Grey Streets. It's inner diningroom and open deck had an ambience unequalled anywhere on this sub-continent. It would not be an exaggeration when I claim that no luxury liner of any distinction ever berthed at our docks without a good number of its passengers seeking out the famed Peter's to savour its legendary curry dishes. And when they went back they told their friends about their gastronomical experience, who in turn told their friends.

"Unfortunately, the property that housed my father's restaurant was inherited by a shortsighted young man who lacked his late father's business acumen. In a moment of monumental stupidity he concluded that it was the property, and its location, that was responsible for my father's success. In a show of bravado he rashly doubled the rent, overnight, and smugly invited my father to humbly negotiate a lease.

"Old Peter, however, was not a man to be trifled with. Displaying a dignity befitting an aristocrat he simply bowed courteously and walked out. Before the day was over he had secured a lease on the property we are now sitting in. Within a further two weeks, with a team of highly skilled artisans working twenty hours a day, under his personal supervision, he miraculously converted the rundown old mansion to what you now see around you. In under a month he had relocated the entire kit and caboodle with a panache that left the town breathless with admiration.

"The harebrained youngster, furious at my old man's audacity and frustrated at having lost a valuable tenant, threatened court action. And on what grounds? Simply that the name Peter's Lounge was an invaluable appendage of his property, part and parcel of the masonry and could not be used elsewhere.

"Old Peter refused to be fazed, nor did he choose to stoop to the level of a fishwife. There was little doubt that he could have had his day in court, had he cared to pursue his rights. Instead, he ignored the interdict and, in a gesture of ironic goodwill, he renamed this place 'Goodwill Lounge'.

"The rest is history."

For the first time in the entire discourse Pumpy paused for a deep breath and sipped on a glass of orange juice.

"Of course, others tried to emulate his achievements at the erstwhile premises, deluded by the assumption that brick and mortar, rather than hard work and acumen, were the formula that ensured success. They lasted only until their purses were empty, then unceremoniously folded. What you see there today is a shell, a fitting epitaph to a man unequal to his inheritance."

Pumpy raised his glass of orange juice in a gesture that was both a salute to the portrait of his sage father, that was prominently displayed on the wall in front of him, and a toast to the beautiful ladies who accompanied their men around the table.

"To Peter then," Sandy responded, smiling at his gorgeous wife. "And one more to the lovely Kathy. Nits, are you ever going to cause the rafters to ring and join the noble club of happily married souls? Kathy, surely you can't deny Nits the pleasure of such a union? I take it, Nits, that you have popped the question?"

Kathy was blushing furiously. "It's not Nits' fault," she protested.

"Just this once, Kathy," Sandy insisted, "let Nits speak for himself."

Nithin remained silent, smiling as he sipped from his glass.

"C'mon, Nits," Jake prodded. "Drop the silent man act. How long is it now? Eight years? You're not school kids anymore. What are you two waiting for?"

"It's not like that, Jake. You know our problem ..."

"What problem? Look! Sandy is a Hindu, Maliga a confirmed Catholic. You see a problem?"

"It's not that simple. Kathy's parents will never agree and ..."

"That's nonsense," Sandy cut in. "I heard you had converted. Even Jake here, and I don't know when he ever goes to the mosque, says he's seen you there."

"Nits has converted?" the girl with Jake asked.

"Later, Shirley, later," Jake said, patting her hand.

"But if Nits can do it, why can't you?"

"I'm already a Muslim, my dear."

"You know what I mean, Jake."

"Okay. If you must insist. I have no intention of marrying you and if Nits, who was always a firm atheist, thinks religion is good enough for him I reckon it's good enough for me."

"You're being mean," Shirley flared.

"Jake has never lied to you, Shirley," Maliga said, going to his defence. "In the few months he's known you he has always made that clear."

"Cut it out, all of you," Sandy said. "We're talking about Nits and Kathy."

"Nits will never talk, Sandy," Jake said, then added, "The only time he'll move is when something moves in Kathy's ..."

"Jake!" Maliga, outraged, slapped him on the shoulder. "And look at what you have done. Kathy is crying. God! You're stupid."

Before Jake could respond she hustled Kathy to the ladies room. Jake, chagrined, spread his hands in apology, his face crestfallen.

"I'm sorry ... hey, Nits, I didn't mean to upset her ... you know how I feel about ..."

"It's not your fault, Jake," Nithin murmured, his face sombre. "Kathy isn't crying because of what you said. Let's leave it at that, please."

"No, Nits," Sandy said, angry now. "We are your friends. We're entitled to more than that. Kathy burst out crying because she's unhappy. And that's your fault and not, as you pointed out, something that Jake said."

Pumpy held up his pudgy hand, requesting a moment's silence. "A respite, gentlemen, from the turn in the conversation." He flicked his fingers imperiously as he turned in his chair and a waiter magically appeared at his side.

"I intend breaking a house rule," Pumpy smiled, turning to the waiter and whispering in his ear. The waiter disappeared.

"For the first time in the history of the Naidoo establishment liquor will be served before dark, albeit in its mildest form. I have ordered champagne from my private stocks. I'm not sure what we're celebrating, if anything. But whatever, the moment is appropriate. Ah! Our purveyor of good cheer has returned. Place the bucket on my right, my good man, and bring us the appropriate glasses."

The girls returned and Maliga angrily re-arranged the seats so that the three females were seated next to each other, Kathy in the middle. She relegated the men to one end of the table, close to Pumpy, and proceeded to ignore them.

"Kathy, I didn't ..."

"Keep quiet, Jake!" Kathy said furiously. "You too, Sandy. And don't give me that innocent look. And what do you guys think you're celebrating? What's the champagne for?"

"Just a bit of the grape, my dear," Pumpy quietly attempted to pacify her. "My idea entirely. Simply an attempt to re-introduce a little good humour to the somewhat discordant mood that has overcome us. A little of the bubbly to raise our good spirits, yes?"

"I don't drink liquor, thank you," Kathy said, pushing her glass away.

"And as for that big oaf next to you," Maliga added, "he has been raising more than someone's good spirits. Nits, I think you're mean and spiteful and a cheat to boot. Now drink that, you big bully!"

"Hey, hang on babe," Sandy said, "What has Nits done that's so bad. Sure, he hasn't married Kathy yet, but he did say there's a problem."

"They are married," Maliga almost spat out. "Kathy just told me."

"Whaaat!" Jake's mouth almost fell open.

"Yes. And for once close your big mouth. Nits, you had better do some fast talking. Right now!""

"Hey, Nits," Sandy asked, unable to hide the surprise from showing. "What's Maliga talking about?"

"Well ..." Nithin began, somewhat shamefaced. "We couldn't go through life without ... you know. We're both adults and couldn't keep fighting our natural urges ... I mean, well, Kathy wouldn't sleep with me until we were married. So we did it ... I mean, we got married, by a *moulana* and witnesses and all the proper ... hey, Kathy, help me here. I'm not sure what's going on. Did I do something wrong?"

"No," Maliga said, "You did everything right. Except you can't be married in the eyes of God only. You have to declare your marriage to all men and women."

"But we both agreed to keep it a secret for a little longer. We had to. I tried to explain earlier ... our society ..."

"And how did you expect to keep it a secret?" Maliga asked acidly.

"Well, hey Maliga, Kathy told you about it, I didn't. Why are you chowing me? Kathy, please, you made me promise not to say anything ... I didn't say a word."

"No, you didn't say a word, that's true. But you did plenty. How did you plan to keep that a secret?" Maliga shot back.

"Did what? Keep what a secret? I don't understand ..."

"She's pregnant, you big oaf! You didn't know that?"

"Huh? What! Pregnant? Kathy?"

"He really doesn't know, Maliga," Jake said. "Look at his face. Have you ever seen anything so stupid?"

"Kathy, you didn't tell him?" Maliga asked.

Kathy shook her head. She looked so miserable that Maliga quickly threw her arms around her and patted her shoulders.

"She's pregnant?" Jake asked no one in particular. "Kathy, you're preg ..."

"Shut up, you big ox!" Kathy cried. "It was your big mouth that started this in the first place."

"I'm sorry, Kathy. I apologise again ..."

Before they could continue Pumpy burst out laughing, huge belly shaking boisterously. "Oh, the web we weave," he began to say, saw the stunned look on Nithin's face, and promptly decided to shut up.

"Kathy," Nits said, his voice barely audible. "I thought that you being a doctor ..." he shook his head, mumbled something, shook his head again, raised his hands and looked beseechingly at Maliga, then turned to Kathy again.

"I suppose," Sandy said hesitantly, "If it comes to that, Kathy is a doctor. I guess she can arrange a ..."

"She can't, Sandy," Maliga said. "It's against her religion. Against all our religions."

"I don't want to hear about it," Nits said quietly, his voice firm. "We're going to have our baby. Kathy, I think I understand why you didn't say anything to me. Look, don't worry about my mother. I'll find a way around her. If her society can't accept ..."

"Nits, I'm going to have our baby. But I will not be a party to hurting anyone, not your mother, not my parents. When the time is right, before it begins to show, I'll go on a long holiday. I'll come back after the baby is born."

"And the baby?"

"The baby is ours. We'll find a way ..."

"That's it," Pumpy broke into the conversation, no longer the benevolent host. "The charade ends here. Now! I think you misjudge your parents and grievously insult their intelligence.

"I have heard both of you refer to the society your parents circulate in. Society? What society? There is no such thing. It's a sham. What you are referring to are social misfits who have failed to assimilate into the real world, the wretched and miserable dinosaurs who represent nothing more than mentally sick individuals who gang up to obtain solace in their numbers. For a group of that sort to survive they must have victims, lest they turn upon themselves in an orgy of soporific frenzy. If you choose to be their victims — fine. You are capable of deciding for yourselves and paying the price of your folly. That is no concern of mine.

"But have you considered the unborn child whose future you are now contemplating? It's the child's birthright to have the love and affection of both sets of grandparents, to have a balanced upbringing, free of the trauma and trials that you two are now experiencing. What sort of life are you now relegating this child to? I suggest you think about that. It does not deserve the netherworld you wish to confine it in.

"Forget about this nebulous society you keep referring to. Think of your parents' peace of mind, by all means. But do not pre-judge them. I have lived longer than you, I have observed the phenomenon from a distance, often. I have come to the conclusion that striding forward openly, laying your cards on the table face up, is the only way. They love you, in a way no society can. That is your trump card.

"Go ahead. Do it for the child you are soon going to bring into this world. Do it now. Today. And do it together, each of you supporting the other in your respective environments.

"If I am wrong, if it does not end up as I envisage it will, you will have the consolation of knowing that you have done the right thing. In everything you've done so far you have behaved honourably. Now complete the process. If it achieves nothing else, it will bring an end to the misery you are presently subjecting yourselves to. It will be done with, for ever and a day. Your comfort will be the knowledge that both of you, and your child, will at least live your lives without looking over your shoulders all the time.

"This country limits our freedom in a thousand different ways and subjects us to indignities of unbelievable proportions. Do not add to those limitations by imposing some of your own. Now go, this very minute, and do what you should have done a long time ago. Come back again and join us over supper at seven. It'll be my treat. You have three clear hours to do what you must sometime in the future. Do not prolong the agony."

As Pumpy reached for the champagne bottle Nithin lifted his eyes to Kathy. A message passed between them, then she nodded as she stood up.

When they had passed through the door Pumpy raised his glass, "It's now in the hands of the gods and fickle fortune. It'll be interesting to see who wins. In the meantime we eat." He beckoned to a waiter in his usual peremptory manner, seemingly having forgotten everything that had transpired.

"But Pumpy," Maliga said, "we promised to wait ..."

Pumpy shook his head with a dismissive gesture. "If they come back at all, my dear, they will be more than an hour late. By then we will be hungry again. I suspect they're in for a few surprises."

∞

Jake, Pumpy and Sandy were on their second bottle of champagne. The ladies hadn't touched their glasses. The wine had restored some of the harmony around the table, established a camaraderie that had earlier mildly threatened to slip away from them. The mood amongst the ladies was still a little depressed — they had empathised deeply with the unhappy couple and were now waiting with some trepidation for the outcome.

"Why did you say they may not come back?" Maliga asked Pumpy.

"Because I expect the outcome will follow one of two courses. Either their respective parents will threaten to banish them from their family circles, forbid them to ever darken their hallowed doors again, or they will be too stunned to make any response and will seek refuge in silence and tears. I expect the initial reaction to be the former scenario, in which case cooler heads will eventually prevail and the inevitable accepted. After all, they are married already. They simply seek their parents' blessing. If that is how it develops then the chances are they will get around to discussing the manner in which they will interact in future — and that could go on all night."

"But if it's the latter?" Maliga asked, drawn in spite of herself.

"The route of emotional blackmail, of moral extortion, will simply delay the lovers' exit. Both Nits and Kathy are strong willed but have allowed themselves to be swayed by emotional considerations. Having taken the painful step of full confession they will be strengthened and simply walk away — unhappy, perhaps, but free at last. Ah! I see our intrepid couple has returned. Their hangdog expression makes me fear the worst-case scenario has triumphed."

Both Maliga and Shirley had jumped up. The men simply looked on expectantly.

"It's okay," Kathy said to Maliga. "I'm okay."

"I need a drink," Nits said, to no one in particular as he lowered himself into a chair.

"No liquor," Kathy shot back. "Not now and not ever again."

"Okay," Nits said placatingly. "I can live with that. How about the wine."

"No wine. Drink the water if you're so thirsty."

"Hey," Jake asked. "Are you two fighting or what?"

"What happened?" Pumpy asked. "We are waiting with bated breath."

"Nothing," Nithin answered, somewhat flippantly.

"Nothing?"

"Well, we have to get married. Kathy's parents insist on it."

"Again?" Jake looked confused. "Didn't you tell them you're already married?"

"They want us to do it properly, whatever that means."

"And your mother?" Pumpy asked.

"She wants us to get married too. The Hindu way."

"So, basically, you have been accepted as a couple and everyone's happy, so to speak?"

"No one's happy. Least of all Kathy."

"But my dear fellow, what, as Jake would say, is the problem?"

"Ask Kathy."

"Kathy? Oh, I begin to understand. It's the Hindu ceremony ..."

"That's not all."

"No? You begin to lose me ..."

Why don't you ask Kathy, dammit! Just when everything settles down she bloody well decides to act up."

"Don't swear, Nithin," Kathy snapped. "And I'm not acting up. I tried to explain my reasons."

"Ya, sure."

"Don't worry about it, Nits," Jake said, smiling sagely. "It's the pregnancy. They get that way ..."

"I'm going to empty this jug of water on your head, Jake," Kathy threatened, her eyes flashing.

"Okay, okay. I was only trying to help."

Maliga turned to Kathy, ignoring Jake. "Kathy, you want to talk about it?"

"I refuse to get married again or go through any kind of ceremony. It's not only stupid, it's sacrilegious. It makes a mockery of the vows we've already taken."

"And that's the only issue now? Everything else is resolved?" Pumpy asked Nits.

"It wasn't easy. We went through the usual ordeal by fire. But, in the end ... yes, that's the only issue."

"Kathy, my dear, surely ..." Pumpy started to say.

"I will not discuss it. I promised myself that I will not obtain my happiness by hurting my parents. I broke that rule. I will not break another."

"Not even if it restores a semblance of their peace of mind?"

"You make it sound as if that would be the end of the matter. It won't. You said earlier that the charade ends here, today. Well, it has. I will not replace it with another lie."

"Did you explain all this to your family?"

"I tried. But that big *gadha* there shut me up. Suddenly, he was the great pacifier, the epitome of the ideal son-in-law."

"You see what I mean," Nithin said, his voice frustrated. "I try to be everything to everybody. And for who? Damn! If God's rules are demanding, women's leave them in the shade."

"I'm going to hit you, Nithin Vania!"

"I'm married to a bloody thug."

"Whoa," Sandy quickly intervened, "Hold on. Sit down, Kathy. Please."

"Whoa yourself, Sandy Murugen! You tell your friend there to stop swearing or I'll break this bottle on his head."

"Nits, stop swearing," Sandy obliged cautiously, looking worried.

"Okay, I surrender." Nits was eyeing the bottle at Kathy's elbow. "Will somebody please move that out of her reach!"

"I'm beginning to lose track of this discussion," Pumpy said in a voice of sweet reasonableness. "Kathy, you were saying something about no more lies. Yes?"

"That's it. No more lies. Don't you see, Pumpy? What was it you said, about the web we weave? Well, let's think about that."

"Can't we just cool it for a second," Jake asked. "All this thinking is turning my ..."

"You keep talking and I'll turn your pretty face," Kathy flared. "Do you guys think this is a street corner discussion ..."

"I give up," Jake muttered, "Nothing I say is right. I guess I'll just shut up."

"Thank you," Kathy said sweetly. "Now you, 'mister-great-everything-to-everybody', you feel I should agree to their ridiculous demands? Go through with the farce and marry you again?"

"I'll go along with whatever you say is right."

"Okay. I'll do it. When?"

"You mean that?"

"Sure. When?"

"Well, .. I don't know. I mean ... the families will have to decide ..."

"No! Come on. Let's give them their moment. When? How about later next month?"

"Why are you pushing me, Kathy? You're up to something. I know you. You're going to put me in a corner ..."

"Answer her, Nithin," Maliga said with a laugh. "You're faffing now."

Nithin stared into Kathy's eyes for several seconds. Finally, he shrugged. "It's a trap. I'm not going to step into it."

"Okay, fine," Kathy said. "I'll make it easier for you. I agree to go through all the rituals at the end of next month. Let's say on the last Saturday. Only, you tell them, both our families. Tell them you made the decision and insisted I go along with it, play the dutiful female."

"Why me? Why can't you say it?"

"Because you already told me to shut up once. Remember? At my mother's place? I'm simply following the dictates of my lord and master."

"Sandy? Jake? Look at her. I'm telling you something's fishy here. That sweet smile doesn't fool me."

"Nithin," Pumpy said a little loudly, then lowered his voice, "Put a lid on it. From what I gather, you wanted to go along with it, not Kathy. It's only fair that you should now convey the message to both families."

"Okay, Pumpy. But I'm telling you, you don't know Kathy."

"Lovely! Now we've settled that you can also tell them that by then I'll be four months into my pregnancy."

"They already know you're pregnant. You told them yourself."

"Yes. But not how far gone I am."

"So?"

"So they need to tell all the guests now, before the farcical ceremony. It'll save them the agony of having to lie later and explaining away what all the world will be able to see."

"I knew it," Nithin exploded, throwing his napkin on the table. "I told you guys it was a trap."

Of your own doing, not mine," Kathy retorted pertly. "I tried to tell them earlier. You start with one lie, it leads to another. Why do you think I insisted that we stop this nonsense now?"

"I can't handle her," Nithin said, looking at the table. "The streets are simpler. I told you okes, we're out of our league here."

"Maybe you should leave all this to me, then, my love," Kathy suggested calmly.

"Okay," Nithin surrendered. "You take over. Whatever you say. I'll back it up."

"And you won't tell me to shut up again?"

"You're the boss. Hey, I'm saying it openly. You have witnesses here."

"That's it, then," Pumpy interjected. "Now, before you two start off again. I have a suggestion. Kathy, you set it up. I'm offering my place for a reception for the two of you. Invite as many guests as you like. Let the old people have their day, leave the guest list to them. And if you arrange it for early evening, on the fifteenth of next month, I promise you and your friends a treat later that night that anyone in this town will give his right arm for. And for that session you can invite whomever you wish. I give you *carte blanche* to do that."

"What happens on the night of the fifteenth?" Maliga asked.

"Oh, just that Tony Scott, the world's greatest jazz clarinettist, will be my guest. He'll be giving a one-off, a solo performance, at the Shah Jehan at six the same evening. After that, at around ten, he'll be right here ..."

"Tony Scott!" The awe in Jake's voice was unmistakable. The girls' eyes were shining. Even the normally inscrutable Sandy couldn't hide his excitement.

"Consider it my present to you two," Pumpy smiled. "It's all on me."

"That's damn generous of you, Pumps!" Jake said.

"Oh, don't mention it. I'll make sure you hoodlums return the favour someday. You can bet on it," Pumpy said drily.

∞

The Tony Scott night was a sellout. The house-full signs were up long before he was due to perform. A huge throng of disgruntled fans crowded into the elegant foyer of the Shah Jehan Cinema, onto the pavements and across the wide expanse of Grey Street. Tickets priced at a rand were changing hands at five and ten times their value and there was nothing the scrupulously careful management could do to stop it. The Rajabs had kept the black-marketers out, the only cinema in town to operate on an advance booking system that made it impossible for anybody to exploit the patrons, but on this occasion it was the patrons themselves who couldn't resist the temptation of making a quick killing.

The show started an hour late, the two thousand seat cinema packed to capacity, with even the aisles crammed with eager fans who considered themselves fortunate to simply sit on the floor and be a part of the audience.

When the clarinettist appeared on stage the roar was deafening, when he raised his instrument to his lips a single sheet of paper fluttering to the ground would have been heard throughout the auditorium. As number followed number the audience swayed with ecstasy. Jake and Sandy, occupying prime seats in the front row, were enthralled, hypnotised by the incomparably superb rendition, the rhythm and tone of a master musician.

"Nithin must be eating his heart out at what he's missing," Sandy whispered in Jake's ear.

"His choice," Jake whispered back. "He gave his heart to Kathy ..." Although they were speaking in low voices several sounds of "hush" and a few hisses shut them up.

Scott hit a high note, held it for so long and with such clarity that Jake found himself holding his breath in sympathy. When, at last, the musician gradually faded, Jake could contain himself no longer.

"Hey, Tony," Jake shouted, "You play the blues so well how come you ain't black?"

The front of the hall erupted with laughter. Scott's eyes twinkled as he bowed to Jake, acknowledging the compliment. As he straightened up Pumpy strode across the stage and whispered something in his ear. Jake saw Scott's mouth form the word "Now?", saw Pumpy nod, and watched as they left the stage.

"Something's wrong here," Jake said to Sandy.

"Hey, what's going on?" someone in the back row shouted.

The audience began to fidget, their voices mounting in frustration. Just as it seemed that things were about to get out of hand, Pumpy returned and spoke into the mike.

"Ladies and gentlemen. Please remain seated. Tony will be back, I promise you."

He raised his hands high, demanding silence. As the audience settled down, he continued, "We have just received a call from New York. The legendary Charlie Parker has died. The 'Bird' is no more."

A low moan rose in the aisles, was picked up by the audience in the front and began to spread.

"I know how you feel," Pumpy said, his eyes sad. "But think of Tony now. He was a great friend of Charlie's, they played several duets together, participated in many jam sessions. Tony needs a few minutes alone. Please grant him that wish. He asked me to tell you that, pained as he is, in the best tradition of showbusiness the performance must and will go on. Thank you."

When Scott came onto the stage again his face was drawn, ashen. Someone clapped, once, and was hushed into silence.

"My friends," Scott said, "you have all heard the phrase 'Bird is God'. He is gone now, but his music will live forever. In the past ten minutes I have composed an epitaph to my friend and mentor. And like all jazz music it is an improvisation from the heart. You, in Durban, will be the first to hear it. I have named it *Blues for Charlie*."

Tony Scott played, and he played his heart out. He made his clarinet talk, he made it wail a tale of woe and sing a song of hope, of love, of glory, and towards its conclusion a salutation to a man who had become a legend in his own lifetime. And as he finished, the tears that coursed down his cheeks told another story, a story that made a mockery of colour and racial prejudice. When he took his final bow for the evening, the audience rose as one and silently filed out, black and white, who had spurned the law that night to share a common desire and were now joined in mutual grief.

It was not only jazz history that was made in Durban that night.

⧉

"I've got a job," Nithin said mysteriously, "at a leading financial institution."

"You're crazy," John Farley said. "What the hell for? In the past few years we've made more than we ever dreamed of. We're set, man. We make more in one day than you could probably earn in a job in a year."

"I know, John. It took a bit longer than I thought but we're there, exactly as we planned it. It's time to learn some new tricks, find out how the big money boys operate. Before we graduate to the big league we must know the rules of the game."

"Don't you ever stop planning, Nits?"

"We have to keep moving, *bra*. The time will come when the escalator effect will take over and we can sit back and reel it in. But if we don't master the playing field we'll be like babes in the woods, the next two wise guys that come along will push us aside and we'll start sliding back to the gutter. And if we ever end up there again that'll be it. We'll never make it back again."

"Well ... I guess you've never called it wrong yet. What next?"

"You control our joint operations during the weekdays. We'll handle it together in the evenings and over the weekends. It'll only be for a few months. If I keep my eyes open I'll learn enough to talk the language of big money. Then we open our suite of offices, exactly as we discussed that day at Kapitans."

"And maybe live a little, huh?"

"Nothing to stop us. We've acted like the poor cousins long enough. When we show our hand we have to have the trappings to go with it. We can't lose, John. We're sitting with a royal flush and the pot won't get much bigger, not in this school."

"So when do you start this new job, then?"

"On Monday. I have to hand over my first month's salary to the guy that's in charge of hiring the darkies. But that's okay. I guess everybody has to have something on the side to take home to his family. It's the only way to get in there anyway."

"Common practice," John said matter of factly.

Four months later, over a beer, Nithin told John, "I can't hang in there much longer. I've learnt all I ever will and I had to hustle to even pick up that much. The darkies there are whitewashed, completely intimidated. Would you believe it when I say they can't even go for a crap without being shat on? And if you find that pun funny let me tell you something else: there's only one toilet, to serve something like twenty of us *bliksems*, and it's located way up on the top floor, literally on the roof. By the time you get there you have to think of rushing back. And you have to use the stairs, buddy. The lifts are reserved for the *wit ous* only. God help you if the toilet is occupied. In all those four months I never once found it vacant. There're usually two or three okes doing a soft shoe shuffle while they wait for their turn. It would be a funny sight, if you weren't yourself hanging in there."

"So tell me what's new," John grimaced.

"What's new is the way they talk about productivity all the time, without even realising that it takes almost twenty minutes to simply take a pee. It's not the law that stops them from allocating a few more toilets to us, in a more accessible place. And there are a few guys, *charos* that I work with, that I really feel sorry for. Chaps like Harry Samuels and Abie Sardiwalla who are highly qualified, with degrees in accounting, who are simply pen-pushing and doing clerical work. They come from good homes and deserve better. In a few years they'll end up like the others, begging for scraps from okes that can't even hold a candle to them."

"So it was a waste of time, huh?"

"Not quite. I've learnt a lot, no thanks to management. Mainly from the literature that's all over the place and talking to some of the *wit ous* who aren't too bad. If I could stay a little longer it would be really useful, but I can't take the arrogance of those bastards anymore. Especially the women who stink like shit and when they open their mouths it's even worse. And it's not only their breath that turns you away — they treat us like we're not human, like you're only being employed to serve them."

"I reckon you should call it a day before you *neuk* one of them."

"*Neuk* someone? You can't even look them in the eye, John, and you're on the firing list. Anyway, there's a staff Christmas party next week, a segregated one for us *charos*. Some of the okes in management will come along, to lend it a bit of status by throwing in a few white faces. I'd like to see how that turns out. If I can stay a few months longer ..."

"Up to you, Nits. I've got the carpenters lined up for our new offices. I'd still like to tackle the job myself."

"You won't have the time, *boet*, not with looking after both our operations. But play it by ear, okay?"

"I guess you're right. I checked our books, Nits. We've got over thirty grand floating around out there. Brings in over fifteen hundred a week. And we're far from fully lent."

"Keep it like that. When we move onto the big borrowers, the business guys, we'll need every cent we can lay our hands on."

∽

It had been left to the Indian staff to decide where they would like to have their Christmas lunch. Because they weren't allowed into a white hotel or restaurant they had to settle for one in their own area and that presented a problem. Most of the good ones were fully booked. Finally, Nithin quietly pulled a few strings and secured a booking at the prestigious Asoka Hotel in Reservoir Hills. The Indians were allowed to leave the office early to give them sufficient time to take a bus from the city to the suburb. Once again Nithin stepped in. There was no way they could get to the Casbah bus rank and also get to Reservoir Hills in the time allocated to them. He arranged for several taxis to take them over, claiming that they were friends of his and no one would have to pay. The taxidrivers were, of course, Nithin's friends, but they expected to be paid. He privately settled the bill out of his own pocket.

Even travelling by taxis they barely made it on time, with no more than ten minutes to spare before the five white staff members arrived in a company car.

Josiah, who was in charge of filing in the archives and who loved to regularly offer home-made samoosas and pies to the few whites who deigned to acknowledge his existence, rushed over and opened the car door. He was welcoming them and generally behaving like the Asoka was his private domain and he the gracious host who had invited them over to spend a few pleasant hours in his humble abode.

Nithin and Harry watched Josiah's antics from a terrace above the car park. Nithin, his face set in disapproving lines, was saying, "There are three types of Indians: there are those that openly defy the system, to the point of losing everything they possess. They deserve our admiration. There is a second group that is so completely intimidated into servitude that all they have left to fall back on is their dignity. Old man Soobiah in the postal department is a good example. He stoically accepts the reality of his existence and, denying himself even the simplest of pleasures, commits himself to providing the best education possible for his children. He forfeits his own future comforts to the realisation of an all-consuming dream — that his offspring will, hopefully, escape the miserable existence to which he himself has been relegated. He deserves our sympathy. Then there is the third kind, the despicable wretch who energetically reduces himself to the level where he resembles a clone that not only imitates his oppressors but actually outclasses them in his effort to emulate their behaviour. His every action, even his private thoughts, are solely devoted to obtaining his master's approval. It is by his behaviour that the rest of us are judged. To treat him with contempt is not enough. He should be completely ostracised from our ranks.

"Which of the three categories do you think Josiah belongs to?"

Throughout the lunch Josiah excelled himself, even by his own low standards, at ingratiating himself with the pompous middle management that Gordon Grenville had inflicted on the Indian clerks. The single female amongst them, who was responsible for personnel and public relations and was in effect the most senior official present, was distinctly unamused. As far as Nithin was concerned she was the only genuinely decent white he had encountered during the short time he had been with the company. Privately, Barbara Homan's colleagues referred to her as "that coolie lover", whilst to her face they turned on the charm — they knew full well that their own career paths were subject to her evaluation. Nithin often wondered whether she was aware that the two that nuzzled up to her the most, the bigoted Maureen Wallace and the treacherous Joan French, were quietly undermining her with senior management out of both jealousy and in an attempt to usurp the position they so dearly coveted. Nithin had long ceased to be amazed by the brazen hypocrisy and the overtly bold actions of the two women — in many ways they resembled the *scotens* in the Casbah. And, unlike out on the streets, he had concluded, in the eyes of these people we don't exist and as a result they never bother to conceal their slimy machinations whenever an Indian is within their hearing. And because they don't see us they fail to realise how much we observe and how perspicacious we are.

Listening to Josiah's performance now Nithin decided that not even the most ultra-rightwing racist from the *platteland* would have failed to approve of his antics. Here is one "Sammy", they would condescendingly conclude, who certainly knows his place and can kow-tow to his masters with supreme self-negation. Josiah, on the other hand, truly believed that he was really making a big hit — he was the star of the show, the pick of the litter, top of the heap.

He wouldn't have lasted an hour on the street.

Throughout his entire act Josiah never once looked directly at his Indian colleagues. Whenever his eyes involuntarily flicked towards Harry or Aby Sardiwalla, he quickly looked away. For this afternoon they were simply not there. This was his day, his chance to prove what great guys they all were, how very equal they could be when given the opportunity to mix with such illustrious gods.

"It's quite funny, really," Josiah was saying in his affected accent, "the poor old guy just didn't know he wasn't allowed to occupy those seats. And when the bus conductor patiently explained 'It's apartheid', the old codger, confused, looked at his watch and said, 'huppart eight? No! no! Hit huppart nine now!'"

Woolf and McFarlane laughed uproariously and Josiah, encouraged, continued from there, basking in the limelight that shone exclusively on him now.

"You heard this one?" Josiah asked, his eyes twinkling with mirth, "How do you get twenty blacks to fit inside a Volksie? Easy, man. Put a white man in first and the darkies will simply creep up his backside. Ha! Ha!" He doubled up in a fake paroxysm of laughter, his eyes actually watering as he held his stomach with both hands.

Nithin, his eyes icy and the anger beginning to show in his face, glanced at Harry. Harry's lips were in a straight line, the fork in his fingers trembling slightly. Aby was looking at his plate, his face flushed. Suddenly, McFarlane sensed the discomfiture amongst the clerks, the absence of laughter, the embarrassed glances they threw at one another.

"Tell me," McFarlane asked patronisingly as he turned towards Aby Sardiwalla. "Do you chaps go much to the theatre? You know, the live shows, not the movies?"

Aby gave a small shrug. "Sometimes," he replied non-committedly, reluctant to be drawn.

"Really, old chap? So you do have them in your areas? I wouldn't have thought so, you know. I suppose it's mainly your ethnic stuff, the Bharata Natyum and that sort of thing, would you say?"

Nithin flicked his eyes at Aby, and then, casually and with extreme care he folded his napkin and deliberately threw it in a bowl of curry in the middle of the table. Slowly, he leaned back in his chair. He let the silence build up before turning in McFarlane's direction with a mocking smile.

"Actually, *old man*," Nithin said, mimicking his host, "we're beyond all that now. Quite cultured these days, in the Western way, if I do say so myself, what?"

McFarlane missed the irony. It was the first time Nithin had spoken and he had deliberately aped Josiah's gestures.

"Really now," McFarlane purred. "So you guys know something about *Madame Butterfly* and ..."

"Come on, old chap," Nithin smiled thinly. "Of course we do. I've personally known Madame Butterfly since she was a moth."

"What!" McFarlane's jaw was hanging, his mouth a big "O". He wasn't sure whether Nithin had cracked a joke or was simply displaying his ignorance. Josiah guffawed at the top of his voice, slapping his thighs. "Hey, Nits, you know what ..."

"No, I don't know what," Nithin snapped, shutting him up, his voice cold. "But I'll tell you what you don't know, you poor fool. We've had enough of the performing monkey act for one afternoon. And as for your organ-grinder there," Nithin glared at McFarlane, "who is so skilled at winding you up, it's time he wised up to the rest of us here."

In the ensuing stunned moment of shock, McFarlane, unsure of what was going on, looked at Woolf whose face had turned beet red.

"Bit tacky of me, wouldn't you say?" Nithin smiled mockingly, looking Woolf in the eye, "Not quite the done thing, eh? Bad table manners, what? But then, hey, what can you expect. Didn't Josiah warn you that you can take a coolie to the cutlery but you can't keep his cuticles out of the curry? Shame on you, Josiah. Anyway, what about you, *Mister* McFarlane? Have you heard Beethoven's Second Opera, the one he wrote immediately after Fidelis?"

"What!" McFarlane spluttered, completely flummoxed. "What! Yes, yes, of course. Often."

"Really now? Well, what do you know, considering Beethoven never wrote a second. But I guess you wouldn't know that, old boy. I would imagine you're more into vaudeville, the sort of show you were hoping we'd put up for all of you this afternoon. After which you could have gone home and told your wives all about your accomplished coolies and what a great bunch of arse-creepers they are. That would really boost your ego and impress your women no end. I mean, how else could you give them a thrill ..."

"Nithin," Barbara cut in, "You've made your point. You asked for that, Colin. All of you did, with your patronising attitudes. Now, let's just drop it."

"But I haven't even warmed up yet, Mrs Homan," Nithin protested mildly. "It's my turn to jump through the hoop now and ..."

"Don't, Nithin. Please stop. I understand your anger but let it ride now." There was a pleading look on her face and her eyes seemed to be conveying a message to Nithin, imploring him to back off, a hint of a warning behind the words.

"Thank you," Nithin murmured. He had been about to add, "my dear" but thought better of it. "Thank you, Mrs Homan," he repeated. "But you really needn't worry. I could have done something quite barbaric, like plastering good old Josiah all over the smarmy Mr McFarlane's elegant backside, where he has been dying to be all afternoon. Now that would give good old Colin here all the ammunition he would need back in the office tomorrow, without stretching his non-existent eloquence. Sorry, Mac old chap, for being such a spoil sport."

"Listen here, Vania," Woolf said ominously, "There's a limit to everything. I must insist ..."

"Ah! The wooden-faced Mr Woolf. I wondered when the Sphinx would open his mouth. That's what they call you, by the way. The shrewd Sphinx, the office rat that scratches through all the secretaries' desks at night, looking for God only knows what. Did you wish to say something, Sir?"

In spite of herself, Barbara Homan couldn't quite hide the smile on her face.

"This has gone far enough," Woolf said, rising.

"Sit down, old man, sit down," Nithin said, his tone relaxed, conciliatory. "After all, we're both men of the world, we can let our hair down a bit without giving offence. Mrs Homan is right, I may have gone too far."

As Woolf reluctantly lowered himself into the chair, Nithin continued, "I'll tell you what, by way of apology, I'll do the gracious thing and resign first thing in the morning. How's that? Of course, I'll do it all very humbly and with the greatest of respect. It's the least I can do. Matter of discipline, an old teacher of mine once called it."

Woolf didn't respond, ignoring Nithin's expectant look. Suddenly, Nithin smiled hugely, arms stretched wide. "Come on now, Mr Woolf. Let it not be said that you failed to play the game, especially one where you set all the rules."

Woolf studiously ignored Nithin, making a point of helping himself to the food on the table, carefully selecting a few choice morsels of meat from a bowl of curry. Guy Wilson, at the far end of the table, straightened up and growled, "I think you're obnoxious and ill mannered and ..."

"Ho, *poepol*, ho! Time to rally around the flag, what?" Nithin almost applauded.

"I don't have to take this," Wilson said angrily. "I think you should leave before I ..."

"If you can't stand the heat, my man, you should stay out of the sun. And before you do what, you creep?"

"Stop it, this minute," Barbara Homan said. "This is ridiculous."

"Go on," Nithin challenged Wilson, "Finish what you were going to say. No? Bit out of your depth suddenly, are you?"

"Nithin, I think you're exceeding the bounds of decency," Mrs Homan said, almost sadly.

"You're right," Nithin said, smiling genuinely for the first time. "I offer you my apologies. You don't deserve this. I'll leave now. But first, may I ask you for a favour? Nothing that will put you out. I promise."

Barbara Homan nodded, then said, "You don't have to go."

"I agree. Not because of what took place this afternoon, anyway. But I've overstayed my usefulness with the group, or perhaps it's the other way around. Whatever, it's time I made tracks. Now, will you grant me the favour?"

"What is it you wish?"

"Simply to avoid dramatising this day and to spare everyone's sensibilities. I have no desire to draw out their agony till the morning. Will you accept my resignation? If I hand it to you now?"

"No, I won't."

"Why not? You have the authority to accept it."

"Because I'm not satisfied it's called for. You were provoked ..."

"Say no more, madam. For what it's worth, I expected you'd say that. I just needed to be absolutely certain."

The look that passed between them was a mutual acknowledgement of respect, a salutation to the rules of fair play. Nithin bowed slightly, then looked around the table, his eyes stopping on Woolf.

"This presents us with a minor problem. If I show up tomorrow we risk getting embroiled in a post-mortem on this afternoon's debacle. Oh, I'm aware it would only be a routine affair, an observance of form, so to speak, before I'm shown the door. Then again, the superior Mrs French may consider it presumptuous of me to ask for an audience with the Great One, and whilst she ensures that I cool my heels sufficiently to satisfy her pride, the tongues in the typing pool would be wagging furiously. I have little doubt a highly embroidered version of today's events will be communicated to at least a few of them before the night has passed."

Nithin spoke as if he were commenting on some casual disturbance, a matter of little significance, a passing disagreement to which they were all no more than mere spectators.

"I'll tell you what," he continued, still looking at Woolf, "I won't sour your moment tomorrow or spoil Bill's thunder. I'll leave it entirely to you. Handle it however you care to. After all, who here will dispute your presentation of the case? Only Mrs Homan has the strength of character to do that and what would be the point in it. I'd be gone anyway and your combined weight will only cast aspersions on her version of events. Shall we say it's settled then? I'd be truly grateful, of course."

Woolf opened his mouth to say something, closed in, opened it again before finally clamping his teeth together.

"Think about it," Nithin continued in his matter of fact voice. "You'll get all the credit for getting rid of an uppity coolie and at the same time entrench your authority over the department you so fondly refer to as 'Little India'. Just add me as another feather to your cap, together with those of your many colleagues that you so smoothly worked out of the company. I'm sure I can depend on you for this small favour. Okay with you too, Mac?"

Throughout, Nithin had been sprawled in his chair, appearing to all the world as if he were discussing a soccer match. He stood up now and looked at Josiah who was busy massaging one hand with the other in petrified silence, eyes frantically darting from one white face to another.

"My biggest thanks go to you, Josiah. You'll never appreciate it but today you helped me on the road to understanding myself. A dubious honour but one you truly deserve."

Nithin pushed his chair back, bowed once again to Barbara Homan, then took a backward step. From behind him he heard a single pair of hands clapping, sounding unnaturally loud in the silence. Startled, he turned around.

"Bravo! Now that was something to warm my heart." Rabbi Bhugwandeen, the owner of the hotel, stood near the doorway grinning.

"I will consider it an honour if you will join me in a drink."

As Nithin and Rabbi were walking out they heard the click of heels and then Barbara Homan's voice, "Does that invitation include me?"

∞

The three of them were sitting at a table in an intimate bar on the second floor. Rabbi was personally pouring from a twelve-year-old bottle of whiskey. "I came in to see if everything was okay. That was about the time you said something about 'coolies and cutlery'. I considered beating a hasty retreat but I was hooked, couldn't have left if the kitchen was on fire."

"I'm concerned about you, Mrs Homan," Nithin said as he took a sip. "When you left there with me you made a pretty damning statement. Those guys will hang you tomorrow."

"I don't doubt it. I'm leaving the company anyway. I've had an offer from a hotel group that's quite tempting. I just couldn't make up my mind whether to accept it or stay on. I guess the clincher was when you thanked Josiah for helping you to understand yourself. It made me do a bit of soul searching of my own."

"Do you think it'll be any different in your new job?"

"No. But at least I will have made a stand with this particular lot."

"For a white, you're okay," Nithin grinned.

"I'm going to assume that's a compliment. That bit about Beethoven and the Second Opera? Is that true?"

"I'm quite certain it is. Any credit, however, for that bit of knowledge must go to my wife who is forever trying to correct my recreant ways. She's the opera buff in our relationship."

"It was a pretty effective squelch. Did you see Mac's face when you threw it at him? It's been a long time since I've seen anything funnier."

"I couldn't help noticing the look on your face either," Nithin laughed. "To be honest, I didn't exactly expect you to be amused. And that reminds me, what are you doing here today? Mac and his bunch are nowhere near your kind of people, Mrs Homan."

"It's Barbara. And since you asked, I have a confession. The whole purpose of this party was entirely my idea. It started off with the office Christmas party planned for next week. Since it's going to be held in the company's boardroom this year, I pointed out to the MD that there was no law stopping you guys from attending. Gordon's not too bad a guy but he was scared stiff that there'd be an uproar from the whites, especially the women. Today was the compromise we agreed on. I thought it would be a start, at least. I came along to oil the wheels, to help break the ice. I had no idea it would turn out the way it did."

"Well, Mrs Homan ..."

"Barbara."

"Barbara. You should have obtained our opinion first. There was not one Indian there that was comfortable with the idea."

"Which begs the question," Rabbi joined in, "Nits, what the hell are you doing with this lot? From what I've heard about you, you don't need the job."

"It's a long story, Rabbi. But you're right. I don't need the job. I'm saying this for your benefit, Barbara. In case you leave here with any guilty feelings about today."

"I was beginning to think that way. I feel better knowing that your next meal is not an issue."

Nithin couldn't stop the chuckle from forming, then laughed outright. "You know what I do with the miserable salary I earn at this company? I give it to the *scotens*, tell them to go buy a few perks for themselves."

"*Scotens?*"

It was Rabbi's turn to laugh. "Street kids, Mrs Homan. You see what different worlds we live in? Nits and I could have a whole conversation here, in English, and you wouldn't even begin to make sense of it."

"I'm fascinated. Try me."

"You *smark* the *stekky*, my *bra?*" Rabbi asked, turning to Nithin.

"A *vukker* step, *charo*. But I don't *simmer temba* seven *jarrers* on my ace," Nithin replied without batting an eyelid.

"Okay, okay," Barbara butted in, her eyes twinkling. "Explain, please."

"So soon?" Rabbi asked, smiling.

"I think you were talking about me. But I don't know if it was good or bad."

"I asked Nits if he liked you a lot. He answered that you're a pretty neat chick but he had no wish to serve seven years in solitary confinement in the local jail."

"You're right," Barbara said. "We live in different worlds. But isn't this some kind of street slang?"

"Not at all, we speak it all the time. Amongst ourselves, of course."

"All of you? Even the businessmen and the academics?"

"I'm a lawyer, madam. When I'm not in court, most times this is how we talk. And when I say 'we' I include many of my white colleagues."

"I'm amazed. And you say some whites talk that way?"

"It's the ghetto patois, Barbara. And more than just a few whites are adept at it. At least, those that mix freely with the rest of us."

"Goes to show. I didn't even know that kind of mixing went on. But wouldn't there be a great risk in that? Surely the Security Branch must be aware of it. Even I know that mixing of the races, even socially, is not allowed. Don't they hassle you?"

"They do, of course. All the time. But they can't stop it. And many of us have paid dearly for it. One of the best lawyers in the land, Rowley Arenstein, got himself struck off the roll for doing just that."

"Simply for socialising with you guys? You're making me wonder which is the criminal here. The law or the people. And how does this Mr Arenstein earn a living now that he can't practise?"

"Oh, we have ways of getting around these laws. At the time when I qualified there were very few Indian legal firms and the whites didn't want to know about us darkies. Rowley, in the face of massive opposition from his own fraternity, took me on and helped me to serve my articles. He lost half his clients in that first year, some of his very good buddies made sure of that. Didn't bother Rowley, though. He was worried about its effect on me, can you believe that? Used to keep telling me to hang in there, not to cave in. There was no happier man in this town than Rowley the day I got my ticket to appear in court, in my own right.

"How does he earn a living now? To put it badly, he works for me. In reality, my office serves as a front for him to pursue his own cases, what few he still has. Between his colleagues and the Security Branch, they've broken him financially but they can't touch his spirit."

"I'm sure you must have paid a heavy price yourself."

"Part of the overhead, madam. You learn to live with these bozos. A raid these days is not much more than a slap and a shove. A pretty routine affair all round."

"I think it's disgusting, an infringement of your basic rights."

"What rights, Barbara? There's only one law in this country — the law of the gun in the hand of the cop. The rest is academic."

"But they should be stopped. This is a democracy."

"Stop right there, lady. I won't take offence at what you just said. I'll simply put it down to ignorance on your part because I don't doubt your sincerity. As to stopping them? Who do you think can do it? Nithin? Me? We don't have the vote. You? Rowley? Sure, you have the vote. But your kind are not even a minority. You are insignificant, voices in the wilderness."

"I can't buy that, Rabbi. I'm a white, I know there are many whites, far more than you suggest, that would be horrified if they knew exactly what is going on."

"That's just my point, my dear. If they knew what's going on. And who do you think is going to tell them? Certainly not the media — they only scratch when their master itches. Oh, they're very strong on the question of freedom of speech and so on but that's where it stops. When it comes to the printed word, where it counts the most, like everybody else they do as they're told."

"I still find it difficult to accept that there are no whites who are brave enough to buck the system and stand up to these monsters."

"There are, Barbara, there are. Unfortunately, they're either behind bars or in some shallow grave somewhere in the bundu. And if that sends a chill up your spine allow me to add another. For every white there are a hundred darkies condemned to the same fate. Try reading *The Leader* sometimes. It's the only newspaper with the courage to print the truth."

"I've never heard of it. And how come they haven't shut it down yet?"

"You answered the question yourself — when you said you had never heard of it. The government can afford to ignore it because they know that no white has heard of it, let alone read it. They probably figure it's a good form of catharsis for us darkies and can't harm them. They'd shut it down overnight if only a hundred whites started subscribing to it."

"The editor must be a brave man."

"It's a family-owned enterprise. Yes, they're brave. More than anyone can believe possible. Anyway, let's drop this topic, Barbara. It's beginning to get a bit depressing."

"Yes, perhaps. But I can't help feeling a little angry too. Nobody should be allowed to get away with such horrid atrocities ..."

"There was a time ..." Rabbi said, so softly that both Barbara and Nithin had to strain their ears to hear him. He was looking at the liquid in his glass, swirling it absent-mindedly. "A time when, if a person did something decent, indulged in an act of spontaneous honesty, the automatic response was 'That's pretty white of you'. Whatever happened to your people along the way, what happened to those noble value systems?" Rabbi shook his head, his face desolate. "It's not fair to say that to you. It's a rhetorical question. There's no answer."

"Greed, Rabbi," Nithin said. "And a lust for power. Barbara, before I leave I have to say this: I got to know you a little today. I enjoyed the experience. A few hours ago I wouldn't have believed such a thing was possible. I also have some advice for you — don't ever repeat what you did today. They'll break you so fast you'll never recover if you live to be a hundred."

Nithin shook Barbara Homan's hand, then, on impulse leaned forward and kissed her on the cheek. He threw a ragged salute at Rabbi Bugwandeen as he turned to leave.

"What about you, Nithin?" Barbara asked. "What makes you so confident you can get away with today?"

Nithin stopped in mid-stride, then half-turned towards Barbara. When she saw the look on his face it almost chilled her.

"Because numero uno, madam, is Nithin Vania. Society, politics and the law can stuff themselves. I live by my own law: if anyone tramps my toes I tramp their face, period. Isn't that exactly how your government operates?"

∞

It was more than two years later, and Nithin was at the Club Lotus having a drink with Jake. Several of the regular members had joined them at their table. Dawood Rasool, a youngster of about eighteen and a first year university student, was elaborating on what he had learnt of the Theory of Money. When he paused to sip his coke Nithin held up his hand and, like a schoolboy in class, requested permission to speak. When the laughter subsided Nithin made what he thought was no more than a casual observation. It ended up as a prolonged discourse.

"Tell me, Dawood, what percentage of what they teach you do you consider has a basis in reality? Do you think this theory of money that you just regurgitated is all encompassing, covers all the angles?"

"How should I know?" Dawood laughed. "I'm still a student."

"Okay," Nithin smiled back. "Shall I tell you what money really is all about? Over and way beyond what the textbooks say?"

"Sure. Can I go back and repeat it in class?"

"I'm not sure it'll earn you any kudu points ..."

"If you repeat what Nithin tells you," Harry Samuels cut in, "you can be sure they'll label you a reactionary. You'll end up completing your studies here at the Lotus."

Nithin chuckled. "Money," he began, "is a synonym for greatness. The manner of its acquisition has little to do with the status it bestows. It levels the playing field and elevates even the most pompous ignoramus and places him on a par with his betters. It's the only thing that can, overnight, provide an entrance to the private salons of a hollow society bereft of any value. Give the most despicable slob a million in hard cash and watch him bloom into society's newest and most welcome member. The fact that he becomes even more insufferable ceases to be a handicap — it becomes the yardstick by which his success is measured. That's the value of money. It's purchasing power is incidental and overshadowed by the newfound status enjoyed by its possessor." Nithin had been smiling throughout. Any sign of humour, however, was restricted to his lips, his eyes were as cold as chips of ice.

"Take this club we're in now. It's a good example of the philosophy I've just enunciated. How many of you guys here know the purpose for which it was created? It started off as an answer to the illustrious white-owned Durban Club. At the time of its inception the membership consisted, amongst others, of some of the oldest money in the city. To belong to the Lotus Club was like wearing a badge of honour, a recognition of having served your people and your community with dignity. Monetary wealth alone was not the criteria; academic excellence and the ability to converse rationally was. How much of that do you see around you today?"

"The founding members have all disappeared," Dawood admitted. "My father was one of them but he doesn't come here anymore. And I hear that Pumpy Naidoo, to whose vision this place owes its existence, has declined the chairmanship for the coming year. That will surely sound its death knell."

"Oh, it will go on, my friend," Nithin said matter of factly. "Never fear. The very people responsible for its deterioration will ensure its continuation. What honest money created will be propped up by the ill-gotten gains of the rabble. Money, however obtained, keeps many doors open."

"So the origin of money as a store of value has been replaced by its power to elevate incompetents and place them on a pedestal. Is that what you're saying?"

"I'm a product of the University of the Street, which confers experience rather than degrees. What I said is merely my observation. Anyway, I'm sorry, I didn't mean to steal your thunder. Please carry on."

"But I like what you said," Dawood went on. "What I want to know is whether the other functions of money, such as a medium of exchange, are a fallacy?"

"Of course not. It serves that purpose admirably, but it's a secondary function. Its prime qualification is that of making giants out of intellectual midgets and bestowing dignity on fools."

"Careful, Dawood," Jake chuckled. "Present that as a thesis and you'll spend the rest of your days on the street corner."

"If there's one thing I'm very good at," Dawood smiled, "It is regurgitating textbook theories. The very first thing I learned in varsity was the knack of behaving like the archetype "Sammy". It didn't take me long to realise that with the correct amount of bowing and scraping and licking whiteys' backsides, I couldn't fail to graduate summa cum laude! Then, with a display of a bit more of the humble appreciation I'll be appointed to the post of junior lecturer. Just about then, I reckon, your children will be ready for me and I can nurture the next generation of servile citizens. I've figured it all out, buddy. No way old Nits here can sway me."

"Listening to you I doubt you'll last that long," Jake chuckled. "Your cynicism — no, that's the wrong word — perhaps your appreciation of the realities of your life will be your undoing. Better for you to get out now and save yourself a fortune in fees and lost earnings."

"And do what, Jake? Sell hankies in Grey Street?"

"You'll only replace one master with another anyway," Nithin said drily. "You'll still be bowing and scraping. The difference will be that the new puppeteers will be from amongst your own people — the Grey Street tykes."

"So either way I lose?"

"Not at all," Nithin smiled. "You haven't been listening to me. What have I been saying for the past half an hour?"

"What? You guys talk in circles ..."

"Dawood, obtain the Great Equaliser!"

"What the hell is that?"

"It's what we have been talking about all this time. Money! With a capital 'M'. It opens all doors and makes heroes out of has-beens. You've heard the old saying about money, that it talks for you? Well, it does more than that, a hell of a lot more — it sings arias for you in places you didn't even know existed. People whose names you haven't even heard of will be singing your praises and claiming your friendship in the hope that, somehow, by that simple act, some of your good fortune will rub off on them."

"So I'll be every bum's hero. I'm not sure I like that."

"It's the price you pay. A small price indeed, depending on your perspective. But you can be sure of one thing, you'll never be another man's lackey."

"So," Dawood asked, "this thing, the Great Equaliser, how do I go about obtaining it?"

"I'll tell you how not to go about it. Academic excellence or working for somebody else won't do it. Show me a moneyed man who tells you that's how he obtained it and I'll show you a liar."

"So how do I go about getting it?"

"Nobody can tell you that. The answer is between your ears. Go into yourself. Plot, plan and puzzle. Set a goal, put a timetable to it, make it an all-consuming passion, be ruthless with yourself in the pursuit of it and presto! your brain will provide the answer."

"Ya? Just like that? You read this somewhere?"

"I lived it, buddy. You don't listen. I told you earlier, nobody can provide you with a formula. That comes from within you. Anyway, you ask too many questions."

"Okay, Nits, okay," Dawood said, putting up his hands. "Plot, plan and puzzle, huh? The three Ps. I'll remember that."

"Why didn't you tell me that when you walked out of that finance company?" Harry Samuels asked plaintively. "I could have been on my way to being wealthy by now."

"I did, my good friend. I told all the *charo*'s that. You guys just weren't listening."

"I don't remember you saying all this ..."

"Sure I did. Not in as many words, perhaps. Remember when I thanked Josiah that day? Did you understand it? His 'good old Sammy' act should have been your redemption, you should have realised the direction in which you were headed if you stayed a minute longer. I joined that company to learn something. It was part of my plan. I suddenly realised I could end up paying a higher price than the lesson was worth."

"But you had a plan. You could afford to walk out. We couldn't."

"Of course not. Why did you not see that it was time for you to make a plan? Wasn't it obvious to you that those *vit okes* were no more than weak snivelling *chutyas*, hitching a free ride on your abilities? That was your clue, the way they folded in the face of my anger. Were these the kind of people you were going to play second fiddle to for the rest of your life?"

"I should have simply looked for another job."

"Then you miss the point of my argument. If you work for a white man you must accept their rules. One place is no different from another."

"That's what Vasi Nair, our old teacher, would have said," Harry added.

"A very wise mentor, Harry. We owe Mr Nair a hell of a lot. That was one man who didn't think much of whitey."

"Why do you say that?" Dawood asked. "Why keep dragging the whites into every discussion? Does our entire life have to boil down to that?"

"Sadly, yes," Nithin said quietly.

"What Nits is saying," Jake explained, "Is that all white businesses, and if there's an exception I haven't heard of it, operate on the same basis. It's the way they have evolved. Changing jobs does not solve the problem."

"Then maybe we should all work for our own people," Dawood suggested.

"Come on, Dawood," Nithin said, his eyes flashing. "You can't be so naive. If it's a question of race with the white man then it's a matter of caste with our own ..."

"I don't buy that," Arvind Bhoola, from a prominent Indian family, said a little loudly. "You can't equate racism with caste."

"Okay, maybe you're right," Nithin said with a disarming smile. "Perhaps it's all a tribal thing."

"Listen you guys," Jake said, looking around the table. "Let's get this in perspective. The Grey Street merchants are almost entirely Muslim or Hindu, nearly all of them from the state of Gujerat. Let's not kid ourselves. Within each of those two groups their own kind always have an advantage over the others."

"But it isn't a religious thing," Arvind said. "A South Indian Hindu, working for a Gujerati Hindu, would still suck the hind tit. The same applies to an Urdu-speaking Muslim working for a Gujerati Muslim. It may be a tribal thing, as Nits said, but dig a little deeper and what do you find — a business environment that does not completely preclude us from prospering or our abilities from going unnoticed.

"We're comfortable in it. We're amongst our own kind. We understand each other, we can empathise with each other. We can, to say the least, hold our heads high and not feel stifled by their condescension. And, very occasionally, if we have the ambition to do so we can even go into business for ourselves with their assistance.

"We know each other's psyche. The different groups, whether it be Surti, Memon, the Bunya, Tamilian or Hindustani, all mix at a social level and on the sports field. Of course, there will always be distinctions, but these are the distinctions created by wealth and differing income groups rather than by race or the colour of our skins. The contact between all of us, at the family or neighbourhood level, provides a certain rapport and a court of last appeal — if you wish to call it that.

"The Europeans, on the other hand, interact with us on a distinct master and vassal basis. The illiterate and obnoxious white hobo enjoys a social status, and for that matter a legal one, that is far superior to our most highly qualified academics. They have refined the system to the point where it has now become a religious conviction. Even their church now preaches separation by colour."

"This is all very enlightening," Samson Naidoo said airily, "And now that we have identified the common enemy can we all go home?"

"Seriously, Sam," Arvind continued, refusing to be deterred, "what does the white man know about us? If we work for them we are relegated to some dingy back room to spare their sensibilities. Our only contact with them is restricted to the martinet they place above us, usually some incompetent buffoon who grows fat on our efforts. The rest? We don't see them, either because we are partitioned off into some corner or, as good coolies, our eyes must always be cast downwards.

"And outside of that stifling environment? Is there any acknowledgment of our existence? At the end of the day they head for their leafy suburbs and exclusive area apartments and we wind our weary way to our ghettoes. Their weekends consist of leisure — sunshine, sailing and sosaties. Ours consist of a second job to supplement the meagre scraps they throw at us."

"Look, Arvind," Dawood leaned forward angrily, "This constant regurgitating of the inequities of our existence achieves blow all and only sours my mood. Wherever you go in the city every conversation comes back to this."

"Do you really believe that?" Nithin asked easily, "that it achieves blow all? If you do then you deserve all you get. Perhaps more. This is what being Indian is all about. It's what we do best. Instead of spending our time simply drinking and carousing we are forever ..."

"Look at it this way," Jake interrupted, "Just imagine for a moment that a white man is that fly on the wall. What do you think would be going through his mind now? Would he be astounded at our ability to think at this level, to reason things out rationally and eloquently?"

"I doubt he'd home in on our eloquence," Samson said, his eyes dancing. "The only words that he would hear are the ones that reflect our opinion of him and, in his anger at our impertinence, he would lose his grip on the wall and splutter to the floor."

"Uppity bloody coolies!" John Desmond mimicked. "Just *klap* the little shits. They'll soon know their place."

"Ja, but," Samson grinned, a naughty look on his face as he pointed towards Jake and began to sing in a smooth clear voice, "One sword at least thy rights shall guard ..."

"One faithful harp praise thee," Jake joined in, smiling.

All at once, the others around the table took up the refrain, their voices melodious. John's youthful tenor rose above the others as he played the conductor, his cigarette serving as a baton.

"The minstrel boy to the war is gone
In the ranks of death you'll find him

His father's sword he has girded on
His wild harp slung behind him."

Jake signalled to the waiter who was grinning at them from a distance. With a sweep of his hand around the table he indicated a repeat of the last order.

"And get one for the fly," Samson shouted over his shoulder, "Make sure it's the best ambrosia in the house."

"Huh?" Marnie, the waiter, mumbled as he came towards them, the ever-present tray held high, his eyes all screwed up. "What you say, *maatie*?"

Samson burst out laughing. "Get one for yourself, bro."

John lifted his glass in salute to Marnie and sang, "For he's a jolly good fellow ..."

He was still drawing out the last syllable when Samson cut in with, "But oh, why did he have to be so bee-yoo-ti-fulll."

They collapsed in their chairs, the sounds of mirth rising above their table and spreading over the room. Somebody from a group across from them stood up and, infected by the humour of the moment, started singing *Swannee River* in a somewhat off-beat voice. His mates joined in and, halfway through the song, several more stood up, their glasses held at arm's length:

"Massa beneath de shade would lay
While we poor niggers toiled all day
Pass de bottle when him dry
brush away de blue-tailed fly ..."

Suddenly, Swart, the burly licensee, burst out of his office and screamed, "Shut up! Just shut up!"

It was as if a revolver had been fired in the air. Without a single exception the group subsided in unison, subdued.

"I'll have none of your focken treason songs in my place! You hear me!" Swart bellowed.

"Christ!" Samson said, "The poor bastard can't distinguish between a lament and ..."

The Afrikaner swung his massive shoulders around violently, his eyes darting all over in an attempt to locate the speaker. "Who said that? *Kom*, stand up! Which of you shits called me a bastard?"

In the silence that followed no one looked directly at him, no one moved. Emboldened by his subjugation of them, he screamed again, "Who the *fock* said that?"

Apart from Samson, who was smiling at him sardonically, most of the eyes remained averted. When Swart looked at the group that had been singing the refrain from the Deep South, they began to fidget with their glasses, eyes downcast. The contempt in the Afrikaner's face became more pronounced and he began to strut around the tables. "Bloody cowards!" he spat scornfully, then added, "*Focken* coolies!"

The words were barely out of the Afrikaner's mouth when a dark lanky figure slowly uncoiled from a chair at the far end of the room. In a voice as smooth as melted honey he asked, "What was that you just said?"

The licencee spun around angrily, noted the attitude of defiance and said, his voice lower, "I wasn't talking to you. Sit down."

"But I'm talking to you. Repeat what you said."

"Look here, just ..."

"Repeat it."

"I'm warning you ..."

"Say it again, tough guy."

"You're asking for trouble ..."

"Mister Swart," the voice was soft, measured, "I don't hear too well. Did you say something about coolies and cowards? I don't like that. I don't like boershit either!"

In the hush that followed, Swart's face turned red as a tomato, his shoulder muscles bunching.

"That *charo* is dead meat," Dawood whispered.

"Watch this," Jake said in an undertone, "You're in for a treat."

"What did you call me?" Swart asked in a strangled voice.

"Boershit!" the tall Indian repeated, in the same quiet voice that carried across the room.

"I'm gonna *donner* you ..."

"Okay," the Indian said, his eyes flat. "This is one on one. Just you and me. Upstairs. On the roof garden." With exaggerated care he pushed his chair away, then addressed the room. "The rest of you guys stay here."

Suddenly, Swart scuttled towards his office, muttering something about a revolver. The Indian silently stared at the retreating figure until it disappeared into the office and, as the door slammed shut, he casually resumed his chair.

"I think he's calling the cops," Dawood said.

"He'll brood in there, but he won't make another move," Nithin chuckled. "He won't risk the consequences."

"What consequences?" Dawood asked. "The cops won't ask any questions. They'll haul that guy out of here like a sack of potatoes."

"He tries that and it's the last move he'll make," Jake said. "Don't worry, boy. That hairyback will simmer but that's all he'll do."

"You okes are talking in riddles again," Dawood complained.

"Look, this is a cushy job for him," Nithin explained. "He gets a fat paycheck for sitting in his office and swigging free booze. You think he's going to throw that away for temporary satisfaction?"

"But the club can't fire him," Dawood argued. "He's appointed by the government."

"He's a moocher, paid by the club. But he can't collect a salary if he can't set his foot in this part of town again. He pushes his luck and he'll wake up one dark night with his neck broken. He's been here long enough to know that."

"Ya? But Swart's a big guy and very fit. How come he backed down like that?"

"Dawood, have you seen that *charo* in action?" Jake asked.

"I have," John Desmond said. "And so has Swart. That guy flattened a few heavies here not long ago, so fast they were still talking when they hit the floor. Take it from me, Swart wouldn't last ten seconds and he knows it."

Sam Naidoo nodded as he half rose in his chair and waved. "Hey, Sandy! I didn't see you there earlier. Come on over. You playing white or what?"

Sandy's easy laugh floated across the room. "Be with you in a minute, buddy. The next round's on me."

"Not a chance," Nithin shouted back. "You earned the treat."

Someone shouted, "Play it again, Sam."

Amid sporadic laughter Sandy stood up and ambled over to Nithin's table.

"Big game tomorrow, Sandy," Jake said as he pulled a chair for Sandy. Swart was already forgotten. "The Avalon boys are going to be out for blood."

"You're sharing joint second position with them but they have the edge on goal average. You okes need a two-goal victory to take the lead," John Desmond added.

"They're a hard team to beat," Sandy confessed. "And that guy, Dharam Mohan! How the hell do you hold him down?"

"Break his legs," Samson laughed. "Only chance you got."

"We'll work on it," Sandy chuckled. "If we can catch him on the field. He zigs when you expect him to zag and weaves when he should bob. Before you know it you're flat on your back and he hasn't even tackled you. As for the ball, lemmie tell you, you'll swear it was tied to his bootlaces."

At that moment Chota Essop, the "Aces" Secretary, walked through the door. "Oh, oh," Samson Naidoo said, "That's your lot for today, Sandy. Big John is in town."

"What the hell are you doing here?" Chota almost screamed at Sandy. "You should be at home sleeping."

"I was just leaving," Sandy said, not moving. "Join us."

"We're laying on a big celebration. After the game tomorrow," Chota announced.

"More likely it will be a wake," Josh Jhavary chuckled as he joined the group.

"If good looks could win a ball game," Chota sneered, "We'll sign you up tomorrow."

"Same goes for a big mouth," Josh said, still smiling.

"Put your money where your mouth is," Chota challenged.

"I never bet on a sure thing," Josh continued good-naturedly. "Not much fun. Too much like stealing candy from a baby."

"You should have stayed in the States. They're the world's experts at wisecracks," Chota responded.

"I'll take that as an admission of your shortcomings," Josh mocked. "But don't feel too bad. Soccer administrators are not renowned for their wit."

"You know, Josh," Chota shot back. "For a fallen star you're still full of shit."

"What can I say," Josh grimaced. "You're hitting a bit below the belt. But what the hell, your legendary devotion to the sport entitles you to that."

"I take that back," Chota said, genuinely contrite, "But damned, if I don't play dirty pool you'll eat me for break ..."

Suddenly, both burst out laughing and clapped each other on the back. It had been a bit of friendly banter, perhaps with an edge to it, no more. Their arms were still around each other's shoulders as Chota asked, "Come to the game tomorrow, Josh. C'mon, make an exception. Be my guest."

"Thanks, pal. But I'll take a raincheck. Can't stand the violence."

"You?" Chota asked unbelievingly. "The ex-US Marine? Go on, pull the other one."

"You overrate the Marines," Josh chuckled again in his infectious way. "It's the movies, I suppose. But you got the 'ex' right. And look who just walked in."

Chota gawked. He couldn't believe his eyes. "Louis Nelson! He's got guts coming in here the night before the big game. Hey, Uncle Lou, over here."

Louis Nelson, his deceptively muscular bulk moving smoothly, walked over and shook Chota's hand.

"You sure you in the right place, Uncle Lou? We're the opposition this time, or have you forgotten you're in the lion's den."

"Just checking," Louis Nelson said easily. "Thought I'll give your spirits a lift. But you seem to be doing okay. With the spirit, anyway."

"Better get back to base fast, Louis," Josh said. "These boys are raring to go."

"Good for the game, then. Don't get over-confident, Sandy. You should be in bed by now."

"I'm on my way," Sandy winked.

"Where have I heard that before," Chota grumbled, his eyes rolling.

"Well, I'll be a son of a bitch!" Josh burst out laughing. "Hey, Chota, another of your stars just walked in."

"Papoo!" Chota almost screamed. "What the bloody hell ..."

"Take it easy, bossman," Papoo Akbar said. "Just came to pick Sandy up. I promised him a lift home."

"At nine thirty?" Chota exploded. "The night before our biggest ..."

"I like that," Louis Nelson cut in, "I really love it. Finally you're showing some respect. But you're right. These two better move it."

"Paps, Sandy," Chota said, his voice ominously soft, "You okes sure you're not looking to be dropped from tomorrow's game?"

"Let's make tracks, Sandy," Papoo said as Sandy stood up. Chota was still shaking his head in frustration as they left.

Louis Nelson settled into Sandy's chair and indicated to a waiter to bring another for Josh.

"Our supporters are beginning to drift away, Chota," Louis Nelson said. "If you guys don't do something fast ..."

"It's the white soccer, Uncle Lou," Chota complained. "They're drawing our fans in the thousands. All I hear about these days is Durban City and Norman Elliot."

"They're playing progressive soccer ..."

"Why not, Louis," Josh interrupted him. "With government backing and financial support from the big businesses they can afford to import the best coaches in the world."

"That's one side of it," Louis Nelson said, "But I reckon the press has a lot to do with it. They glamorise those boys and give them extended coverage. When it comes to black soccer it's as if we don't even exist."

"It's not fair," Chota moaned. "Look at our guys. Dharam, Lall, Civvie Dass, Streni Moodley, Excellent Mthembu, Blondie Campbell. What about the boys from Jo'burg, like Scara and ..."

"Chota, nobody is disputing their abilities," Louis Nelson said, holding up a hand. "Those chaps and a dozen others can give the best of the white players a run for their money. But you listen to me, boy. I've lived longer than you. Find some answers. Now! Otherwise in a few years they'll join the legendary Matambo, James Oliver, Cassim Akbar, Kondiah and a hell of a lot of others into ignominy. Who remembers those guys today?"

"We've tried," Chota groaned in despair. "God knows we've tried. Officials from our league even obtained a firm financial undertaking from the Moosas — the cinema family — and several others for a friendly against Durban City. Elliot and his bunch hedged for a while and then claimed it'd be a violation of the law. What more can we do?"

"Smuggle them out of the country," Josh suggested.

"Are you crazy, man. Look what happened to the table tennis boys when they tried that. The harassment when they returned home was enough for them to hang their bats on the wall. How do you expect our players to give of their best with a threat like that hanging over their heads?"

"But why think of bringing them back?" Josh asked. "Look at guys like Precious Mackenzie, Basil D'Oliviera, and a stack of other chaps. They were the best in the land, in their respective fields. They were stifled here but were snapped up overseas."

"Those are decisions made by individuals, Josh. Administrators can't take on such a responsibility. There are families involved here, jobs, and a lot besides."

"Tell me something, Chota," Jake asked. "Did you really believe that a friendly against Durban City could have been pulled off?"

"Well ... we had high hopes. In fairness to Norman Elliott he honestly did everything in his power to make it happen. But the moment word spread of what he was trying to do someone whispered a word in his ear — 'call it off or face a ban forever'. Not only Norman but the whole Durban City team was in danger of being taken off the field. What could the poor guy do?"

"That's my point, exactly," Jake said. "Can you imagine the embarrassment to the State if you ended up winning? Remember the sensation Slumber David caused when, as a sparring partner, he knocked out Vic Toweel? Vic went on to become world champ, but what happened to Slumber? And how about Papwa, Uncle Lou? He licks the pants off Gary Player and what happens? Who knows about what they did to Papwa better than you do. What good did all your efforts do for him? Both of you nearly ended up in jail."

"But the world got to know about it," Louis Nelson said, "Every time something like that happens it drives our point home. The alternative is to lie down and rot."

"The alternative is to blow the State to hell," Jake said coldly. "Give those bastards a taste of their own medicine."

"Violence is not our way ..."

"Bulldust!" Jake said bluntly. "You, Uncle Lou, are like my father and my grandfather. You're all dreamers. Your way has failed. It's time you accepted it and stood aside."

"To achieve what? To stand and watch our children die from their bullets?"

"You think this is living? We were born to be the white man's bumboys? It burns me up when I hear fighters like yourself talking that way. It only delays ..."

"Jake, Jake," Louis Nelson almost groaned. "Give us a chance. There are better options than ..."

"What? After a hundred plus years? You still believe in options?"

"Listen to me, son. It may take another hundred years but we will lick these bastards. Believe me when I say that."

Coming from the old man, to Jake it sounded like the last defiant growl of a mortally wounded animal refusing to acknowledge defeat.

chapter eight

Durban: 1986

Early on Friday morning fate decided to intervene. Rushda had just left with the tea tray when the red light on Sam's private phone began to blink. Idly, he lifted the receiver and was about to answer when Sally's voice came over the wire.

"Salim?"

"Yes, Sally?"

"You alone?"

Sally's voice was hushed. Something, some slight tremor, a soft edge to the way she had said his name, made him sit up.

"You okay, Sally?"

"*Baji* didn't wake up this morning." Sally sounded breathless, a hint of hysteria beginning to enter her voice. Sam felt the blood drain out of him.

"Yes ... okay. Sally, hang in there, girl. How's mother taking it?"

"You know mother ... she's already sent for the *Moulana*."

"I'll be over right away. Make the necessary calls. Inform everyone."

"Sam ...?"

"Yes?" he asked gently.

"Is there any way we can get Jake out?... Just for the funeral?"

"I'll try."

Sam replaced the receiver and took a deep breath, then raised his hands to his face and pressed the trembling fingers against his eyelids. He remained that way for a full minute, then lowered his hands onto the desk and whispered, "Man makes a plan. God makes a plan. God's will prevails."

When he reached for the receiver again the trembling had stopped. He dialled rapidly and when Karan answered he said, in a firm voice, "Karan, *Baji* just passed away."

He heard the sharp intake of Karan's breath, followed by a few seconds of silence. When Karan spoke again there was a break in his voice. "I'm sorry, Sam. Where are you?"

"At the office. I'm about to go home."

"Shall I pick you up?"

"I'm okay. But there is something you can do ..."

"Of course. Just name it."

"You think there's a chance we can get Jake out? Just for an hour or two?"

"I'll get on it," Karan replied, his voice doubtful. "Let me make a few calls ... and Sam?"

"Ya?"

"I was about to get in touch with you ..." Karan hesitated. "Perhaps it can wait till later ..."

"What is it, Karan?"

"You don't need to hear this right now ..."

"What can be worse than what I just told you? What is it?"

"Well, it seems as if your old man read the signs, made his preparations. He signed the documents yesterday. The deal is sealed. The completed agreement is in the possession of the buyer's attorneys. I'm afraid that just about takes the matter out of your hands."

For the second time in a few minutes Sam's world came crashing down around him. "God's will," he said quietly.

"You didn't need this, not on top of everything else."

"You know what the old guys used to say, my friend — sometimes it's sunshine, sometimes it rains. Both these elements live in the same town. Some things you have to take the way they come. Like it or not, you play the cards that are dealt to you."

∞

Dara's funeral procession was the largest ever seen in the Casbah.

In spite of the speed with which Muslim funerals were conducted and the shortness of notice — less than five hours had elapsed from the time Dara took his last breath and the time his body left the mosque on its final journey — news of his death had spread with a swiftness that would have shamed the famed bush telegraph.

The mourners came from everywhere and every section of the Indian community: Muslim and Hindu, Christian and Parsee, the Gujerati and the Memon, Tamilian and Hindi. A fair number of African and coloured, together with a sprinkling of whites and even several from the Chinese community joined the crowds, both inside and outside the Grey Street mosque. Street sweepers touched shoulders with businessmen, market gardeners walked alongside academics in quiet harmony. Farmers from as far north as Stanger, and every little village in between, came to pay their respects, and many brought their field-hands with them.

By the time the pallbearers reached the cemetery in Brook Street, along the way passing Dara's humble birthplace and the silent women lined up in front of it with the baskets placed on the pavement in front of them, the mourners were still streaming out of the mosque a quarter of a mile away and joining the tail end of the procession, fifteen and twenty to a row. The hustlers were there too, together with the *Motas*. Only Jake was missing.

Sam, even through his grief, was stunned — Dara's name had never appeared in print, he had never made a speech in public or addressed a crowd. As far as Sam was aware his father had always been a loner, his only friend his wife, his only audience Madhoo Daya, and occasionally a neighbouring shopkeeper. And, even after the last prayers had been read and Dara's body interred, the vast crowd of mourners refused to disperse. They quietly gathered around the cemetery and conversed in low voices, Dara's name seemingly on every lip.

Over the next few days Sam began to understand the phenomenon of his father's demise. Strangers streamed in and out of the store, shook his hand and mumbled a few words about Dara's charity and generosity. Many simply looked at Sam mournfully, shook their heads in sorrow, and silently left.

"I need money," a middle-aged garbage collector said to Sam. "My mother need operation. Who I turn to? Your father see me collecting rubbish, see look on my face, ask what wrong. I tell him. What he do? He give me money, more than enough. You know what he say? Doan worry 'bout paying back. Can't care for mother with debt on head! Next time he see me he ask me how mother. I say she okay. He smile and say good, very good."

An old lady, in a sari almost threadbare through repeated washing, told Sam, "He give me school uniform for my daughter, tell me take two of everything so there is always clean change of clothes. When I say I can't

381

pay he only laugh and say, 'Oh, I'll be paid, Umma, when I see your daughter become doctor.' And she did, *thumbi*. Become doctor, I mean. That only last month. And when she come to thank him he tell her go home, to kitchen, where she belong. My daughter still laugh when she tell me that."

And so it went on, day after day. Strangers, people Sam had never seen before in his life, stopped him in the street and offered their condolences, repeating over and over, "Good man, that. Real good man. Yes."

Not all were labourers and simple working people. The managing director of a huge firm of wholesalers, a Mr Brown, came over to Sam's office, shook his hand firmly and said, "He was a strange man, Sam. My despatch boys once erroneously sent over an extra carton of jerseys and failed to invoice him for it. There was no way we would ever have picked up the mistake. When your dad made payment he simply added on the amount for the additional items and forwarded the cheque without any explanation. Of course, my accounts department couldn't reconcile the figures. And it was a substantial amount, believe me. When they rang him he simply pointed out the error and slammed the phone down. I came over personally to thank him for his honesty. I'll never forget what he said to me: 'You want to thank me? For paying what I owe?' The look of astonishment on your old man's face was incredible to see. Now you know why we have never placed a limit on your account."

Finally, when a tenant from a small block of flats owned by Dara knocked at Shaida's door and handed her a home-cooked pie, Sam turned to his mother and asked, "Did you know what he was doing all these years?"

Shaida shrugged. "Your father was not a man who talked about these things. But, yes, I knew some of it. Mostly about businessmen who came here to ask for loans or extensions of time when they were unable to pay their debts. About the ordinary people who went to the store I knew nothing."

"And that man that just left?"

"He was in arrears with his rent. For many months. He asked *Baji* to speak to the lawyers, to give him time. The man had lost his job and was unemployed."

"What did *Baji* say?"

"You know your father. He simply tore up the summons or ejectment notice or whatever it was. Then he gave the man a little money and told him to go to Pravin-dada's store in the morning. This pie? His wife sends it to us regularly, once a month, without fail. Have a piece, it's quite tasty."

Sam was dumbfounded. For days after that he kept shaking his head from time to time, unable to understand how this could have been going on, literally under his nose, without him noticing any of it. At last, over dinner with Karan one evening, he mentioned the incidents in some detail.

"I had no idea what was going on, Karan. It's not as if I would have objected or anything like that. But *Baji* was such a martinet, so hard on us at home, I would have sworn he was a miser of the worst kind. Sure, he didn't deny us the essentials, but anything that even smacked of being a luxury was out. He never even bought us a cheap toy. And unlike Yahya, he hardly ever gave a thing to the established charities and berated me harshly whenever I did. And now I find out he was playing 'Good King Wencesles' all the time."

"Your father, Sam," Karan said, "Like many of our old guys, had strange values. The clerks in my office used to go crazy with frustration whenever he phoned and instructed them to suspend some action or another, often at the last minute, just when the matter was about to go to court. That tenant you mentioned? The guy who brought your mother the pie? Your old man gave me a blast about it, called me a stupid *chootya* and then ordered me to give the guy a job by way of penance. He made me feel as if I had been guilty of some great act of stupidity."

"What did you do?"

"What could I do," Karan laughed. "I employed the oke. He's still there and I hear he's doing a pretty good job too. And, of course, he pays his rent on time, without fail."

"What would have happened if you had simply ignored Dara's orders?"

"Are you crazy? He always followed up on these things, in his own quiet way. He would have hung me from the nearest rafter and my grandfather would have stood by and applauded the action."

"I don't doubt that," Sam nodded, smiling. "It's funny, though, how their way always worked out for the better in the long run."

"Those are pretty big shoes you're stepping in, Sam. Better get used to it."

"I'm no good at this sort of thing, Karan. Those old guys acted like saints. Can you see me behaving like that? I wouldn't know how to even ..."

"Maybe they were saints, Sam. We'll never know. I like to believe they were just simple men, of the old school."

"You reckon there are any more of them left?"

"A dying breed. Perhaps Dara was the last of them. And that reminds me, it's decision time, pal. I've used every trick I could dream of to delay transfer of the properties. In fairness, the purchasers have been patient, out of sympathy for your grief. And the conveyancing attorneys have gone along with me up till now. They can't risk their reputation any longer ..."

"I understand. Go ahead, Karan. Proceed."

"Do you realise what that will mean, Sam? It'll be the end of Solomon Brothers, everything you worked for, built up over ..."

"Nothing lasts for ever, my friend. Sooner or later, everything comes to an end."

"So you're going to give up? Just like that?"

"There are some things that are within our control, and some that we can do nothing about. Why delay the inevitable. You know how it goes: if you can't avoid rape you may as well lie back and enjoy it."

"That's pure crap, Sam! And you know it. Look, use your influence. Talk to the buyers, pull in a few favours. Use your connections to prevail on these guys. We still have a few days before the papers are lodged at the Master's Office. It's a simple matter of returning the *uplung*. You can bring it back today."

Sam quietly shook his head from side to side. "The only thing I would have wished to save is the building housing my retail business. The rest, the investment properties — the office and industrial complexes — were just that, investments. I can always buy others, invest the proceeds elsewhere."

"So why not save Solomon Brothers. At least, obtain a long lease. There's still a good chance of ..."

"Karan, Dara made a deal. I have to honour it."

"But the guys he dealt with, there must have been a tacit arrangement that your family will continue to trade from your traditional base. Dara could never have agreed to move out. He probably didn't ask for a formal lease because it wasn't part of his long-term plan. But you can be sure there was a gentleman's agreement there. All we are asking is for them to honour it."

"We can't prove that. And if those guys choose to renege on it, and you can bet they will, we don't have a leg to stand on."

"The courtroom is not always the sole arbiter ..."

"Do you realise what you just said, Karan? Since when ..."

"Okay, okay. Just drop that subject for now. Tell me something else. Are you going to bring the money back? All of it?"

"I haven't thought about it. Let's just see how things pan out over the next few months."

"All right, Sam," Karan said wearily. "But I'm not going to let you lose the Queen Street property. After all, it represents more than a base for

your retail operations. It's your grandfather's bequest, something that he
and Pravin-dada ..."

"You are the executor of Dara's estate. Do what you like. If you can pull
something out of the bag, great. If not ... well then, that's the end of it."

"Fine," Karan said. "I'll see you again on Sunday, then."

"Good. After the prayers for Dara are over we'll spend some time
together. Nits and Sandy will be there too."

∞

"Cancel all my appointments for the rest of the day," Karan instructed his
secretary. "When Mr Vania and Mr Murugen arrive bring them directly to
my office. I don't want to be disturbed after that. Not even a phone call.
Okay?"

"Yes, Mr Naran. Do you want me to wait if your meeting takes longer
than ..."

"No. You go on home. I'll be quite late."

"Oh! Mr Naran, the two gentlemen just arrived. They walked right
past me."

"It's okay. I'll take it from here."

Karan had barely opened the door when Nithin and Sandy walked in
and settled down in the easy chairs.

"Make yourselves at home," Karan said, a little sarcastically.

"Nice of you to offer," Nithin responded, grinning.

"You guys must be wondering why I sent for you. It concerns Sam."

"We figured that," Sandy said. "We wouldn't have come otherwise."

"Sandy, I'm not sure if you know anything about what Sam's old man
was up to. I am aware that Nithin had a damn good idea and helped Sam
with one or two things. Anyway, I'm going to put you in the picture and
bring the situation up to date."

Karan explained the position in full detail, including his last
conversation with Sam. He left nothing out, not even his own thoughts, on
the matter.

"The purchaser is an investment company, two of the shareholders are
well-known Durban businessmen. The third is a wheeler-dealer from
Jo'burg. The local boys are from two of the oldest business houses in
Durban — the Jhaveries and the Moosas. They are extremely decent
chaps and readily agreed to my proposal to exclude the Queen Street
property from the package. They even offered, in their personal capacities,
to pick up any costs incurred as a result of the re-arrangement."

"So you're home and dry," Nithin said.

"Not quite," Karan said, "There's still the third guy."

"You've got two out of three," Nithin said bluntly. "In my books that's a majority."

"Let me finish," Karan requested. "The Durban okes are only minority shareholders. Ninety percent of the company is owned by the Jo'burg honcho. In my opinion he simply conned the other two into joining him. All he really wanted was the leverage their good names would give him. They may have been somewhat trusting but as they said, when this guy approached them he came with impeccable references from some of the best families up north.

"There is also another angle to take into account. Neither of these two families deal in *uplung* — they are past that stage. When I mentioned it to them, in passing by the way, they were quite astonished, and that's putting it mildly. They were, in fact, on the verge of pulling out of the transaction altogether. I have no reason to doubt their sincerity, more so when you realise that by distancing themselves from it they can only lose out because they would receive no refund in the event we come to some arrangement."

"This oke from Joeys," Nithin asked. "Do you know him?"

"Very little, really. It's possible he may be quite a straightforward businessman. After all, *uplung* is a way of doing business all over the world, even the whites here are quite adept at it, though they refer to it in different terms."

"In any case," Nithin added, "As the majority shareholder he would have funded the bulk of the *uplung* portion. If he chose to carry the balance, knowing his partners would not approve, well ... you can't hold that against him."

"No, you can't," Karan agreed. "Anyway, there was little point in asking the chaps here to place our case and obtain the Jo'burg okes view on the matter. They're obviously totally disenchanted with him and are, at this moment, considering ways in which they can extricate themselves totally from the association."

"So where do we go from here?" Nithin asked.

"Will you let me finish?" Karan retorted angrily. "The Jo'burg player goes by the name of David Cohen — possibly a corruption of Dawood Khan. But that's only a guess on my part, his real name could be anything. But I know for certain that he's an Indian."

"Nothing wrong with that," Nithin said. "A lot of our guys assume such names. It oils the wheels with the authorities, on paper anyway."

"Sure," Karan agreed. "Happens all the time. I'm simply placing all the facts before you. Anyway, I contacted this *ou* early today. To put it plainly, he told me to go and stuff myself, and I'm saying that somewhat elegantly."

"Good for him," Nithin laughed. "You need to be brought down a peg or two."

"I'll keep your sentiments in mind," Karan snapped. "You want to hear the rest?"

"Sure. I find all this very interesting. And you're only warming up, I can see it in your face."

"That's very astute of you, considering you're not normally ..."

"Karan, please cool it," Sandy said. "What is all this leading up to?"

"Well ... he's in a pretty solid legal position. In a court of law we don't have a foot to stand on. He is acting perfectly within his rights. There is no reason, not a solitary consideration, moral or otherwise, why he should not act on them."

Karan stopped talking, took a deep breath, then said angrily, "I don't like his attitude, I don't like the manner in which he's gone about this business, and I don't like the way the bastard spoke to me. I want to sort him out. Now!"

"Well, well, well," Nithin smiled widely. "Welcome to the real world."

"And I don't like your wisecracks either," Karan said, his face flushed.

"Just pointing out the realities, pal," Nithin shot back. "It's easy to be principled when ..."

"So fuck the principles," Karan almost shouted.

"Cut it out, you two," Sandy growled. "Our concern here is Sam. Am I right, Karan?"

"First and foremost," Karan answered. "My personal feelings are secondary."

"Does Sam know all this?" Nithin asked Karan.

"No. And he won't approve of where this conversation is heading either."

Sandy nodded his head several times, acknowledging Karan's assessment of Sam's stance on such matters. "Okay, Karan. Is that it? Are you saying it's over to us now?"

"That's up to you. You are both, in your own way, as close to Sam as I am."

"But you have no objection to the way we respond to this information?"

"Far as I am concerned, we never had this talk."

"You're a bloody fake," Nithin said coolly.

"I'm not denying it," Karan replied, with the beginning of a smile.

Nithin and Sandy burst out laughing, with Karan joining in.

"You're okay, Karan," Nithin conceded. "When the chips are down you're there for your mates."

"If I remember," Sandy added with a grin, "When we were *lighties* in Dutchene you always stood by us, never knew when it was time to run."

"And always ended up with the worst beating," Karan said ruefully. "I was one *Bunya* boy that never learnt the art of getting out of the way."

"But you did," Sandy chuckled. "By the time you were fourteen you disappeared into your own world. It's nice to know that world didn't completely knock the spots off you."

"They're all still there, Sandy. I've just disguised them skillfully."

When they stopped laughing Sandy said, "Okay, Karan. We understand the situation. You have your professional status to protect. Leave this to us."

"Just one thing ..." Karan started to say.

"There's always one last thing with you," Nithin cut in. "Now what?"

"Nothing you can object to. Sam must never know about your involvement in this matter. And I insist on paying my share of any costs that may be incurred."

"What the hell do you think we're going to do?" Nithin asked. "Put a hitman on the job?"

"Well ... no... but I thought that if you two are going to ... you know, sort of talk to the *Motas* ..."

Nithin and Sandy looked at each other, then simultaneously erupted into laughter. Karan looked confused, staring at them in absolute bewilderment, his face betraying his inability to see anything funny in what he had said.

"Karan," Sandy said at last, his eyes still twinkling, "There are no real *Motas* anymore. They lost their clout a long time ago, when most of our people were forced into the townships. It's places like Chatsworth, Phoenix, Wentworth — you name it, that's where the action is. The gangsters there are more vicious, more deadly, than anything that existed in this city. Many of them are still kids, fifteen and sixteen year olds, all packing a *gat* and quick to use it. There's no sophistication in their methods, no style. They'll kill a guy for you for as little as a clip, then turn on you just as fast. Talk about principles — they've never even heard of words such as honour or diplomacy. As for friendly persuasion, you can forget about it. All they understand is vengeance and survival, in that order. Dealing with them is looking to end up with bigger problems than you started with. They relegated the *Motas* to the shade a long time ago."

"Stick to your world," Nithin put in. "It may be far more rotten but the smell won't kill you."

"Okay," Karan said, somewhat chagrined. "Thanks for the education."

"Remember that the next time you decide to bill us for your advice," Nithin said. "But, to be fair, we were only laughing at the awe in which you mentioned the *Motas*. In spite of what Sandy said, we will approach them, but not in the way you think. This Cohen character, he could have the backing of some of the Jo'burg *Motas*. From the way he spoke to you I reckon that's a fair assumption."

"So the *Motas* still wield a fair amount of influence?" Karan asked.

"Make no mistake about that," Sandy replied. "They can be as vicious as they ever were, but that's mainly when they're protecting their territory. Otherwise, they prefer to keep a low profile. They are no longer the final arbiters in matters of this nature. There are too many players for that, and everybody seems to be connected to some player somewhere."

"So what do you hope to achieve by turning to them?"

"I wouldn't quite put it that way, that we will be turning to them. It's simply an obvious first move to make, to suss out Cohen's strength. If his only backup is the Jo'burg *Motas* then our guys here can oil the wheels for us with them, so to speak. It'll serve to show Cohen that he's not dealing with *garachs*, tone him down a bit."

"And if that doesn't work?" Karan asked.

"Don't ever allow what we told you to underestimate the *Motas*," Sandy replied. "That would be a serious mistake. They're still pretty well organised and have connections such as you wouldn't believe. But let's assume that that option doesn't work, that Cohen has a bunch of thugs from the townships ready to back him up. If it comes to that I guess we'll just fall back on our own resources. But let's not second guess the outcome. Let's see how it develops."

"Karan," Nithin said, "you don't want to know more than that. Like I said before, stick to your world, what you're good at. Leave this to us, it's our scene."

"But you'll keep me in the picture, sort of inform me from time to time on how things are develop..."

"No," Nithin said bluntly. "From here on the only time you'll hear anything will be through Cohen's attorneys, requesting the necessary changes to the original deal. It's better for you that way."

∽

The Five Aces was humming with activity, operating at a frenetic pace, the patrons absorbed in winning, and as often losing, enormous sums of money in a matter of a few minutes. Generally referred to as a nightclub, the name was a misnomer — it remained open twenty four hours a day, although the really heavy action usually commenced after six in the evening when the big money rollers strolled in.

It had come into existence in the late fifties, in a small room on the top floor of one of the oldest buildings in the city, at the corner of Grey and Victoria Streets and immediately above the world famous Victory Lounge.

Its founders, a small group of businessmen seeking a safe haven in which to indulge their gambling habits, had miscalculated the venue's attraction. In the very first week the tiny place was packed solid with hopeful newcomers seeking an equally respected hideaway. The tables were pushed closer, the air became a bit heavier, but the quiet dignity of the predominantly rummy games continued undisturbed.

A few months later the Big Five moved in, commandeered the whole of the top floor, renovated the premises and moved into business. Before the year was out it was established as the safest gambling den in town where only the cardsharps had cause for fear. The wide boys from the other gambling schools were allowed to participate on the strict condition that their every move would be carefully observed, and the slightest display of strong-arm behaviour would lead to dire consequences. The businessmen were happy, their safety assured by the Big Five's connections with the Vice Squad and the protection afforded against being roughed up by the usual "sharks".

When the *Motas* moved on to more lucrative pastures, attracted by the huge profits in underground casinos and escort agencies, Sandy struck a deal with them and, together with several carefully selected investors, took over the Five Aces. In his usual quiet way he immediately began upgrading the facilities and creating an ambiance in which the gamblers felt comfortable and moved about with a sense of belonging verging on ownership. By the end of the decade it was the place to go to and, in the early eighties, the only school where the sky was the limit, with free food and liquor always available to any gambler provided he was seated at a table.

The facilities had been expanded enormously. The vast floor was hived off into specific areas: "The Snooker Room", with two of the best maintained tables in town, was soundproofed and restricted to only the most adept cueists. A minimum bet of a hundred rands a corner was imposed and welcomed by the patrons — the side bets alone exceeded that amount several time over; "The Bucket Shop" placed no restriction on the size of the bet. Two rands wagered on a horse were as welcome as a thousand, and at odds equal to the best available at the racetrack itself; "The Centre Court", where the sudden death and quick result game of "call card" catered to the hardened veterans, guaranteed every side bet in the event of a dispute between players. At any given time there was never less than five thousand rands scattered around the huge playing table; finally, there was the sedate "'Rummy Room" where the more patient and laid-back gamblers participated at their own lazy pace around a half dozen tables each accommodating seven to eight players.

Of the original shareholders only Sandy and the elegant "Zorro" Khan were still in existence, the others had either gambled their interest away in a fit of passion or sold out to the remaining two. Zorro, a cardsharp of great repute and even greater skill, never participated in any session of "call card": it would have sounded the death knell of that particular activity faster than a raid by the Vice Squad. What Zorro could do to a pack of cards was pure magic. You could riffle them, shuffle them, cut them every which way and mix them in whatever manner you cared to — hand the pack to him and he would call out each card, by suit and number or name before he placed it face up on the table. Only the legendary Jimmy Fredericks, the pied piper of the card game, was equal to Zorro's remarkable ability. The comparison was a tribute to the affable Jimmy and a compliment to Zorro.

Late on the Wednesday evening following the meeting in Karan's office, Nithin was in Sandy's private glass -fronted room, gazing out at the activity around the hall, the subdued hum emanating from the exterior all but obliterated by the hiss of the airconditioning unit. A casual look at his face would have suggested he was absorbed in the activities of a big winner on the other side of the glass, totally disinterested in the proceedings around him. Sandy was doing all the talking, addressing three elderly *Motas* seated in front of him.

"It's the end of the road for Sam," Sandy said. "If the sale goes through he will no longer be able to trade from those premises. Sam was hoping to pull a fast one on his old man by buying the properties himself. A pal of his, a lawyer, was in the process of floating a company that would have served as a front to make that possible. Nits had the finance laid on. When the old *topee* kicked the bucket he also killed Sam's plans. Nits and I are trying to put in place a rescue operation. This is where you come in."

"The buyer, what's his name?" Bull Pillay asked in his rasping voice. The others had to strain their ears to hear him.

"Some guy from Jo'burg, goes by the name of David Cohen. But he's a *charo*, we know that for sure."

"And the purchase price?"

"For the trading property? A mil even, plus another two hundred gees *uplung*."

"And the total deal? How much is involved?"

"It has no bearing on our discussion. I don't know anyway. All we require is to pull this one property out of the package." Sandy leaned back in his chair, giving the trio a chance to digest what he had said. Nithin continued to look through the window.

A full minute went by, then Boxer Miller said, "This Cohen, I know him. He's nothing. He's a *cachela*, a tube for the Hayaat family, their front man."

"You okes better understand something," a short, thickset man known only as "The Somali" spoke up. "The Hayaats are under the protection of Faizoo. You pressurise the Hayaats and you declare against Faizoo. You know what that means."

"Why talk of declaring," Sandy said. "We're only asking for a simple favour, just the one property. And we're prepared to refund every cent they've paid on it so far, including whatever costs the lawyers charge for re-drafting the documents."

"You will have to offer them a sweetener, say ten percent of the total value," The Somali suggested, a sly look on his face. "That way Faizoo won't consider he's being pushed. He's not a guy that likes being *neuked*."

"If anyone was *neuked* here it was Dara. You guys know what he was like. If he had known who the real purchaser was he wouldn't even have entered into any discussions, let alone a sale. *Dakus* and Dara just didn't mix."

"You can only use that argument from a position of strength. You want to tell Faizoo that yourself? You reckon you have the arse to do that, boy?"

Sandy's eyes flashed, then hooded over. He ignored the insult. "That's why we're talking to you," he said quietly.

It was a calculated statement. Sandy knew the men before him were the most powerful of all the *Motas*, their fires perhaps a little dimmed, but still a force to be reckoned with. Their reputations preceded them, even amongst some of the feared township ganglords. He was deliberately putting them on the spot, forcing them to prove themselves.

"You want us to handle this for you?" The Somali asked with a cunning expression on his face.

"We're putting you in the picture," Nithin said suddenly, turning towards them, his voice ice cold. "We're ready to move on Cohen. If Faizoo decides to step into the shit he'd better be prepared to eat it."

"You're saying you don't need us?" Boxer asked, the menace in his voice unmistakable.

"We're saying there's nothing in this for you," Sandy said softly. "This is for Sam, for family. If Faizoo owes you a favour and you choose to call him on it, fine. If you can get his cooperation, we'll owe you one in exchange. It'll save a lot of grief all round. But as for handling it for us, the answer is *no*."

"Look," Nithin said, "We're not talking deals here. This is something personal, no bucks in it for anyone. Okay, I want to say something else, just so we all know where we stand. Sandy and I are talking to you now as your equals, but that relationship depends on what you say next."

"I don't like your tone, *boy*," Boxer snapped. "I've been watching you and your sidekick, that *bruin ou* Farley ..."

"Try talking that way to John," Nithin said with a sneer. "Right now I'm saying you're either with us or you're against us. That's it. There's no middle road. We're drawing the line here."

"Those are strong words, boy," The Somali said, his voice flat. "I don't see you smiling."

"Then you're getting the message. If you're not with us on this don't expect us to be there for you next time around. For now you can leave here in peace. We didn't call you over to ..."

"You're telling us we can leave in peace? We need this from *you*?" The Somali was leaning forward, his face contorted with rage.

Sandy gently pushed his chair back, then draped an arm over the backrest. When he spoke there was an edge to his voice. "We've been reasonable. We gave you all the facts. How come you guys suddenly talk to us like we're *garachs*? When you talk about handling this for us do you think we don't understand what it means?"

"You're talking big, *boy*," The Somali growled. "You reckon you're ready to make a move against us? You want to try your luck now?"

"*I'm telling you to go get fucked*! You got any other questions, *Mister*?"

"Hey," Bull Pillay said, his voice gritty. "What's happening here? We've always understood how we operate. You guys are a part of our team, Sandy. Why do I feel we're declaring here? You boys got a problem, you reckon you can solve it by making enemies?"

"I'm trying to find out who our friends are. I don't see any around this table."

"But this talk, this language, you think it's necessary? When we offer to handle it for you we're saying we can cut your costs. You see something wrong with that? Sure, we're talking big money here. We're all in it for the bucks. We have to cover Faizoo too. It's the name of our game. I don't have to explain this to you, you know how these things work."

"I thought I explained our interest in the matter. I told you Sam is family."

"Ya, sure. Hey, I got no problem there. But you two, you're getting out of hand. Look, you cover us and we cover Sam. Why quarrel about it?"

"How about you cover us and we cover you?" Sandy asked.

"How's that again?"

"This guy Faizoo. You're sure he won't be a problem?"

"We guarantee it."

"His word is final?"

"I said we *guarantee* it. Consider it done. Leave it to us and you get what you want."

"Okay," Nithin said. "You guys handle it. But you offer Faizoo the deal, exactly as we set it out earlier."

"Ya, sure," Bull said expansively, spreading his hands wide. "You see, Sandy. That's what I like about Nits. He's a businessman, he's got style. Come, let's shake on it."

"Aren't you forgetting something?" Nithin asked.

"Ya? What?"

"What you okes get out of it."

"Like I said, *boy*. You got style. Sure, let's talk about that. We're satisfied with ten percent, like we already said."

"Sandy has something better in mind. Remember what he said earlier, you cover us and we cover you? I think Sandy can explain that now."

"Ya?" Bull was beginning to look confused, not sure where the conversation was headed.

"Let me make myself clear," Sandy said, placing both his hands on his thighs. "The three of you, you control what? Three underground casinos, four of the best escort agencies in town, two of the snazziest discos ..."

"Hey! Why talk about that? Our ..."

"You're not listening, *boy*," Sandy said bluntly. "You still want to be in the rackets by the weekend, you deliver. *Fast!*"

"Shit!" The Somali exploded. "You little ..."

Nithin stood up. "You cover us and we cover you. That's what you get out of it."

Sandy followed Nithin's lead, got to his feet and took a step forward. "*It's that time*, gentlemen. We're calling the shots now. You don't like it, you lump it. But you do what we tell you."

"You boys are making a big mistake, Sandy," Boxer said, his voice even.

"You okes made the mistake," Nithin said, matching Boxer's tone. "It didn't have to be this way."

"So it's war, ya? You got the guts to tell us this, just like that?"

"It's up to you," Sandy said. "Think about it. Go to the 'Oceans', check out your showpiece. We'll still be here."

Boxer looked at The Somali, then at Bull Pillay. "You guys are dead meat," he said as they walked out.

The *Motas* were barely out of sight when both Nithin and Sandy reached for the telephones and began to dial.

"Camps?" Sandy said into the phone, "Move the boys out — the security, the bouncers, everybody. Start with the 'Oceans'. That's your first target. Move the *lighties* in, tell them to cause it. Follow the plan, we only have a few minutes, okay?"

"... and John," Nithin was saying, "Tell the heavies to make themselves scarce. Stick to the deal we made with them, lay on a bit extra. Make certain the *Motas* can't contact them." Nithin listened for a minute, the receiver pressed to his ear, then began to chuckle. "You're ahead of the game, John. Keep it going. I'll see you later."

Nithin cut the connection, then turned to Sandy. "John Farley, he's something else. He's got all the *Motas*' top muscle at the beach cottage in La Mercy. He's laid on the best booze and the hottest chicks. I guess he sussed the *Motas* correctly."

"Nothing to do but wait then," Sandy grinned. "Your man John, he's pretty fast on the uptake."

"John's the best, Sandy. And he's never failed me."

Nithin was dialling again, then held the phone loosely, waiting for the call to be answered. A second later there was a click and he began to speak. "Captain, how you doing? Ya, I reckon your Vice Squad can make that raid now. Yup, the 'Oceans' first. But put a few extra men on the job, close all their operations down for a while ... Thanks, Cap. I'll be seeing you."

"Now we wait," Nithin said, relaxing. "I could do with a drink."

"We can both do with one. I reckon it's time to crack a bottle of Royal Salute."

Sandy poured for both of them, then handed a goblet to Nithin. As they settled back he said, "Hell, Nits. It's times like these that I miss Jake. You could never tell when he'd step through that door, with that cocky walk of his ..."

"Like he owned the world," Nithin finished the sentence for Sandy.

"I hate to think what they're doing to him in there."

"Jake always had what they call true grit. He's a lot tougher than all of us put together. Those *Motas* tonight — can you hear what Jake would have said: 'What's to talk about. Time for you *chachas* to shine up and fuck all this jive!'"

"That sounds like Jake, all the way. Remember that time in Verbena Road? When we were about ten years old? Jake walked straight up to those okes from Etna Lane and said, 'Me, I'm Pathan Khan. When I was born my father said I got a cock, I'm a man. Come, you bastards, two at a time'."

"How could I forget," Nithin grinned. "We ragged him for years after that. I just hope he's not saying that now, to the Security Branch."

"Let's not talk about Jake right now. I don't think straight when I'm worried about him. I reckon the *Motas* must be just about getting the message. In another hour they'll get into a huddle, consider their options. When they realise they're on their own they'll move fast, get hold of Faizoo and get him to deliver."

"Bull is our best bet. The other two, they'll be at each other's throats, accusing the other of handling it badly. There's a lot of hatred between those two, Sandy. They've been forced to bury the past, in the interest of the common good. But the graves are shallow. What happened tonight could just be the spur for them to go for each other."

"Maybe. But those *Motas*, they didn't survive up to now by being stupid. We'll have to watch our backs for a while. I wouldn't be surprised if they have some back-up boys in reserve."

"I don't think so. If they had planned that far ahead in their game they would still have been here, laughing in our faces. I've kept close tabs on their moves, Sandy. I reckon I've summed them up pretty accurately. But, okay. Let's not be too confident. You going to stick around here?"

"I have to. The place is buzzing. How about we meet here in the morning, say at eleven? I'll lay on the chow."

"You're on. Watch your back, bro."

"You too, buddy."

⊗

Bull Pillay rang just after twelve noon, his voice full of bonhomie, all friendly and charming. "How you doing, Sandy? Just thought I'd keep you guys in the picture, you and Nits. He's with you?"

"He's here."

Sandy signalled Nithin to pick up the extension.

"Good! That's good. Sam's lawyer, he should be hearing from the other party anytime now. All done, Sandy. Nice and sweet. Didn't I tell you to leave it to me, let me handle it? When I guarantee something you can bet your *ezie* on it, ya?"

"So it's agreed, exactly as we asked?"

"Sure, Sandy, sure. It'll all be done, in writing. Just like you want it. They're preparing the changes right now, in fact."

"No chance of a hitch? No comebacks?"

"Hey, c'mon. You know me, Sandy. I wouldn't *charf* you. You got what you want, no shit."

"Okay. How's business, Bull?"

"Bit quiet. But you know how it is, midweek and all that."

"I reckon it should pick up tonight. Matter of fact, I *guarantee* it."

"Hey, nice of you to say so, Sandy. By the way, I've been meaning to talk to you, both of you. Let's get together, soon. What do you say?"

"We're a bit busy ..."

"C'mon, think about it. Just the three of us, somewhere nice and quiet. I reckon there's a lot of *kachev* to be made, you know, like in the old days. I like your style. And Nits there, he's sharp. It's time you okes moved to the top, got what's due to you."

"What about your partners?"

"Nah ... I reckon they're losing it. You heard them last night. They got short memories. They forget where you guys come from. Now me — you heard me, ya? Did I say no? Didn't I guarantee I'll do this for you? And hey, it's done, just like that. Did I move fast for you okes, or what?"

"Bull, look after what you have. Nits and I have other plans, but they don't affect you. And you're right. You delivered. We have no quarrel with you. Good luck to you."

Sandy replaced the receiver, grinning widely. "You read those okes correctly. There's trouble in the camp and Bull is looking to move in. He's seen our pull, the way we neutralised them. He reckons that with us on his team it'll be a walkover."

"He's edgy too, Sandy. He's not sure of our next move. He's trying to draw us out, get a lead on whether we're aiming to move in on him."

"I reckon I cleared his mind on that. But he's slipping, Nits. He stayed in this game too long, became too complacent. There's a lesson in there for us."

"A year or two, maybe a bit more. That's all we have. By then the township *brazos* will start maturing, begin to eye the city centre. I've met a few guys from out there and they're like we used to be. They've got the brains and the muscle to back up any move they make. What we called on last night? It's nothing. They could put us in the fridge."

"I've seen them operate," Sandy said, nodding seriously. "The only reason they're not here already is simply because they haven't thought of it. They're still *lighties* and full of themselves and the *kachev* is pouring in from their drug deals. All it needs is one oke with the right motivation — a thirst for power — and he could mobilise all the different gangs into one powerful force. Think about it. A little Caesar with a bit of vision and careful planning, with all the resources already there. He'd be on fertile ground. With that kind of clout we'd be farting against thunder."

"Their first target would be the *Motas*. That's where the glitz and the glamour is. Those discos will provide them with a massive market to peddle their drugs and that's not counting the other spin-offs. And they'll buy the cops off so fast they'll make us look like *kachelas*. They already have the cash flow, compared to which we're a backyard card game."

"What are we saying, Nits? That all it'll take is one guy, maybe a dreamer with a sudden flash of foresight followed by a few weeks of thee and thy and he'll own the city?"

"Maybe more than a few weeks but certainly a hell of a lot less than five years. But that's it, I reckon. In a nutshell."

"Okay, buddy. So what does that tell us?"

"We could don the mantle of Caesar ourselves, move into the townships and put it all together. It can be done. But those guys are like vicious dogs. They're a new breed. I'm not sure we could control them in the long run. I'm not even sure I want to."

"That's because we're not the same guys we were when we started off. We aren't lean and hungry anymore. In this game, when you lose that you're a sitting target. It's the point the *Motas* missed."

"Of course, now that we've sussed out the situation we could pre-empt them, or try to. Prepare for their move and be ready to meet them head on. But that means a bloody war. I'm not sure I have the stomach for that. Last night was a good example. When the *Motas* caved in this morning we both gave a sigh of relief. That's a bad sign, my friend."

"You're right," Sandy said thoughtfully. "If you can't take the heat you get out of the sun. But where does that leave us?"

"We start making tracks, begin to ease out. Very quietly and very cagily. We cash in our chips without showing our hand. We take care of those who have been loyal to us. You've got Zorro to think about, maybe others. I only have John Farley, and he's already set for life. But when I walk away from here he comes with me. We've been together from the very beginning. I wouldn't even think of ditching him."

"I like what I hear, Nits. I like it a hell of a lot."

"Let's plan it then. Let's also consider what we do afterwards. Maybe we can pool our capital into a joint venture, something more laid-back. That is, if you don't mind John Farley on our team."

"John's more than welcome."

"Zorro?"

"No problem there. He's into religion now, in a big way, has been flirting a little with those Tabliq characters, on and off. I guess he can take care of himself."

"Okay. I have a suggestion. You want to hear it now?"

"Ya. Sure."

"We need a bit of perspective on this, input from someone who knows us and who we can trust, whose commitment to us is ..."

"Sam!"

"Right. Let's throw this around with him on Sunday after Dara's prayers are over. It can do no harm."

"The more you talk, old buddy, the more I like what you say. Okay, you're on. In the meantime, can you follow the last step with Karan, make sure Sam is truly covered all round?"

"Done."

For the first time in almost forty years, Sandy and Nithin actually shook hands.

The Seven Gods of Luck, however, were in deep slumber. The prayers for Dara's soul would be combined with another before Nithin and Sandy could pursue their retreat from the underworld.

chapter nine

*L*ionel Peterson emptied his glass before accepting a refill from Karan Naran. "I don't know where these Saturday night sessions are taking us. We have to formulate a plan of action, do something ... I don't know what ... but we can't keep talking for ever, fiddling like Nero whilst our world collapses around us."

"They serve a purpose, Lionel," Karan said. "It brings us together and gives us an opportunity to discuss what's going on. That's a lot better than just sitting around and twiddling our thumbs. And look how we have grown in size. Remember when there were only about a dozen of us? These days we seldom have less than thirty at any one time. We've already moved out of my study and into the lounge. I'm seriously considering moving over to my offices in future, where we won't be so cramped."

"I think that would be wise, and not only because we are getting squashed in here. A public venue would be even better, like say a private room at one of our hotels. You're too vulnerable here, Karan. I can't help thinking we'll be raided one of these days. If that happens you, more likely, will be the first to end up behind bars."

"What can the Security Branch prove? What would we be guilty of anyway. It's not as if we are plotting against the State or planning something subversive."

"Do you think they have to prove anything to lock us up? We're here, a bunch of Indians and coloureds, we're talking politics — it's always the central topic. That's enough for them. Case closed."

"And point taken," Karan laughed softly. "Let's put it to the others later tonight and we can agree on a new venue."

"It would be a wise move. Is Sam coming over tonight?"

"You never know with him," Karan replied. "Sam hates to commit himself to any kind of routine."

"How is he taking his father's death?"

"Philosophically, I guess. Sam's pretty contained about his emotions. Always has been."

Lionel nodded. "That's Sam alright. What's the latest on Jake?"

"Not a lead. Nothing new on his wife either."

"How long has it been now? Two, three weeks?"

"Almost two months."

"My God! Any news on how they are?"

"News? The cops don't even acknowledge that they're holding them."

At that moment Sam came through the door. When he caught sight of Peterson, his eyes lit up with pleasure and he walked over to them.

"Howzit, Lionel," Sam said, holding out his hand.

"Sam, how are you?" Peterson asked warmly, taking the outstretched hand in both of his. "We were just wondering how Jake and his wife are."

"Hannah's okay," Sam replied. "We know that much. As for Jake ..."

Their conversation was cut short by Harry Maraj, who had approached them, accompanied by Rohith Singh.

"Hi, Sam," Rohith called out as he broke away and headed for the makeshift bar Karan had set up. "Get you something?"

"A coke will be fine," Sam said.

The room had started to fill up and was becoming a little noisy. Sam had missed more sessions than he had attended and was surprised to see the number of new faces.

"How's Devi taking all this?" Sam asked Karan. "I just spoke to her in the kitchen and she didn't seem too pleased."

"She isn't. Lionel and I were just talking about changing venues. For a different reason, actually. That should keep Devi happy."

"Karan, what's the purpose of all this? Do you really need this sort of thing in your life?"

"Lionel here mentioned something similar a while ago. It all started off as a marketing exercise, an opportunity to meet my major clients informally. Pretty soon my university pals joined in. It wasn't long before politics became the only topic under discussion. That's natural, I suppose, considering the climate we live in. Lionel feels that we should be doing a little more than just talking."

"What do you think?"

"Can't say I disagree with him entirely."

"Be careful, Karan," Harry Maraj said. "Be very, very careful."

They were standing a little distance away from the others and had kept their voices low. Rohith came back with the drinks and picked up the tail end of the conversation.

"Harry's right, Karan. Those SB guys have ears everywhere. You'll be surprised at some of the places they've bugged. Some of these new faces ..."

Sam broke away from the group and began to move around, stopping occasionally to talk to an acquaintance. A few minutes later he headed for the French doors that led to the garden. He was beginning to feel claustrophobic and needed a breath of fresh air. As he reached for the doorhandle he heard something that froze him to the spot.

"... died whilst in detention," someone said. "The body was released with the strict instruction that the family make no fuss about it."

Sam's eyes darted in the direction of the voice, identified the speaker as Raymond Desai, a surgeon and close friend of the Petersons.

"Did you see the body, Ray?" Peterson asked.

"Not in my professional capacity. Only as a friend of the family."

"What was its condition? Any signs of ..."

"Lionel, let it ride," Desai said, his eyes passing some kind of message. "It's not something I want to talk about."

"I understand," Peterson nodded. "Well, they've certainly learnt a lot from the Biko experience. They won't make the same mistake again."

"Only in the sense that they've tightened up on the information channels," Harry Maraj said, lighting a cigarette. "The Emergency laws give them pretty wide powers."

"Do you have to smoke that thing in here," Desai cut in irritably as he waved his hands in front of him, dispersing the smoke.

"I'd rather die from this than at the hands of those bastards," Harry retaliated, smiling as he puffed away.

Sam moved closer to Desai, hoping to get him alone for a minute. The buzz of conversation around them continued, but Sam heard nothing. He seemed to be in a vacuum, alone in a room full of people. Even his eyes seemed remote, although they were fixed on the medical specialist. A moment later Sam threw caution to the winds and gently led Desai to a far corner.

"Ray, you know my brother and his wife are in the hands of the SB. Can you tell me anything about the guy that died?"

For a little while Desai looked at Sam speculatively. He seemed to be wrestling with his conscience, uncertain how much he wanted to say.

"Sam, what do you want me to tell you? Even the papers aren't allowed to report on those things. What more can I say?"

"Okay. But how long was this person in jail?"

"Just over four months."

"Was his family allowed to visit him?"

"No."

"Did they know officially that he was detained by the SB?"

"No."

"So the only time the SB came into the picture was when they informed the family of his death?"

"Yes. Look Sam, I'm sorry. Really sorry. But there isn't much I can tell you about this. I've heard that somewhere in the region of twenty five to thirty thousand detainees are being held by the SB. And I believe that's a conservative estimate."

Sam nodded as Desai moved away, heading towards a group in the centre where a speaker that Sam hadn't heard before was angrily moving a finger in the air.

"... we have to do something ourselves instead of leaving it to the workers and the schoolchildren. We can't allow the whites to continue doing this to us forever. If we don't rise now and pull them down, allow our anger free rein ..."

"I may be seething with anger," Harry Maraj cut in, "But I'm not sure I want to translate that into a bloody revolution. In any case, we keep saying the whites this and the whites that, and in the process dehumanise all whites. And that's just not true."

"If you are right," Peterson said, "Can you tell me why the Nats are repeatedly voted into power by an ever-increasing majority? I find it strange that every white I meet, on a one-on-one basis, is extremely vociferous in his denunciation of apartheid and loud in his condemnation of the government's policies. And yet, at the polling booths, those same guys vote the Nats in time after time."

"You must be meeting only the immigrants," Harry said. "The freeloaders who are as guilty as hell and know it. They're only here to fill their pockets and get back home to a cushy life. At least the Afrikaner is honest. He doesn't bulldust you. He believes in the separation of the races and he says it, loud and clear."

"That's a fair comment," someone in the back said. "Meet an Afrikaner and he looks you in the eye and says it like it is."

"I like that," Peterson said caustically. "Just great. Tomorrow I'll go out there and commit grand larceny, then look you in the eye ..."

Whatever else Lionel Peterson was going to say was drowned by the loud laughter, Peterson himself joining in.

Sam decided he had heard enough. The talk was beginning to depress him. He was about to slip away when he saw Devi standing near the door, signalling frantically in an attempt to catch his attention. Sam quickly walked towards her. As soon as he was at her side she pulled the door behind them, shutting them off from the others.

"What is it, *bhabi*?" Sam asked.

"Sally is outside with a friend of Jake's," Devi answered. "She asked me to bring you out. This friend, I think she has a lead on where Jake is."

"Where are they now?"

"In the back garden, near the swings."

"Okay, thanks." Sam half walked, half ran, down the long passage leading to the back door. As he reached for the doorknob he stopped, took a deep breath and pulled himself together. When he stepped out he was outwardly calm, his face composed.

Sally was standing near a garden fence, a little away from the brightly lit rear porch, talking to a slim, well-dressed woman who appeared to be in her mid-forties. As he approached them Sam was sure, even from a distance, that he had never seen the woman before. When he was close to them Sam put his arm around Sally's waist and looked at her questioningly.

"Sam, this is Shirley Barnes," Sally said, by way of introduction. "She knows Jake well and she asked to see you urgently. I thought it would be better out here."

Sam nodded and smiled at Shirley, not quite succeeding in hiding his apprehension.

"Sam, I've known Jake for a long time and I'm a very good friend of Hannah's. I'm a matron at King's and I saw Jake there this afternoon."

Sam felt a chill run down his spine. "Shirley, is he ..."

"He looked okay. I barely caught a glimpse of his face from the side as they took him into a private ward. There were four uniformed guards around him."

"Shirley, you sure it was Jake? No chance of a mistake?"

"It was Jake allright. I have no doubts about it."

"And he looked fine? Not sick or in pain?"

"I can't be absolutely positive, but he moved in his usual way. You know how Jake struts around sometimes, daring the world to take him on." Shirley couldn't help smiling as she said it.

"But he must have been in hospital for a reason," Sam said, more to himself.

"I know from past experience that they never bring a detainee to hospital unless it's something serious. But he was moving okay, that's all I know."

"Did he see you?"

"No. I'm sure of that."

"Is there any chance of seeing him, talking to him?"

"I'm sorry, Sam. There's absolutely no hope of that. I explained that to Sally earlier. Those guards will stick to him like velcro and none of the regular nurses are allowed to enter that particular ward. They even have their own doctors, people we have never seen before."

"There must be some way ..."

"There's no way, Sam. We're not allowed to talk about what we see. And we could lose our jobs, just like that, if they even think we are acting curious. Please, don't try to come near the hospital. If they suspect ..."

"Okay, Shirley. I won't jeopardise you in any way. As it is you're taking a terrible risk talking to me. I appreciate it."

Shirley placed a hand on Sam's shoulder, her voice very soft. "Jake's my friend, Sam. He used to speak often about you, in the days when he was courting Hannah. I'll never regret what I've told you today."

"Thank you, Shirley," Sam said, covering her hand with his own. "And I can tell you this much — Hannah is fit and well. She's at the Point Prison and someone there brings me a regular report. But that's all we know."

"I'm so glad to hear that. I was crazy with worry thinking about her." Shirley's eyes had gone moist and she dabbed at them with a tiny hanky that she had pulled out of her handbag. "I have to go now."

"You'll keep in touch?"

"It would be better if I don't see you folks for a while. You don't know these people, Sam. They're organised like nothing you could imagine. They watch all of us like hawks. They've been known to follow the nurses that they suspect may have seen something. I'm not worried about tonight. I was very careful. But I wouldn't chance it again."

"Okay. Maybe someday I'll be able to thank you properly. Is it safe for Sally to take you home?"

"I'll direct her to a point near my house. I'll be okay from there."

Sam watched as they walked around the side of the house. When they were out of sight he sat on a bench and lit a cigarette. For the next ten minutes he remained engrossed in himself, oblivious of the cold biting wind that had come up. When it began to rain he walked back towards the house, making no effort to cover himself.

Once inside the house, Sam headed directly towards Karan's study and reached for the phone. He dialled, held the receiver to his ear and waited. When Nithin answered, he began to speak. "I have just received information that Jake is at King Edward Hospital. He walked in unaided, but with Jake that doesn't mean much. They've got him under tight security."

"He's there now?"

"Yes. But we can't try anything, not even go near the place. We could put someone else in danger."

"We don't have to. I know he'll be back in prison before morning. And I'm about to find out where."

"What!"

"Take it easy, Sam. I've been working my butt off on this. I'm busy tying up a few loose ends right now, at this very moment. In the next few hours I'm hoping to set it up so you can see him, for a few minutes. But it's touch and go right now. You listening?"

"Yes."

"Okay. Get some sleep and leave me to do what I can. I'll see you in the morning."

∞

"Sam," Rushda said over the intercom, "Mr Vania is on his way to your office."

"Okay. I'm expecting him."

He was halfway out of his chair when Nithin opened the door and walked in.

"Sit down, Sam. This may take some time."

Nithin carefully closed the door and leaned against it for a moment, his eyes taking in the office. There were dark patches below his eyes and his face looked drawn, the weariness apparent in every move he made. Sam had never seen Nithin look so bushed.

"How private is it in here?" Even his voice sounded tired.

"The street is behind me and Rushda is far enough away ..."

"Is there any other way into here?" Nithin was eyeing the washroom door.

"Not unless you pass her."

"Ask her to leave the room and lock the door behind her."

"Nithin, why all these ..."

"Please do it, Sam."

Sam pressed the intercom and spoke into it. "Rushda, take an early lunch break and lock the door behind you. Instruct switchboard to hold all my calls."

Nithin opened the door an inch and listened. He heard the door to the outer office slam shut, then the faint click as the key was turned. Satisfied, he walked up to the desk and pulled up a chair.

"Sam, I'm going to give you some advice. I suggest you take it seriously. When the SB guys pick someone up the rules of the game are very clear — the family is expected to shut up, make no fuss and ask no questions. All you're allowed to do is pray, if you're so inclined. Ignore those rules and you find yourself on some deserted farm, tied to a tree. You don't want to know what happens to you next."

"I guess we've already broken that rule, several times."

Nithin nodded, then continued speaking in his odd monologue. "These new Nats are not like their predecessors, as bad as those guys were. They're vicious in the extreme. And they have a spy system, backed up by well-paid informers, that is the envy of every intelligence agency in the world. It's common knowledge that much of their training was conducted by Mossad.

"Don't attempt to find out but if you ever get to know who shopped Jake and Vusi it'll shock you. And if you forget what I just said we could both end up where Jake is, okay?"

Sam nodded as Nithin inserted a cigarette between his lips.

"I've got a lead on where Jake is being held. There's a chance I can arrange for you to see him."

Sam felt his heart jump a beat and he leaned forward, smiling.

"Nits, that's good ..."

"Don't get too elated. Things could still go wrong. Even now, I'm only beginning to get no more than an idea of how powerful the State is. Just to get a lead on where Jake and Hannah could have ended up I pulled every string of my not inconsiderable resources, called in every favour owing to me. I begged like I've never done before and short of going down on my knees I've done everything humanly possible, including outlaying large sums of money."

"I'll make it good, Nits. Just name ..."

"This is for Jake, Sam, for what he means to me. The only reason I'm telling you all this is to impress on you what we're up against. There's a special division of the SB that is not unlike Hitler's SS. They have no conscience, they cannot be bought and taking a life means nothing to them. They operate independently of any court of law. They are absolutely untouchable. All political detainees end up in their hands."

"I have some idea ..."

"You have no idea, Sam. Outside of their circle, very few do. These okes can shoot you in broad daylight, in the back and while you're standing still, in front of a thousand witnesses, and take a cool walk. There'll be no questions asked, the press won't report it, and there won't be an inquiry or inquest into the matter. They are the law. And there are no apparent chinks in their armour, no way of penetrating their ranks.

"We had every hustler, every newspaper boy and reporter, the bent cops and even some honest okes, the night workers, the cleaning services, garden workers and a hell of a lot of others working for us. If we had been looking for an unmarked fly we would have found it. But as far as Jake and Vusi were concerned there was not even a whisper.

"In the end, I guess I just got lucky. There's no other explanation. The break came from an unexpected quarter.

"A black prossie told her pimp she'd been with some honky who had been trying to impress her even as he abused her. In an unguarded moment, probably as he was blowing his mind, he mentioned something about having *Aza Kwela* in his clutches. I gather he clammed up pretty fast. The prossie dismissed it at the time as bullshit, but she mentioned it later in the day to the pimp. *Aza Kwela* is, after all, every black's hero. It's not something you forget. The pimp mentioned it, in passing, to a buddy of his. The buddy in turn laughed about it over a beer in some pub. By the next morning it found its way to me. That's where the luck came in. In that long chain it could have died down very easily, at any point.

"I put my best men on the job to check it out."

Nithin stood up, went to a bar fridge and extracted a can of coke. He took a few deep swallows, then resumed his seat.

"What my guys dug up was pay dirt: the honky is a senior warden in some obscure prison in the city which is reserved exclusively for transient political detainees, on their way to their handlers. The oke himself is crazy about black *ezie*, he just can't keep away from it. It's like an obsession with him, a psychological thing. How the hell he hid it from his superiors is beyond me.

"I called in the sharpest *scotens* I could find and put them on the job. It had to be done at that level. Anyone higher up and our target would have clammed up. The *scotens* know the ropes. I supplied them with the hottest chicks in town, the best booze available, a stack of bucks and clear instructions that I wanted this honky someplace where I could get at him easily. The *scots* were in their element, it was the name of their game and this time they were backed up with solid resources. It was our best shot.

"And, after all the disappointments, a damned sexual pervert comes up trumps."

Nithin gulped down the last bit of the coke, placed the can on the desk, and sat back.

"To cut it short, Jake is right here, in this town and under this guy's nose. But he'll only be there for another day or two. They brought him in for some kind of a check up, from a farm not far away. That's how come he was in hospital last night.

"I've offered the warden more money than he will ever own at any one time, and all the chicks he can handle. Right now he's drooling worse than a hungry marabunta ant.

"When I mentioned Jake to him he nearly crapped in his pants, his eyes jumping with fear. It was obvious that trying to smuggle Jake out of there would be suicidal, for all of us. I settled for what we have now, and even then this warden guy was trying to hedge his options. In the end lust and greed overcame caution. He's agreed to a short visit, no more than a few minutes. The man's paranoid about security, scared witless.

"Anyway, there are moments when the security can be sidetracked, possibly late at night when the guards ease up a bit. According to this oke the prison is like a vault anyway, you couldn't break in with a tank.

"Now, what I've arranged with him is this: he'll phone me on my private line, anytime after eight tonight. If it takes us longer than ten minutes to get there the deal is off.

"That's it, Sam. Get hold of whoever will accompany you and show up at my office by not later than seven thirty. We may have to bunk there."

"Nits, I don't know how to say this but ..."

"Then don't say it."

"Okay. But I'd like you to come with me."

"I'll have to take a back seat on this, Sam. I'll see that you get in and out, and the timing is vital. I can't trust anyone else or put him in danger. The prison is solid, but small. Visitors are unheard of and there are very few inmates to talk about. Jake is probably the only one there. Follow my lead on this and we may come out of it without problems."

"Whatever you say. Perhaps I'll just go in alone."

"Fine. And, Sam? If you change your mind, decide to bring someone along, don't choose your mother. I got the impression that Jake doesn't look too good at the moment. If that's true I'd like to spare her the agony."

"Okay, Nits. My old lady's as tough as they come, but you're right, she doesn't need this."

"Now get me the hell out of here. I need to sleep."

Sam explained the situation to Sally then added, "I'll have to go alone."

"I'm coming with you."

"Look, it'll make Jake wonder why Hannah didn't come instead. It's fair to assume he doesn't know she has also been taken in."

"I have to see Jake," she said stubbornly. "I'm coming along."

When Sam hesitated, she said pleadingly, "Sam, don't deny me this. I'll find a way to cover for Hannah."

"Okay. But not a word to Ma. Let's see him first."

When they entered Nithin's office he greeted Sally warmly and pointed at an easy chair. "It could be a long wait. Might as well be comfortable."

Sam stretched out on a reclining chair in front of Nithin's desk. For a while they made desultory conversation, talking in snatches about the old days and old friends who had settled in the UK, Australia, New Zealand, Canada and the US.

"There are South Africans all over the world," Nithin said. "Practically every family has someone who has skipped the country. The close-knit family unit has been ruptured, perhaps forever. Siblings have lost that special bond and first cousins have become strangers. I find that very sad."

"We saw something similar with our own fathers and grandfathers. My father never got to see, let alone know, his grandparents. All my own grandfather knew about his brothers' children were their names, and he used to cry sometimes that he had forgotten even that."

"The South Africans overseas, I've heard that they hang on to each other and pine for home. Can you imagine what an asset they would represent if they all came back. With their skills they could make this country boom."

"For whose benefit?" Sam scoffed. "Aren't you forgetting why they left?"

"When I think of Jake and Hannah I can't help thinking that those who left were wise."

"Dara's way of thinking, exactly. It's strange how we come back to that. But it has to stop sometime, this destruction of entire communities. Those countries we mentioned earlier, where the South Africans have settled, prosper because they are genuine democracies. Human rights is a value not restricted to one single race group, their courts of law are not packed with stooges and lily-livered hypocrites acting on the dictates of a ruling tribe. Is it any wonder that a visitor from those places is invariably horrified that no person of colour has a right to a vote."

"To be able to vote is considered by them to be a birthright, not an issue for politicians to tamper with. It's a basic, a given. They learnt a long time ago that you take that away and you destroy society as a whole — it gives the gangsters a mandate to rule."

"And this country of ours is proof of the accuracy of that statement."

Sally had dozed off, her feet coiled under her. Nithin brought in a small urn from an outer office and began to brew coffee. And continued to chain-smoke.

"Luck is a funny lady, Sam," Nithin said over his shoulder. "Just when you're about to call it a day she deals you a royal flush and puts you back in the game. How you play it from there is up to you. I won't be surprised if something concerning Hannah comes up, perhaps another lucky break."

The phone rang loudly, shaking them out of their lethargy. Sally jerked awake, then quickly stood up. Sam looked at the time, noted that it was a minute past ten. Nithin lifted the receiver.

"Yes?" Nithin said into it, listened for a few seconds, then slammed it back in place.

"Let's go," he said. "We have to move fast."

Nithin was through the door before Sam or Sally could react. They caught up with him as he reached his car and unlocked it. They had barely slammed the doors before it moved away from the kerb.

The streets were relatively free of traffic and Nithin made good time. Within six minutes he had turned into Fisher Street and a minute later he pulled up a short distance away from an old, whitewashed building that stood by itself and isolated from its surroundings. He led the way around a corner, Sally and Sam close on his heels. When he reached a huge steel door he held up his hand and waited. The watch on Sam's wrist said it was ten minutes past ten. Sam was thinking that Nithin must have covered the route several times earlier when he heard the bolts behind the door rasp as steel scraped on steel. The door began to open. Nithin stepped back into the shadows, indicating with a short movement of his hand that Sam and Sally should go in.

They entered a tiny, spartan room. The cement floor was caked with grime and the paint on the walls peeling off in patches.

"You Solomon?" a hulking Afrikaner asked in a thick accent, from behind the door.

"Yes," Sam said, turning to face the man.

"And the *poontang*?"

"My wife," Sam replied, ignoring the crude reference.

"*Goed*! Now you *focken* listen to me. There's a cell in the next room.

You'll meet your *boet* there. When I tell you to move out, you move your *huckters* fast. No hugging, kissing or last goodbyes. You scheme what I'm saying?"

Sam nodded.

"My name's Blackie. You know why they call me that?" he asked, throwing a wink at Sally.

"Just take me to my brother," Sam said evenly, keeping his temper in check.

"*Kom*," Blackie said, crowding Sally and sniffing appreciatively as he led them into the next room. It was fairly large and halfway down it were thick steel bars, from floor to ceiling and running across its entire width. Behind the bars, at the far end, there was a door clad in thick iron sheets.

On Sam's side of the room, near a wall, an elderly African lady with a broom and a steel bucket silently gazed at them.

"That's my kaffir," Blackie said, pointing at the woman. "She's going to keep watch at the end of the passage, look out for the guards. She knows what to do. Give her a few bobs." He disappeared into an adjoining room.

Sam was reaching into his pocket when the woman held up a hand, restraining him.

"No money! I happy to do this, to help you. *Aza Kwela*, he your brother?"

"Yes," Sam replied.

"They bring him from hospital, in morning, early. They push him to door there, he push back. They hit him. He fall, get up, try to fight. They hit him again. He get up. Again they hit, again he get up. You know what he do then? He laugh, spit in their face. *Hau! Aza Kwela*, he a real man! Now you tell him stay down. They leave him then .."

The door at the end of the cell opened and somebody, pushed from behind, stumbled in. It wasn't Jake. Sam's heart sank, someone had made a mistake. The woman next to him placed her bucket on the floor, raised her fist in the air, and said softly, "*Mayibuye, Aza Kwela! Mayibuye, Mkonto!*" Then she saluted, picked up her bucket and walked swiftly towards the corridor.

Sam heard Sally gasp, then the sharp intake of her breath as her hand flew to her mouth. He looked closely as the battered figure walked towards the bars. It was the walk that did it. It was Jake.

"Hey, *lighty*," Jake said. "*Howzit.*"

"Jake!" Sally cried, "What have they done to you?"

Jake's face was swollen, two large bumps on his forehead. The whites of both eyes were bloodshot, with dark spots at the edges. When Jake curled his hands around the bars Sam noticed that his knuckles were encrusted with blood, the one behind the index finger of his right hand a little skewed, off centre and pushed back.

"Jake ..." Sam said, his voice tight.

"Just a few dents, my bro," Jake said. "You should have seen me yesterday."

There was a rasping sound emanating from Jake's chest when he spoke and he seemed to be having trouble with his breathing. Sam also thought he detected a slur in the voice.

"Jake, we're trying ..."

"Sure, *lighty*, sure. Hey, take it easy. I'm getting to know these guys. They're not much."

"Jake," Sally said softly, "Don't fight back, please."

"Don't know how to do that, *Bhabi*. Have to get in a few licks now and then, just to keep in touch. Not much else to do around here."

Sam thought Jake was grimacing with pain, then realised with a shock that he was actually smiling. And there was something wrong with his peripheral vision, he had turned his whole body when he looked at Sally.

"The old man," Jake asked. "He's okay?"

"Yes, fine." Sam lied. "Ma's okay too."

"How's my *lighty*? He miss me?"

"He's like you, Jake. Full of himself."

"You tell him I'm coming home. Soon. Tell Hannah I love her, Sally."

There was something odd in the way Jake uttered the last few words, making it sound like a question, looking for some sort of confirmation. His eyes were fixed on Sally, watching her carefully.

"She loves you too, Jake. The last thing she said was, 'Tell Jake I'm waiting for him,'" Sally was crying, the tears rolling down her cheeks.

"She couldn't make it?"

"She had to stay with Zain," Sam quickly added, a little lamely.

Jake turned to Sam. "You look great, *lighty*. Ma taking all this okay?"

"She's fine. Proud of you."

"That's some lady, Sam."

"Did they say anything to you. About when they'll let you out?"

"Promise it all the time. They say I can walk out of here tomorrow if I play ball with them."

"Go along with them. Pull a fast one. Once you're out we can move you ..."

"You want me to be their tube-lighty? Knock it off, *boet*. I can't sign on for their team. I can't be the tube to their tyre."

"But it'll get you out of here, give you a breather."

"Sam, what do you know about these *ous* ...? They can teach the *Motas* a few tricks. I try something like you say and I expose all of you to danger ... When I fail to deliver they'll turn on the family."

"They could turn on us anyway."

"Maybe. But there'd be no point in it ... then."

The slur in Jake's voice was becoming more pronounced and he seemed to be having difficulty forming words. His body was beginning to sway a little and his grip on the bars was tighter, as if his hands were holding him up.

"Sam ... tell the old man ... to hang in there. Too many good people ... have died in ... this struggle. If he takes the family out now ... it'll be ... like a betrayal, of everything ... we fought for ... like ..."

"Don't think about it now, Jake." Sally quickly cut in, covering Jake's hands with her own. When he winced she moved her hands to his wrists. "We're going to get you out of here. I promise you that. These bastards are not God!"

Jake actually laughed, loudly. In spite of the rasp in it Sam could sense the amusement. Jake released his left hand and touched Sally's face. What Sally had said seemed to have revitalised him and when he spoke his voice sounded a little stronger. "The women in our family," he said, turning to Sam, "They're the real fighters. Put them in the front line and the war ..."

There was a loud clanging noise, like the sound of metal falling on concrete. Sam realised, with dismay, that it had to be the woman with the bucket, sending a warning.

"Out!" Blackie hissed, suddenly beside them. "Move! Now! You, get your black arse back in there."

Blackie swiftly hustled them into the outer room towards the steel doors, his face distorted. Sam turned his head, trying to get a last glimpse of Jake through the bars.

"Out, you *focken* coolies!" Blackie snarled under his breath as he pushed the bolts back. He pulled the door open, then shoved them out onto the pavement. The door silently closed behind them and a second later Sam heard the bolts rasp home. Nithin emerged from the shadows.

"Keep moving," Nithin whispered to them. "We can't be seen around here."

In the car, Sam glanced at his watch. He couldn't believe it. It was barely ten twenty five. Sally sat silently in the back, curled into a corner.

"Jake okay?" Nithin asked.

"He isn't looking good, Nits. His face is full of globes and I think a few ribs may be broken. But it's more than that ..."

Nithin nodded, his face set in tight lines. "I tried to warn you, why I told you to keep the old lady away."

They drove the rest of the way in silence, Nithin keeping to the speed limit. When they reached Sam's home Sally jumped out, went over to the driver's window and, leaning in, kissed Nithin on the cheek. "Thanks, *bhai*," she said, then disappeared into the house.

Nithin reached for a cigarette as he turned towards Sam. "What's it like in there?"

"It's a fort. Impenetrable. That steel door is not the only problem."

"But we got you in. That's a start. It may have been uphill all the way but the dice are rolling for us. There has to be someone at the top that we can work on."

"You don't let up, do you?" Sam said, smiling affectionately.

"What else is there to do. Jake, he was always there for me, no questions asked. Trouble with him, he didn't know when to take the gap. I took the gap when I stayed out of politics. So did Sandy. You took it when you moved into the business world, walked off the street. Jake and Vusi ..."

"Nits, what about Vusi. Any leads at all?"

"A complete blank. Each time I put out a feeler for Jake and Hannah I included Vusi."

"I don't know what to do next." Sam sounded desolate, defeated.

"Get some sleep." Nithin started the car. "I'm out on my feet. Let's get together in the morning. We can throw it around then."

Sally was in the kitchen, waiting for the kettle to boil, her shoulders slumped. Sam hugged her from behind.

"I botched up on Hannah, Sam," Sally murmured, her voice small. "I could see Jake didn't quite believe me."

"You did okay. Forget it."

She turned around, placed her hands on Sam's shoulders. "We've got to get them out, and quickly. They'll kill Jake in there."

When Sam didn't say anything, Sally added. "Every man has his price. These people can't be any different. Make them an offer. Sell everything we own and put it on the table. Call in one of the government stooges, whoever is right up there with them. When the hypocrite sees the size of the bundle he'll kill his own mother to get Jake out."

"Sal, you heard what that woman called Jake. He's *Aza Kwela*. If you know what that means you'll understand why he's so valuable to the SB."

"So Jake's *Aza Kwela*. But what are they? Jake has the courage of his convictions, what do they have? They must know they're guilty as hell, they know their actions are base and immoral. People like that are inherently weak. They're scum. And scum can be bought if the amount is large enough."

"Okay, Sal. I guess every man has his price, sometimes all you need to know is his currency. That guy Blackie, his currency is women, especially ..."

"The man is a pig, Sam. The bastard felt me up when he pushed us out. Stuck his hands up ..."

Sally clammed up when she saw Sam's face grow dark, his jaw tighten with anger.

"Forget him, Sam. He is nothing. Concentrate on Jake and Hannah. Get the priorities sorted out first."

They slept fitfully that night, and were up before the break of dawn, lying quietly next to each other, not moving.

chapter ten

"You look like hell," Nithin said, looking at Sam.

"I feel like it," Sam responded. "I've asked Karan to join us. I'd like to brainstorm this thing."

"We need to look at it from a different angle. All of us are too emotionally involved. Perhaps a new perspective, from someone less intense, could be useful."

"The problem is that no one is prepared to even listen to us. The moment you mention the SB their faces close up, you can see the fear coursing through them. If they don't have a commitment they don't want to hear about it."

"Here's an odd thing, Sam. The only okes that don't freeze when you talk about the Special Branch are the thugs and the hustlers. It's almost as if you're referring to a rival gang, like a powerful mob, someone to be wary of and no more. They can identify with them, a sense of kinship. It may not be so strange after all, considering that fear is the stock in trade of both those groups."

"If fear is their stock in trade, what is their business? What are both those groups after, what is the common denominator between them?"

"To obtain by force that which does not belong to them — money, or its equivalent."

"Exactly. When you boil it down to its bare essentials, it's all you come up with. There may be degrees of sophistication in their methods but the aims are essentially the same. Our rulers are the equivalent of the Mafia, a hell of a lot more organised and far better armed, with far better representation in the corridors of the world powers for the simple reason that they've conned the world into believing that they are the legitimate government of a country, elected by a democratic system."

"What democracy? A selected five percent of the population? It's laughable. But until the world sees it for what it is, that's the reality."

"Sure. And that's one of the reasons why they're always offering their victims all those sterile forms of representation, which they attempt to legitimise by bestowing glorified titles called the House of Representatives and the House of Delegates or some such garbage. And the ten percenters amongst our own people, the sell-outs, smell the *kachev* and see the pot at the end of the rainbow and fall over themselves to become the Don's henchmen."

"This gangster state, which is all it really is, has beaten the Mafia Dons at their own game. It has usurped the *law of the land* and made it subservient to their greed. To attempt to topple them from within the country is suicidal, a non-starter."

"But it's evil nevertheless, and it's a fact of history that evil never lasts."

"So what else is new. Look, you and I may not have their firepower but we know the rules of their game. If we are going to get Jake out of there we have to play by their rules. I think we should stop trying to gain access to the handful right at the top — those okes can't be bought, their vaults are already bursting at the seams. Their god is power and we have nothing to offer them there. Let's aim a little lower, concentrate on their henchmen, they are the guys who are still lining their pockets. The route to them is through our own guys, the sell-outs. I'm convinced of that. If we can buy freedom for Jake, Hannah and Vusi, even for a day, our underground machine can go into action. We will get them over the border so fast even the gods will nod with admiration."

"It's the route Sally recommended last night, and she came to that conclusion without all this convoluted analysis we just ..."

The extension on Nithin's desk buzzed. He listened for a moment, then said, "Send him in."

"It's the honky from the *tronks*, here for his 'see right'."

"Nits, I have a score to settle with that punk, something he did to Sally last night. Will it cause trouble for you?"

"That shit? He's just a minion, small potatoes. Besides, we own him now. You know the first rule — you take the king's penny, you become the king's lackey. As of last night he's on our payroll, our bumboy. What did he do?"

"Ran his hands over her. I'd like to straighten him up."

"Take him!" Nits snarled.

The door opened and Blackie walked in. He was bouncing and smiling widely. Nithin didn't say a word. He opened a drawer, removed a thick envelope and threw it on the desk. "It's all there. Check it."

"Don't need to, *kerels*." He slipped the envelope into a back pocket, then added, "You coolies try to short change me and I'll break your necks."

"Hey, Blackie," Sam smiled. "You remember me?"

"Sure. You and that hot *bokkie* of yours. That's a lekker ..."

"That's what I wanted to talk to you about. My wife asked me to give you a message."

"Ya?"

"She didn't like what you did to her."

"What the fuck, *yong*. Just having some fun."

"Well, it's like this. That lady doesn't like a *Jahver*'s filthy paws to touch her. You know what I'm saying?" Sam was still smiling easily.

"You jiving me, *bliksem*? *Khoing kuk* at me?" Blackie spat, his eyes narrowing. Sam's fist caught him on the cheek, sending him staggering backwards. Sam had deliberately pulled his punch, giving Blackie a chance to defend himself.

"What! Hey, fuck man. What you doing? You fancy yourself ..."

Sam stepped closer, then threw two short punches. The first one caught Blackie squarely in the eye, the second split the lips open. A roundhouse swing landed flush on his temple and Blackie began to go down, his knees buckling, when the uppercut caught him just below the jaw. It lifted the man in the air and sent him flying backwards. He landed in a heap, his breathing ragged, his body unmoving.

Nithin opened the door and called out, "Mojo? Claw? Take this creep and drop him where you picked him up."

When Nithin's men lifted Blackie to his feet, Sam smiled with satisfaction — one eye was swollen tight and a huge lump had formed on the temple. The lower lip had ballooned grotesquely, a thick line of blood running down the chin and into his neck. As Blackie was hauled through the door, Karan walked in. "What happened to him?"

"He tripped on the carpet and fell," Nithin said, winking at Sam.

"You guys don't change," Karan grimaced. "They can take you off the street but they can't take the street out of you."

"Let's get down to business," Nithin said bluntly.

"Only if you promise that I'll walk out of here on my own two feet."

"Karan," Sam cut in quickly, "Nithin and I feel we should try one of our government stooges again. Only this time we lay it on the line, offer him enough to put his *ezie* off centre and tempt him to play for us. What do you think?"

"It's worth another try," Karan said slowly, "They're in it for the money, we all know that. But how far are we prepared to go? They'll want us to be specific before they bite. What's our limit?"

"None! I'll pay whatever it takes. I'm prepared to sell everything I own, bring back the money from Dara's deal with the union guys, everything. Even Sally's jewellery."

"You're talking big bucks, Sam."

"Double it," Nithin growled. "I'll cover the difference."

"Guess I can do no less," Karan added. "If that doesn't buy us the keys to the kingdom we may as well join those stooges ourselves."

"It's agreed then," Nithin said. "But let's not each of us act independently on this and mess things up. How about we make a list during the day, a separate one for each of us. We get together tomorrow and compare notes, select the most likely target and go to work on him."

"Fine." Sam stood up. "I'll get onto it immediately."

"I'll work on it as soon as I get back to my office," Karan added.

The break, when it finally came that night, left all three of them stunned and a little shamefaced. It also forced them to revise their attitudes towards those they considered as no more than adjuncts to their lives.

∞

Sam had just finished his supper when Sally said, "You know that lady down the road, the one who sells samoosas?"

"Mrs Vaiz?"

"Yes. Now listen to this. I visited her this afternoon and we got to talking about her business. She delivers her samoosas twice a month to a Mrs Seepye in Chatsworth."

"I didn't know you dealt with her. I always thought you made your own samoosas."

"I do. Does that mean I can't call on a neighbour?"

"Of course not. I can't see what you find interesting about her, though."

"Stop being snobbish and listen to what I have to say."

"Okay."

"I remembered this morning that she had, a few months ago, mentioned that she had delivered a larger than normal order to the Seepyes. I also recalled that she had said, in passing, that when she was leaving there a car had pulled up in their driveway. Two men got out of the car. One was an Indian, the other was General Geechie."

"What the hell would Geechie be doing in Chatsworth? And, in any case, how would this Vaiz woman know who he was?"

"Mrs Vaiz."

"What?"

"I said Mrs Vaiz, not 'that Vaiz woman'."

"Okay. Mrs Vaiz."

"Sam, because she sells samoosas doesn't mean she's stupid. She has a Bachelor's degree in Arts. She couldn't get a job so she started selling ..."

"Okay, Sally, okay. But how would she know Geechie?"

"In the same way we do. She reads the papers, she watches television, his photograph is often in the papers and because, on her next visit, Mrs Seepye told her. Satisfied?"

"Sorry, go on." Sam was paying careful attention now, suddenly aware that Sally was not making idle conversation.

"I asked her about it again today. She confirmed that it was definitely Geechie."

"Sally, this could be a lead. Geechie is one of the top SB men."

"I know, darling. I've already arranged through Mrs Vaiz for you to meet Seepye."

"Good work, girl. You amaze me sometimes. When do I see this guy?"

"It's seven now. If you rush you'll make it to Chatsworth in time. Seepye is expecting you at seven thirty. Here's the address."

Sam grabbed the slip of paper and headed for the door, then turned back and kissed Sally. "Why did you only tell me now?"

"Because Mrs Vaiz confirmed the appointment just before you came in. I wanted you to eat first."

Sam squeezed her arm, then rushed out.

Seepye's house wasn't difficult to find. It was just off the main Chatsworth road. Sam got there with time to spare. Seepye himself opened the door and led Sam to a spacious lounge. When they were seated Seepye asked, "How can I help you, Mr Solomon?"

"Please call me Sam. You don't know why I'm here?"

Seepye shook his head from side to side. "I only know my wife insisted I meet you tonight. She didn't know why except that it was a matter of someone's life and death."

Sam nodded. On the way over he had worked out his approach, had decided to be blunt with Seepye, to get straight to the point and lay it on the line. He had intended to offer the man a huge sum, straight out, and take it from there. Now, he found himself hesitating. There was something about Seepye, a dignified bearing, an old-world courtesy and charm, that just did not fit in with Sam's assessment of a stooge. Everything about the man was gentle, serene. Even the way he walked, the way his lounge was furnished, was faintly reminiscent of Dara. Sam decided to change tactics, to feel his way through before getting down to specifics.

Seepye, sensing some conflict in Sam, said quietly, "What is it, Sam?"

"My brother and his wife are in the hands of the Special Branch, have been now for over two months. I have reason to believe that he is being treated brutally, that his life could be at risk. I suspect my brother couldn't survive further physical abuse. I was given to understand you know General Geechie. I am here for your help."

"Mr Solomon, let me explain something to you. I am a businessman. I own a string of stores around here. I have few friends. My wife and my children are my only companions.

"Geechie was here, certainly. But he was foisted on me at the instigation of a man called Aman Munchie. Do you know him?"

"No. I may have heard the name somewhere."

"Then consider yourself lucky. I was asked, instructed may be a better word, to host a dinner for Geechie. I was specifically told to invite at least twenty wealthy individuals from this area, and to make certain that they attended the function. A list of those invited was to be forwarded to him in advance. Amongst other things, the insistence that I let him have a list in advance implied a subtle threat, a form of insurance, if you like, to ensure that those invited did not fail to attend.

"You can imagine my consternation. Munchie was barely an acquaintance, Geechie I don't know at all. To find twenty wealthy men in Chatsworth is not an easy task. And whatever else, I am not a fool. It was very obvious to me that no good would come of it. It also left a nasty taste in my mouth, the knowledge that, however obliquely, I would be exposing other people to an unhappy experience.

"I tried to wriggle out of it, requested Munchie to prepare the list himself. I'm afraid that didn't go down too well. In the end, I was given little option in the matter. I did as I was told but I forewarned each guest that Geechie would be present. Whether they attended or not was up to them. Naturally, amongst ourselves, we tried to analyse their purpose, what it was that they expected of us. We settled on the possibility that

Aman Munchie intended to stand as a candidate for the House of Delegates and that Geechie would strongarm us into ensuring he received enough votes to ensure not only his legitimacy but also the legitimacy of the State's tactics.

"The reality couldn't have been further removed."

Seepye had paused to gather his thoughts.

"Mr Seepye," Sam said sincerely, "I apologise for reawakening unhappy memories. You don't have to go into the details ..."

Seepye held up a hand, brushing Sam's request aside. "I'm almost finished. At the end of the dinner, which didn't last long, Munchie made a speech, something about a fundraising campaign for the boys returning from the border. Most of us didn't see the point or how it concerned us. Those were white boys, Geechie's troops. If anything, we despised them. In any case, we were not allowed to ask any questions, the few feeble attempts were slapped down by Munchie himself. Geechie simply chain-smoked and used one of the dinner plates for this purpose, despite the fact that an ashtray was close at hand. He didn't say a word, not once during the course of the entire period that he was here.

"Munchie placed a stack of blank cheque forms on the table, payable to the bearer on demand. He told us to fill in the name of our banks, the branch and the amount, to insert the current date and to sign it. He stipulated a minimum figure, made it clear that we were to exceed it, and sat back.

"We were not threatened in any way, it was all apparently very friendly. The implication, however, was very clear. Pay up and shut up.

"It was extortion, whichever way you choose to look at it.

"They walked out of here with well in excess of a quarter of a million rands."

"I appreciate your frankness. Thank you."

"Before I became a businessman, I was a lecturer until they kicked me out for insubordination. I have learnt that my first impressions of people are usually very accurate. I like the look of you, Mr Solomon, the cut of your jib, as they used to say in more halcyon days. I wanted to make absolutely certain that you understand the kind of people you wish to turn to for help."

"That kind may just be to my advantage. They are people who can be bought."

"They'll take your money, you can be sure of that. Whether they'll deliver is far from guaranteed."

"Yes ... well ... what choice do I have. Will you help me, open the door so to speak?"

"I'm not comfortable with the idea of exposing myself to Munchie again. But, yes, I'll do it if it helps you."

"My family and I will always be grateful to you. Please believe me when I state that I am not in the habit of saying such things lightly."

"Sam, anybody in the hands of the S. has to be a fighter for human rights. When one man, one solitary individual, wherever in the world he may be, stands up for what's right, he speaks on behalf of every decent human being throughout the universe — white, black or whatever colour in between. He automatically enters the fraternity of the followers of truth. And that fraternity represents a bond that is stronger than blood ties, it is bound together by a principle far more powerful than the unguent that blood represents."

"Jake is not a man of words, Mr Seepye. He has little use for them. He is convinced that the State is no more than a bunch of well organised gangsters, that gangsters are not noted for being rational people who respond to reasoned arguments. He opted for violent solutions. It was not an option that civilised people approve of, but Jake is of the clear opinion that barbaric people do not deserve, nor are they swayed, by civilised behaviour. He acted on those beliefs."

"I consider myself a civilised man, in my heart I abhor violence. My religion forbids it, but I would be lying through my teeth if I said that I had never considered it as the only route open to us. I would hate to count the number of times I almost succumbed to that temptation. I'm still not convinced as to whether I was opting for civilised behaviour or that I lacked the courage of what we are now assessing as your brother's convictions.

"He must have known, deep down, what the ultimate result of his actions would be. I would like to believe he was registering his protest in the only way he considered would be effective."

"It's a debate that sages and saints indulge in. Ordinary mortals like us can only speculate ..."

"You're wrong there, my boy. Take your own case. If you were convinced that your brother — that Jake — was guilty, would you right now be exposing yourself to what the end result of your quest could be? What it could do to you and the rest of your family? And whilst you think about that let me tell you that I had already considered my own position when I agreed to help you. Nothing you have told me gives me cause to deviate from that decision."

"Thank you. How do you suggest I go about contacting Munchie?"

"I'll ring him, now if you wish. But that, unfortunately, is as far as my courage goes. Once I get an appointment for you that's the end of my participation in the matter. Fair enough?"

"More than fair. You don't have to do it."

"It's the least I can do," Seepye said firmly as he stood up. "I'll have to look in the directory for his number. I was afraid that if I entered his name in my index book the others in it would have walked out in disgust."

Sam contained the chuckle as it rose in his throat. Seepye, as he flipped through the directory, did not give the appearance of a man who thought he had said something amusing. He located the number, dialled, waited a few seconds, then spoke into the phone.

"Is Mr Munchie in?"

He waited a full minute, then spoke again. "Mr Munchie, this is Ramnath Seepye ... yes, I'm fine. I have someone here who would like to see you, on a matter he feels you could assist him with. I understand he is prepared to pay well for your help ... yes, he's with me now ... no, I have no idea ... I'm sure he'll accommodate whatever time suits you ... right now?" Seepye raised his eyes at Sam, who nodded back. "Yes, that's fine. He'll be with you in about fifteen minutes ... What? Oh, Mr Solomon."

Seepye replaced the phone and reached for a pen, copied the address on a slip of paper, then gave Sam clear directions. "It's not far from here."

"Mr Seepye, I consider myself obligated to you. This is my business card. If ever I can be of assistance to you, in any way, I would be honoured to serve you."

Seepye held out his hand and Sam took it in his.

"I wish you luck, Sam," Seepye said. "May the Lord Krishna guide you."

Sam inclined his head, shook Seepye's hand firmly, and walked out.

It took Sam considerably over half an hour to find the house. He had taken a wrong turn and was forced to double back. The roads were badly lit and some of the street names were non-existent. On several occasions he had to stop and ask for directions. When he finally found Munchie's house and stepped onto the verandah, a short, dapper man, a little on the heavy side, was sitting in a wicker chair and smoking a cigarette.

"Mr Solomon?"

Munchie neither stood nor offered to shake hands. When Sam nodded he indicated a chair nearby and waited for Sam to speak.

Sam sat down and crossed one leg over the other. He said nothing. He was thinking that his presence here was a mistake, that he should have asked Nithin to handle it. Munchie looked like the sort of man that was right up Nithin's street — one look would have been all Nithin would have required to turn Munchie into putty. A minute passed, then another. Munchie stubbed his cigarette in an ashtray and grunted.

"Well?"

"My brother and his wife," Sam said evenly, his voice revealing no emotion, "are political detainees. I have no idea where they are being held. I am prepared to pay a huge sum to have them released immediately."

"Why tell me? What makes you think I can help?"

"I'm here to find out if you can. If I have come to the wrong place I'll apologise for taking your time and leave."

"Did Seepye suggest you speak to me?"

"Mr Seepye had no views to express either way. I met him for the first time tonight."

"What made you approach him?"

"A friend of a friend mentioned that you and a General Geechie had dinner at Seepye's place. Mr Seepye neither confirmed nor denied the dinner and did not ask me why I wished to meet you. I didn't consider it necessary to tell him."

"And?"

"Because I was at his house he granted me the courtesy of looking up your number in the telephone directory and calling you. His participation in this matter began and ended there."

Sam was deliberately drawing it out, trying to get the measure of the man. Munchie said nothing. He reached for another cigarette, flicked an expensive gold lighter with a stubby finger, and drew the smoke into his lungs. Throughout, he studied Sam carefully, his eyes probing. Sam met his eyes and held them without wavering. Munchie looked away and puffed at his cigarette several times.

"Why do you think the general will listen to me?"

"I have no reason to believe he will. I simply felt it was an avenue worth exploring."

Munchie nodded and continued smoking.

"Naturally, I don't expect you or the general to forfeit your valuable time for nothing. And there may be people down the line who may not share your sympathies. I can understand that. After all, I am a businessman. I am prepared to pay a large sum of money in exchange for this favour."

Munchie quickly lowered his eyes, but not before Sam caught the flash of greed as they jumped at the mention of money. Got you, Sam thought. You're hooked. You may shake and jump a bit but you won't break the line.

"What do you consider a large sum of money?"

"Whatever it takes," Sam replied airily, at the same time reaching into his pocket. "My business card. Ask around. I'm sure any enquiries you make will not disappoint you."

Munchie looked at the card, then placed it on the table between them. "Have you approached anybody else regarding this matter?"

"No."

"Have you discussed your visit to me tonight with anyone else?"

"No."

"So, besides Seepye no one else knows you're here?"

"That's correct."

Munchie stood up. "Sit. I may be a while. Smoke if you wish."

Munchie was gone for a little over half an hour. When he returned he found Sam seated patiently, his arms folded across his chest. Munchie settled into his chair and leaned far back, looking at Sam appraisingly.

"I may be in a position to assist you. Of course, I can guarantee nothing. If I am able to do this ... favour, how much are you prepared to outlay?"

"I will discuss that with Geechie."

"That's not possible. I'm not saying I have spoken to him, but I can tell you he will not see you."

"Then we can't do business," Sam said flatly, not moving. "I will not part with what I am satisfied will be an immense sum of money without Geechie's promise, directly to me, that he will release my brother and his wife."

The moment Sam had said "immense sum of money" the avaricious gleam flashed again. This time Munchie didn't even attempt to hide it.

Suddenly, Munchie was smiling patronisingly, leaning forward like an old friend.

"Trust me, Sam. There are ways these things are done. Let me handle the negotiations with the general. I know how he thinks. Tell me how far you are prepared to go, your topmost limit. I'll do my best to convince the general not to exceed it. Like I said ..."

"No, Mister Munchie," Sam said firmly. "I am a wealthy man. The money is unimportant to me. However, I am a suspicious man by nature. It may be through no fault of your own but if I lose the money without obtaining satisfaction, I may do you the injustice of holding it against you.

By talking to Geechie direct such suspicions will be removed. I have no doubts that you are an honourable man. Why sully that belief unnecessarily?"

When Sam leaned back he said to himself: I can play this game better than you, my friend.

Munchie seemed to be thinking it over. Sam pressed his point home. "Once Geechie gives me his word I will hand over the money in cash or whatever other form he stipulates. I'll pass it over to you, to Geechie himself, or to whoever he may wish to nominate. I am prepared to do this in advance, before my brother and his wife are released. Can I be fairer than that?"

"All right," Munchie said, "I'll try it your way. Give me the names."

"Yacoob Solomon. His wife's name is Hannah."

"Can I get you at this number?" Munchie asked, pointing to the card.

"That is not a card I normally hand out. The number on it is a twenty-four hour contact."

Sam rose before Munchie did and, without offering to shake hands, walked out.

∞

It was close to midnight by the time Sam reached home, Sally was awake and waiting. He told her as much as he could recall about his discussions with Seepye and Munchie.

"Seepye is an honourable man. Munchie is motivated by greed, a man who would sacrifice his soul for a pot of gold."

"How much do you think they'll settle for?"

"Like you suggested, I laid it on the table. I had to hook their greed to make sure they take the bait." Sam was stretched out on a sofa, his feet spilling over the armrest. "I'm satisfied Munchie has swallowed the hook with the bait."

"And Geechie?"

"The first thing Munchie asked after he returned from what was obviously a call to Geechie was how much I was prepared to pay. And from what Seepye told me about those two they're out to bleed anyone they can. You can be sure they will aim to make a killing. My gut feeling is they will also deliver. What supports my instincts is Munchie's insistence that he deals with Geechie alone. Apart from the fact that he was probably hoping to pocket a large share for himself, he wouldn't expose himself if there was no possibility of Geechie playing ball."

"But he must know there's nothing you can do to Geechie if he reneges on his promise."

"Maybe. But Munchie is not Geechie. He lives amongst us and he's vulnerable. If they intended to pull a fast one, giving me access to Geechie would be his insurance. When he tried to bypass that I felt encouraged."

"Both Karan and Nithin phoned while you were out. I told them about Seepye."

"Good. I'll see them tomorrow."

They threw it around for a while, feeling alternately hopeful and discouraged. Somewhere along the way Sam drifted off to sleep.

The sun was rising above the skyline when he jerked awake. Sally had thrown a light rug over his feet. He stood up and stretched, massaging his back and removing the kinks in the muscles. He heard Sally moving around in the kitchen.

"Didn't you sleep at all?" Sam asked as he entered the kitchen.

"I tried for a while and finally gave up. To give myself something to do I baked a few pies. I'll get you a cup of tea."

Sam took his time as he shaved and showered, the hot water loosening the knots in his shoulders. Just before he finished he turned on the cold water full force. When he stepped out of the shower, he felt refreshed and ready to face the day.

A little before seven he rang Karan and filled him in on the latest developments, promising to update him as things progressed. When he spoke to Nithin the response was more optimistic.

"You handled it perfectly. You'll hear from Munchie sooner than you expect. These guys believe in moving fast, the prospect of easy money is like a spur up their arses, goading them into action. They'll take you to the cleaners but they'll keep to the deal. What you need to insist on is an undertaking that they won't arrest Jake again a few days later."

"You think they'll do that?"

"The way I see it, Jake is too valuable a catch. You can bet a few medals were passed out after his capture. Geechie can't act on this alone and set Jake free. There's no way he could justify such an action. His only hope is to con his superiors into believing that Jake was allowed a few days to visit his family, in exchange for playing ball with them."

"Nits, gimme a second ... we need to think this through. Look, you make sense, a hell of a lot of sense. But ... if I make his freedom conditional on a blanket amnesty ... won't Geechie back out completely?"

"Sam, let's take this slowly. Maybe I should come over and ..."

"Hang on a sec, Nits. I hear my private line ringing."

Sam lifted the receiver. Before he could speak into it a voice said, "Solomon?"

"Yes."

"Munchie here. I'll see you in your office. In an hour."

Sam heard a click, then the line went dead.

"Nits, you there?"

"Yep."

"That was Munchie. Wants to see me in my office in an hour."

"Doesn't give us much time. Okay. I suggest you drop the freedom clause. Don't even mention it or give Geechie a hint that it's on your mind. You do that and you'll be showing your hand. Just give them what they want and get Jake and Hannah out. In the meantime I'll work on the angles. You better get going."

"You think Munchie will bring Geechie along?"

"Maybe. Get in touch with me at the first opportunity."

Sam skipped breakfast and was in his office in under twenty minutes. A few minutes later Rushda buzzed him.

"A Mr Munchie is here to see you."

As he replaced the receiver Sam glanced at his watch. Munchie was almost half an hour early. Nithin had been right, these people believed in moving fast.

Munchie stepped into the office and Sam silently indicated a chair, inviting Munchie to sit down.

"We don't have time," Munchie snapped. "My car is waiting. The general will see you, immediately. He flew in early this morning from Pretoria in a military jet. As it happened he had some private business to attend to in Durban. I was able to arrange a few minutes for you. Let's go."

The journey was concluded in silence and when they entered CR Swart Square the driver seemed to know his way around. There was a small complex set apart from the main buildings and the car turned into it. They passed several guards, armed with rifles, who watched them closely as they drove slowly by. Sam had the impression that they were expected.

The driver pulled up near an imposing block. Munchie stepped out of the car and indicated, with a nod of his head, that Sam should follow him. A greater number of soldiers, in combat uniforms, were in evidence, all alert and on their toes.

The main door was manned by a muscular, officious-looking young man with a thick beard. Munchie walked up to him, smiling obsequiously and rubbing his hands together. Sam couldn't hear what Munchie was saying but it was obvious that he was not quite finished when the doorman unceremoniously motioned him to wait and then spoke into the intercom. Munchie took a step back, the smile still on his face. Sam joined Munchie and waited.

A minute later the door opened and Sam and Munchie were allowed to enter. There was a reception desk at the end of the foyer. A tall, blonde woman glared at them, then turned away and ignored the visitors. About a minute later the lift doors opened and a man in military uniform emerged. The blonde indicated, with a toss of her head, where Munchie and Sam were standing.

"*Kom,*" the aide said arrogantly as he stepped back into the lift. Munchie hurried over, motioning to Sam with his right hand that he should move faster. Sam followed at his normal pace, refusing to be hustled. There were no introductions, no sign of a welcome, and they rode the lift silently.

They exited on the third floor, followed the aide down a richly carpeted corridor with Munchie frantically signalling with his fingers and exhorting Sam to step up his pace. At the far end the aide opened a door and, just before entering he pointed at the floor and brusquely indicated that they should wait at the entrance. He went in, leaving the door open. Sam took a step closer but before he could move again Munchie quickly shot out his arm and whispered, "Wait! Wait!"

Sam could see their escort as he gently tapped on an inter-leading door and listened for a second. He opened it a few inches and stepped back. Then, without as much as a glance at the visitors, he motioned with his thumb that they should go in.

Munchie scuttled forward and mumbled over his shoulder, "Come! Come!"

They entered an opulently furnished office, the walls lined with photographs of various cabinet ministers and past prime ministers. In pride of place was a huge enlargement of Hendrik Verwoerd, in many ways the architect and leading exponent of white supremacy. Sam recalled a conversation at one of Karan's meetings when someone had bitterly claimed that the man was not even born in the country, had in fact migrated to South Africa from Amsterdam. After a previously unsuccessful attempt on his life he had been stabbed to death in the parliamentary chamber. As far as Sam was concerned, it was a fitting end to a man responsible for most of the recent apartheid legislation, and whose hands were stained with the blood of those that died at Sharpeville in 1960.

Behind an unusually large desk a slight, startlingly pale man was paging through a file, occasionally stopping to read a few lines before moving on. He neither looked up nor gave any acknowledgement that he was aware of the two men standing in front of him. Sam recognised Geechie.

After several minutes had passed, with the only sound the slight rustling of paper as Geechie perused the file, Sam turned to his left and began to study the photographs on the wall, to Munchie's apparent disapproval and discomfort.

When Geechie finally spoke Sam had the impression that the man was speaking to himself.

"I have studied the file," Geechie muttered in a thick, guttural Afrikaans accent. "The woman seems harmless but this chap, Solomon, is a *blerry skelm!*"

Geechie paused. He did not look up and did not raise his eyes. He turned a few pages at random, then continued. "Men like him are a danger to law and order. They deserve to be eliminated."

Geechie's eyes remained hooded. He seemed to be waiting for a response from Sam. To hell with you buddy, Sam thought. I've dealt with *Motas* like you before. He allowed the silence to build up.

Geechie suddenly slammed the file angrily, the sound abnormally loud in the confined area. "You will ensure his full co-operation in future?" He continued to look at the folder in front of him.

Sam was aware that Geechie was attempting to intimidate him, to extract an undertaking that would assist in Jake's interrogation at a later date.

"I do not make promises that are beyond my ability to fulfil," Sam replied bluntly. "All I can do is try to keep my brother out of politics if he is returned to me."

Geechie's eyes shot up and locked onto Sam's. "It is your patriotic duty to act in the interests of the State. The family must always remain subservient ... "

"I have no desire to debate these issues with you. I am not a politician."

When Geechie's eyes narrowed Sam continued, smiling thinly, "The only promise I can make is to remain silent about his treatment whilst in detention. And, if he is released, to forget completely that we ever had this discussion."

Geechie placed his hands flat on the desk and lowered his eyes. He remained that way for a few seconds, in deep thought.

"The chances of releasing him," Geechie said, his voice unnaturally loud. "Are a million to one." He looked at Munchie for the first time. "You understand? A million to one."

Geechie dismissed them with a wave of his hand. "Now, get out. Go!"

Munchie immediately led the way out of the office, taking Sam by the arm and pulling him forward. Sam hesitated, considered telling Geechie what he thought of him, then shrugged his shoulder and followed Munchie. The escort remained with them until they passed the reception desk and walked through the door.

As soon as they were alone Sam turned to Munchie and said furiously, "What the hell was that all about? Why bring me here to listen to ..."

"Later," Munchie muttered, "Later. Just trust me."

When they pulled up at the entrance to Solomon Brothers Munchie turned to the driver and ordered, "Take a walk."

The moment the driver was out of hearing Munchie leaned towards Sam and passed an envelope to him.

"Open it later. You will find in there the name of a bank in the Principality of Liechtenstein and the name of a company. You will arrange to deposit the equivalent of two million rands, in Swiss francs, into the company's account."

"A million to one!" Sam repeated softly, imitating Geechie's accent. "I understand. It will be done. When will they be released?"

"Soon after confirmation that the money has been deposited. Your brother will be delivered to your door but only after the sum of a further two hundred thousand, in cash, has been handed over to me, as my commission." All pretence of a "favour" had now vanished. Munchie's tone was blunt, matter of fact.

"And my sister-in-law?"

"Of course. Naturally. It's a package deal."

Munchie turned away, dismissing Sam with a wave of his hand.

∞

The second Sam entered his office he opened the envelope and extracted a sheet of ordinary paper. It contained a single line typed on an old-fashioned ribbon typewriter: the name of a bank followed by the name of a company. Nothing further. Not even an account number.

Sam stuck his head through the door and said, "Rushda, please arrange a pot of coffee. But first ring Mr Vania and Mr Naran. Ask them to come over and impress upon them that it's urgent."

Sam phoned Sally, told her briefly about what had taken place and promised to fill her in later. He was on his second cup of coffee when Karan walked in, followed almost immediately by Nithin.

Sam explained, as accurately as he could recall, including all the subtle nuances, of his interaction with Munchie and Geechie. Finally, he sat back and waited for their comments.

"Geechie must have had a tape-recorder hidden somewhere," Nithin mused. "To cover his arse in the event something goes wrong after Jake is released. He can always say that you got back to him later in the day, promised to get Jake to co-operate with them all the way down the line in exchange for a few days with his family — perhaps even to give you an opportunity to convince Jake that it was in his best interests to do so. It's the only explanation that makes sense."

"Then it confirms your suspicions that they plan to take Jake back into custody," Sam added.

"This Geechie oke is one smart cookie," Nithin almost smiled in admiration. "The only mistake he made was that he figures us to be a bunch of suckers, typical *garachs*, ripe for plucking."

"And Munchie had the envelope, with the slip of paper, on him all the time."

"As for that," Karan said, "You did insist on dealing direct with Geechie."

"Sure, but it also tells us that the amount came as no surprise to Munchie. It was all settled in advance. For all we know, he'll probably get a cut of the two mil. He couldn't help but cream a bit more for himself by adding on the payment to him direct."

"Does it matter? I don't see how that helps us."

"Just adding a bit of perspective," Sam smiled.

"No harm in knowing how the opposition thinks," Nithin threw in. "Now, Sam, how do you plan to proceed?"

"The two hundred gees I can put together in an hour. The best way to handle the overseas transaction is to access Dara's foreign account ..."

"Too scrappy!" Karan said. "That account was under Dara's sole control. It'll take a few days to verify your signature and time is ..."

"I agree," Nithin cut in. "I can get that amount over by tomorrow ..."

"Nithin," Karan cut in. "With respect to you, I can tie this up with one phone call. In a few hours Geechie or Munchie or whoever will have their confirmation."

"Fine," Nithin agreed. "Why don't you get on it straightaway. I'll go over the ground with Sam, assist him with Munchie's end of the deal."

Karan stood up and nodded. "You'll hear from me in a short while."

When Karan had left, Nithin asked, "This oke Geechie, any peculiar inflections in his voice, anything you could have missed out on?"

"Can't think of anything else. Apart from the 'million to one' bit, and

Chapter ten

I only tumbled to that later, when I was with Munchie in the car. There was little else in it."

"What about Munchie? Nothing more there?"

"Nope. He didn't talk much. Is something bugging you?"

"I don't know. My instincts are probably running wild. But somewhere, when you were telling us about what took place, something flashed through my mind and was gone before I could latch onto it. It's still there, lurking in my brain and making me uneasy. Maybe it will come back. Maybe I've been in this game too long, seeing ghosts behind every door. Forget it. Let's get back to Jake."

"We'll have to move him out of the country."

"The faster the better. Give him a bit of time with the family, no more than four or five hours, then move him to a neighbouring country, together with Hannah and their *lighty*. For starters, that's our best solution. Between Sandy and I we can work out some plan, okay?"

"Do it, Nits. We'll all sleep better for it."

"Leave it to me. You still sure you can put Munchie's parcel together?"

"It's as good as done."

"Then leave the delivery to me. Some of my best men will call on you here in an hour. They're used to moving huge sums around, they'll take care of it. We don't want any last minute hitches."

They parted on an optimistic note, for the first time in what seemed an age.

∞

By two that afternoon Karan confirmed that the overseas transaction had been concluded. By three Nithin phoned to say that Munchie had been handed his money, or, as Nits put it, "The stooge is crapping gold."

Sam took the rest of the day off and headed home.

"Everything they asked for has been done," Sam told Sally. "All we can do now is wait."

"I trust Nithin *bhai*'s judgment," Sally said. "I'm trying not to get too excited."

Sam nodded, weariness beginning to seep into his bones. He walked onto the balcony and stretched out in an easy chair. After a while he dozed off, picturing the reunion with Jake and Hannah.

It was a brief respite. An hour later he was pacing the floor, having difficulty containing his impatience. Karan phoned at six to ask if there was any news. Nithin popped in and simply said that they should be prepared for a long wait.

437

"It could take a day or two," Nithin continued. "Geechie has no reason to jump to it."

At eight Sam's phone rang. It was Munchie.

"Expect a call sometime tomorrow morning. Your brother and his wife should be with you soon after that."

Munchie cut the connection before Sam could ask any questions. When Sam turned around Sally was at the door looking at him expectantly.

"Tomorrow morning," Sam smiled ecstatically, for the first time in ages. Sally flew into his arms and they hugged each other.

"I think we should inform the family now, ring Hannah's parents, call ma home from *foi*'s place."

Sally thought it over for a few seconds. "Let's wait till they're home, Sam. Remember what Nithin *bhai* said, Munchie's 'soon' could mean anything. I don't want to put ma through a long vigil. It'll also give Jake a chance to freshen up, look good so that ma won't be too shocked by his appearance."

"I like that. And I'm beginning to feel hungry."

"About time. The food around here has been going to waste."

Sam had a huge meal, the first in several days. When he reached for a cigarette, for once Sally didn't ask him to leave the room. He stretched his long legs and looked at Sally expectantly.

"What?" she asked, smiling.

"Just thinking. In a day or two, when this is behind us, we could maybe go on a holiday overseas, take Jake and Hannah — and Zain — with us. Perhaps settle them there. Rashid and the Friedmans can handle the store perfectly well. And Hannah could even meet her long lost relatives ..."

Sally burst out laughing. "You're beginning to sound like the boy I married."

"Sound like him? Want me to prove I am him?"

"*Choop, sala!* And if you're going to light another cigarette, go outside."

∞

It wasn't long before Sam was restless again. He was torn between the urge to get out of the house and the need to stay close to the phone, just in case there were further developments. He sighed with relief when Sandy and Nits walked in an hour later, Karan trailing them.

They sat around for a while, making small talk, until Sally went off to bed. When they were alone Nithin said, "Everything is in place. Sandy's arranged for a four-wheel drive and insists on taking them to Botswana himself. Someone he knows in the PAC has given him the directions to a safe house in the mountains there and they will be taken good care of. There's also some top doctor there to see to Jake's injuries."

"The PAC oke has given me clear directions, even a road map. He has pinpointed a place where I can cross over and bypass the border post," Sandy added. "I also have a long list of local activists along the route, any one of whom will give us cover if the need arises."

"Sandy," Sam said with feeling, "You've always steered clear of this sort of thing all your life. Politics has never been your scene. You're sticking your neck out now."

"This is not politics, Sam. And I've not quite steered clear of it anyway. Which darkie can. The bottom line here is Jake and his family. Anyway, what the hell, we all need to stand up and be counted sometime. If I can't do this for Jake you know someone else I could do it for?"

"The trick here, Sam," Nithin stressed, "Is to get Jake and Hannah out of this house without anyone noticing. You can be sure Geechie's men will have this place staked out. How they'll do it and what their cover will be is beyond me. But you can bet your life they'll be out there somewhere."

"You guys don't think we're being paranoid about this?" Sam asked.

"No, Sam," Sandy replied. "Nithin, Karan and I spent the past two hours at Karan's house throwing this around. All three of us feel we can't be too careful."

"This is what we finally settled on," Karan said, entering into the discussion. "We should have a homecoming party an hour or so after Jake gets here. Get as many people over as we can, make it a real celebration, with lots of cars and people coming and going all the time. My mother, Devi and my *lighty* will be here throughout. Somewhere along the way Jake will finally go to his room without making a fuss of it, claiming to be tired. He'll put on my mother's clothes, Hannah into Devi's sari, and Zain into my *lighty*'s clothes — they're about the same age and build. Maliga and Kathy will leave at the same time as Jake and his family does, through the front door. I'll be with Jake, of course. Each group will head for their own cars. We'll make sure mine is parked closest to the door. With a bit of luck, Geechie's men, if they're out there, will notice nothing unusual."

"I can't agree to that, Karan," Sam almost shouted. "There's no way I can expose Devi and your mother ..."

"It was my mother's idea anyway," Karan grinned. "We didn't know she had been listening to us discussing different ways to get them out, and she finally barged in and told us this was the way to do it. Devi was only too happy to back her up."

"My God!" Sam exclaimed. "These mothers of ours ..."

"I tried to dissuade her," Nithin smiled. "You know what she said?"

"*Choop, Sala!*" Sally said, emerging from the kitchen.

"You're right," Nithin confessed a little shamefaced. "That's exactly what Karan's mother said."

"Sally," Sam said, a little taken aback. "What are you doing there?"

"What *kaki* was doing earlier, listening to you idiots."

"But I thought you had gone to bed ..."

"What else could I say? None of you trust our judgment."

"Put the women in the frontline; that's what Jake said that night," Sam softly added. "Will we ever learn?"

∞

The phone rang at exactly nine the next morning. Sam pounced on the receiver. "Yes?"

"Mr Solomon?"

"Yes."

"My name is Van Heerden. I will be with you in under an hour. Your brother and sister-in-law will be brought over."

Sam couldn't help noticing that the voice was surprisingly courteous. "And, Mr Solomon, I have been instructed to inform you that you are to be alone when you receive them. Only you. No one else must be present."

"My wife is with me now. Surely she ..."

"My instructions are very clear. I'm not allowed to deviate from them."

"There are only the two of us here. I can't see the harm in that."

There was a moment's silence. Van Heerden seemed to be thinking it over.

"Fine, *Meneer*. I'll take the chance. You'll have to give me your word that it is done without my permission — if it should ever come up."

"I promise. Thank you."

Sam was elated. He couldn't keep the excitement from showing as he took Sally in his arms. "They'll be here in an hour, both of them." He did a little jig as he lifted Sally clear off the floor.

"Sam!" Sally laughed. "Put me down. I must phone ..."

"Not yet. Only after they're gone. They made it very clear only you and I are to meet them. Let's keep to their rules, for now.""

"I think I'm going to cry. I'm so happy."

"Woman, you ..." Sam said, imitating Dara.

"*Choop, Sala!*" Sally shot back, in Shaida's voice, then burst out laughing as she headed for the kitchen.

For the next half an hour Sam straightened out Jake's room, located his favourite books and placed them next to the lamp. He went over to the wall cupboard and selected a pair of casual pants and one of Jake's favourite shirts and placed them on the bed. He went into the bathroom, noted that there were fresh towels in place, straightened a few of Hannah's shampoo bottles, then looked around. Satisfied, he entered Hannah's dressing room, opened her cupboard and suddenly realised he didn't know where to start. He had never been in there before.

"Sally!" Sam shouted at the top of his voice. He was about to call again when he realised that she couldn't hear him. He re-entered the bedroom, moved around idly for a while, then pulled the curtains as far apart as they would go and opened a window, letting the sun stream in.

Sam was heading for the kitchen when the doorbell rang.

"Mr Solomon? I'm Van Heerden." He stuck out his right hand. Sam took it in his and briefly returned the greeting. He could hear Sally's soft footsteps behind him. Van Heerden was simply dressed, in a dark civilian suit. He was spare, of medium height and displayed none of the arrogance that Sam had recently encountered. His thin, long face was sombre, a little sad, and strangely respectful. When Sally joined them at the door Van Heerden inclined his head graciously and stepped back.

Sam walked down the driveway, Sally close to him. His heart was pounding furiously and he took several short breaths to control his breathing. Two cars were parked halfway up the driveway, the second considerably larger than the first. The windows of both were tinted and he couldn't see into the interior. Four well-built men stood near the larger car, at strict attention, their hands folded across their chests. Suddenly, one of the doors was flung open and Hannah ran towards them. She flew into Sam's arms and he held her tightly, patting her shoulders. Hannah was sobbing and saying something, her voice indistinct, muffled by Sam's chest. Sally quickly took over and embraced Hannah, both stumbling a little. Sam steadied them, his eyes fixed to the open door, waiting for Jake to emerge.

Van Heerden gave a signal and the men moved to the rear and opened the large doors in the back. It's an ambulance of some sort, Sam said to himself, Jake must be on a stretcher. He was about to take a step forward when the casket emerged.

Sam's heart froze. He was stunned into immobility, one knee still bent, his body at an angle. He heard Sally scream, the wail penetrating through him, cutting into his brain and shaking him out of his stupor. Somewhere, from an immense distance, he heard Van Heerden's voice.

"I'm sorry, *Meneer* ... I wasn't aware that you didn't know. Please believe me, it pains me to see this. I'm truly sorry ..."

All Sam heard was "Sorry .. It pains me .. truly sorry." Sam shook his head a few times, as if to clear his mind, then turned to Van Heerden and quietly looked at him. The man's face was immensely sad, deeply etched with lines that had not been apparent a moment earlier.

"This is not the way of the Afrikaner," Van Heerden muttered, his voice hollow. Suddenly, he straightened up to his full height and shouted, "Not on the pavement. Take it inside!"

The four men, who had been in the act of lowering the casket, grunted and hefted the heavy load.

"Gently," Van Heerden said, "with respect!"

Sally followed the men, her arms around Hannah, holding her up.

Sam stared straight ahead, not looking at Van Heerden whose head was bowed now, eyes fixed on his shoes. The men returned and entered the car. Van Heerden saluted, held it for a second, then left.

∞

Shaida was the first to arrive, her head high, eyes clear. Ayesha, her face set, was a step behind her mother. The Friedmans, who had collected Zain from school, walked through the door a minute later, followed by Heera Daya and Karan's family. The house began to fill up with family, friends and neighbours, the men beginning to overflow into the garden. Nithin and Sandy walked in together, hugged Sam silently and stood back. Karan, for the first time looking dishevelled, his long hair uncombed, simply stood in a corner by himself. By eleven thirty the large lawn was packed with mourners.

"Hannah's okay," Sam said in response to Sandy's enquiry. "She told us that she had been given firm instructions not to open the casket. They warned her that it had been sealed and that we will be watched all the time. They obviously know that we bury our dead on the same day. They insisted that it must be over before three this afternoon. They threatened to pick her up again if their instructions are not followed."

"How do we know Jake is in ..." Nithin started to ask.

"Hannah identified the body and was present when they placed it in the coffin."

"Can we meet their deadline?"

"Rashid and Mr Shaikh are attending to it. We'll make it."

At that moment Sally stepped into the garden, looked around until she located Sam, and walked over. When she was close enough she whispered, "Come with me. You too, Nithin *bhai*, Sandy." She led them to a spot a little away from the crowds and quietly told them, "We've spotted one of the SB's people."

"Are you sure?" Sam asked, startled. "How can you tell?"

"Ayesha noticed that one of the women in the lounge was behaving in a strange way. She had a Koran in her lap but her eyes were elsewhere. Every once in a while she turned a page and pretended to read. The odd thing was that she was turning the pages the wrong way, the way you read an English novel, from the front to the back. And Ayesha asked around, no one seems to know the woman."

"Okay, Sal. Let's play it cool for a while."

"Ayesha is on her way to tell mother."

"There's no way of telling what mother will do" Sam muttered. "Sally, get back in there and try to contain mother if she attempts to approach the woman. We'll go in through the back and onto the balcony."

Sam, with Nithin and Sandy, stood near the french doors and looked into the lounge. The casket was in the centre, covered with a large velvet shawl embroidered with verses from the Koran. The first few rows of women were seated in a circle around it, quietly reading from the Koran placed on cushions in front of each of them. They could see Ayesha leaning over Shaida's shoulder, saying something and pointing with her eyes.

Shaida stood up, her eyes flashing angrily. "Bring Zainul Aberdeen to me," she said, her voice clear as a bell, carrying all over the room.

"That's torn it," Sam muttered. "Anything can happen now."

"But why did she send for Jake's *lighty*?" Sandy asked.

"I can't even begin to guess," Sam replied. "Those two are very close to each other."

"I didn't quite follow the bit about how the Koran is read," Sandy said.

"The Arabic text," Sam said, "is read from back to front. You start from what in the west is the last page and you move towards the beginning ..." Sam stopped talking when Zain entered the lounge, in his stockinged feet, and approached his grandmother. Shaida whispered something to him, then pointed towards a woman near the door. The woman was beginning to get to her feet, obviously in a hurry to leave. Suddenly, Ayesha and Sally were standing in front of her, blocking the exit. Zain nodded at his grandmother, said something to her, then straightened up.

"You, lady," Zain said, "You desecrate the sanctity of my father's funeral and violate the privacy of our house. You are a disgrace to every person of colour in this country. It is good that you are standing, that everyone here can see the Judas in you and point you out to their friends in the streets. My father will rest in peace, you are damned for ever. Now go! Get out of here and tell your white masters what I said and then find a hole to creep into."

"I'll be damned!" Sandy whispered in awe, "Jake's not in the casket. I swear that's him standing there, when he was fourteen years old."

"Where the hell did the *lighty* learn to talk like that?" Nithin asked.

"I guess he is his father's son," Sam smiled, his eyes moist.

When the woman scuttled out of the house, someone began to sob loudly. Shaida immediately looked up. "There will be no overt display of grief in my house," she said sternly. "Our religion forbids it. If you cannot maintain your dignity you will leave this room."

The sobbing stopped immediately.

You were right again, Jake, Sam said to himself. The women are the real fighters. They don't pussyfoot around and they mould us in their image.

∞

A dozen men grunted as they hoisted the casket to their shoulders and entered the iron gates. The freshly dug grave, adjacent to those of Dara and Yahya, was ready to receive Jake's remains.

Sam and Rashid removed their shoes and entered the grave. A second later Zain was beside them. Sam patted his shoulder and nodded. The casket, still covered with the velvet shroud, was placed on several strong nylon straps that those on either side of the grave carefully payed out. Sam and Zain at one end, Rashid at the other, steadied the casket until it touched the ground. Under normal circumstances it would have been the body itself, wrapped in white calico tied at either end, that would have been lowered. Caskets did not form part of an Islamic burial.

Strict procedure now required the body to be turned to its side, facing towards Mecca. Those proceedings could not be observed today and Sam said a silent prayer of regret. Somebody reached down, took Rashid by the hand and hoisted him to the top. Another hand reached out to Zain, who looked at Sam beseechingly. Sam nodded, took the outstretched hand in his own, and pulled himself out of the grave.

One at a time, the wooden slats were passed down to Zain, who carefully slotted the grooves in place, ensuring that they rested firmly on their counterparts on either side. Finally Sam hauled Zain to the top and the mourners began shovelling the sand into the grave as the priest reverently read the appropriate verses from the Koran. At last it was done and they stepped back.

The priest, a young man in his mid-twenties, stepped onto a small hillock and quietly surveyed the gathering. In a carefully modulated voice, just loud enough to reach the farthest mourner, he intoned the opening chapter from the Koran.

"In the name of Allah, most Gracious, most Merciful.
Praise be to Allah, the Cherisher and Sustainer of the worlds.
Most Gracious, most Merciful, Master of the Day of Judgment.
Thee do we worship and Thine aid we seek.
Show us the straight way.
The way of those on whom Thou has bestowed Thy Grace.
Those whose portion is not wrath.
And who go not astray."

A chorus of "Ameens" responded in unison.

Several more verses from the Koran followed, then the priest asked for forgiveness for all of mankind, paused, and took a deep breath.

"We have come here today to pay homage to our Creator and to pray for our dearly departed brother. My duty to God and to those of you here today goes beyond that.

"The pursuit of justice is what separates us from the animal world, it distinguishes civilized man from the savage and sets honest men apart from the criminal.

"There is no principle on earth that supersedes justice. Ignore it and you ignore the power of reason, of decency, and you destroy the very foundations on which civilised society rests. You revert to the days of darkness and of savagery. If you do not hold firm to this principle, if you make the tiniest compromise, you take the first step towards your own eventual destruction.

"Take a penny that you have not earned honestly, by the sweat of your own brow, and you take the first step towards breaking that law. You cannot abrogate to yourself the fruits of that which you have not yourself produced.

"When the leaders of a country deviate from this principle they sentence all those who voted them in power to perdition.

"It is a law. The first law of God and the first law of survival.

"I know of no religion on earth that preaches anything that is contrary to what I have said. The government of this country will have to give me the name of the mysterious religion that they follow, the religion that gives them the right to behave in the manner that they do, that allows them to violate this principle.

"Yacoob Suleiman gave his life in pursuit of that principle.

"The followers of Satan must not hide behind the veil of the *munafiques*, the hypocrites who pretend that they serve God, when in reality they serve their own avaricious goals. And those who enjoy the proceeds of those ill-gotten gains must not claim ignorance of the source of their bounty."

The priest paused, looked around him, then continued.

"I am constantly reminded to be careful of what I say, that the agents of this Satan State are all around us. I have been told that they are here today.

"For them time is running out. It is they who should leave here in fear, not I. It is they who have been parties to the murder of the man whom we have buried today.

"God in his mercy always gives us one last hope of salvation. To save their own souls those agents should leave here now and dedicate themselves, each of them, to save one life which, but for their intervention, may otherwise be lost. And when they have done that they should pray that the angels around us today, who have noted their names, will also note their acts of atonement and intercede for them on the Day of Judgment.

"If they fail to do that before the angel of death taps them on their shoulder — and no man can guarantee that death is not around the next corner — it will be too late for them.

"Go with God."

※

By eight, with the exception of family and close friends, most of the mourners had left. Sam, Sandy and Nithin were sitting at a table in the back garden, having coffee.

"The best laid plans of men and mice, as the poet Burns said, ..." Nithin murmured.

"You just have to take it as it comes," Sandy added. "Geechie pulled a sharp double bluff. He was way ahead of us."

"It's the way they have continued to maintain their grip on this country. When I saw Jake that night in jail, he told me these guys can teach the *Motas* a few tricks. I'm beginning to understand now what he meant.

I should have kept that in mind that morning in Geechie's office. I didn't play it cool. I allowed myself to get angry. It was stupid."

"I must be getting old," Nithin muttered, a distant look in his eyes. "It was staring me in the face and I couldn't see it. Remember, Sam, when you recounted your conversations with Geechie and Munchie? I told you something was bugging me, something I couldn't put my finger on?"

"I remember," Sam was leaning forward, his eyes quizzical.

"It's only surfacing now. The way Munchie phrased it: 'Your brother will be delivered to your door'. It's a strange way to put it. Why didn't he simply say 'released' instead of 'delivered to your door'? People don't talk that way normally. Munchie knew he was double-dealing, that Jake would be put away, you'd never see him alive. The bastard was hedging his bets."

"That was Geechie's doing, then. Or maybe the guys who were interrogating Jake, they went too far, maybe Jake was dead already."

"I don't buy that. He wanted to ensure Jake's co-operation. What would have been the purpose if Jake was already dead? He was still alive at that time. The decision was made right then, just after you refused to promise Jake would play ball with them."

"In that case Munchie couldn't have known about it. I was with him all the time."

"Then why the odd phraseology?"

"You know what I think," Sandy said. "The decision was made the night you first approached Munchie at his house. When the stooge phoned Geechie the honky must have told him that there was no way he could do that, that releasing Jake alive was out of the question. That's when the decision was made. They just couldn't resist the loot. Why else was he on the phone for so long? It doesn't take over half an hour to decide whether they could free him or not. The bit about Jake's future co-operation? That was simply part of the double bluff. To lull your suspicions in case you asked to see Jake first, before parting with the dough."

"There's one way to check it out," Sam said. "It's a long shot but Munchie's an arrogant swine, he may just give himself away. Let's go to my study."

Sam located Munchie's number and picked up the receiver. He pressed a button on the cradle before dialling. "I've released the 'mute' button. You'll be able to hear both sides of the conversation." When Sam stopped dialling they could all hear the phone ringing at the other end.

"Who is it?" It was Munchie's voice.

"Munchie, this is Sam Solomon."

"So?"

"You failed to honour our arrangements, when my brother reached me he was dead."

"Listen, Solomon," Munchie snarled. "The arrangement was to deliver him to you. I said that clearly. His death has nothing to do with me. I've never seen him in my life. If you don't like it, ask Geechie. You know where he is. Don't ring me again if you know what's good for you." Munchie slammed the phone down.

Sam lowered the receiver slowly, his face a grim mask.

"That's it," Nithin said. "All the confirmation we need."

Sandy and Nithin exchanged a strange look. A message of some sort passed between them, an understanding arrived at. It happened so quickly that only a close observer would have picked up on it. Sam, his back against the wall, had not missed it.

"Okay, *lighty*?" Sandy asked.

Sam nodded, once. "Okay," he said.

Two days later, on a hot still night, Munchie's body was found slumped in his chair, a bullet hole between his eyes.

chapter eleven

*I*t was a rare evening, the likes of which none of them could remember enjoying since their early youth. Sam, Nithin, Sandy and Karan were together socially, the result of pure chance.

Nithin and Sandy, with Kathija and Maliga, had popped in after an early dinner at a restaurant. Sam and Sally were at a loose end and were delighted to see the foursome. They had barely settled, Nithin stretched out on a sofa, when Karan and Devi popped in unexpectedly.

"Oh! Oh!" Nithin said, loud enough for Karan to hear, "Father Angelino, the paragon of virtue, goody-two-shoes himself, has arrived to save us from our wanton ways."

"You leave Karan *bhai* alone," Sally scolded Nithin mildly.

"He doesn't bother me, Sally," Karan said with a smile. "But I am intrigued. Where did this erstwhile urchin of the streets acquire the ability to be so flowing in his speech, considering the only school that he is acquainted with is a gambling den."

"A den of iniquity would sound better, more in keeping with your la-di-da pretensions," Nithin shot back.

"You two guys!" Sandy shook his head in despair. "I keep telling you Sam, it's some *Bunya* thing."

"Sounds more like mutual envy to me," Kathy laughed.

"Who asked you, doctor?" Nithin asked in mock anger.

"We seem to have touched a sore spot, Sandy," Kathy smiled. "Must have struck the nail squarely ..."

"Go and make us some tea, woman," Nithin dismissed her with a wave of his hand. "Karan, help her. You women can be nice and cosy where you belong — in the kitchen."

"The word is 'brew', Nithin," Karan scoffed, "you know, brew, like in beer. Your repertoire of phrases seems to be easily exhausted."

"Go on," Nits said, wagging his fingers. "Flounce off. To the kitchen with you, you flunky of the law courts."

"Not a bad comeback," Karan goaded him, "Now, with a bit more polish in your presentation ..."

"That's it," Maliga ordered, "Cut! Wrap it up. And you guys, all four of you, can make — brew — the tea."

"And walk in a straight line," Kathy ordered. "Any physical jerks or shoulder swings and you're dead."

"Let's go," Nithin scrambled to his feet. "Karan I can handle. As for these witches of the heath, their ill wind stifles me."

In the kitchen, all but Karan settled around the breakfast table, stretching comfortably.

"What about the tea?" Karan asked.

"Come and sit down, Karan," Nithin muttered irritably. Karan hesitated, looked at Sam and Sandy, then shrugged his shoulders.

"This is what I like about the joint family system," Sandy said. "Everybody is together and yet on their own. Each house is a miniature village, with all the support and security it provides."

"It's fast disappearing," Sam said, with a touch of regret. "In another ten years it will be an anachronism."

It wasn't long before they were in a huddle, even Nithin and Karan laughing at each other's jokes. They were just getting into their stride when the ladies walked in. "I'm out of here," Nithin grumbled, standing up.

"It's Saturday night, Nithin. Relax, we won't bite," Sally reassured him.

"Why don't you chauvinists go into Sam's study," Kathy suggested. "We girls have a lot to talk about and Hannah is going to join us in a minute. If you little boys are good, and don't make too much noise, we might even make the tea."

Pretty soon they were sprawled on the floor in Sam's den, their mood mellow, and had drifted into an easy banter, occasionally ragging each other until the jokes began to wear thin.

"I've always wondered about that business," Sam was now saying, "about reading the signs ... I mean, what signs? I'm not saying it's crap, that would be stupid. We've all been exposed to someone who apparently read the signs. And poof! He's gone. But hell ... *what signs?*"

"From what I've heard," Karan said seriously, "It's like you see this one bud, in a field of blooming flowers, and it's a sign, or one of them anyway. When you see it ..."

"But Karan," Nithin waved his hand vaguely, "everyone sees it and ..."

"No! That's the point. No one else sees it. Only the one person whose time is up."

"That's a bit fanciful," Sam scoffed. "How does he *know* that he's the only one that can see it?"

"I don't know, Sam. It's what I heard ..."

"I think I know what you mean." Sandy came to Karan's rescue. "Like the perfect stranger who passes you in the street and stares so hard, without saying a word, that you wonder if you forgot to zip your fly or something."

"So maybe that's what you should do," Nithin chuckled. "Zip up your fly instead of preparing your will."

"I guess the next chick that gives me the eye ..." Sam began.

"Can't you guys be serious," Karan complained.

"I was going to add that she could be the Grim Reaper," Sam smiled, "Good old '*Malekul Mort*' herself."

"Joke about it if you like," Karan sniffed. "But what about the knock on the door, at midnight? And nobody's there when you open it?"

"But anybody can open the door," Nithin said. "There's no guarantee that ..."

"You okes are not listening to me," Karan was truly cross now. "Nobody else *hears* the knock. That's the point. Are you telling me that none of you, in all your lives, have seen someone open a door when you heard nothing yourself?"

"I think I have," Sandy said. "But I can't remember if the guy kicked the bucket afterwards."

"Okay, fine!" Karan conceded. "But how about when, on a perfectly hot day someone, and it's only just the one person, suddenly feels cold and begins to shiver? A minute later he's okay. You've never come across that?"

"Are we speculating here?" Sam asked. "Are all these actual ... what? guidelines?"

"I'm only telling you what I've heard," Karan replied. "And what Sandy said about the perfect stranger ... well, I've heard of that too ..."

"What I'd like to know," Sandy asked, "is do all these things have to happen ... you know ... sort of immediately one after the other, over a short period of time?"

"These aren't the only signs," Karan explained. "But a combination of them, or a certain number, are sufficient to get the message across ... you know ... sort of prepare you ..."

"I'm beginning to get the drift here," Sam said, "The day before my old man died? My mother told me afterwards that just after lunch, as he sat back, he suddenly went white as a sheet and said something like 'I've been stupid. Careless. Now it's too late!' Then he hurried to his room and was busy doing things he never did before at that time in the afternoon, like shaving and spending a long time in the bath, that sort of thing. And that evening, he was on the phone for hours, talking to people he cared for. Not saying anything important, just making small conversation. It was also the night he called me into his room and told me about the family treasure — I told you okes about the dagger. The next morning he was gone. My mother only thought about these things days later, when the grief had subsided."

"The signs were there," Karan said smugly. "What he was saying to your mother, when he told her he was careless, was that he hadn't paid attention to them."

"How come they don't talk about it, then?" Sam asked. "Tell their loved ones and whoever else. I mean, why the big secret?"

"Your grandfather told mine," Karan replied. "And my grandfather told your dad. We both know that."

"Yes, sure," Sam agreed. "But that was like ... well, he said it in confidence. We only heard about it in passing, much later, when my old man was reminiscing with someone."

"Hey, Sam," Nithin laughed, "What do you expect? You want them to run around town telling everyone 'I saw this bird, it came to my window, my time's up, goodbye, goodbye.'"

Everybody, even Karan, couldn't help laughing loudly. They were still chortling when Devi walked in with the tray and smiled at them. As soon as she was gone they dug into the *bhajia* and samoosas, smacking their lips with pleasure.

"This is another of life's mysteries," Sam said. "How the hell do our women prepare these things so fast, almost without effort?"

"No mystery there," Nithin smiled mischievously, "My grandmother told me all about it. It's like that story about the shoemaker's shop, you know, when in the middle of the night the goblins come over and help him with his ..."

"You never had a grandmother that you knew," Karan chirped. "In fact, I sometimes think you weren't even born. When I look at you I'm convinced there's a stork somewhere in your ancestry."

"Well, maybe the stork told me then," Nithin said cheerfully. "The same stork that told you all those fairytales about buds and strange knocks at midnight and ..."

"So you don't believe that the old guys had advance warning?"

"I'm not saying that. And you still haven't answered Sam's question. What's the big secret? How come they don't spell it out to us?"

"That's because we don't listen to them anymore. When they talk we think it's all fairytales. In any case, when you know your days are numbered you have other things on your mind. You have to see to unfinished business. Like they say — 'start preparing'."

"You're right," Nithin was suddenly very serious, his face grim. "It was that way with my old man. He stopped drinking just like that, cold turkey. For a man who guzzled a bottle a day, maybe more, it was like a miracle. And the booze was there, right next to him all the time. I know, I threw it in the bin after he died."

"Maybe he just got sick," Sam offered.

"There's more to it, Sam. On the day after he went on the wagon, he asked my mother to call me. I refused to go to him. I thought: shit! He stops drinking for a few hours and he expects me to congratulate him? To hell with that jive. You okes must remember something — I hadn't spoken to him in what? Thirty years? Longer?"

"You should have gone to him," Karan looked at Nithin accusingly.

"In any case, my mother spent that night in his room — they had slept in separate rooms for as long as I can recall — and he was talking all the time, sounding kind of tender. I could hear the soft murmurs, it was like they were lovers whispering undying love to each other. I remember that night as clearly as I'm sitting here now. And I was mad as hell, with my mother mostly. I sat up most of that night, in the adjoining room, which was my mother's room, and fumed, like a jealous — anyway, I guess I was sad too, sort of angry-sad, you have to experience it to understand the feeling."

They were silent now, not wanting to interrupt Nithin. He wasn't with them anymore, his eyes were far away, glazed over. They had never seen him in that mood before. He seemed to be talking to himself.

"There were times when I wanted to barge in there, to grab hold of her and shake her, to break the spell I was sure he was weaving, to remind her what a bastard he had been to us. Once, when there was a lull in their conversation, I swear I thought they were making love. I was so beside myself I peeked through the crack in the door. They were just lying there, next to each other, a little apart.

"I felt a little guilty then. I kept repeating to myself that they were married, that if they wanted to make love it was their right to do so. The guilt didn't last. Back in the other room, I could hear their voices again. Then she gave a soft laugh. That was it for me. I felt an immense sense of betrayal, as if she had been deceiving me all through the years. I decided then and there that if I didn't get out of the house I'd end up killing him, maybe both of them.

"I got the hell out of there. He may have stopped drinking, but I made sure I got drunk that night — or tried to. When that didn't work I looked for the biggest, meanest looking oke in the pub, and picked a fight with him. The poor guy didn't stand a chance. I beat the hell out of him. But the hell in me was still there. I guess I went on some kind of rampage. I woke up hours later in some strange room in a backyard in Fountain Lane, in some prossie's bed."

All at once, Nithin shivered, violently. When he spoke again his voice was normal.

"I guess that prossie saved my life. I was still on the warpath when she sent for Sandy and Jake."

Nithin was smiling now as he looked at Sandy. "You remember? I waded into Jake. He took all I threw at him and then hucked me over his shoulder and you okes took me home.

"Anyway, the old man died two days later, in his sleep. I guess he must have read the signs."

None of them had seen Kathy standing at the door. Her stance gave the impression that she had been there a long time. Her eyes were misty.

"You okay, Nits? Want to go home now?" There was a slight break in her voice.

"I'm okay, babe," Nithin said.

Kathy nodded, leaving them alone again.

"I'm surprised," Sandy said, trying to sound frivolous, attempting to relieve the emotional tension, "that he was ever sober enough to read the signs."

"And that's no lie," Nithin chuckled. "But I guess they're there all right. If the message is meant for you, you can't avoid it."

"I reckon we've lost the knack of it now, become too Westernised." Karan's voice had a note of regret in it.

"What about the West?" Sam asked. "Do the *wit ous* ever experience this sort of thing?"

"If any of them are prone to it," Karan said, "it's probably the Irish. The Emerald Isle is steeped in mysterious folklore."

"There must be others. I mean, look at their poetry. You chaps remember Abu Ben Adam? That was clearly ..."

"I would hardly call that Western, Sam," Nithin corrected him.

"But it's a poem written in English, Nits."

"Probably a translation. In any case it's not quite relevant to our discussion."

"Well, it's full of angels going back and forth ... okay, how about the Ancient Mariner? Wouldn't the albatross qualify as a sign?"

"What the hell do we know about the *wit ous* anyway? They're all in their ivory towers, so far removed from us that I don't even know if they catch a crap."

"If they do," Sandy laughed, "they probably think it flows straight to the perfume factory."

"Hey," Karan asked, "anybody remember old man Sanjee?"

"Old 'attar of roses' himself," Sam grinned.

Nithin gave an involuntary shiver. "Remember him? Hell, there were days when, after listening to his stories, I didn't sleep all night. Every shadow in my room was a ghost, every time the wind moved the curtain I was ready to yell."

"Old Sanjee was really something," Sandy nodded. "Remember that story about the devil and his disciples?"

"The - day - will - come," Karan began, in imitation of Sanjee's voice, whispering each word as he drew it out from deep inside him and pausing pregnantly at the end. "When *khyamat* will be upon us — the day the world will come to an end. The devil and his hordes are behind the Great Wall that keeps them out of our world ..."

The room had grown silent. Karan's rendition of the old man's story had them transfixed, taking them back to their childhood. Karan took a deep breath, then continued in the same deep bass voice:

"They have no tools with which to break the wall down, not even a simple nail with which to pick at it. But they have their tongues. And there are millions of them, and they take turns licking that wall, over and over and over again. They go on all night. But that wall is thick and their mouths are dry. Just before dawn, just before the sun comes over the mountain, when the wall is almost as thin as a wafer, they can lick no more. They are also creatures of darkness, daylight is not their friend, the sun blinds them.

"They take a break, go back under the ground, into their holes, and hide. They are excited too, now. They know that when darkness comes again, a few good licks and the wall will crumble.

"The next night, when the shadows are around them, they leave their holes and approach the wall, ready to crash through it. But they bounce off it, they can't go through. Like a miracle, the wall is thick again — like it was the night before. They scream with anger, they wave their fists at the sky, they curse God. But they don't give up! They start licking again. Just before daybreak, they lick that wall till it's thin as paper, then they jump back into their holes. They are sure now that when night comes they can break through and destroy the world.

"Again there is a miracle, again the wall is thick. They swear, they shout, and then start once more. And so it has been going on, right up to now, night after night, since God put Lucifer and his followers behind that wall, away from us.

"And do you know why that wall always grows back each night? Because the *shaitaan* does not have faith in God, when he says 'tomorrow night we will break through' he does not say 'God willing'. But one night, on the night he remembers to say 'God willing', then they'll break through and they will attack all of us.

"That will be the night of *Khyamat* — the end of the world!"

Karan paused, then continued in his normal voice, "Damn, Sam, I wish Sally would break her rule about no liquor in her house. I could use a drink now."

Sandy clapped softly. "Bravo! You did that beautifully. Not quite the language Sanjee used to say it in, but I can't fault the content."

"When I closed my eyes," Sam added, "I could actually see and hear old Sanjee, just like when we were *lighties*."

"For years after that," Nithin said, "I stayed awake most nights shivering in bed and praying like mad that the devil would not remember those two words — 'God willing' — and when I saw the sun rise, and all was well, I finally went off to sleep with a sigh of relief."

"Ya, I guess I had nights like that too," Sam said. "I used to keep repeating, 'God willing they won't break through' as if I was trying to beat the devil to it, sort of beat him to the draw."

"That guy Sanjee," Karan chuckled, "put the fear of God in more people than a drunken bus driver ever did."

"Thugs and tycoons," Maliga said from the doorway, "Talking about God and fear. Now I've heard everything."

"That's it!" Nithin jumped up. "Nothing to drink, eavesdroppers at the door and now I'm being insulted too. I'm on my way."

"Me too," Sam said, getting to his feet.

"Not you," Sandy laughed. "You stay here. I reckon you're stuck for life."

"I'll teach you all about 'stuck' when we get home, my boy," Maliga winked.

❦

Later that night Sam lay in bed, unable to sleep. Vivid images of his childhood were flashing through his mind like disjointed stills from a badly constructed motion picture. The harder he tried to fix a particular scene the faster the pictures seemed to roll. When, at last and in sheer frustration, he gave up the ghost and allowed his thoughts free rein, suddenly the focus took hold and he was back in Verbena Road. He could see himself clearly, playing a game of marbles with his pals in somebody's back yard. The next moment they were playing soccer in the street, followed by "policemen and robbers". Then it was evening, the sun had gone down and he was participating in the sport of "stingers", deftly avoiding the tennis ball as it sped towards him.

In another minute the flashbacks began to slow down and Sam succumbed completely to their lure. Now he was into a particular Sunday evening, a sultry, lazy evening with all the kids in the neighbourhood gathered on the Solomon's front verandah. The Reid boys from next door were there, as were two of the Sallies — Talip and Braim from Verbena Court — together with Lionel and Douggy Sebastian. Eric and Alan Spies were seated next to Isaac and Billy from the John family who lived across the road. Solly Martin was there too, huddled between Yacoob and Ebrahim — the "Cowboy" brothers from the corner house. Even "Pie" Lawton, from way down in Milton Road had joined them, together with the daring Ali Bey who was forever getting into trouble and equally as often punished by his parents for being involved in some scrape or another. Baboo Kajee and Mohan Govender, with Bala Pillay, were sprawled on the stairs nearby.

The verandah of No. 15 was packed solid; Nithin, Karan and Sandy were in the far corner, somewhat aloof from the others with their usual mocking grins. And, of course, old Sanjee was there — his face typically mournful. According to Sam's mother Sanjee was at least eighty although no one, least of all Mr Sanjee himself, knew for sure when he was born. All he could remember was that he had come into the world on the same day that the steamship Vijli sank in the Indian Ocean.

"My father," he would always say sadly, "was passenger on that ship. That name, Vijli, it mean lightening, like storm in sky. Maybe it unlucky name, see? Mr Hajee Cassim give my father free passage from India. They good friends, you know. Great friends! They from same village in India. Porbandar. You hear of that place? Everybody know Mr Hajee Cassim he own that ship and very wealthy man. He even come to forty-day *khatam* for my father and stay till all prayers over. Great man, him. Yes, great man!"

Sam could see Sanjee clearly now, on the verandah, his straggly beard tinted red from the henna leaves. "Sanjee *Bapu*", as he was called by all and sundry, never ventured beyond that front verandah. "Not right, you know," he always repeated mournfully from the low wicker chair that was his favourite resting place, his bony knees sticking up in the air like stilts. "No, not right, you father not yet home and all! People talk." He quite forgot that he was a geriatric and beyond the age where anyone cared to speculate about his intentions.

The flashback was so vivid that Sam could clearly see old Sanjee constantly glancing at his wrist and muttering through his beard. "Must go. Can't waste time. Life short." The fact that the watch had stopped ticking years ago and that everyone was aware of that fact didn't seem to bother him. And he didn't move either. If anything, he settled more comfortably in his chair. The words were no more than fillers, as if the silence embarrassed him. And when Solly Martin asked for a story it didn't take much persuasion from the others to get him talking.

"Tell us about the old days," Nithin urged, keeping his voice respectfully low. "Tell us about Durban when you first came here, *Bapu*." Nithin knew the old man liked being called *Bapu*. It would put him in the right frame of mind to reminisce and, when in full stride, his stories were highly entertaining.

"What there to tell," Sanjee said, spreading his hands deprecatingly. The boys' faces immediately lit up. It was a standard response, a prelude to a few spellbinding anecdotes from the dim past, some of which were really amusing though, more often, deliciously frightening and sending a shiver up their spines. When he saw the young faces staring at him expectantly, Sanjee grunted with satisfaction.

"What there to tell," he repeated. "This place all bush. People stay in town. Young one like you work hard, make money, look after mother and father. Now ..." he sighed, shook his head, then continued, "Well, children still good, only I grow old. Sit in sun and dream. Don't understand many thing now happening.

"Look you now. Those days, Badsha Peer, you hear 'bout him? Yes? Those days, maybe 1890, he ordinary man, walk 'roun' town like beggar. But take money from no one and mind own business, not talk much. He know many thing, some not yet happen. You think that can't be? Listen nice now, you learn something.

"Everybody know 'bout time when rich shopkeeper in Grey Street say something nasty to him. You know, tease him. That happen one 'clock in afternoon. Badsha Peer, he say 'you got time make joke? When you brother in village in India dead? Better you go mosque now and pray for him soul?' See now, no phone that time. Shopkeeper get telegram nex' day. It say brother dead, yesterday, twelve 'clock. That when town find out that man, Badsha Peer, he not ordinary man.

"But that nothing to 'nother time what happen. See you now, old lady ask rich man for help, ask money to pay rent. What he do? He say 'Go 'way, old woman, money not grow on tree!' Badsha Peer, he very far away but everybody hear him shout 'Look in you bag, ma!' When old woman look in bag she find gold coin. It not there before. Look you now, how he hear old woman when he other side street? How gold coin get in bag? Not stories, boys. All true. Ask you father. Whole town talk 'bout that for long time.

"Many time it happen people see Badsha Peer in Durban. Same time he in Newcastle, Ladysmith, somewhere far. But same time he in Durban too. How that can be? And look you, lot time he cook in small pot, everybody come eat, food never finish. Never! Okay. Now he saint. You go him shrine in Brook Street, ask help, everything come right. If sick, you better. If no money, it come. If you ..."

Suddenly, from a window on the second floor of Verbena Court, a piercing whistle cut through the air. It was the summons from Uncle Tainy and had to be instantly obeyed. The Spies boys, Alan and Eric, jumped up as if prodded by an electric rod and ran towards home. With the spell broken, the boys all stood up at once.

The picture faded, as if the reel had come to an end, and Sam was back in the present. He lay immobile, desperately trying to hang on to the scene from the past, attempting with all his will to go back. It was useless. He couldn't recapture a brief second. Finally, he sighed with regret. The magic of that day was gone forever.

Sam sat up, propping a pillow in the small of his back and resting his shoulders against the wall behind him. An immense sadness coursed through him as the years sloughed off and long-forgotten memories invaded his mind and ran rampantly through his emotions. With an effort he pulled himself together. We would still have been living there, he mused, a community of good solid citizens with strong family and neighbourhood ties, if they hadn't thrown us out of our homes and forced us into ghettoes, to live with strangers. Where are they all today? The Reids, he seemed to recall, were somewhere in Woodford Grove. Sheila, their only daughter had married and settled in Germany. The Spies family was scattered all over — Alan, the eldest, was in Wentworth, the coloured ghetto. He remembered hearing that the Sebastians had emigrated to either Canada or England, he couldn't be sure where. And Solly Martin? The Lawtons? All the others? Only God knew where they were.

What sin were we guilty of, Sam asked himself. Was the colour of our skins, even when we were amongst our own kind and out of sight, really so obnoxious? Who were we a threat to, whose lifestyle were we tainting with our existence? Would not all of us, white and black and every colour in between, have been perfectly happy today if everything had simply been left alone and undisturbed?

Sam was alternating between anger and futility and knew that sleep was now impossible. He left the bed and walked through the french doors and out into the garden. For the first time in years the urge for a cigarette almost overpowered him. He fought the craving by channelling his thoughts into formulating a plan to do something positive. I must talk to Karan, he promised himself. Sandy and Nithin too. If we put our heads together, we could trace at least some of the old families. Maybe arrange some kind of a get-together.

He was standing in his bare feet, oblivious of the moist grass, staring into the distance, when he was suddenly overcome by an irresistible impulse, an urge to be somewhere else. He rushed into the house, changed into street clothes, grabbed a bunch of keys and hurried towards his car.

He was driving fast, almost in a stupor, as he left Reservoir Hills and headed towards the city centre. A powerful magnet seemed to be drawing him, pulling him against his will and relentlessly hurtling him towards the old neighbourhood. The force was so strong it had frozen his mind and overpowered his will to resist it.

Twenty minutes later he parked at the furthest end of Wills Road, near the Old Dutch Road intersection, and stepped out of the car. The street was gloomy, the lampposts dark sentinels pointing at the sky, the bulbs either shattered or burnt out. It was an alien landscape, resembling a ruined civilisation whose former glory had been destroyed by some catastrophic event. Nature had reclaimed the land, the grass knee high and littered with the concrete debris of what had once been human habitation.

As Sam looked around he could see the remains of a few of the stately residences that he had so vividly visualised earlier that night in bed: a crumbling boundary wall; a sagging roof canted dangerously towards the ground and resting on nothing but a few wooden posts in an advanced stage of erosion and deteriorated to the point where they were on the verge of giving up the losing battle and crashing to earth.

As he peered into the gloaming Sam had the eerie sensation that he was the sole survivor of some monumental upheaval that had wiped out every other living being. Nothing moved. Not a stray dog or cat was in sight. No sign of human existence was in evidence, not even a crumpled sheet of an old newspaper or magazine. And the silence was almost audible, disturbing in its absence.

He took a few hesitant steps back in the direction he had driven up from, and was attracted towards what seemed to be a black spot considerably darker than its surroundings. As he drew closer a vague shape rose before him and he suddenly stopped, rooted to the spot. He couldn't believe his eyes. There, before him, looking incongruous in the dark, was the Pather home, intact, solid and well-maintained in spite of its age. Sam was certain he was hallucinating, looking at a mirage from the past, created entirely by his imagination and his disorientated brain. He approached the structure with trepidation, expecting that at any moment his eyes would clear and all that would remain would be an empty hole before him.

He stepped a little closer, noted the well tended garden, flowers blooming in profusion, and realised that what he was looking at was no figment of his imagination. It occurred to him that people must still be living there, possibly the Pathers themselves. Even as the thoughts raced through him he had the eerie sensation that at the next moment Dicky Pather would come bouncing through the door, sail effortlessly over the hedge and land lightly on his feet, ready to take a bow.

Only the fact that the home was in absolute darkness and the unholy hour stopped Sam from knocking on the front door. He walked alongside the hedge and, at the corner, stared down the length of Lutman Avenue. He could dimly see the double storied building at the edge of the cul-de-sac. In spite of the bad light he could see that it was sadly neglected and in an advanced stage of deterioration. It was difficult to tell if people lived in it, there was a haunted aura around it and he quickly moved on.

Sam crossed the road and headed towards Hampson Grove, walked alongside bare land where homes had once stood, stepped across Douglas Lane and, when he reached Milton Road he crossed over again. All around him the destruction was complete, with not a soul in sight.

Syringa Avenue seemed to have survived the passage of time, the double storied buildings on either side still intact, some with a light glowing dimly through the windows. Sam smiled grimly as he recalled that it was a street that had been occupied by whites and had not been subject to the mass removal of its inhabitants.

A short distance to his left the grand old Wills Court still looked as it had over thirty years ago. He remembered with a deep pang of sadness that its coloured and Indian tenants, who had lived there for over half a century, had been forcibly evicted by the police to make way for white municipal workers and Italian immigrants.

Sam quickly looked away, dispelling the anger welling up in him, and found himself looking at a narrow lane just off Syringa Avenue. "My God!" he almost said aloud. "Alfred Avenue! And the small block of flats is still there!" He searched his memory; he used to know all the tenants of years gone by, remembered the Haupts and suddenly, in his mind's eye he could see Desmond grinning that confident grin of his and daring anyone to take him on. And, without fail, Desmond took on the best in the district and always walked away unmarked and smiling in the mocking way that was almost his exclusive trademark. Sam thought of Maryna Haupt who, together with June Lawton, was probably the loveliest of all the girls in the neighbourhood. He sighed with deep bitterness when it struck him that he couldn't even be sure whether he had got their names right. "Damn," he said, loudly this time, "they used to be my friends!"

He felt a faint thrill of regret as he walked back towards Verbena Road. Then he saw another house that had miraculously survived the destroyers — the old Coovadia residence. Next to it was an empty lot, the only sign that a home had once stood on it was a lopsided section of a wooden fence holding up a rusty, low steel gate almost torn from its hinges.

Sam passed his car, walked up to the very end of Wills Road, and was suddenly disorientated — there was no sign of Verbena Road, not even a solitary landmark. It had simply disappeared, as surely as death obliterates life, leaving only the memories that live on in the minds of those that still remember. He cast his eyes around him, pinpointed the spot where Goodwill Court used to be, traced an imaginary line across the road towards where the Seedat house should have been, and gave up in despair. There was nothing there except concrete bollards cutting off access to the freeway that used to be Old Dutch Road. All he was left with was the memory of a haunted era, gone forever.

With a start Sam realised that the sky was lightening. He looked at the pavement below him, read the names that had been etched deeply into the concrete by children who had, in another age, inhabited the area. He saw the faint outline of squares, circles and oblongs created by some sharp instrument. Somehow it had survived the passage of time.

He went down on his haunches and inspected the scratches, ran a finger over them, the rough concrete gritty to his touch. His memories went into free-fall. In vivid detail he could see the girls in knee length blue poplin dresses and white bobby sox, doing the hop, skip and jump as they played hopscotch. His ears acquired a new dimension, echoing the laughter of the schoolgirls as their dresses billowed in the air. His body responded to the thrill of recollection, involuntarily trembling as long forgotten images surged through him. Sam would swear later that he had distinctly heard the happy voices of Lorraine Sebastian and her older sister Joan as they flew gracefully over the forbidden lines and landed in the centre of the squares. This was not his memory reliving the past, he was physically there with them, in form and substance.

The image faded and he stood up reluctantly, his eyes misty. His fingers touched a steel lamppost and he leaned into it, closing his eyes and savouring the moment even as it faded. He stayed that way for a full minute, anger and sadness mingling within him, then opened his eyes and raised them to the sky accusingly, seeking an answer to how such atrocities had been allowed to pass with impunity. His gaze latched on to something that was stuck at the very top of the lamppost, in the bend that formed the elbow that jutted into the street. It resembled a mass of rusted wire rings and looked out of place.

For a little longer he stared at the concentric circles of metal with no more than mild interest. Then, overcome by curiosity, he stepped into the street to get a better look. It was quite high and he had to crane his neck and angle his head way back to focus on it. Suddenly, as if nature or some higher power had decided to lend a hand, the clouds shifted and the object was bathed in light and began to glow with a luminescence that was out of harmony with the dimness of its surroundings. Slowly, as his gaze adjusted to the change, he became aware that he was looking at the circular inner steel radials of a bicycle tyre, the rubber long worn away until only a few threads of hemp remained, blowing in the light breeze.

Sam's body began to shake uncontrollably and he had difficulty maintaining his balance. Recollection of a dim incident from his past swept over him and he shivered spasmodically, like a man overcome by some strange spell. With a supreme effort of will he forced his feet to move, stepped back onto the pavement and braced himself against the lamppost, taking in huge gulps of air and tensing his muscles to suppress the fit of shakes.

"Ivan!" Sam croaked, his voice trembling. "Ivan Reid! Can you hear me, old friend? Do you remember that day, so long ago, when you were rolling that tyre down the road and I grabbed it and flung it in the air? How we marvelled when it soared over the top and landed into that bend in the lamppost! Oh my God, Ivan! It's still there, after all these years. And where are you now? Do you remember that day, old *maat?*"

Sam felt the trembling start again. From deep inside him a surge of anger began to rise and stilled his body. He stumbled towards his car, fumbled frantically at the door, then jumped into the driver's seat.

"Too many ghosts," Sam whispered hoarsely as he turned the ignition key and the engine burst to life. "Too many ghosts," he repeated several times. "They're still here, all my old friends. And I'm somewhere there too, caught in a time warp, forever a part of this environment."

As the car began to move forward Sam suddenly began to laugh. It rose from his stomach, filled his chest and burst through his lips. He threw his head back and let the sound fill the car and reverberate off the windows.

"You poor fools," he chuckled as he sped off. "It's no wonder you couldn't settle here, in homes that you so zealously looted from us. The spirits of the living, not the dead, drove you back to wherever you came from!"

chapter twelve

Sam was in the kitchen talking to Sally when the doorbell rang. "I'll get it," he said over his shoulder as he headed for the front door.

There was something vaguely familiar about the slim visitor who stood diffidently before Sam with his hands behind his back. Sam was still trying to place him when the man spoke.

"*Goeie naand, Meneer*. May I speak to you? Only for a few minutes? I would be most grateful."

As recognition penetrated Sam's mind his jaw tightened, his lips stretched thinly across his teeth and the fingers of both hands curled into fists.

"Please, Mr Solomon, I'm here in my private capacity. I promise not to be long."

"What do you want?" Sam snapped.

"I'd like to speak with you about your brother."

"We have nothing to say to each other."

"I understand. For days I have debated with myself the purpose of this visit. I expected your anger but I had to come. I wouldn't have been able to live with myself otherwise."

"Is that something that should matter to me?"

"No, sir. My personal feelings are no concern of yours."

"Then why call on me? Why revive unpleasant memories?"

"To give me an opportunity to set the record straight. I am requesting that you grant me a few minutes to explain ..."

"You have had your few minutes. Be grateful that you are still on your feet. Now go."

"Mr Solomon, I am requesting, in the name of everything that's decent in this world, please grant me an audience."

"In the name of decency? Do you even begin to understand what that means? Coming from you it sounds obscene. Leave here, now."

Sam heard footsteps behind him, then felt his mother's presence at his side. "Who is this person, Salim?"

"He is just leaving, mother. Come."

"Who is he?" Shaida repeated, not moving.

"My name is Van Heerden, *mevrou*. I had to see you, to talk to you."

"Why are you two standing here? Come in."

"Ma, this man brought Yacoob's body home. They are the people who killed him."

Shaida's body went rigid, her eyes narrowed as she raised her chin, her head tilting backwards. The Afrikaner remained silent, his eyes fixed on the ground, both hands still behind his back, looking curiously vulnerable.

"You have the arrogance to come here again?" Shaida said coldly. "To knock at my door, like we are some insignificant vermin who have no business to be here?"

"No, madam. I do not think that. It was not my wish to upset you further."

"No? You brutally murdered my son. You handed his broken body to me in a sealed casket. I wasn't even allowed the consolation of a last look at his face. Now you say you have no wish to upset me any more. How can that be possible?"

"*Ja, mevrou*, what you say is true. I understand a little the pain in you. I am a father too. Only God knows how I feel about what you went through. But it is not sympathy I have come here to offer you. Even I can see how ridiculous that would sound." There was a peculiar timbre in the Afrikaner's voice, a sincerity that could not be denied.

For what seemed an eternity the three of them stood there, not speaking, unmoving, each face reflecting a different emotion: Sam, eyes blazing, cheeks flushed; Shaida, anger dissipating into sadness, a tinge of curiosity in her face; the Afrikaner, head bowed, eyes hollow, seemingly humbled by some inner conflict. Sam was the first to react, was about to speak, when Shaida silenced him with a motion of her hand.

"Come in," she said simply as she turned and led the way to the visitors' room. Sam reluctantly stepped aside.

Van Heerden followed Shaida silently until she stopped, pointed to a chair and said, quietly, "Sit."

The government man lowered his body and sat on the edge of the chair, hands on his knees, and continued looking at the ground.

"My son sometimes forgets his manners. It is not our custom to be rude to anyone who comes to our door in peace."

"I don't blame him. In his place I would have been less restrained."

"Why are you here?"

"To apologise on behalf of my people. To let you know that I had nothing to do with his death. And to try and make you understand that this is not the way of the Afrikaner ... what was done to your son ... we are not like that."

"And that is supposed to make me feel better?"

"No, Madam. It is my conscience that I am attempting to set at rest. And to let you know that I was unaware that you had no knowledge of your son's death. I brought him here in the sincere belief that you had been prepared to take possession of his body."

"Why do you feel differently now?"

"I realised ... when I brought him here ... the shock on your family's face ... I was deeply upset to witness such a thing."

"And you feel your salvation can be obtained by saying this to me?"

"No — I bear no guilt for his death. None of that was of my doing. Nor do I ask you to forgive those who were responsible for it. But it would be unfair to blame the Afrikaner nation for such atrocities."

Sam, who had remained silent throughout the exchange, raised an eyebrow sceptically. He was standing just inside the entrance to the room, arms folded, one shoulder leaning against the wall. Shaida, who had asked her questions in a soft voice, continued to gaze at the visitor.

"We are not animals, Madam," Van Heerden continued in a low voice. "The actions of a few mavericks must not be held against the majority who do not condone such brutalities. It is on behalf of the decent white man that I am here today."

"I didn't know such a person existed."

"I assure you, *mevrou*, there are many."

"And you would have me believe that you are one of them?"

"As God's my judge."

"So you do believe in Him."

"That is unfair, madam. The Bible has always been my guide, the basis on which all my actions are judged."

"Which bible?"

"Pardon? I do not follow you ..."

"Which bible? The one the Dutch Reformed Church expounds and which I take it you belong to, or the true word of God?"

"There is only the one Bible ..."

"Never mind. Do you work for the Security Branch, Mr Van Heerden?"

"Yes."

"And you have always voted for the National Party?"

"Yes."

"And it was the majority white vote that put these people in power?"

"Yes."

"Then how do you reconcile that with what you would have me believe?"

The Afrikaner nodded, raised his hands helplessly, nodded again and lowered them to his sides.

"What you have just said, *mevrou*, I have asked myself as I lay in bed unable to sleep, night after night and into the early hours of the morning. When I do sleep for a few hours I repeat those questions in my dreams. There is an insanity loose in this country that is beyond my comprehension."

The hollow voice, the tremor as he uttered the words, his entire bearing, reflected a man defeated by inner ghosts whose power was greater than his ability to wrestle with them.

"I have tried prayer, I have walked for hours in the park, I have gazed at the steeple of my church, and now I have come to you. If coming here ... to seek I know not what ... was a mistake, then I apologise."

"This is our home, *Meneer*. We expect no apologies from anyone who comes to us in peace."

"For those words alone, I thank you."

"But I must ask you this, out of curiosity only. Tell me, at the next elections? How will you vote?"

"How do I answer you, *mevrou*? There are issues, questions of my people's security, that go beyond what we have discussed. It would be easy for me to lie to you. But in this little while I have come to know you, to understand your own feelings and to respect them. I did not come here to deceive you. My people have suffered much at the hands of the *Engelse*. We, too, have suffered from the atrocities they inflicted on us. But to say this ... it is not why I came here either. All I can say now is that if you cannot believe all I have said then at least accept that I am sincere about my feelings."

"Mr Van Heerden, as a courtesy to your sincerity, I have to say this to you: I was very close to my son. I loved him with a mother's passion. I wasn't privy to all his actions but there were times when I was aware that he was in deep pain over whatever it was that he was forced to do. I silently shared that pain with him. There may have been a rare occasion on which I may have disagreed with his methods but I can tell you that I would have defended to the death his right to do so. I believe you are sincere in your beliefs. It is necessary for you to understand mine. My consolation is that my son was fighting a just cause — in the eyes of both man and God. Can the people responsible for his murder claim the same right?"

"I don't know, madam. I truly don't know ..."

"There will be no peace amongst our people, yours and mine and all those who live in this beautiful land, until you face up to that question honestly. If you and all your people — you who voted these *dakus* into power — cannot face God with a clear conscience what salvation can insignificant people like my family offer? The power to change things is in your hands, not ours. My people do not have the vote."

"I am a simple man. I do not know how things reached this stage. All I ever wanted for my family was no more than what I believe is their God-given right — a decent home, the ability to earn an honest living and the freedom to enjoy all that He has given us. I've never asked for more than that."

"These are exclusive rights? For your people only? God allocated his generosity to you alone and to no one else?"

"No, *mevrou*. I do not believe that. Everything on earth is there for all of us. My people have always accepted that."

"But your church promotes a different dogma. Is it necessary for me to spell it out for you? Your government enacts laws that are in complete contradiction to what you've just said. How do you reconcile that with what your people believe in?"

"There are many of us, more than you believe possible, that are tormented with these questions."

"But not enough to vote these *dakus* out of power."

"Perhaps not many understand, or are aware of, what's happening."

"And whilst they plead ignorance, we are being systematically destroyed."

"These things, *mevrou* ... I do not have the capacity to understand them ... I feel things ... your grief ... what do I say? To say I'm sorry is meaningless. ..."

Shaida stood up, her hands folded low in front of her. The Afrikaner, his eyes bleak, the face deeply lined, slowly rose.

"You strike me as an honest person. I accept what you have said as an apology from the heart. If that provides you with any comfort then I am happy for you. Go with God."

"Thank you, *mevrou*. If we meet again I pray it will be in happier circumstances."

Shaida inclined her head, turned to leave the room, hesitated, then turned back again. Silently, she held out her right hand and, as Van Heerden took it in both of his, smiled sadly.

"How is it possible," she asked quietly, "that you can empathise with us as individuals and yet, collectively, hate us so much?"

Before the Afrikaner could answer Shaida nodded at Sam, then left the room.

At the door Van Heerden extended his right hand, held it out for a moment, then lowered it when Sam didn't respond to the gesture. "May God forgive us all," he said, with a hint of despair.

As the visitor walked towards his car Sam sensed a presence behind him. He turned around and almost bumped into Zain.

"That man killed my father!" Zain spat out.

"No, son. His hands are clean. Don't blame him for the actions of the Security Branch."

"Is there a difference?" the boy asked, his face grim. "Is the man who loads the gun less guilty than the man who pulls the trigger?"

"Nothing in life is that simple ..."

"It is to me, Uncle Sam. If you willingly sup with the devil you must relish his soup. Why then complain afterwards of an upset stomach?"

"Did you hear the conversation between him and granny?"

"Every word."

"I didn't see you ..."

"No. I kept out of sight."

"You don't think he's sincere?"

"Will whatever remorse he now feels bring my father back?"

"No, it won't. But that doesn't make him personally guilty."

"Then why come here? To apologise for his people? Is that what he said? Can you apologise for killing someone?"

"So many questions. Your father was like that."

"If I sound like my father then I'm flattered. I take it as a compliment."

"And you should. He did nothing for which we should be ashamed."

"Then there can be no objections if I continue where he ended. I have to see granny now, Uncle Sam. She sent for me a few minutes ago. Can I borrow your car later? There's a rally at the school this afternoon."

Sam simply nodded, expelling air slowly from between his lips. His eyes followed Zain as he walked down the passage, noted the broad shoulders, the narrow waist and Jake's cocky walk. What he was seeing was a much younger Jake, from the days when he used to badger old Madhoo dada with a million questions. The strong sense of *deja vu* was followed by a shiver that ran up Sam's spine. "Dear God," he muttered, unaware that he was saying the words aloud. "Not again. Please!"

∞

Sam, his thoughts still pre-occupied with Van Heerden's visit, was on his way to his room when he heard the voices. They were emanating from an alcove to his right, a little in front of him. It was his mother's favourite corner, to which she often retreated when she wished to be alone. Without thinking, he automatically stopped, listening.

"... but I need to know more than that," Sam heard Zain saying. "I want to know about my father's dada, and his father before him. I have to know their history and what made them into the men they were."

"You spent a lot of time with your father," Shaida said. "Did you not talk about these things?"

"No ... not about our ancestry. But I do recall that he said to me, more than once, 'If you don't know where you come from how can you know where you're going!' I've often thought of that. It's why I am asking you now, dadima."

"Yes ... I can understand that. Over the years I have told you many things, tried to inculcate our values into you. You have been a good listener, quick to understand concepts that I sometimes felt were beyond your years. In that, you resemble your father. But you now ask me about your ancestry, where do I begin? With your great grandfather Yahya? With those who came before him?"

"With all of them, dadima, and beyond that too. I have to know their beliefs, their philosophy, where they came from."

"Then listen, and listen very carefully. I only have the strength to say this once ..."

Automatically, Sam lowered himself to the floor and folded his legs under him, listening as if his mother was talking directly to him and not to Zain, in another room and out of sight.

"You, my son, are an Indian — first and foremost. In this country the other groups behave as if that is something you should be ashamed of. Don't ever allow that to affect you. It is always a loser, the envious person,

471

who resorts to such tactics. It is his own failings that he tries to justify by insulting the abilities of those who are more successful than he is.

"But you are a Pathan too — the product of a tribe whose heritage is as glorious as its history. You are the descendant of legendary warriors who bow before no man and bend their knees to God alone. Their ancestral homeland is the North West Frontier Province, on the border with Afghanistan.

"No one, not even the great Moghuls who were themselves renowned for their fighting prowess, not the British after them whose imperial ambitions knew no boundaries, nor, more recently, the Russians, ever subjugated your people.

"But do not be misled by your militant background. You are an upholder of the rights of man, not some kind of savage animal that bares its teeth at every imagined insult. Your actions must be based on the concept of *Paktünwali*, the code by which every Pathan lives.

"What is this belief — this *Paktünwali*? It is your *nang*, your honour, without which you are nothing. Without *nang* you are less than an animal — you do not deserve to live. To maintain your honour you must, if necessary, be prepared to sacrifice your life. Allow no man to belittle your *nang* and walk away. Protect it zealously. And if you have no other alternative then resort to *badal* - obtain revenge, or lose your honour.

"But *Paktünwali* is not some primitive tribal belief that advocates violence at the slightest pretext. Be very sure that you have done nothing to invite others to insult you. The way to do that is to hold your tongue, to talk only when it is absolutely necessary and then to do so sparingly.

"You asked me earlier how I could allow that man, Van Heerden, into our house. Let me explain something to you. An integral part of our code is the concept of *maelmastya*, which requires us to display the utmost hospitality to anyone who calls on us in peace, even when that visitor is a sworn enemy. And it goes further than that — he becomes our responsibility whilst he is under our roof, we are beholden to protect him with our lives if need be. Don't ever violate that rule in the years to come.

"*Paktünwali* also means that you are the equal of all men, that you are in fact the first among equals. Up to your dying breath make certain you do not concede one inch of this code.

"Now listen very closely. To be a male is an accident of birth, to be a man amongst real men goes beyond that which dangles between your legs. If you wish to be counted amongst those who hold their heads high, to look at any man no matter how powerful without blinking or taking a backward step, requires more than mouthing brave words. Leave the heroic oratory to those who are good at it. It is not what you are cut out for. A Pathan is not a man of many words.

"Pin what I am now going to tell you, fix it to your heart: you must always observe the time honoured traditions of your forefathers, amongst which the central tenet of their very existence, their foremost duty, is the protection of that which belongs to us. It is your bounden duty to allow no man to interfere with your *zan, zar* and *zamin*. It is the prime reason for your existence. These three sacred things — your women, your wealth and your land — they are your personal responsibility, to cherish and protect with all your might. Fail to do that and you cease to be a man.

"Your father chose to forfeit his life rather than compromise his honour. You, Zainul Aberdeen, can do no less ..."

Sam slowly straightened his body, a far away expression in his eyes. He could still hear his mother's voice but it was a distant drone. From somewhere deep within him an accusing voice had replaced his mother's, taunting him, the tone scornful, mocking. Like loud jungle drums the words "*zan, zar, zamin*" boomed in his head, repeated over and over. The last, *zamin*, louder than the other two. "*Zamin, nang, zamin, zamin, nang nang honour nang*" rose to a crescendo and enveloped his body. Unable to stand the throbbing beat any longer he rose to his feet and headed for his room, flung himself on his bed and covered his face with his hands. In less than a minute he was sound asleep.

"Sam! Wake up! What is it?"

Sally's voice, Sally's hands. He could sense her body, leaning over him.

"Sam! Stop it! Sit up!"

He opened his eyes, saw Sally's face — a blur that he found difficult to focus — and looked around him. He was totally disorientated, his mind numb, his body soaked with perspiration.

"You were having a bad dream," he heard Sally say, from somewhere far away.

He rolled off the bed, looked through the window, saw that it was pitch black outside, and croaked, "What time is it?"

"Almost three in the morning. You've been sleeping for hours. The nightmare started ..."

"Wait. Give me a minute."

He willed himself into full consciousness, shook his head violently a few times, then took a deep breath. Before he could expel the air from his lungs the drums started again "*zamin, nang, zamin, zamin!*"

"Sally, there's something I have to do. Somewhere I have to go."

"Now? It's three in the morning, Sam!"

He shook his head, said, "No!" Shook his head again and repeated the word several times. He looked down at himself, noticed that he was fully clothed, and headed for the door.

"Sam!"

∞

He was back in Dutchene, at the intersection of Wills and Old Dutch Roads, the wide expanse of the recently constructed freeway behind him. At that hour of the morning the roads were deserted, not a single thing moved. Even the early commuter buses would not pass by for several hours.

In the deathly silence that engulfed him he strained his eyes in the half-dark in an attempt to find a familiar landmark, failed, and began to pace the road, moving in one direction before abruptly turning back and veering off at a tangent. He seemed to be measuring distances with his eyes, his memory serving as a yardstick, directing him one way, then another. At last he stopped, took several steps backwards, then stopped again.

This has to be it, he muttered to himself. This is number 15 Verbena Road. I'm standing on the very spot where my bedroom used to be. My *zamin*, the house my father would have left to me if it hadn't been looted from him. *If I hadn't allowed it to be looted.* Even as the bitterness coursed through him, threatening to overwhelm him, he heard the voices as clear and distinct as the day on which he had first heard them. From somewhere above him old Sanjee was saying:

"Someone take you valuable thing, they pay. Maybe their chillun pay. Someone take you neighbour thing, same punishment. But first you fight, for you, for neighbour. Nev' mind you lose. That not important. What important is you fight — for you right, you HAQ!"

Sanjee's voice had barely faded when another replaced it:

"Anybody in the hands of the SB has to be a fighter for human rights. When one man, one solitary individual, whoever in the world he may be, stands up for what's right, he speaks on behalf of every decent human being throughout the universe — white, black or whatever colour in between.

He automatically enters the fraternity of the followers of truth.
And that fraternity represents a bond that is stronger than
blood ties, it is bound together by a principle far more
powerful than the unguent that blood represents."

Ramnath Seepye's dignified voice was still ringing in his ears when he heard the priest take over, speaking from the little hillock near Jake's grave:

"*The pursuit of justice is what separates us from the animal*
world, it distinguishes civilized man from the savage and
sets honest men apart from the criminal.
There is no principle on earth that supersedes justice.
Ignore it and you ignore the power of reason, of decency,
and you destroy the very foundations on which civilized
society rests. You revert to the days of darkness and savagery.
If you do not hold firm to this principle, if you make the
tiniest compromise, you take the first step towards your own
eventual destruction ..."

Sam, his head tilted to one side, listened to the priest, half his mind hearing the words, the other half lost in thought.

" *... Yacoob Suleiman gave his life in pursuit of that principle ...*"

"*Nang*, Jake!" Sam shouted to the sky, his fist in the air. "You kept your faith with honour. What was it ma said to your son? 'Your father chose to forfeit his life rather than compromise his honour. You can do no less.' Dammit, *bru*, I've been what *baji* would have called recreant — I forgot where I came from. How the hell can I know where I'm going?"

∞

"Where are you off to, Zain?" Sam asked.
"There's a rally tonight at the Orient Hall, Uncle Sam. A protest meeting. Nothing that would interest you ..."
"Well ... I don't know. Who is the key speaker?"
"Alan Boesak."
"Is he good?"
"Is he good! Uncle Sam, what kind of a question is that? When Boesak speaks the world listens. Even God holds his tongue."

"Don't blaspheme. You say he's good?"

"He's better than Dadoo, Fatima Meer, Naicker. Maybe even Dr Goonum."

"Whoa! Hold on. What do you know about those people?"

"More than most. I know every word they uttered. My da told me all about them."

"And you've heard Boesak speak before?"

"Often. And not often enough."

"That good, huh? Maybe I should hear what he has to say. How about if we go there together. Okay with you?"

Zain was delighted, the look on his face alone warmed Sam's heart. In the next second Zain began to look doubtful.

"Uh ... Uncle Sam ... you know ... it's not safe at these rallies. The SB is always there in full force, they're not particular who they use their whips and batons on."

"But you're still going?"

"Yes."

"Then I guess I'd better tag along, sort of keep an eye on you. Can't have anybody pushing my nephew around ..."

"You sound like you mean it. You really want to go there, in spite of the danger?"

"Yup."

"Way to go, Uncle Sam! Let's make tracks."

The Orient Hall was packed to capacity. Sam was forced to park at the top end of Sydenham Road, close to the Botanic Gardens, and they walked all the way down to Centenary Road. As they neared the hall Sam saw Father Gabriel emerge from St Anthony's Church, still in his cassock and his dark skin glowing radiantly. Not far behind a number of his parishioners followed, their peaceful faces suggesting that they had just completed evening mass. As the priest stepped onto the pavement he smiled at Sam and headed for the hall.

With Zain leading they pushed their way towards the front, past the huge crowds that overflowed onto the car-park and the driveway. Sam couldn't help marvelling at Zain's confidence — where others held back he forged ahead, leaving Sam to trail in his wake. Before long they had forced their way through the main doors and, ignoring the protesting mutters of those that Zain casually elbowed aside, they ended up halfway inside the hall.

Alan Boesak was at the podium, leaning slightly forward on his elbows. An elderly Indian woman in a faded sari was on her feet, her fist raised high.

"Mr Boesak," the woman shouted at the top of her voice, "you listen to me now. For too long this govinment treat us like we rubbish. You tell those blady fools to boesak! You tell them ..."

"It's not 'boesak', you silly woman," someone nearby shouted. "It's '*voetsak*'. You're confused ..."

"Boesak, *voetsak*, same thing," the woman yelled back as the friendly guffawing arose around her. "This blady govinment is full of sheet. Me? I say boesak to all of them!"

The applause started from the back, filled the hall and rolled over the audience.

"You tell them, Umma," someone screamed mockingly.

"You take me there, bubba, I tell them. Mebbe I old, but I not cold like someone I hear shouting."

"Way to go, ma," Sam heard Zain yell. "Give him hell!"

The laughter rose again and Alan Boesak raised his hands for silence. Abruptly, even before his arms had fully extended, the noise subsided.

"Okay," he said, lowering his hands. "Now you all know how we feel. But we don't talk to this government anymore. We stopped doing that a long time ago. We don't waste our breath on people who are too stupid to listen. And even if they did listen to us why should we talk to them in the first place? Who are they? Who put them in power? You? Me? The large majority of the people of this land, the voteless millions?

"In the eyes of every democracy in the world they are an illegitimate government. They are a bunch of criminals whose only hold on power is the gun they point at our heads. And they know this. They know it better than you and I do. What they don't know is that that gun also represents their greatest weakness. And the moment we tell them 'Go ahead, shoot!' at that moment their power over us is blown away, like the flame of a matchstick in a gale.

"They have corrupted every value on earth, including their religion, to maintain their hold over us. They make a mockery of God's word, they distort the Bible in an attempt to justify their criminal behaviour and smugly sit back as their confused followers applaud them and grab with both hands the booty thrown in their laps. When they do these things do they realise that is it not only us that they are insulting, that it is God whom they are reviling?

"Are they aware that they are DECLARING WAR ON GOD!

"And these are people we should be speaking to? Do we enter into debate with the devil? No! We do what that lady there said. We tell them to *voetsek*, to crawl back in their hole and then we cover it with a huge block of concrete and keep them down there until the Day of Judgement.

"But we can't do this by acting as individuals. We have to unite, to move forward in a solid phalanx. We have to be God's Soldiers! How can we fail? HE is on our side. HE is our leader! The Mass Democratic Movement is HIS army.

"We are going to wage a war, my friends. For God and all that is beautiful, against the devil and all that is evil. We must extinguish the flame of their flimsy matchsticks ..."

Sam heard a "pop" somewhere behind him, then saw what looked like a large soft drink can float above his head and fall on the crowd ahead of him. Before he could fully register what was happening several more cans flew overhead and landed in the aisles, on the massed body of humanity that occupied every inch of space.

"TEAR GAS!" someone screamed from the front. "They're firing tear gas!"

What followed was sheer pandemonium, a wild surge towards the entrance, a mindless lunge for safety. A number of the more agile men were climbing onto the seatbacks and recklessly hopping from one backrest to another. A number lost their footing and fell flat on their faces, landing on the shoulders of others who were hemmed in and unable to move.

Sam, on his feet in the aisle, moved against the crush of bodies, craning his neck for a glimpse of Zain. Against his will he was being pushed back, his toes barely touching the ground, desperately trying to retain his balance.

"Not that way, Uncle Sam. Turn around. Use your elbows!"

"Take care of yourself!" Sam shouted back, then realised he couldn't be heard over the noise of someone screaming from the floor. He turned around, caught Zain's eye, made a sweeping gesture with his right hand and mouthed, "Go! I'm okay!" To his horror Zain began to push forward, swinging his wide shoulders from side to side and coming closer with each movement. A shift in direction, a lateral surge towards a side door, cleared a space on his left and Zain was there, miraculously still on his feet. Fingers of steel locked onto Sam's wrist and steadied him.

"Don't fight it, Uncle Sam," Zain shouted into his ear. "Let the crowd push you forward, use their momentum. Go with the flow. Concentrate on keeping your feet on the ground."

It was sound advice. Within a minute they were at the entrance and spilling into the foyer. Sam was still wondering where Zain had learnt how to react in such a situation when he heard the first explosion, followed by several more. The staccato sound of gunfire reached his ears, a man next to him clutched his chest, muttered something, then sank to the floor.

"What the hell ..." Sam started to say and cut himself off as a searing pain lanced through his left shoulder. Stunned, he looked down, saw the blood beginning to soak through his chest and realised that he had been shot. Before he could fully grasp what was going on he saw Alan Boesak move in front of him, his arms spread wide, his voice grim.

"What do you think you're doing! These people are defenceless ..."

"Fuck you, hotnot!" a grinning riot cop spat back. "You okes asked for it. Didn't you say 'Go ahead, shoot!' We're matchsticks, ya?"

The cop, a youngster, no more than twenty, his hair cropped short and his skull glistening, raised his rifle and pointed it at Boesak's chest. "Time to die, you *focken kleurling*."

In the deafening silence that followed, all movement stopped, not a soul stirred. A line of policemen flanked the youngster, looking uncertain and a little shaken.

"Well?" Boesak asked calmly. "What are you waiting for? Go ahead, big guy, finish it. Pull the trigger."

Suddenly a burly individual, wearing the stripes of a senior official, leapt forward and slapped the rifle out of the youngster's hand. A collective sigh went up.

"*Gott, yong!*" The official bellowed. "Can't you see this is what they want? You *domkop!*"

Alan Boesak took a step forward, leaned into the senior official's face and, in a clear voice that could be heard across the courtyard, said, "You have lost control of your wild dogs. How much longer before they take to the streets and ..."

The backhanded slap caught Boesak high on the side of the face, the military academy ring splitting the skin open. A thin trickle of blood began to run down his cheek.

"Bravo!" Boesak said, a mocking smile on his lips. "Not long now, my friend. I'll return the compliment, soon. Your days are all but numbered."

The official, his face suffused with anger, moved closer to Boesak. Sam was beginning to feel lightheaded from loss of blood. He sensed the crowd in front of him preparing to surge forward, to support Boesak. As the confrontation came to a head he felt his legs begin to give way.

"I've got you. Take it easy. I've got you." He thought it was Zain's voice, couldn't be sure, then felt his body being lifted and carried forward. A wisp of fresh air passed over his face, he saw the grim faces around him, looked up and gazed at the stars. Then he felt his eyes grow heavy, the pain beginning to subside and a curious vacuum replace it. He wanted to say something to Zain, parted his lips and, with the breath leaving him, his chin slumped onto his chest.

"You're going to be okay, Uncle Sam. *You're going to be fucken okay!*"

∞

When Zain walked through the door Hannah took one look at his face, saw the blood on his shirt and struggled to stifle the scream that rose in her throat.

"I'm fine, ma. It's not my blood."

Hannah was looking at him doubtfully, one hand on her lips, when Shaida asked quietly, "Zainul Aberdeen, are you sure you're not hurt?"

"Yes, dadima."

"What happened?"

"There was an incident at the rally. Shots were fired ..."

Shaida walked over to Zain, pulled his shirt over his shoulders and examined his chest. Satisfied, she asked, "Whose blood is that?"

"It's ... what happened ..."

"Zain! Where's Uncle Sam?" Sally asked, her voice almost cracking up.

Zain looked at Sally, then at his mother, before finally turning towards his grandmother. "Dadi, Uncle Sam is at the hospital."

Sally gasped, Hannah took a step forward, Shaida raised a hand and stopped all movement. "How badly hurt is he?"

"Pretty bad," Zain replied in a low voice. "He's still in the theatre, has been for the past two hours. I'm going back now."

Shaida nodded, taking control firmly. "Go and wake Uncle Rashid. The two of you go back together. Which hospital is he in?"

"In Centenary Road — at Saint Aidans."

"Fine. Go now. Sally, ring Karan. Ask him to meet us at the hospital. Hannah, get the car out of the garage." She swept past them without another word, head high, eyes straight ahead.

Karan met Shaida in the waiting room, his face grave. He took both her hands in his and led her to a chair. "I've just spoken to one of the doctors. I'm sorry, but it sounds very bad. They're still operating on him. Sally, we must be prepared for the worst."

"Do they say what his chances are?"

Karan was about to look away when Sally said, "Karan bhai, tell me the truth. Will he pull through?"

"The doctors are not optimistic, Sally. They're doing their best."

"Where is Zainul Aberdeen?" Shaida asked Karan.

"Outside the theatre. He won't budge from there."

"Leave him there. Time enough to find out what happened. We'll wait here."

"It'll be several hours before ..."

"We'll wait here," Shaida repeated, firmly.

Three hours later Karan came back and reported, "The doctors have done all they can. It's out of their hands now. All they could tell me is that he is still breathing."

"Do we know any of the surgeons?"

"Yes. You've often met Manna Pillay at my house. He's the head of the surgical team that worked on Sam."

"I'd like to speak to him."

"I've already asked him to come over. There he is now."

An extremely tall, gaunt looking man in a white coat came up to them and walked straight over to Shaida, pulled up a chair and sat down, facing her.

"Are you all right, ma?" he asked as he placed a hand over hers.

"Yes. Thank you. And thank you for attending to my son."

"I'm just glad that I was here when they brought him in. Not they, really. Just your grandson. He carried Sam in his arms, all the way from Orient Hall. That's quite a walk, several hundred yards, and Sam's no lightweight. When Zain walked through that door the tears were pouring down his cheeks but his face was a set mask, emotionless. All he said to a passing doctor was: 'This is my Uncle Sam. Fix him up.'

"When the doctor pulled up a trolley, Zain refused to lower Sam onto it. He carried him all the way to the theatre. Those who witnessed it say they've seen nothing like it in their lives."

"And my son? He will live?"

"All we can do is pray, ma. He's beyond human help."

"Where is he now?"

"In the intensive care section. He ..."

"I have to see him."

"You can't do that just yet, ma. You see, he's ..."

"You listen to me, young man. We collected his grandfather's body from the mortuary. His brother was brought home to me in a casket. Now they may have killed my son, but right now he is still alive. I have to see him while he is still breathing. Can you understand why?"

"Yes. Yes, I understand. Come with me."

∞

"Sam's barely hanging in there, Sandy," Karan said. "Seventy two hours have passed since he stopped that bullet. The doctors don't know what to make of it. They gave up hope long ago."

"What the hell was he doing at the rally anyway?" Nithin muttered, looking at his shoes and shaking his head. "That's not Sam's scene. Never was."

"Only Jake's *lighty* can answer that," Karan replied. "And he isn't talking much. Except for an hour or so he hasn't moved from this place since he carried Sam in. He's still there, sitting in a chair across from Sam's bed."

"Has Sam ever regained consciousness?" Sandy enquired.

"Once only. But very briefly, then went under again very quickly."

"And Sam's old lady? How is she taking it?"

"Like a warrior. And she told me the same thing she told you."

"And what was that?" Nithin asked.

"That old lady," Sandy said, "She's something else. You want to know what she said? 'There's not a Pathan in the world that can be killed with just one bullet.' And she sounded as if she believed it."

"She believes it. You can bet your life on it," Karan added.

"I still want to know why Sam went to the rally," Nithin repeated.

"Sally said something to Devi yesterday ..." Karan volunteered. "Something about Sam not being himself a few days before that protest meeting. He was sleeping badly, having nightmares that left Sally shaken. And on one or two occasions he took off on his own, in the middle of the night, without any explanation. And when he came back he looked like death itself. Does any of that sound like the Sam we know?"

"There may be a simple explanation," Nithin suggested. "On the other hand ... Sandy, do you think Sam was taking over from where Jake left off? Jake used to do that, disappear from time to time ..."

"Whatever," Sandy said. "We won't know until Sam decides to tell us himself. Zain may know something but that *lighty* is like his old man ..."

"I can tell you one thing for sure," Nithin said. "It's a phenomenon I've observed from a distance over the years. The SB okes *khup* one of us and, before you know it, two more take his place. And each succeeding guy is more of an extremist than the one before him, often more violent and less inclined to listen to the voice of reason. I sometimes feel as if the SB is breeding violent revolutionaries, as if they themselves have a death wish somewhere in their subconscious, a guilt they cannot face up to."

"Sounds a bit fanciful to me ..." Karan began to say when Sandy cut him off.

"You think so? How many voices of reason are there now? When last did you hear a moderate speech? Compare the Dadoos and Goonums of the past with the speakers of today. The difference is glaringly obvious. It is inevitable that when the soft voice of reason is brutally suppressed then the angry shouts of violence will always replace it."

"If that is true," Karan said, "Then we're heading on a course fifty times worse than Sharpeville. This state is ruthless and not influenced by world opinion."

"That may well be," Nithin spat out. "But these bastards are not invincible. One way or another they're reaching the end of the road. Their time is running out, pal. They're losing their grip."

"You talk like they're a bunch of mobsters," Karan said.

"What the hell do you think they are?" Nithin retorted. "A lot more sophisticated in their methods, sure, and a damned sight better organised. But thugs nevertheless."

"I don't know ..." Karan shrugged. "Seems somewhat far-fetched to me. I mean, they do hold elections, their people do vote, even if it is restricted to their own kind."

"And that is the sophistication in their methods. They've conditioned their people to respond to certain stimuli, whether that be fear, the loss of their beautiful perks, whatever. Nothing clever about it, though. The Mafia operates on the same basis."

"It's still a bit over the top," Karan said doubtfully. "I mean, to condition a whole race ..."

"What the fuck do you think Hitler did?" Nithin demanded. "Are you forgetting that these guys are the Führer's disciples, the very bunch that voted against waging war against that madman? And don't tell me that's history, because those are the facts and the passage of time can't alter them."

"But Hitler was a one-man show ..."

"You don't know that he had his own henchmen? That his cabinet or government or whatever the hell he called it was packed with his trusted lieutenants."

"But it was still a one-man show. What we have here is a government, with different leaders from time to time ..."

"That doesn't change anything. If Hitler was a one-man show, these guys are a syndicate. Same difference."

"Well," Karan smiled, raising his hands in surrender, "It's a plausible theory, I'll grant you that. But I thought politics and you were poles apart. Now you sound more like a revolutionary than the most die-hard speaker I've ever come across. Since when have you felt so strongly about these things?"

"I've been wondering about that myself these past few days," Nithin smiled back, then laughed softly. "But don't start getting any ideas, old pal. The name of my game is still money, and *numero uno* is still *moi*, whichever way you cut it."

"From the way you sounded a minute ago I would have given odds to the contrary. The anger in your words didn't strike me as if you were passing the time of day."

"Perish the thought, my friend. Politics and I don't share the same bed. Never have and never will."

In spite of the confident way Nithin said it, Karan couldn't help feeling as if the words sounded hollow, forced. He looked like a man who is suddenly faced with some great truth that he had no desire to acknowledge.

∞

"I've seen some strange things in my life, Sandy," Nithin was saying. "But this beats everything. Whilst all the experts — the surgeons, the doctors, anyone who is qualified to judge — have all given up hope, three people stand rock solid in their belief that Sam will walk out of here."

"Zain, his granny, and the priest," Sandy added. "I know, I've been watching and listening to them."

"That priest," Nithin said speculatively, "is a real oddball. He comes here several times a day. I've been observing him through the window. He doesn't seem to be praying or raising his hands in entreaty. He just stands there, in his pointed cap and white shirt, and stares at Sam silently. What the heck is he doing?"

"He's a Sufi. They're some sort of a mystic order. They spend more time in their mosques feeding the poor than they do praying. It's the same guy who delivered the eulogy at Jake's funeral."

"He's a gutsy guy, I'll say that much for him."

"Ya. Him and that Reverend Boesak. They don't mince their words, don't pussyfoot around. They say it like it is, tell the SB to go get fucked and take their bosses with them ... Well, not quite in those words ..."

"They're *vilt*, for sure. Not many of these so-called men of God have the courage of their commitments. They mouth their inane sermons and pocket the *marcher* — a bunch of snivelling fakes. That Sufi guy, and Boesak, they can play on my team anytime. They're *skrik* of no one."

"Some hope. Can you see them with a pack of cards in their hands? Perhaps you should consider playing on their team."

"I've never prayed in my life."

"I didn't say that, you know what I'm referring to."

"What about you?"

"I've been doing a bit of thinking. Let's talk about it later, here comes Jake's *lighty*."

"Hey, Zain," Sandy called, stepping forward and hugging him.

"Hi, Uncle Sandy," Zain said, returning the embrace and smiling over Sandy's shoulder at Nithin. "Hello, Uncle Nits."

"You okay, son?" Nithin asked.

"Ya. Sure."

"Uncle Sam? How's he doing?"

"Uncle Sam is fine. Coming home pretty soon."

Nithin was delighted, smiling widely. "That's the best news I've heard in a long time. The doctors ..."

"Don't know about the doctors, Uncle Nits. But my gran and I are taking him home as soon as he wakes up. No *Jahver's* bullet is gonna kill my Uncle Sam, you can be sure of that."

"Okay, Zain," Sandy smiled. "We're with you, son. Just ease up a bit, okay?"

"You guys were my da's best buddies. You loved him like a brother. Did you ever ask him to ease up?"

"Your da wasn't the sort that listened to anybody ..." Sandy started to say.

"That's because he knew the time for talking and listening was over," Zain cut in. "He left that to the *chachas*, who'll still be talking when they walk through the pearly gates."

"Okay, Zain," Nithin grinned. "But don't go off half-cocked. Play it cool, okay?"

"I aim to do that. Like Boesak says, 'It would be stupid to underestimate the enemy's strength.'"

"Okay, fine. But talk to us," Nithin pleaded. "We won't try to stop you. Maybe we can guide you a little, be there when you need someone. Hey, we're family ..."

"I know that, Uncle Nits. And I'll keep what you said in mind. But I have to go now. My gran's waiting. You'll be coming home tonight?" When Nithin and Sandy nodded he patted their shoulders and hurried off.

"The *lighty* makes me feel like shit," Sandy growled. "And look at what he did. He patted our shoulders. Like we were some bloody *chachas*. We're taking lessons from kids, Nits. Listening to him makes me feel guilty, like I failed to do something important ..."

"Let's get the hell out of here. I've always hated hospitals. And don't talk to me about feeling guilty. I hear enough of that crap from Kathy."

"Sore spot, huh? Well, Zain just touched mine. Let's get a bite to eat. There's something I want to talk to you about."

"I know what you're going to say. But okay, dammit! Let's go."

∞

They were seated at a table at the Mermaid Restaurant, on the first floor of Teachers Centre in Albert Street. The subdued lighting, muted decor and soft music were having a soothing effect on their somewhat discordant mood. They were beginning to relax, allowing the atmosphere to seep into them.

"Soobry's son has done a great job on this place," Nithin said as he looked around. "Came back from London with his MBA and settled down to hard graft straightaway. Did his old man proud."

"That old guy worked his ass to the bone to give his *lighty* the breaks in life that he himself didn't have. From a lowly barman to a hugely successful businessman is no small achievement."

"I doff my hat to him. Remember the old days, Sandy? At the West End? At the first sign that we were even slightly tipsy he'd hustle us out of there, call a taxi from across the road and instruct the guy to take us home. Paid him too, out of his own pocket."

"And as soon as old Soobry turned his back we took the money from the taxi driver and walked home!" Sandy laughed loudly.

"Better not let him hear that." Nithin grinned. "He's still around and still full of himself."

They finished their meal in silence after that, savouring the superb curry dishes and the crisp, flaky rotis. Nithin stopped eating first, pushed his plate away and placed his napkin on the table.

"Okay, Sandy. Let's hear it."

"Before I go into that, there's something I have to say — I don't think Sam is going to pull through."

"I hate to say it, but I agree."

"Which brings us to Jake's *lighty*. He's got nobody now. Rashid's a *garach*. There's no man around him. And he's a walking time-bomb."

"He's got us."

"And that's my point, where this conversation is heading."

"I remember a time, when we were still shit *lighties* ourselves ..." Nithin mused, barely audible. "Jake and I were in Verbena Road, sitting on the wall outside that block of flats next to his house. We were talking about the *Motas* and their strengths. Jake had the idea that I was plotting to take them on someday. I can't recall the exact conversation but I remember he mentioned that we were family and then warned me against any such move, told me that the *Motas* were too powerful to buck. I promised him that I would watch and play. I don't think he was happy with that answer because the next thing he said, and I remember it as clearly as if he had said it this morning, his exact words: 'In a push Sandy and I will back you, all the way and against anybody. But we won't like it. It'll be a losing hand — aces and eights.' What he was telling me was that you guys would give your lives for me even though it was a no-win situation."

"Jake spoke to me about it. I recall we were both worried about what you would do next. And you're right, we meant to stand by you and fuck the odds. We knew it was pointless talking to you, that you wouldn't listen anyway. All we could do was be there when the shit hit the fan."

"And now there's Jake's *lighty*. And he's not listening either. The circle has made a full turn."

"Only I've never felt so old in my life."

"We are old, Sandy. Maybe we're past it."

"I wouldn't quite say that."

"No, I reckon not. So, what do we do? Are we sitting with dead man's cards again?"

"Well, we're still here, aren't we, in spite of the losing hand? Who says we can't win again?"

"But do we want to sit in on this game?"

"Do we have a choice? And if we're in the November of our lives, we may as well make sure that when December comes around we go down in glory."

"Getting a bit poetic in your old age, as Karan would say."

"More like Tennyson would say. Remember that poem? *Ulysses*."

"Remember it! Old Vasi Nair made us memorise it, word for word. Hang on a sec, I know where you're going:

You and I are old
Old age hath yet his honour and his toil
Death closes all, but something ere the end
Some work of noble note may yet be done
Not unbecoming men that strove with Gods!

And how's that for a good memory?"

"Quoted with feeling, maestro. Now let me round it off for you:

Tho we are not now that strength which in old days
Moved earth and heaven, that which we are, we are
One equal temper of heroic hearts
Made weak by time and fate, but strong in will ..."

"Shit, help me here, Nits. I seem to have lost it. I can't remember ..."

"No need, pal. You just said it all. But you can't make a bullet proof vest out of Tennyson's poems."

"Okay, let's cut the cackle. What do we do about Zain?"

"You know how it goes: if you can't lick 'em, join 'em."

"You're crazy. I've done my bit for the Resistance. I have no ..."

"Wait, Sandy. *Un momento*, my friend. Let's take this slowly. What have we really done? When it came to the bottom line we simply took a walk, like it wasn't any business of ours."

"And it wasn't. Still isn't."

"Then why do you feel guilty, like you failed to do something important?"

"Did I say that?"

"Stop hedging. You said it all right."

"Then put it down to a moment's weakness. Reason has prevailed."

"For what purpose? Where do we go from here? We've both achieved what we set out to get. We talked about it being time to move on. To where?"

"We were talking business. You're talking suicide now."

"You think so? How many chances have we taken over the years, really bad moves, any of which could have killed us?"

"That was survival, buddy."

"Ya? And when we bucked the *Motas* to help Sam? Was that less suicidal?"

"We had a fighting chance. It was a pretty even playing field. And we had the edge on them. There's no comparison with what you're proposing."

"So the odds are a bit skewed. It didn't worry us in the past."

"Remember what Sam said Jake told him? Something about those guys teaching the *Motas* a thing or two? We'd be farting against thunder, Nits."

"Boesak doesn't let that stop him, that priest oke doesn't. All the guys before them didn't. Even our Goonum didn't. I reckon we're better qualified than all of them, we know how those guys in the SB think. As you often used to say, we're third cousins to them."

"Ease up, Nits. You're moving too fast for me."

"Okay. But let me say this. There's nothing noble about what we're proposing here. But we've never run from a battle in our lives. If we were protecting our turf then, we need to protect Zain now. No difference. The fact that we can't do that without some participation in the fight for freedom may be unfortunate, but it's the reality nevertheless. And the thought isn't so unpalatable. We can't deny we've always hated the State and their stooges amongst us. Maybe it's time we took the bastards apart, to whatever little extent we can."

"Like we did that swine Munchie."

"We got a lot of satisfaction out of that. It went beyond his double dealing act, possibly beyond Jake even. How different is what we're proposing now from the early days, when we used to go to all the rallies with Jake, at the Red Square?"

"Sort of like a grand finale," Sandy grinned crookedly.

"Maybe. Maybe not. We don't have to go out with our guns blazing. We don't have to go out at all. We watch and play."

"Not much like what Tennyson was waxing lyrical about."

"Fuck Tennyson. He was a *garach*."

Sandy chuckled, poured himself a drink and chuckled again. "Okay, he served his purpose. And you're right, nothing much need change."

"Not a lot that it would affect our safety. Jake lasted a long time. If he hadn't been sold out he would still be here today. We can learn from that. Make certain we trust nobody, always cover our tracks. But hell, we're good at that, been doing it all our lives."

"So did Jake. You have to trust somebody, sometime."

"Sure. But most of the time Jake was a loner, a one-man show. We can cover each other."

"You're talking as if we're in it now. Have we come to a decision?"

"You know we have. You knew it when you asked me to join you here. All you've been doing so far is testing my resolve."

Sandy burst out laughing, so loudly that several amused diners turned in their direction.

"You're one smart cookie, Nits. I'm glad we're friends. I'd hate to make an enemy of you."

"The feeling's mutual, old pal. Now, if Zain won't listen to us, let's go over and listen to him."

❧

"He's locked into a mighty struggle with the messenger of death," Sam's mother said, so softly that Sandy had to lean forward to hear her. "He's willing himself into Sam's mind and pulling him away from the clutches of death. It won't be long now before the outcome is decided."

"That priest ... these mystics ..." Sandy muttered, his voice somewhat dubious, "They're beyond me. These Sufis and their strange philosophy ... I don't know ..."

"You believe in it or you don't. Those who do require no explanations."

"But for someone, even a priest, to fight the messenger of death ..."

"He isn't fighting him, Sandy. He's arguing with him, convincing him that Sam's time isn't up, that he still has much to do."

"So it's a sort of ... what — a silent debate?"

"If you wish to call it that."

"I don't know, ma. It's hard to believe such things are possible."

"That's because, like so much else, your generation has lost it. Spend a few months in India, get to know what it's all about. Nobody there considers this sort of thing as being mysterious, or even unusual."

"I have heard the old people talk of these things," Nithin ventured tentatively. "At the time I put it down to fairy tales, village myths and old people talk. But I remember once, when I was about ten or so, my sister was bitten by a snake or scorpion and my mother sent for some holy man. It wasn't a Sufi, I'm sure of that. All I know was that my sister was going to die — she was shaking and convulsing in pain and frothing at the mouth. And then this guy came into our yard and started chanting something, in a language I didn't understand. I found out later it was Sanskrit. Pretty soon my sister stopped moving, her eyes were no longer jumping wildly, she just lay there quietly like she was in a trance. I tried to ask my mother what was happening but she pushed me behind her, and said in Gujerati: '*Vitchi ne utarè chè.*' The strange chanting frightened me, I reckon I was so scared that I ran away from there."

"It's the normal way of describing what was being done," Sam's mother said. "It must have been a scorpion that bit your sister, a *vitchi*. He was calling the scorpion and also draining the poison out of your sister's body."

"But he didn't use his hands or anything else," Nithin said. "All he did was chant something ..."

"But your sister lived through it," Shaida stated.

"She sure did. And she's still around."

"And you still have doubts?"

"Not me," Nithin said with a laugh. "The story was for Sandy's benefit."

"You should have stayed there," Shaida said seriously. "Quite often the viper responsible for the sting comes forward to account for its actions, to justify its behaviour. Of course, people like us can't hear the communication, but you can be sure it takes place."

"Are holy men like those still around?" Sandy asked Shaida.

"A few. But people don't turn to them much these days, they prefer to call a doctor or go to a hospital. Even our medical knowledge, the miraculous healing powers that certain herbs and roots possess, are seldom available here now. In this country the *hakim* is obsolete, an endangered species."

"Well ..." Sandy said, settling into the couch, "whatever works for Sam, pulls him back from the jaws of death, is good enough for me."

"Ultimately, it's up to God," Shaida started to say when the telephone cut into their discussion, the shrill tone startling them. As Sally went off to answer the call, Shaida stood up and walked towards the kitchen.

"Is Zain still at the hospital?" Sandy asked, turning to face Hannah.

"He won't budge from there."

"Do you think he holds himself responsible for what happened?"

"I'm sure he doesn't," Hannah replied, shaking her head. "He loves Sam and what they did to him is fuelling the anger in Zain. The anger ... it's not much different from the way Jake used to be. It's eating into him, tearing him apart. And you know, Sandy, unlike Jake, who had no time for the white man but differentiated between the State and the man in the street, Zain makes no such allowances. To him they're all the same — the enemy."

"Hannah," Nithin asked gently, "Did you know that Zain was going to those rallies?"

"Certainly. There are no secrets in this house. We've always been open about our opposition to the government."

"Did he always go alone. I mean, before Sam joined him?"

"Sometimes. More often he was accompanied by Haroun and Pradeep. All three belong to the same ANC cell. On the night of the shooting, the other two split up to attend a protest meeting at their school. Zain wanted to hear Boesak speak. They were supposed to meet here later that night."

"But Sam and Karan are not political people. How did their sons get involved in these things?"

"Their sons and everybody else's sons. The schools, Nithin. Haven't you heard? That's where the real resistance is now. Didn't Mariam ever talk to you."

"Mariam? My daughter?" Nithin looked stunned.

"You really don't know? No, I can see you don't. The schools have been closed down, Nithin. For over a month now. The kids are on strike. Where have you been?"

"They're on strike? Against what? Their studies?"

"Against the lack of facilities, the distorted syllabus, the ..."

"Sandy," Nithin said helplessly, "Your kids ... you know about this? Kathy usually sees to ..."

Sandy, however, seemed to have withdrawn into himself, eyes closed, his head slowly shaking from side to side. When, at last, he spoke his voice was hollow. "Nits, we have failed ... we have been too caught up in our own little world ... we missed the big picture. It's time now to ..."

"That call was from Manna Pillay," Sally said as she re-entered the lounge, a slight break in her voice. "Sam's fading fast. We must go over immediately."

Hannah went over to Sally. Nithin and Sandy simultaneously stood up. Shaida slowly walked towards them, leaning heavily on her cane. "There's no need to rush. Sandy, Nithin — you go ahead. We'll follow you in a few minutes."

Nithin nodded as he followed Sandy, patting Sally's shoulder as he passed her. As they entered the car Sandy slammed the door and muttered, "The old lady doesn't accept that Sam's not going to make it."

"Faith, Sandy," Nithin responded. "And perhaps trust in ancient beliefs."

"Ya. Like that business of the signs," Sandy added, turning the ignition. "This is more Karan's field than ours."

"That Karan," Nithin chuckled. "For a university graduate, he's still got one leg in the past. And he's devastated at the thought of losing Sam."

"He's closer to Sam than we are, I guess. It's understandable."

"But Pradeep ... how the hell did Karan ever spawn a revolutionary!"

"Isn't there another question somewhere in there, Nits old buddy? One a little closer to home?"

"Ya ... shit, man! Looks like everyone and his son is into it!"

∞

"So many visitors," Nithin grumbled. "They're cluttering the bloody corridor. There should be some control over the numbers."

"Sam's a popular guy," Sandy observed. "And most of them are close family. I guess they have more rights than we do."

"Have you been watching Zain and his grandmother? Damned! You can't help admiring their courage. Makes you feel kinda proud of them."

"Nits ..." Sandy whispered, his fingers curling around Nithin's arm. "Look! Manna just stepped out of Sam's ward. Look at his face. I reckon Sam's lost the battle."

The surgeon surveyed the crowd, his expression grave. He caught Sally's eye and walked towards her. Nithin and Sandy edged closer.

"Sally, I'm sorry. It's all over. He's gone."

Sally nodded, pushed her hair back from her face as she secured a scarf over her head, and closed her eyes. Hannah silently hugged herself and swayed a little. Karan collapsed into a chair and covered his face. Nithin and Sandy simply looked at each other. Sam's son folded his arms around his mother, his face grim, cheeks flushed, eyes glinting angrily.

"They butchered my grandparents," Haroun said softly, Sally's head buried in his shoulder. "They murdered my Uncle Jake. Now they've killed my pa. This won't break my heart!"

"And that," Sandy growled quietly to Nithin, "says it all. I'd like to hear any *wit ou* explain to that *lighty* what civilised behaviour is all about!"

From somewhere in the crowd someone let out a low sob. It sounded abnormally loud in the stillness that had descended over the corridor. It was followed by a muted cough, then a choking sound.

Manna Pillay, his shoulders slumped, turned towards Karan and leaned over him, his hands resting lightly over Karan's shoulders. He murmured something, his face solicitous. Suddenly, the door to Sam's ward was flung open and Zain stepped out.

"Where's the doc!" Zain shouted, then saw Manna begin to straighten up. "Hey doc, come back in here. My dadi wants you."

As Manna walked back into the room, Sandy muttered, "Now what? I hope the old lady is okay!"

"Probably just some formality," Nithin whispered. "I guess there's nothing more here for us. Let's make tracks."

"No, wait," Sandy said, his voice strange. "Just a little while ..."

A few minutes passed, then five that stretched into ten. After what seemed an age, though in reality no more than twenty minutes had elapsed, the surgeon came through the door and closed it behind him. The expression on his face was that of a man who had just received an electric shock.

"There's no scientific explanation ..." he was saying to himself and shaking his head. "I was there ... his heart stopped ... some doctor I am..."

"Manna, talk to me!" Sandy demanded. "What the hell is going on?"

"I reckon it's that Sufi guy," Manna said, more to himself and still shaking his head. "If this don't beat everything. I guess I've seen it all now, but no medical journal will ever print ..."

"Manna, come on! You're not making sense," Sandy said.

Karan was out of his chair, his hands clutching the surgeon's lapels. "Manna, are you saying ..."

"Yes, Karan. Your buddy's alive and looking better than he did the day they brought him here."

"But you said ..." Karan was smiling, hope surging through his face.

At that moment the priest walked out of the room and paused for a second. He looked suddenly gaunt, his eyes dark and sunk into their sockets. His shirt was drenched with perspiration and clung to his chest. Suddenly, he squared his shoulders and said loudly, "God is Great!" When he walked down the corridor his steps were steady, firm.

"Can't argue with that," Manna whispered. "You live and you learn."

∞

They were sitting in the rear garden, Sam stretched out on a recliner; Karan, Nithin and Sandy around him.

"Don't talk to me," Nithin grinned widely. "I don't want to hear anything you have to say. I don't *temba* zombies."

"Do I look like a zombie?" Sam smiled.

"You're a zombie. You can't fool me."

"Okay. Let's say I am. Do you think it's infectious?"

"Just keep your distance. I'm not taking any chances."

"You can't escape me, *bru*. When I beat my voodoo drums ..."

"Can you okes stop kidding," Sandy snapped. "Can we be serious here?"

"Ease up, Sandy," Nithin laughed. "We're just letting our hair down a bit."

"Thank God it doesn't happen often. Sam, three weeks ago I would have given odds of a thousand to one that we'd never be sitting like this again. What did that priest do?"

"Prayed, most of the time, I guess. I don't know. I was out of it completely."

"Seems to me you're still out of it," Nithin grimaced.

"Why? Because I justified my presence at the rally?"

"No. Our answer to that may surprise you. Anyway, what are your plans now? Are you going to take an active interest in politics?"

"Well ... it was no passing urge."

"Why should you guys care?" Karan scoffed. "The system doesn't stop you okes from cashing in."

"Is that what you think?" Nithin asked harshly. "That we cashed in on the system?"

"Well, perhaps that was a bit unfair ..."

"A *bit* unfair? You can do better than that, pal!"

"You want *me* to apologise, for how *you* make your money?"

"Go on, pal. Exactly how do you think we made our money?"

"Look, to hell with it. I don't want to talk about ..."

"To hell with you, man! And I don't talk to *garachs* ..."

"I'm a *garach*?" Karan bristled. "You calling me a *garach*? Hell, I've dealt with bigger dons than you. They didn't say anything clever either."

"Tell me something," Sandy asked reasonably, "What is it with you two? From as far back as I can remember it's been like this."

"Fuck him!" Nithin growled. "He's just a shitassed *bunya*."

"And you," Karan threw back. "What kind of an asshole *bunya* are you?"

Sam and Sandy burst out laughing, their unrestrained mirth taking the edge off the angry exchange.

"Care to share the joke with us?" Maliga asked as she came over and placed a tray on the table.

Kathy, a few feet behind Maliga, a plate in each hand, said. "Don't ask, Maliga. Because then we'll have to ask them to tell us when to laugh."

"Hey," Hannah called out as she stepped through the kitchen door, "Why wasn't I invited to the party?"

"Because your job is to look after the business," Karan joked. "Not to flirt with us."

"Flirt with you?" Nithin mocked. "There are better prospects at the graveyard."

"You leave Karan bhai alone, Nithin," Sally shouted through a window.

"I wouldn't touch him if I was an old *juntu* from Point Road," Nithin replied, but softly, so Sally wouldn't hear him.

"You're not such hot stuff yourself," Kathy shot back.

"I used to pray that this woman would mellow in her old age," Nithin said sadly. "I was prepared to believe in God if just that one prayer was answered."

"God doesn't know you exist. I sometimes feel as if even the devil prays for your soul."

"Ja. And while God and the devil are negotiating over who owns me, you're busy giving me hell on earth."

"Kathy," Sam said, smiling, "I think you should give Nits a break. You're killing the poor guy."

"But I love him. I'm keeping him alive. If I ease up he'll become suspicious, maybe start believing that I'm having an affair."

"I sometimes wish you would," Nithin snapped. "It'd take the heat off me for a while."

"This is like old times," Sandy grinned. "See what you would have been missing, Sam?"

"I'm not so sure. That hospital was mighty peaceful."

"If Sally hears that," Kathy said, "You'll have to send for that priest again."

"I always said the street was safer, Sandy," Nithin threw in.

"You and your so called street," Kathy scoffed, rolling her eyes. "You make it sound like Sunset Boulevard."

"My mother was right," Nithin complained mournfully. "Once an Indian girl gets a bit of education ..."

"She becomes a thug," Sandy finished it for him. "Or so you always said."

"Why do we bother with these chauvinists, anyway," Maliga said to Kathy. "Let's join Sally and Devi. We can at least have an intelligent conversation."

"You forgot to add 'pig'," Nithin shouted at their retreating backs, then turned to Sam and asked, "Now that the sideshow is over you want to talk to us about what happened before you stopped that bullet? Why you really went to that rally?"

"I overheard my mother talking to Zain," Sam explained. "What she was telling him made me feel guilty as hell. That led to a few other things, memories of people like Sanjee and a conversation I had with Ramnath Seepye ... it's a bit involved and I'll go into it some other time ... in the old days it was Goonum and Dadoo, now it's the kids who have taken over. They're fighting the battle that we seem to have abandoned. I reckon it's a sad indictment of all of us sitting here."

"I look at my son," Karan said, "and I see a sixteen-year-old with the eyes of an adult. He doesn't talk to me a lot. Most of the time he just avoids me, like I'm part of some problem. He makes me feel ashamed of myself, as if I've let the side down ..."

"I know the feeling," Nithin added, his face grave. "Sandy and I were talking about something similar. We felt as if everyone was actively participating in the battle, except for the two of us."

"It's not just the kids," Sandy said. "It's our mothers too. They're there in the background, quietly prodding us. I remember when I used to go home late at night and my old lady would wade into me, but the moment I told her I'd been to a rally then everything was okay. It was as if I'd been to the temple or something."

"Yup," Sam added. "It's like Tata down the street, Strini Moodley's old man. He lost every last cent he had, including the house he lived in together with his wife's jewellery. It all went towards legal costs and assisting Strini in his fight against the *jahvers*. Strini still ended up in Robben Island but that old man didn't even blink an eyelid. Once, when I tried to offer him my sympathies, all he said was, 'It's okay, bubba. My son is fighting for the people. For that I would sell the shoes on my feet!' Things like that make me wonder what the hell we've been doing all this time."

"I guess we've always had the convictions, what we lacked was the courage." Karan said.

"I wouldn't say it quite like that," Nithin interjected. "But yes, we lacked something. Perhaps it was a commitment, a failure to totally involve ourselves."

"This guy Boesak," Sam said, "you want to hear him talk. Nothing scares him. He bluntly tells the State that its days are over, that they had better get out of the way. He's declaring war on them and they're shitting themselves. You can see it in the faces of the SB enforcers. They're running scared, facing violent opposition for the first time — the kind of opposition that's not appealing to their reason any longer. Boesak's openly saying he's going to turn this country into a bloody battlefield and then tells them that they've lost the battle already because God is on our side."

"They'll put him away fast," Sandy said. "These guys operate like the *Motas* used to. They wipe out the opposition before it becomes a problem. And they have the equipment to do it."

"And what happened to the *Motas*, Sandy?" Sam asked. "Not long ago you said something about half-baked township *lighties* that could blow them away."

"We're not talking about anything even vaguely similar," Sandy argued. "You can't even begin to compare the two in those terms."

"The difference," Karan said, "is Boesak. Good against evil, God against the devil."

"First sensible thing you said," Nithin jeered. "You're learning fast."

"Hold it," Sam said quickly, "before you two start your act again. Whilst I have been lying around recuperating, I've been doing a lot of reading and watching a few video tapes of the cops beating the kids up, stuff that Hannah gave me. How about you guys running through this stuff?"

"What are we saying here?" Karan asked. "Are we getting actively involved?"

"We were always involved," Sandy said. "In one way or another. There isn't an Indian around who didn't lose his home, his business, his job or someone he loved when the government's hatchet men moved in. Nits and I have done our bit, from time to time, in our own quiet way. We've provided a sort of back-up to the guys in the field. Jake was something else altogether. He *was* in the field, he blew those bastards to hell without blinking an eye."

"I didn't know ..." Karan muttered. "I never thought that you guys ..."

"Us guys *what*?" Nithin spat out. "Okes like you have this opinion of us, like we're thugs creating hell on the streets. Well, it's time you wised up to a few facts — we've been a part of the resistance from the days of Red Square right up to now. We may not have been up front about it and we could certainly have done a lot more but we did do something. Unlike mama's little sugar lumps like you and your kind."

"All I was saying was that I didn't know ..."

"Why *should* you know? Where were you when we were following Dadoo and Goonum around? Who the hell did you think were our heroes? Al Capone? Dillinger? Get the fuck out of here! It's no wonder your son makes you feel ashamed of yourself. You *are* a part of the bloody problem, with your goody-two-shoes attitude."

"Okay, Nits," Karan said quietly. "I apologise. Not because I thought what you said but because I led you to believe that I did. And, for whatever it's worth, I want to say this: the day I heard that Jake was the famous *Aza Kwela* I was so fucken proud of him that I actually cried. From that day on he was my hero. Whatever your opinion of me may be, please believe that."

"Hey, Karan ..." Nithin began softly, "okay ... I guess it's my turn to say I didn't know ..."

"Now we all know," Sandy smiled. "It was good to hear you talk like that, Karan. Makes us all feel a lot better. You two should shake on it, put an end to the ongoing feud."

"My pleasure," Nithin shot out his hand and Karan took it in his own. "But don't expect me to hug you."

"I won't respond to that," Karan chuckled.

"Okay," Sandy said. "What we do now is play it very cool. There're a hundred Jakes in the making out there, and they're all loose cannons. Our Jake, with all the anger in him, never aimed at a civilian target. Not that he believed there was such a thing as an innocent white, it's just that his anger was more focused. These *lighties* now, they don't believe in such niceties, they've seen too many of their buddies killed brutally. They're a new generation and, like Boesak, they're declaring war. But unlike Boesak, they're on a hair-trigger; and they're not afraid to die. What I'm scared of is that our own *lighties* are right there with them. I'm not sure I can handle another Jake brought home in a casket."

"We can't stop them," Sam said.

"No, but we can contain them," Sandy pointed out, "control their actions."

"They're not listening anymore, Sandy," Sam said in despair. "They follow Boesak because he is one of them, he speaks their language. It's a question of either you agree with them or you're the enemy."

"Which means what?" Karan asked. "Another Belfast? Right here?"

"That pot has been bubbling for a long time," Sandy said softly. "If it boils over it won't be because we stoked the fire."

∞

"The one day of the week," Karan complained as he walked into Sam's office, "when I can let my hair down and enjoy a game of golf. And what happens? I listen to you and end up traipsing all over the old neighbourhood, with these two *dakus* for company."

"It'll do more for your soul," Sam laughed, "than a hundred games of golf ever will."

"Certainly did something for his spine," Nithin said laconically, pulling up a chair. "It's the first time in years I've seen him looking to strangle somebody. The second time, actually."

"Strangling people is your line of business," Karan threw back. "Mine is a more civilised world."

"Ya? Civilised?" Nithin jeered. "You reckon it was a civilised response when you wanted to *khup* Cohen ..." Nithin caught the warning look in Sandy's eyes and quickly stopped talking. Fortunately, Sam seemed pre-occupied and hadn't picked up on the by-play. Nithin grunted with relief and changed the subject. "What the hell ... forget it. You don't need guts to become a lawyer."

"It takes courage to become a loan shark?" Karan asked with a sneer.

"I'm a financier, you bloody goody-two-shoes. You never borrowed money? Sure, you went to so-called legit bankers but what rates did you pay and what was their risk? Whatever they lent you those honkies insisted that you invested an equivalent amount with them and then gave you peanuts on your investment. On the loan? You paid the maximum they could squeeze out of you. What is it now? Twenty percent? More? The difference between their rates and mine is reflected in the additional risk I took. That's normal business practice — the greater the risk the greater the rate of interest. And I ask for no collateral security. Those okes took no risk and bled you dry nevertheless."

"There was no choice."

"And that's my point. The fact is they treated you like dogshit and made you go to them hat in hand. They screwed you royally even as you bent over backwards to show how grateful you were. And who were these bank managers that you kow-towed to? *Lighties*! Little shits who were promoted through the ranks by the system and the colour of their skins. The rest they learned as they went along. And you made it easy for them each time you went down on one knee. Don't give me that crap about not having a choice."

"You don't think I knew this, Nits? You reckon I liked what they did? At least they didn't resort to a bunch of enforcers when their clients fell into arrears."

"They didn't have to because they were lending you your own money. As for enforcers, the law is their henchman. They chopped and changed it to suit them, as and when they needed to. There was a law that applied to you, another that applied to a white. Surely even you can see that, you poor fool."

"Call me that again and we go to the roof garden."

"I told you guys," Nithin said mockingly, raising his hands in surrender, "he's got his spine back."

"What makes you think I ever lost it, you ...?"

"You two ..." Sandy said, "you shake with one hand and swipe with the other. Anyway, what's this all about, Sam? Why the tour of the ruins of apartheid?"

"You needed to see what it's like out there. It'll save me a lot of background description."

"It's like a damned war zone," Karan snapped. "It almost broke my heart to see what's become of the old district."

"I felt the same way," Nithin muttered, his voice suddenly subdued.

"I have to admit," Sandy confessed, "It shook me. What is it with these *wit ous*? Why snatch it from us if they didn't want it for themselves?"

"Oh, they wanted it allright," Sam said, "but the spirits wouldn't allow them to settle there."

"What're you talking about, Sam?" Nithin asked, "you sound like someone that's lost his marbles."

"Okay. Let it ride for now. But the Dutchene is not the only place that has been destroyed. Go down Mitchell Road, First Avenue, May Street — where there were lovely homes once all that you now see is bush and a few foundations. Go out of town, to Riverside, or Cato Manor — you'll see the same result."

"I'm damned if I'll ever understand how the honkey thinks," Nithin said.

"They certainly cashed in on Florida Road," Karan added. "The same goes for Cowey Road and all the avenues leading off it. Whitey is certainly living in clover there."

"You know what really blows my mind?" Nithin asked. "In the centre of all that bush they stick this sign that says: NO TRESPASSING. DEPARTMENT OF PLANNING AND DEVELOPMENT. Who the hell are they addressing that to?"

"Not the white-owned business houses," Karan observed. "Some couldn't wait to dive in and build their fancy layouts. And you can bet they picked up the land for peanuts."

"I've heard all this before," Nithin interrupted. "I don't know where this discussion is going. Sure, it makes me madder'n hell, but look ... what I'm saying is there's no point bellyaching about all this crap. Far as I'm concerned the honkey is one big shit and I don't give him space in my mind. I've survived by believing that the foot that goes gets there. And unlike the *wit ou* I didn't *skit* anything from anyone. I force nobody to do business with me. If you don't like my face you're free to get out of it and chuck. Some other time, some other place, we can shoot the breeze about the system in this country. For now, I'd like to know what's on Sam's mind. Make it short and sweet, Sam. Why are we here today?"

"Okay. You want it in a nutshell? I'll give it to you in two words: 'our *lighties*'."

"I figured that," Nithin said. "Is this a follow up on that talk we had in your garden."

"Ya. What we were just talking about, it was essential to set the mood. That's why I allowed you okes to freewheel without interrupting. Now I think it's time to listen to the *lighties* themselves."

"That's great! I can have that chat with Mariam at home. I have no problem with that ..."

"They're here, Nits. Waiting for us in the boardroom. Mariam, Haroun, Pradeep and Zain. Sandy's two boys are doing their thing in Joburg, but Zain told me they have been okayed to speak on behalf of Selvan and Vincent."

When the others followed Sam into the boardroom the kids were huddled in a corner, talking softly. They immediately stood up and waited for Sam to give them a lead.

"Okay ... look," Sam said, "let's keep it informal. I'm sorry we kept you waiting. So ... you guys want to tell us what's going on?"

"Can we talk freely?" Mariam asked.

"Say whatever you like. We're here to understand why you're doing the things you are."

"Uncle Sam," Zain said, "if we are being asked to justify our actions then we're not interested in ..."

"No, Zain. There'll be no recriminations. You just say it like it is."

"But only as equals."

"I'm not sure what you mean."

"I'm saying that, for purposes of this meeting, we want to be treated as your equals. That's the only way we can talk freely."

"That's okay too, Zain," Sam replied, waving Karan back into his chair.

"Okay. Maybe you should ask us some specific questions. Let's start from there."

"That's fine. How about telling us why you kids are boycotting school."

"That's easy. School is no longer a school. The State is using it as a centre of indoctrination."

"Would you care to elaborate on that?" Karan asked.

"I'll do that, dad," Pradeep replied. "Forget about the distorted syllabus and the poor facilities. Ignore the fact that fifty of us are crammed in one class. We won't even elaborate on the funding — that they spend ten times more per student in white schools. Let's not talk about the State insisting on using Afrikaans as a medium for instruction, much as we hate the language of the oppressor ... before I go on, I have to ask ... were you aware of this?"

"Not all of it," Karan replied. "But yes, we were not entirely ignorant of the distortions."

"It didn't occur to you to do something about that?"

"Hey, I'm not on the stand here."

"Nobody is, Karan kaka," Haroun said. "We're just talking, as equals, remember?"

"I want you *lighties* to accept something," Sandy said. "We admit we were not very supportive. It's why we're talking to you now. To learn where we fell short and to find some way to correct it."

"I reckon that's fair," Zain conceded. "It doesn't exonerate you from your lack of interest but it's a start, at least."

"You guys are not making this easy, Zain," Sam said. "But we accept that. Can we proceed on that basis?"

"We did agree that this was a discussion amongst equals," Pradeep pointed out. "We're not arguing though. We hear you."

"I like the way we're talking," Sandy said. "Now, you said it was more than those things you mentioned earlier. So, what was the final ... shall we say, the last straw?"

"It was all of them. And more. The last straw? That was when they decided to hammer us into submission. When they sent their bully-boys to the schools to subdue us."

"To stop you from doing ... what?" Karan asked.

"Talking! They wanted us to shut up and lie down," Zain answered. "Only, they made one big mistake — they treated us as adults."

"You're losing me, Zain," Sandy said. "Why was it wrong to treat you as adults?"

"Because, unlike you guys, we're not scared. The adults, they run when the cops arrive. We stand our ground."

Sandy nodded, his hands at his sides, palms up. "We must have given you reason to think that. But I'm still in the dark about how you organised yourselves. I mean, this boycott, it can't be something spontaneous ..."

"It's not. All of us here belong to the same ANC cell. Each of us has more than a hundred students under our orders. A similar situation exists all over the country. But this boycott, of schools, you have to understand something, it's a short term action. We will go back, soon. But it won't be for study reasons. The school is an ideal venue to mobilise all of us, to plan our next move."

"And your aim?" Karan asked. "Is it equality of education for all ..."

"That's simplistic thinking, dad," Pradeep cut in. "What we're aiming for is a democracy, a universal franchise. When the people of this country are liberated, education will follow."

"Pradeep said earlier that the State sent in the bully-boys," Nithin said, "Exactly what did those guys do?"

"They beat us up," Pradeep answered.

"That's it?" Nithin asked. "They beat you up? Just like that?"

"I'm not sure what you mean when you say 'just like that' so I'll spell it out for you," Zain said. "They came with their dogs, their whips and their guns. Those Alsatians are trained to kill; and they sjambok us with wild abandon, like we're a bunch of stray cattle. When we say 'they beat us up' that's what we're referring to."

"Have any of the kids been killed by them?"

"Scores — more than that. Not at our school ... not yet anyway. But it's simply a matter of time, Uncle Nits. It'll happen."

"We should have been told of this," Karan said.

"You never gave me the space at home to talk about anything," Pradeep answered. "There was never a forum for such discussion."

"You were pretty liberal with us, dad," Haroun added, "but it was easier to talk to dadi or mom ... I'm sorry ... but that's how it was ..."

"You've always been a good father," Pradeep said, "But when it came to politics... well, you know how it was ..."

"Okay," Sandy said. "We stand corrected. My boys are not here but I reckon they'll say the same as you boys have. I haven't forgotten that you said you have their permission to speak for them."

"They're not in Joburg on holiday, Uncle Sandy," Zain said. "They're at a meeting of organisers ... maybe you should talk to them when they get back."

"I intend to. And I'll listen, I promise you that."

"All this is going on and we know nothing about it," Karan said, sounding somewhat bewildered. "There's been nothing in the papers ..."

"Forget the press," Zain said dismissingly. "They print only what suits their masters."

"But you boys could have been killed, or badly hurt. Surely we have a right to know."

"Those who are a part of the struggle have always known it," Mariam said bluntly. "Sorry, dad, but mom always knew. If she chose not to tell you ..."

"I think she tried," Nithin said apologetically. "I guess I wasn't listening ..."

"Uncle Karan, did you say we could have been killed or badly hurt?" Zain asked.

"Sure. I mean ... only luck and ..."

Zain turned to Pradeep and looked at him pointedly. Pradeep nodded, stared at his father for a few seconds, opened his mouth to say something, then changed his mind and shook his head.

"Go ahead, Pradeep," Zain urged.

"Okay. Dad, I want to show you something." Pradeep said in a quiet voice. He pulled his shirt over his head, then turned around. Pradeep's shoulders and back were covered in deep scars, a half dozen livid welts criss-crossed each other and disappeared under his waistband. Karan gasped, rose in his chair, his face stunned, and took a step towards his son. Before he could touch him, Pradeep lowered the shirt and turned around.

Sandy, who had let out a low whistle, pulled his lips together and slumped in his chair, eyes blazing with anger. Nithin's fists were clenched tightly, the knuckles white. He swore under his breath, then looked at Sam who shook his head and silently conveyed the message that he had had no foreknowledge of what they were seeing.

"It's okay, dad. As you said, I could have been killed."

"But when did this happen ..." Karan whispered. "Why wasn't I told ..."

"You were away on business for a few weeks. Ma got the doctor ..."

"But when I came back ... you didn't say a word to me. Even your mother ..."

The anguish in Karan's voice was so obvious that Pradeep said, softly, "It's okay, dad. It's not your fault ..."

"You should have told me, I'm your father. Do you think I don't care?"

"I want to be honest with you. I'm not sure what you would have done. I expected you to ground me or take me out of school altogether."

"I think you're wrong, Pradeep," Sam said. "Your dad has a right to know."

"Okay. But what about you, Uncle Sam?"

"I'm not sure I understand ..."

"Dad," Haroun called, then turned around and dropped his pants. Just below the cheek of his left buttock, half hidden by his briefs, was a lump of scar tissue, several deep teeth marks around it. Across both calves the skin was raised, two ropes of hard scar tissue standing out vividly.

Sam looked dumbfounded. His eyes began to blaze, then flattened out as two red spots suddenly glittered on his cheekbones. He turned slowly, looked at Zain questioningly, his head tilted to one side.

"You don't want to see it, Uncle Sam. Uncle Nits, don't ask. Mariam's back is not very pretty. Those swines don't differentiate between the sexes."

"We're leaving now," Mariam said, taking the lead. "Dad, I promise I'll answer all your questions at home. I'm sorry we didn't put you fully in the picture, Uncle Sam. We had no intention of showing you what their dogs and whips did to us but when we realised you were sincere in your approach today we felt we had to be equally frank with you. For now, we've arranged something else. There's a man, not more than five minutes walk from here, and he's waiting for your call. Here's his number. Phone him, ask him over and hear what he has to say." She placed a slip of paper in front of Sam, then nodded at the boys, who followed her out of the room.

As soon as the door closed behind the kids, the men looked at each other, no one prepared to lead the discussion. They sat that way for a long time, then lowered their eyes. The anger was still there, apparent in their faces, but there was something else too, a hint of overt guilt and a fleeting sense of regret. The minutes ticked by, then Sam walked over to a fridge and extracted several cans of coke. The others accepted it silently. When they snapped the lids the sound was startlingly loud in the still room. Finally, Sandy, his voice tightly controlled, asked, "Is there a name on that piece of paper?"

Sam lifted the slip off the desk, gazed at it silently, then nodded. "I wouldn't call it a name, all that's written here is the word 'doctor' followed by a number."

Sandy smiled thinly, then rubbed his forehead as he said, "If that's who I think it is then I can promise you guys we're in for a lot more than what our kids told us. There was a time when I didn't want to hear what he had to say. I wanted no part of him. Now, I reckon I'm just plain scared. Whatever, give him a buzz, Sam. We've been out of the rain for long enough. I guess *it's that time* for all of us here."

∞

When the doctor walked in and saw Sandy he immediately smiled widely and stretched his hand. "Well, Sandy? Life plays some funny games, ya?"

As they shook hands, Sandy said, "Can't say it's a pleasure to see you, doc."

"I've waited a long time for this day, my friend. I see you're as brutally honest as always."

"It's the only way to be. Do you know everyone here?"

"If I'm not mistaken, that's Nits there."

When Nithin inclined his head Sandy said, "This is Karan Naran. The oke across from you is Sam Solomon ..."

"Ah! *Aza Kwela*'s brother! This is indeed a pleasure, Sam. And it's good to see you looking so well. You Solomons are hard to keep down."

"You know about ..."

"Naturally. Your children kept us updated on your progress."

"We've just been talking with them ..." Sam added, a little lamely.

"Tell me something, Doc," Sandy said. "These kids ... I got the impression they were more deeply involved, that they were into much more than a school boycott. Am I on the right track here?"

The doctor nodded, then said, "Look, we'd better all sit down. This could be a long session. I don't know what your children told you but they made it clear to me that I was not to pull my punches."

"We'd appreciate that," Sam said. "We're trying to understand what makes them run, exactly what's going on out there."

"Where do I start ..." the doctor said, looking at his hands. " ... okay. This is not about your children only. They're a microcosm of every child of colour in this country. They have more political savvy than the large majority of our adults. And they're impatient, they want results and they want them now. Strange as it may sound, they are leading the way. Even guys like me often have to give in to them. It happens that at times we are the followers, they the leaders ..."

"Are they absolutely clear about what they hope to achieve?" Karan asked, "some sort of definite aim?"

"Far beyond what you would expect from anyone that age. There's nothing wishy-washy about them. They have a set agenda, they are organised, they know exactly what they want, and they'll settle for nothing less."

"So they're not ... what did you call them, Sandy? Loose cannons?" Nithin asked.

"Quite the opposite. But there is a hardlined militancy about them, they don't think twice about being in the frontline, the possibility of death does not frighten them. They're the product of the '76 Soweto uprising. They're lean, mean and focused. Loose cannons? Far from it."

"They told us they're a part of an ANC cell." Sam said.

"There are hundreds of these cells all over the country," the doctor responded. "The government's clampdown on our leaders simply resulted in the children taking over. It is the kids who formed these cells, became members of the ANC and took over the reins. After '76 the schools became swiftly politicised, the schoolchildren became more articulate and increasingly better organised. They demanded to be heard and made it very clear that they were joint and equal partners in the liberation struggle. You're either with them or against them. There's no middle ground."

"But at their age," Karan said. "They're kids, damn it! As parents they must respect our authority."

"Try and understand ... Karan? ... okay, try and see it from their point of view. They have no respect for authority. Don't take that personally. To these kids authority and the system that oppresses us is one and the same. With our most charismatic leaders thrown into jail, in exile, or killed by the government's lackeys, the kids had no effective leadership — they had no one to turn to. So what did they do? They produced their own leaders."

"But we were always there ..." Karan started to say.

"Were you? Really? Okay, tell me this: exactly what sort of example have you set for them? You are politically more sophisticated than the man in the street, you understand exactly how evil this government is and you paid the price when their henchmen grabbed your properties and your businesses. But what did you do?"

"Hold it, Doc,"" Sandy said, a touch angrily. "Nits and I have always done our bit for the movement, more than ..."

"And I'm the first to acknowledge it. But was it enough? Your family, Sam, gave us Jake, the legend of *Aza Kwela* will live on long after we are all gone. But what did you personally do? Don't misunderstand me here, your children have not been slow to put themselves on the line. But you asked me to explain how they think, their opinion of you. That is the question I'm addressing."

"I'm beginning to understand something here," Sam said. "When you mentioned that the kids subscribed to the view that you're either with them or you're their enemy, that I reckon, is the bottom line."

"Quite! Your children are comparing you to your predecessors, and they don't like what they see. The Dadoos, Goonums, Pahads, Naickers — hell, a hundred like them lost everything they possessed but stood their ground and refused to compromise. These *lighties*, they see people like Dadoo's mother, an old lady in poor health, out there in the frontline with them, and then they come home to you. What are they supposed to think?"

"I get the picture," Sandy said. "Even our contemporaries show us up for our shortcomings. Compared to Jake we're miserable failures, non-starters. We need to examine our own consciences."

"When you talk about Jake and conscience," the doctor said sadly, "that's something I'll live with all my life — it was a slip of my tongue, an act of pure stupidity, that led to his capture; and ultimately cost him his life."

"The Americans have a nice way of putting it," Sandy said, "their phrase 'that's the way the cookie crumbles' says it all."

"I saw the scars on our children's backs," Karan muttered, "what on earth does the State think it's doing? These kids are not rioting or running wild. They're protesting peacefully."

"Let me tell you something," the doctor said, his voice suddenly fierce, "have any of you heard of Roodeplaat? No? It's the largest dog breeding centre in the world. A German professor there combined wolf and Alsatian genes to produce a vicious wolf-dog, for the sole purpose of setting it loose on our people. It's a huge animal requiring several powerful handlers to contain it, the teeth alone are an awesome size, like nothing you've ever seen in a dog. The jaw of this hybrid creation is so powerful it can crack your thighbone and reduce it to splinters in a second. They've been trained to hate blacks and rip into them, without any provocation.

"The German guy, who is employed by the Defence Force, imported that wolf from the mountains of Russia, an animal called Big Red, and cross-bred it to produce the monsters we're talking about. A dozen Alsatians can't stand up to one of them. These are the superdogs they set upon our children, who are defenceless and unarmed. Even their damned handlers don't go near them without specially made protective clothing and custom built equipment to protect them from those long teeth."

"But Doc," Karan protested, "these are children, not some terrorists from across the border bent on creating mayhem and chaos."

"Am I shocking you? I haven't even started. Have you heard of the Boerbul? It's the proud creation of the Afrikaners' mastery of genetic engineering, the result of what they learnt from their Nazi tutors — a creature that weighs far more than the largest of us here, perhaps ninety kilograms or more. These canine freaks are products of the apartheid regime, a symbol of white supremacy, their only purpose to kill and maim our people, which they do with great enthusiasm. This is what your kids face on a daily basis."

"For doing what?" Nithin asked. "Standing up and peacefully demanding their democratic rights?"

"I'm glad you're getting the picture. Maybe you'll understand your children better because of it."

"I've never doubted that these okes are anything other than disciples of the Nazis," Sandy said. "That place, Roodeplaat, I've heard it's a chemical research centre, that it produces tons of chemicals that induce cancer and heart attacks and even result in sterilisation. Not long ago some of my runners were offered drugs like mandrax and coke, at a fraction of the going price, on the strict condition that they were distributed to the public at a tenth of the price the merchants sell them for. They wanted to flood the market, turn every other guy into a hophead. They didn't say so, of course. But it didn't require a genius to work that out."

"Of course. And the ghettoes and townships would be effectively subdued, all resistance nicely eliminated."

"The kids, Doc," Karan said, "Do they know all this? I mean, it's all news to me."

"They know a lot more. They made it their business to find out."

"That probably explains their militancy," Sandy said. "I guess you have to admire their guts. With odds such as those stacked against them they're still out there, fighting back whilst we ... shit! We've been living in a blinkered world, and we thought we had all the answers."

"What's worse," Nithin added ruefully, "is that we thought that we could guide them, as if they were stray sheep needing some direction."

"I'm beginning to understand where Boesak comes from," Sam said. "I can appreciate his anger, why he says that the time for talking has passed."

"Jake worked that out when he was still a *lighty*," the doctor said, "nearly forty years ago."

"Okay, doc. I'm glad you came here. I can see my boys' point of view," Sandy said. "But the ANC? Can you give us a broad outline of what they are all about, what their aims are?"

"I can answer that in one sentence: the destruction of the apartheid state and the establishment of a people's democracy."

"This people's democracy, it includes the whites?" Karan asked.

"South Africa belongs to all who live in it. We have always rejected racism."

"This can be done?" Sandy asked. "A democracy is possible?"

"Within ten years. You're a betting man, Sandy. I'll give you odds of fifty to one on that."

"Through an armed struggle?" Nithin wanted to know.

"Why not, Nithin. Since 1912 we have talked of peaceful solutions. We've tried petitions, deputations, non-violent protests. Damn it, the concept of passive resistance was born in this country. What was the government's response? You know the answer. They resorted to violence, imprisonment and murder."

"And the ANC was banned," Karan said.

"Sure. What they were saying was that peaceful protest was being denied to us."

"So responding to violence with violence is the only option?" Sandy asked.

"They use violence and force to stay in power, they are not democratically elected, they have no legitimacy as a government. There is not a single democracy in the world that can justify their existence. They made the rules, they chose brute force as the only option and rejected any peaceful negotiation."

"So, as Boesak says, we're going to war now," Sam said.

"We're going to war, yes. We intend, as a start, to target government personnel and installations. That includes the white farmer, who is a part of their army units. This is not a war that will take place in the townships, it will be conducted wherever whites live."

"So there are no innocent whites, is that what you're saying?" Nithin asked.

"They are the real terrorists, Nits. Do you ever hear any howls of protest from them when thousands of us are killed by people they elected into power? In any case, in a war civilians die. We don't like it but there you are."

"There are no other options left?" Sam asked.

"Of course there are. All that the white people of this country are required to do is instruct their government to unban the ANC, release Mandela, allow our leaders to come home and set up a National Convention. No sincere person can have any difficulty doing that."

"I can't see any white voting for that," Karan said emphatically.

"Then they vote for war. What can we do? Any self-respecting people can't fail to respond to that in like manner. But, in any case, that debate is now academic. Our children have taken up the cudgels. Their attitude is you either fight back or die a coward."

"And that," Sandy said quietly, "brings us back to the beginning, why we all came here."

"But how do we support our children?" Karan asked. "Look, today was an education for me, but I don't even know where to go from here. When I go home, when all of us do that, those kids will be waiting to hear what we have to say. What can we say?"

"I'll answer that for you, Karan," the doctor said, "and I guarantee your kids won't be a problem after that."

"Ya? You have a magic wand?"

"No. Just a magic phrase," the doctor said with a smile, "four simple words."

"I suppose you'll get around to telling us what they are," Sandy said.

"Just tell them this: 'We've joined the ANC'"

∞

"The street's changing, Sandy," Nithin sighed. "Look around you. There was a time you could spot half a dozen scotens with one sweep of your eyes. Not anymore. And the cinemas — the Vic, the Royal, the Avalon — all no more than a memory. What happened to Dhanjees Fruiterers, Victoria Furniture Mart, Kapitans, that noisy Royal Tinsmith Company ... hell buddy, I could go on forever."

"Things change, Nits. Nothing stays the same," Sandy said matter-of-factly

"Does that include us? Or are we like the dinosaurs, living in a blinkered world."

"The doctor got to you, huh?"

"That, and our kids."

The two of them had walked down from Sam's office and were standing with their backs to the Victory Lounge. Sandy was puffing on a cigarette, Nithin staring around him bleakly.

"Sam said they'd wait for us at his place."

"I asked him to give us an hour or so. I need to think this through," Sandy responded. "I also want to visit someone, maybe get a better perspective on things."

"I've heard more than I can handle in one day, Sandy."

"You won't mind this call," Sandy said as he waved to a parked taxi driver, who immediately started the engine and rolled over.

"Hey there, Sandy. Howzit Nits," Haffy said as they jumped in.

"Howzit, *bru*," Nits and Sandy said in unison.

"Where to, *maat?*"

"Overport," Sandy directed. "*Leader* offices."

"Got it," Haffy said as he changed gears. "Don't see much of you guys these days."

"You know how it is," Sandy said absentmindedly. "How's Choonie?"

"Same as always. You can't keep a good man down."

"That's one tough *bunya*," Sandy agreed. "Have to be, in your business."

"Gets tougher as the years go by. The *lighties* don't show much respect."

"Go with the flow, pal. The locals know you okes' reputation. Trade on it. Don't allow them to test you. You fail once you don't get a second chance. Every shit *lighty* piles in, wanting to make a name for himself."

"They try their luck once in a while. You know Choonie, never slow to shape up."

"He'd be wise to play it cool."

"It's a living, *maat*. Don't know any other way to do it."

They made small talk for a few minutes then, as the noisy engine laboured up Sydenham Hill, they fell silent. It wasn't long before they turned into Sparks Road and, a short while later, pulled up alongside the pavement.

"The safe part of your journey is over, gentlemen," Haffy chuckled. "See you around ..."

"Thanks, buddy," Sandy said as he passed a note over. "Say howzit to Choonie from me."

As the taxi roared off Nithin asked, "What now?"

"Now we meet a very special lady."

When they entered the foyer Sunil Bramdaw spotted them through the glass and walked over, his hand outstretched. "Hello Sandy, Nits. Nice to see you."

"Good to see you too," Sandy said. "How's the newspaper business?"

"Chugging along," Sunil replied, his right hand dipping from side to side.

"We need to see the old lady. She in?"

"You know her Sandy. Never missed a day in her life."

"She must be in her late seventies now. When does she rest?"

"Never ask her that," Sunil laughed as he led the way. "She keeps us on our toes. Thinks rest is only for the wicked."

Saraswati Bramdaw stood up as they entered her office, a smile lighting her face. In her neat sari and trademark string of pearls she looked barely sixty and the way she moved made her appear even younger.

"You two playboys still kicking?" she asked affectionately. "You have a story for an old friend?"

"No stories today, ma. We're here to listen to you," Sandy said.

"What can I say that can interest you sharks," she said dismissively. "You boys are where the action is."

"That's not what our children think. Far as they're concerned we're not even on the playing field."

"And what field is that?"

"The Special Branch, the government ..."

"Ho there, my boy! Hold it right there. Grab a chair and get real."

"Why do you think we're here," Sandy smiled.

"Find another ballpark, boys. Stick to what you're good at."

"It's not our choice," Sandy started to say, then took a deep breath. "Okay. Let me explain." For the next fifteen minutes he told her everything — the school boycott that led to the discussion with their children, the scars on their backs and their attitude towards their parents, then ended with what the doctor had said. He left nothing out. He finished by saying, "We thought we knew what this government is all about. Seems now as if we weren't even touching sides."

"Why are you talking to me, Sandy? You could have picked a lot of that out of almost any issue of *The Leader*."

"Well ... we came to you for some corroboration, and hopefully some advice. After all, who better than a veteran journalist to get the facts from."

"You'll get them. Whether you'll like them is another matter."

"We want to hear it anyway."

"Listen, I'm going to say this to you boys just once — you're dabbling with dynamite. Stick to your world, it's a lot safer."

"Do we have a choice? Our kids are out there, they're our world."

"Supposing I can add to what you already know, what then?"

"We haven't thought that through yet. But Nits and I, we've never confronted an enemy without first sussing him out. This is no different."

"Let me tell you something right now: you boys are out of your league. I never thought I'd ever say this to you but the truth is you're just not ruthless enough. You don't have their muscle and you don't have the organisation. Back off! You'll be biting off more than you can chew."

Sandy sighed. "If only it were that simple. If we don't move on this our children become the enemy. It's heads we lose, tails we lose."

Mrs Bramdaw looked at them speculatively for a while, then asked, "Weren't you two very close to Jake Solomon?"

"He was a brother."

"I knew him well. My husband knew him better. People in this town used to think he was a gangster. My husband and I subscribed to the view that he was the most moral person we had ever met."

"Did you know that he was *Aza Kwela?*"

"Not with certainty. We suspected it. That only upgraded our opinion of him."

Sandy nodded. "Jake was a loner. He didn't talk much."

"He was a friend of *The Leader*. He always said that he admired our courage, that we printed what no other newspaper dared to do. In the context of courage, he had no equal. And he was the one that pointed me in the direction of the government's secret installations, their experimentation centres. In some respects Jake knew more about their dirty tricks campaign than anyone outside of the government's close confidants."

"You obviously knew Jake intimately. You know what a tight knit team we were. Take that a little lower down the line and you'll know where Nits and I are coming from. I'm not saying we had his courage but please believe me when I say that we shared the same convictions."

Mrs Bramdaw inclined her head in acquiescence, then asked, "Jake's murder didn't seem to deter his brother. Has Sam fully recovered from the shooting?"

"Back to his old self. He's in the same dilemma that we're in. And there's Jake's son ..."

"I've been watching him. The boy is a chip off the old block, possesses the same daring and, like his father, walks boldly where, as the saying goes, even the angels fear to tread."

"Then you'll understand what we're up against. These are the children who are now questioning our participation in the struggle, silently judging our failure to stand up and be counted."

"Okay. I'm beginning to understand your concerns. But tell me, before you heard about Roodeplaat from the doctor, did you have any inkling of its existence?"

"No."

"Perhaps that's understandable. It's a closely kept secret that not even our top journalists have heard of. Incidentally, this man you call 'the doctor', do you know his real name?"

"No."

"Then I can't tell you. But I can say this: he is a dedicated fighter for the people's rights and not a man given to exaggeration. Now, I'll tell you about that place, the evil laboratory called Roodeplaat ..."

As she spoke, the old journalist's face underwent a remarkable change. From the quiet, dignified and soft spoken woman, the epitome of everyone's mother, she suddenly became an angry and bitter woman. Her voice lost its sweet reasonableness, it acquired a timbre that contained both a fiery passion and a fierce fury that shook her audience. And yet, somewhere within it there lurked a tinge of sadness, a regret that decency could be reduced to such abysmal depths.

"As far back as the early fifties a heinous plot was devised, its sole purpose to eliminate, or, at the very least, neutralise every black person in this country. To this end, they somehow smuggled in a few of the remnants of the Gestapo's most brilliant minds — those that had somehow survived the Allies' interrogators and escaped detention; and, of course, their just deserts.

"Those wolf dogs that the doctor told you about? They are the product of a German scientist, a geneticist actually, a professor by the name of Geertshen. I don't know his history, he may merely be of German descent and not from among those brought here, but he can't escape the fact that he must have been aware that he was breeding killer dogs whose sole purpose was to rip people to pieces. But that is only one example of what is going on at that research laboratory.

"There are scientists there who are busy developing sophisticated poisons, anti-fertility vaccines and biological weapons. Others are experimenting on embryo transfers between different species — baboons, chimpanzees and related animals. And they're using humans, hobos kidnapped from the ghettoes, people who won't be missed. They're subjected to horrendous tests, heinous experiments that reduce them to screaming sub-humans, mindless lumps of flesh and blood. Their supply of such guinea pigs is unlimited — when the government's recruitment agents can't deliver fast enough to satisfy these maniacal professors, they simply turn to the prisons.

"This is a Defence Force programme, funded by the State — the people that your children are committed to destroying."

"You know all this," Nithin said in a hoarse voice, "and you're sitting on it ..."

"Hold it right there, Nits! Don't you dare question where my duty lies! I'm certain of my facts. But proof? Documentation that can stand up in the courts? That's another matter."

"But you're an investigative reporter, the best in the country."

"Nithin, listen. A wall of secrecy surrounds that place, a fly can't get in or out without permission. These people who rule us, they're masters of the art of deception, lords of the lie. They have conned the world into believing that this is a Western style democracy, that it subscribes to the rules of the United Nations Declaration on Human Rights. And behind this elaborate facade, like their hero with his Heydrichs and Himmlers, they have their infamous CB with its C10 killers, their rabid human dogs and hit squads."

"I know how the CB operates ..."

"You know nothing, my boy. Do you know of a place called Vlakplaas, their Third Force? Have you heard of a man called Prime Evil?" The old lady laughed harshly, her eyes burning with a bitter anger that made Nithin recoil with shocked surprise and forced him back into his chair. "It's not a name given to him by his victims, that's what his colleagues call him. Cross his path, just once, and that's the last breath you take."

"Okay, ma," Sandy said. "We hear you. How you live with this, bottled up in you ..."

"Now you can live with it too. You'll soon know what it feels like."

"In the US they would give you the Pullitzer Prize," Nithin muttered. "Here, I guess you'll be presented with a coffin, with you inside it."

"This is not conducive to a good night's rest," Sandy said, trying to make light of it.

"Oh, I'm used to that, my boy. Not sleeping well is something quite normal to me. It started way back, in my early days, when they took away my properties. Those were prime lands, substantial blocks a stone's throw from the Maritzburg City Hall. They reduced me to penury, contributed to my husband's death and almost brought *The Leader* to its knees. But we kept it going, losing more money than we could afford. These pearls are all that's left of my jewellery, the rest kept the printing press rolling. A good night's sleep — it's a luxury I can't remember.

"Would you like to know what keeps me going? Where I get my strength from?"

Sandy and Nithin, unsure of how to respond, simply gazed at the now tired face and quietly waited. They watched the play of emotions on the lined cheeks, saw the neat grey hair and the veins on her hands and marvelled at the strength that emanated from the eyes.

"For what they have done to our people," Saraswati Bramdaw said harshly, "THEY WILL PAY! For every drop of blood they have spilled, every property they have looted, every life they have taken, THEY WILL PAY! So long as I breathe, that is my mission and God will be at my avenging right hand. Then I will sleep."

"Hey, ma," Sandy said in awe, "you're some lady. Shit! You can play for my team ..."

Suddenly, Saraswati smiled, and the world righted itself. Sandy and Nithin thought they hadn't seen anything as lovely in all their lives.

"Don't be vulgar, my boy. Besides, you're amateurs. I set my sights a little higher."

∞

"You've been too long with the hens, Uncle Sam," Zain said. "You've forgotten that you were once an eagle."

Sam laughed as he rocked the Lazyboy that he was sprawled in. The boys, Zain, Pradeep and Haroun had stretched out on the floor. Mariam was leaning against the picture window, her hands deep in the pockets of her jeans. Karan was at the far end of the room, rummaging through Hannah's collection of books and tapes.

"Maybe," Sam said. "But let me tell you guys about an old Gujerati saying: when you live in the river, don't make an enemy of the crocodile."

"There's another saying," Pradeep smiled amiably, "Something my granny once told me: when you have a viper in your stomach you have to regurgitate it before it destroys you. Which of the two sayings do you think applies to our situation?"

"Well ... I don't know ... wise men say these things, I guess. Fools like us repeat them."

"That was neatly done, dad," Haroun shot back. "A lovely lesson in the art of evasive tactics. Anybody got anymore gems here?"

"I have one," Mariam said, winking at Haroun. "How about 'a fool and his friends are soon parted'."

"That's not how it goes," Pradeep grinned. "You just made it up."

"You don't think it's appropriate?" Mariam asked, a little pointedly.

"I'll tell you what," Sam said, "Let's try this one on for size: get to know your enemy, think like he does, then outwit him. How's that sound?"

"Think like he does?" Zain repeated. "Now you want us to lose our minds too?"

"Who the hell said that anyway?" Pradeep asked.

"Confucius. And mind your manners."

"Confucius said nothing of the sort," Zain scoffed. "Sounds more like that Chinese general, the guy who wrote *The Art of War*! Somebody called Zon Zhee or something."

"Whatever. It's still applicable to our problem."

"We've identified the problem, Uncle Sam," Zain said. "We're talking about implementing the solution."

Sam was still thinking of a response when Sandy and Nithin walked in, their faces grim.

"Just in time," Sam breathed a sigh of relief. "These kids are chowing me. What kept you guys anyway?"

"Don't get up," Sandy signalled to the boys. "Nits, you want to take the lead on this one?"

"You tell them, Sandy. I don't have the stomach for it."

"Okay. We've just been talking to the editor of *The Leader*, getting a different perspective ..."

Sandy repeated, almost word for word, the entire conversation and what they had been told. He concluded with, "I know evil when I see it. But this ... it goes beyond that ... it defies credibility. 'Heinous' wouldn't even begin to describe these monsters. There's no single word in the English language that even remotely conveys their despicable behaviour."

"Try 'megalomania'," Karan said as he walked over.

"Doesn't come close," Sandy said. "But okay, I guess it's decision time. We have to take a stance here. No point pussy-footing around."

"Whatever we decide," Nithin said firmly, "We can't act on our own. We don't have the firepower."

"Get that doctor guy back in here!" Karan hissed. "I've heard enough!"

"Before we do that," Sandy suggested pragmatically, "I think we should identify how far we can commit on this."

"After all we've heard today?" Karan asked. "Can we limit our participation to specific levels?"

"I just don't want to start shooting from the hip. Let's examine this carefully. The oke we call 'the doctor', I've met him before. When a

Bramdaw clears anyone I don't argue. But you need to know this: he's a radical, a man of action. From what he once said I got the impression that bombs and mayhem are what he deals in. We're talking about death and destruction here, not speeches and peaceful marches. We should keep that in mind before we go off half-cocked. There'll be no turning back."

"Sandy ... look ... what they did to our kids, and we know they're not isolated instances .. that's not all that gets to me," Nithin said. "Those places ... Roodeplaat, Vlakplaas ... okay, that blows my mind. But what's eating me up is the feeling that time is running out on us, that events are overtaking us and all we're doing is talking ... hey, does that sound familiar? Damned! I've never felt so helpless in my life ..."

"No harm in talking," Sandy said, "long as it doesn't go on forever. I hear what you say, Nits. I know the feeling. All I'm saying is that we think about this carefully, no more than a day or so. That way there can be no regrets later."

"Uncle Sandy," Mariam said. "I'd like to ask you something: how many black families in this country are having a similar conversation today? Do you think any of them feels there are any options left?"

"If there's one thing I learned from the Jews," Zain said, "It's that you can't reason with a Nazi. Civilised responses lead to the gas chambers and death camps. You fight evil with evil. You stop them in their tracks, stamp their faces into the ground. You blow their military apparatus off the face of the earth. And if you die in the process, that's okay. Because they're going to kill you anyway. At least you get to go down with dignity. As for talking about it — I guess we just finished doing that."

When Zain stopped there was a stillness in the room, an eerie silence that froze the adults in their tracks.

"That's the reality of it, Uncle Sandy," Pradeep said, not unkindly. "Looking for options is, in our opinion, simply an excuse for doing nothing."

"We're not telling you what to do," Mariam said quietly. "You must be guided by your own consciences. But you sent for us, you asked for an explanation. We've given you that. What you now do with what you have learnt today is for you to decide."

"However you choose to act," Haroun added, his voice low, "we want you to know that we love you. Whether you stand with us or not, nothing will change that. But until you arrive at a clear decision we are saying that you ask us no more questions. We consider that a fair request."

"Nothing could be fairer," Sam said, slowly standing up. "You asked to be treated as equals. I believe we've done that. Now it's our turn. Give us till the morning to absorb this and revert to you. Just the one night, okay?"

When the youngsters nodded, Sam turned to the others and said, "Let's take a walk. My joints are stiff."

❧

"The kids don't trust us to do the right thing, Sam," Sandy said as they walked towards the pool.

"I used to think they were a bunch of brats," Karan said, shaking his head sadly. "Now ... well, they make me feel sort of ... inadequate. Like I'm the child."

"You're not alone there, pal," Nithin added.

"It all came too swiftly," Sandy reasoned. "We suddenly found ourselves at the deep end. Of course, we were foolish. It was always there, staring us in the face, from the time we were their age."

"What took us so long?" Karan asked. "We weren't stupid. We did discuss it ... is that it? Did we just talk all the time ..."

"This may sound trite," Sandy smiled, "but I reckon we had other priorities, like putting the food on the table. Our *lighties* don't have that distraction."

"Maybe," Sam mumbled. "Or perhaps, as my old man used to fear, we were a recreant generation."

"I don't know," Nithin muttered. "Jake was one of us. It didn't distract him in any way."

"Jake will always be our conscience," Sandy concluded. "Funny how I'm only beginning to understand him now. I used to think there was an anger in him, that he was acting on hate alone. Only now do I realise that he was motivated by justice. It came home to me when Mrs Bramdaw called him the most moral person she knew."

"So what do we do now?" Karan asked as they stopped under a tree.

"I think we're forgetting a fundamental issue here," Sam suggested. "Our wives. I think we should throw this around with them, tonight, one on one. I'm not forgetting how, in every calamity, theirs was always the voice of reason."

"Let's do it then," Nithin agreed. "All we have is tonight. Don't expect an easy ride. But what the hell, when was life ever an easy ride?"

❧

They had been talking for hours. Finally, Sandy ran his hands through his hair and shook his head. "Whichever way you cut it, it'll always be a no-win outcome. I didn't survive by playing that game. If I can't call the tune I don't get on the dance floor. I learnt that very early in life.

"My old lady sold veggies on the pavement to feed us. Rain or shine, from early in the morning to sunset, she sat on that cement floor and froze her ass off. There was that day, I was maybe ten or so, when a bunch of honkey cops drove up in their van and booted my ma off that pavement, then took her baskets and pulled out. We didn't eat that night. I was hardly a *lighty* then and I couldn't do much to help her. What I did was make a promise to myself — as soon as I could I'd get her off the pavement.

"I learnt to fight by getting beaten up. Pretty soon I got down to some serious thinking. Wasn't long before I used my brains and my fists to fight my way to the top. Once there I decided I liked the scene. There's only one law up there: when a man is down, you tramp him — you give him a hand up and he either pulls you down or tries to muscle in. When I dealt with the *Motas* I learnt another rule: you lead by following. You still with me, babe?

"I've never expected life to give me a fair deal — that's like trying to catch a falling star, okay for the *garachs* and the romantics. All I wanted was that my ma — and after that, you and the boys — always had the edge over the rest. I made it happen. I did it without help from anyone. I took care of me and mine. The rest could take care of themselves, I didn't see them as my problem.

"Now I'm expected to make a stand. For what? To die a hero? Who the hell remembers a hero? They come and go and after the first bunch of roses, the memory withers with the petals. Not long after, when the grave starts to flatten out, some passing bum pisses on it and moves on. That'll happen anyway but it won't be because I fought a stupid fight.

"So? Where do I go from here? Shit, Jake! You were my buddy. You and I were a symphony in motion, we were a team. Who were the ghosts that drove you? Was the fight worth it? What did you achieve? Where the hell are you now? Talk to me!"

When he buried his head in her shoulder, Maliga shivered from fear of what the day would bring.

∞

He was sprawled on the sofa, his hands hanging limply at his sides. There was a look on his face, the things that he was saying — she had never seen him like this before and it frightened her. The peculiar timbre in his voice, the hint of uncertainty in the way he spoke, his posture — they were all alien to the confident and bold creature she had mated with. It shook her centre of gravity and threw her off balance. She felt her heart go out to him, reached out and took his hand in hers and silently raised it to her lips.

"I've never loved anyone as I've loved you. I wasn't even attracted to any girl before I met you. My ma, my sisters — they were my responsibility, I would have given my life for them. But that was different ... Did I tell you about the time when a bully fondled one of them? I blew him away and I didn't lose any sleep over it. Now these bastards have whipped my daughter and here I am debating what I should do. Some big deal I am!"

He began to ramble, saying things out of sequence, jumping from one thought to another.

"Those merchants out there, they kiss my ass when they see me. When I'm out of sight they blackball me. Do I go to them when I have a problem? Do I turn to them for help? When they need me they call me the lender of last resort, when their problem is solved they wriggle their miserable bums all the way to the bank that kicked them in the first place. Do they thank me? Do they realise that, but for me, they would be insolvent today? When things are sweet again they invite those same bank managers to their houses for dinner and parade their wives' *ezies* before them. And when they talk about me to their fat aunties they call me a bloodsucker — they boost their egos at my expense. Those were the milksops that made my mother kow-tow to them. Are those the *garachs* I am expected to fight for?

"When I was a *lighty* a bunch of honkies pissed on my face. That night I swore an oath that no man would be my master. That my fate would be determined by me alone. I gave my loyalty to no man ... except to Jake ... and later John.

"Do you know how I got my start in life? Hell, I almost forgot about it. But what the hell ... it's all history now ... you make your own luck, you stand or fall by the decisions you make. The Big Guy up there — all he gives you is a brain and then he sets you loose, you're on your own. He doesn't give you another thing. Why should he. Isn't that enough for any man?

"Jake ... he had no time for all this philosophising — he didn't like you, he *khupped* you. If you were his *maat* he was there for you, all the way down the line. Like John, he was a man of honour. What did it do for him? It's not his statue that graces the Town Gardens. Don't talk to me about 'the unknown soldier', the 'grain of corn' and all that *kuk*! That's just there to keep the *garachs* in line.

"What am I saying here? When did those *gamoolas* out there become my people? You with me here, Kathy love? Ya? Am I supposed to reduce myself to cannon fodder now?

"Oh shit! Shit man! To hell with this jive!"

When she felt his body tremble Kathy folded him in her arms and held him close to her. She wasn't aware of the solitary tear that rolled down her cheek.

∞

"My father once ordered me to choose: '*daku* or *dukan*, for now and forever'. He didn't fully appreciate the limitations in that statement. There was no contradiction there — he was simply missing the big picture. The real decision I should have been making was either death or survival.

"When they killed Yahya and Nadia and Kantha kaki — we did nothing. When the state's intransigence broke Dara's heart — we did nothing. When they murdered Jake we did nothing! And now? When they almost put me six feet under the ground? Am I to continue playing the humble martyr?

"I walked off the street ... I thought that was a moral decision ... I didn't know what the word meant. Now it's my son that's asking me to choose — he's become the father to the child in me. What does he know about me? Does he think I'm a coward escaping a confrontation? Does he realise that what we're proposing is like shouting against thunder — the fight's over before it's even begun. Zain says that they'll kill us anyway, the question is whether we go down with dignity ... nothing wrong with that.

"You remember what Dara said, in this very room — 'Am I now to be their meal, the bones off which they partake their last supper?' Was he right all along? Are our children now the idealists? Were all of them wrong — Yahya, Madhoo dada, Dara? And what about Gandhi? Is passive resistance just an excuse to avoid the real issue — the violent confrontation? If that's true then Jake saw it before wiser men than us did. What did he know that we don't? What made him so wise?

"So ... what do I do now? Blow up everything in sight? Is that what it all boils down to — an eye for an eye, a tooth for a tooth? All these questions - is that the one answer that applies to all of them? And how long do you think we will last? A week, two weeks? And how long can we live with ourselves if we do nothing? Can we say 'I breathe, therefore I live?'

"Talk to me, Sal. You always come up with the right answers. Hey! Why are your eyes moist?"

∞

"I'm a *bunya*, Devi. We don't go around planting bombs and blowing people to pieces. Life, any life, is sacred to us. Must I be like the chameleon now — changing colour as my environment changes?

"Pradeep says looking for a civilised solution is simply an excuse for doing nothing. Haroun says that even if we decide to do nothing they will still love us. But this is not about love, this is about killing. And what if we really do nothing, is that the end of it? Can we absolve ourselves of responsibility for the actions of our children?

"What I see are heads rolling in the gutter, broken bodies in the streets, blood in every corner — this is an option? But today I found out that that is happening anyway. What these thugs in government are doing is beyond belief, they're tearing decent people to ribbons with those killer dogs of theirs, they're using their sjamboks to scar children for life and their elaborate laboratories are workshops of the devil!

"When they massacred my father in '49 I didn't go looking for revenge. When they looted our many properties I didn't blow up theirs. Now they're destroying our children and I'm talking about non-violence. They've persecuted us for over a hundred years, and their teeth get sharper and their cruelty progressively worse as the years go by. Must we wait another hundred years before we say 'enough is enough'?

"Dara — we all called him that in his absence — foresaw the arrival of this day. He told me to take our family and get out. How could I do that? I saw it as an act of a coward. So? What does a brave man do? I asked Sam the same question today. What did he tell me? 'Bravery has nothing to do with it. It's simply a question of seeking justice.' What kind of answer is that?

"Jake was ahead of the game, he worked it out without all this verbal bulldust. He knew that survival, when confronted by a killer beast, couldn't be obtained by appealing to its sense of decency. Listen to me now! I sound like I've already made up my mind!"

When Karan's head slumped on his chest, Devi quietly stood up and led him to the prayer room. As she lit the lamp she struggled to hold back the sob that threatened to escape from her lips.

❦

It was the first taste of winter. The chill wind that had swept over the snow-covered Drakensberg brought with it a hint that the coldest season in living memory was on its way.

They were huddled close together in an attempt to conserve their body heat. The greater coldness, however, was in their minds, which were frozen with uncertainty and the fear of what the morning would bring.

"What do you think they'll decide to do?" Mariam asked.

OTHER TITLES FROM STE PUBLISHERS

Cultural history
The world that made Mandela by Luli Callinicos
Johannesburg — One City Colliding Worlds by Professor Lindsay Bremner

Photographic
In the Company of God by Joao Silva
Jo'burg by Guy Tillim

Film
Come Back Africa by Lionel Rogosin

Biography / Autobiography
Makeba — the Miriam Makeba Story by Miriam Makeba in Conversation with Nomsa Mwamuka
Timol — A Quest for Justice by Imtiaz Cajee
All My Life and All My Strength by Ray Alexander Simons
Now Listen Here — the Life and Times of Bill Jardine by Chris van Wyk
Comrade Jack — The Political Lectures and Diary of Jack Simons, Novo Catengue Edited by Marion Sparg, Jenny Schreiner and Gwen Ansell

Reference
The South Africa Yearbook 2004/05 by the GCIS
Pocket Guide to South Africa by the GCIS

Art
Images of Defiance — South African Resistance Posters of the 1980s by the Poster Book Collective of the South African History Archive

Education
Turning Points in History series by Various
Turning Points in History cd-rom by Various

Literary Criticism
Indias Abroad by Rajendra Chetty & Pier Paolo Piciucco

Fiction
The Lotus People by Aziz Hassim
Bite of the Banshee by Muff Andersson

Esoteric
Afternoon Tea in Heaven — Conversations with the Spirit World By Nanette Adams

Self Help
My Life Your Life — Steps to Heal the Heart By Michelle Friedman

To order contact: www.ste.co.za OR angela@ste.co.za